Illegitimate son of a Chinese mother and Irish father, he built a fabulous trade empire and dared anyone to defy his rule . . .

SIR CHARLES

Profligate and flamboyant, he put lust before honor and married a woman he could neither understand nor dominate . . .

MARY

She married into an alien culture and discovered the depths of her passion in adultery and the heights of her glory in a man's world . . .

JAMES

A child of shame and love, he grew to manhood to become a leader in a land divided by politics and blood . . .

DYNASTY

A NOVEL BY

Robert S. Elegant

FAWCETT CREST • NEW YORK

DYNASTY

THIS BOOK CONTAINS THE COMPLETE TEXT OF THE ORIGINAL HARDCOVER EDITION.

Published by Fawcett Crest Books, a unit of CBS Publications, the Consumer Publishing Division of CBS Inc., by arrangement with McGraw-Hill, Inc.

ISBN: 0-449-23655-2

Selection of the Book-of-the-Month Club
Selection of the Playboy Book Club

Printed in the United States of America

10 9 8 7 6 5 4 3 2 1

For Kitung—

and for Moira, again and always

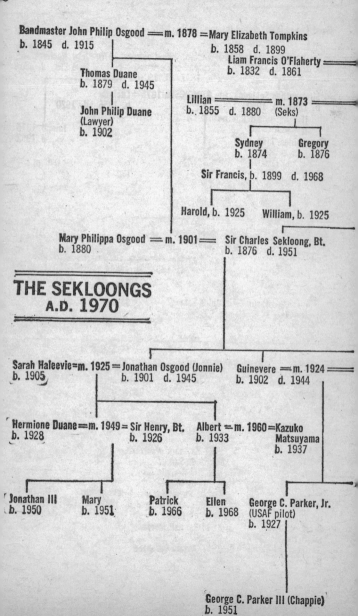

Bandmaster John Philip Osgood === m. 1878 === Mary Elizabeth Tompkins
b. 1845 d. 1915   b. 1858 d. 1899

Liam Francis O'Flaherty ===
b. 1832 d. 1861

Thomas Duane
b. 1879 d. 1945

Lillian === m. 1873 ===
b. 1855 d. 1880   (Seks)

John Philip Duane
(Lawyer)
b. 1902

Sydney   Gregory
b. 1874   b. 1876

Sir Francis, b. 1899 d. 1968

Harold, b. 1925   William, b. 1925

Mary Philippa Osgood === m. 1901 === Sir Charles Sekloong, Bt.
b. 1880   b. 1876 d. 1951

THE SEKLOONGS
A.D. 1970

Sarah Haleevie=m. 1925 = Jonathan Osgood (Jonnie)   Guinevere === m. 1924 ===
b. 1905   b. 1901 d. 1945   b. 1902 d. 1944

Hermione Duane===m. 1949 = Sir Henry, Bt.   Albert === m. 1960 === Kazuko
b. 1928   b. 1926   b. 1933   Matsuyama
   b. 1937

Jonathan III   Mary   Patrick   Ellen   George C. Parker, Jr.
b. 1950   b. 1951   b. 1966   b. 1968   (USAF pilot)
   b. 1927

George C. Parker III (Chappie)
b. 1951

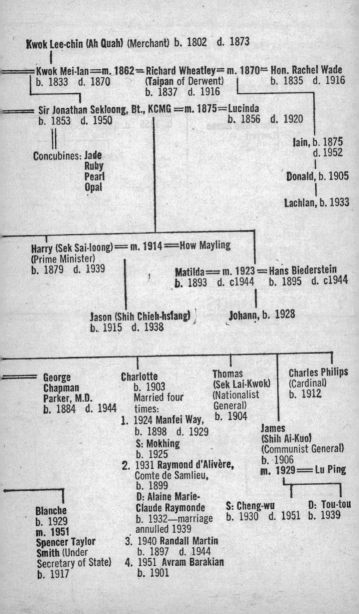

Kwok Lee-chin (Ah Quah) (Merchant) b. 1802 d. 1873

══ Kwok Mei-lan══m. 1862 ══ Richard Wheatley══ m. 1870 ══ Hon. Rachel Wade
   b. 1833 d. 1870   (Taipan of Derwent)   b. 1835 d. 1916
                            b. 1837 d. 1916

══ Sir Jonathan Sekloong, Bt., KCMG══m. 1875══Lucinda
   b. 1853 d. 1950   b. 1856 d. 1920

   Concubines: Jade
               Ruby
               Pearl
               Opal

                                                          Iain, b. 1875
                                                               d. 1952

                                                          Donald, b. 1905

                                                          Lachlan, b. 1933

Harry (Sek Sai-loong)══ m. 1914 ══How Mayling
(Prime Minister)
b. 1879 d. 1939
                        Matilda══ m. 1923 ══Hans Biederstein
                        b. 1893 d. c1944   b. 1895 d. c1944

      Jason (Shih Chieh-hsiang)   Johann, b. 1928
      b. 1915 d. 1938

══ George   Charlotte   Thomas   Charles Philips
   Chapman   b. 1903   (Sek Lai-Kwok)   (Cardinal)
   Parker, M.D.   Married four   (Nationalist   b. 1912
   b. 1884 d. 1944   times: General)
                       1. 1924 Manfei Way,   b. 1904
                          b. 1898 d. 1929
                          S: Mokhing   James
                          b. 1925   (Shih Ai-Kuo)
                       2. 1931 Raymond d'Alivère,   (Communist General)
                          Comte de Samlieu,   b. 1906
                          b. 1899   m. 1929 ══ Lu Ping
                          D: Alaine Marie-
   Blanche   Claude Raymonde   S: Cheng-wu   D: Tou-tou
   b. 1929   b. 1932—marriage   b. 1930 d. 1951 b. 1939
   m. 1951   annulled 1939
   Spencer Taylor   3. 1940 Randall Martin
   Smith (Under   b. 1897 d. 1944
   Secretary of State) 4. 1951 Avram Barakian
   b. 1917   b. 1901

Contents

PRELUDE
JUNE 27, 1970 / 7:30–8:30 P.M.   13

Part I
Mary
MAY 28, 1900–DECEMBER 26, 1900   31

INTERLUDE
JUNE 27, 1970 / 8:30–10:30 P.M.   131

Part II
Mary and Charles
FEBRUARY 4, 1905–NOVEMBER 16, 1906 145

Part III
Mary and Harry
NOVEMBER 13, 1908–SEPTEMBER 11, 1909 213

Part IV
Mary and Jonathan
DECEMBER 6, 1911–JUNE 18, 1916   285

Part V
Thomas and James
MARCH 2, 1924–DECEMBER 15, 1927   373

Part VI
James and Harry
JULY 7, 1937–DECEMBER 9, 1944   497

INTERLUDE
JUNE 27, 1970 / 10:30 P.M.–12 N.   651

Part VII
The Sekloongs and the Lao Pai-Hsing
NOVEMBER 28, 1950–FEBRUARY 22, 1959   667

Part VIII
Albert and the Red Guards
OCTOBER 24, 1965–SEPTEMBER 26, 1967   749

POSTLUDE
.JUNE 28, 1970 / 1:04 A.M.–4:31 A.M.   835

All novels have their basis in reality. This is particularly true of a novel that deals with specific historical events and characters. I hope, however, that the reader will forgive me for having taken some literary license with the chronology of certain events and with the personalities of certain historical figures named. For example, General Morris Abraham Cohen did not appear in Hong Kong at the precise time he does in the novel, nor did the Duke of Gloucester.

All the fictional characters in the novel represent a composite of many real people from the various periods covered. Nevertheless, I hope these fictional personages will reveal the greater realities of the turbulent life of China and Hong Kong from 1900 to 1970.

R.S.E.

Prelude

June 27, 1970

FOGHORNS wailed from burnished-white liners and rust-scabbed freighters tethered to massive buoys. The oily swells barely rocked the big ships. Hong Kong harbor was as forebodingly flat as a pitted black mirror, and the greasy fog crept implacably down the surrounding hills to enshroud the bay.

The last ferry to Kowloon cautiously picked its way among the moored ships. Its horizontal rows of lights cast a pale nimbus in the encroaching darkness, and its siren lamented the coming of the night. A bat-sailed junk drifted like a ghost on the breeze. The ferry's coxswain muttered Cantonese obscenities and spun the six-foot wheel to avoid the unlighted vessel. Grimy wal-la-walla motorboats skittered through the murk, their horns shrieking mournful warnings.

Typhoon Linda was racing toward the smug British Crown Colony at 30 knots in the early evening of June 27, 1970. Though the haze was still spreading and the rain still came in gusts, the Royal Observatory's forecasts were ominous. The typhoon's breath would soon blow away the fog, and the rain would stream across the bay in opaque sheets.

The Colony's communications were sophisticated: the tilted white bowls of the satellite earth-station shone on the Stanley Peninsula; the enormous grids of white-and-red checkerboard radar antennae perched on the hills; and a forest of radio masts sprang from Cape Collinson.

But all movement across the harbor would cease within an hour. Despite man's technological cunning, no man could move from Hong Kong Island to the Kowloon Peninsula jutting from the mainland of Asia when the angry winds stormed out of the South China Sea. The 200-foot breadth of the runway of Kaitak Airport extended 8,350 feet into the eastern arm of the harbor, but the West's wondrously complex aircraft were earthbound by the rage of Tien Mu Hou, the Empress of Heaven and Goddess of the Sea.

Air Force One squatted unlighted on the tarmac before the Royal Air Force Terminal. Defying the weight of their four Pratt and Whitney engines, the silver wings of the Boeing 707 tugged against the wire cables that secured them to ring bolts set in concrete. Before the Civil Aviation Terminal, eleven jetliners flanked a 747 Jumbo. All were similarly tethered against the oncoming cataclysm, and the bright symbols on their tail planes were intermittently obscured by the rain-bursts that presaged the typhoon. Three smaller private jets huddled near the airliners like eagles beside friendly dragons.

The immobilized aircraft had already disembarked their passengers. Twenty-three had been summoned to the British enclave on the periphery of the Communist People's Republic of China by the same command. Air Force One had borne Under Secretary of State Spencer Taylor Smith to the Crown Colony despite his misgivings. The spacious first-class compartments of Japan Air Lines, Swissair, and TWA jetliners had disgorged fifteen of his relations by marriage into the torrents of rain. Five others had alighted from their private jets, and obsequious attendants wielding umbrellas had escorted them to limousines.

Alongside Air Force One, a British Aircraft Corporation Trident also stood aloof from the covey of civilian jets. Occasionally revealed by the writhing fog, its tail plane displayed five clustered golden stars on a crimson rectangle. Flying direct from Peking, the Trident had carried a reluctant General Shih Ai-kuo, member of the Central Committee of the Communist Party of the People's Republic of China and Deputy Political Commissar of the Chinese People's Liberation Army. Incongruously paired, the transports of the United States Air Force and the Chinese People's Air Force were heavily guarded. Sergeants and constables of the Royal Hong Kong Police wearing black slickers crouched in drenched misery under the broad fuselages.

Through the squalls, illuminated signs shone faintly from the shadowy bulk of Hong Kong Island across the bay. The neatly squared, pale-blue letters on the left read: HONG KONG HILTON. On the far right a scrolled yellow M marked the Mandarin Hotel. Between those pleasure palaces of the self-indulgent West, four angular Chinese characters pierced the night with glowing red rays. They proclaimed: LONG LIVE CHAIRMAN MAO!

In his suite five stories below the scrolled M, the Under Secretary of State peered into a mirror to adjust his bow-tie. Finally satisfied, he slipped the crimson-and-white star of the Legion of Merit on its rose-red ribbon around his neck and pinned a row of miniature decorations to the silk lapel of his tailcoat. He contemplated his slightly florid, slightly corpulent handsomeness with approval.

"Damn it, Blanche!" Spencer Taylor Smith growled to his honey-haired wife. "What the hell have you gotten me into? The old lady's all right. But why do we have to get mixed up with this bunch of chinks and yids? Worthy Orientals and Hebrews, I suppose I should call them. And what in God's own name am I supposed to call General Shih? 'Uncle James'?"

The slight woman with the deep-set blue eyes rose from the mirrored dressing table. Unperturbed, she clasped a diamond-and-sapphire necklace around her slender throat.

"Now, Spence," she said equably, "please zip me up."

The Under Secretary muttered ill-temperedly as he inched the zipper up to the green brocade curtaining her ivory back.

"You can call him whatever you damned please, as far as I'm concerned." Blanche Smith's voice was edged. " 'General Shih'—'honored colleague'—'Uncle James'—or 'You Communist bastard.' Don't talk to him at all if you don't want to. All I asked is to come for Lady Mary's birthday—I don't complain about your interminably boring state banquets."

17

"Could be damned embarrassing," the Under Secretary grumbled.

"I'm sure you'll manage, dear. You always do. You can even charm the cranky French. And don't forget you married one of those chinks and yids."

"Sorry!" The Under Secretary was momentarily abashed. "Shall we go?"

In the anachronistically plush penthouse atop the Bank of China, General Shih Ai-kuo was alone with his forebodings. His wife, Lu Ping, alternate member of the Communist Party's Central Committee, had declined to accompany him to Hong Kong. Of her own will, he wondered, or on the Party's orders? But the Premier himself had insisted that the General attend the celebration of his mother's birthday. Were *they*, he brooded, setting him up for "criticism" and subsequent dismissal? The Premier's instructions had been deplorably vague, merely: "Observe and report."

General Shih scowled as he pulled his high-collared, blue-gray tunic over his bulky shoulders. His hazel eyes narrowed, and his high forehead wrinkled above his aquiline features. Only the slight slant of his eyes and the faint golden cast of his skin were markedly Chinese. Comrades ignorant of his background assumed that he was part Turkyi from Central Asia, and he rarely bothered to enlighten them.

"Ninety she is," he muttered in English. "And I'm practically sixty-four, and I haven't seen her in twenty-odd years. Of course I want to see the old girl. But why the decorations? Nobody's worn them in years."

Distastefully, he weighed two medals in his broad palm. Brilliantly chased in red-and-gold enamel, each was as large as a silver dollar. Squaring his shoulders, he pinned the Order of a Hero of the Chinese People on his breast and, beside it, the Order of August First. He would have been happier with a simple plastic button displaying the benevolent features of Chairman Mao Tse-tung. But his orders were quite precise in that respect: he had been specifically instructed to wear the orders that had been out of fashion for a decade.

"Like a damned Russian comic-opera general," he complained. "And why wouldn't Ping come? Meeting of the Standing Committee of the Women's Association, hell! She's skipped them before when it suited her —or them."

The General's Mercedes 280SE waited in the cavernous garage, whose exit ramp to Bank Street was guarded by the Party's plainclothesmen. Though he could not delay much longer, he parted the purple satin drapes and gazed up at The Peak. Clustered lights from the beehive apartment houses on the lower slopes overbore the fog by their profusion, and segmented orange glowworms marked the zigzag road to the heights. He felt he could almost see the sharp turnoff to Sekloong Manor, that monstrosity of bourgeois ostentation where he had been born. A semi-opaque curtain of haze and rain swept across the mountain, obscuring all but the hint of distant luminescence.

On The Peak itself, the leaden fog blotted out all the works of man and nature. The gross gray mass flowed over villas and mansions, over broad roads and narrow byways, over trees, flowers, and rocks. In the feeble orange glow of sodium streetlights, motorcars crawled along Magazine Gap Road into Peak Road. Drivers craned their heads through the windows, searching for the white centerline to avoid the precipice on the left. Only the diffused loom of lights warned of oncoming traffic. Automobiles appeared like gleaming spirit cars, to be ingested again by the blackness.

Turning sharply right, a stately Rolls-Royce Phantom IV shone its locomotive headlights on the leering tortoise gargoyles astride the arch guarding the private road to Sekloong Manor. Greasy tentacles of fog coiled around the upturned eaves of the twenty-five-foot-high gate, and its canary-yellow tiles gleamed insubstantial when the mist momentarily parted. On the broad crossbeam, illuminated by the Phantom's uptilted lights, a golden dragon writhed in high relief. The supreme beast's black claws clutched white clouds, and its outspread wings shaded from pale azure roots to the broad, bright carnelian tips. Its crimson eyes fixed on the pearl shimmering before its open jaws; the great reptile appeared in the shifting light to lunge toward the unattainable gem.

Each of the beast's feet had four claws, since only the Emperor's dragon might display five claws. But its hue was indistinguishable from the Imperial yellow, and the carving was as fine as any outside the Imperial City in Peking. The dragon represented the Emperor's temporal and spiritual power, for he was *Tien-tze*, the Son of Heaven.

Jonathan, founder of the House of Sekloong, had taken the winged dragon as his own symbol almost a century earlier, when the Emperor still reigned. The gesture was then not merely presumptuous; it verged upon blasphemy. But Jonathan Sekloong spurned his contemporaries' shocked remonstrances. He had, he said, been born in Sekloong, which means Stone Dragon, and had taken both the town's name and its symbol as his own. His Chinese mother could not give him a name, and his Irish father would not.

During the ensuing years, the ultimate symbol of grandeur had come to seem no more than Jonathan's due. The Emperor had been dethroned, and the *Ta Ching Chao*, the Great Pure Dynasty, had been overthrown. But Jonathan Sekloong had flourished, building a great commercial empire and founding a dynasty that endured. His achievements recognized by two British knighthoods and, subsequently, by a baronetcy, he had died Sir Jonathan at the age of ninety-seven, in 1950.

The older passengers in the limousines crawling along Peak Road remembered Sir Jonathan's imperious temperament. Even before his death twenty years earlier, he had been more myth than man. His own life and his descendants' lives were themselves the chronicles of more than a century of the tumultuous history of both modern China and that unique anomaly that had profoundly influenced the violent course of the world's most populous country—British-ruled, Chinese-inhabited Hong Kong. Despite the approaching typhoon, almost a hundred descendants and several hundred guests were assembling to pay tribute to his daughter-in-law on her ninetieth birthday. Their homage was tendered equally to the spirit of the colossal figure who had spanned the Orient and the Occident. Though Lady Mary Sekloong was herself legend, the Matriarch maintained that she was but the legatee of the Old Gentleman. When Hong Kong spoke of the Old Gentleman —or any Sekloong anywhere used the term—it meant only Sir Jonathan.

The stately Rolls was the first vehicle of the motorcade that passed under the arch. Sweating Chinese constables halted oncoming traffic with swinging yellow flashlights to clear the turn into Sekloong Manor. Eldorados and Imperials, Rolls-Royces, Jaguars, and Mercedes 600's rolled under the rampant winged dragon. Gaudy sportscars, driven through the murk with more dash than skill, revved throaty salutes to the mythical reptile. The English police inspector commanding the traffic detail counted two Ferraris, four Jensens, six Lotuses, and three Maseratis. When the stream dwindled, he enviously calculated that he had waved on more than $3 million worth of finely tuned machinery.

Battered Minis, Morris Minors, and Volkswagens mingled with those ostentatiously expensive toys. For her ninetieth birthday Lady Mary had summoned not only her own children, her grandchildren, and her great-grandchildren, but all known descendants of the Old Gentleman by his two wives, his three concubines, and his numerous liaisons. The Matriarch could not herself count their exact number, though she knew that the Old Gentleman had fathered nineteen children as far as he was aware. His children and their children had procreated enthusiastically—with and without the sanction of Holy Church or the law.

The air-conditioned, deep-cushioned dimness of a Lincoln Continental enclosed Lady Mary's younger daughter Charlotte and her fourth husband, Avram Barakian, whose accountants could not precisely calculate his wealth in ships, oil, factories, and land. Charlotte Sekloong Way d'Alivère Martin Barakian's sixty-six-year-old eyes roved hungrily over the sprawling compound where she had known her happiest days —if she ever had been truly happy since leaving the security of the Manor.

The motorcars rolled through the cascades of light that played along the triangular road leading to the Main House. Banks of spotlights lanced the fog, and many-colored lanterns gyrated in the wind-battered trees. Strings of incandescent bulbs outlined the three Small Houses, themselves mansions by ordinary standards. Floodlights on the lawns carved balconies and overhanging roofs into geometrical patterns of alternating brilliance and blackness. At the apex of the triangle stood the Main House, which successive generations of Sekloong children had called The Castle.

Only the children had explored all The Castle's remote corners, clattering noisily up spiral staircases to the eight towers that raked the sky. Soaring from the corners of the four-story central structure and its lower wings, their tops invisible in the fog, the towers were both turrets and minarets. The crenelated battlements connecting the spires were spectacularly incongruous above green-tiled roofs with out-flared eaves. Sir Jonathan's implacable will had not only built his own monument, but had imposed an improbable harmony on the curious structure. Though The Castle was grotesque, it was as overwhelmingly impressive as he had intended.

The Castle contained forty bedrooms. But Sir Jonathan's daughter-in-law, the second Lady Sekloong, lived in the central structure alone except for twelve servants and their broods. Two other dowagers shared her state, each reigning over her own household in its own wing.

Sarah Haleevie Sekloong was darkly vivacious and still compellingly attractive at sixty-five. Proudly self-assured, the daughter of the most powerful of the four great Iraqi Jewish families that had virtually built modern Shanghai was accustomed to her solitary state. Her husband, Jonathan II, the Matriarch's eldest child, had died in 1945 when a young sergeant-pilot brushed the wingtip of his RAF Dakota against the mountainside

22

that guarded the approach to the old landing strip at Kaitak.

The widow Sarah was revered in Israel for the lavish endowment that maintained the Haleevie-Sekloong Hospital and its attendant research institutes on the slopes of Mount Carmel. She was honored in Hong Kong for the benefactions of the Jonathan and Sarah Foundation. Intelligent distribution of the Foundation's abundant funds had transported the people of eleven villages in the rural New Territories on the mainland from medieval squalor to the era of electric light, modern sanitation, and primary schools. Above all, the Foundation offered those farmers the opportunity to remake their own lives by raising new strains of pigs, chickens, and rice.

Still, Sarah affected an inconsequential light-mindedness that verged on frivolity. She delighted in marathon sessions of Mah-Jongg and bridge to the counterpoint of mildly malicious gossip that spanned the fashionable world. That night, she wore a long aqua dress cut with expensive simplicity by Dior. Her only jewelry was a necklace of massive, square-cut emeralds set with barbaric ostentation in heavy red-gold links.

Beside Sarah in the circular reception hall of The Castle stood the third "dowager empress." She was called simply Opal. She did not know her parents' names, and she was a widow only by courtesy. She was, at forty-six, a statuesque Polynesian goddess in a flowing bronze silk robe splashed with orange hibiscus. Opal had come into Sir Jonathan's bed as the last of his acknowledged concubines in 1939, when she was fifteen and he was fast closing eighty-six. When his yacht visited Tahiti for a long weekend, the Old Gentleman had bought her for $38 from the French official with whom she was living. She had been fiercely devoted to him, and, irrepressible Hong Kong gossip insisted, she had nourished him with her own milk in his senescence.

Opal was obsessively independent, for Sir Jonathan had left her a large trust fund, carefully secured against her compulsive generosity. Having freely transferred

23

her devotion to Sarah and Lady Sekloong, she brooded over the older women's comfort, scolding and cosseting them as if they were her own mother and her grandmother. They, in turn, overlooked her full-blooded amours.

Sarah and Opal waited in the great pink-marble-floored circle of the reception hall. Hand-rubbed teak paneling glowed in the soft light of candelabra, and incense wafted through the central air-conditioning. An embossed blue-and-white carpet covered the broad central staircase that divided at the landing into two arms. Above the fork of the Y hung an intricately curved Chinese character ten feet high. Its sinuous gilt loops invoked the blessing of long life.

The double doors on the landing swung open under the hands of a manservant wearing a white coat, black trousers, and cloth slippers. A couple descended the stairs, reflected in the polished brass of the long-life symbol. The gentleman's left arm was crooked to support the lady's hand, and their slow progress was a miniature royal procession.

Swarthy and stocky in full evening dress, the man wore two rows of medals. They included the American Silver Star and China-Burma-India Service Medal, as well as the British India Star. The jeweled Order of the Phoenix hung from his neck on a rainbow ribbon, while the broad pink-and-pearl sash of a Knight Commander of the British Empire diagonally bisected his starched shirtfront. The Chinese decoration had been conferred by Generalissimo Chiang Kai-shek in 1941, the K.C.B.E. by King George VI in 1947, when its wearer left the post of Ambassador of the Nationalist Republic of China to the Court of St. James's.

He had been christened Thomas Sekloong, but he called himself General Sek Lai-kwok when he executed special missions for his commander-in-chief in exile in Taiwan. As a young lieutenant he had briefly commanded a platoon in action more than forty years earlier. During the following decades he had rarely heard shots fired with intent to kill from a distance of less than twenty-five miles. He was a political general, a

24

diplomat in uniform, adept at maneuvering among rival factions. His devotion to Generalissimo Chiang Kai-shek transcended fanaticism; it was an unquestioning, total commitment.

The General's broad face was flushed with anger, and his arm trembled under his mother's fingers. Though he was sixty-five, the Matriarch could still reduce him to impotent fury with one softly murmured sentence. He had, he knew, never been her favorite. Sometimes he suspected that she actually disliked him.

She had, once again, enraged him by her instructions that evening. His wide eyes, normally placid, smoldered above his broad cheekbones. He was not sure that he could follow his mother's wishes, though his personal credo placed filial obedience above even loyalty to his leader. The General looked down at the small figure beside him with more awe than love in his dark-brown eyes.

The crown of her head was thick with abundant hair drawn back into a soft knot. At ninety, Lady Mary's frost-white hair was her chief vanity; she had delighted inordinately in its flaming red-gold profusion when she was twenty. Her high forehead and wrinkled-petal cheeks were translucent ivory, while her withered-crepe throat was concealed by the high collar of her red-gold-and-green Chinese silk jacket. Three strands of graduated apple-green jade beads strung between diamonds cascaded onto her breast. She still treasured her jewelry, above all the four-inch-square jade plaque carved in bas-relief with the arrogant Sekloong dragon that hung below her necklace. Her loose-cut gown, red-gold-and-green like her jacket, was faced with embroidered strips of mauve asters, each minuscule blossom so realistically embroidered it seemed to shine with dew.

Beneath the finery, she was as fragile as a wax figure, but she was still vain of her small feet and her slender fingers ringed with diamonds and jade. Her gold-embroidered pumps sought each tread with caution. She was an old, old lady, and she strove for decorum. But the majesty of her bearing was dispelled when her eyes

25

sparkled with joy or anger like an eager young child's.

Sarah Haleevie Sekloong stepped forward to claim the Matriarch's right hand, and Thomas happily relinquished his featherweight burden. His mother's violet eyes flashed imperiously to remind him of her wishes.

"Good evening, Mother. A very happy birthday." Sarah spoke with unaccustomed formality as she leaned forward to kiss the crumpled-velvet cheek.

"Good evening, Lady Mary. A hundred more for our sake!" Opal's dark voice still echoed the silver-starred skies over her native isles. She enveloped the frail figure in her strong arms, half-bearing Lady Mary to the black wood chair from which the Matriarch would receive her guests. All Hong Kong—and half the world, it seemed—called her Lady Mary. As the widow of a baronet, she should have been called Lady Sekloong. But the former title was peculiarly her own.

"Good evening, Sarah. Good evening, Opal." Lady Mary, too, spoke with unwonted formality, her high-pitched voice still carrying traces of her North Country origin. "Good evening, girls. But don't wish that on me. I don't think I could bear another ten, much less a hundred. And, for Heaven's sake, don't fuss."

"It's your party, Mother," Thomas reminded her, "and a grand occasion."

"Yes, it is. Perhaps foolish on my part, but we'll go through with it now. If you do something foolish, then go the whole hog."

The ponderous front doors opened to admit a tendril of intrusive fog and a flashing glimpse of the crimson-and-gilt crown that marked the vice-regal Rolls-Royce. The servants' half-bows greeted Sir David Trench, Governor of Hong Kong. His bulky figure was the self-conscious embodiment of the fading grandeur of his sovereign half a world away in London. Runnels of sweat ran down his weathered cheeks, and he eased the stiff collar under his white tie with a spatulate forefinger.

"Good evening, Lady Mary," he said formally. "Her Majesty the Queen has asked me to convey her warm wishes and her admiration. She hopes to see you again in London soon. And may I add our own heartiest congratulations and best wishes for many more?"

"Thank you, David—and Margaret." Lady Mary nodded to Lady Trench. "I shall write the Queen to express my deepest gratitude and loyal devotion. But to old friends—my joyous thanks and my love."

More than practiced charm, the Governor concluded as he had in the past, much more. When she spoke to you, all her mind was fixed on you alone and her every word was deeply felt, whether the words were pleasant or unpleasant. He was relieved by her omitting his title. She had known him since he was a twenty-year-old cadet in the Colonial Service. He would have felt chilled if she had again addressed him formally as "Sir David" because of their continuing argument over the Hong Kong Government's land policy.

"Bunch of thieves you're conniving with," she had snapped at their last meeting. "That lot at Victoria Landholdings are all thieves—always have been. And you're letting them drive land prices up so high, not just the poor, but the middle classes will suffer desperately. Then we'll be for it. Theft, yes, Sir David, theft by all means. Hong Kong's built on theft. But intelligent theft with moderation, if you please, Sir David."

The Governor flushed at the memory as he bowed over her hand. He knew that she was right, and he also knew that he was powerless. He stepped aside in relief when a high-pitched voice called over his shoulder.

"Mother! Mother darling! All our love and so many happy returns."

Charlotte Barakian descended upon Lady Mary, a whirlwind incarnate in a mink stole over an extravagantly draped, pale-green dress. The shock of her *décolleté* slashed almost to the waist was dimmed by the single 112-carat diamond that hung between her breasts on a platinum chain. The Star of Jaipur was her husband's latest and most publicized gift. Gorgeously and unabashedly tinted its original color, her hair flamed red-gold, and she moved with the exuberance of a woman a quarter century younger than her sixty-six years.

As his wife enfolded her mother, Avram Barakian bowed gravely. The shipping magnate was tall, and his dark features were saturnine despite his jutting, aggressive nose. Only his carefully waved white pompadour revealed vanity; with his tailcoat the billionaire wore unadorned black-onyx studs and cufflinks.

"Enough, Charlotte, enough," Lady Mary laughed in mock protest. "We all love you, too. But don't smother me or I'll never see another birthday."

Following the Barakians, Joe Sek, a seedy clerk in a third-rate import-export house, was ill at ease in his mossy-green dinner jacket. Lady Mary offered him a particularly warm smile because she could not recall exactly where the seedy clerk fitted on the convoluted family tree. The poor relation was followed by the rich Seks, Harold and William, twin great-grandsons of the Old Gentleman and his first wife, whom he had married under traditional Chinese law. The twins rivaled the fortune of the main line with wealth accumulated through arms-running, gold-smuggling, and the drug traffic. Behind them bowed Sir Mosing Way, Hong Kong's premier Chinese knight, who was almost as old as Lady Mary herself and serenely dignified in a blue silk long-gown.

Lady Mary held out her arms to her son James, whom the world knew as General Shih Ai-kuo, Deputy Political Commissar of the Communist People's Liberation Army—though Lady Mary would not call him Ai-kuo, she was stirred to pride by his air of distinction, even in the austere, gray-blue tunic.

"We must talk later, James," she whispered when he bent to kiss her. "It's been too many years."

General Shih Ai-kuo's eyes misted. He nodded distantly to his eldest brother, the Nationalist General. Yet James Sekloong, not General Shih Ai-kuo, took his place beside Thomas Sekloong behind their mother's chair. Communist General Shih Ai-kuo contemplated the ceiling when the American Under Secretary of State Spencer Taylor Smith stepped forward, but James Sekloong smiled with unfeigned pleasure at his niece Blanche, the Under Secretary's wife.

The guests were arriving in waves, and the reception hall was filled with a babbling sea of greetings. Lady Mary's memory catalogued each guest automatically, but her thoughts strayed to contemplate the tumultuous panorama of the past. She was still surprised by the size and vigor of the unruly clan she had dominated since the Old Gentleman's death.

The Sekloongs, themselves insecurely straddling two antagonistic worlds, were an unstable compound of arrogance and insecurity, generosity and baseness, talent and mediocrity. Their blood was a volatile mixture of East and West. Though they considered themselves at home in both worlds, some of the elder Sekloongs lived in perpetual unease. The "touch of the tar brush" at which Lady Mary's father had sneered made them alternately uncertain and assertive. But the younger Sekloongs, her grandchildren and her great-grandchildren, gloried in their mixed background. As did their great wealth, their exotic heritage attracted admirers—as well as sycophants, toadies, and spongers. Horrifying to her own contemporaries, their mixed races were attractive to their new milieu. The jet set, she had heard them called. She shuddered delicately at the barbarous term.

The older generation bolstered its self-esteem by pursuing money, fame, and social position; some had even learned that hard-won achievements brought solace. Titles, too, they pursued, decorations, honors, and even notoriety. The Old Gentleman's compulsive drive still animated his descendants, and almost all were avid in their desires.

She had assured herself that her own children would never forget their Chinese heritage. They knew that the Westernized cities of Asia—Hong Kong, Singapore, and Shanghai—had been built by Chinese brains and Chinese brawn. They knew that the Sekloongs had played a decisive role in shaping both those cities and China itself. They uninhibitedly utilized their Chinese connections, skillfully manipulating the network of power and wealth that encompassed not only Asia, but Europe and the United States as well.

The foreigners—the Europeans and the Americans—

were an impermanent force in Asia, and the foreigners felt themselves less secure each day. Almost all finally retired to their own home countries, subtly defeated by Asia. The Sekloongs themselves might some day become superfluous to an aggressively nationalistic and racist Asia. But that day could be long postponed, for they had representatives in all camps.

It had been totally different when she first came to Hong Kong. The white man's rule seemed permanently fixed, while the Asian seemed forever doomed to subjugation. Yet both the proconsuls of the expanding white empires and the Mandarins of the decaying Chinese Empire had been equally arrogant and complacent.

She remembered, and her eyes were soft as morning-dewed violets. Cherished as lovingly as her collection of ivory, jade, bronze, and porcelain figures, her memories, though clear as ever, had acquired luster with the passing years.

She recalled her first landing in Hong Kong seventy years earlier—before The Castle was built, before she had even heard the name Sekloong. She remembered the flurried emotions that bewildered a callow girl, and she saw again the holystoned teak decks of the Peninsular and Oriental Steamship *Orion*.

Part One

Mary

May 28, 1900–December 26, 1900

May 28, 1900

MARY Philippa Osgood was four weeks removed from the twentieth birthday that would, by the rigid standards of the late Victorian era, transform her from a young woman into a spinster. Never during the preceding nineteen years and eleven months had she been as acutely aware of her own body as she was at 8:15 on the morning of May 28, 1900. Dancing across the ruffled Pearl River Estuary, the gusts that swelled the vestigial sails of the *Orion* molded her ankle-length dress to the curves of her bosom, her hips, and her legs.

Before leaving England seven weeks earlier, she had bought a new dress for £5, her Aunt Margaret's generous going-away gift. The motherly wife of the major commanding the home depot of the Royal Wessex Fusiliers had helped her select the long-wearing dark blue serge the Stepney mercers recommended as "eminently suitable for summer." But the "lightweight" fabric was a sackcloth torment in the 92° heat and 93 percent humidity when the *Orion* left the fresh sea air behind on entering the western approaches to Hong Kong.

She had daringly discarded her camisole along with two of her three petticoats, and she wore her lightest stays. The major's wife had confided that the corsets suitable for the English summer could be agonizingly confining in the faraway, subtropical Crown Colony. Nonetheless, Mary was uncomfortably aware of her nipples' swelling under the chafing serge. Perspiration dripped between her full breasts, trickling down to tremble on the secret tendrils of hair that covered the parts she thought of as "the place between my thighs." Though she remembered shameful dreams, she had never known such intense awareness of her body before this voyage. Was this, she wondered uneasily, the spell of the sensuous, sinful East? She was profoundly conscious of being a woman, not only a woman in all her parts, but a white woman surrounded by men of color.

33

Soft-padded fingers grasped her elbow to steady her against the ship's motion with excessive concern, though her own hands gripped the foredeck rail. The pressure was light and deferential, but, she felt in her heightened awareness, somehow predatory. Abruptly, her North Country common sense asserted itself. She laughed at her fancies and brushed back a tendril of red-gold hair. The gesture strained her breasts against the light serge, and her companion caught his breath.

"Miss Osgood, there it is, just over the horizon. You can see the loom against the clouds."

Hilary Metcalfe's deep voice recalled her to a reality different from any she had known. *Orion* was steaming among rocky islets veined with emerald vegetation, which lay upon the wind-brushed sea like meteorites. In the distance on her left a wisp of smoke rose, and a dark shape that might have been a small craft bobbed beneath an elongated, vertical shadow that might have been a sail. She saw no other sign of human life. Yet her nostrils were assailed by unfamiliar odors that swamped the clean tang of the sea: wood-smoke and incense; an unpleasant mustiness and the reek of corruption; a nauseatingly fecal stench and a garlic-laden, many-spiced scent.

"The fragrance of the East, essence of the Orient," Metcalfe rumbled in her ear. "They call it Hong Kong —the Fragrant Port. There's the stench of decay, of course, but mainly the effluvia of the chief Chinese occupation—eating. There's wood-smoke, garlic, coriander, anise, vingear, oyster sauce, dried fish, and barbecued pork. And, over all, dark brown, pungent soy-sauce."

She had learned early in the voyage that Mr. Metcalfe was a pedant. She knew the type well, for she had earned her keep as a governess since her mother's death two years earlier. As she would not a few months earlier, she applied the word to a man who seemed venerable at fifty-six. The journey had taught her that she was quicker, more forceful, and more perceptive than most young women in the sixty-second year of the reign of Her Most Excellent Majesty, Victoria, By the Grace

34

of God of the United Kingdom of England, Scotland, Wales, Ireland, and of Her Other Realms and Territories over the Sea, Queen; Empress of India; Defender of the Faith. She guarded her knowledge of her capabilities, and she could flutter her eyelashes as fetchingly as the most helpless Victorian miss. Besides, she had learned much from Hilary Metcalfe, who was neither patronizing nor importunate. She had also learned that she could bend Metcalfe and the ship's officers to her wishes, not only by feminine guile, but by calm persistence.

"Perhaps the Chinese don't have enough to eat, Mr. Metcalfe," she teased.

"Sometimes, Miss Osgood. But they're devoted, religiously devoted to their bellies—pardon an old man's directness. More than family, more than their gods, more than their Emperor, more than their . . . anything else, they're devoted to their bellies."

"And to nothing else, Sir?"

"I didn't say that. The Chinese're also devoted to gold, and acquire wealth in many devious ways. They'll also labor hard—if they must. They are an ingenious race and a desperately industrious race, when all else fails. But they are also different from all other races."

Hilary Metcalfe paused to formulate his words precisely, straining instinctively to give his best to his eager pupil.

"We have moved slowly over the seas and through the weeks from one pole of civilization to another. The curious sights you saw in the Mediterranean, the Near East, India, and the Straits Settlements were but a gradual transition. You have now arrived at the true Antipodes. Even the Japanese are not more strange."

"How so, Mr. Metcalfe?" she asked.

Orion's captain had told her that the Metcalfes possessed much wealth amassed in the India trade. But Hilary Metcalfe worked as a clerk-interpreter in the Hong Kong trading house of Derwent, Hayes and Company, rather than tending his fortune in fashionable state. His occupation afforded him both opportunity and leisure to study the culture, the history, and the language of the

Chinese. Though he might have taken a swift Peninsular and Oriental mail steamer that guaranteed passage to Hong Kong in just thirty-four days, his eccentricity had led him to sail on *Orion,* which was finally closing port on the fiftieth day after leaving the Pool of London.

Mary had been granted no such choice. The War Office, reluctant to disburse £60 for her passage on *Orion,* had flatly refused to pay a surcharge of ten guineas for a mail steamer. Only the cajoling of the major's wife had spared the lonely girl the rigors of a troopship, since her father was no more than the Bandmaster of the Regiment.

"How," Mary persisted, "are the Chinese different?"

"How?" Hilary Metcalfe echoed her question. "It's not just the claptrap you've heard—men wearing skirts and women trousers, soup at the end of the meal, brides wearing red, mourners wearing white—though all true enough. Their minds are made different . . . antipodean, the other pole from ours. They'll scramble for a handful of coppers today, but disdain to plan to gain a bag of gold tomorrow. Hong Kong was a barren rock before *we* made it the world's third busiest port—soon, perhaps, the second."

Mary gasped in pretty wonder, though she was as much concerned about commerce as the dark side of the moon.

"We had to force the Chinese to trade," Hilary Metcalfe continued, "though they could've made Hong Kong or Canton their own goldmine. But they virtually compelled us to seize Hong Kong. And we get the lion's share. Some don't do badly, too shrewd not to. But the ruling classes, the Mandarins, profoundly despise trade —and despise us too."

Hilary Metcalfe pondered the inner resonance of his own words. The broad head beneath his checked deerstalker cap withdrew like a turtle's into his heavy shoulders. He gestured toward the surrounding islands.

Two objects bobbing on the water caught Mary's eye. One was pale gray, and its swollen curves glittered repellently. The other, equally distended, was a livid black. From each four small posts thrust upright like warped tables abandoned to the sea. She caught her breath, when a rising wave displayed the bloated carcasses of a pig and a dog keeping strange convoy in death.

The horizon was speckled with islands. Some barren gray, others richly green, all seemed to appear from the depths as the broom of the wind dispersed the morning mist. The *Orion* was winding through a narrow channel. On her right two shoe-shaped boats lay on a dun-brown beach. On the left, a cliff loomed on the verge of a large land mass.

"Hong Kong?" Mary asked. "Hong Kong, finally? No, it can't be. It must be China, the mainland, there."

"Neither, Miss Osgood," the Sinologue answered. "That's Lantao, Rocky Mount. It's bigger than Hong Kong, the biggest island. The Portuguese, who settled Macao three hundred and fifty years ago, called these islands the Ladrones—Thieves. They were home for a nest of pirates until we began cleaning them out sixty years ago. Pirates are still about, though they'll not bother us. But these islands are still the Ladrones. The big thieves've driven out the little thieves. Haphazard Chinese theft's given way to organized European theft."

"You sound as if you too hated the English. Do you really despise us?"

"Despise the English, Miss Osgood?" Mr. Metcalfe rallied. "Hardly. It would hardly do to despise myself. We've done fearful deeds here, but we've also done some magnificent things."

"Fearful *and* magnificent things, Mr. Metcalfe?" Mary prompted.

"Yes, both. Hong Kong was a barren, fever-ridden island of a few hundred fishermen and pirates, no more. We made it a great port. But we taught the people to hate us—and to fawn on us. We forced opium on them. The mansions you'll see aren't built on rock, but on the noxious juice of pretty poppies.

"You know, Miss Osgood, at this moment in Peking, the Chinese are rising. The Boxers, we call them. The Righteous Harmonious Society, they call themselves. A devil-worshiping sect that claims esoteric powers is stealthily backed by the Court of the Empress Dowager. The Boxers claim they can't be killed by our bullets. Nonsense, of course. But they know what they want. No nonsense about that. They're sworn to expel us from China. They want our blood."

"Our blood, Sir?"

"Our blood, *your* blood, Miss Osgood. We've forced their hands, forced the Chinese to trade with us when they wanted only to be left alone. We've done so with guns and arrogance, with rapine and destruction and slaughter."

"My father wrote we had to keep the upper hand or they'd be at our throats."

"He's right, perhaps. So most people believe. But why? In part, because we've always kept them apart in Hong Kong, even farther apart than they wanted to keep us in China—the Chinese and the British are two different species, not different races. Between the two —a few Chinese we've won over, a few who cooperate for gain, a few déclassé Portuguese, and some Eurasians . . . mixed bloods, your pardon, Miss Osgood. We've driven the Chinese, but they've done the work. They've sweated to build this British paradise in the Orient."

"You feel very strongly."

"That I do!" Mr. Metcalfe forced a chuckle. "Your father tells you we must keep the upper hand. He'll probably tell you the Chinese all hate us, that we can't trust one of them. He may tell you that a single drop of Chinese blood in a great Eurasian gentleman like Sir Jonathan Sekloong or the promising young man, Robert Hotung, makes him less than a man—neither proper Chinese pagan nor good British Christian.

"But such men have served us well—and served China well. Ten centuries ago, their ancestors were living with civilized grace on the mainland just over there to the north. No hive of bandits, thieves, and pirates, the mainland was a cultivated community. Yet I grow too heated—and there is Hong Kong."

The gray mass on the horizon had resolved into an island studded with irregular hills around a summit

Mary knew was called Victoria Peak to honor the young Queen who had ascended the throne only four years before Hong Kong formally became a Crown Colony in 1842. *Orion* was passing a miniature island with a whitewashed lighthouse on its summit and two small houses clinging to its slopes. It was called Green Island, she knew from the maps she'd studied. On Hong Kong Island itself, rows of hovels built of bamboo, wood, and woven reeds descended in tiers like ramshackle steps to the harbor's edge.

Miniature high-pooped galleons tossed in the white-capped waters. Their tattered sails were crazy-quilts of stained yellow, rusty brown, and faded purple stretched on frail bamboo ribs. She marveled that the fragile patchwork did not shred, but drove the clumsy vessels through the waves. They surged purposefully toward *Orion,* trailing twisted white wakes behind their square sterns.

Orion turned majestically to starboard, and her siren shrieked repeatedly. In Mary's bemused ears the wild ululation sounded both mournful and joyous. The ship was keening her sorrow at the long voyage's end while crying exultant greetings to the goal finally attained.

Mary shuddered involuntarily as the vista of the harbor opened before her. She would, she knew, stay no longer than a year before the Regiment was posted home to England. But her blood throbbed as if she had come to a long-awaited rendezvous in a place that was outlandishly strange, yet redolent with ancient memories. She was, at once, exhilarated and terrified.

"Quite different from what you pictured, but still somehow familiar, isn't it, Miss Osgood?"

Mr. Metcalfe's voice in her ear was almost drowned by the shrieking siren. She looked up half-fearfully at his blunt features dominated by the brooding gray eyes that had uncannily discerned her own feelings.

"I'll leave you now," the deep, gentle voice said. "It's better to see Hong Kong for the first time alone. Please don't forget you can reach me at Derwent's if you can find time from the round of gaiety—or if you need help."

She nodded abstractedly. Why, she wondered, should she possibly need Hilary Metcalfe's help? But the unease evoked by his remark was forgotten when she gazed upon the panorama of Hong Kong.

The harbor was forested with masts: the rope-and-wood tracery of sailing ships' masts crossed by square yards; the blunt masts of steamers; and the light-gray warships' tripod masts like little Eiffel Towers. Multitudes of wooden Chinese junks skittered through that forest under their patchwork sails. The all-pervading medley of odors was already as warmly familiar as the aroma of new-baked bread. For the first time, Mary told herself self-consciously, she knew that she had come to China.

Coolies wearing only flapping black trousers streamed through wide gates into the cavernous warehouses along the waterfront. Mary sensed the tension in the distant bronze figures that bore their burdens on bamboo poles across sweat-filmed shoulders. The scene shimmered in the heat waves rising from the stone pavements.

In the central district, buildings with crenelated façades offered shelter from the harsh sun beneath marquees supported by ornate pillars. Two strolling ladies in flowing dresses were obscured by the artificial gloom beneath the marquees, while white-clad gentlemen strode purposefully. Two signs in English stood out amid a welter of contorted Chinese writing: QUEEN'S BUILDING on the broad front of a four-story structure across the road from the seawall and the familiar legend PENINSULAR AND ORIENTAL.

A narrow path wound up The Peak, still half obscured by the veil of the morning mist. Two cathedrals dominated its lower slopes. The Catholic edifice on the right was mock-Gothic with half-buttresses; the Anglican was austere in its whitewashed simplicity. Between the churches stood a four-square mansion with sweeping steps set amid broad grounds. She recognized it from the photographs she had seen as Government House, the residence of the Governor of the Crown Colony.

Smaller villas dotted the winding roads. Most were white, but some were painted green or pink like those she had seen at Malta. All in all, Hong Kong was reassuringly, familiarly British, despite its faintly Mediterranean air. But the photographs had depicted neither the damp heat—a palpable entity as real as the stone buildings—nor the enveloping, pungent odors.

The anchor chain clattering through the hawse pipe recalled Mary to reality. But she was relieved of the multitude of tasks a journey's end normally entailed. Sweating profusely in a high-collared red uniform with silver facings, a sergeant of the Fusiliers appeared like a devil popping through a trapdoor in a Christmas pantomime. His heavy-featured, florid face and his brass badges were blessedly familiar.

"Miss Osgood?" The sergeant's smile revealed discolored teeth. "Your Dad—pardon, Miss—Bandmaster Osgood presents his compliments. He can't meet you. The band's playing at Government House for the nobs. But I'm told off to look out for you. Sergeant Howells, Miss."

Coolies' bare feet slapped on the white-sanded deck. Mary flinched from the acrid stench of sweat, and her steamer trunk, swaying on a bamboo pole, swung sideways brushing her skirt.

"Hi, there Johnnie, makee slow, makee slow!" Sergeant Howells slashed at the nearer coolie with his bamboo stick. "Damned yellow fellow—you can hurtee Missy."

A broad welt appeared on the bronze back as if a crimson-dipped brush had been drawn across the corded, straining muscles. The coolie did not look up.

"Only language they understand, Miss," the Sergeant grinned. "Lazy lot of buggers—beggin' your pardon, Miss."

At the foot of the gangway a squat boat bobbed. Its canvas awning sheltered wicker chairs, while her steamer trunk and her carpet bags lay on the foredeck. A sturdy woman wearing black trousers and tunic plied the single long oar that extended over the stern. An infant hung in a red sling on her back, its head lolling, and Mary wondered why it did not break its neck. The woman's husband squatted on the foredeck. His head was shaven bare, but a thick braid hung from a patch of hair at the crown.

"Is this a sampan?" she asked. "Is that a queue?"

"Don't rightly know, Miss. Don't rightly know what they call them things. All the Chinamen wears suchlike braids. Damned foolishness. Pigs' tails the men call them. But they could be real tails. They're a bunch of devils—thievin', cunnin' devils. I swear they're not human, not like us, Miss. More like clever monkeys. Can't even speak proper, jabber away like monkeys."

The sampan crabbed alongside a wooden wharf under a sign-board reading: BLAKE PIER. Green-slimed steps led to a dim cavern sheltered from the glaring sun by a peaked roof of woven-straw mats. The ground rocked beneath her feet, and Sergeant Howells caught her arm.

"Easy, Miss, easy!" He soothed her like a fractious mare. "Been a long time on ship. Take a while to get your land legs."

On the pier, coolies with impenetrable faces shifted heavy loads. Dark-lipped mouths emitted high-pitched warnings like the complaints of overburdened camels: "Hoo-hoo! Hoo-hoo!" Chinese women in rusty black bore lighter burdens. Other women shoveled mortar and carried bricks, their faces half-hidden by grimy pennants hanging from crownless circular hats of woven bamboo two feet across. The fetid stench of unwashed bodies made Mary's head reel, and the moist air drenched her clothing.

Oblivious to the tumult, two British clerks in white suits tallied the bales that coolies bore up a rickety plank from a square-built lighter. Chinese gentlemen in blue-cotton long-gowns strolled aloof, their brightly colored paper fans fluttering like captive butterflies before faces glistening with perspiration. Hawkers raucously called attention to wares spread on grass mats: gold jewelry and bright porcelain bowls, black iron pots and gaudy fabrics, umbrellas and walking-sticks, dried fish and heaps of colored spices. A blue-black Indian snatched importuningly at her skirts. When Sergeant Howells flourished his bamboo stick, the hawker drew back.

The Sergeant breasted the throngs as if wading a mountain stream, and Mary followed. Dazzled by the crush of humanity, she halted abruptly and the Sergeant turned.

"What's wrong, Miss?" he asked solicitously. "Tired? You can go it easier in half a mo'."

Mary pointed mutely. A stocky Chinese wearing only short, baggy trousers was hobbling through the crowd. His flat features were distorted with pain, and his shaven head was twisted at a bizarre angle by the three-foot-square wooden collar around his neck. A placard scrawled with black Chinese writing hung on his bare chest. Behind him, a plump Chinese constable in white uniform self-importantly fondled the hilt of his long sword.

"Oh, that!" The Sergeant's good-humored features crinkled in laughter. "That's what they call the cangue. Bloke's a thief—one they caught. Maybe that's what's wrote on that there sign. It's not so bad's what it looks. You'll soon get used to it. Anyway, their own people treat 'em worse. We got to treat 'em rough. Only thing they understand."

She followed the Sergeant into the incandescent sunlight, and the damp heat smote her unprotected head. She closed her eyes against sudden, dizzying blackness and clutched the Sergeant's arm.

"Touch of sun, Miss?" Howells asked. "You'll soon get used to it, too. Where's the blasted chair?"

She barely heard his rough reassurance. Out of the bright-haloed darkness swirling around her, a tableau appeared, dominating all the other sounds, smells, and sights that assailed her senses.

Seven British gentlemen leaned casually on their walking-sticks while a small Chinese photographer craned under the black hood of a boxlike camera on a tripod. At the gentlemen's feet was strewn a row of trussed bundles. Before each bundle a small round packet lay amid red-splashed rubble.

Sergeant Howells whistled, and his ruddy face paled.

"I wouldn't look if I was you, Miss," he advised.

"But what is it, Sergeant? What are those bundles?"

"Pirates, Miss, pirates. They caught 'em trying to pirate a steamcoaster up northways in Bias Bay."

"And—"

"And off with their heads. Only way to stop 'em. Give 'em a quick trial and off with their heads. Same way their own people punish 'em."

"But," she protested, "twelve men executed right here in the center of Hong Kong! And the bodies left lying!"

"To show the others, Miss. These chinks think they can make free with us. Only way to show 'em. They'll leave the bodies there for a week."

He took her arm and gently led her away.

"Beggin' your pardon, Miss. You looked downright funny. I thought you was fallin'. Rough things happen in old Honkers. But here's the chair."

A pair of long bamboo poles lay on the cobblestones, a coolie standing at either end. Between the poles, a seat and a foot-rest hung from ropes like a child's swing.

"Now, if you'll just settle yourself, Miss, they'll carry you along—all comfortable and safe as a kiddie in a pram. Too hot for a lady to walk."

Mary gathered her skirts and gratefully leaned on the Sergeant's arm to step between the poles. She felt the swing-seat rise beneath her and scrabbled to place her feet on the foot-rest. Chanting "Hoo-hoo! Hoo-hoo!" the chair bearers broke into a half-trot, and she was swaying three feet above the ground.

The pendulumlike swing of the chair intensified her nausea at the barbaric execution scene. Striving for composure, she looked around.

Sergeant Howells waved reassuringly from his own chair. She had heard that in Hong Kong a sergeant, even a private, was a privileged being because he was white. In England, the Sergeant would have walked on his own broad feet—and stepped into the roadway to let gentlemen pass. In Hong Kong, he was privileged, one of the white lords of the Orient.

The sedan-chair bearers, she surmised perceptively, ranked above the bare-chested coolies who groaned behind with her luggage. They wore tunics of beige nankeen clasped with cloth frogs, and the Regiment's badge hung from their necks. The trotting legs, bare beneath short trousers, were corded with taut muscles over knobby bones. At each step, swollen purple veins writhed like snakes beneath dark skin.

Mary's white-knuckled hands gripped the poles in fear, but she ventured a wider glance. The broad street ended at a white clock tower, its hands showing thirty-three minutes past twelve. The chair bearers turned a corner, and she was thrown to the left. They resumed their steady trot down a road sheltered by spreading trees. Red-painted rickshaws lined the curb, their green oilcloth hoods raised against the sun. Some rickshaw pullers scooped rice into their mouths from small bowls with short sticks. Most squatted between the shafts like dray horses awaiting the crack of the driver's whip.

Mary shuddered, acutely, viscerally aware that those men were beasts of burden—and that she herself was being carried by human beings. Her tumultuous arrival had obscured that abhorrent reality, as had Sergeant Howell's breezy assumption that all Chinese were lesser beings divinely appointed to carry superior beings like herself.

She suppressed the impulse to bid the chair bearers to set her down. It was so hot she might truly faint if she walked. The chair bearers, she consoled herself, were accustomed to the climate and had freely chosen to earn their living by such demeaning labors. Only fifty or sixty years earlier, ladies had been carried through the streets of London itself in sedan chairs. She must go slowly, as her father had warned her. "Nothing is considered more ludicrous," he had written in his stilted manner, "than the horror of the newcomer at the established ways of the Colony. And nothing is more futile than his feeble attempts to set things to rights according to his lights by dictating to the old inhabitants who have built Hong Kong and established its proper customs."

Resolutely, Mary turned her gaze to buildings, at once reassuringly familiar and piquantly exotic. The upper stories extended over the footpath to provide a shaded promenade. Across one façade, she noted with pleasure in the familiar, was painted: QUEEN'S DISPENSARY. But deep open drains extended alongside the roadway, and pedestrians crossed to the footpaths on precarious wooden planks.

The yellow-brown faces of the passersby were faintly menacing, and their clothing was extraordinary. Black-trousered maidservants trotted intently along the footpaths, their long pigtails flopping rhythmically against their white jackets. Chinese ladies in calf-length tunics over loose, purple-embroidered pantaloons swayed past a pillared gray-stone building carved with the legend COURTS OF LAW. Their gait was mincing, and their embroidered slippers were no larger than an English three-year-old's. Those slippers must encase "golden lilies," the miniature club-feet produced by the barbarous custom of female foot-binding she had read about.

The chair bearers were slowed by the incline before a parade-ground dominated by a square, dun-colored building with shaded balconies encircling its upper stories. Soldiers in the Fusiliers' new khaki undress uniforms were just breaking ranks to disperse into stone-built barracks, fanning themselves with white solar topees. Threading a lane between the bungalows like the married officers' quarters at the Regiment's depot in England, the chair bearers finally halted. The white-painted front of the bungalow bore a small sign: J. P. OSGOOD, BANDMASTER.

"Well, here we are, Miss," Sergeant Howells boomed as she disentangled herself from the sedan chair. "Home, sweet home, at last. Mr. Osgood says he'll be along this afternoon—early as he can. But that luncheon could go on to late afternoon. Fearsome lot they eat and drink here, the nobs."

"Thank you, Sergeant," she answered, coolly discouraging his familiarity.

"Well, Miss, I'll just see the coolies get your boxes

into the house and then leave you to rest. Old Ah Sam'll look after you. He's Number One Boy. Used to be a pirate, they say. But he's reformed now—maybe saw some snick-snack as light near the pier and re-formed chop-chop."

A burly figure wearing a white, high-collared jacket and black trousers stood in the doorway. His round face was twisted into a fearsome grimace that displayed a treasure-vault of gleaming gold teeth. He was, she re-alized after her instinctive, fearful recoil, smiling broadly, and he was at least fifty if the lines in his brown cheeks and the grizzled stubble on his shaven head told true. But his thick queue was jet-black and shining with pomade.

Its windows shaded with bamboo screens, the bunga-low's dim interior was a delightfully cool refuge. The furniture, she noted, was primarily light wicker. But a mahogany sideboard bore an array of English crockery, and the light of familiar oil lamps flickered through ponderous glass-beaded shades. Above the fireplace hung her father's favorite picture, Landseer's *Stag at Bay*. With unanticipated nostalgia, she sniffed the pun-gent scent of his Bulldog pipe tobacco. The reassuringly familiar odor mingled with the dank mustiness that seemed to pervade the Colony.

"Come long this way, Missy," the Number One Boy said in a curious sing-song parody of English. "Master say come back by 'n' bye. But I makee you very fine curry tiffin."

"Thank you, Ah Sam," she smiled, speaking for the first time to one of the strange denizens of Hong Kong. "I'll just wash first."

She had, she reflected wryly, come home, though home was ten thousand miles from England.

July 22, 1900

THE bone-handled knife sliced through the two-inch beefsteak, and crimson rivulets puddled on the coarse

47

white plate. Bandmaster John Philip Osgood smugly inspected the singed chunk impaled on his fork before popping it into his mouth. Blood stained his fox-red mustache, but his napkin remained crumpled on the table. He drained a bumper of claret and belched contentedly.

"Nothing like a good breakfast to set you up in this devilish climate."

Mary Philippa Osgood sipped her tea pale as straw, and fought off nausea. Even tea with milk and sugar was too rich in the moisture-drenched, mid-July heat of the bungalow's cramped dining room. Mesmerized by revulsion, she watched her father's fox-furred fingers manipulate the knife and fork. Having already devoured a papaya, he was avidly consuming a pound of steak and a half dozen kidneys. Washed down with two pints of claret, that was his accustomed breakfast.

At seven in the morning she herself could barely face a boiled egg and a piece of toast. After almost two months in Hong Kong, she found the climate exhausting; the thermometer hovered in the high nineties and the humidity inexorably kept pace. The light cotton wrapper over her nightdress was stifling. She had tossed almost all night under the tentlike mosquito net, sleeping briefly and awakening periodically between sheets sodden with perspiration.

"You're looking peaky, Mary," her father observed. "No . . . female problems?"

His ponderous delicacy irritated her. She assumed that she loved the heavy-set, insensitive man whose incongruous passion for music had brought him to his present impasse. Otherwise, why should she have undertaken the long, wearying journey to the end of the world? She suspected, but could not fully acknowledge to herself, that she had been moved not so much by love of her father as by the bleak prospects she faced in England. She could no more tell him that she detested the climate, which left him untouched, than she could admit that the lure—and the hope—of the unknown, rather than filial affection, had drawn her to Hong Kong.

"No, Father, I'm fine," she answered. "But it was hard getting to sleep. I'm a bit tired."

"Um . . . takes some getting used to, this climate. It's harder for the ladies, I suppose."

At forty-six, John Osgood was almost as totally ignorant of the female character as he had been at sixteen. Mary had no sisters, and her parents had not lived together since she was two and her brother Thomas a year older. Her mother had flatly refused to join her father on overseas postings. He had been an occasional visitor, rather than a husband or parent.

"Don't worry, Father. The climate's wearing, but Hong Kong *is* fascinating. I'm so glad I came."

"Well, that's good. But what's all that fascinating?"

"Everything's different and fascinating—but mostly the people."

"Now, see here, Mary. You mustn't get mixed up with the chinks. Don't mind your dabbling in chink painting; that's ladylike enough. But this learning chink talk—I don't like it."

He slapped down his knife and fork emphatically. Their ends were propped on his plate, and their bone handles dribbled gravy onto the cheap lace tablecloth. Mary winced at the clatter and immediately reproached herself for a priggish snob. Coarse table manners did not reveal a man's true nature. Besides, she reflected bitterly, fine manners were superfluous in the circles her father frequented—and would always frequent.

"And another thing, my girl. Your mother was a lady all right. Her father was a schoolteacher, not a poor greengrocer like mine. But your mother knew her place —didn't get above herself. You're flying high, too high. You may come down with a bump."

Mary suppressed rebellious irritation. When her father was excited, his native Yorkshire tones thickened. "Coom doon wi' a boomp," he'd said. She knew his lower-middle-class accent shouldn't annoy her so, but she would not allow him to dictate to her. She placated him with a smile, carefully measuring her geniality to avoid fanning his anger.

49

"It's only Mr. Metcalfe, Father. Tea with his sister . . . and some officers."

"Exactly what I mean. Yon Metcalfe's a nob . . . an odd sort of nob, but an important man in the Colony in his own strange way. Pots of lolly, he has. I don't like you getting above yourself. After all, I've a father's responsibility."

"I'll be good, Father." She had learned how to manage men even more irascible than her testy parent. "I won't push myself forward."

Partially mollified, Bandmaster John Osgood tucked his solar topee under his khaki-clad arm, reverently lifted the baton that was his badge of office, and strode heavily through the minuscule front hall. For three minutes after he had vanished into the heat haze of the parade-ground, the strings of glass beads hanging in the doorway to deter flies chuckled their farewell.

Mary meditatively took up her teacup. Mercifully, her father was lunching at the Warrant Officers' Mess, and she need not again cajole him into letting her have her own way. After breakfast, she would bathe, then dress in the cool dimity and brief undergarments that were acceptable in the Hong Kong summer, though she still felt half-naked in that attire. After lunch, Mr. Wong would come by to teach her Chinese painting and the Cantonese dialect. Her father called him "that fancy old chink." She herself addressed him as *Sin-sang*, "Teacher," though Ah Sam, the Number One Boy, hovering in elaborately casual chaperonage, frowned his puzzlement.

When Mr. Wong left, she would stroll through the relative coolness of the late afternoon to the Metcalfes' small house on Upper Wyndham Street. The Colony was already a substantial city. Some fifteen thousand Britons and other "foreigners," chiefly Eurasians, Indians, and Portuguese, lived among a quarter of a million Chinese. But essential *British* Hong Kong—those who really mattered—was a village of no more than five hundred. The Metcalfes mattered.

Nothing, Mary thought, could be more respectable and homey than the Metcalfes' house, despite her father's admonitions. Elizabeth Metcalfe was a plump and comfortable spinster, a few years younger than her brother. Her only eccentricity was the numerous strings of rose quartz, lapis lazuli, and onyx necklaces that cascaded onto her massive bosom, where they jangled like the glass beads in the Osgoods' doorway. Her only passion was her brother. She chided him "for failing to use your intellectual gifts fully and for failing to take our proper place in society." The Metcalfe name and the Metcalfe fortune would open every door, she complained, every important door from Bombay to Peking, but he was content to serve Derwent, Hayes and Company as a "kind of glorified Oriental secretary." She meant, of course, every important European's door, for Miss Elizabeth Metcalfe was outwardly a model of propriety.

Walking among the glowing marigolds, asters, and dahlias displayed in the street stalls, Mary smiled. Her father would, she imagined, disapprove of Elizabeth Metcalfe—should they ever meet. She was beyond question a "real lady" by his standards, but she was also an "educated lady," a type he abhorred. There was, he had observed, too much "high-falutin' argy-bargy" in the Metcalfe household that had become her refuge, "too much worryin' about the chinks."

Mary's pleasure in the gorgeous colors of the banked blossoms was diminished by a vague feeling that something was amiss. The flowers, she realized abruptly, gave off only the faintest aroma. Half their number would have overwhelmed with their fragrance in England, but these Oriental blooms were almost scentless. The earth tilled so intensively for so many centuries had long ago yielded almost all its abundance. It was exhausted by producing color alone.

"Come in, my dear," Miss Metcalfe welcomed her. "Hilary'll be down in a minute. I believe you know Captain French and Lieutenant Williams."

"Servant, Ma'am," Captain French drawled, his exaggerated bow almost tumbling his gold-rimmed monocle onto the golden Tientsin carpet.

"Good afternoon, Miss Osgood," Lieutenant Williams bubbled. "I'm delighted to see you."

The officers were at ease in cream linen suits. The light fabric was a concession to the climate, though the unshakable complacency of the British Army in the waning days of the reign of the great Queen Empress insisted that no officer wear uniform off duty. But the formality of the age required them to imprison their throats in high, stiff shirt collars even when they doffed their jackets for the picnics attended by dozens of servants that were a principal diversion of late Victorian Hong Kong.

The British Army was itself suspended between the nineteenth and the twentieth centuries. The moral and practical lessons of the Crimean disaster forty years earlier were, at that moment, being reiterated by Britain's gory bumbling on the South African veldt. But few officers' minds ranged beyond the parade-ground, the grouse moor, and the ballroom. Lord Jackie Fisher was remaking the Royal Navy, and even the Army was reluctantly acknowledging the necessity for efficient staff work and an effective logistical apparatus. Though the purchase of commissions had been abolished in 1860, the social criteria for rank and promotion remained virtually unchanged. The inborn arrogance of the British ruling class, who were the corps of officers, had been further reinforced by victories in tribal wars on the frontiers of the Empire. The Hong Kong Garrison believed itself an invincible unit of the best army that had ever marched across the world. The officers knew beyond a doubt that a platoon of British soldiers could disperse a full regiment of the Chinese Emperor's gaudily clad "Braves." That judgment was not wholly wrong, though irregular "commandos" of hard-riding farmers were humiliating the flower of the British Army in South Africa. The primitively armed Chinese troops were far less effectively trained and even worse led than the maltreated British infantryman. Yet the Chinese officers, like their British counterparts, were totally convinced of their own superiority, the convictions of both

52

not merely unshaken, but untouched by cruel experience.

Mary had been fascinated by the extreme differences between the two young officers since first meeting them at the Metcalfes'. Captain Lord Peter Comyn FitzHubert French, equinely handsome with sleeked-down black hair, epitomized the British officers' hauteur. He wore his well-cut suit with negligent grace, and his manner blended languid formality with casual arrogance—more like a slim Regency buck than a man of the new twentieth century.

Lieutenant John Williams was awkward in a suit cut with more concern for economy than style, and his blond hair bristled under its coating of pomade. At six foot two he towered over his superior's elegant figure by four inches, but he was gauche beside that self-assured prig of the aristocracy.

A son of the lower-middle class, Lieutenant Williams was one of the new officers the British Army was hesitantly commissioning—after repeated near disasters salvaged by the stolid bravery of the British private soldier and the rough ingenuity of the British noncommissioned officer, both as often Scots or Irish as English. He had won his commission by gaining a place at the Royal Military Academy at Sandhurst through merit. Even the Royal Wessex Fusiliers looked askance at such qualifications, and the Fusiliers did not stand high in the Army's social hierarchy.

Worse, John Williams lived on his pay or, at any rate, tried. Hong Kong expected every officer to maintain a household staffed with at least six servants who could, at an hour's notice, provide a seven-course dinner for twenty-four with the appropriate wines and liqueurs. Fortunately, the Chinese money-lenders were accommodating, and Williams escaped the fatal charge of cheese-paring. But he winced when he contemplated his debts.

Mary knew of the Lieutenant's difficulties from the gossip that continuously circulated through the Colony's small European community by "bamboo telegraph"—

though she was denied entry to the upper reaches inhabited by the ladies of generals, colonels, senior civilian officials, and directors of the great trading companies, the *hongs*. Besides, her father had forthrightly sketched the prospects and the characters of both officers before warning her to see them infrequently or, better, not at all. As always, the Warrant Officers' Mess knew more about the Regiment's officers than did the Regiment's colonel.

Lieutenant John Williams might himself become a lieutenant-colonel some day—if he was lucky. He would always be pressed for cash, and he would never be fully accepted by all his brother officers. Her father had pronounced the final verdict: "Too much schooling, too little breeding—and a bad seat on a horse." There was little else to say.

Captain Lord Peter French was a bird-of-passage in both Hong Kong and the Royal Wessex Fusiliers. He was serving out a term of banishment from his own regiment, the elite Coldstream Guards. He was the younger son of the sixth Marquess of Langweyten; the first Marquess, a country baron, had been elevated when his sister was briefly mistress to King Charles II. Lord Peter would undoubtedly attain the rank of major general and a knighthood—unless he was most unlucky. With a touch of good fortune, he would end his career as a full general, endowed with a peerage of his own.

Meanwhile, he was enjoying the limited diversions of the Colony. When he had done penance for his indiscretions, he would return to London to mount ceremonial guard on his Sovereign. He was eager to taste again the delights of the metropolis, which offered the most deliciously depraved pleasures of an age remarkably dissolute behind its granitic façade of respectability. Only the "damned prudishness" of his father and his colonel, Lord Peter complained, had required his exile. Goaded beyond the patience inspired by recollections of his own youthful escapades, the sixth Marquess had refused to settle his son's gambling debts, some £7,000.

"I've bailed out the puppy for £24,000," he swore. "Let him wait and sweat it out hard in Hong Kong for a while."

Amid the whaleboned respectability commanded by the aged widow on the throne, the Army made its own rules, as did the self-indulgent aristocracy and the New Bohemians. The rigid conventions of Victorian society were observed chiefly by the middle classes. The colonel of the Coldstream Guards was, therefore, normally tolerant of his young officers' pranks. But his tolerance had been strained beyond immediate forgiveness when Captain French smuggled two prostitutes in transparent tights into the wild hilarity of a regimental guest night. Too many outsiders were present. Lord Peter was offered the alternatives of resigning his commission or secondment to Hong Kong until the scandal cooled. He had astonished both his father and his colonel by choosing temporary exile.

Mary Osgood warmed to both young men—against her own good sense and in defiance of her father's heavy-handed good counsel. They were a pair of endearing puppies: John Williams a clumsy, loving St. Bernard; Lord Peter a high-strung, mischievous pointer. The big, blond lieutenant was as comfortingly familiar as her brother's school friends. The slender, witheringly self-assured captain offered a dazzling glimpse of the aristocratic milieu she would never have seen on even remotely equal terms in England. She greeted them with a smile that was just a shade too warm.

Hilary Metcalfe hurtled into the parlor, shattering the light social chatter and rattling the delicate teacups. His entrance stirred the humid air more than did the fringed punkah that swayed from the molded ceiling when the small, Chinese boy half-dozing outside remembered to pull its string. The green plush horsehair sofas, the geometrically patterned Chinese rug, and the deeply carved ebony tables all seemed to tremble.

"Afternoon, Miss Osgood—French—Williams," he boomed. "Have you heard? Li Hung-chang's in the Colony. Supposed to meet Kang Yu-wei. Sun Yat-sen may turn up too."

55

Languidly astonished, Lord Peter contemplated the older man's excitement through his polished eyeglass.

"Li Hung what?" he asked. "And Kong? Kong? Sound like a firm of rice merchants and a brass band. Who are these fellows, Metcalfe?"

"Can they call off the Boxers, Mr. Metcalfe?" John Williams asked. "Will we be too late? You know the Regiment's alerted to sail for Peking."

"Well past time we took a hand," Lord Peter added. "That German fellow who's usurped command hasn't arrived yet, and the others are dithering. Even *this* regiment could disperse those howling savages around the Legation Quarter in fifteen minutes!"

"You're quite an expert, French, even if you don't know the name of the most important man in China—Li Hung-chang," Hilary Metcalfe exploded. "It'll take more than the sight of the Fusiliers to disperse the Boxers—not to speak of the Imperial troops and the fierce Moslem cavalry."

"I say, Sir," Williams protested. "Surely any well-armed, well-disciplined modern troops could cope with that rabble, however fierce."

"Tell me, Mr. Metcalfe," Mary quickly interposed, "who is Li Hung-chang, and what would he want here with—with—you said Kang Yu-wei? I know Sun Yat-sen's the rebel who was released from imprisonment in the Chinese Legation on Portland Place. But it's all so confusing."

Metcalfe's gray eyes glinted, and his sister observed plaintively: "Hilary's on his hobby-horse again."

"Sun Yat-sen, you know, wants a republic." His irritation forgotten, Metcalfe was eagerly didactic. "He's determined to overthrow the Empire, thinks it's rotten beyond redemption. Besides, he's American-educated. Wants to make China a modern nation. I assume even Lord Peter's heard of Sun Yat-sen."

"Not really, Mr. Metcalfe," the Captain drawled.

"Do go on, Sir," Lieutenant Williams urged. "We should know about them to fight the rotters."

"I *shall* go on." Metcalfe's vigorous recital rode over the antagonism between the young officers. "Li Hung-

56

chang is the Viceroy of Canton and China's greatest statesman. He likes the Boxer Uprising no more than you or I. He's a reasonably loyal servant of the Empress Dowager, and he thinks it's a disaster for the Empire. Besides, he knows Chinese troops are no match for the European and Japanese forces."

"And Kang Yu-wei, Mr. Metcalfe?" Mary persisted.

"Now there's an interesting chap, Mary . . . Miss Osgood. A great scholar, one of the last great Confucian scholars. But a man of today. The Empress Dowager sent him packing in '98 after he talked the young Emperor into decreeing major reforms. The old lady locked the Emperor up, and Kang Yu-wei was sentenced to death. Took refuge right here. Almost all forward-looking Chinese've fled to Hong Kong or Shanghai one time or another."

"And so the Boxers?" John Williams prompted.

"And so the Boxers, Lieutenant! A band of wild fanatics who think they're immune to shot and shell. Called Boxers from their shadow-boxing exercises before battle and their own boastful name: Righteous Fists. Encouraged by the Empress Dowager, who believes she can drive all the foreigners from China. That's why the Queen's Minister, Sir Claude MacDonald, along with more than two thousand others, including scores of ladies, are cooped up in the Legation Quarter under siege—eating horses, camels, and donkeys. They may be eating rats by the time the brave soldiery gets a move on—if they're eating at all."

Mary shuddered, and Miss Metcalfe interjected: "Hilary, you're being crude. And you're exaggerating."

"Devil me if I am, Liz," Metcalfe retorted. "The irony is Li Hung-chang hopes our estimable Governor, Sir Henry Blake, will hinder his going north. Li doesn't want to get directly involved, but thinks he and Kang Yu-wei could contrive a compromise here to save the Manchu Dynasty—and the Empire.

"But Sir Henry's been told to pass the Viceroy through quickly. Whitehall doesn't want to mix in internal Chinese politics. As if we weren't already embroiled —with our missionaries slaughtered, our diplomats

57

under siege, and our troops marching on Peking with traditional British pluck . . . and traditional British sloth."

"The damned niggers are holding things up," Lord Peter interjected. "An eight-nation force, Japs, wops, frogs, and what all. It'll never work, you know."

"I hear, Sir—" John Williams ignored the interruption—"that Government fears disturbances in the Colony. It's reported Sun Yat-sen and Kang Yu-wei are raising men in South China for a new rising against the Manchus and collecting funds from wealthy Hong Kong Chinese."

"Disturbances, twaddle," Metcalfe exploded. "Three posters bravely demanding: EXPEL THE BRITISH! RESTORE THE GLORY OF THE CHINESE EMPIRE! It needs more than posters to incite riots—just yet. But later!"

He hunched his head into his shoulders like a great sea turtle.

"Hong Kong *will* erupt if the Boxers massacre the diplomats—or the Allied forces take Peking and massacre thousands of Chinese. Then you'll see your Hong Kong disturbances—full-fledged, gory riots. Best way out is encouraging Kang Yu-wei and Li Hung-chang to put their heads together. But London, in its wisdom, thinks we can wash our hands of internal Chinese politics. Might as well stick our heads in the sand while we're at it. At least it'll keep our ears warm and unsullied—though the part sticking up might get singed."

"Hilary," his sister remonstrated, "your language!"

"Are we really in danger, Mr. Metcalfe?" Mary asked.

"Not just yet, Mary . . . Miss Osgood. But we will if we don't act sensibly. You see—"

"Hilary," Miss Metcalfe interrupted firmly, "you're frightening Miss Osgood. Gory politics are no more fit for young ladies' ears than your language. And here's Mrs. Wheatley."

An elongated woman in her late fifties swept into the parlor. Her sallow, scaly skin was drawn taut over sharp cheekbones; her bony nose was a parrot's beak; and her small black eyes were reptilian dull, the left squinting through a disfiguring purple birthmark. The splendor of her mauve silk dress attempted to compensate for nature's unkindness. The confection was pinched tight at the waist to thrust out a meager bosom, while the inadequacy of her scrawny hips was accentuated by rows of pink braid draped around a bustle of jutting immensity last seen in England in the mid-1880's.

"Rachel, may I present Miss Osgood?" Elizabeth Metcalfe said. "Lord Peter and Lieutenant Williams I believe you know. Mary . . . Miss Osgood . . . may I introduce you to the Honorable Rachel Wheatley? As you know, Mr. Wheatley is *taipan* of Derwent, Hayes."

"Miss Osgood." The Honorable Mrs. Wheatley inclined her head minutely. "Lord Peter, how terribly nice to see you again. Good afternoon, Lieutenant."

"Miss Osgood's father is with the Regiment, Rachel," Miss Metcalfe said. "She's just arrived. We find her charming and hope to make her stay in Hong Kong very pleasant."

"Osgood? Osgood?" The thin lips mused. "I have not had the pleasure of his acquaintance. Your father—a major at least to have such a grown-up daughter—is he also a new arrival, Miss Osgood?"

"No, Mrs. Wheatley," Mary answered. "He's been here for some time."

"Mr. Osgood is the Bandmaster," Miss Metcalfe explained, "whose music gives us so much pleasure."

"Oh, I see," pursed lips acknowledged. "Tell me, Hilary, do you fear that demonstrations and violence will mar the visit of His Royal Highness?"

Mary's heart shriveled. Her precarious self-confidence was shattered by three icy syllables. She had been casually snubbed in the past, but she had never suffered such a brutal dismissal. The grotesque woman whose husband controlled Hong Kong's chief *hong* would not even acknowledge her existence.

The Metcalfes had, perhaps, been too kind. Perhaps, as her father warned, she had been flying too high in Hong Kong's caste-obsessed society. In the anachronistic Crown Colony, the distance between the consort of

59

the leading man of commerce and the daughter of a warrant officer was almost as great as the distance between herself and a rickshaw coolie. Taking refuge behind downcast eyelashes, she feared she was indeed "coomin' doon wi' a boomp."

The visit of His Royal Highness Prince William, Duke of Gloucester, grandson of the old Queen Empress, could have only one effect on her own life. She would see her father even less frequently. The Regimental Band would parade for the twenty-six-year-old Prince and would play at splendid balls and receptions. *She* would be invited to none—certainly not to the grand ball at Government House. Though presentable unmarried young ladies were few in Hong Kong, she was not a young lady in the eyes of the Honorable Rachel Wheatley. She was a "young person."

Anger at the scarecrow woman's arrogance overcame Mary's practical discretion.

"Certainly," she smiled brightly, "no trivial political disturbances could possibly mar the Prince's visit. We must keep a sense of proportion. A few Chinamen carrying on in their normal barbarous fashion—so unlike the cultivated British!"

Mrs. Wheatley ignored Mary's words as she would a beggar's whining, but Elizabeth Metcalfe cast her a troubled glance. She was hurt by the open snub her protégée had suffered, and she was dismayed by Mary's pertness.

"No, Rachel, Miss Osgood's right." Hilary Metcalfe cast the radiance of his goodwill over Mary's dejection. "You can rest easy. No serious disturbances quite so soon. You'll certainly enjoy your big balls."

Mary blushed at his crudeness, though it was employed in her defense. She rose and gathered her skirts.

"I'm afraid I must leave now." She forced a smile. "Thank you so much, Miss Metcalfe. Good-bye, Lord Peter, Lieutenant Williams. It's been a unique pleasure, Mrs. Wheatley."

The reptilian eyes flickered, but the Honorable Rachel Wheatley's thin lips remained pursed.

"Come back soon, Mary," Hilary Metcalfe grinned. "You're a joy, a ray of sunshine in this gloomy place."

"Yes, do," Elizabeth Metcalfe echoed dutifully.

To Mary's surprise, Lieutenant Williams also rose.

"Miss Osgood," he asked formally, "may I see you home?"

The blond officer's good-humored gray eyes glowed in unaccustomed anger, and his fair cheeks were flushed as they left the small house together. He took a nosegay of asters from a young flower seller and dropped a ten-cent coin into a grubby hand.

"May I give you these, Miss Osgood? They're pretty little flowers, I think."

Mary murmured her thanks, astonished at John Williams's challenging the power of the Honorable Rachel Wheatley embodied by seeing her home. The *taipan*'s wife had the ear of the General Officer Commanding, and John Williams had his way to make. It was a rocky way for a young officer who possessed neither influence nor wealth. Yet he had chosen to make a powerful enemy on her behalf. She had, of course, noticed that John Williams was "castin' sheeps' eyes," as her father said. Did he, she wondered, feel more than the kind of interest aroused by any young woman who was neither outstandingly homely nor intolerably shrewish in a community where young bachelors outnumbered unmarried young women by twenty to one? She herself liked him well enough, but that was all. Yet she could easily grow to like him much better if she did not restrain herself.

"That woman's a menace, a nasty, rude old trout," John Williams erupted. "I'm terribly sorry."

"Thank you, Lieutenant," Mary replied. "You're very kind."

They strolled down the hill toward Queen's Road Central in awkward, embarrassed silence. Despite John Williams's kindness, Mary was still raging at the Honorable Rachel Wheatley's snub. Her unappeased anger searched for an appropriate vengeance. But she was, she knew, a cipher in Hong Kong, a powerless nonentity who could no more strike back at the lofty Mrs. Wheatley than she could permit herself to become fond of the penniless Lieutenant Williams.

"Miss Osgood," John Williams gulped, "Mary . . . if I may?"

"Mary, please. Better than Miss Osgood, less like a governess."

If John Williams was not smitten by her, he was obviously very much interested. His gauche approach was endearing, and she warmed to him.

"Mary," he stammered, "I don't—don't quite know how to say—but—"

"Yes, John?"

She was intrigued. They had known each other no more than a month, having taken tea together in the Metcalfes' parlor three times and chatted when they met on the parade-ground. Elsewhere his bashful preliminaries might presage a proposal of marriage that would not be wholly unwelcome, though he was hardly her heart's desire. In topsy-turvy Hong Kong, his clumsy approaches could presage—what? She simply did not know. They could presage almost anything. Still, a scheme was forming in her own mind. She was, after all, fond of him, and all the young officers were bidden to the Governor's Ball for Prince William. The ladies of the inner circle and, above all, their daughters required dancing partners.

"Mary, I'd like to—to see more of you."

"John, I'm flattered. And I am fond of you, too. But it's so difficult in Hong Kong."

"Difficult? I don't understand."

"It's difficult for us, the Bandmaster's daughter and a commissioned officer. You do see, don't you? There are so few opportunities with propriety."

"Blast propriety!"

"We can't really, can we? Neither of us."

"I suppose not," he conceded glumly.

"Of course, there is . . . but, no, it's impossible."

Mary put her words forward as skillfully as a chess player advancing his key pieces. Her scheme was fully shaped. In archaically caste-conscious Hong Kong attending the Royal Ball would automatically elevate her social position. Her presence at John's own invitation, though itself unorthodox, would create the circumstances under which they could meet with propriety and would, simultaneously, pay off the insufferable Mrs. Wheatley. She felt no compunction at using his newly awakened sympathy for her to attain a purpose they both desired.

"What," he pressed, "were you thinking?"

"Just that there is a way. But I couldn't—"

"Whatever it is, I'm sure you could. Do tell me, Mary."

"It's too much, John, really. But the Governor's Ball. If, somehow, I were invited, then there'd be no problem —no difficulty in our seeing each other."

"Capital idea. But how?"

"I don't know, John. I just don't know."

"Of course!" he exclaimed. "You'll come with me."

"But the Colonel and the officers' wives. What would they . . . ?"

"Blast the Colonel and the wives. Mary, you must come with me."

Having precipitously gained her end, she was momentarily abashed. She thought first of her father's anger and next of the inescapable complications. John Williams would be embarrassed by squiring the daughter of the man on the bandstand. She would herself invite snubs beside which Mrs. Wheatley's iciness might appear cordial. But she replied recklessly.

"Yes, John, I will. I'd love to go with you."

"Oh, Mary," he blurted, "that's splendid."

Perhaps he was already regretting his impulsive invitation. But, she reflected coolly, she must leave that concern to his own conscience. She had received a normal invitation from an attractive young man, and she had accepted with normal grace. And she desperately wanted to dance at the Governor's Ball. Her immediate problem, she concluded practically, was twofold: wheedling a suitable ballgown from tight-fisted John Philip Osgood and placating his wrath.

John Williams left her at the glass-beaded doorway after clasping her hand in both his own.

Her father was out again. After dinner, as she prepared for bed, Mary wondered idly how he spent his evenings—and was fleetingly ashamed of her curiosity. The Chinese merchants who catered to the band constantly pressed invitations upon the Bandmaster, and he accepted most. Their hospitality was, she suspected, not limited to sumptuous banquets laved with claret and brandy, but was capped by visits to the flower boats in Causeway Bay.

Hilary Metcalfe had told her forthrightly that the girls on those floating bordellos were normally no younger than twelve and no older than eighteen. After repaying the proprietors who bought them from impoverished parents, most accumulated a small dowry and married respectable farmers or artisans who accepted their past and their dowries without recrimination. A fortunate few would be taken by wealthy merchants— as concubines or even as second or third wives. "Some," Metcalfe had explained, "stay in the game because they like it. In time, they can become entrepreneurs who buy lucky young country girls out of toil and privation. The system is more humane and less hypocritical than Europe. There are no *ruined* girls." Respectable—even respected—prostitution and the equally respectable—even honored—opium trade. Perhaps she already knew too much about Hong Kong.

Mary twisted on the hard bed under the tentlike mosquito net. Sleep was repelled by both the stifling humidity and her agitated memories of the day. Her restless thoughts passed to British Hong Kong's stratified social structure and her own place—or lack of any place—within the rigid framework. The stern realism instilled by her lonely upbringing told her that she was an embarrassment to the Crown Colony's prim matriarchy.

A half-century earlier, the rise of the new manufacturing and professional classes had breached traditional social barriers in England. The breezy permissiveness of the embryonic Edwardian era was at that moment

64

shaking their foundations. Yet Hong Kong had not merely preserved, but had raised and strengthened caste distinctions that were cracking at home. Chivvied by their pretentious wives, the middle-class merchant-adventurers had erected even more formidable barriers of their own design. "A female cabal," Hilary Metcalfe insisted, "really runs the Colony—by gossip, innuendo, and slander. More careers and lives have been destroyed over the teacups than by the law courts, the counting-house, or the battlefield."

Her father's position and, therefore, her own were equivocal. He was British, and the lowliest Briton was virtually a lord compared to the Chinese. Yet John Philip Osgood was neither a commissioned officer nor an "other rank," an enlisted soldier. Either grade would have precisely defined his position—and her own. But he was a warrant officer, a hybrid creature. She could mingle unconstrained with neither the sergeants' wives and daughters, who, in any event, bored her beyond tears, nor with the officers' ladies, who were hardly more stimulating. She was not welcomed by the self-anointed civilian elite, who were at least as tedious—and much ruder. Only the Metcalfes' hospitality offered her surcease from stark loneliness.

If she had been overwhelmingly beautiful, much might have been forgiven her by the matriarchs, as well as their men. She might have swept all before her if she had typified the ideal of the age. Had she been either a languid blonde or a dark-haired beauty with regular features, insipid conversation, and a taste for the genteel flirtation, she might have overleaped the barrier of her father's position.

But she was not beautiful. She was, she knew dispassionately, attractive, though her features lacked classic symmetry. Her nose was acceptably high-bridged, but her mouth was too wide. Her glowing auburn hair, a flaming crown Burne-Jones would have rejoiced to paint, was her chief beauty, and her figure was striking. Yet she was too vivacious, too "pert and outspoken," too "strong-minded and intellectual" for the small-minded ladies who ruled the Colony's society. Her manifest deficiencies—social and personal—had already compelled her to resign herself to living on the fringe of proper British Hong Kong. Since the domineering hostesses could forgive neither her origins nor her manners, she had not hoped to attend the Grand Ball hallowed by Royalty's presence, *the* event of the new century.

Her attendance could make a vast difference in her status, but she could not be as certain as she had intimated to John Williams. She knew without vanity that the young officers, civil servants, and gentleman clerks of the great trading *hongs* found her attractive. But did they consider her anything more than, at best, a pleasant diversion or, at worst, a casual conquest? Some were betrothed to "suitable" young ladies in England, while others were searching for brides whose connections and wealth would advance their careers. Really, she concluded, Mary Osgood had only one thing to offer. Some suitors would persevere—until she either yielded or decisively rejected them.

"Maybe I should take myself to a flower boat!" She laughed aloud in the moonlit bedroom. "I'd be a sensation, a red-haired flower girl. And think of the money —I'd be a very rich woman in a few years."

The ebullience of youth had overcome both her depression at the Honorable Rachel Wheatley's cruel snub and her agitation at having maneuvered John Williams's invitation. She turned on her side and composed herself in renewed invitation to slumber.

July 23, 1900–August 1, 1900

THE clatter of crockery woke Mary Osgood. Ah Sam coughed softly as he placed the teacup on her teak bedside table. His elephantine tread normally aroused her before that morning ritual, but exhaustion had granted her deep and dreamless sleep.

The Number One Boy's entry at dawn no longer disturbed her. A manservant's awakening a single lady was unthinkable in England. But respectable Hong Kong thought nothing of it, for the Colony's mores unabashedly combined prudishness and license. Some matrons, gossips whispered, summoned their boys to scrub their backs as they sat in their deep baths. Mary found it hard to imagine of a harridan like the Honorable Rachel Wheatley, but the tale was often told.

"After all," the ladies observed, "you can't consider them 'men.' They're just Chinamen."

Ah Sam's features grimaced in his customary ferocious good humor, but his manner was heartily disingenuous.

She knew she had found an ally, perhaps even a friend, in the piratical-looking Number One Boy. After his initial suspicion, he volubly approved of her studying his language, and they chatted in improvised Cantonese, reverting to pidgin English to bridge the gaps in her new knowledge. She had apparently won the regard of one member of the race most of her compatriots derided as "the beastly Celestials, not quite human."

"Good morning, Ah Sam," she said in Cantonese. "It's a lovely morning."

The stocky servant normally contented himself with echoing in his clacking tongue, *"Jow-sang, Siu-jieh, Tin-chi ho-ho ah."* But this morning he lingered, adjusting the curtains with deliberation and flicking imaginary dust from the dressing table.

"Ve'y good mo'ning," he said in pidgin, apparently determined that she should not miss his meaning. "But mans not so good. Have got bad Englishmans in Hong Kong. Also have got many bad Chinee mans."

"How so, Ah Sam?"

"Yeste'day," he answered, "I hear bad words at teahouse."

Ah Sam's teahouse usually meant the hole-in-the-corner food shop where he observed the ritual called *yum cha*—drinking tea. *Yum cha* really meant playing Mah-jongg and gossiping while consuming a variety of succulent dumplings with the fragrant tea. But "teahouse" was also Ah Sam's euphemism for the divan where he occasionally smoked a few soothing pipes of

67

sticky, black opium. Mary had read de Quincey's and Coleridge's reminiscences of "opium eating," but the word "divan" still conjured up images of dark evil in her mind.

"What teahouse, Ah Sam?" she pressed at the risk of straining the tenuous confidence between them.

"Oh, *othah* teahouse, Missy," he replied without hesitation. "Not reg'lah one. You know what teahouse. Sometime, *othah* teahouse have got bad mans. They say young—what you say—g'andson of g'eat English Queen come Hong Kong next week—and they say maybe some bad mans want chop him. Say Englishmans behave ve'y bad up no'th Shanghai mo'e fah—shoot many Chinee mans. So they wanchee chop g'eat English Queen's g'andson."

"You told Master?"

"Oh, no need speak, Missy." Ah Sam's face closed stubbornly. "Some British mans know al'eady. I go now, see to b'eakfast."

Mary knew she would learn no more from Ah Sam, despite their useful alliance against her father's rages. He revered the "g'eat English Queen" almost as deeply as he did the Dowager Empress in Peking, who was sixteen years younger than eighty-one-year-old Queen Victoria herself. But his ultimate loyalty necessarily lay with his own people.

Could she dismiss the matter as casually? She pondered the question as she stripped the nightdress from her body, sticky with sweat, and reveled in the cooling breeze blowing through the shutters of the tiled bathroom. She stood naked for several minutes, stretching luxuriously and letting the air play on her bare skin. Since coming to Hong Kong, earthy despite its outward prudishness, she was no longer shy of her own body. She felt pleasure in the rough caress of the bath sponge on her breasts and the firm swell of her belly above the inverted triangle of flame between her thighs. She suddenly blushed and seized the pannikin floating in the porous earthenware water butt.

Mary flung dipper after dipper of cold water over herself, delighting in the successive shocks. Was her enjoyment of the bracing drench, she wondered guiltily, lust of the flesh? She vigorously toweled herself dry, but was half-drenched with perspiration by the time she'd finished dressing.

To resolve the dilemma Ah Sam had posed, she wrote a brief note. Emerging from her bedroom, she saw with relief that her father had already left the bungalow. She summoned the coolie, the man of all work, to the front door and instructed him to carry her message to Mr. Metcalfe.

While she was sipping her pale tea, the coolie returned bearing Hilary Metcalfe's familiar blue envelope with his seal's red Chinese characters impressed on the flap. The message was brief: "M.O., Matter under control. Come see us soon. H.M."

She had done all she could, for Hilary Metcalfe's voice commanded attention in Government House. She was subsequently to wonder if she had truly done all she could. But that was much later.

At 6:47 on the morning of August 2, 1900, Her Majesty's Ship *Defiance,* heavy cruiser, steamed past Green Island into the drifting mist of Hong Kong harbor followed by H.M.S. *Persephone,* light cruiser. The squadron was on passage to Taku Bar to join the flotilla supporting the Allied force that was still girding itself to march on the capital of the Chinese Empire. Tientsin, the chief seaport of North China and the gateway to Peking, had finally fallen to naval gunfire and infantry landings in mid-July. But there the relief force had stuck after one weak thrust was repulsed by unexpectedly tenacious Chinese resistance. Fearful confusion in Tientsin had prevented a lightning sweep like that which took Peking in 1860. At that moment, the commanders of the eight-nation array were finally resolving their own disputes. Goaded by the self-confident British, they had finally agreed to march in force on August 5, waiting no longer for full complement of cavalry and artillery or the Balloon Section that had just embarked from Southampton.

The Legation Quarter of Peking was being squeezed

behind its contracting perimeter by the pressure of the fanatical Boxers, unofficially supported by the motley regular troops of the Empress Dowager. Wholly committed to their own bloodthirsty oaths and totally confident of their invulnerability, the Boxers were slowly wearing down the will of the besieged; the passage of time was consuming both the provisions and the ammunition of the few soldiers and the armed civilians who defended the foreign legations. For the first time since 1839, Chinese forces were engaged in effective military action against Europeans. China was striking back at the arrogant barbarians who had almost effortlessly imposed their will on the decadent Empire for more than forty years, extracting vast sums, humiliating concessions, and immunity from Chinese law that chipped away China's essential sovereignty. Exultation outside was matched by suffering within the Legation Quarter. If the Allied forces did not rescue them soon, the besieged would be slaughtered in expiation for the transgressions of their predecessors—the women raped repeatedly by filthy fanatics, the men barbarously mutilated before sword strokes ended their agony.

Nonetheless, Hong Kong apparently believed that the chief purpose of the gray ships' long voyage from the Mediterranean was to honor the Colony with the presence of His Royal Highness, Lieutenant Prince William, Duke of Gloucester, navigating officer of *Defiance*. Sirens howled from steamers; whistles shrieked joyous paeans from square-rigged sailing ships; hoarse foghorns reverberated jubilantly; and bells pealed from churches. Fusillades of firecrackers punctuated the pounding of drums and clashing of cymbals from junks and sampans. A solemn twenty-one-gun salute thundered from Jardine's Wharf as the cruisers dropped anchor.

The Colony was *en fête,* the board *praya* along the waterfront a kaleidoscope of gaudy bunting. Bamboo-and-matting towers swayed in the light winds, their many-colored paper streamers dancing in the morning sun. Arches flung across the streets bore the scrolled initials VR for Victoria Regina, as well as fulsome declarations of loyalty in red Chinese characters. Blake Pier was smothered by sunbursts of rosettes, bunting, flowers, and banners—all dominated by the great signboard: HONG KONG WELCOMES H.R.H. PRINCE WILLIAM!

"Once again," Hilary Metcalfe observed sourly and portentously, "this jewel of Empire has managed to transform a crisis into a revel. One would think *Defiance* had come to celebrate a great victory, rather than to assist a squalid, mismanaged, minor expeditionary force. If this little lot had lived in Pompeii, they wouldn't have fled. They'd have danced in the streets as the lava engulfed them."

Mary Osgood and Elizabeth Metcalfe indignantly reproached the Sinologue for his cynicism. Like their own, every feminine heart in Hong Kong fluttered in hope of actually beholding the dashing young prince. A martial demi-god, his divine chariot the armored ship, Prince William embodied not only Britain's Imperial might, but the perfection of British manhood.

Those ladies favored with invitations to the receptions planned for His Royal Highness's three-day visit fluttered in a frenzy of preparation. Dressmakers, milliners, and perfumers were overwhelmed with custom; harried clerks and gratified proprietors, pale tailors and consumptive seamstresses worked through the nights by the flickering light of gas lamps and kerosene lanterns. Merchant princes and senior officials retreated behind the blue-and-white arches of the Hong Kong Club to escape the hysteria. But the waiters inside, like the rickshaw pullers outside, flaunted red-white-and-blue rosettes.

Many maiden pillows were drenched with tears of disappointment. The glorious culmination of the Royal visit was to be the Grand Ball given by the Governor, Sir Henry Blake. That imperious arbitrix of fashion, Lady Blake, had pruned the guest list with ruthless shears. Only those unmarried ladies might attend whose standing was unchallengeable—by the Colony's particular standards. Besides those few who asserted special claims because of noble connections or wealth, the chosen few included only the daughters of: senior officers, majors and above; superior civil servants, under secretaries and above; and the ranking executives of the great trading houses, the *hongs* that actually ruled the Colony.

Derwent, Hayes and Company was assured of invitations. The Honorable Rachel Wheatley's attractive daughter Cynthia would curtsy to the Prince among the daughters of the other great *hongs*: John Swire and Jardine, Matheson foremost among them. But Lady Blake had rigorously excluded Kelley and Walsh, booksellers; Halliday and Wise, provision merchants; and Lane Crawford, ships' chandlers. Their daughters would *not* be presented to the Prince.

Those firms traded at retail, and Lady Blake would not permit the presence of "tradespeople" to sully the Royal occasion. It did not matter that the original wealth of the great *hongs* came from forcing opium upon the Chinese at gunpoint. It did not matter that they had been smugglers, tax evaders, and, when expedient, pirates. Nor did it matter that they still shipped opium to China, despite the expressed disapproval of the Queen Empress's prime minister. The *hongs* were, most obviously, not engaged in *retail* trade.

Mary Philippa Osgood hugged her secret in delight. Because of John Williams's impulsiveness and her own gentle wiles, *she* would attend the Royal Ball, whatever Lady Blake might say. Her tears, not all feigned, had leached reluctant and admonitory consent from her father. Bandmaster John Philip Osgood had stormed up and down their small parlor, firing admonitions like a ship-of-the-line repeatedly going about to loose successive broadsides.

" 'Twill be t' end of you, my girl—mayhap t' end of me," he'd thundered. "What'll the Colonel say—or t' Colony's lady—when you're seen where you never belong? Comes of mixing with your betters."

"Father," she'd pleaded, "it's the most important thing that's ever happened to me."

"Aye," he'd replied, his North Country accent thickening, "and likely t' most important thing ever happened to me—t' end of me."

"But, Father," she'd sobbed, "Lieutenant Williams would be offended if I didn't come."

"Lass, he only asked you like a stray pup he pitied. He's a good-hearted lad—even if no proper officer and too hasty."

The battle had raged at intervals for three days while Ah Sam shook his heavy head in amazement. Mary had finally triumphed.

"If you must, you must," John Osgood had reluctantly agreed. "And, if you must, you'll do't handsomely. Who's t' best dressmaker in this heathen place?"

"Madame Rachelle, they tell me. But she's frightfully expensive. I wouldn't dream of—"

"Off you go, lass! Off you go! If you're bound to play t' fool, you'll be dressed as well—or better—than t' damned nobs' daughters."

Elizabeth Metcalfe took Mary to Madame Rachelle's *atelier* on Wellington Street. To her surprise, Hilary Metcalfe accompanied them. His forceful personality —and, no doubt, his wealth—prevailed upon the temperamental, overworked French-Russian couturier to promise her gown on the afternoon before the Ball. Mary suspected that he had supplemented the Hong Kong $150, about £15, her father thought ample for the grandest dress. Hilary Metcalfe gently rebuffed her protestations and her thanks.

"Madame Rachelle owes me some favors," he said cryptically. "I'm just collecting a bit on account."

Mary had heard snide whispers when promenading at Scandal Point, the grass-covered junction of Kennedy Road and the Garden Road footpath where European ladies in their Sunday finery gossiped after church. At Scandal Point she was accepted, if only by the wives and daughters of retail merchants who knew that the Metcalfes received her. Feminine love of scandal leveled social barriers, and feminine malice wafted spiced rumors to her ears.

"My dear," Mrs. Wise had confided. "It's said Mr. Metcalfe set Madame Rachelle up in business. They say he brought her down from Shanghai, but tired of her. Whatever—it was a handsome gesture."

Mary had feigned shocked disbelief, though a spring of pleasure bubbled in her heart at learning that gruff old Hilary Metcalfe had once played the ardent lover. But she forgot all else when she displayed her ballgown to the Metcalfes in Madame Rachelle's crowded *atelier*.

Daringly omitting the customary train, the floor-length gown was, Madame Rachelle rhapsodized, "in the Grecian mode." The fine white silk, gathered above the waist, flowed into a full skirt. Her shoulders were covered, and the flying panels of the gown's sleeves danced in the air with every movement. The deep *décolleté* was outlined with antique strips of gold-and-green Chinese embroidery crossing beneath her bust. Otherwise unadorned, the dress's simplicity set off the jewelry Elizabeth Metcalfe had insisted upon lending her. Ruby eyes shining, a white-jade butterfly danced atop its gold spring on the hairpin thrust into her red-gold hair. Identical jade bracelets set with diamonds encircled her slender wrists, their green-and-crystal iridescence shimmering.

"You're lovely, my dear," Miss Metcalfe sighed. "The frock's different, quite different—and *so* striking. But *do* remember a modest manner. And *do* set a guard on your tongue!"

"Liz wants you to be a movable doll, my dear, but just be yourself," Hilary Metcalfe boomed above his sister's advice. "You know I've sometimes thought it'd be better if you were a boy. You've got three times the spirit and brains of any of our local coxcombs. But right now I wouldn't wish you anything but what you are—the most beautiful girl in Hong Kong. Not just Hong Kong—the most beautiful girl on the China Coast."

She was still tingling with pleasure at that gruff accolade—and John Williams's sharp intake of breath on first beholding her when his hired carriage clattered through the gilt-iron gates of Government House. But she braced herself as they alighted before sweeping steps guarded by Fusiliers in red-and-gold dress-uniform crowned with plumed shakos. Her stomach was an icy pit, and her palms were damp within long kid gloves. She felt a hot flush and knew with fearful certainty that her face was glowing red beneath its discreet dusting of rice powder. She leaned on John Williams's extended hand.

If you're doing something most people will disapprove, she told herself, then do it with a flair, my girl. If you're being foolish, go the whole hog.

Government House floated on a fountain of light. Torrents of brilliant rays streaming from every window transformed the squat structure into a crystalline fairy palace. Lanterns glowed in the surrounding trees, like rainbow-hued butterflies. The pungent-sweet scent of frangipani drifted on the gentle breeze that fluttered ladies' skirts and rocked the lanterns amid the green leaves. From the center of the grounds a great flame-of-the-forest tree thrust its crimson fire into the blue-satin sky. An orange moon nestled in the hills of Kowloon across the bay.

John Williams offered a red-sheathed arm, and Mary's fingers lightly touched the gold piping. The hard muscles beneath the fine barathea trembled. They joined the queue on the steps to the entrance hall, and she saw with sudden dismay that Captain Lord Peter French stood beside her. The encounter with that arrogant son of the aristocracy in a setting so different from the informality of the Metcalfes' parlor was her first trial of an evening that would be an ordeal.

"Good evening, Lord Peter," she smiled her sweetest. *If you will be foolish, do it well*—and be damned to everyone.

"Your servant, Miss Osgood," Lord Peter replied with cold hauteur. "Good evening, Lieutenant."

The perfumed, perspiring queue shuffled into the entrance hall where Sir Henry Blake was receiving his guests. The Governor's white uniform was a panoply of gold epaulettes, rainbow ribbons, and jeweled orders. Lady Blake's low-cut chartreuse ballgown fringed with bobbles at the neckline, hips, and hem was, Mary felt, an unfortunate accent for her plump shoulders and sallow cheeks. Prince William stood beside the Blakes, a gracious Royal smile pasted slightly askew on his high-bred features like a made-up bow-tie. Cut high in front, the gold-encrusted jacket of his formal evening uniform swept to long swallowtails in back. A silver-hilted dress sword hung from the blue-and-white cummerbund girding his waist, and the pale-blue riband of a Knight of the Garter crossed his chest. Around his neck hung the Knight's Cross of the Iron Cross with Swords and Diamonds bestowed by his cousin Kaiser Wilhelm II. The two golden stripes of a lieutenant on his sleeves enhanced his youthful dignity. His Royal Highness's petulant lower lip belied his smile of state, but curved in honest pleasure when he glimpsed Mary awaiting presentation to Lady Blake.

"How d'you do?" the formidable matron snapped unsmiling when John Williams presented Mary Osgood. Oblivious to his wife's frosty eye, Sir Henry beamed in welcome.

Prince William extended his hand to help Mary rise from her deep curtsy. Though she had practiced for a week, her heel momentarily caught in her hem.

"Steady there, Miss!" The Prince's light tenor had charmed a thousand debutantes and their mothers. "Can't have the prettiest girl of the evening hurting herself. The butterfly in your hair dances charmingly."

"Thank you, Your Royal Highness."

As she stepped aside, Mary's head swam with delight. The sailor-prince was not only as handsome as his repute, but regally gracious. As if from a great distance, she heard John Williams's voice.

"A charmer, isn't he? I suppose it's his job. But he's right: you are the prettiest of all."

"Thank you, John," she murmured, still bedazzled.

"But I don't think we'll be seeing him again. We're far below the salt, practically in the kitchen."

They sat down to dine amid streams of light cascading from hundreds of candles in crystal chandeliers. Mary barely heard John Williams's whispers and she pecked at the profusion of courses: dressed crab in the shell, cold lobster mayonnaise, turtle soup, Macao

76

salmon garnished with tiny shrimps, roast duckling, stuffed goose, a lemon sorbet, a baron of beef, lamb-en-croute, a mango sorbet, crown-shaped *gâteaux,* a multitude of cheeses, and a cornucopia of fruit.

The mixed bouquet of perfumes was almost as exhilarating as the hock, the claret, and the champagne. Among the gentlemen's black tailcoats and dark-hued uniforms, the ladies' pastel gowns shimmered like a painter's palette. Their silks, satins, and taffetas were tortured into panniers, drapes, trains, and bustles. Her own simply cut, virtually unadorned white dress, Mary realized, made her most striking and, perhaps unfortunately, obtrusive. If her mere presence was in truth foolish, it was undeniably spectacular. She shrank into herself.

The apparently interminable dinner finally drew to a bloated close. Lady Blake's eyes swept around the table. Their trains swaying, the chosen ladies withdrew to a smaller parlor. Mary was left standing indecisively with the fourteen other young women who were excluded from the charmed circle. The gentlemen were already passing the port along the polished mahogany table.

John Williams looked up in impotent apology as she fled with the other outcasts to the shelter of the powder room. An overdressed blonde with an enormous bust encased in purple silk sat before the mirror, tears trickling silently down her cheeks. Mary sank into a wicker chair, waving off the aged amah's proffered assistance in refreshing her toilette. She should not, she realized with cold self-contempt, have defied propriety by coming to the Royal Ball. High-spirited daring was one thing, deliberately playing the fool quite another. And she had played the fool in the most public manner possible.

She passed a half-hour of dull misery before the orchestra struck up to summon the party to the dance-floor. John Williams claimed Mary as Prince William led out Lady Blake for the first waltz.

"The old cow's had His Royal Highness with her cronies, formally presenting each of them," he whispered. "You'd think he was a performing bear and she his keeper."

When the first dance ended, Lady Blake firmly led Prince William to a corner behind a veritable stockade of chairs which kept all but the elect from approaching the Royal presence. The Prince dutifully partnered matrons selected by Lady Blake or the few younger ladies she judged worthy to repose briefly in the formal Royal embrace. The slightly protuberant Royal eyes grew glazed with boredom, and the Royal lower lip drooped in undisguised irritation.

The evening that appeared a minor disaster for Mary Philippa Osgood was a protracted ordeal for the handsome Prince, who was condemned to dance with Lady Blake's hand-picked Gorgons. Despite her own misery, Mary almost laughed aloud as she watched Prince William steering the angular and Honorable Rachel Wheatley around the dance-floor. At least she herself had John. She smiled into his eyes and pressed closer to his brilliant red tunic. The heart beneath the gold braid quickened its beat.

Despite the glowing decor and the spirited music, a heavy dullness settled over the ballroom. The Prince's displeasure was apparent to even the least sensitive—to all, it seemed, except Lady Blake herself. When a diversion presented itself, the relieved guests rushed with a single will to the open french doors. A joyous dissonance from the garden sounded—the beating of drums, the clashing of cymbals, and the shrill lilting of pipes.

The surge separated Mary from John Williams and swept her into the garden. A gaudy paper dragon danced among the lantern-hung trees, twisting in serpentine coils, capering sideways at the drums' command, and bounding high on fifty pairs of brown legs. The red-painted jaws in the enormous head grinned gleefully beneath pop-eyes glowing with lantern light. Around the cavorting monster, Chinese musicians sounded their gay cacophony on drums, gongs, pipes, and flutes.

The crush forced Mary into a *cul-de-sac* in the red brick wall surrounding the garden. When the dragon

78

darted mock-ferociously in her direction, a gentleman backed into her, treading on her toe.

"So sorry. Terribly sorry."

Mary looked up into Prince William's blue eyes, which were alight with amusement. She bobbed a curtsy, but his hand was under her arm.

"Do you know what this dragon's all about, Miss—ah—Miss?" he asked. "Lady Blake didn't tell me about his performance."

"Yes, Sir," she answered tremulously. "The dragon is the symbol of China, the symbol of majesty and joy —and he's dancing just for Your Royal Highness."

"Pleasant custom, Miss—Miss—do forgive me. I've forgotten the name of the most charming girl here. Where did she hide *you* when we were dancing?"

"Osgood . . . Mary Osgood, Sir."

"Well, Miss Osgood." The Prince spoke over the din of gongs and drums; the dragon, having found its Royal prey, was jubilantly weaving its coils around them. "I want to know more about this. Does anyone talk the lingo? Could someone ask that headman-looking fellow what it's all about? Grandmama would want to know."

"I could try, Sir," Mary ventured.

Prince William beckoned to the dragon's leader, who was immensely stout in flowing green-silk robes.

"He says," Mary interpreted timorously, "that the dragon always dances to honor great occasions. It's a royal dragon, an Imperial dragon, and it rejoices at your presence. He also says—but I don't think . . ."

"Carry on, Miss Osgood. Tell me everything the old boy says. This is the best fun I've had since this damned—pardon, Miss Osgood—this glorious ball began. A whacking great dragon that practically talks —and the prettiest girl in Hong Kong."

"He also says, Your Royal Highness," Mary blurted, "that the fierce dragon is loyal—utterly loyal to yourself and the great Queen Empress. But he hopes there will be peace between the Queen Empress in London and the Empress Dowager in Peking."

"Does he, by Jove? Tell him I'm all for peace, Miss Osgood."

Mary essayed a farewell curtsy, realizing that it was not merely foolish, but foolhardy to monopolize the Prince's attention. But his hand clasped her arm as the dragon capered away, and she yielded to the temptation.

"I mustn't keep you from your dancing partners, Sir."

"You won't escape me so easily," Prince William laughed. "I command you to dance with me. My prerogative, you know. You can't refuse."

"As a loyal subject," Mary coquetted over her fan, "I wouldn't dream of disputing a Royal command." *If you're being foolish,* she thought, *why not foolhardy?*

Dancing with a Royal prince, Mary found, was much like dancing with any other young man of twenty-six. He held her too close, and she strained away as gracefully as possible. She was aware of only two other persons as they whirled to the lilting song "Poor Little Buttercup," from Gilbert and Sullivan's newest light opera, *H.M.S. Pinafore.* As if the Gorgon had turned herself to stone, Lady Blake sat frozen on the chair guarding the entrance to her Royal stockade, her small eyes fixing the twirling couple with a basilisk glare. Bandmaster John Philip Osgood stared from the bandstand with horror stamped on his heavy features. An eternity passed before the music stopped and the Prince stepped back laughing.

"Capital, Miss Osgood. You're a feather in a breeze. We'll do it again, but now duty calls. Can I take you to your friends?"

Friends? Mary looked around desperately. John Williams was nowhere in sight. With overwhelming relief, she saw the Metcalfes seated with a slender, middle-aged man in a full-dress suit.

"Thank you, Your Royal Highness. My friends are there."

Prince William offered his arm, and she was suddenly aware of the enormity of her offense. In her misery, she was barely aware that he acknowledged the Metcalfes' homage with a nod and commanded: "Now promise you'll save a dance for me."

When she looked up, Hilary Metcalfe was beaming at her, and his sister's smile was joyous.

"I've done it now," Mary said in low-voiced despair. "Everyone'll hate me for dancing with the Prince. It was better when they just ignored me."

"Mary, you still don't understand Hong Kong." Hilary Metcalfe's laughter resounded. "You've *done* it, indeed. You'll be deluged with invitations. The middle-class matriarchy can't resist the Royal touch. You're not just acceptable, but the belle of the year. It's mad, but it's true."

"But I thought—"

"Hilary's right, Mary," Elizabeth Metcalfe assured her. "You should be very happy. Even that jade hairpin is hallowed. I'd like you to keep it for remembrance."

"But I thought—I couldn't—I don't see—"

"Liz has a whim of iron, Mary. Keep the bauble. But I'm forgetting my manners. May I present Sir Jonathan Sekloong and Mr. Charles Sekloong?"

The name wrenched Mary from her preoccupation, dispelling the storms of self-recrimination, which had been abruptly transformed into elation. She had first heard of Jonathan Sekloong from Hilary Metcalfe on the *Orion*. Later, her father had grumbled: "Now they've done it. Made a chink a Knight in the last Honors list. Next thing Ah Sam'll be a Lord."

Jonathan Sekloong was not wholly Chinese, but half European, and his services were invaluable to Derwent, Hayes and Company. He was the "comprador," the essential link between the British trading firm and its Chinese customers. He had also proved an invaluable channel between the British Government and the Imperial Government when China was forced to lease three hundred and seventy square miles—the so-called New Territories—to Hong Kong for ninety-nine years in 1898. He had been knighted for those services, only the second Chinese to be so honored. But he had refused to accept his knighthood unless he was permitted to build a residence on The Peak, which was tacitly reserved for Europeans. Sekloong Manor was already rising, its vast foundations dwarfing Government House

81

itself. Hilary Metcalfe hoped Sir Jonathan's elevation would show both communities that their interests were linked and, further, that Chinese and British need not always live apart.

The man himself was almost dwarfed by the flamboyant tales told about him. He was praised by his friends for his acumen, his benevolence, and his energy; he was vilified by his enemies for his cunning, his rapacity, and his "bandit-connections." In his late forties, his erect form was spare under the Chinese long-gown, and his features were oddly more European than Oriental. His nose was straight and slender with a thrusting Irish-arched bridge; his forehead was high, and his hazel eyes were only slightly almond-shaped. His air of assumed authority contrasted with Prince William's petulant self-assertion. Yet the Eurasian could not conceivably have been invited to the Royal Ball, however impressive his accomplishments and however great his wealth, if he had not recently received the accolade of knighthood.

"Congratulations, Miss Osgood." Sir Jonathan's courtesy broke into Mary's revery. "May I boldly say that you are the handsomest young lady here tonight?"

Mary smiled her gratitude. Sir Jonathan's English was marred by the faintest lilt. His accent might have been Welsh, except for the slurred s's, incomplete vowels, and stilted diction characteristic of Hong Kong's English-educated Chinese.

"Charles wants so much to dance with you," Sir Jonathan continued. "Before he takes you away, may I ask if you will soon dine with me and my good friends, the Metcalfes?"

"I'd be delighted, Sir Jonathan."

"We must celebrate," the Eurasian continued. "We two broke into Hong Kong's social fortress tonight. Perhaps it's less impressive inside than seen outside."

"Will you dance with me, Miss Osgood?" Charles Sekloong asked formally.

His intonation was slightly more lilting than his father's, slightly more Hong Kong, and his pronunciation was marred by similar minor flaws. Charles was taller than his father and darker, his skin a golden olive. But his light hazel eyes were set squarely under heavy black brows, and his nose was imperiously arched. Mary surreptitiously studied the long, clean run of his jawline, taking pleasure from the sculptured sweep under the fine skin she had never previously felt looking at a man. His powerful shoulders strained the fine broadcloth of his tailcoat, which had obviously been made on Savile Row, not by any Hong Kong tailor.

Madame Rachelle's ballgown suddenly seemed dowdy under Charles Sekloong's disconcertingly direct gaze. She was also intrigued. His manner breathed a passion for living, in which her countrymen were notably deficient. Neither the puppylike John Williams nor the pampered Lord Peter French had ever looked at her with such unabashed, intense admiration. No young man she had ever known carried Charles Sekloong's aura of self-assured command.

"I'd love to dance." She smiled.

From H.R.H. Prince William to the son of a Eurasian knight—the spectacle would keep tongues wagging for months. *But,* she told herself, *do what you will —and, even if it's foolish, do it thoroughly.* If the Osgoods possessed a family crest, that would be her motto. She very much wanted to dance with the compelling young man who seemed only a year or two older than herself.

His encircling arms were more powerful than the Prince's or John Williams's. She felt herself yielding to their implicit demand. His determination was a full-grown man's, and his emotions were frankly expressed, regardless of the world's opinion.

"Magnificent, Miss Osgood, you were, and very beautiful. I reveled watching you with the Prince. You made them look sick—the fools who think they rule Hong Kong."

"You flatter me, Mr. Sekloong," she murmured.

"Not flattery, just good observation. You're like me. You don't care about these fools, and you won't let them put you in place—where they'd like to put you."

"I never thought of it," she answered half-truthfully.

"You know that hairpin was my mother's? She gave it to Elizabeth Metcalfe. But she'd love you to wear it. It's already a bond between us."

Mary smiled. Charles Sekloong was, in his way, as imperious as Lord Peter French. But nicer, much nicer —and much more exciting. He was quite different from all the young men she had ever known—a man, rather than an overgrown boy.

Mary's evening passed in a golden haze. She would, she knew, afterward never quite recall the separate details of that night, only the sensation of joy.

Having escaped the stockade Lady Blake had erected around him, Prince William called for more champagne. He danced with Mary twice again, and once, she saw, with the Honorable Rachel Wheatley's daughter Cynthia. John Williams claimed Mary for three dances. His eyes were bright with pleasure at her success, but his mouth was sulky when she danced with Charles Sekloong.

At half past three in the morning, Prince William at last yielded to Lady Blake's glances, at first commanding and finally pleading. The orchestra swung into "Good-Night Ladies," and John Williams claimed Mary from Charles Sekloong for the last dance. When Royalty withdrew, the other guests made their farewells, the older yawning for sleep, the younger bubbling with exhilaration.

John Williams drew Mary's arm under his own as the open carriage clattered down Garden Road, the driver swaying half awake on his perch. She laid her head sleepily on the red-clad shoulder, finding it comfortable rather than stirring.

"Thank you, John. Thank you for taking me."

"Mary," he said softly as they alighted before the bungalow, "Mary—I wonder—"

"Yes, John," she prompted imprudently.

"Mary, I—I wonder—but no, not yet. Just this."

His blond hair blotted out the stars, and his lips pressed hard on her own. With a sigh, she responded, her arms around his neck drawing him down to her.

But she slipped out of his embrace as his arms tightened possessively.

"Good-night, John. Thank you for a lovely evening."

"Good-night, Mary." The melody of the chiming glass beads in the doorway obscured his soft farewell. "A beautiful night."

August 14, 1900–September 18, 1900

BEHIND its battered brick walls, the ancient metropolis lay heavy on the ocher North China plain. Seen from hillocks outside the walls, the golden-tiled roofs that sheltered the Imperial Palaces were as literally square within a broad border of red-and-gray tiles as building blocks in a child's sandbox. Powdered yellow dust mingled with pale-gray smoke to cast a gauzy canopy over the Legation Quarter in the southeast corner of the capital of the Manchu Dynasty. Already seared by the late summer heat at eight A.M. on August 14, 1900, Peking was uneasily preparing to receive her new masters.

The seven Western nations that had joined with the Japanese to rescue their beleaguered citizens from the fanatical Boxers and avenge their humiliation were the latest in a cavalcade of conquerors that had begun more than 3,000 years earlier. Before that time, even the Chinese passion for historiography had not recorded the city's travails. But wandering marauders had undoubtedly assailed the Bronze Age settlement—just as other armies would take the city in the decades still in the womb of the future.

Ever since Peking, which meant "Northern Capital," had become a city known as Yenking, the capital of the Duchy of Yen in the second millennium B.C., such invasions had been mounted against it by non-Chinese "barbarians" or by Chinese rebels intent upon taking the city to assert their rule over, first, the original feudal state, and, later, the nation. The Manchus, themselves "northern barbarians" from outside the Great Wall, had conquered the city in A.D. 1644, driving out the Chinese peasant-rebel who deposed the decadent Chinese Ming Dynasty and proclaimed his own dynasty—one that endured for only a week.

Similar rebellions had been endemic to the Manchu realms since the reign of their greatest sovereign, the Chien Lung Emperor, in the latter half of the eighteenth century. That Emperor had in 1793 contemptuously rejected the request of the British envoy, Lord Macartney, that China enter into free trade with Europe. The British emissaries who followed Macartney had exacerbated the misunderstanding between the "overseas barbarians" and the Supreme Empire. Nonetheless, the Court still permitted the British to trade with China—as long as they continued to adhere to rigid conditions, formalized in 1759, that included voluntary confinement to an area of some 8,500 square yards in Canton.

Peking assumed that the aggressive British intruders would again reconcile themselves to restricted commerce conducted on China's terms, as had the pioneer Portuguese and other early European and British merchants since the sixteenth century. But the Manchus had underestimated the commercial ardor of the British, who became the vanguard of the foreign intruders.

Ignoring the wishes of the isolationist Manchu Empire, the British, Europeans, and Americans had, by the middle of the nineteenth century, asserted their right to trade on their own terms through military campaigns somewhat inaccurately called the "Opium Wars." Brief clashes between the Chinese and foreigners were used as a pretext for dispatching Allied expeditionary forces to wear down Chinese resistance, and in 1841 the British took Hong Kong. A few years later, the European powers had not only seized Chinese territory, but had also forcibly opened many Chinese ports to Allied trade, exacting the right of residence in those previously forbidden ports for their own commercial and diplomatic representatives.

Angered by Chinese hauteur, an Allied expeditionary force had taken Peking in 1860 and sacked the Summer

Palace of the Emperors to the northwest of the city. But none of those incursions had produced such cataclysmic effects upon the decadent Manchu Empire as were wreaked by the righteous campaign to relieve the siege of the Legation Quarter—and that climactic campaign was finally going well.

The inept Imperial forces had already sacrificed hundreds to halt the Allied columns that finally thrust out from Tientsin on August 5, 1900. The impassioned bravery of the ill-armed, ill-trained Chinese forces had been swept aside by the quick-firing guns of well-disciplined foreign units—and the Chinese general had taken poison. Most resistance within Peking had already dissipated before the threat of the foreign banners which had subjugated the Empire's capital four decades earlier. The soul of the Dynasty, embodied in its sovereigns, was poised for flight that had, characteristically, been too long delayed. The strong-willed Empress Dowager Tzu Hsi had finally released her nephew, the neurasthenic Kuang Hsü Emperor, from the confinement that she herself had imposed. Accompanied by a bedraggled cloud of complaining courtiers, the sixty-five-year-old princess and her twenty-nine-year-old puppet were to jounce in unsprung carts along deep ruts carved through the millennia by turning wheels. Their destination was the ancient former Imperial capital called Sian, "Western Peace." Peking's regular garrison was also fleeing the bumbling but implacable advance of the Allied forces.

Small bands of the Righteous Harmonious Fists still held strongpoints around the Legation Quarter they had almost taken, while the foreign armies dragged their unwieldy length from the coast of the Yellow Sea less than one hundred miles away. Those Boxers who had neither fled nor died still believed that their amulets and incantations rendered them invulnerable to foreign bullets: they awaited the assault of the overseas devils with confidence enflamed by the lust for inevitable victory. The Boxers—the besiegers who had become the besieged—were as certain in August that they would slaughter the sacrilegious intruders on the holy soil of

China as they had been in May when their protracted uprising closed upon the Legation Quarter.

Company C of the Second Battalion of the Royal Wessex Fusiliers marched toward the pall of dust and smoke over the Legation Quarter. Having come late to the expedition, the English unit was contending not only with British-led Sikhs and Rajputs of the Indian Army, but with the hard-bitten American Marines, the tireless Imperial Japanese Infantry, the Czar's swashbuckling Cossacks, and the enduring Tonkinese of the French Colonial Army for the glory of entering Peking first.

Captain Lord Peter French, commanding C Company, and Lieutenant John Williams, his second-in-command, communicated in curt and hostile words. They had, for the moment, subordinated to their common purpose the mutual detestation that sprang from their mutual interest in the same young woman. Both were sweating profusely in heavy khaki drill uniforms belted about with field-glasses, map-cases, revolvers, and water bottles. Lord Peter retained an air of insolent elegance, though his eyebrows and mustache were caked with yellow dust and his lean face was smudged with black powder. John Williams wearily rubbed his forehead, smearing sweat and grit into a gray swirl, but his heavily muscled body appeared inexhaustible.

"Sar'nt-major!" French's high-pitched command voice pierced the din. "Dress ranks. Load with ball. Quick march."

John Williams loosened his Scott-Webley revolver in its leather holster. Magazines clicked in metallic menace before rifles snapped to khaki shoulders.

The infantrymen's spines stiffened, and their clumsy boots, marching at one hundred and twenty paces a minute, kicked up spurts of ocher dust that enveloped them in a golden cloud. The Fusiliers advanced across the alien plain as if on parade: the khaki files die-straight; the red-white-and-blue Union Jack whipping in the morning breeze; the officers' swords sparkling in the sunshine. A crystalline ray pierced the golden cloud.

Puffs of black smoke from a volley ballooned above the city wall, and the battle flag dipped with solemn grace. The flag-bearer's jaw was shattered, and bright-red arterial blood spurted from splintered white bone. Before the flag-bearer fell, the corporal beside him seized the banner. A second rattle of shots exploded from the wall.

"Maxim gun section, halt, mark target, and open fire," French ordered. "Riflemen, follow me."

The panting soldiers advanced at a trot. On C Company's right flank the Maxim guns coughed in staccato rhythm, and lead raked the bricks beneath the smoke-puffs. A field-piece lobbed a shell, and the wall cracked minutely. The Boxers fired another ragged volley, and the sergeant beside John Williams, clutching his stomach, sank into the yellow dust.

"Jingals," French remarked conversationally. "Open ranks."

The khaki rows accordioned outward while maintaining their forward momentum. The Boxers were firing nails, chains, bolts, stones, and broken bottles from the jingals, their bell-mouthed brass cannon. Resembling outsized, muzzle-loading shotguns, those hand-forged culverins were the only heavy weapons the defenders mustered after the Imperial troops had withdrawn with their few quick-firing Krupp field-pieces. The primitive jingals were, however, deadly at close range.

The Boxers' fire ceased when the Fusiliers stood safe in the shadow of the wall, for the Chinese could not depress their muzzles to rake their assailants. Few of the British troops looked back at the plain where four khaki-colored heaps were just visible against the dun earth, marked by gouts of crimson flesh and the white faces turned upward to the pitiless sun. Their enemy's barricade was the Fusiliers' best protection. Even the intoxicated Boxers would not expose themselves to the Maxims' scything bullets in order to fire down into the British ranks. The shells of their own field-pieces were a greater danger to the Fusiliers. But the wall's battered bricks were slowly crumbling under the explosions that would breach a fortress built long before modern artillery was invented.

"Lieutenant, see the men through," Lord Peter directed. "Follow with the rear platoon."

John Williams bit back a protest against the order that would make his company commander the first man into Peking. Stifling his resentment, he watched in bitter silence. Lord Peter's scarred, begrimed riding boots, lovingly crafted by John Lobb of St. James's Street, clambered over the red-brick rubble. A fifteen-foot-wide section of the wall tumbled to the ground. The narrow breach had become a gate through which a platoon could march. The rasping coughs of the Boxers' muskets were overwhelmed by the mechanical bark of the Fusiliers' Lee-Enfields. Transferring his sword to his left hand, John Williams drew his revolver and led his men through the gap.

"Damned thoughtful, Sah," his sergeant grinned, "this dirty great hole. Bloody well as easy and come-into-my-parlor as changing guard at Aldershot."

The Fusiliers advanced through the breach into the unsuspected trap of an oblong courtyard surrounded by unpierced walls. At the far end, the round opening of a traditional moon-gate had been bricked shut. The masonry stubbornly withstood the repeated blows of a half-dozen rifle butts. Standing insouciantly in the center of the courtyard. Captain Lord Peter French was exposed to raking fire from the Boxers atop the surrounding walls. His pale sergeant major relayed commands to soldiers sheltering beneath the walls.

"Follow me," John Williams ordered, sheathing his sword.

Running all out at the moon-gate, he stumbled on an abandoned jingal and, recovering in midstride, scooped up the crude weapon. At a full run, he smashed the jingal against the bricks that sealed the moon-gate. The fresh mortar was already flaking, and his third blow yielded a broad crack. Bricks tumbling inward, the barrier collapsed after three more blows.

Williams stumbled through the gate into a second

courtyard. A tile wall emblazoned with writhing dragons guarded a second moon-gate from evil spirits, which can only move in straight lines. For the first time, John Williams beheld the previously invisible enemy. Four die-hard Boxers faced him. Painted amulets hung on their bare chests, and cloth bands adorned with red Chinese characters encircled their foreheads. A dark-faced Hopei farmboy stared incredulously at the overseas devils, loose lips gaping to reveal stained, broken teeth. His face exploded into red pulp when the Fusiliers fired, and the Boxer fell beside his three companions. His last sensation was astonishment that the bullets could actually injure him.

The morning was as abruptly silent as a concert hall after the final crescendo. John Williams smelled the sweet stench of blood and the musky tang of the yellow earth, the acrid odor of gunpowder and the heavy fragrance of incense.

A musket's throaty rasp punctured his exhausted preoccupation. His sergeant spun around and fell to his knees, dropping his weapon. The next instant, the sergeant stood erect, ruefully contemplating a rifle butt shattered by an iron slug. Greasy smoke drifted over the tiled wall's guardian dragons.

"Cover me," Williams commanded and sprinted toward the spirit wall. He flourished his sword above his head, his revolver dangling forgotten from its lanyard.

Twenty yards separated him from the spirit wall, and he ran as he had never run on the rugby field. Ten yards from the gaudy spirit wall, a blow to his left shoulder checked his momentum. He gathered himself and hurtled across the intervening space.

Behind the wall, a Boxer in a scarlet silk robe was reloading his musket. Williams was astonished to see that his enemy wore a massive necklace of sea-green jade and gold. The Boxer raised his musket in a vain parry as the Lieutenant's sword descended on his head. A gush of bright blood stained the jade necklace. His sword dangling by its retaining knot, Williams caught the dying man and tore the jade circlet from his neck.

He was stuffing his prize into his pocket when he collapsed from the delayed shock of the musketball embedded in his shoulder.

"Rapine and pillage," Hilary Metcalfe said heavily, "rapine and pillage. The brave British soldiery foremost in the fray—and the looting. We maintain our hallowed traditions in the new century."

"Greater evil will spring from the deeds of the past months," Sir Jonathan Sekloong observed somberly. "Gunpowder and swords have hewn a chasm between Europe and China. Torrents of blood will flow in that chasm."

Elizabeth Metcalfe looked up from her embroidery in surprise. Sir Jonathan, who was normally fluent in English, was obviously translating as he spoke from the formal Chinese of his thoughts.

"Such vehemence in your home violates good manners." He nodded apology to his hostess. "We Chinese were ashamed. Our cheeks were red with shame for the barbaric Boxers—though many sympathized in their hearts. What are we to think now of the barbarism of the enlightened European troops?"

"It was a mission of mercy," Mary Osgood protested. "The Boxers would have slaughtered the diplomats just like the martyred missionaries."

"And to the victors belong the spoils?" Metcalfe asked ironically. "The rape and the killing are justified?"

"The Boxers would've been less merciful, much less merciful," Elizabeth Metcalfe countered. "I shudder when I think of what might have happened. They got what they deserved."

"And the Fusiliers first into the breach," Mary added. "They fought bravely. You can't make an omelet without breaking eggs."

"Ladies! Ladies!" Metcalfe threw his hands up in mock supplication. "Why so bloodthirsty?"

The women spoke simultaneously, ignited by common indignation. Mary began, but yielded to the older woman.

"Mr. Metcalfe, that's not fair—"

"Hilary, you *are* provoking," Elizabeth said. "You yourself argued the expedition must move fast or the Chinese would massacre the Europeans in Peking, and then when the Allies finally arrived, you said they would slaughter Chinese."

"I commend your political acumen, Liz, Mary." Metcalfe smiled. "Since it had to be done, 'twas better 'twas done quickly. But afterward?"

"You're right, Hilary." Sir Jonathan nodded. "Have the ladies seen Dr. Morrison's cable to *The Times?*"

"You, too, have an understanding with the Great Eastern Telegraph and Cable Company, do you, Jonathan?"

"I'm a simple Chinaman, Hilary," Sir Jonathan laughed, "but I did arrange for my own copies. Think of the *cumshaw* we'd save by buying the company."

"When is a bribe not a bribe?" The pair chanted in practiced chorus. "When it's *cumshaw* on the China Coast!"

"You two could always do a music-hall turn," Elizabeth Metcalfe said tartly.

But she smiled at the overwrought middle-aged men who were boisterously relieving their pent-up tension in her cluttered drawing-room. The chorus goaded the dozing Chinese boy on the veranda, and the punkah's frantic flapping stirred the cloyingly moist heat.

"What," Elizabeth asked, "did Dr. Morrison say in the dispatch you've stolen?"

"Let me recall," her brother answered. "Siege lifted, as you know. Heartfelt welcome for relieving troops— Britain's might displayed as first assault mounted by Royal Wessex Fusiliers—light resistance crushed—the Manchu Court, including the Empress Dowager and the Emperor, fled toward Sian . . . Allied troops pacify Peking, after regrettable instances of looting of abandoned mansions by both Boxers and Allies . . . . widespread reports of alleged (Morrison *is* cautious) killing and torture by Allies . . . three young women came forward to complain they'd been outraged . . . inquiry ordered . . . discipline restored and troops now marching to relieve missionaries isolated in small villages (if any survive). Negotiations offered to Manchus—that's about all."

"And the Regiment?" Mary asked. "Anything more?"

"I believe there may be," Metcalfe teased.

"Miss Osgood," Sir Jonathan interposed, "casualties were light. Four privates, a lance-corporal, and a sergeant killed, another sergeant severely wounded. But, otherwise, only minor wounds. Captain French was the first man into Peking, and Lieutenant Williams fought well. Both are mentioned in dispatches. Lieutenant Williams is making good recovery from his wound."

"His wound?" Mary's heart lurched. "John wounded?"

"Slightly, my dear," Metcalfe reassured her. "No more than a flesh wound, Dr. Morrison says."

"And my father?" Mary asked. "No word?"

"None, I'm afraid," Metcalfe answered. "But no word means he's safe. And the young Lieutenant, I imagine you'll hear more directly when the post comes in."

A flush crimsoned Mary's throat and cheeks. Her heart had resumed its normal rhythm, but her hand trembled when she set her teacup down.

"As the English poet wrote, it was a famous victory." The heavy irony was intensified by the lack of emphasis in Sir Jonathan's voice; his lilt was hardly noticeable, and his lean features were expressionless. "My fears for the faraway future may be too great. But repercussions in Hong Kong are no idle fear. Viceroy Li Hung-chang in Canton is worried. His own hotheads, you know. . . ."

"What do you expect, Jonathan?" Metcalfe asked.

"The usual: demonstrations, posters, perhaps riots. After seizing the New Territories, the British despoil Peking. The hotheads can't let it pass."

"Damn it, Jonathan," Metcalfe objected, "you know more than that."

"Well, perhaps I do. It won't be good for trade. I've heard . . . that is, I'm advised to warn that . . ."

"Hilary, please don't bore us to death with talk of trade," Elizabeth Metcalfe interjected. "You've already frightened Mary to no purpose. But she might as well spend the night here, not alone in her bungalow."

"Capital idea, Liz, though there's nothing to fear. Now, if you'll excuse us—"

Mary's concern for John Williams was overlaid by curiosity roused by Sir Jonathan's tantalizing hints. She wanted to hear the men's talk. Perhaps ungraciously, she resented Elizabeth Metcalfe's assertive maternalism, the arbitrary decision as to what was best for herself. But it proved well that she did not return to the bungalow off Murray Parade-ground for three days.

Staying with the Metcalfes was like living in a command-post during a battle. Hilary Metcalfe sat at the center of his web while civilian officials and military officers brought reports and sought advice. Sir Jonathan was often present, and Mary saw that he and Metcalfe exercised great power, though they held only the relatively modest appointments of comprador and secretary to Derwent, Hayes and Company. Theirs was the power of knowledge that was intelligently applied and actually solicited by the authorities in the emergency. Only a few others in Hong Kong, men like Robert Hotung and Mosing Way, understood the psychology of both sides in the confrontation between self-righteous Chinese indignation and equally self-righteous British anger.

Her most vivid memory of that time in later years was, however, not her elders' wisdom. Toward the end of the second afternoon, she was sketching her impression of the Regiment before Peking with a fine brush in Chinese ink on rice paper, when Charles Sekloong hurried into the drawing-room. His nankeen silk suit was soiled and torn. A stained bandage swathed his left hand, and his hazel eyes flashed.

"Called me a damned Chinaman," he raged. "Me—a damned Chinaman! Who do they think messed me up?"

Mary extended her hand in quick sympathy. Charles grasped it with both his own.

"What happened, Mr. Sekloong?" she asked. "You're not badly hurt?"

"No, Miss Osgood. Just bruised. But it's so unfair."

She wanted to comfort him. Like a small boy who had just discovered that not all the world loved him, he was more bewildered than angry.

"Unfair?"

"A crowd of patriots—Chinese patriots, they claim —attacked me. 'False foreign devil,' they called me. 'Running-dog of the British' and—and other things I can't repeat."

Mary knew instinctively that the insults Charles could not bring himself to report were not merely obscenities, but jibes at his hybrid ancestry. He was, she had already learned, almost morbidly sensitive about the mixed blood that made him an outsider to both the Chinese and the British.

"I finally broke away. Just down the street, fifty yards down this street, I bumped into an insolent puppy —an English subaltern. He said: 'Out of my way, you damned Chinaman!' "

Mary realized that Charles was wounded chiefly in his self-esteem. His loyalties were already fixed—by both circumstances and choice. The Sekloongs of necessity exerted all their influence to bolster British law and to sustain the established order. Yet their position was equivocal. Formally esteemed by both the British and the Chinese authorities, they were suspect to both the Chinese mob and the British plutocracy.

Elizabeth Metcalfe cleaned the gash in Charles's hard cricket-player's palm. Mary mouthed almost the same consoling, meaningless syllables that had in the past soothed small boys whose feelings had been outraged.

"I deeply appreciate your kindness, Miss Osgood." Charles thanked her effusively. "Miss Metcalfe, you have always been very kind to me. Now I must see Mr. Metcalfe."

"Mary, my dear, Charles is uncommonly grateful for a small service," Elizabeth Metcalfe observed slyly when the young man had bounded up the stairs.

"You think so? He was shocked, and he needed sympathy from . . . from one of *us*."

"You mean because you're white?" Elizabeth could be as forthright as her brother.

"I imagine so. And he was very grateful to you."

"Fiddlesticks. He's used to me. I've always been around, just like an extra mother. But you're another matter. Of course, he knows you're white, and that's important. But he's also very much aware that you're a girl—a very pretty girl."

Elizabeth's pronunciation "gel"—the new manner—cleansed the common word "girl" of both familiarity and offense. Mary bent over her painting to hide her confusion. In any event, Elizabeth's insinuations were temporarily relegated by violent events outside the sheltered house behind the flower market. Messengers reported battles and bloodshed. Public demonstrations shook Hong Kong and Kowloon, while gory clashes rocked the New Territories that had lately been leased to Britain by a reluctant but impotent Imperial Government.

Gangs of Chinese youth tramped through Victoria, overturning sedan chairs and rickshaws, burning wooden buildings, and posting placards that demanded British withdrawal from not only the New Territories, but the entire Crown Colony. The street-gangs dispersed before the loyal Sikh police, but soon coalesced again. The demonstrations were apparently not spontaneous. Sir Jonathan spoke of an alliance between, on the one hand, the gangsters, pirates, and brigands who considered the New Territories their private kingdom and, on the other, the Triads, the quasi-criminal Secret Societies originally formed to resist Manchu rule two hundred and fifty years earlier. Clandestine encouragement, financial support, and overall direction, he felt, came from resentful young Mandarins at the Viceregal Court in Canton. Their strategy of disruption concentrated on the unsettled New Territories.

The Governor, Sir Henry Blake, moved decisively when he received a report that Chief Superintendent of Police Francis May was "besieged with six Sikh and ten

Chinese constables by a mixed Chinese force in a mat-shed police-post in a hamlet at the head of Tolo Harbor" on the mainland sixteen miles from Victoria. Sir Henry was charged to maintain order—and he was determined to disprove whispered accusations that he had been too lenient with the natives. For the moment, his dream of bringing Hong Kong's Chinese inhabitants into equal partnership with the British was superseded by the necessity to maintain British power.

Dated midnight, August 17, 1900, Sir Henry's hasty note instructed the Commodore Commanding Hong Kong Naval Forces to dispatch two steam frigates to Tolo Harbor to rescue Superintendent May.

H.M.S. *Whiting* sailed first with a hundred and ten Sepoys of the Bengal Regiment and twenty-eight Sikh policemen. Since Government had reverted in the emergency to its distrust of the small Chinese contingent in the police force, no local constables were embarked. H.M.S. *Fame* followed to serve as a command and dispatch vessel. *Whiting* grounded on a shoal at the entrance to Tolo Harbor, but the troops landed from small boats and routed the irregular Chinese force. Superintendent May and his small unit were rescued, though two Sikhs were killed and the flimsy mat-shed police-post was burned. The British held the field, and their enemies were dispersed. But the next day saw worse conflict. Later the British major commanding the two-hundred-man detachment of the Volunteer Hong Kong Regiment (recruited from Europeans, Eurasians, and Indians) at Taipo, just three miles southwest of Tolo Harbor, recalled:

It was damned unpleasant for a while. At dusk, more than a thousand "Braves" in Imperial uniforms appeared on the ridges encircling our camp. They discharged jingals, muskets, a few rifles, and what they call fire-arrows, small rockets. My men stood to and fired in volleys. We held till two in the morning. Fortunately, there was a bright moon. Then the ships came up and began shelling the reverse slope. Well, the buggers scuttled—and that was that.

That was not quite that for the Hong Kong Government. Though rejecting the hotheads' demands for a punitive expedition against Canton, the Governor was determined to impose firm British rule upon the restive New Territories.

"We've had enough of expeditionary forces," Sir Henry snorted. "Viceroy Li wants a direct confrontation no more than we do. But our writ must run in the New Territories."

The military and the police were to be occupied for months rooting out the brigands who treated the wild New Territories as their own domain, defying both British and Chinese authority. Though complete "pacification" was to take decades, more potent forces than arms were already at work. As implacably as—and, of necessity, even more slowly than—the Allied Force had moved on Peking, Western civilization was on the march in the border territories that had known no orderly government since the Sung Dynasty some seven centuries earlier. Supported by scattered troop encampments and police-posts, civilian officials imposed, first, their own summary will and, subsequently, the rule of British law leavened by traditional Chinese laws and customs. Ferry services were established, and roads were laid. Pagodas were leveled, and their stones were used to build houses, barns, and pigsties. Postmen, those heralds of modern civilization, defied the brigands' harassment to serve isolated mountain villages. Commerce came in their wake, and farmers in remote valleys gave grudging obedience to the new order that offered them new markets and new goods. The obvious benefits of British rule, backed by the manifest superiority of British arms, were slowly to win over a suspicious, illiterate, superstitious, and stubborn populace. Nonetheless, two towns on the east coast of the New Territories, accessible only by sea, were to hold out as virtually autonomous pirate havens until the year 1923.

Protracted negotiations dealt with the larger issues between the Western powers and the Manchu Dynasty. Those issues were ostensibly settled after a year—to no one's complete satisfaction. During that time, Sir Jonathan Sekloong was, as Hilary Metcalfe said, "almost constantly on his travels, like a new Charles Stewart with nothing to gain for himself." Trusted as much as anyone by both sides, he played his essential conciliatory role in the shadows. He loathed some of the messages he carried, particularly the Western powers' arrogant demands on the Chinese. But he knew the satisfaction of mitigating the harsher conditions the West wished to impose; and he served China further by persuading haughty Imperial officials, who had learned little from successive debacles, to moderate their own imperious language.

"It could have been worse, much worse," he later told Mary. "But it could have been much better."

It could, indeed, have been worse for China, which at least endured as an independent nation. Two years before the Boxer Uprising, China's chances of survival had been dubious, for the Empire was about to be "cut up like a melon" by the alien powers. American Secretary of State John Hay had then proclaimed the Open Door Policy, which promised all foreign nations equal access to China's markets and bound them to eschew all further territorial claims. The Europeans sneered that John Hay had put forward those conditions because the United States, alone among the great powers, possessed no territorial holdings in China. But the Open Door Policy, backed by the U.S. Navy's Great White Fleet, helped prevent destruction of the *Ta Ching Chao,* the Great Pure Dynasty. Even the fanatical ferocity of the Boxer Uprising, exacerbated by the stubbornness of the wily but ignorant Empress Dowager and the rapacious greed of the West, could not yet destroy the Empire. China's best defense was her immensity and diversity, which inertly frustrated colonization. Still, the final settlement could, as Sir Jonathan said, have in justice and in good sense been much less humiliating to China. A more lenient settlement might also have resulted in less sanguinary strife in the future.

Under duress, Peking accepted the West's terms: Public apologies for the foreigners killed by the Boxers, the missionaries in general and Japanese and German diplomats assassinated in Peking in particular. (Those culprits who were apprehended were sentenced by Chinese courts of law convened by the same Imperial Government that had encouraged the Boxer Uprising.) Memorials to the martyred diplomats and missionaries were erected at Chinese expense. All sales of arms to China were banned, depriving the Empire of a good measure of its sovereignty. The Legation Quarter in Peking became a self-governing enclave occupied by foreign troops. Finally, China undertook to pay indemnities totaling $335 million over a forty-year period; the pledge was secured by liens on the Empire's customs dues and salt taxes, its two chief sources of revenue. China, thus, remained a sovereign state—barely.

At last the chief issues seemed settled, and a new, stable relationship between China and the outside world was apparently created. The Chinese emissaries wept after signing the agreements, and Chinese resentment was not notably mitigated by the benevolence of the United States in using indemnities to establish "Boxer Scholarships" that educated Chinese students in America and to endow universities in China. The Boxer Settlement evoked not only hatred of the West, but deep suspicion of all Western motives and actions. Though Chinese liberals were already turning eagerly to Western models of thought, science, and democracy, the Boxer Settlement poisoned those intellectual currents at their source. The Marxist Soviet Union, apparently untainted by such extortion, was later to be the beneficiary of widespread suspicion of the liberal West.

In the fullness of time, retribution was to be exacted on all foreigners in China. That harsh revenge would, nonetheless, appear mild to vehemently nationalistic Chinese when compared with the foreigners' original misdeeds.

Mary Osgood was a spectator to those great events. The subsequent consequences of the gory summer of 1900 unfolded so gradually that she did not comprehend their full import for some years. Besides, the

101

quickening pace of her own life demanded all her concern.

Six days after she returned to her father's bungalow, Ah Sam padded into the cozy parlor with unwonted ceremony. He presented a silver-plated salver on which lay a small parcel wrapped in stained burlap. It was subscribed: MISS MARY PHILIPPA OSGOOD, OFFICERS' LINES, MURRAY BARRACKS, HONG KONG—BY COURTESY OF COMMANDER M. R. E. EDWARDES, R.N.

She cut the rough stitching with her nail scissors that seemed infuriatingly blunt to reveal heavy folds of cream silk tied with a crimson cord. When her fumbling fingers finally undid the knot, a necklace of massive sea-green jade stones set in gold spilled into her lap. She caught her breath in delight. Clasping the necklace around her throat, she admired herself in the mirror. Finally she opened the accompanying envelope engraved with the familiar crest of the Regiment. The sender was John Williams, V.C., Captain, Royal Wessex Fusiliers. It was, she realized, the first time she had seen his small, neat handwriting.

Peking
26 August 1900

Dearest Mary,

I write you as a rough soldier unskilled in the literary arts, though I long for the pen of a Tennyson or a Shelley. Only the lyric passion of a poet could tell you how I truly feel. [Inarticulate John Williams had not written those phrases without assistance from a brother officer of literary inclinations, she surmised—and then was ashamed of her own coolness.]

But I must haste. *Persephone* sails within the hour, and Commander Edwardes stands impatiently beside me. You may have heard that I was wounded slightly in the unpleasantness. I am happy to be able to allay whatever unease (perhaps I flatter myself!) you may feel. I am recovering well, and I shall be returning to troop duties in a week or two. It will be longer, perhaps months, before the Regiment returns to Hong Kong, since we are ordered to root out all the remaining Boxers.

You may have heard that I was fortunate enough to

102

be in the forefront when we met with some resistance. They have given me the Victoria Cross, though many of our brave fellows deserved the honor much more than I. I shall wear it for them. They have also promoted me to captain. The step came before its time, and I am grateful.

You must pardon me if I presume—or flatter myself unduly—in feeling that you will be concerned with my affairs. However, I can say that my prospects are now much better than they appeared only a few short weeks ago. The Colonel has assured me that a "Career" is now truly open to me. Apparently I am to be forgiven my professional studies because I have demonstrated the traditional rashness of the "fearless" British officer.

I hope devoutly that these tidings will interest you.

Mary, dearest, for the first time, I am in a position to put to you the question I have so long yearned to ask. Will you marry me when I return? I long for our union more than any honors our Sovereign can bestow.

I pray that you will find it in your heart to accept my suit. I shall presumptuously close by sending,

All my love,
John

Mary avidly reread the letter through a mist of tears. Yes or no—she could not know what her answer would be, but a wave of tenderness rose in her breast. She gently lifted the magnificent necklace from its silken wrapping. She knew instinctively that the costly jewels were a product of the looting Hilary Metcalfe denounced, since John Williams could never have found the funds for its purchase. But it was no more than a paltry reward for the suffering he had endured and the courage he had displayed. And, she reflected, admiring her image in the looking-glass, it *was* magnificent.

October 3, 1900–December 26, 1900

FIVE high-pooped junks circled the anchored ketch like sportive whales. When the cumbersome craft turned, their patchwork sails swung across decks strewn with fishing-nets, cooking pots, dog kennels, wooden tubs, and tangles of ropes. Fishermen and their wives shouted earthy jests in their own rough dialect, and naked infants tottered across the cluttered decks.

"Don't the children ever fall overboard?" Mary Osgood asked lazily.

"Sometimes," Charles Sekloong laughed. "But they don't drown."

"Why? Divine protection?" she persisted idly. "Does the Goddess of the Sea save them?"

"That's not the secret," he replied. "Look more closely. They're tied to Chinese life-preservers—empty wooden kegs."

"How ingenious!" Mary sustained the light conversation, though her thoughts were engaged elsewhere.

"They're Tankas, the outcasts of the sea. The brats swim long before they walk. Most Tankas never touch land—except for burial."

Mary shuddered at lifetimes spent amid the putrid reek of fish on junks that tossed like walnut shells, sheltered from the blazing summer sun and the cruel winter rain only by threadbare tarpaulins. Consciously complacent, she contemplated her slim legs stretched in the deck-chair under the green sun-umbrella. The squared neckline and puff-sleeves of the bodice of her blue-serge bathing costume were far less revealing than a ballgown. But the lace-frilled pantaloons under a mid-thigh skirt ended just below the knee, and in the fierce heat her calves were not covered by the long stockings that were essential to modesty in England.

Sprawled on the holystoned deckplanking of the fore-deck, Charles Sekloong slitted his eyes against the glare. Unobserved, she appraised the strong features dominated by his arrogantly arched nose and the tautly muscled body revealed by his striped-jersey singlet and blue trunks. Faintly tinged with gold, his olive skin glowed with health. Mary had met Welshmen and Scots who were darker than Charles. He was actually fair compared to the Spaniards and Maltese she had seen on the trip out, though they were considered "white Europeans."

She had met few such vitally attractive male animals. But she felt instinctive, unreasoning revulsion at the thought of his mixed blood. It was foolish, she reproached herself. Worse, it was atavistic and bigoted, but she could not quite suppress the feeling. Yet the man himself fascinated her, in part, she admitted, because he was so different from all the other men she had known. His body's hairlessness alternately attracted and repelled her. Her hand reached out of its own will to touch his smoothly rippling shoulder, and she consciously checked the movement. There was, she had been brought up to feel, something weak and womanish about a man whose torso, arms, and legs were utterly hairless. But there was nothing remotely womanish about his trained athlete's powerful grace. His sinuous muscles, she knew, had been trained by horseback riding, cricket, rugby, and hard slashing tennis. And his hazel eyes were charged with wholly masculine desire when they frankly assayed her.

"Why do the junks keep circling?" Her words remained completely detached from her thoughts. "I've heard so much talk about pirates."

Charles laughed reassuringly, happy to press his undeclared courtship by parading his knowledge and his power. Despite his father's outspoken opposition, he wanted this woman—and he would have her. Uncharacteristically self-analytical, he reflected that he had never been thwarted during his entire life—except when his wishes clashed with his father's will. At the age of twenty-four he had never been denied by a woman he desired, and he had never seriously considered marriage, though his mother constantly impressed upon him the splendid virtues of the daughters of the leading Chinese families of Canton and Hong Kong. This woman, he knew, he could possess only in marriage, though his feelings about her race veered wildly, one moment enhancing her attraction, the next provoking revulsion. He had been brought up as Chinese, with all the Chinese pride of blood. His parents had fervidly encouraged that pride—in part, he suspected, because his father hated the memory of his own Caucasian father.

"The junks?" Mary's laughing reminder pierced his reverie. "You *are* in a brown study."

'Oh, yes. They're waiting for the tide to change. Fataumun, the strait there's studded with underwater rocks. They must pass through just right. They can't beat against tide and wind like us. But no need to worry even if pirates were all around us, not just fishermen."

"Why not? Why have the boat-boys hidden rifles in the ventilators?"

"They always do. A safeguard against kidnapping. But *that* is our sure protection."

He pointed to the mizzenmast, from which fluttered a royal-blue banner embroidered in golden thread with the winged Sekloong dragon.

"Everybody knows that emblem, every fisherman, merchantman, and pirate from Hainan in the south to Dairen in the north. Even the wild sea brigands of Taiwan pay homage to the winged dragon. Only madmen could defy it. We Sekloongs have many friends—and much *kuan-hsi,* many connections. I'll tell you more some day."

Mary knew that assertively male note well, for he was obviously deploying his words to impress her. They had been much together since August; she had heard the welling peacock tones frequently, and, more often in the last few weeks, a yearning, tender tone. She knew, too, that Charles was exaggerating only slightly, if at all. The Sekloongs lived like princes, rather than merchants, and innumerable convoluted tendrils connected them with the sources of power in both Hong Kong and China. Hilary Metcalfe, who sat ponderous and rubicund in white linen shirt and trousers beside Lady Sekloong under the sun-awning on the afterdeck, had told her much—and hinted more. Charles's tone was the familiar courting display of the male, but his braggadocio proceeded from a splendid reality.

The sailing ketch *Orchidia* alone would have been beyond Mary's imagining if the Metcalfes had not introduced her to this glittering new world that evoked Coleridge's line, "In Xanadu did Kubla Khan a stately pleasure-dome decree." Called *Orchidia* after Sir Jonathan's mother, whose name, Mei-lan, meant "beautiful orchid," the vessel carried twelve crewmen smartly turned out in gold-striped blue jumpers. The ketch was one hundred feet long, a bare ten feet shorter, Charles had told her, than the racing yacht *Britannia* His Royal Highness Albert Edward, Prince of Wales, was building at Cowes.

Orchidia was just one of the three pleasure craft that flew the winged-dragon pennant. The newest, *Lucinda,* fifty-eight feet of gleaming steam-pinnace, normally lay at anchor off Blake Pier so that Sir Jonathan could stroll across the *praya* from his offices in St. George's Building for lunch and a catnap. *Regina,* eighty-five feet in length, broad in proportion, and powered by new twin turbines, had been a present to Lucinda, Lady Sekloong, on the birth of her youngest son Harry almost twenty-one years earlier.

"Mother doesn't like *Orchidia,*" Charles had explained. "Sailboats make her stomach queasy, so father built *Regina* for her."

Yet plump Lady Lucinda sat enthroned on a deckchair between Elizabeth and Hilary Metcalfe on *Orchidia's* afterdeck, her fingers mechanically telling a Buddhist rosary. Why, Mary wondered, had she joined them on the sailboat? The daughter of a prosperous Cantonese gold-merchant was normally self-indulgent —except when her children's interests were involved. Surely Elizabeth Metcalfe's chaperonage would have satisfied convention. And why was Harry Sekloong lounging indolently on the afterdeck?

A few months older than herself, Harry was slightly darker, a shade taller, and definitely more exuberant than Charles. The three had been much together, since he normally accompanied Charles and herself for propriety's sake. Laughing at Harry's antics, Mary felt the warm affection she might toward a mischievous twin brother who was her only companion of her own age.

107

Though Harry could rarely resist baiting his serious elder brother, he was keeping his distance from the foredeck.

"There they go," Charles broke into her sunlit musings. "Look."

The five junks pointed their prows toward the Fataumun Strait and the open sea.

"Does that mean the tide's changing?"

"Must be." He consulted the gold pocket-watch that lay with its heavy chain beside his cigar case. "And right on time. We'll have to buck the tide. I told the coxswain not to try to catch it."

"Why, Charles?" Mary asked provocatively. "What's special about today?"

"Oh, nothing particular, though it might—it might, perhaps, be, but—"

"Be what?"

"Just pleasanter to sail back in the cool dusk." His voice was uncertain, the assertive, demanding note muted. "I'm sure it won't be cold for you. Anyway, the saloon's snug."

"I shan't be chilled," she smiled. "You always take good care of me."

Charles did not rise to the opening, but silently trickled his watch-chain through his fingers. Mary was momentarily abashed. Was she too blatantly flirtatious? Charles himself had been hinting so broadly she felt it not unseemly to trail her petticoats with a provocative swirl. It was, after all, only a game she was playing—with greater freedom because her choleric father was still in Peking with the Regiment two months after the relief of the Legation Quarter. No, she decided, her manner was not wanton. How could she possibly be wanton under the vigilant eyes of Elizabeth Metcalfe and Lady Lucinda? Besides, the prospect was absurd —unlikely to arise and unthinkable if it did.

"Why so pensive, Charles?" she teased. "What're you brooding about, a great business coup or winning the Kwangtung Handicap at Happy Valley? I'd like a tip, you know."

"Neither, Mary. Dragon Prince is a good bet—if I

can convince Harry *not* to ride him," Charles said in jest. "It's more important."

"*More* important than business or racing? In Hong Kong, nothing's more important."

"Some things are. My parents feel—that is, I've discussed—"

Mary's relief was marred by a chill of disappointment. She knew then that she would not face the dilemma she anticipated and feared, though she had already decided on her answer. She had given Charles no reason to presume that his suit would be successful, though she had noted all the signs indicating that he would propose marriage to her. But, she realized at that moment, he would not do so: his prickly pride, which verged upon arrogance, arose, she had discovered, from a conviction of superiority that was not founded upon absolute certainty. He could not bear to appear ridiculous or less than wholly in command of himself and those about him. She could not believe that he would discuss with his family the prospect of marriage to her until he had first assured himself that she would not reject him.

Watching the junks' tattered sails recede into the clouds, she lowered the guard on her tongue and her heart she had automatically raised when Charles's conversation seemed to veer toward the proposal she feared. No longer directly involved, she could quite properly coax him to express the thoughts at which he shied for some reason.

"Since you've talked about this mysterious something, why not tell me? I'm just a convenient ear."

"Never, Mary. Not just a convenient ear."

"That's kind, but—"

"Mary, I could never take you for granted. You're too—too kind and too good, too beautiful and exciting. But I've discussed with my father and Hilary—"

"You've really been collecting opinions, Charles," she teased.

"I have really." His solemnity reproached her light-mindedness.

Enthroned on the afterdeck, the Metcalfes and Lady

Lucinda appeared to her inflamed imagination a jury sitting silent in judgment. Even the scapegrace Harry was perched quietly on the bulwarks, his vivacious features quite expressionless. She knew she would always remember the moment.

"Mary, we talked about it very much these weeks. My father now finally says all right. Mother still doubts very much. The Metcalfes say they can't say."

Charles Sekloong was, this once in his life, determined to be totally candid, though his suit might be impeded by candor. The decision, he felt, was too important for the innocent dissimulation or deliberate evasion that had so often attained his purposes. Still, he felt no compulsion to tell Mary of his fierce quarrel with his father when he first suggested marriage to a European. It would serve no conceivable purpose to tell her that Sir Jonathan had recoiled in unfeigned horror or that he and his son had argued bitterly for weeks thereafter.

Mary Philippa Osgood was misled by her own quick intelligence and by her ignorance of Chinese customs. Instinct told her that Charles was approaching a proposal of marriage. But she could not conceive of his pride's permitting him to engage in lengthy discussions with his family, much less the Metcalfes, before expressing his wishes to herself. Nor could she conceive that he might be so insensitive to her own pride and dignity as to make a public debate of an intensely personal matter. She was, quite simply, puzzled.

"Charles, what is it?" she asked. "Nothing's as grave as all that."

"It is. It certainly is."

"Then say it," she prompted impatiently. "Whatever it is. Be easier after you've said it."

"I will. But I'll do it my way. These last few months, Mary, we've been together a lot and I've enjoyed every minute, deeply."

"I've enjoyed it, too, Charles. Very much."

"I'm glad, Mary. I know how much I'm asking you to give up; your rightful place in England and—"

Along with her initial surprise that Charles was, after all, proposing, Mary was incongruously amused. What rightful place? The shabby gentility of a governess, an upper-servant? What place at all had she in England? Then realization came flooding in, realization that he was speaking the words she had feared and, perversely, hoped for.

"—and to live with strangers." Charles's words were carefully rehearsed. "Different blood, different ways—it won't be easy. I'll make it up to you. We'd travel, though we must live in Hong Kong. My father insists, and I agree. For me, Hong Kong would be barren without you. I—I love you very much."

"Charles. You're—dear—very dear to me, Charles. But I can't be sure—"

Mary was again startled by her own words. Her voice sounded coolly composed, but she was not speaking as she had when she rehearsed the scene in her mind.

"You're not sure," Charles interrupted forcefully. "You know what you're really saying? You're not saying no. I'm sure you're saying 'yes, but not just yet.' You will finally say yes. I know it."

"Perhaps, Charles. Perhaps that's true. But, for now, I must say no. I'm not certain . . . of anything."

Her confusion deepening, she listened intently to her own voice as if it were a stranger's. She should really not be encouraging him in any way, for she knew she must, finally, refuse him. Even if the prospect of such an alien marriage were not intrinsically impossible, his family's opposition required her to refuse him.

"Charles." She strove again to explain her bewildering emotions. "It's not what I thought. Like all girls, I've thought about a moment like this . . . and you flatter me greatly. I was so sure I could say no quite firmly —without hurting you. But, now, I care more about not hurting you than anything else. I don't know what that means—"

"Then you will say yes." Charles was, once again, utterly confident, his self-assurance almost overcoming her doubts. "I know it. I'm very happy."

"Happy? I don't know. I'm so confused. I certainly can't say yes. But, somehow, I can't just now say no.

Charles, please don't press me. Just don't press . . . for a while."

"For a while, all right. But later, I'll press you again and again and again. And you will say yes."

Mary almost yielded to Charles at that moment. His lean, aristocratic jawline was set in determination, and his clear hazel eyes glowed. He was, she realized, offering her not only his own dynamic self, but a position in his own society equivalent to a countess's in England. If only that society were less outlandish to her, not so different and, somehow, frightening. He engulfed her hand in his own hard palm and her pulse quickened. At a great distance, she heard chains clank as *Orchidia*'s anchor came up. The rising sails filled, and the bowsprit pointed west into the amethyst twilight. She felt enclosed in a glowing crystal sphere, elated by successive thrills of joy and tenderness.

Yet her wayward thoughts pursued their own awkward surmises. Did she feel conventional triumph at his proposal—and no more? Were not all young women so instilled with yearning for marriage, the true proof of their triumphant femininity, that they might respond as she had to a proposal by any man for whom they felt some fondness? Was she, perhaps, deluded by her own instinctive response and the gorgeous setting Charles had chosen?

Why, she pondered uneasily, had Charles assiduously conferred with his family before speaking to her? She had apparently been appraised in the clan's councils like a plot of land whose acquisition the Sekloongs were considering. Such cold calculation was, perhaps, normal among families of great wealth but was nonetheless demeaning to herself. Mary indignantly reaffirmed her decision: she would reject Charles because she must.

For the moment, though, she deliberately ignored the nagging voice of both reason and indignation to abandon herself to the pleasure any young woman might properly feel upon receiving such a proposal. Properly, quite properly, could she enjoy that pleasure. She was a female, even before she was a lady, though perhaps, though only an aspiring lady; she was a female before she was the Bandmaster's daughter. Besides, she was so deliciously secure within her crystal sphere.

Charles was startled but not discouraged by Mary's equivocal response. He was utterly convinced that he would in time possess the woman he wanted. He had, above all, already borne down his dictatorial father's violent opposition, for the first time in his life defying *the* Sekloong—and winning. Charles relived his fierce arguments with his father after he declared his determination to marry Mary. Though the Sekloongs thought themselves at home in English, they had gone at each other in Cantonese tirades like fishermen bickering over their share of the catch.

"You're not serious, can't be," Sir Jonathan had shouted. "She's nobody—common as yesterday's cold rice. Worse, she's a *European* nobody."

"That's rotten hypocrisy, a dog's head on a sheep's body. You're always telling me Chinese must get along with Europeans," Charles rejoined. "Otherwise no stability—and no business."

"But not *marry* them. Offhand I can think of a dozen virtuous Chinese girls of good family who—"

"So you and Mother're always telling me. Good family—meaning good gold bars."

"Nothing wrong with gold either," Sir Jonathan observed. "But I'm thinking of our position. If we chase after them, the Europeans'll despise us."

"I'm not chasing. Mary's willing; I can tell."

"Willing? Why not? The Bandmaster's daughter is doing well for herself. The Sekloongs are very important and very rich. She's no fool—don't think she hasn't thought about gold. I've made our name deeply respected by both Chinese and Europeans. Go your way—and both'll despise us."

"It's my life, Father. I've pondered ten thousand hours about this. You're prejudiced, rotten prejudiced."

Despite his rising anger, Charles carefully skirted the explosive central issue. He could not taunt his father with their own mixed blood. Himself half-European, Sir Jonathan almost invariably appeared in public in the Chinese gentleman-scholar's long-gown because his

Caucasian features appeared so wholly European when he wore Western clothing. He not only retained Chinese nationality, but fought as a *Chinese* against the social and legal restrictions Hong Kong imposed on the race which made up more than 98 percent of its population. In part because of his mixed blood, he battled for acceptance on his own terms—Chinese terms. But the older man again surprised his son.

"You mean," he asked hotly, "because of my Irish father?"

"Yes, I do, since you've said it. You're not logical."

"Not logical! By the Nine Dragons, not logical! Is it logical to go crawling after the Europeans? Is your spear so finicky it must pierce a European target?"

"You're talking about the lady I'm going to marry."

"Marry, hell! Just bed her and get it out of your system."

"Wonderful advice from a good Catholic father!"

"Don't come the religious line on me. I know your habits. You've had half the sing-song girls between here and Canton. Don't try piety on me."

"Mary's different. She won't be a concubine or a mistress, not this woman. I don't want her that way, and she'd never—"

"Try gold," Sir Jonathan advised curtly. "Enough gold and jewels make even a female Buddha surrender."

"She won't take anything but marriage," Charles reiterated. "And I don't want—"

"*You* don't want. *You're* suddenly so damned moral. *I've* spent my life building a kingdom for you and your descendants. A Chinese kingdom needs a Chinese crown-princess, not the fortune-hunting daughter of an English mummer—a musician, practically a strolling actor."

"That's rubbish. Her father holds rank. They call him Mister. He's a gentleman."

"Some gentleman, a boozy, beery old devil-head always rutting on the flower boats. But no European can make you a proper wife. We need—*need,* I tell you— an alliance with a great Chinese family."

The battle had raged for more than a week, while Lady Lucinda and Harry walked wide of the angry father and son. Sir Jonathan had finally yielded, prudently withdrawing from the battle he realized he could not win. He was, Charles suspected, convinced that his son would relinquish his purpose if his father appeared to acquiesce—or that, alternately, he could buy Mary off or frighten her away. That was his way, as it was also his way to wring every advantage from circumstances he disliked but recognized he could not prevent.

"If you must, you must," Sir Jonathan sighed. "Somehow I'll make the best of it."

"Father, I swear. I won't marry for years—if ever— if I can't marry Mary, if you block it."

"Ever? A long time indeed! But I yield to your blackmail. You know I want many grandchildren, many heirs as soon as possible. Go ahead, then."

"Thank you, Father."

"For what? Giving in to the inevitable—if it's really inevitable? You know I don't want a breach between us. You can't afford a breach either, for all your brave talk. The family comes first."

"I feel thankful—"

"It's not for you, but for the family, the Sekloongs. I'll even assist your suit. Then, if she won't you can blame only yourself."

Sir Jonathan's reluctance had not abated, but his over-riding realism had forced him to give his grudging consent. Armed with that consent and elated by his first victory over his father, Charles Sekloong thereupon proposed marriage to Mary Osgood in the twilight over the South China Sea.

An impassioned proposal was, Mary had been taught, every young woman's brightest dream. It was perhaps every other young woman's dream; it had become her own particular nightmare.

Not one, but two, ardent suitors sought her hand. The first was a hero, his dauntless courage attested by the Realm's highest award for valor. John Williams was also a man of solid value, totally dependable as well as valorous. The second suitor was more attractive—darkly handsome, masterful, and passionate. Charles Sekloong was also the heir of a wealthy knight who would certainly grow even richer. She need but choose between them. Yet Mary Osgood could not decide which she wished to marry—if, indeed, she wished to marry either. John Williams and Charles Sekloong each posed practical problems as well as offering different prospects, and the North Country common sense of the daughter of a penniless warrant officer counseled her to choose very carefully.

John Williams was part of her own world, the Regiment she knew too well—and the England she knew well enough. She could accurately assess her feelings toward John in the light of her own direct experience. However unromantic it might seem, she must also assess her prospects with John in the same clear light.

She did not really know Charles Sekloong's world, which she had entered less than six months earlier. Colonial Hong Kong was far removed from all her previous experience. His background and his blood were both mixed, and she had seen only the glittering surface of the Sekloong clan. Marrying Charles would mean not only taking a husband, but entering a wholly alien milieu. She would assume responsibilities and enjoy privileges within a complex structure of which she knew only the exterior. Little in her experience qualified her to weigh Charles's proposal as deliberately as she must. She did not even fully understand her own feelings, the reasons for the passionate attraction Charles exerted upon her. How much was she drawn to the man himself and how much was she lured—as well as repelled—by his exotic background?

In her perplexity, Mary turned to her mentors, the Metcalfes. Since Charles had talked with them even before speaking to herself, she could quite properly consult the brother and sister who had, despite the brevity of their friendship, become beloved surrogate parents.

"You want counsel on a matter of the heart?" Hilary Metcalfe boomed. "I'm flattered, but it's not really my line. Who am I to advise a young lady on matrimony?"

"You *and* Miss Metcalfe." Unabashed, Mary appealed to his affection and to his loquacity. "It's not just my heart, but my life and—I hope I won't shock you —my prospects."

"You couldn't shock me," Hilary Metcalfe replied. "Only a damned fool forgets the harsh, practical questions, and you're no fool. Far from it. Only a brave girl'd admit she's worried about the prospects."

Elizabeth Metcalfe's plain features were suffused with concern, and her cascade of necklaces was, for once, silent. She sat quite still in the woven-cane chair beside the embroidered screen that masked the fireplace.

"Well, what do you want?" Metcalfe demanded. "Am I to decide for you? Are we?"

"Just advice," Mary smiled. "You're not usually mean with advice."

Hilary Metcalfe hunched his big head between his shoulders, momentarily stricken by the laughter sparkling in her violet eyes and the soft swirl of the red-gold hair that tumbled around her shoulders in blithe defiance of fashion. He contemplated the swell of her breasts beneath the tight, high-necked bodice of apple-green shantung, and he admired the curved sweep of her legs outlined by her light skirt.

"And advice you'll have. You may even take it. Hong Kong's a little far for the Fishing Fleet to venture; but you've got a fine catch—two fat fish on the line."

Mary had heard heavy jests about the young ladies of good family, but uncertain matrimonial prospects, who sailed to India in the autumn to pass the season with friends or relations—and, they hoped, to catch a husband. They were ungallantly called the Fishing Fleet.

"Hilary, stop playing the goat." Elizabeth Metcalfe leaned forward indignantly, and the beads on her deep bosom clucked their own admonition. "Mary's not amused."

"Well, then, to our muttons—or your fish, my dear," Hilary Metcalfe resumed. "I've known Charles since he was a baby. Good chap, somewhat too malleable, but

117

bright—and prospects almost unlimited. If Jonathan's worth less than two million at this moment, I'm a longshore coolie. Two million pounds, not Hong Kong dollars. Soon he'll be richer—much, much richer. . . . Charles, as I said, good chap. Mind you, he's not his father. Jonathan's extraordinary, damned near a commercial and political genius—no more than a fly's whisker between Jonathan and genius. Charles, now, Charles. A few peccadilloes with the ladies, but that's expected. Make you a willing, wealthy husband."

"And what would you advise?" Mary had known instinctively that her hot-blooded suitor was not inexperienced, and the confirmation of that knowledge enhanced rather than detracted from his animal appeal. "Shall I say yes or no?"

"That *is* a direct question, isn't it?" Metcalfe temporized. "Damned direct. These modern misses don't mince words, do they?"

"Hilary, what *would* you advise Mary—yes or no?"

"If I must, then I'd say . . . No. Jonathan's my closest friend, but I can't say I know him—really know him. It's almost thirty-five years since we studied Mandarin together . . . met him then, when he was less than fifteen. We've worked together ever since, and I'm closer to him than anyone else outside the clan. But sometimes you reach a certain point—and the shutters come down. He's my closest friend, but I don't really know him."

"But, Mr. Metcalfe, you're talking about Sir Jonathan—and I'm asking about marrying Charles. It's not the same thing."

"It is, you know. Exactly the same thing. I'm talking about a family—a Chinese family, despite the Western blood and the Western influence. The son *is* the father, since the family's indivisible. I'd say no, definitely no."

"Why, Mr. Metcalfe?"

"Because they're completely foreign to you. It's not merely a matter of children of mixed blood. Time's hardly ripe for them to be easy in their hearts—won't be for generations, I fear. Look at Charles. Look at Jonathan himself. It's not just race, but entirely different customs. Did you know Jonathan had a brace of concubines—and a half-dozen mistresses?"

"But Charles doesn't," Mary objected.

"Not yet. Maybe never, maybe very soon."

"You must think of that, my dear," Elizabeth interjected.

"Also, the Sekloongs are Catholics." His initial reluctance was overcome, and Hilary Metcalfe's opinions tumbled out. "Don't know how much it means to you, but the offspring'd have to be Romans. Lucinda promised, though she's a devout Buddhist."

"How did they become Catholics?"

"Because only the Jesuits gave the young Jonathan consistent, even-handed affection and discipline. His father, you know, was an Irish adventurer who abandoned Jonathan's unwed mother. The boy was brought up between two worlds. Neither proper European nor proper Chinese. His wealthy Chinese grandfather sometimes cosseted him, but most of the time ignored him. Except for the Jesuits' care, Jonathan had to make his own way. He missed the advantages of Chinese wealth —and the privileges of European blood. Do you wonder he's a hard man, a driven man? Hardest on himself, but very hard on his family. Charles has borne the brunt. In some ways, he's now almost as hard as Jonathan. But I can't in conscience tell you the other things only I know, information I learned in confidence."

"I want a strong man, not a namby-pamby."

"Above all," he ignored her interjection, "the time's not ripe for mixed blood. Jonathan's an example of the damage, even if, you may think, an extreme example. This kind of marriage, an amalgam of East and West, it's my dream of the future. But not yet. When *you* ask me, Mary, I'm fearful. I don't want you sacrificing yourself in the Eurasians' agonies."

Metcalfe cocked his head as if listening to an inner voice before adding: "And Charles . . . well, Charles is Charles. You must finally judge him for yourself. Don't rush your fences. But, if you must marry, take young Williams and an easier life."

"May I ask something?" Elizabeth said. "Do you love Charles Sekloong, truly love him?"

"I don't know," Mary mused. "I don't actually know. I don't really know about love. But I *do* think so."

Harry Sekloong was as definite, though not as vehement as Hilary Metcalfe. He called at the Osgood bungalow when the autumnal sun was just receding from its zenith, and he and Mary strolled to the wooden-roofed Peak Tram terminus. Drawn clanking over steel rails by its great cable, the green carriage bore them to the top of The Peak. Sedan chairs waited to carry them through the green wooded heights on winding footpaths.

"The White Highlands," Harry laughed, handing Mary into her chair. "Inviolate till my old man broke the taboo. When the Manor's finished, we'll be the first wogs on The Peak."

Mary laughed in response as he swung into his chair. She knew that Sir Jonathan had refused to accept his knighthood until he could build on The Peak, previously reserved by inflexible custom for the Colony's British overlords. The epithet "wog"—abbreviation of the derogatory term, "Worthy Oriental Gentleman," would have grated if anyone else used it, however flippantly. But Harry Sekloong, just approaching his twenty-first birthday, possessed a talent for lighthearted laughter that purged his words of bitterness. Hilary Metcalfe had observed: "Harry Sekloong has no sense of the serious. Is that his affliction—or ours?"

Harry's crisp hair fitted his broad head like a black cap. The hazel Sekloong eyes, the legacy of distant Celtic ancestors, twinkled disconcertingly above his high cheekbones, and his wide mouth smiled in gentle mockery. Mary felt a glow of affection for Harry. So nearly her own age, he was totally undemanding and intuitively sensitive to her feelings. She could relax and enjoy Harry's gamin charm as she could not wholly relax with his passionate older brother.

"We're coming to the sacred site," Harry called from his swaying chair. "Just like building the Pyramids, only in Hong Kong. Every stone, every board hauled up

Peak Road by bullocks—and carried the last five thousand yards on coolies' backs."

Mary nodded her interest.

"Five hundred tons of stone, ten miles of timber, three acres of slates—my old man's got it all worked out. When he's finished, Buckingham Palace'll look like a poorhouse."

Mary chuckled at his curiously belittling hyperbole. Yet she gasped when their chairs swung through a cutting in an earthen bank and settled gently to the ground.

The scene truly recalled an imaginative engraving of the building of the Great Pyramids. Laboriously leveled by cutting away the steep hillside, the site occupied ten acres. Across the raw-red patch of earth, hundreds of coolies were deployed like teams of Hebrew slaves. The gray-stone walls of the main house, which jesting Harry called The Castle, enclosed half a London block. The second story was rising amid a tracery of bamboo scaffolding, on which workmen swarmed like monkeys, and massive cut-stones swayed upward on ropes pulled by fifty men. The din was overwhelming—grinding machinery, resounding hammer blows, squealing pulleys, and, above all, the coolies' shouting in raucous Cantonese.

"Modest, isn't it?" Harry smiled. "My old man builds big—and leaves room for bigger."

She nodded, smiling, and Harry led her behind a grove of pines that filtered out the tumult.

"What'd you say when Charles asked you?" he inquired abruptly. "He thinks you said 'Maybe yes.' I guess you said 'Possibly no.' What'd you really say?"

"I suppose I said, 'Well, perhaps we'll see,'" she answered, surprised by his intrusiveness, but not resentful. "I certainly didn't say 'Maybe yes.' More like 'Possibly no.'"

"Tell him no, Mary! Tell him no!"

"Harry," she bridled, "I'm fond of you. But isn't that our business—his and mine?"

"No," he said hotly, "it's family business, big business. You know Charles fought and haggled with the

121

old man before he even asked you? Afterward, the old man finally granted you might do. Healthy, intelligent, not too flighty. He's still not really happy with a *gwailo,* a foreign devil person. You'll do—just."

"I'm flattered," Mary snapped.

"You should be, I suppose. They all looked you over. Charles had fancies before, but never talked marriage."

"I am not interested in Charles's past fancies." Mary turned her back in anger. "It's time we left."

"Now, Mary, don't fret." Harry was genuinely abashed. "After all, you've talked to no one but the Metcalfes. And they're really too old. If there's anyone else, perhaps a girl friend our age, you can really talk to, I'll stop."

"No, Harry." His conscious charm placated her. "There isn't."

"Will you talk to me then? Or, at least, listen? I'll never repeat a word."

"But why do you feel so strongly?" She was genuinely puzzled by his opposition, his obvious concern for herself, rather than the Sekloong clan.

"Because, Mary, because—"

He was deliberately exerting all his charm. Though Mary knew he was playing to her weakness for him, she gave way and asked, "Because what, Harry?"

"Because I do care about you. Like a sister, of course. And I don't want you swallowed by the Sekloongs or sacrificed to my old man's ambitions. He's afraid of tearing the clan apart by opposing Charles on this marriage, so he's given in. But, next thing, he'll start remolding you, trying to make you no more than a docile breeder of the next generation of the Sekloong dynasty."

Harry silenced Mary's incipient protest.

"Another minute, and I'll be quiet. If you accept their terms, they'll give you the world wrapped in silk. But I don't want you humiliated—or broken."

"Thank you, Harry." She was so wholly mollified that she missed the implications of his final words and failed to pursue them. "I can see you do care about me.

I'll think about your advice. Honestly, I haven't made up my mind."

"I'm glad," he said. "One last question?"

"You might as well. But you promised. Our conversation will remain . . . our own conversation."

"What," he asked baldly, "about the alternative?"

"The alternative? Oh, you mean—"

"Captain John Williams, the so-called Hero of Peking. All Hong Kong knows the tale of your magnificent necklace. The girl who captivated Prince William also captivates the glorious Hero of Peking."

"What else does all Hong Kong know about me?"

"Well, of course, that the necklace was—ah—the spoils of war and that the brave Captain's becoming rich by looting."

"And what more?"

"They say he's also asked you to marry him."

"We do correspond, Harry. . . ."

She gratefully took the opportunity to speak with total candor, neither cloaking her feelings with maidenly reserve nor fencing with another young woman who was implicitly a rival. She could always talk more easily to a man, and Harry was a most satisfactory confidant.

"And," he pressed, "has he—"

"I haven't said yes. I haven't even said 'Maybe, yes.' "

"Nor 'Possibly no'?"

"No, not even 'Possibly no.' Just pleasant little letters. I must think further about Charles and John. I'm alone in the whole world, not just in your world."

"That's why I'm taking such liberties—confidently expecting you to forgive me."

"I'll tell you truly. I feel much affection for John, though he doesn't stir me, not like Charles. But, now, I've shocked you. Such fleshly feelings."

"Nothing you said or did could ever shock me."

"Let's walk up the road." She took his arm. "I'll answer you, but then we must end this kind of talk."

"Agreed."

"My mother spent half her life waiting for my father to return from abroad," Mary recalled. "To my brother and me he was a vague, bulky figure, occasionally pop-ping up like Punch. Mother spent all her life waiting for his promotion. But it never came—he'll die a warrant officer."

"Captain John Williams," Harry interrupted, "is marked for great things. London needs a story-book hero to glorify that squalid adventure."

"Perhaps he is. But John is still penniless—and low-er-middle-class. I will not spend my life like my mother —scrimping, pretending, and toadying to senior ladies. In England, I'm nothing—and I'd remain nothing."

"Charles isn't an escape-hatch."

"You don't understand," she flared. "I'd never marry Charles—or any man—just to find a new life if I didn't love him. But I won't condemn myself to follow an end-less, dreary road to nowhere, no matter how much I loved a man."

"The choice, then," Harry probed, "is hard. An alien world, exciting and glamorous, but strewn with pitfalls. Or your own world, which chills you. Am I right?"

"You put it well," she smiled. "But you've left out love. I *can* choose not to choose between them. I'll take no man rather than choose between two I may or may not love—but may not want."

Mary's frank discussion with Harry was grueling, de-spite her impulsive need to confide. She was accus-tomed neither to examining her emotions minutely nor to revealing them to others. But she was later to recall their talk as a light interlude during a period when she was the objective of an implacable campaign.

Harry was proved correct. The Sekloong clan was a powerful, disciplined force that maneuvered to break down her resistance as if she were a city under siege. Once he had given in to Charles, Sir Jonathan directed the campaign as if Mary's marriage to his son were his own cherished desire. Only he himself knew whether he truly wanted the match or whether he hoped her ulti-mate refusal would disillusion his headstrong son and make Charles more amenable in the future. In either event, he had to show enthusiasm in order to repair the breach he had opened with Charles and to regain his sway over his first-born.

The Sekloongs' pressure constantly intensified. Their unrelenting assaults on Mary's emotions sapped her will. Their entertainment and presents sought to overcome her resistance while simultaneously displaying the clan's wealth and power. Later, she could not recall every intimate dinner, lavish dance, and luxury-cushioned excursion. At the time, she could not refuse the tasteful presents without appearing churlish—even to herself.

A carved-jade bracelet or an amethyst ring set with chip diamonds from the avuncular Sir Jonathan. A cloisonné powder-box from Lady Lucinda or a roll of gorgeous "tribute silk," the stiff, embossed fabric shimmering gold as befitted an offering to the Emperor. And from Charles himself—Charles, who normally refrained from any gesture more pressing than an eyebrow lifted interrogatively or a murmured intimacy—expensive trifles: a silver-embroidered scarf from Laos; a minuscule pot of caviar from Persia; a spray of orchids clasped by an enameled seventeenth-century brooch from Peking.

Only once did Charles breach his promise not to press her. Neither did he pine like the wan romantic lovers of Victorian convention; that was no more his way than was the ancient Chinese convention of the worthy young scholar-official who hopelessly adores his superior's daughter. Never denied by a woman, Charles saw himself as the bold warrior on a "thousand-league horse" who seizes what he wants. Seeing Mary home from dinner at the Sekloong mansion off Bonham Road, he dismissed the rickshaw coolies and accompanied her to the door of the bungalow.

"When do I get your answer?" he demanded. "When do I say yes?"

"I still need time, Charles," she countered. "I'm sorry."

"Time's almost up. So's my patience. I love you, Mary, I want you, and I will have you. I swear that to you. I'll break with my family if you insist. We'll make our own way. Penniless, if that's what you really want.

But I won't wait much longer. And you *will* marry me!"

"But, Charles, I can't be . . ."

"You will be sure—and very soon. You *will* say yes —very soon."

He grasped her shoulders, and she gave herself gladly to his demanding kiss. Abruptly, he released her.

"I can tell," he said curtly, "even if you can't. It won't be long before you agree. So go and think again. But not too long!"

On Christmas morning, a coolie brought her a packet with a brief note: "From all the Sekloongs, with much affection." The 1,200-year-old ceramic duck, just four inches high, glowed in its silken nest with the unique three-color glaze of the Tang Dynasty. It was obviously valuable, but not quite so valuable that she could return it without gauche discourtesy.

"Not a bribe," Hilary Metcalfe observed, admiring the small masterpiece of the potter's art, "but very strong persuasion."

Mary still pleaded for time, time to reflect and find her own way. But she was subjected to another pressure almost as intense. John Williams wrote stiltedly passionate letters from Peking, pressing his suit, and he sent his own tokens: a Manchu bridal gown of brilliant red-and-green silk, embroidered with yellow chrysanthemums; a miniature tree, its leaves, flowers, and fruit carved from varicolored jade; a cobalt-blue-and-cream-white vase of the Kang Hsi period, two centuries earlier. Mary acknowledged those gifts and replied to those letters as graciously as she could without committing herself.

"They're beautiful, John, and I'll keep them safe for you. [Such was the burden of her letters.] I look forward keenly to your return. It's always good to see old friends. And I rejoice at your good fortune."

Not a single word could he construe as accepting—or unduly encouraging—his suit. But, his ardor undiminished, John Williams replied as if she were already his acknowledged fiancée.

On the day after Christmas, Mary sat alone at her painting in the cramped parlor of the bungalow, glad of a respite from the hectic holiday season. She had attended four dinner-parties and three elaborate luncheons in one week, culminating with a Christmas feast at the Sekloong mansion. Not only the Sekloongs besieged her with invitations. As Hilary Metcalfe had predicted, she was a minor celebrity because of the attentions Prince William had paid her at the Grand Ball. Aside from the Honorable Rachel Wheatley, every hostess in Hong Kong was eager to lure "His Royal Highness's dancing partner." As was apparently inevitable in the Colony, her popularity made her the center of intrigue. Resentful of Sir Henry Blake's attempts to placate the Chinese community, conservative *taipans* and officers tried to transform Mary into a symbol, "the young lady who defied Lady Blake." Her own sympathies lay with the Chinese and the Eurasians, but she had learned to hold her tongue while treading the convoluted maze of Colonial Society. After the first rush of pleasure at her popularity, she was, she realized, slightly bored.

It was therefore a joy to lunch alone on broth and cold chicken before resuming her long-neglected painting of misty gray-green mountains sundered by an azure waterfall. That tranquil occupation allayed the depression induced by fevered festivities in a climate where giant poinsettias flaunted their crimson petals in the sunlight on every veranda in the 75° heat of Christmas Day.

Heralded by the chiming of glass beads in the doorway, Captain John Williams strode into the quiet room. He was overwhelming in red-and-gold dress uniform with the crimson ribbon of the Victoria Cross on his left breast and the three silver pips of his new rank on his epaulettes. But he had lost much weight, and new lines creased his bluff cheeks. He had also lost the diffidence she had found endearing before the Regiment sailed for Peking almost six months earlier.

"Mary, my dear," he declared. "I've longed to see you. Finally wangled convalescent leave after all these months."

"John!" she gasped. "John, it's so good to see you.

We were all so happy when we learned you weren't badly wounded. And we drank champagne to your medal and your promotion."

"My dear Mary! It's been so long. I came as soon as I could."

His arms gathered her up, and she tasted tobacco and whiskey on his lips. She slipped out of his embrace, her heart hammering.

"You look lovely, absolutely lovely. I've dreamed about this moment."

He kissed her again, and she yielded for an instant before again evading his arms.

"It's delightful to see you," she laughed. "But you must be good—or I'll have to ask you to leave. Only Ah Sam's about, and it's not proper—"

"All the better!" His new confidence spoke. "All the better—a man should be alone with his fiancée after so long away. Mary, I do love you."

She seated herself behind the sturdy teak dining-room table as a barrier to his ardor.

"John," she reminded him, "we're not affianced, you know."

"Not affianced? Nonsense! I could tell from your letters."

"What could you tell?" She intended to be stern, but feared that she was involuntarily coquetting. "What?"

"Just that I could tell. You never said no. So I knew you meant yes, though you were too shy, too diffident."

"I never said yes, either, did I?"

"Just what are you getting at?" he demanded. "You led me to believe—Mary, do stop your teasing."

"I'm not teasing, John. I never said yes, and I didn't mean yes. Perhaps I didn't say no directly. Perhaps I wanted to say I didn't know, but how could I—"

"Then it's true," he glowered, "the rumors I've been hearing—but couldn't believe. You've been playing fast and loose with me and that . . . that Eurasian, Sek-loong."

"Hardly fast and loose," she replied coldly. "I wrote you as I'd write any friend . . . any good friend. But I didn't lead you to believe—anything. Besides, what

128

makes you believe it must be another man if it isn't you?"

"And my presents?" He ignored her question. "You kept them, didn't that mean something?"

"I kept them for you. I wrote that I was keeping them for you."

"Well, then, Mary, where do we stand? Can I hope or shall I leave?"

"I'd hate to send you out alone just after you've returned. But you must see—"

"You're not—you're not committed—not promised to that half-caste chink? I've had my bellyful of chinks."

"No, I'm not committed to anyone . . . to Mr. Sekloong or to you, Captain Williams. And don't call Charles a chink. He's a fine gentleman—a good deal more sensitive and more gentle than you."

"A chink's a chink, however he's dressed up—or his father hung with a title. You're mine, Mary, not his."

"I'm my own woman, John. Can't you understand?"

John Williams shifted his weight in the creaking wicker chair. Perplexed anger rose like a red tide across his open face.

"I'm trying to understand, Mary," he said grimly. "If you're not promised to him, then marry me before the week's out."

"I'll marry no one until I please." Her temper finally broke. "I'm not a prize for valor awarded by Her Majesty's Government."

"But you are for sale to the highest bidder!" Williams's voice thickened with choler. "And the highest bidder is the chink."

Mary's vestigial self-control snapped. The decision she'd evaded was taken in one searing instant. Forced to weigh her suitors, she unhesitatingly chose the absent one. Her fiercely possessive defense of Charles showed that she did truly love him very much.

"No, Captain Williams, I'm *not* for sale to the highest bidder, and I won't be browbeaten into marriage. No, Captain Williams, I won't marry you. I *will* marry Mr. Sekloong."

"Mary," he interrupted contritely, "Mary, just listen to me."

"I've listened too long, and now it's too late."

"Marry Sekloong or his father's money?" Williams shouted. "A Queen's officer's not good enough for you. Must be a nabob, even a chink nabob."

"Think what you will, Captain. I *will* marry Charles Sekloong with all my heart—and I *will* make him the best wife I can."

Interlude

June 27, 1970

8:30–10:30 P.M.

THE muted ringing Lady Mary heard as she fingered her necklaces was a haunting echo of the past. Amid the quiet joy of a ninety-year-old dowager, she remembered the exhilaration of a twenty-year-old girl after her first Grand Ball and the same girl's dismay at the wrath of a rejected suitor. The gentle chiming of the glass beads in a vanished doorway and the spiteful rattle of those same beads on an angry afternoon almost seventy years earlier reverberated in her mind. The sounds her ears heard were the clatter of ivory chopsticks against porcelain bowls above rolling waves of conversation and the soft tinkling of her own strands of jade.

Her immediate family, forty-two in all, was seated at the broad oblong table in the Great Hall of The Castle where medieval European wood-carvings stared blindly at thousand-year-old Chinese scrolls. Her back was to the doors, and Sir Mosing Way, himself eighty-five, sat in the place of honor directly opposite his hostess. Lesser members of the House of Sekloong and the Crown Colony's dignitaries sat at nine identical tables, while battalions of waiters presented the fifty-six courses of the Imperial Manchu Banquet. The feast included extravagant delicacies like hummingbirds' tongues, bear's paws, and elephant's trunk, as well as the more familiar shrimp in rice-flour wrapping, crackly Peking duck, sharks' fins with minced chicken, crabclaws with black beans, delicate baby corn with conch, roast young squab, crisp chunks of pomfret in a sweet red sauce, and eight-treasures soup in a hollow wintermelon. Mary had made only one stipulation when Sarah and Opal suggested the menu first conceived for the Empress Dowager Tzu Hsi. Afterward, the guests were to be served traditional birthday noodles, their length symbolizing long life—but the feast was to end with

133

jook, the rice-gruel that was the staple of the poor in South China.

"Remind them of their origins," she snapped. "Remind them how all this grandeur and mock-grandeur began."

The gesture would probably pass unnoticed amid the ostentatious splendor. The ten tables set with a gold-mounted service for more than four hundred were dwarfed by the immensity of the Great Hall. As The Castle dominated Sekloong Manor, The Castle itself was dominated by the Great Hall, one hundred and fifty feet square, three stories high. A Peking carpet commissioned in 1921 covered the waxed parquet with patterns incised in blue and gold on a beige field. From one of six carved-wooden galleries, a chamber ensemble played Mozart.

The wooden figures of angels, saints, knights, and ladies adorning the galleries had come from *châteaux* in France, *Schlösser* in Germany, and manor houses in England. Recesses in the teak-paneled walls displayed the porcelains of three Imperial Dynasties: the softly glowing celadon of the Sung, the brilliant blue-and-white of the Ming, and the varicolored, six-foot-high vases of the Ching. A time-darkened Rembrandt study of his mistress Saskia hung in a pool of light on the far wall. Extending ninety feet along the opposite wall, a minutely detailed painting depicted the sixty-mile-long sweep of the Yang-tze Valley from Wuhu to Nanking. The artist had spent twenty-three years painting the procession of musicians, cavalrymen, courtiers, officials, and palanquined concubines accompanying the Emperor Kao Tsung of the Southern Sung Dynasty to his capital seven hundred and fifty years earlier.

The past was too much with her, though the chiming was not swaying glass beads. She was fingering the four-inch-square jade pendant that had been Sir Jonathan's gift, her fingers tracing the winged dragon rampant on the cool, sepia-striated stone. She stroked the plaque and set her necklaces ringing whenever she brooded on the plans her great-grandchildren called "Lady Mary's diabolical schemes."

Toying with necklaces was a universal feminine gesture. Even proper British matrons—once attired in flowing, pinch-waisted dresses, but now uniformed in skirts and twin-sets—fingered their pearls unaware. The proper, proper British! She had lived with them and quarreled with them, despised them and loved them all her life—as she had the Chinese. Henry, the eldest son of her own eldest son Jonathan, was proper British. He was Lieutenant Colonel Sir Henry Jonathan Osgood Sekloong, Baronet, and chain-mail epaulettes glittered on his dark-blue formal uniform of the 17/21 Lancers. The skull-and-cross-bones insignia of the Regiment on his lapels were to soon be exchanged for the red tabs of a Brigadier. Despite his clouded background, Sir Henry had been gazetted to command the Armored Force Training School at Bovingdon in Surrey. That was rapid promotion for an officer of only forty-three in a shrinking military establishment.

For the British, position was a great leveler. But wealth was an even greater leveler, and he was the extremely wealthy third Baronet. Yet they could never quite forget his origins. His dark good looks owed more to his mother, Sarah Haleevie, than to the Sekloongs. The Jewish strain was marginally more acceptable than his Chinese blood, though Sir Henry had inherited the Old Gentleman's slimly erect figure and inborn dignity. But he had learned to mute both the Sekloong brilliance and the Haleevie vivacity. The firm molding of the Jesuits at Stonyhurst College and the discipline of the Royal Military Academy at Sandhurst had made him the model of a proper British officer.

By God, there were too many soldiers in the family! Perhaps the inclination was passed along by her father's frustrated genes. A figure in a light-blue uniform sat across the table from Lieutenant Colonel Sir Henry. The twin stars of a major general of the United States Air Force shone on his shoulders, and four rows of miniature medals hung below the laurel-wreathed-star that crowned the silver wings of a command pilot.

Her eldest grandson, Major General George Chapman Parker, Jr., was just forty-four. His breezy manner

135

was very American, as was his occasional earnest solemnity. Blanche Taylor, wife of the Under Secretary of State, was his sister, younger by two years. Lady Mary's daughter Guinevere had married Dr. George Chapman Parker to found the American branch of the family and to die with her husband in 1944. Her son George was heavy-set and grizzled blond, his intent hazel-green eyes his chief inheritance from the Old Gentleman. He had flown fighter-bombers in Korea and had commanded a wing in Vietnam.

Sir Henry had also fought in Korea. Lady Mary wondered again if the grandson she had never seen might have died under Henry's cannon fire or George's bombs. Her son, James (she simply could not call him Ai-kuo) had dutifully written to report his own son's "heroic sacrifice in defense of the Motherland" on a nameless, half-frozen hill in North Korea in the spring of 1951. James himself—addressed, of course, as Lieutenant General Shih Ai-kuo—had commanded the corps of the "Chinese People's Volunteers" in which his son served as a political commissar.

A fleeting frown marred the translucent skin between Lady Mary's eyebrows. The romantic girl of twenty had dreamed of bringing East and West together, united in the fruit of her own body. The wise old lady of ninety reflected with sorrow purged of bitterness that East and West were still irreconcilable. Rather than finding harmony in their common blood, her grandsons had warred against each other. The apparently irrepressible conflict between two worlds had erupted within her own family—as it might again.

She twisted on the red-velvet cushions of her gilt-carved chair. The lesser dowagers, Sarah and Opal, watched uneasily. They knew how feeble she had grown during the past four months. She smiled reassuringly and turned her eyes to the array of statuettes shielded by a glass case.

The figurines buried with a Tang Dynasty nobleman 1,300 years earlier always comforted her. Their eternal beauty salved the sting of mortality by reminding her that men's works endured, though men's bodies perished. Fierce warriors mounted on arrogant, long-necked horses guarded a caravan of camels, pack-horses, and donkeys; green, brown, and yellow glaze glowed on their flanks. A pair of Mandarins escorted three hook-nosed Central Asian traders, one holding a bird, the second cradling a dog, the third hunched under a heavy sack. Dancing girls, servants, and a covey of small birds played around the caravan.

The display-case was protected by its own burglar alarm, for the figures had been valued at more than $5 million by London's most conservative auctioneer. But their imperishable beauty was far more to Lady Mary than their presumed worth. Money, once the key to life and freedom, had become almost meaningless over the years, breeding on itself to produce amounts so vast they defied her perception. The men and women assembled in the Great Hall represented more than $3 billion in personal assets; they controlled corporate assets running into tens of billions.

Passions even stronger than acquisitiveness moved the assemblage. Angry shouts broke Lady Mary's contemplation of the Tang figures' perfection. Her sons Thomas and James were on their feet shouting insults at each other in the harsh Cantonese that was their childhood tongue.

"Liar and betrayer," the Nationalist General screamed at his younger brother. "You sold China to the Russians. You betrayed the Generalissimo. You've destroyed China's culture."

"Lackey of the imperialists," the Communist General shouted. "Running-dog of the Americans. Your corrupt lot of thieves squeezed the people 'til blood ran from their fingernails! Your Generalissimo is no more than . . ."

"Thomas! James! That will do!"

The two aging Generals sank abashed into their seats, silenced like errant schoolboys by Lady Mary's high-pitched voice.

The Under Secretary of State stared into his gold-rimmed rice-bowl as if the shimmering porcelain might reveal the solutions of the world's most pressing problems. The first cousins, Colonel Sir Henry Sekloong and Major General George Parker, chatted animatedly across the table. Charlotte Barakian laughed nervously. Her husband was impassive, deliberately withdrawing himself, for he did business with both Peking and Taipei. Sarah Haleevie Sekloong and Opal watched Lady Mary in renewed concern.

The waves raised by the brief clash spread far from the main table in concentric circles. The heavy-shouldered Shantung plainclothesman behind General Shih Ai-kuo stepped forward, his hand on the holster under his loose-cut tunic. The crew-cut young man in the dark suit standing behind the Under Secretary raised his miniature transceiver to his lips. Six waiters pushed through the throng, their hands in the pockets of their white coats. They were the elite vanguard of the Hong Kong detectives assigned to the most splendid banquet the Colony had seen since the visit of H.R.H. Princess Margaret the preceding year, when 1,500 sat down to dinner. Compared to that state occasion, this gathering was potentially more important politically, and much more volatile.

The waves spread outside The Castle itself, and the uniformed policemen moved toward the great carved-teak main-doors. The cordon was assigned to direct traffic and to exclude the uninvited. But two blue-bereted platoons of the Riot Company waited in slat-sided lorries, and the British Assistant-Commissioner commanding all police on Hong Kong Island sat in an unmarked car fitted with four radio antennae.

His chief, the Commissioner, had warned the Governor that the power and wealth assembled in the Great Hall could attract thieves, kidnappers, and assassins. The Governor had ordered maximum security precautions, for he was acutely sensitive to the danger of any incident or—his nightmare dread—killing. Both Peking and Washington, not to speak of London, would scream for his head, and the Colony's crowded streets could erupt in vicious rioting worse than the violence of 1967. The big Alsatians and the watchmen who normally patrolled Sekloong Manor had, therefore, been supplemented by 150 men of the Royal Hong Kong Police Force. The shock waves raised by a serious incident could extend far beyond the compound, beyond Hong Kong itself, to imperil the precarious balance of the great nations.

Apprehension swept the Great Hall. Even the sculpted Tang warriors appeared alert.

Old Sir Mosing Way rose to quell the unease, supported by his grandson, forty-six-year-old Mokhing Way, the fruit of Charlotte Sekloong Way d'Alivère Martin Barakian's first marriage. The old man in the Chinese long-gown and the younger man in the tail-suit poignantly reminded Lady Mary of her first meeting with Sir Jonathan and Charles. Sir Mosing was not a blood relation, and his son Manfei, Charlotte's first husband, had been killed by kidnappers decades earlier. But no general assembly of the Sekloong clan could exclude him. The family-obsessed Chinese called them *chin-chia*, "members of the same house."

"To our hostess and to family harmony," Sir Mosing intoned reedily. "As the only other member of the eldest generation present, I claim the privilege of the first toast. To Lady Mary, much joy and long life."

Cups rose to lips, and the tension broke. Partaking of the toast in the Chinese manner, Lady Mary raised her gold-chased cup to sip the rice wine specially brewed and aged twelve years for her. Compared to the harsh yellow-wine of Shaohsing or the fiery, medicated *maotai* of Kweichow, it was as a Taittinger *blanc de blancs* champagne to a raw Algerian red.

"To the family," she responded. "To all my family here gathered and to those absent. To all our friends from all quarters of the earth. To all within the four seas and all under Heaven. I drink to love and peace —this night and forever."

"Amen and amen!" a baritone voice concluded. "Blessed be the peace-makers."

Lady Mary turned in delight. Charles had finally arrived—Charles, perhaps her favorite child and certainly equal in her affections to her prodigal, the alternately sullen and affable Communist General, James Sekloong. Charles Cardinal Sekloong's spare figure and the serene determination that suffused his lean, regular features made him a living replica of his grandfather, Sir Jonathan. She could not look at him without a conscious thrill of pride and love.

He had warned his mother that he would be delayed, because the Colony's large Catholic community insisted that the visiting titular Archbishop of Chungking celebrate a High Mass. The fifty-nine-year-old churchman was at least as eminent as any other person in the Great Hall. As secretary of the Roman Curia's Council for Public Affairs, he was the Vatican's effective foreign minister. The only mark of that eminence was a bishop's purple square beneath his Roman collar.

All her living children were now gathered with her for the first time in decades, and Lady Mary sighed with joy. She would need them all for her latest "diabolical scheme." It might be the most foolish she had ever conceived, but that was all the more reason for executing it with vigor. Cardinal Charles, she believed, would be her strongest support; but she needed them all.

If united, the family and its manifold connections could be a major force in the international mêlée, the unending contention of nations and beliefs. *If* the family could be united, for the diversity that was its strength spontaneously operated to prevent unanimous action. Sir Jonathan had in truth founded an almost imperial dynasty, its members occupying seats of power throughout the world, disposing of almost incalculable riches, and exercising immense influence. Like all dynasties, the clan was riven by personal, political, and ideological rivalries. The House of Sekloong embodied not only the relatively new contest between East and West and the old antipathies between Occident and Orient, but actively participated in the violent clashes between those forces.

Lady Mary was determined that the family would not dissolve in conflict. Though the House of Sekloong was disunited, her summons had brought all its major parts together, for all acknowledged the common bond of

140

blood. She must now prevail upon them to recognize their common self-interest. By doing so she would crown her own life, which had given life to so many in the company while bestowing treasure and power on so many more. She envisioned a daring enterprise, and she prayed that her will would be strong enough to unite the House of Sekloong in that audacious endeavor.

Lady Mary closed her tired old eyes, seeking strength in recalling the origins of the contentious, glittering assembly. It had begun with a marriage between a young man and a young woman of wholly different worlds. Splendid to a nervous bride, that beginning was dwarfed by its overwhelming consequences. As Harry Sekloong had warned her, Sir Jonathan was determined to found a uniquely powerful realm inhabited by his descendants.

"He'll fashion it out of chaos—if necessary!" Harry's irrepressible mockery added, "We can only hope that he'll rest on the *eighth* day."

The initial act of creation was Charles's marrying Mary on February 18, 1901. Their wedding was the first unofficial ceremony in Hong Kong's history that both races attended as equals.

The Governor, the Colonial Secretary, the General Officer Commanding British Forces, and their ladies had all been present at the nuptial mass in the Cathedral. So, too, had Richard and the Honorable Rachel Wheatley, the latter sniffing beneath her veil at the portly Cantonese merchant seated beside her and gazing in frosty disapproval at the rows of Chinese faces in the pews.

Sullenly unforgiving, Bandmaster John Philip Osgood had refused to attend. He was infuriated by Mary's defying his will and "marrying that jumped-up Roman chink." Only his daughter regretted his absence —and she only fleetingly. On her wedding morning, she received a lengthily expensive cablegram from York signed by her frugal brother Thomas. The message pleaded with her to reconsider, and she knew that her father had contrived that jarring note. After expressing conventional regrets, Sir Jonathan had not attempted to conceal his relief that Hilary Metcalfe, rather than John Osgood, gave the bride away. The new realm he was creating required its crown-princess—auburn-haired, rather than black-haired if she must be. It required neither the presence nor the blessing of her somewhat seedy, beer-flushed father.

The marriage service, performed by the Roman Catholic Bishop, was a haze of incense, solemn chants, and many-colored vestments, Mary shining white in their midst like a lily in a field of wild flowers. She could recall only brief flashes of the lavish reception, for which Sir Jonathan had provided two hundred cases of Dom Perignon. Captain John Williams had already slipped away on a long leave. He had avoided Mary since she rejected him, and, in his bitter haste to be gone, had reclaimed none of his gifts, not even the gorgeous jade necklace. Unabashed, Captain Lord Peter Comyn French had donned the skin-tight regimentals of the Coldstream Guards and polished his gold-rimmed eyeglass to a high gloss to dance at the reception before taking his leave of the bride and the Colony.

The formal reception was the Sekloongs' courtly bow to European customs, since they realized that they would thenceforth necessarily live with "a foot unequivocally in each camp," as Sir Jonathan remarked dispassionately. Mary could not tell whether he was pleased at that prospect or merely resigned to it. The counterpoint to the reception was the time-prescribed Chinese wedding banquet at which she appeared first in a gown of crimson satin, the color of the traditional Chinese bridal costume. The same custom required her to change her dress six times in the course of the evening to display the lavish trousseau with which the Metcalfes had endowed her. But Charles refused to allow her to wear a Chinese-style dress, enigmatically insisting that it would be "inappropriate."

The frustration of her own desire to compliment the Sekloongs' Chinese ancestry and their Chinese guests by her costume had not marred Mary's intense pleasure in that day and evening of exuberant excitement. To her surprise, she had actually found much pleasure in

142

yielding to Charles's wishes, since she thus honored her promise to "love, honor, and obey."

That same night she further realized why marriage was every young woman's dream, for she delighted in her voluntary submission. Her lusty response in bed first surprised and soon captivated her husband, who delighted in teaching her the arts he had obviously learned from skilled partners. Her fleeting jealousy of his past experiences was submerged by the rising tides of her own sensuality and by her knowledge that thereafter he belonged only to her. Their joy in each other's bodies made luminous the first year of their marriage, which was passed in his parents' mansion off Bonham Road while they waited for The Castle and their own Small House on The Peak to be completed.

Mary was simultaneously gaining understanding of the intricacies of the Sekloongs' world, the world in which she had chosen to live. Bulbously pregnant as the year 1901 entered its second half, she was pampered as if she were carrying a prince or a princess. For the first time, she truly comprehended the grandiose ambitions that inspired both her husband and her father-in-law. At the end of that year, she congratulated herself on her graceful adaption to her new milieu. After giving birth to a son in late November, she was virtually venerated—almost as if she had performed a miracle. Each day, she felt, she was penetrating more deeply the unique customs and compulsions of her new world. Later, Mary was to realize that she had at that early moment merely been dazzled by the glittering façade that concealed the Sekloongs' complex hearts and subtle minds.

Part Two

━❚━❚━❚━❚━❚━❚━❚━❚━❚━❚━❚━❚━❚━❚━❚━

Mary and Charles

February 4, 1905–November 16, 1906

February 4, 1905

MARY Philippa Osgood Sekloong shivered and drew the pastel-embroidered cashmere shawl around her shoulders. Early evening had wrapped The Peak in a cold-gray cocoon on Saturday the fourth of February, 1905—by the Chinese lunar calendar the last day of the thirty-first year of the reign of the Kuang Hsü Emperor of the Great Pure Dynasty. Staccato fusillades from the heights of Sekloong Manor replied to the unremitting barrage of New Year firecrackers in the valleys below. Despite the crimson-and-yellow flames dancing in the Adam fireplace, the overfurnished drawing-room of the Small House was chill and damp. The walls and ceiling were still settling behind their elaborate moldings, and the dank air reeked mustily of drying plaster. She had rarely felt as miserably cold in the England she had not seen for almost five years as she did at that moment in subtropical Hong Kong.

Dreading the formal dinner at The Castle, she decided, this once, to take enough yellow rice wine to warm her blood, despite the inevitable headache the next morning. It was still virtually impossible to heat the brick-and-plaster Small House Sir Jonathan had built as the first of the three mansions he planned for his children by Lady Lucinda. It would, for decades, be totally impossible to defeat the damp cold weeping from the stone walls of The Castle.

In England, they expected the raw, pinching winter that always took Hong Kong by surprise. She longed for the coziness of the shabby-genteel gas-heated parlors she had hated when her mother trailed her brother Thomas and herself from one furnished lodging to another. She even yearned for the English fog, the friendly, brown English fog that shut out the intrusive world and accentuated the cheery warmth of small rooms. The alien gray pall outside seemed to extend thousands of miles over the sea and across the vast

147

land-mass where hundreds of millions of outlandish yellow and brown people swarmed.

Dr. Alex Moncriefe, a hearty, red-faced Scot, had offered a ready answer to her continuing depression after the birth of her fourth child—her second son—just two months earlier.

"Tropical neurasthenia," he diagnosed, "a feeling of despair induced by no particular cause—except living amid people with different features, strange pigmentation, and peculiar customs. Ladies are specially susceptible. Most get over it spontaneously. For those who don't, there's only one cure—ship 'em back home. Meanwhile, take an occasional brandy, my dear."

Neurasthenia perhaps—but hardly tropical. The only thing tropical in His Majesty's Crown Colony of Hong Kong in February was baskets of fruit from Malaya. The Chinese New Year was the most depressing time for Mary—the obligatory gaiety, the exchange of ostentatious gifts, and the constant visiting and receiving. It was not and would never be her holiday. Besides, her depression stemmed from a most "particular cause." Mary feared that she had, just four years earlier, wholeheartedly done something that was not only foolish, but irrevocable.

Her twenty-fifth birthday still four months distant, she was a settled matron with four demanding children and a querulous husband. Of course, the children were darlings, particularly the girls. Two-year-old Guinevere and one-year-old Charlotte had inherited both her auburn hair and her normally irrepressible temperament. Her eldest, Jonathan, was a sturdy, sunny, four-year-old with Sekloong hazel eyes that flashed imperiously at the servants. Only baby Thomas, barely two months old, was a disappointment. His skin was sallow; his hair was coarsely black; and his dark brown eyes were markedly slanted. Somehow, he looked so Chinese.

She should not, Mary reproached herself, express such misgivings, even in her secret thoughts. She had freely chosen to make herself part of an essentially Chinese family. She had known that Lady Lucinda's

148

wholly Chinese blood and Sir Jonathan's half-Chinese blood were likely to shape her children's appearance, just as their Chinese manners and customs would shape her own life. But that choice, taken in substantial ignorance of its true consequences, was an abstraction beside the reality that oppressed her. Despite her deep interest in Chinese culture, she was a child of her times and the child of her fiercely prejudiced father. After four years of marriage, she should have resolved the conflict between her intellectual enthusiasm for the exotic way of life she had chosen and her instinctive shrinking from its alien demands. Instead, the internal conflict was becoming more acute and more distressing.

She had never before her marriage truly appreciated the joys of solitude, the opportunities to reflect undisturbed. The Sekloongs were inured to never being out of sight or earshot of another human being for more than five minutes. The multitude of servants were integral to their lives, and they would probably long for the habitual bustle if it should magically vanish. The gardeners, coolies, chair bearers, and houseboys were cheerful and ubiquitous, but her own worst irritation was the loud quarrels and gossip of the maidservants. They were called amahs, the word itself a typically Chinese evasion, for it meant literally "esteemed mothers." The household included wash-amahs and coolie-amahs, cook-amahs and baby-amahs. The latter jealously disputed her interference with their management of her own children, though deliberate spoiling better described the way they pandered to the infants' whims.

Sometimes, Mary just wanted to be alone. Solitude was the simple boon the Sekloong wealth could not buy: that lack, too, was typically Chinese. She suspected that Chinese nerves had developed insensitivity to the constant noise that lacerated her less robust European nerves.

She could, she mused, have borne all the worries of her new life happily if she had been sustained by her husband. But Charles was himself the chief cause of her

149

ill-defined unhappiness, despite her love for him. She was unhappy with Charles for a number of reasons, some quite general—and one most specific.

It was, above all, a matter of attitudes. His character had changed greatly since their courtship. He was peremptory and inconsiderate, upon occasion petulant if his wishes were not obeyed immediately. The attentive, dashing young man she'd married seemed to have aged appreciably, though he was only twenty-nine. He was putting on weight, and, worse, he was growing magisterially pompous—as if his spirit were becoming obese. It really came down to the difference they had discussed, and dismissed, during their courtship. She herself had not reconciled her own wearingly contradictory feelings toward the Chinese. Charles and she had not reconciled his increasingly Chinese cast of mind and behavior with her own attitudes and actions, which were in self-defense becoming assertively more English.

Charles had been sulking for more than three weeks, ever since she had dared to assume the prerogative of the "new woman" whose advent English intellectuals were noting. She had told him that there must, for some time, be no more babies; she insisted upon a long pause in her constant replenishment of the mansion's nurseries in the sacred cause of enlarging and perpetuating the Sekloong clan. Charles had protested that he was a good Catholic, who was not only repelled by the crude devices available for contraception, but morally debarred from their use.

"What," he'd asked plaintively, "will we do?"

"That, my sweet, is as much your problem as mine," she'd answered, and he had slept on the chaise-longue in the dressing room ever since. "No," she'd said, "no, nursing the infant doesn't prevent conception, whatever tales your mother's told you." Besides, she had no intention of breast-feeding Thomas much longer. "You can please yourself," she had concluded, "but you must take the appropriate measures or stay out of my bed."

Charles was deeply shocked—as much by her frank language as by her resolute decision. He still could not quite believe that she was successfully defying him.

Only his father, the founder-lord of the dynasty, commanded the crown-prince. Charles simply could not apprehend that a woman had presented him with an ultimatum. He was wilfully blind, deliberately refusing to recognize the strength of character and mind of the woman he had married. He simply could not see that she was as capable as she was strong-willed. Nor could he conceive that her searching intellect, her own attraction to power, and her restless energy would pose grave danger to himself and their one-dimensional relationship after she had cast off her enforced preoccupation with their children—unless her talents found suitable employment.

Despite their superficial Westernization, the Sekloongs still considered a woman little more than a female animal. The crown-princess was pampered because she performed the essential function of producing children to carry on the line. When related to that prime function, her whims were unchallengeable commands. Beaming his delight at her fecundity, Sir Jonathan occasionally introduced subjects unrelated to procreation. Exhausted by constant reproduction, Mary half-attended to his chief themes: commerce, politics, and the Chinese past. She was deeply interested, but she was too tired. Except for the devoted Harry, she felt all the Sekloongs looked upon her as a reliable brood-mare, best loved when gravid and docile. They had deprived her of her dignity as an individual. Nothing could compensate for that deprivation: not the luxury that cushioned her; the instant obedience to her female whims that pampered her; or the family solidarity that sheltered her.

Mary shivered and stretched her hands to the fire. The doors opened, and a draft fluttered the twin red paper signs inscribed in golden characters with the invocations: MAY OLD AND YOUNG DWELL IN PEACE TOGETHER! FILL OUR HALLS WITH GOLD AND JEWELS!

Ah Sam entered, imposing in his high-collared white tunic. The old pirate's rough ebullience had not been quelled by his translation from the Number One Boy in a warrant officer's bungalow to the major-domo of a millionaire's mansion, and he still walked with a porcelain-rattling stride. Before her marriage, six months before her father's departure with the Regiment on regular transfer he had announced: "I go with Missy."

She could not have refused his services if she had wanted to. Though Charles would have preferred a factotum of his own choosing, at the time he still granted her slightest wish. And Ah Sam had remained her firm ally.

"*Goong-hay, Tai-tai! Goong-hay fat-choy!*" He boomed the traditional New Year greeting. "Congratulations, Madam! Congratulations and prosperity!"

"*Goong-hay fat-choy,* Ah Sam!" Mary replied absently for the sixth time that day. Ah Sam was obviously determined to miss no opportunity to remind the spirits of their duties in the coming year. He would allow them no pretext for neglecting those duties.

The cooks, she knew, were welcoming the Household Spirit's return to his crimson niche after his trip to Heaven to report to his superiors. His old portrait had been removed, his lips smeared with opium and honey to insure that he would arrive in Heaven befuddled and utter only sweet words. His new portrait, painted on rice-paper, was at that moment being forcefully instructed that he would be rewarded handsomely for looking after the family's fortunes, but punished by exile if he were remiss. Given the Chinese preoccupation with money, it was not remarkable that he did double-duty as the God of Wealth.

Ah Sam squatted to poke the fire. As always, he cleared his throat to signal an important remark.

"Eve'ything a'right, Missy?" he asked in pidgin. "You quite happy?"

"Yes, Ah Sam, thank you," she replied, amused by his clumsy circumspection. "Everything is quite all right."

"Good, ve'y good. New Year time, eve'yone must be happy. . . ."

"*Aiyaa! Aiyaa! Dai-siu lay-la! Aiyaa!*"

The cry of distress echoed in the outside corridor, and the doors opened to the hobbling progress of Ah

Ying, the Number One Baby-amah. She hurled an unintelligibly rapid stream of colloquial Cantonese at Ah Sam.

"Missy! Missy!" he said. "Mastah come home. He not ve'y well. Maybe little bit hurt a bit."

Charles Sekloong shuffled into the drawing-room supported by a wiry chair coolie. A deep cut in his cheek oozed blood; an angry laceration reddened his smooth forehead; and his gray-worsted suit-jacket was torn. He slumped into the yellow brocade sofa beside the fire. All her resentment forgotten, Mary knelt beside him.

"What is it, Charles?" she asked. "Are you hurt badly? What happened? Shall I send for Dr. Moncriefe?"

"It's all right, Mary. I'll be all right." He smiled, and the passionate youth she had married peeped over the stolid façade of the preoccupied businessman. "It's really nothing."

"Hot water and cotton-wool," she directed. "Bring Dettol—and a brandy for Master."

"I could take a brandy," he sighed. "But don't make a fuss. And, for God's sake, don't tell the old man."

"What happened, Charles?" Mary persisted.

"Thugs set on me. Came out of the fog at the Peak Tram. It was dicey till the chair coolies came up. Fog all over and no one around. Don't worry, I'll be fine."

He tossed back the brandy, exhaling in satisfaction, and color began to return to his face.

"But why you?" she persisted.

"Could've been anyone who'd been carrying lots of the ready. This time of year, thieves come out. Even thieves have to pay their debts before New Year."

"Dr. Moncriefe must see you. This cut looks nasty —I'll send for him."

"No," he commanded. "No need—and, remember, tell the old man I fell. No need to worry him."

Out of the corner of her eye Mary saw Ah Sam shake his head in melodramatic dismay. She ignored his pantomime, dabbing gently to wash the grit from Charles's cheekbone to the corner of his eye.

"Aiyaa! Aiyaa!" The baby-amah declaimed again like the narrator of a Cantonese opera. "Old Master come."

Sir Jonathan strode into the drawing-room. His hazel eyes were coldly angry, and red spots glowed under his cheekbones.

"What the devil?" he demanded in rough Cantonese. "What the devil is it *this* time?"

Suddenly aware of the audience, he pointed to the doors, and the goggling servants pelted out.

"What *this* time?" Sir Jonathan demanded, speaking English to frustrate the ears that might be pressed against the door. "What's the new tale?"

"I tripped and fell in the fog." Charles evaded. "Really, it's nothing."

"You act the fool, but don't take me for a fool!" Sir Jonathan shouted. "Knives don't slash your cheek falling in the fog. Who beat you?"

"Well, actually, thugs. Tried to rob me. I didn't want to worry you on New Year's Eve."

"Very considerate. I've told you a thousand times—be careful. But *you* know better."

"Know better, Father?"

Mary stood silent, forgotten by both father and son. Charles still smiled, but his temper was rising.

"You've been playing with that glorified flower girl again, haven't you? Golden Lily."

Charles's face was a mask of outraged innocence.

"She belongs to Tai-Foo, Tiger Chung, and he set his Green League Braves on you, didn't he?"

"Yes," Charles acknowledged.

"You know damned well how tricky things are," Sir Jonathan said angrily. "The Red League's behind us, but we need neutrality—not hostility—from the Greens. Without the Triads I'll never shake loose of the Wheatleys. You and your women!"

Mary Sekloong's heart lurched at the double shock. She had suspected that Charles might seek elsewhere the pleasures she was forced to deny him. But confirmation of her fears wounded both her pride and her love for Charles. As a superior male, a Chinese male,

154

he demanded that *she* be perfectly chaste, while custom granted him complete self-indulgence. He considered it in the natural order of life that he should satisfy his desires as he wished. Worse, Sir Jonathan's reproaches told her that Charles had been unfaithful for some time, certainly long before she had denied him her body.

Her chronic sense of insecurity was further heightened by Sir Jonathan's mention of his relations with the Triads, the powerful Secret Societies. Founded to oppose the Manchu usurpers after the Chinese-ruled Ming Dynasty fell in 1644, the Secret Societies were divided into the Red and Green Leagues, which contended against each other, but united against outsiders. Hong Kong called them Triads, after their chief branch in the Colony, the Three Harmonies Society.

She knew something of the Secret Societies from Charles and from Hilary Metcalfe. Swearing their members to life-long loyalty by fearsome blood-oaths, they used their great extra-legal power to enrich and protect their adherents. Some, like the Association of Elder Brothers in distant Szechwan, virtually ruled parts of China. Elsewhere, the Societies were hardly more than interlocked, organized gangs of evil-doers. Their depredations recalled the Black Hand Society of Sicily, which had extended its activities into England during the past decade. Irresistibly drawn to political action and reassuming their original patriotic purposes, the Societies were allied with the numerous rebels against the decadent Manchu Dynasty. Though she knew little more of the Secret Societies, Mary instinctively recoiled from the Sekloongs' involving themselves deeply with their devious and often violent Oriental intrigues.

Awareness of Mary standing pale beside the fireplace had penetrated Sir Jonathan's rage.

"Won't you leave us, Mary?" he demanded. "No need to mix in this mess."

The angry father and son silently awaited her departure, and she longed to remove herself from their confrontation. But instinct warned her to remain. As much for Charles's sake as her own, she must not leave the room like an obedient schoolgirl. Whatever he had done, Charles was the husband she had taken, even if unwisely. She could not leave him to be browbeaten or, more likely, to flail out at his father. Though it was she who was most deeply wounded, only her presence could restrain the bristling men until volatile Sekloong tempers cooled.

"For God's sake, Mary!" Charles spoke testily. "This is between us. It's men's business."

"My business, too, I think," she parried.

"Charles and I must talk this out before the party." Sir Jonathan's persuasive lilt was pronounced. "We both ask you. Just leave us to sort it out, so we can say the right words to the right guests."

"Let her stay." Charles was grim. "If she must hear, better now than later."

"It's my future—and my children's," Mary insisted.

"God preserve me from clever, stubborn women!" Sir Jonathan's outward equanimity was largely restored. "But then you'll let us sort it out?"

"When my husband wishes."

"Thanks be for small mercies and great signs of grace, as the good fathers would say." Sir Jonathan's lilt was cajoling; his self-assured pride was so great that he no more disdained flattery to gain his ends than he shrank from intimidation.

"It's your scheme, Father," Charles said. "You tell her."

"You know," Sir Jonathan explained, "I'm not over-fond of my—let's call them step-kindred—the Wheatleys, for good reason. My wonderful mother married Richard Wheatley after my own father, O'Flaherty, died. My grandfather, Kwok Lee-chin, then got Dick Wheatley into Derwent's. Then, after Mother died, Wheatley married again, chiefly to consolidate his position in the *hong*. What he couldn't steal, he took by marrying."

Mary looked up in surprise. She had never heard Sir Jonathan speak frankly of his illegitimacy or his strained, yet intimate, relationship with the Wheatleys.

"Right now I'm Derwent's comprador, the go-between, a glorified native-guide for the big white chief." Sir Jonathan's bitterness edged his voice. "But I want independence, want what properly belongs to me. To get it, I need the backing of the Green Band and the Red Band, the patriotic, anti-Manchu societies."

"They're other things, too." Mary couldn't resist the gibe. "Or so I've heard. Hatchetmen and gangsters, too."

"Perhaps," Sir Jonathan conceded. "Regardless, your husband has now tossed a spanner into the works. We can't offend the Green Band, but he's made a good start. Now, will you please leave us to make running repairs?"

"In a moment," Mary temporized. "But what precisely has Charles done?"

"That you can ask *him*." Sir Jonathan smiled thinly. "I'm sure you will . . . vigorously. Will you leave us to it? Time's short."

"Charles," she asked, "will you be all right?"

"I'll explain later, Mary," he replied firmly. "But do as Father asks."

"I'll do as my husband wishes."

She gathered her skirts. As the teak doors closed behind her, she heard Sir Jonathan's voice.

"The best thing that ever happened to you, boy, is that young woman. But you're too foolish to . . ."

Mary trod the fixed measures of her evening routine like an automaton. Determined not to brood, she gave herself instead to the sensual pleasure of nursing the infant Thomas. But his greedy gums pulled at her nipple, and she abruptly decided to stop feeding him just as soon as she could find a wet-nurse. Or he could go on the bottle, though Lady Lucinda would frown. The Dairy Farm was soliciting her custom, promising to provide "absolutely disease-free and sterile milk" from their new herds at Pokfulam. Though Dr. Moncriefe's hearty conservatism might advise otherwise, she'd still do as she thought best.

She kissed the girls good-night and tucked in their teddy bears. Her heart stirred beneath the ice that sheathed it when she closed the door on the two red-gold heads beside the toys' furry yellow ears on the white pillows. Young Jonathan demanded a story and bellowed in four-year-old anger when she preferred to read from *Alice's Adventures in Wonderland*. That evening, she just couldn't invent new adventures for the miraculous winged dragon, the continuing tale he loved. Jonnie was already petulant because she'd rejected his grandmother's suggestion that he attend the New Year's banquet. But her familiar voice soothed him with the White Rabbit's giddy disappearance down the burrow. Mary's thoughts wandered in spite of her resolve.

To her surprise, her first emotion was wry satisfaction at having faced down Sir Jonathan. Her father-in-law's proprietary assumption that she, too, would honor his every command had been increasingly galling. Sir Jonathan finally knew where they stood and, she suspected, welcomed her defiance for his own reasons. She had learned, above all, that she could not permit the Sekloongs to dominate her. But, it would be criminally foolish to provoke a decisive confrontation.

Mary had no intention of altering her circumstances radically, since she could only alter them to her detriment. The children were hers—and must remain hers. That imperative meant she must remain with Charles and his overwhelming family. Besides, she was not prepared to exchange her life with Charles for the uncertain, déclassé existence of a divorcée. Despite his follies, she realized anew that she still loved Charles. She stoically acknowledged again that he was inclined to rove, though that acknowledgment was a spear in her heart. Not her own self-esteem was most deeply wounded, but her regard for Charles—and the wound was, therefore, more painful. She was stricken by that pain and by the contempt for the man she loved implicit in her readiness to acknowledge his wanton unfaithfulness. She had not thought herself so deeply committed. Was she a modern woman who would not countenance infidelity? Or was she submissively old-fashioned, totally committed to her man, despite his weakness?

She automatically dressed herself in royal-blue velvet with a deep round *décolleté*, and she hung herself with her most ostentatious jewels. Charles and Sir Jonathan were equally barbaric in their desire that she display *their* wealth on *her* person.

Where, she wondered, would the Old Gentleman's new schemes lead? A cavern of insecurity yawned beneath all the Sekloong splendor. Mary's sturdy North Country skepticism distrusted the princely pretension the family considered the normal framework of its life. *If* Sir Jonathan miscalculated; *if* his intricately woven web came adrift; *if* his Chinese allies fell away or the British Establishment turned on him, The Castle could come crashing down into the cavern—burying them all.

When Charles limped into their dressing room an hour later, she was inspecting the jade-and-ruby butterfly hairpin in her hair. Abstractly, she discarded the ornament as superfluous.

"Hurry, Charles," she said evenly, "or we'll be late."

"I'll bathe in a hurry, Mary, but—"

"Do, please," she interrupted. "I'm looking forward to the party."

Surprised, he assessed the cool smile on her full lips and the calm candor of her violet eyes. He wisely said no more, assuming that her manner was a rebuke. His jaws tightened at the prospect of the next day's scene, no way to start the New Year.

Charles Sekloong misjudged his wife. Rather than brooding bitterly on his infidelity, Mary was feeling that he had already suffered too much in a few hours, first the physical assault and then his father's recriminations. She would not now wound him by exacting a stumbling apology. She would not unsex herself—and, perhaps, destroy all remaining chances for their happiness—by humiliating her husband.

Charles wondered at his wife's casual manner as they walked through the torch-lit fog to The Castle. The Great Hall was, for the first time, lit by hundreds of glowing incandescent bulbs. It was, he reminded her needlessly, the first home on The Peak and only the third private residence in the Colony to lay on electricity, at great expense. His words flowed as persistently and as erratically as the current in the thick cables

159

sheathed in gutta-percha. They seemed more like sputtering sparks from a broken cable in the rain.

Sir Jonathan wore his finest long-gown and his silkiest manner to welcome his guests to the Great Hall of The Castle. He exuded the relaxed satisfaction of a man who knew that all his acounts for the Old Year were settled; he glowed with total confidence that the New Year would bring new triumphs. Only four persons in the splendor of rubbed-teak paneling and glowing-crystal chandeliers guessed at the deep anxiety Sir Jonathan's expansive air concealed.

Lady Lucinda sensed her husband's distress because of a sympathetic unease within herself. But her role in his life was so circumscribed that she did not know why she knew. Hilary Metcalfe saw that Jonathan was the too perfect host. He had observed the same manic mood and excessive urbanity during other crises in Jonathan's life. But only Charles and Mary knew precisely why the master of the household was so disturbed, and Charles was himself unnerved by the failure of Sir Jonathan's self-assurance.

Unaware of their host's true mood, the guests trooped into the Great Hall to gape at the Ming and Ching Dynasty porcelains and to exclaim at the miracle of electric light. Gilt and enamel candelabra nonetheless stood on the dinner tables. Lady Lucinda had prepared for the inevitable failure of the electricity she profoundly distrusted. The tang of fresh-sawn wood blended with the fragrance of incense and tantalizing odors from the kitchens, where twenty cooks were preparing the feast. The Great Hall was still incomplete, as it was to remain for another decade, while Sir Jonathan piled superfluity upon perfection. Red-silk banners inscribed with New Year's invocations concealed the bamboo-scaffolding the workmen had left unoccupied during their own holidays.

The guests represented not merely two great realms, the British and the Chinese Empires, but the dozens of smaller realms and semiautonomous fiefs imperfectly conjoined in those enormous organisms. Just three years after The Castle's erection, Lunar New Year's Eve at Sekloong Manor was already a full-blown tradition. The youthful Crown Colony was adept at creating instantaneous traditions. All its divergent peoples met in amicable equality—one night a year.

The Colonial Secretary, still stiffly Victorian five years after the death of the great British Queen Empress, amiably greeted the Delegate of the Viceroy of Canton, whose own Dowager Empress still lived in bitter senescence in the Forbidden City of Peking. Chieftains of the Green Band and the Red Band, their power maintained by ten thousand "Braves" in the labyrinthine slums of Wanchai and Kowloon, toasted the *taipans* of the great European trading *hongs*. The *taipans'* wealth was garnered by dozens of "young gentlemen" European clerks; by thousands of farmers in the opium fields of Laos, Burma, Thailand, and India; by wiry, broad-faced hunters tending their traplines on the frozen plains of Manchuria; and by hosts of sailors, coolies, and agents throughout Asia.

Sallow British ladies bowed to shy Chinese matrons, to whom they paid no more deference than to maidservants the other 364 days of each year. American ship captains laughed with Teocheo smugglers, whom they normally met in backrooms, if indeed they did not send their Chinese supercargoes to haggle over shipments of contraband. French and German diplomats fawned on French and German bankers and merchants, accepting in return exaggerated expressions of respect—*"J'ai l'honneur, Monsieur le Consul-Général!" "Mein tiefste Ehre, Herr General-Konsul!"*—just as they did every week of the year.

Generals and colonels in trousers so tight they could bend no more than three inches without risking social catastrophe exchanged amiable grunts of mutual incomprehension with village headmen from the New Territories. Ageless, wispy-bearded Chinese scholars in worn long-gowns chatted with a few eager young Europeans in Mandarin. Mastery of the northern Court language was almost as unusual among educated Cantonese as it

161

was among the "barbarian devil persons." Eurasian and Jewish entrepreneurs drifted easily through the throng, greeting most men in their own languages.

All the multifarious guests ritually praised the Sekloong hospitality, which was as remarkable for its scope as for its lavishness. Sir Jonathan was making a new world that would blend East and West. He was its creator, the object of its devotion—and its benevolent ruler.

"Sometimes," Harry Sekloong observed, "the old man confuses God with himself. He may know he didn't create Eve, but he's determined to use her."

Hilary Metcalfe was irritated by that quip, though Harry's subtle deflation of Jonathan's pretensions usually amused his old friend. Harry's pointed jest distressed Hilary, who traced Sir Jonathan's changing attitudes to Mary's entry into the family. A fiercely chauvinistic Chinese patriot before 1901, despite his expedient cooperation with the British, Jonathan Sekloong was beginning to accept that cooperation as a virtue in itself. The guiding principle of his new realm was gradually being transformed from straightforward exaltation of the Sekloongs and China to exaltation of the Sekloongs and the Sino-European endeavor to bring China into the modern comity of nations.

Four years after Mary's marriage to Charles, Sir Jonathan's realm was asserting its unique power, with Mary as the pampered crown-princess. She was ostentatiously displayed to the throngs that had assembled to savor the Sekloong hospitality and to pay tribute to the Sekloongs' increasing power. Hilary Metcalfe knew that Sir Jonathan esteemed his daughter-in-law more highly than he did the artistic wonders that adorned his palace, if, perhaps, a shade less than the grotesque edifice itself.

That evening, however, Jonathan's attentions were patently excessive. A resentful Charles reflected that his father, whose motivations were as complex as his ambitions were grandiose, sought to attain not one, but several diverse purposes by his fulsome introductions. Why else should he commit the gaucherie of not merely presenting Mary as the mother of his four favorite grand-

162

children, but intrusively recalling her social triumph with Prince William in 1900?

The master of the House of Sekloong was deliberately strengthening his ties with the British by recalling an incident that would in retrospect appear trivial anywhere else than Hong Kong. Royal approbation had, however, not only established Mary's status in Colonial Society, but had touched her with imperishable glamour. Sir Jonathan, who had weighed Hong Kong's essential pettiness, was catering to his British audience. His guests, in turn, courteously affected to remember only Mary's social triumph, while forgetting her father's lowly position. At the same time, Sir Jonathan was impressing upon his Chinese associates the high esteem in which the British held the Sekloongs; prestige that in no wise vitiated the clan's loyalty to China and Chinese customs. He was also, Charles assumed, placating Mary's outraged dignity.

The extravagant introductions, Charles felt, punished him. They relegated him to second place by demonstrating that the House of Sekloongs' continuity did not depend on a weak reed like himself. Though still a vigorous fifty-two, Sir Jonathan was displaying his possession of legitimate grandsons to succeed him and legitimate granddaughters to form new alliances by marriage.

As etiquette dictated, Charles played host to the second table when the forty-eight honored guests sat down to dinner after the others had left. As their own protocol further dictated, Lady Lucinda sat at her husband's left at the first table while Mary sat on his right. Like the family itself, Sekloong etiquette was a unique mélange of Eastern and Western practices. The Old Gentleman's personal force made the mixture unexceptionable—if not wholly palatable—even to the Honorable Rachel Wheatley. She fumbled with her chopsticks on Charles's left, and greedily downed repeated thimble-cups of warm rice wine.

After the traditional New Year's dumplings, when the guests were toying with glasses of aromatic tea in

163

silver-gilt holders, the host signaled to his intimates. Those outside the inner circle made their farewells, for a Chinese dinner sensibly ends with the food. The ladies withdrew in deference to British customs. But Sir Jonathan grasped Mary's arm with playful insistence.

"Tonight, we defy both Western and Chinese etiquette." He raised his voice to carry. "You must sit with us and endure my tales."

Sir Jonathan led his guests into the rosewood-paneled library and settled them in deep leather chairs before a granite fireplace large enough to roast a whole calf. Hilary Metcalfe sat beside his host, Mary on his other side, while Charles perched on the arm of her chair. Crotchety Richard Wheatley, an acidly ambitious seventy-one, sipped his brandy. Mosing Way, Sir Jonathan's young protégé, abstemiously balanced a cup of tea on the ebony sidetable, but appreciatively drew on a Havana panatella. After taking aboard a heavy cargo of wines and spirits, the plump Colonial Secretary was somnolent beside a bright-eyed young man introduced as Mr. S. Y. Tong. He had returned from studies in the United States and Britain to represent both the decaying Viceregal Court at Canton and the republican rebels who were determined to destroy the Empire. The conversation was slow-paced and seemingly casual.

"The Japanese are grinding down the Russians," Sir Jonathan remarked, gazing into the fire. "The Russo-Japanese war is all but over, and the balance in the Far East is shifting rapidly. The Russian fleet is finished, and Japan's Home Fleet—Britain's ally, they say—is almost as strong as the British Far East Fleet. But the contract for the Canton-Kowloon Railway is still unsigned."

"I've told London a dozen times already," Wheatley said testily, "if we don't build that railway, Hong Kong is finished. Without that link, Hong Kong perishes as the entreport for South China."

"And if the fleet withdraws . . ." the Colonial Secretary ventured.

"If the British fleet goes," young S. Y. Tong said hotly, "all China will be open to the Japanese dwarfs."

"Well, it's not going tomorrow, Mr. Tong, is it?" Metcalfe interjected. "But in a few years, perhaps. In a few years, we might just decide to leave it to the Japanese."

"A disaster for China," Sir Jonathan interjected, "and for Britain."

"Unless we get that railway started!" Wheatley spoke with singleminded commercial insistence.

"I remember when Britain was supreme," Mosing Way observed gently. "Then came the Boxers and Britain's alliance with the other powers. It was folly. Britain's now just another country scrabbling for a place in China."

"It's not that bad, Way," Wheatley interrupted. "We're not leaving just yet. We're expanding. And we'll get those duffers in Whitehall off their bums—pardon, Mrs. Sekloong."

Mary smiled abstractedly, too immersed in the conversation to bother with the pretense of ladylike fluster at the rude word.

"And are the Japanese our allies, truly?" she asked disingenuously.

"Yes, Mary, but for how long?" Hilary Metcalfe answered. "Bigger question is the size of their appetite. Can't have an ally who's determined to devour all he sees. He'll end up eating us, too."

"After he eats all China," young Tong said bitterly. "The dwarfs made a good start in the Sino-Japanese War in '95. How many years do you give the Manchus, Mr. Metcalfe? How many years before they collapse of their own weight and corruption? How many years before China 'dissolves like a sheet of sand,' as Dr. Sun Yat-sen puts it?"

"Not many, Mr. Tong." Sir Jonathan spoke with grave authority. "The Civil Service examinations are abolished, and the Imperial Civil Service must disintegrate. Who then will rule China—even badly?"

"You know the answer as well as I, Sir Jonathan," Tong replied. "Only one man can pull China together —Dr. Sun Yat-sen. Build your railway by all means,

165

even maintain Imperial rule for a while to prevent anarchy, but put your money on Dr. Sun."

"You've come to plead for Dr. Sun, Mr. Tong?" Mosing Way asked sleepily.

"Not to plead, Mr. Way. He'll win in any event. Just to advise you to act in your own self-interest—and China's."

"A few rag-tag bare-bummed—pardon, Ma'am." Richard Wheatley spoke sharply from the leather depths of his chair. "A few rebels scattered around the world. They'll inherit China? I'll bet on the Manchus or any one of a dozen viceroys and generals loyal to the Imperial tradition."

"Those ragged rebels *will* inherit China, I assure you," Tong rejoined. "And don't you forget it, Mr. Wheatley. The Empire is dying, in protracted, unseemly throes. Seven rebellions threaten the Manchus at this moment. But the republicans will triumph. You've all drawn your own conclusions, I'm sure."

"And with what guarantees of commercial access?" Metcalfe asked. "Where will this group stand? Where will Hong Kong stand?"

"Dr. Sun is a republican, not an anarchist or a socialist. Trade will be bigger and more profitable when modern-minded men rule China."

"Worth thinking about, eh, Jonathan?" Metcalfe observed.

"Certainly, Hilary, certainly. We must look to our trade and our profits. Otherwise, we serve neither Britain nor China."

"Well, we'll just have to see," the Colonial Secretary pronounced magisterially, rising from his chair. "It's getting late. Wonderful dinner, Sir Jonathan. But I must be at the salt mines early. Only time I get any work done is on holidays—no one to bother me."

"The salt mines," Charles whispered to Mary, "are the new golf course at Fanling."

Charles and Mary joined Sir Jonathan and Lady Lucinda to bid the guests good-night. The party milled about the brass-bound doors to the front courtyard. Attentive servants helped the ladies with their wraps and barked peremptorily at chair coolies and torchbearers.

The Wheatleys left first, for the Honorable Rachel asserted her own precedence and her husband's primacy as the preeminent *taipan* over even the complaisant Colonial Secretary. As they stood in the doorway waiting for their sedan chairs, Mary heard the Honorable Rachel's high-pitched whisper.

"Did you see, Richard?" she asked. "Did you see that woman?"

"Eh, what woman?"

"That Vorobya woman who left before dinner with young Spriggens. Calls herself Countess Vera Vorobya, but I know she's Madame Rachelle's niece, the dressmaker's niece. Richard, she's carrying on with Charles Sekloong. They've been seen entering Dick Daley's Owl Grill—and you know what that means."

The shrill voice became muffled as the Honorable Rachel drew the curtains of her sedan chair. Mary stood frozen.

The barrage of firecrackers that had sounded intermittently all through the evening rose to a booming, deafening crescendo to hasten the Old Year's passing. Distant bells pealed and cymbals crashed to proclaim the midnight. The guns of the warships in the harbor flashed in thunderous welcome to the Year of the Snake.

February 5, 1905

CHARLES Sekloong ostentatiously devoted himself to creating a perfect knot in the dove-gray tie that complemented the velvet lapels of his pearl-gray suit. He had already eaten a full breakfast of spiced rice-porridge, preserved eggs, and grilled kidneys in the morningroom on the ground floor, while his wife crumbled honeyed toast and sipped tea on the first floor in the big bed they had not shared for three months. Mary was curled catlike on the chaise-longue in their dressing room. In a violet-sprigged robe over a satin nightdress, her slender, full-breasted body was still exciting, even after four pregnancies. Her husband peered into the mirror on the dresser, avoiding the level glance of her violet eyes beneath the burnished auburn hair caught in a loose knot at her nape.

"Charles," she said evenly, "I'd like a word."

"Yes, Mary, what is it? I'm in a hurry. New Year's calls, you know. A devil of a day. The old man says he and Mother will receive callers while I trot around town like a messenger boy."

"I'm sorry I can't go with you," Mary said. "But next year, I'll surely—"

"Count yourself lucky to be out of it. Couldn't the talk wait? Some teapot tempest, I suppose."

"Yes. Certainly a tempest, but not a tempest in a teapot."

"All right, Mary," he sighed. "But make it fast, will you? I'm already overdue."

"Charles, who is Countess Vorobya?"

Mary's light-voiced question shattered the pretence that they were merely chatting. Charles braced himself for the onslaught he had been dreading since the previous night's revelations.

"Vorobya? Vera Vorobya?" he said. "I'm not sure I—"

"Vera Vorobya. Who is she, Charles?"

"Calls herself 'Countess'—maybe she is. Some distant relation of Madame Rachelle's, the dressmaker, you know. Why?"

"Charles, you're too casual. You're always too casual when you've got something to hide."

"Nonsense. Look, can't it wait 'til this evening? I'm late already."

"No, it can't wait." Mary's tone was frosty. "I want to know now. Who is she, and what is she to you?"

"To *me*?" he exploded. "What's the matter with you? Who gave you that idea?"

"*You* did. Just now!" Her tone grew icy. "I wasn't sure before. But your nervousness proves what I heard. The Golden Lily is one thing . . ."

"Ah," he interjected, "I wondered when you'd throw that teahouse rumor in my face. There's no truth—"

"Not for want of trying, I'm sure," Mary snapped. "But I'm not talking about Golden Lily. I want to know about Countess Vera Vorobya and your assignations at Dick Daley's Owl Grill."

"You seem to know all about it," he sulked. "Or think you do."

"I'd rather not know, Charles, much rather not. But it's true, isn't it?"

"If you insist—yes. What the hell do you expect? You pregnant all the time, and then throwing me out of bed."

"And whose fault is that? I didn't marry you just to breed heirs for your sacred family. You know I want you. But I simply won't have more children for a while. It's up to you anyway; there are things you can use."

"And I've told you a hundred times that as a Catholic I can't do anything about it."

"And that justifies your philandering?" she demanded. "How does *that* go with your precious Catholicism?"

"Sometimes a man strays, especially when his wife . . . but I can't break the Church's fundamental law on contraception."

Mary's gaze dropped to her hands tightly clasped in her lap. Her rage was so overwhelming she did not trust herself to speak. Mistaking her silence for yielding, Charles pressed his counterattack.

"Why *did* you marry me, then?" His cheeks flushed crimson with self-vindicating anger. "Did the Sekloong money make you overlook the Sekloong blood? I suppose a damned chink was all right—as long as he had the brass."

"Charles, I loved you. I still love you."

"Love!" His defensive anger fed itself. "Love! More like love of money. Why a man should have to run after tarts. . . . Men are different than women."

"That I've learned. Your attitude disgusts me, your Chinese contempt for women. We're playthings or brood-mares. But you will not create a public spectacle. I won't have it, Charles!"

"You bloody well will," he shouted. "You think you're so pure, so British, so white, so far above us. But you squirmed and squealed in bed like any other tart before you turned into an icicle."

Mary rose to face her husband. She drew her hand back and slapped him across the cheek.

Charles stood stunned for a moment. A crimson tide rose from his choker-collar to his hairline. He grasped her shoulders and shook her violently.

"Bitch!" he cried. "Bloody British bitch! Bloody, bloody—fortune-hunting, British bitch!"

Mary went limp in his grasp. Her head snapped back and forth, the pain so great she thought her neck would snap. Since she offered no resistance, he flung her onto the chaise-longue.

"Bloody, useless icicle!" He screamed at her bowed head. "White-skinned tart!"

His arm swept the crystal bottles off her dressing table. Powder, scent, and rouge exploded against the golden fleur-de-lis on the wallpaper. Her jade-and-ruby hairpin fluttered to the blue carpet, the butterfly trembling on its golden spring.

"Damned frigging British bitch," Charles shouted. "The devil with you!"

The door slammed behind him; the impact reverberated through the dressing room. Beyond emotion, Mary lay numb where he had flung her.

The pendant, light-pink flowers called hanging bells glowed in the Metcalfes' heavy drawing-room. Livelier Edwardian taste had not yet displaced solid Victorian furnishings in distant Hong Kong. But thick shrubs of peach blossoms and the "great luck" plant—miniature orange-trees promising good fortune in the new year— brightened the heavy teak tables, horsehair sofas, and betassled glass lampshades. Unthinking as a wounded doe, Mary had retreated to her one certain refuge.

The Metcalfes' calm sympathy and candid good sense was balm to her pain. Apparently ageless, Hilary was gruffly perceptive as always, his head tucked tortoiselike between his heavy shoulders. Elizabeth was slightly grayer, but just as energetic, and the familiar beads cascaded on her deep bosom.

"It's not really the end of the world, Mary," Hilary Metcalfe counseled, deliberately filling his pipe. "Worse things happen at sea, as the soldiers say. You yourself will live through worse things."

"That's cold comfort, Hilary," his sister chided. "You're a true Job's comforter."

"Dammit, Liz, it's true! But how can we help, Mary? Liz is right. Talk's no help just now, though I'm convinced your best course is the Taoist recipe—*wu-wei*, do nothing."

"You will help me, Hilary?"

Mary clutched the damp scrap of her handkerchief. She had not cried when Charles left her like a discarded ragdoll; she had not cried as she dressed; and she had not cried as she made her way by sedan chair, Peak Tram, and foot to the house on Wyndham Street. She had wept only when she told the Metcalfes why she had come to them. She had wept for her marriage, for her children—and for her husband.

"I'll do anything I can, Mary," Hilary Metcalfe promised. "But what can I do?"

"Get that woman out of the Colony. I want her out immediately."

"I dare say that can be managed without too much trouble. I'll have a word with Madame Rachelle. You just want her removed instanter, not punished in any way?"

"No!" Mary shook her head. "It's not her fault. But I couldn't bear her being in Hong Kong, the constant humiliation."

"Good girl! Good girl!" Metcalfe muttered approvingly as if gentling a nervous filly. "You've got the stuff. Only point of revenge is to teach a lesson. Remove Miss Countess Vorobya and the lesson'll be clear. Jonathan, I'm sure, will deal with the Golden Lily."

"Hilary," his sister protested, "you're talking about a woman's heart, Mary's entire life, not a business deal."

"You always had a taste for toffee melodrama, Liz," Metcalfe smiled.

"Hilary, what nonsense!" Elizabeth Metcalfe protested.

"Mary," Metcalfe continued, "I hate saying I told you so. But I did advise against this marriage. I'm reminding you because it may help if I—"

"Do you want to leave Charles?" Elizabeth asked impulsively.

"I don't know. No, not really. I just don't know if I can live with him."

Mary tucked her handkerchief into her purse. She closed the jeweled clasp with a decisive snap before speaking.

"Please give me a brandy, Hilary, and I'll try to explain. I know I'm imposing on you, but I'm very grateful and—"

Metcalfe growled in embarrassment as he unlocked the gold-mounted mahogany tantalus on the sideboard: "If *you* can't impose on us, who can?"

"No, Elizabeth," Mary resumed more calmly, "I don't want to leave Charles—the children. What would I do? How could I support them?"

"Jonathan won't let them go," Hilary interjected. "He'd never part with them."

"I suppose I know that, Hilary. Besides, there's no place for me elsewhere. I chose and I must abide by it." She paused, stricken, remembering her father's dire warnings. "Elizabeth, you understand. It's not just a matter of . . . not just what's best for me. I still love Charles. I do love him. Perhaps it's weakness. But I don't want to leave Charles, for his sake and, I suppose, for my own."

"Well, that's clear enough." Metcalfe handed her a dark amber glass of brandy-and-soda. "Now I can go on. I reminded you I'd opposed this marriage because I want to tell you a story. I think it'll help you understand what you're up against, understand why Charles is what Charles is. Jonathan'll no doubt tell you more, when he chooses."

"He must never know," Mary exclaimed.

"Oh, he'll know. No question about it. The old fox knows everything that touches him. And this affair touches him closely—most closely."

"Yes," Mary conceded, "I'm afraid you're right. But the story you want to tell me?"

Hilary Metcalfe incinerated five wooden matches before his pipe drew to his satisfaction. He sipped his brandy-and-soda before speaking from the center of a blue smoke cloud.

"Imagine, Mary, Hong Kong in 1853. Fifty, let me see, just fifty-two years ago. A small group of foreigners, mostly British, say eight hundred civilians and the same number of troops. Those adventurers perched on a rocky, barren island utterly dependent on, say, forty thousand Chinese for everything. For the profitable trade that lured them here, of course, but also dependent for food, for labor, for all services, for life itself. Hong Kong no more than a carbuncle on the flank of China, twelve thousand miles from Britain, three months by sea. The Manchu Empire still powerful and arrogant, despite the pinprick defeat in the First Opium War thirteen years earlier that forced the Chinese to cede the Colony.

"Imagine an insidiously hostile climate, the Chinese inhabitants tacitly hostile, overwhelmingly prejudiced, though some recognize the advantages of working with the 'devil-heads.' And nature itself viciously hostile. Typhoons that crush flimsy buildings. Dysentery that kills strong men in a few weeks. Worst of all, the 'fevers.' Malaria rampaging for months, cutting down half the community like a volley of grapeshot. Cholera, a mysterious illness that strikes without warning and kills in a week. Plague, yes, the Black Death itself. You've seen the dates on the gravestones here and the old cemetery in Macao. They died young in those days."

"Hilary," Elizabeth interrupted, "we've all seen the cemeteries. Mary needs helpful advice, she doesn't need a history lesson."

"Oh, but she does. A history lesson is precisely what she needs. I'll go on after I've recharged our glasses. And, Liz, you have a small one."

Hilary Metcalfe rose slowly. His blunt fingers busied themselves with the cut-crystal decanter and the silver-mounted syphon. In every other foreign household in Hong Kong, even the warrant officers' bungalows, serving drinks was a ritual. A white-coated Number One Boy responded to a tinkling bell and made great play with clanking bottles and tumblers. He presented his creations on a salver—gold, sterling silver, or silver-plated brass, according to his master's pocketbook. Mary appreciated the Metcalfes' bland disregard of such ceremonials of Colonial Society.

"Small ones, Hilary," Elizabeth Metcalfe instructed her brother's burly shoulders "Drinks for ladies, not for dragoons or navvies."

"As you wish, Liz. The strong one stiffened Mary's backbone—this one'll put the roses back in her cheeks. I'll make my story short, just the bare bones. Let Jonathan tell her the whole story, when he's ready. After all, it's *his* story."

"Your bare bones, my dear, are anyone else's epic. But do go on."

"So there we are, a half century ago, in this insignificant Colony torn from China by ruthless merchant-adventurers—and forced on the government in Whitehall . . . a poor little waif . . . a bastard waif neither Peking nor London really wants. Sustained by a few Chinese canny enough to see the future—and the profits. The *co-hong* merchants of Canton, a baker's dozen of them, were a monopoly chartered by the Emperor in 1757 to cope with the insistent foreigners, who buzzed like a swarm of mosquitos . . . irritating but, it appeared, no great danger. Peking reckons it a good idea to allow a few Chinese to go through the motions of trading with the foreigners and keep them at arm's length that way.

"One of those *co-hong* merchants, the greatest if not the wealthiest, is a man named Kwok. Kwok Lee-chin, scion of an old trading family from the town of Sekloong on the West River. For their own inscrutable reasons, the British call him Ah Quah. After '40, after the Opium War breaks the *co-hong* monopoly, he joins

174

forces with Derwent, Hayes and Company—not yet the biggest, but the most aggressive *hong*—most aggressive in pushing its opium and finding new Chinese products for Europe to discover it needs.

"The Derwent *hong*—in Mandarin *Teh Wan*, which means 'universal virtue.' Well, this appropriately named firm employs a young Irish adventurer called Liam Francis O'Flaherty. Just nineteen, but already cashiered from the Bengal Artillery for seducing his major's wife! Imagine a nineteen-year-old ensign with flowing blond locks and hazel-green eyes, shoe-horned into a commission to get him out of Ireland, and the languorous, bored major's wife. A parson's daughter who subsists on a diet of romantic novels—like my sister's secret vice!"

"Hilary, you don't know a thing about the major's wife," Elizabeth chided. "Stick to your story!"

"Well, it's a good story, and I'm pretty sure it's true." Metcalfe grinned. "But, fair enough, I'll stick to what I definitely know. . . . Because of his charm and quick wit, O'Flaherty becomes a sort of liaison officer. Day-to-day dealings with Ah Quah are his line, and he's constantly in and out of the merchant's house. Now, Ah Quah has a twenty-year-old daughter called Mei-lan, 'Beautiful Orchid,' and he's a modern-thinking man. He indulges his only daughter. After all, the family are only merchants, next to soldiers the lowest form of human life in a Confucian society. He doesn't keep her locked up like the daughters of the country gentry or the Mandarins. It's even whispered, scandal of scandals, that her feet aren't bound.

"Need I draw the full picture, Mary? The inevitable happens—and the result is an infant you now know as Sir Jonathan Sekloong, Knight Bachelor. O'Flaherty flits away; young Jonathan's brought up by his doting mother. Desperately in love with O'Flaherty, she wants the boy reared a Catholic like his father. And the good fathers of the Society of Jesus are delighted to oblige."

"I wondered about that," Mary interjected. "I've heard snippets of your story. But I never fully understood the fierce Catholicism."

"It's simple, my dear," Metcalfe resumed. "The Jesuits gave young Jonathan the only sustained affection he knew. In 1862, Mei-lan, 'Beautiful Orchid,' marries Richard Wheatley—the old stick you sat with last night was a young man on the make. He marries a Chinese because of her father's influence with Derwent, breaking the taboo against intermarriage to secure the indispensable Ah Quah's support for his ambitions. Mei-lan becomes preoccupied with her new husband and neglects the boy. Ah Quah, before he dies in 1866, is of two minds about his bastard mixed-blood grandson— sometimes mildly indulgent, most of the time a hectoring martinet, presumably to make up for his laxity toward his daughter. The only real security for young Jonathan is the Jesuits, who educate him with even-handed affection. He's the scion of an important commercial house, but on the wrong side of the blanket. That galls deeply, particularly since the cash and the business'll go to his legitimate cousins. Besides, he's a Eurasian, not proper Chinese, not proper European, but floating between two worlds like Mohammed's coffin between Heaven and Earth.

"Jonathan grows up with one overwhelming determination. After old Ah Quah leaves him a pittance, he'll turn his hand to anything to make his fortune. He'll ruthlessly use his grandfather's connections and his mother's special relationship with Derwent. But Jonathan'll call no man master. He *will* make his own way, create his own world, establish his own impregnable position. And he will wield enormous power.

"His own family will be ruled justly, but very strictly. There'll be none of his grandfather's laxity and none of his father's scapegrace evasion of responsibility. His own sexual peccadilloes, you'd ask? That's another matter. Chinese men aren't strict about that sort of thing, not for themselves or their sons. Daughters, of course, are different.

"Thus we have the man you know today. Undeniably brilliant, charming, reasonable, but an absolute Tartar with his sons. And this brings us to Charles, brought up by a father who's devoutly Catholic, incredibly ambitious, indulgent in some ways, but terribly demanding. There's Charles, educated in the best English schools of Hong Kong, for what that's worth, but still very Chinese underneath. A Chinese gentleman with a British gloss. And there's your problem."

Mary sipped her brandy-and-soda in silent consternation, having listened to the tale with mounting unease. She had heard other versions, usually in brief snatches. They differed sharply from Hilary Metcalfe's account, for Sir Jonathan was already the focus of extravagant legends. She felt a rush of compassion for Sir Jonathan and for her husband, whose character had been ordained even before his birth. She grieved for a society that could so distort its children.

She would, she knew, some day forgive Charles for his violent tantrum. Understanding the origins of his behavior, she could forgive him. But she would always remember the terrifying scene.

Mary was, above all, perplexed. Coping with the complex man she had married might prove beyond her ability. The Chinese were so hard on others and the men so indulgent of their own desires. The daughters and wives of the rich were also remarkably self-centered and self-indulgent in other ways. For the first time, she wondered if she truly liked the Chinese.

Mary knew she would recall Hilary Metcalfe's story every time she heard firecrackers, since the New Year's fusillades had rattled in constant counterpoint to his deep voice. She would often remember that day, since fireworks marked every festive occasion. Their *feu de joie* frightened away evil spirits. Chinese gods, even the beneficent gods, required ceaseless cajoling—and threatening.

She was immersed in her thoughts when Sir Jonathan came into the drawing-room. His light voice drew her eyes to the spare, commanding figure with the hazel eyes.

"Good afternoon, Elizabeth, Hilary. *Goong-hay fat-choy!* Mary, my dear, how are you?"

"*Goong-hay fat-choy*, Jonathan," Metcalfe answered. "Why I waste spiritual credit on you I don't under-

177

stand. It's really painting the lily to wish you prosperity."

"You mustn't say that, Hilary," Elizabeth counseled. "It's bad joss. *Goong-hay fat-choy*, Jonathan. You'll take a glass?"

"No, Elizabeth, time's too tight. But I couldn't let New Year's Day pass without offering old friends a trifling keepsake. You were good to take my daughter in. Now I must take her home."

Sir Jonathan handed Elizabeth a small parcel wrapped in yellow brocade. After his first warm smile, he had not looked at Mary again. Her obedience was assumed.

The streets and alleys, crowded with holiday-makers, reverberated with the thunder of firecrackers. Sir Jonathan leaned down to speak into her ear.

"Can't talk now. Too noisy. But we *all* want you to come home."

On the crowded Peak Tram, he reminisced inconsequentially about the great changes he'd seen in the vista of hill-girt water that lay below them. But he instructed the chair bearers to set them down before they came to the great double-beamed gate with the winged dragon rampant.

"You won't mind walking from here," he said. "I'd like a little talk."

Mary smiled at him tremulously, responding to the sheer force he exuded. It was the same commanding male strength that, in Charles, had drawn her into marriage.

"I'd want you to stay with us," Sir Jonathan said abruptly. "We need you. The family needs you—I need you. Please give it thought."

He paused for her reply, but she remained silent.

"I won't bribe you to stay or threaten you," he resumed. "If you want to go away for a while to think things over, the children must remain. Otherwise, you can have anything you want. I won't keep you here against your will; you'd be no use to me. Besides, I've grown rather fond of you."

Mary gazed at the stones in the path. The acrid odor of firecrackers filled her nostrils.

"And I of you, Father," she said softly.

"I'm glad to hear that, very glad. I apologize deeply for Charles. But Charles is . . . what Charles is."

"I married him in your Church," she declared, "and I'll stay for now."

"Charles will be discreet. Up to now, you've turned a blind eye, as I have. But that's no good now. I can't guarantee his behavior. He's a young man, and we Sekloongs have our faults. But I promise you one thing. He'll be discreet, very discreet. I'll see to that."

"Father, you don't seem to understand . . ." Mary began, then paused in helpless confusion. "Perhaps you really do. But I'll stay for the moment. I'll talk with my husband. We'll settle our difficulties."

"Good," he said. "The old man has to interfere sometimes, but you've got courage and brains enough for two sons. I'll keep my long nose out of your affairs —as much as Charles permits. *Pax?*"

"*Pax!*"

Mary smiled and extended her hand, but frost lay on her heart. She was grateful for her father-in-law's affectionate concern. But what had he actually promised? Only that her husband would be discreet.

Her anger spent, Mary was quietly appalled. She was equally disturbed by Sir Jonathan's conviction that he could manipulate Charles and by his assumption that her husband was quite entitled to philander—as long as he was discreet. Her father-in-law had promised her no more than freedom from embarrassment, guaranteed by his own determination that Charles's behavior would never again expose them to public humiliation.

That determination was rooted more deeply in his own interests than her own. Even his Chinese associates would be repelled if the heir of the Sekloong dynasty should earn the name of a libertine. Those associates would not, of course, be disturbed by Charles's pursuing high-priced flower girls, but such diversions must on no account interfere with business or family obligations.

179

The European community, for its part, would not countenance a public scandal like Charles's liaison with the Vorobya woman; such light-minded indiscretion evoked suspicion that he was "not solid"—the ultimate condemnation in Edwardian Hong Kong.

Her marriage, her happiness, her life itself, all had been reduced to a tidy commercial proposition. Entering the spacious front hall of the Small House, Mary Philippa Osgood Sekloong reflected bitterly that she was hardly more than a parcel of property that must be managed properly. It would no more do to undervalue her than it would a shipment of cotton goods. But neither must she be overvalued.

February 5, 1905–March 16, 1905

THE dwindling volley of fireworks on the narrow shores below were no more than a distant rumble on The Peak. The first chill evening of the thirty-second year of the reign of the Son of Heaven Kuang Hsü, Emperor of the Great Pure Dynasty, spread its dark robes over the Crown Colony of Edward VII of England, Scotland, Wales, and Ireland and of the Realms and Territories Over the Seas, King; Emperor of India; and (titularly, at least) Defender of the Faith. Behind blue-velvet drapes drawn against the darkness, the drawing-room of the Small House was a snug refuge within the larger fastness of Sekloong Manor.

His husky torso encased in a blue-satin smokingjacket, the master of the house was sipping his third after-dinner brandy-and-soda. Charles Sekloong was totally at ease, apparently affected by neither the brandy nor the emotional storms of the day. His powerful hands were relaxed, and his wide-set hazel eyes were untroubled beneath his smooth, bronzed forehead.

Mary Sekloong was struck again by the animal force that had first attracted her. Like a black panther in repose, her husband appeared totally sure of his male strength. For the first time in almost two years, she felt

180

the liquid ache in her loins Charles had once called forth simply by looking at her.

Charles and Mary sat silent on the twin yellow-brocade sofas flanking the marble fireplace. She was turning the pages of E. J. Eitel's *Europe in China: The History of Hong Kong;* and he was contemplating the leaping flames. Though they were six feet apart, she involuntarily responded as if his fingertips were stroking her thighs. She shifted uneasily on the down-filled cushion, feeling constricted by corsets that compressed her waist to a twenty-one-inch span beneath the low-cut bodice of a panniered burgundy-silk dress. Her breasts swelled under the light caress of her filmy camisole, and a pink flush suffused her shoulders and face.

A rush of shame of her sensuality dismayed Mary. Worse than unseemly, it was unwise. In that moment she hated the female weakness that was so profoundly stirred by the familiar male body that had consistently betrayed her trust. Laying the book down, she stared into the fire. Their gazes intersected, but did not meet.

"Underlying this mixed and fluctuating population of Hong Kong," the historian Eitel had written, "a self-perpetuating amity: the secret inchoative union of Europe and Asia (as represented by China)." Could it, she wondered, be true in any way?

Drawn by her slight movement, Charles looked up from the fire. He sipped his brandy-and-soda before speaking in the liquid baritone that at once soothed and aroused her.

"So you went to the old man?" he asked softly.

"No, Charles, I didn't." Her voice was tense. "I wouldn't. He came to me."

"Whee-oo!" He exhaled with a muted whistle. "Your stock must be high. You're sure he came to you? How did he know about the unpleasantness?"

"Did you really think he wouldn't know?" Mary strove to keep her voice free of asperity.

"No," he conceded without rancor, "I suppose not. You can't keep anything from him. It's uncanny."

"Yes, isn't it?"

"Mary," he said haltingly, "Mary, I'm sorry about this morning. Did I hurt you much?"

"Yes, Charles. Badly."

"I regret most deeply dishonoring myself by violence," he said with extravagant politeness.

Mary did not reply. His unabated arrogance was so characteristically Chinese, and she knew that he was incapable of unbending. Granting him quick forgiveness would therefore mean nothing. Half-hating him, she wanted to draw his head to her breast and say she forgave him. But she remained silent.

"The old man raised the nine devils out of Hell." Charles sought contact with her, unconsciously reverting to the Chinese idiom in his agitation. "He was rough."

"But, Charles, how . . . how could you attack me?"

"I was angry. I've been angry for a long time. I can't live with those rules you make."

"Charles," she said wryly, "whether I'm pregnant or not is up to you."

"I'm sorry, Mary, but I won't use those things. It's wrong."

"And I'm sorry, too, Charles. But I won't bear any children for a while. I'm too young to be a broodmare."

"And too beautiful." His mood changed abruptly, and the flash of his smile lit his hazel eyes. He was playing on her emotions so adroitly she found it virtually impossible to resist. They were drawing closer, groping for contact across the barriers of different backgrounds and different standards. He would, it was blatantly obvious, commit himself neither to using a contraceptive device nor to bridling his wandering fancy. But she could not flatly reject his overtures without imperiling their total relationship.

Her resentment and her self-control were both being eroded. Longing engulfed her, and she lay back on the sofa, languorous as a Siamese cat.

"There is," he ventured, "a right time, I'm told, when the Maiden in the Moon allows . . ."

"So I've told you."

"And might this be the right time?"

"Perhaps." She smiled, her reluctance abandoned.

He came to her, and his mouth touched hers fleetingly. The back of his hand brushed her cheek, and his demanding mouth parted her lips. A tide of warmth swept over her entire body. She felt him rise against her, and yearning surged between her thighs.

"Perhaps," she repeated, rising and taking his hand, "that time is now."

His hand cupped her breast, but she evaded him with a swirling pirouette to open the doors. They laughed like children as she raced up the stairs and he pursued her.

Charles slid the bolt closed, and the red-draped bedroom became a refuge. His arms enclosed her, and his hands grasped her buttocks. They undressed each other in awkward haste, garments falling to the thick carpet in a multicolored ring that encircled them. Her breasts and thighs glowed at his touch, and she longed for his distended maleness.

"Now, Charles!" she cried out, falling back on the bed. "Now, my love!"

He came into her, thrusting and dominant. She enveloped him, lifted by a tide of triumph in surrender. She grasped him within her, and their climax was shattering. All reserve, all consciousness were overwhelmed by waves of crimson fire lanced by golden rays.

Mary longed to hold him in peace inside herself forever, and fiercely pressed her legs together to confine him. After several minutes, they reluctantly disentangled their limbs and lay side by side, exultantly exhausted. She drowsily reminded herself that she must pick up their scattered clothing. But there would be time before Ah Sam brought the morning tea. As the delicious languor of satiation overcame her, she reflected, half awake, that it was, fortunately, the right time of the month. Not only harvest and spring festivals were governed by the stately progress of the waxing and waning moon across the Eastern skies.

The young woman who called herself Countess Vera Vorobya embarked for Sydney on February 7, 1905. The packet Sir Jonathan handed Elizabeth Metcalfe on New Year's Day, he later told Mary, had contained a steamer ticket and £1,000 in notes. Mary was almost grateful to the woman she had glimpsed only in passing; she was almost grateful to Rachel Wheatley for her malicious tongue. They had inadvertently not merely restored her husband to her, but opened the gates of bliss.

The two weeks following her hectic reconciliation with Charles were a kaleidoscopic joy, a carnival of the senses in the big bed with the red-brocade canopy. Charles swore he had never known such perfect pleasure; and Mary knew she had never gloried in such total abandonment. They were besotted zealots, seeking their own earthly paradise in each other's bodies.

For two weeks Mary lived in a golden haze, and Charles was not only an ardent lover, but a model husband. Sir Jonathan and Lady Lucinda beamed their pleasure at the reconciliation and confidently expected that another grandchild would soon enhance their complacent satisfaction.

At the beginning of the third week, the golden glow was fading; desire was giving way to satiation; languid fatigue was becoming exhaustion. Mary had discovered unsuspected and unseemly depths of sensuality in herself. But the overwhelming fleshly passion could not endure—if, for no other reason, because she suffered a constant burning sensation.

Dr. Moncriefe smiled when she described her symptoms.

"Honeymoon cystitis," he said archly. "I congratulate you, my dear, on captivating your husband so. The complaint's most unusual after the first few months of marriage." Himself a devout Scots Catholic, the physician explained again the periodic abstinence the Church called "the rhythm method" for avoiding pregnancy.

Mary would not bear another child so soon, though she had impetuously risked pregnancy in the first raptures of the impassioned reconciliation. She was, moreover, forced to recognize that their new joy sprang chiefly from her surrender to his demands, rather than from new understanding between them or any mutual compromise. Charles was enthralled because she had become the ardent, ivory-skinned houri of his fantasies. But his revived ardor did not acknowledge her as an individual human being possessed of any needs or interests outside the canopied bed.

For nearly four years her womb had been a cornucopia pouring out children to enlarge the Sekloong dynasty. During the weeks just passed she had been hardly more than a receptacle for his seed, and she felt soiled. They cleaved together only physically, while their emotions and their thoughts remained separated. Even their love-making, she reflected with revulsion, had become a set, meaningless ritual, like actors playing fixed roles. Charles and she remained virtually oblivious to each other's hearts and minds; their bodies were reduced to no more than ingenious devices for manufacturing gratification by mutual friction.

Charles was tolerant when she tried to convey her doubts—tolerant and uninterested. Rather than listen, he embraced her and kissed her until, to her disgust, she felt the familiar stirrings and feared that she had become a captive of his sensuality.

"That was glorious," he said afterward. "But, sometimes, silence pleases fate—and talk offends. We say: Do not rouse the tiger by shouting or frighten away the benevolent dragon. Europeans spoil good things by probing them. Besides, bed's no place for intellectual discussions."

She had subsided, silently giving herself to his embrace. The next night, when they lay in the half-darkness under the red-brocade canopy, she kissed him gently and turned away to compose herself for sleep.

"What's this?" he demanded. "My beautiful bed-companion turning her back on me?"

"Charles, I'm tired tonight."

"Oh, is that all?" he responded. "I worried we were going back to the old ways. Well, maybe later or tomorrow."

"No, Charles," she whispered, cradling her head on his shoulder. "Not for a while, at least."

"And why not?" He was still tolerantly amused. "Is something wrong?"

"Well, not really." She weighed her words. "Not really anything wrong, though we *have* been overdoing it. It's been wonderful, but Dr. Moncriefe . . ."

His arm stiffened under her, and he asked harshly: "Back to that again?"

"No, Charles," she reassured him, "we're not back to anything. Only it's not the right time now. Dr. Moncriefe explained. You know I really don't want another child so soon. Perhaps, but not just now. So—"

"More damned nonsense," he snorted, pulling his arm away. "My mother had seven, lost four—and none the worse for it. What are women for?"

"For children, but also for other things."

"The devil with it," he swore. "God save me from intellectual women, all vapors and high-flown philosophizing. Might as well go to bed with a Taoist nun. You still don't understand: we've got to build the clan."

"But Charles," she protested, still hopeful, "you don't really believe that . . . that getting children's the only . . ."

Her words trailed off, for he was feigning the deep, regular breathing of sleep.

The next morning, Charles did not return to their bedroom after his breakfast to kiss her good-bye. That evening, he did not return for dinner. When he had not returned by midnight, Mary bitterly recognized that he would not return at all that night. During the following weeks, his frequent absences gave her much time—too much time for anguished reflection.

Mary realized anew that she did not understand the man she had married. His ostentatious anger, she feared, sprang as much from her daring to oppose his will as from her physical withdrawal. Like his father, Charles demanded absolute obedience. Only the total submission she could not make would mollify him. His moods were beyond her comprehension, and no stable foundation sustained their relationship.

For weeks, the Small House was a fortress where two armies, allied only by expedience, watched each other with deep suspicion barely veiled by formal courtesy. Charles restricted his conversation to brief sentences spoken before the servants. After several vain attempts to break through the barrier he had erected, Mary, too, uttered no more than polite half-sentences.

They coupled twice, no more than brief, uncomfortable writhing on rumpled sheets. He took her contemptuously, without physical or verbal preliminaries, determined to master her body. She yielded, knowing it was the time Dr. Moncriefe called the "safe period." But the physical act meant nothing—in truth, less than nothing. It was destructive. He could not break her to his will, and she loathed his cold determination to do so.

Mary still allowed herself to hope for a true reconciliation. Left alone they could find their way back to love. But they were not left alone: Sir Jonathan was elaborately courteous, but his eyes were agate cold; Lady Lucinda regarded her with pitying uncomprehension. She was, she felt, no longer an individual, but the family's possession. Nor could she turn to the Metcalfes for comfort; some things she would not discuss even with Elizabeth, and no advice could help her. Her spirit and body wracked by tension, she was desperately alone amid the flock of children and servants. But still she hoped.

Her vestigial optimism was blasted by a conversation with Charles in late March after they had eaten their evening meal in awkward silence.

"Mary," he began. "I must talk with you."

"As you wish." Her tone was defensively noncommittal, though her spirit leaped in renewed hope. "I'm always happy to talk."

"Not much else lately but talk."

"Other things are possible—with a little consideration and affection."

"Well, we'll see. But there's something else."

"What is it then, Charles?"

"You know what I promised the old man—no scandals, no public humiliation."

"Yes, Charles."

"There'll be none, no such thing. You won't be affected. Your position remains the same. But I'm obliged to tell you . . . give you notice."

"What *are* you talking about, Charles?"

A chill premonition overcame her. It was inconceivable that he should force an open break. The scandal would badly hurt the clan, when Sir Jonathan was still preparing his coup against the Wheatleys. Besides, divorce was forbidden him by his Church. What notice could he possibly give her?

"I've taken a concubine," Charles said flatly. "Had to."

"You've *what?*" She literally could not believe she'd heard correctly. *"What?"*

"Taken a concubine. You won't give me more children. She will."

Her first rage subsided within seconds. She was beyond anger, beyond surprise, almost beyond despair. As if confronting a dangerous animal, she warily considered her reply. When she finally spoke, her tone was pitched to the offhand politeness of small talk with a casual acquaintance.

"I'm puzzled, Charles."

"Puzzled? That's a queer word."

"Did you expect me to weep? Gnash my teeth and tear my clothing in mourning? I'm truly puzzled. I don't understand your strange customs."

"We're off on the chink business again, are we?" Charles's quick temper flared. "Bloody British superiority."

"By no means superiority. I'm just puzzled by your Chinese customs. How can you take a concubine when we were married in your Church and promised to remain true to each other? Not, I know, that infidelity bothers you. But the law, too, requires monogamy."

"Who's to stop me?"

"No one, I suppose. Only your own conscience."

"It's a sanctioned Chinese custom. When the first

wife can't—or won't—produce children, the husband has a right . . . a duty . . . to take a concubine."

"And Hong Kong law? Does it agree?"

"It doesn't matter. She's a Swatow girl, and Chinese law permits the relationship. We believe big families, many children, are a blessing. And she will—"

"Produce children," Mary interrupted. "I've gathered that. But I'd rather you didn't tell me about her."

"I won't. The old man said you should know. He didn't object."

"How quaint—you're to follow in his footsteps in all things."

"It's my decision. I'm my own master."

"Really?" she taunted. "I'm glad to hear you say so. Is that all you have to say?"

"Since you take it that way, yes. That's all. Except that you remain the Number One Wife, and I won't bring her into this house."

"How considerate of you," Mary replied. "Courteous and considerate as always."

Charles brooded in frustrated silence while Mary methodically turned the pages of S. Wells Williams's thick tome, *The Middle Kingdom,* taking in not a single word. After half an hour, he flung out of the house, and she climbed the stairs to the dressing room. Her steps were as slow as an arthritic old woman's.

Overwhelming weariness weighted her limbs as she undressed and put on her nightclothes. Coldly despairing, she avoided her own eyes in the dim-lit mirror as she brushed her long, red-gold hair. Was this insult, she wondered, any worse than Charles's previous light-hearted philandering? But she was too exhausted to attempt an answer. She automatically slipped between the silken sheets. Her last conscious act of will before sleeping was the decision to put off all further thought. Perhaps this final deed meant that her marriage was over and that she must find a way out. But she was too tired to think, too numb to care.

On an afternoon in mid-April when the sunlight gilded The Peak, Mary was playing with her three older children in the formal garden behind the Small House. Baby Charlotte, not quite a year and a half old, toddled uncertainly under the protective eyes of her sister Guinevere, just a year older. Jonathan, who would be four in November, chased the red-and-white ball his mother threw for him. Ah Ying, the baby-amah, scowled her disapproval of *Tai-tai*'s usurping her functions and gasped with ostentatious anxiety whenever Jonnie stumbled.

"Mary! Hoi, Mary!" A deep voice called from the terrace. "Where are you?"

She drew breath in surprise. The voice was Charles's, and he had come home in midafternoon for the first time in a year. Despite her numbed dismay at his taking the concubine and his methodical neglect, she yearned for a reconciliation. Pride burnt out, she knew that he was all she had. Her heart leaped as she turned to greet him, then plummeted.

Harry Sekloong stood on the terrace. She had not realized how similar were the brothers' voices, though their physical resemblance was marked. Harry was slightly taller, slightly darker, and slightly heavier than Charles. His eyes were a deeper hazel and his nose was straighter, lacking the pronounced arch that gave Charles's and Sir Jonathan's features a predatory cast. Harry also lacked Charles's solemnity, which verged on pomposity. Four years younger than his brother, Harry evaded the full, oppressive weight of his father's will through the lightheartedness that Sir Jonathan, in exasperation, called light-mindedness. Harry was quicksilver, sparkling and irrepressible.

In spite of her disappointment, her spirits rose to Harry's bubbling gaiety. Her own age, he was more brother than her own elder brother Thomas Duane Osgood, ten thousand miles away in England.

"Wotcher, 'arry?" she called, slipping into the mock Cockney he sometimes affected.

"Wotcher, Mary?" he called. "Gotta cuppa char for me? The old man unshackled me early, and I decided to call on my favorite sister-in-law."

"Your *only* sister-in-law!" Her joking protest slipped
190

out unaware, but her laughter abruptly halted. Was the nameless "Swatow girl," Charles's concubine, also his sister-in-law?

"Not to worry!" He ignored her obvious consternation. "You'd be my favorite if I had twenty sister-in-laws. Having only one, you're still my favorite."

He caught her up in a bear-hug and whirled her around.

"Punishment for doubting my sincerity," he said with mock gravity. "And worse to come if you still misbehave."

"Harry! Harry! Let me down!" she protested laughing. "What'll the servants think?"

"The servants think? Good for 'em to make 'em think. Thinking's a rare exercise for 'em."

"Don't do your Colonel Dunderhead act now. Come have that cup of tea."

"Right y'are, luv. Whatever you say."

He set her down with exaggerated care. She took his hand and led him into the morning-room, where Ah Sam stood behind the full paraphernalia of an English high tea—thin sandwiches arrayed on Spode plates before the silver teapot and samovar, the silver strainer, creamer, and sugar bowl knobby with scrolled leaves and flowers. The Number One Boy's features were twisted in a ferocious grin quite different from the forced half-smile he tendered Charles. Always suspiciously protective on her behalf, even Ah Sam could not resist Harry's ebullience. He not only liked the younger brother, but trusted him. Harry satisfied Ah Sam's mysterious standards as Charles did not.

Harry addressed him in Cantonese so rapid she caught only a few words, and the Number One Boy left the room chuckling.

"Harry," she asked with sudden suspicion, "you haven't come from Sir Jonathan, from Father, have you? Why did he unlock your leg-irons early today?"

"Swear to you, Mary, I'm not an emissary from the old man or anyone else. Just from myself."

"No better accreditation," she smiled. "What is your mission, Mr. Ambassador Plenipotentiary?"

"It is a secret mission, *chère Madame*. And it has already succeeded."

"Succeeded!"

"I wanted to see you laugh again. You've been going around like a tragedy queen half the time—and a sick calf the other."

"A flattering description, Mr. Ambassador. Very diplomatic. Do you talk to all your hostesses the same way?"

"*Chère Madame,* I have accredited myself only to you. And I am very diplomatic. I've not come to request explanations of your strange conduct, but to make explanations."

"Explanations about what, Your Excellency?"

"Gimme another crab-and-cucumber sandwich," he answered inelegantly, "and I'll explain my explanations."

Mary laughed and passed the platter. For the first time in months, she was free of self-absorption.

"May I stop clowning for a minute?" His words were muffled by the sandwich he chewed. "You can throw me out on my ear whenever you please. It's not my business, I suppose, but I've made it my business. You've got to talk with someone who loves you as you are—wouldn't change anything about you."

"Go on, Harry," she prompted. "I'm listening."

"You remember I told you not to marry Charles? Later I wondered why. I wanted you for myself. But that's all past now; it's unthinkable. Do you remember I told you the Sekloongs would try to remake you?"

"I remember that very well."

"The House of Sekloong is a hydraulic press. Whatever goes in must come out in the shape the family wishes—to be used as the family wishes."

"They haven't succeeded in remolding you," Mary objected.

"I'm not too sure. But I resist. Yes, I resist. The oldest son can't. That's what made Charles—irresistible pressure and no talent for evasion, for playing the clown. He's malleable—stubborn, yet malleable. But

192

not flexible. Me, I'm not malleable . . . or I've half convinced the old man I'm not. But I'm flexible."

Mary nodded, intrigued by the coincidence between Harry's assessment and her own musing.

"Now you're part of us. No point talking about what might've been or might not've been. You're part of us, a highly valued part. You can't escape—even if you really want to."

"I don't know what I want anymore," she confessed. "But how can you say highly valued? Prettier girls are sixpence a dozen, prettier and more docile girls."

"More docile, yes. More beautiful, more charming, no. And highly valued because of this damned Eurasian complex. Your children are more than half European, and that's the way we're moving."

"But your father objected violently. He wanted Charles to marry a Chinese girl."

"True enough. But once he'd yielded, it was a fundamental change. He knew it'd be; that's why he fought so hard."

"I don't quite understand," Mary said.

"Behind the bluster, the old man's a total realist, isn't he?"

She nodded.

"He's a ferocious Chinese patriot—most of the time. But he's got the Eurasian tic. He won't say it, but his realism tells him the Chinese'll never accept us totally. They're too arrogant, too blood-proud."

"You . . . we . . . we're not quite embraced by the European community, even with his knighthood."

"True again. But the worst Europeans are less rigid than the Chinese, more open. The old man's convinced the Europeans will accept us in time. Maybe another generation or two, but in time—"

"And the Chinese?"

"Not in *this* century. The old man's determined to make the Sekloongs not only respected, but accepted. That's why he wouldn't take the name O'Flaherty. He's determined the Europeans will accept us on his—our —terms. That's why he insisted on building on The

193

Peak. A weakness perhaps in the strongest man I know, but there it is."

"I can't believe he puts so much stress . . ."

"I've told you. Once he gave way on your marriage, it was inevitable. And he's determined it'll work, your marriage."

"It all sounds a bit mad. So different from the way it appears."

"But it's true. Mary, do you know how many children the old man has? By rough count, I'd say fourteen he knows about. Only five strictly legitimate, Charles, little Matilda, myself, and our two half-brothers by his first marriage, his Chinese-style marriage, Sydney and Gregory."

"But he acknowledges them."

"Of course. But they're three-quarters Chinese and married to Chinese. Their mother Lillian was a Shanghai girl, killed by the Green Gang when she'd been married only three years. As far as the old man's concerned, the Seks are déclassé, not quite up to snuff. They're just second-rate treaty-port Eurasians. And you know what that means—scum to both Europeans and Chinese. But you and Charles are the white hopes, the new Sekloongs who'll conquer both worlds."

"You're overstating it, Harry. The Sek brothers *are* running the Shanghai end of the business."

"Yes, the Shanghai end, not the center in Hong Kong. That's reserved for Charles and you . . . maybe me. You, your children are the point of the spear the old man's determined will conquer the European citadel."

"Strange you should say that. The first time we met, he talked of penetrating the fortress of Hong Kong."

"See what I mean?" Harry rejoined. "And it's not just because he can use you—he's got more respect for you than for Charles or, certainly, me."

"Then why . . . why does he allow . . ." Mary faltered.

"Why does he allow Charles his little bit of fluff, you mean? You know any children won't count. That's a pretext Charles invented."

"Then why?" she interrupted.

"Even the old man can't control Charles all the time. You know Charles is hurt, too—deeply hurt. Though I'm sure it's his own damned-fool fault, whatever's going on between you. But he's hurt, and he's striking back at you. Sounds funny, I know, but Charles'd never take a concubine if he didn't care about you and want to get back at you. Otherwise, a simple arrangement, another liaison, but discreetly."

"I don't understand," she protested. "It doesn't make sense."

"It does, you know. Makes curious sense, if you know Charles. The old man respects you, but he'll use you ruthlessly. Same for Charles. He's been molded by that pressure. He kicks up hell once in a while, but always comes to heel. The old man knows that."

"You mean he's counting on Charles to come back to me?"

"Of course. If you leave Charles, that'll tear it. Your children'll be completely unprotected from the same pressure. You've got to stay to protect them. Charles won't. He can't."

"You're very persuasive," she conceded. "But the price is too high."

"So's the cost of leaving. You still love the old fellow, my esteemed elder brother, don't you? You haven't given up, have you?"

She nodded reluctant assent.

"Mary, it's a bad time for everyone. The old man's doing his trickiest maneuvering ever, and his career has, shall we say, not always been entirely straightforward. Legal, yes. He's got great respect for legitimacy, maybe because he's not. But straightforward—hardly ever."

"What's that to do with me? I can't see the connection. One's a family matter, a recalcitrant daughter-in-law in an overwhelming Chinese family. The other's business."

"You're learning, Mary, but you're still incorrigibly British. No Chinese woman would ask that question. There's no dividing line, no distinction between family

195

and business. The business is for the family, the family is for the business. Nothing can separate them. I warned you."

"I see," she said dubiously. "Do go on."

"Briefly, just now. I don't want to burden you with too much too soon. But can you understand that everything that happens between Charles and you directly affects the family and the Sekloong enterprises?"

"I'll try to understand."

"That's my girl!" he drawled. "If you'll take me on as your native guide, you'll learn faster. After all, I know the terrain."

"Gladly, if you'll teach me that terrain."

"Well, just one more glimpse right now. As my jolly step-grandfather Richard Wheatley would say, 'Mustn't worry that pretty little head'!"

"Get on with it, my good man!" Mary's jest did not conceal her impatience.

"All right, though not all today. The old man wants his independence, his own mighty Sekloong *hong*, not Derwent's leavings. Of course, he'll stay their comprador. Saves face on both sides. But he's determined to be the first great Chinese *taipan*, and he's moving fast. There's the railroad, the Canton–Kowloon line. When we get a substantial piece, we'll really be moving."

"Who takes over the opium?" Mary jibed indignantly.

"Opium's a dying trade, but still important. As a Chinese patriot, the old man hates the traffic. But he wants it extinguished properly. Then Dr. Sun Yat-sen's getting five *lakhs* a year, say £50,000, from us to fight the Manchus. Some money goes to the Manchus too. Only sensible to hedge our bet, though the Empire'll fall apart anyway. London thinks it can preserve the Manchu Empire. If old Dick Wheatley caught us red-handed, he could make a damned fine effort to smash us."

"It's all so complicated," Mary sighed. "But I think I'm beginning to understand."

"Good. For now, let's stop with the Secret Society connection. The Greens and Reds hate each other—

when they're not conniving together. But they hate Manchus and Europeans more. The old man's flirting with them; so's Dr. Sun Yat-sen. After all, the societies are patriotic Chinese, even if they are outside the law. We're laying out a packet of tea-money to buy certain immunities for the Triads in Hong Kong."

Harry grinned wickedly and extended his cup for replenishment from the silver teapot.

"Do you follow me?" he demanded. "You see how one misstep—one confidence betrayed—could ruin us? That's why the old man's so tense. P'etty Eng'ish missee savvy poor Chinee fellah he makee talk-talk?"

"In general," she acknowledged, "but not entirely."

"Be a miracle if you did entirely. Let's leave it for now and go see the children. But you will take me on as your native guide?"

"Gladly," Mary smiled, "and at a good wage."

June 19, 1905–November 16, 1906

HARRY'S intervention opened a window to the world outside the nurseries and the overfurnished rooms of the Small House. Mary could again see beyond the high walls that protected and isolated Sekloong Manor. She felt herself vitally alive for the first time since she had been stunned by colliding with the granite obduracy of Charles's character. She had found a strong ally within the family, an ally who might in time even help her arrive at a new relationship with Charles, for the two brothers were close. She still raged in humiliation at the thought of Charles and his concubine intertwined beneath a silken coverlet. But she was less frequently afflicted by yearning for the husband she still loved. Harry buoyed her spirits and often diverted her thoughts from the hateful "Swatow girl."

Mary badly needed a confidant. Charles's self-indulgence and his innate contempt for women had finally made it impossible for her to talk with him except in banalities, while bearing four children in hardly four

197

years had cut her off from almost all contact with outsiders. Moreover, Harry's accounts of the complex role the Sekloongs played in the tense drama of commerce and politics fascinated her. The family was far more influential than she had imagined, though it chose to move in the half-shadows outside the limelight. Her brother-in-law opened the curtains on a vista she had briefly glimpsed before her eyes turned inward upon domestic preoccupations. She felt that she was again becoming a whole human being in a vital, dynamic world, rather than a queen bee brooding in secluded splendor.

They saw each other almost every day, since it was only a three-minute walk to the Small House from The Castle, where Harry lived with his parents like a dutiful Chinese son. He was never loath to escape Sir Jonathan's admonitions that he must apply himself to the business or Lady Lucinda's urging that he take a virtuous Chinese bride.

They often discussed matters outside confined Hong Kong, the great world where the Manchu Empire was toppling of its own weight. That collapse was hastened not only by endemic rebellion, but by the interference of Western merchants backed by Western arms and Western technology. Men like the Wheatleys wished to sustain the oppressive rule of the Manchus, since they felt the rebels against the decadent Great Pure Dynasty threatened stable trade. But the conservative Europeans understood the purposes of those democratic, bourgeois rebels no more than they did the consequences of their own actions. The foreigners sought to preserve the Empire, but their intervention eroded its sovereignty, hastening its inevitable collapse.

Sometimes Harry told her of his own secret missions to deliver funds to the republicans and assist in planning their campaigns. Dr. Sun Yat-sen's following within China was steadily growing, as was his determination to overthrow that living fossil, the Manchu Empire. The Imperial System was based upon doctrines first enunciated by Confucius in the sixth century B.C., when they were already conservative. Sustained by a petrified moral code, that system had evolved only slightly over the millennia. Its essential structure had not altered significantly since it was institutionalized by the Han Dynasty in the second century B.C. Although he was anti-Manchu by conviction, Sir Jonathan originally hesitated to acknowledge the necessity to destroy the Imperial System Harry called "the last survivor of the age of political dinosaurs." He would instinctively have preferred to set a Chinese Emperor on the Dragon Throne to rule China in much the same manner as the Central Realms had been ruled for two millennia. He was finally convinced that reform within the Imperial System was impossible, since no Confucian Empire, whoever ruled, could withstand the brutal challenges of the twentieth century. Sir Jonathan was thereafter totally committed to the rebels, and Harry was his emissary to the "new men" who were determined to transform China into a modern, technological republic.

Sometimes Harry and Mary laughed together at Harry's wry tales of his forced quest for a bride. Sir Jonathan, like Lady Lucinda, was determined that he should marry soon, preferably a young Chinese lady, but, otherwise, the daughter of another great Hong Kong Eurasian family like the Hotungs or, if unavoidable, a suitable European. Harry was, he boasted, "supple as a serpent and twice as wily." He eluded his father's unremitting pressure by pursuing the search with apparent eagerness—and finally rejecting each prospective bride as unworthy. There were fortunately no suitable European candidates, for Mary suspected that one European daughter-in-law was more than enough for Sir Jonathan and Lady Lucinda.

Sometimes Charles was at home, and Harry tried to bridge the abyss between husband and wife. Though mutual communication was tenuous, they could, at least, laugh together when Harry was with them, and Charles would even discuss business matters. He would literally speak over her head to his brother, but he would tolerate her presence—just as she tolerated his presence in her house. Although progress was glacially slow, Harry felt that Charles and Mary were moving toward a reconciliation of sorts.

Sometimes Harry and Mary talked at length of the Sekloongs' campaign to win their own independent commercial empire. She wondered if he would speak so openly without Sir Jonathan's express permission and asked Harry directly late one afternoon, when they languidly sipped gimlets on the shaded terrace.

"I wondered when you'd ask," Harry acknowledged. "Of course he knows. I couldn't talk so frankly if the old man objected. Matter of fact, he *wants* you to know much more about the business. I can't guess why, and he doesn't tell me. But it suits us both, so why worry?"

Theirs was a curious kind of courtship. They rarely touched and then only in boisterous horseplay. Inclination and caution both counseled against expressions of affection that could lead only to guilty frustration. Theirs was a courtship of the mind and the spirit that offered Mary her first experience of an equal relationship with an adult male that was neither intense nor painful. She simply enjoyed Harry's wide-ranging conversation and even-handed comradeship. His penchant for light banter enlivened even their discussion of grave matters. She reflected complacently that, for once, her bravura motto was beside the point. She was doing nothing in any way foolish, and she was certainly not committing herself wholeheartedly.

And Charles, to whom she had committed herself wholeheartedly and foolishly? She could, at least, talk with Charles again, though their words were guarded. Occasionally they slept together, though without passion. Charles insisted that husbands and wives should share the same bed. Besides, he wanted more children. Though they both avoided the prickly subject, Mary knew that any offspring of his concubine, the "Swatow girl," would not be suitable heirs to the respectable solid tradition Sir Jonathan was creating. She followed Dr. Moncriefe's timetable for avoiding conception, and Charles expressed no curiosity regarding her monthly cycle. If he pursued other fancies, he was discreet, as
200

Sir Jonathan had promised. She was spared public humiliation, and, having tacitly accepted the concubine's existence, she was less bitterly jealous of that poor sequestered creature whose children could never challenge her own. Scar tissue was slowly suturing the wounds Charles's blatant philandering had inflicted. If she was still in love with her husband, she no longer suffered constant anguish at his betrayal.

Mary lavished her pent-up love on the children, hovering between relief and resentment at the servants' sparing her the task of attending to their physical needs. She ventured into Hong Kong's stratified society, which received the Sekloongs formally but rejected intimacy. Still, she found women of her own age to talk with, however uninspired their conversation, as well as young men to flirt with, however innocently and tepidly. She fashioned a new, functional framework for her life. By no means perfect, at least it existed, and she was, she told herself, reasonably content.

But such mild diversions did not satisfy her aspirations. Her extraordinary energy and her latent ardor compelled her to explore the strange world in which she lived. She resumed her Cantonese lessons, even started learning the complex brushstrokes of Chinese ideographs, and she seriously studied Chinese history. Her painting, which she had never abandoned, complemented her interest in Chinese calligraphy and the civilization it epitomized. She sometimes lay awake at night, chilled by her empty vision of the future, but her long, cheerful talks with Harry sustained her basically optimistic spirit and kept her fears at bay.

"The old man's so pleased with you," he remarked one afternoon in September, "you'd think he invented you."

"I'm glad," she replied thoughtfully. "Perhaps he did invent the new me. I'm tougher."

"He likes that too."

"Even though he won't get yet another precious grandchild from me?"

"Maybe, but he's as patient as a stalking tiger. Probably thinks time will provide."

"He may be right, though it'll be a long, long time," she conceded. "But he's pleased that I'm tougher? I'd expect the opposite. A daughter-in-law who stands up to him, a puny female who defies his will—the last thing I should think he'd want."

"You do it so gracefully, love," Harry laughed. "Charles either knuckles under or rears up in rage, and I slither away. He needs some toughness in the family."

"Why ever?"

"We'll need to be tough. Rough times are coming. This war between the Japs and the Russkis doesn't look like much, but the Japs have beaten the Russkis hollow. Whatever the little tin-gods of Hong Kong think, things'll never be the same. The Manchus didn't learn a thing when the Japs defeated them in '95, but some people did."

"The Japanese did, you mean?"

"Of course. London backed Tokyo to keep Moscow in line. Whitehall wanted to stop the Russkis nibbling into China like termites. Now it's the Japs' turn. But they won't nibble. They'll bite off big chunks."

"Worse than the Europeans?"

"Much worse. Besides, the Americans're now in the game. That president with the funny spectacles and the big teeth, Teddy Roosevelt—he's shrewd. He's playing the peacemaker, bringing Tokyo and Moscow to a settlement. Remember how the Yanks proclaimed their Open Door Policy a few years ago? Everyone to share in trade. No one to gobble any more pieces of China. The Yanks've outdone the British at good old Anglo-Saxon hypocrisy. They play the peacemakers, but make damned sure they get their share—or more."

"Harry," she interrupted, "I take your point, but don't get swept away by anti-Americanism. We were talking about what it means for China—and for us. I can see the general drift: the Manchus getting weaker under greater pressure, the Western powers and Japan getting greedier and more aggressive. And you were saying—"

"You've got the script right. I'd give the Manchus another decade, no more. Then Dr. Sun Yat-sen, or someone like him, takes over and faces problems ten times worse than now bedevil the Manchus. Instead of cutting China up like a melon, the powers'll try dismembering her with surgeons' scalpels. China has to get modern armaments and industry practically overnight —or perish. That's where we come in."

"I knew the Sekloongs would get their share," she commented tartly. "How, though?"

"The old man's determined to play a major part in that modernization. The House of Sekloong will either amass an immense fortune or go bust. We're big now, but we've got no depth. One major mistake and we're wiped out. That's why the old man's so testy lately. He's got too many strings in his hands. He could bring the whole thing down around our ears if he pulled the wrong string."

"I've felt that," Mary pondered. "How does he think he can run with the Chinese hare and hunt with the European hounds? The principle's sound, mind you, but—"

"As for me," he interjected, "I don't see why all the fuss. I'm happy as we are."

"No, Harry," she replied earnestly, "that won't do. We must either grow bigger or perish."

"So the old man says," he answered. "You two think the same way. And you're both mad about power."

"Don't be mad yourself, Harry," she laughed. "I'm just thinking aloud. Anyway, we've been sitting too long. Let's have a walk. You haven't seen the pavilion since I refurnished it."

She took his hands and pulled him to his feet. He rose lithely, and, for an immeasurable moment, they stood facing each other, two separate, dark figures against the sunlight bridged by their joined hands. The next instant she was in his arms, her fingertips caressing his crisp black hair, her lips brushing his bronzed cheeks.

"Mary, my love," he whispered, "Mary, I've wanted so long to—"

"And I—"

They pressed against each other for an infinity of

203

seconds. He tried to pull away, but her arms around his neck drew his mouth down upon hers. She strained upward, fitting her body to his. Finally, he broke away.

"Mary, for God's sake—"

"We've waited too long already, Harry."

Their lips met again, and she was swept by the raptures of the senses she had thought renounced forever.

"No, Mary," he protested. "We can't. Charles—the family."

"We almost have, my darling," she laughed in delight. "And we certainly shall. I don't care about them. Only about you—about us."

They did not become lovers that afternoon, though she ached to feel her hands on his body. If Harry's will had been stronger, their bodies might never have melted into one in joy. But he could not withstand her ardor or his own longing. She led and he followed, though he evaded her need for total possession. They talked, laughed, and loved with abandon, but she could not quite touch the core of him.

Harry was awed at the irresistible force that drew them together, but he was also deeply troubled. Though he mockingly derided the Sekloongs' dynastic pretentions and affected to take his Catholicism lightly, the clan and the Church were the twin pillars of his life. The enormity of their transgression therefore burdened him far more heavily than it did Mary. She knew moments when she loathed herself for breaking her marriage vows, but she did not suffer the agonies Harry endured. He had been instilled with the belief that the welfare of the Sekloongs was the foremost purpose of his own existence—and he knew that public revelation of their love could gravely imperil the clan itself.

Unlike Harry, Mary was not in thrall to the stringent Chinese code of behavior, as sternly demanding as the unforgiving laws of the Old Testament. She simply did not consider their love-making incest, but Harry knew he violated that fundamental taboo by lying with his brother's wife.

Mary consciously assuaged her guilt by recalling the West's conviction that men and women were entitled to seek individual happiness. Her husband Charles's own behavior had, however, denied her both fulfillment in marriage and human dignity. In her abandoned joy, she consciously cast aside the fear of pregnancy that had precipitated her conflict with Charles. The measure of her love for Harry was the yearning she felt to conceive a child by him. His own fears were borne down by the lure of her bright spirit and voluptuous body. Yet she still felt that the essence of him evaded her passionate possessiveness.

The unacknowledged struggle of wills upon occasion shadowed her joy, but as often made her joy sharper. The pavilion at the far end of the garden became a secret citadel of pleasure, wholly secure because Ah Sam pottered outside, alert against intruders. When the interminable summer came early upon them, bamboo blinds transformed the pavilion into a shadowed cave, and he caressed her breasts and thighs, which were dewed with sweet perspiration. During the brief winter, they lay on raw-silk-filled quilts before the open fire, and her fingertips traced the reflections of the dancing flames on his skin.

The passionate encounters were made radiant by tenderness. During the four or five hours they stole each week, Mary knew the most profound sensual pleasures of her life. But she yearned almost as much for Harry's gentle presence as for those piercing ecstasies. For the first time in her life, Mary longed to be with another human being—not only coupled in passion, but in the sweet communion of repose. She felt herself complete only when Harry was beside her, and then she was gloriously complete, a wholly new, unconstrainedly exultant woman.

"This, I suppose, is love, true love," she mused one summer afternoon in utter satisfaction of the senses and the spirit that shattered all restraints. "True love, I thought, was only in the story-books."

"Of course it's true love," Harry looked at her in unfeigned surprise. "How else could we—"

"It is!" Her fierce affirmation was abruptly pierced by fear. "It is. But how long can it last?"

"Another minute, another week, or forever. Who knows?"

She was temporarily content with that answer. Love discovered transcended past and future, and time was real only when they were together. Summer passed into autumn; petulant winter came; and late January brought the Lunar New Year of 1906, almost seven weeks since they had acknowledged their love. Amid rain and fog, the pavilion was a fire-lit, enchanted cavern beyond time and space. Mary learned that she was pregnant, and the discovery completed her joy. She rejoiced as if the minuscule life in her womb were the first child ever conceived.

The entire family rejoiced with her. Charles assumed that all was well between them. She had yielded to his infrequent advances, feeling neither pleasure nor revulsion, but only a sense of duty fulfilled. Sir Jonathan and Lady Lucinda glowed with satisfaction at the imminent arrival of still another Sekloong. Her past waywardness, Mary reflected wryly, was apparently forgotten, while her new transgression was unremarked. She had redeemed herself by resuming her proper function—strengthening the House of Sekloong by increasing its numbers.

The infant was born on November 13, 1906, three weeks short of full term. The vigorous boy-child was eager to enter the world, and only three hours elapsed from her first pains to his triumphant arrival.

They called him James. Ironically, he looked more like Charles than did any of the other children. In his cradle, James displayed the family's glowing hazel eyes and broad forehead, as well as the grasping Sekloong determination—as if the world were a toy made for his pleasure. The clan noted neither that his Uncle Harry's joy was greater than his father's, nor that his full-lipped mouth was Harry's, not Charles's. Harry was, after all, far less inhibited in expressing his emotions than Charles, and they all knew he doted on his sister-in-law.

When she cradled the fragile, black-furred head in her arms, Mary felt as if James were truly her first-born. She was devoted to her entire brood: Jonathan, the eldest; the two spritely, auburn-haired girls, Guinevere and Charlotte; even the enigmatic, vulnerable Thomas. But, they did not evoke the possessive love, almost adoration, she felt for the spirited mite who was in every sense her love-child, the fruit of the sin she would not renounce.

From her spacious room in Matilda Hospital built on an outjutting spur of The Peak, Mary could see the sweep of the harbor, roiled by the wakes of lighters darting among anchored ships, and, further away, the low buildings of the Kowloon Peninsula, where a new community was growing. Beyond Kowloon lay the broad expanse of the pastoral New Territories, leased to Britain only nine years earlier, its ranges of billowing hills, which still sheltered brigands, covered with light-green foliage. Beyond the New Territories reared the craggy ranges of Imperial China's Kwangtung Province, where corrupt officials, portly gentry, and earth-stained farmers lived just as had their ancestors a thousand years earlier.

The late-afternoon fog was beginning to swirl around her eyrie on the third day after James's birth. Mary lay back in her nest of pillows, indolently content after nursing the infant. She was idly watching the lights flashing into brilliance in Kowloon when Sir Jonathan knocked on the door. He was followed by a young amah carrying a number of cloth-wrapped parcels.

The servant set her burdens down on the white-painted table and scurried from the room after shyly offering felicitations. "*Goong-hay, Tai-tai! Goong-hay sang-la Siu-yeh!* Congratulations, Madame, congratulations on the birth of the Little Lord!"

"Little Lord, indeed!" Sir Jonathan snorted as he unwrapped the parcels. "You'd think it was the first baby ever born."

"It's strange," Mary answered languorously. "I almost feel that way myself. But every baby is the first baby ever born."

"Beware of compradors bearing gifts." A smile warmed Sir Jonathan's austere features. "There're more red eggs, a few of the hundreds presented upon the birth of the Little Lord. And, Lucinda insists, more chicken-soup with *dong-guai*, that magic herb to cure all female complaints."

"I'm already awash with chicken-soup," she protested.

"No matter. Lucinda insists. And a small trinket from me."

Her pink-nailed fingers fumbled with the bone-and-silk hasps of the silver-brocade box. On a bed of white silk glowed a four-inch-square piece of sepia-striated jade carved in bas-relief with the winged Sekloong dragon.

"It's beautiful, Father—absolutely lovely. The most beautiful thing you've given me. But why now? James isn't the first-born son."

"Because you've returned to the family with the gift of James." His manner was elaborately casual. "Pity we can't call him Harry."

Her head bowed in shame, and her heart pounded under the shock. She rallied to smile defensively at the Old Gentleman's grave face. Since her secret was no secret, she would not dissemble.

"Perhaps it *is* a pity." Her voice was steady. "But I'm content with James."

"Only Lucinda and I guessed. I really should've sent Harry away a year ago, but I didn't."

"I'm grateful." Tears clouded her violet eyes. "But I'm not ashamed. I'm proud of James and—and what Harry and I have found. Perhaps I've been very foolish. But I'll be foolish as long as I can, with all my heart!"

"Don't be so damned defiant," he said irascibly. "No need to, though I can't say, 'Bless you my children.' "

"But why?" she asked in apprehension. "Why so forbearing?"

"The reason's there." His fingernails tapped the jade plaque. "The reason's that dragon, *my* dragon."

"I don't understand."

"I'd be lying if I said I didn't object. I do. Much better to've found with Charles what you think you've found with Harry. But divorce is impossible. 'Twould be impossible if we were heathen. Since we're not, it's doubly impossible."

"I've thought about divorce," she admitted.

"Put it out of your mind; I won't have it. I will *not* have a public scandal. You *must* finally let Harry go to marry. But there's time. And you *must* be very discreet. We, the House, couldn't survive a scandal."

"Why, Father?" she asked rashly. "Tolerance isn't really your long suit."

"Because I must put up with your foolishness—can't alter what's done. I need you for the future. And the child is, regardless, a Sekloong—another arrow in my quiver. You're a damned attractive woman. I understand Harry, can't understand Charles."

Her laughter at his heavy gallantry smoothed the double line of strain between her russet eyebrows.

"But I'm thinking of something more important to me and the family, really more important to you."

"Impossible. Nothing could be more important than Harry."

"Let me finish. I know it's not been easy for you these past few years. I can appreciate your joy, though it *must* be temporary. But I'm offering something permanent."

"And," she asked, "that is?"

"I need your help, your capabilities."

A shadow crossed his pale features, momentarily dulling even the silver sheen of his hair. For an instant, he was a tired old man, rather than the vigorous, self-confident figure the world saw.

"The chronicle of a woman's life, the Chinese say, is the men to whom she successively makes submission: father, husband, then son," he resumed. "But for you, I'm convinced, there *can* be much more. Remember, the chronicle of a man's life is not only his women, but other men—the men he challenges and the men who challenge him. Eventually, the old bull must yield to the young bulls. But my young bulls have no fire in their bellies."

"That's not true," she protested. "Certainly Harry—"

209

"You're blind there." He dismissed her objection. "But you have the fire, and it's tempered your steel. I need both your fire and your steel. I need an ally I can trust implicitly. I need an ally with your intelligence and drive. Frankly, an ally who can never turn against me."

"Can't turn against you?"

"No woman could, not even you." His male certainty was absolute. "So my offer serves my needs as well as yours. Anyway, I'm partially to blame for your unhappiness, your foolishness."

"It was my doing. I knew what I was doing when I married Charles."

"Did you? I wonder. I shouldn't have allowed it. But nothing can be done now."

"Harry," she asserted, "Harry and I could—"

"Harry won't." He brusquely dismissed her protests. "You know that, don't you? Harry'll go just so far. He'll never elope with you."

She nodded silent agreement.

"Harry 'til he marries. I'll put up with that, have to. But I'm offering what you really want: your own power, and your own wealth. Much more too, a hand in shaping the next century. Not just in Asia, but in Europe and America. My fight with the Wheatleys is secondary, though it must be won. Even the family's secondary, though it must be bound with steel bands. I'm offering you a role on the stage of history."

"Why should I want that? After all, I'm just an ordinary woman."

"That you're not," he laughed. "You're the most unordinary woman I've met. I *know* you want power because you understand power and the use of power. Even now, your eyes are shining with excitement at the prospect."

If the Old Gentleman thought her extraordinary, how precisely was she to assess him? His actions were widely at variance with both his professed moral standards and his avowed prejudices. He could not only recognize a woman's superiority over men in the male bastion of commerce, but his cold realism could tolerate her behavior, which was both adulterous and incestuous. Those crimes were as heinous to the Confucian morality of his ancestors as they were by the code of his own Catholicism. Was Jonathan Sekloong, Mary wondered, moved solely by his own ruthless logic to acknowledge unalterable circumstances and turn them to his advantage? Or was he also moved by compassion toward three human beings for whose predicament, he had said, he was partially responsible? She simply could not resolve the enigma. Nonetheless, his dominant purpose was clear, however complex his deeds. The welfare of the House of Sekloong transcended all else in Sir Jonathan's calculations.

"But your terms?" she finally demanded. "What exactly must I do?"

"I won't tire you," he replied. "I'd forgotten my new partner's condition, so I'll explain fully later. Of course, you do agree?"

"No, not completely, though I'll think hard. I must know your conditions and exactly what you want of me. But I warn you, my own conditions will be hard."

He laughed and kissed her cheek.

"Then it's agreed, even if you don't know it. You'll find me a hard bargainer, too."

"Now that," she jabbed, "*will* be a surprise."

Part Three

Mary and Harry

November 13, 1908–September 11, 1909

November 13, 1908

HILARY Metcalfe glanced inquiringly at Sir Jonathan and Harry Sekloong, who sipped after-dinner brandies. On the embossed Tientsin carpet of the library in The Castle lay a gold-and-crimson-embroidered, stiff-silk bridal-coat, just delivered by courier from Peking. Mary coveted the gorgeous garment, though its real importance was the tightly rolled rice-paper sheaf Metcalfe had extracted from its hem.

"Don't stop," Mary urged. "It's fascinating."

"The time," he calculated, massaging the broad bridge of his nose with thumb and forefinger, "would be ten P.M. on the thirteenth day of November in this year of Our Lord, 1908."

"Get on with it," Sir Jonathan urged. "Rather you than me translating that damned Mandarin's language."

"Can't you just give us the gist?" Harry asked impatiently.

"No," his father replied. "I want you and Mary to hear it in his own words. Then you'll see why I pay this young eunuch well to report what really goes on behind the walls of the Forbidden City. I want you to understand how precarious Manchu rule is—and why. We must know every detail. Our own future is at stake."

Her Imperial Majesty, being sorely afflicted summoned the Chief Eunuch at the penultimate hour of the 21st day of the tenth month of the 34th year of the reign of the Kuang Hsü Emperor. [Metcalfe resumed his translation of the dispatch from Sir Jonathan's confidential agent at the Court of the Great Pure Dynasty.]

My venerable superior bent low in dutiful attention to the Empress Dowager. Her features were drawn and aged. Despite the charcoal braziers on the dais and the silk-padded quilts on Her rosewood bed, She shivered. Though She thought to speak softly, the habit of fifty years made Her high-pitched voice ring like a bell.

". . . and, so, it must be done tonight. The Emperor,

my sister's son, is very ill. He suffers. It is time He was allowed to rest."

"As you command, Holy Mother."

My superior bowed low. He began to withdraw, walking backward with practiced steps. The Old Buddha raised a hand so frail the lamplight shone through it, and the Chief Eunuch again drew close to Her bed.

The red glow of braziers and the yellow radiance of oil lamps flickered on Her matte-white skin and Her ebony-black hair. My superior inclined his head, and his queue susurrated on his silken back. I recalled that he had by faithful service accumulated vast wealth and become, after the Empress Dowager Herself, the most powerful person in the broad domains of the Great Pure Dynasty.

The events of that night had their genesis ten days earlier, on the morning of Her seventy-third birthday, when the Holy Mother received the Emperor. The Son of Heaven was emaciated; furrows plowed His bloodless cheeks; and He tottered unsteadily between two eunuchs. After paying His respects, the Emperor returned to his yellow-curtained palanquin.

The Dalai Lama next made obeisance to Her Imperial Highness before his return to his many-terraced palace amid the ice-rimmed mountains of distant Tibet. The Eleventh Reincarnation of the God Junresi was attended by six lesser lamas, their red robes stinking of sweat and rancid butter.

The Holy Mother and His Holiness spoke privately for half an hour. He withdrew after knocking his head on the floor nine times in the formal kowtow, groaning audibly and grimacing in outrage. When the barbarians left, we sprinkled the hall with perfume, but their stench lingered.

During the afternoon of The Birthday the Holy Mother disported Herself with Her ladies. Wearing the flowing robes of Kwan Yin, the Goddess of Mercy, in the mode of the Tang Dynasty, She was as beautiful as the sixteen-year-old Manchu maiden who had come into the bed of the Hsien Feng Emperor as a concubine of the third rank more than fifty years earlier to bear Him an heir; become the principal Empress; and, after His untimely death, assume the cares of state on behalf of, first, Her infant son, the Tung Chih Emperor, and, later, Her nephew, the Kuang Hsü Emperor.

The Holy Mother first recalled Her recent visit to the Zoological Gardens, frowning when She spoke of the elephant presented to Her some years earlier. The Mandarin charged with its care pocketed the silver appropriated to feed the great beast's enormous appetite. One morning, the emaciated elephant died, toppling comically from its broad feet. The Holy Mother ordered the Mandarin decapitated, but later commuted the sentence to exile in Central Asia.

I believe even that punishment was excessive. The Mandarin did no more than allocate a portion of public monies to himself—as his responsibility to his family demanded, as we all do.

The Empress Dowager then spoke of Queen Victoria, regretting that the English Queen had never called upon Her. She had admired the older woman, though that Queen's rank was much inferior to Her own.

Convinced by Her own vigorous enjoyment of that carefree afternoon that Her protracted ailment was finally cured, the Empress Dowager consumed three plates of stewed crab-apples and clotted cream. That evening she was severely afflicted with the dysentery that had intermittently weakened Her for the past nineteen months.

The Dalai Lama sent a small gilt Buddha to be enshrined on the altar in the mausoleum prepared for the Holy Mother amid the tombs of the Dynasty in the Fragrant Hills. The Pontiff promised the life of the Empress Dowager would thereupon be greatly prolonged.

However, the Emperor's condition grew appreciably worse after the Imperial pair on November 9 received the Commissioner for Education of the Northern Provinces. Her Majesty sternly charged the Commissioner to suppress the revolutionary intrigues of the students in that last formal audience She was to grant.

Concerned for the Son of Heaven, the Holy Mother called master physicians from afar and summoned all senior Mandarins to the capital. Before lapsing into a coma, the Emperor set His seal to a brief decree prepared by the Empress Dowager's Secretariat. It regretted His inability to attend upon Her and urged Her to appoint an heir to the Throne immediately.

She selected Pu Yi, the infant son of Prince Chun, who was the older brother of the Kuang Hsü Emperor;

she spurned the adult Prince Pu Lun, direct descendant of the Tao Kuang Emperor, who ruled from 1821 to 1850. Since She believed She would live many years longer, She set upon the Dragon Throne an infant who would be attentive to Her wisdom, as would his father, the Co-Regent. The Imperial Council protested, and the dying Emperor contended that an infant should not be elevated to the Throne in a time of turmoil. But the Holy Mother's will prevailed, as always.

The Chief Eunuch summoned me in the early morning of November 14, shortly after our visit to the Empress Dowager's bedside with which this humble account began. The Emperor, he said, was failing fast. Fortunately, a courier had just delivered a previous packet from Lhasa to the Empress Dowager. It contained a root shaped like a tiny man, which grew high on two sacred Tibetan mountains.

The Chief Eunuch gave me a powder ground from the root, instructing me to burn it in saucers placed around the Emperor's bed. The fragrant smoke would immediately relieve His congested breathing, and the Son of Heaven would soon recover.

The Empress Consort Herself at first questioned the remedy. But She knew that the Empress Dowager, who was Her own aunt as well as the Emperor's, cared only to preserve the Son of Heaven. The Empress Consort finally sighed and instructed me to convey Her thanks to the Holy Mother.

I rejoiced as the Son of Heaven's breathing became easier. Yet I was disturbed when I saw on the Emperor's side table a document written in His own hand. I could make out only the first three lines.

"We were the second son of Prince Chun," the Emperor had written, "when the Empress Dowager selected Us for the Throne. She has always hated Us since that time . . ."

Sorrowing that the Emperor's mind was wandering, I retired. I was, however, awakened the next morning to be told that the Emperor could not live out the day. The magical Tibetan herb had failed. He died at 5 P.M., having refused to don the Robes of Longevity in which all His Predecessors had attired Themselves for Their final journey.

You should know that the Emperor's last Decree reviewed His endeavors to harmonize the time-proven

Confucian way of government and life with Western technical and administrative innovations. The Son of Heaven's last rescript further reiterated His thwarted desires to establish an independent judiciary and to give the Realm a Constitution.

The very day after the Son of Heaven ascended the Dragon, the Holy Mother put aside Her natural grief. She rejoiced at having adroitly arranged the succession of the infant Pu Yi, thus averting Court intrigues and public disturbances after the demise of the Kuang Hsü Emperor. She was painfully cognizant of the many threats that menaced the Dynasty: the rebellious southerners who desire a republic; the greedy foreigners with their aggressive religion and their murderous cannon; the heightened tension between Chinese subjects and Manchu rulers; as well as the rivalry between Her own branch of the Imperial family and the senior line.

The designs of even the most puissant of mortals are subject to the Will of Heaven. The Holy Mother's farseeing measures to consolidate the new reign had made Her grandnephew Pu Yi the Hsüan Tung Emperor and His father, Her nephew, Prince Chun the Younger, Her Co-Regent. But the Motherly and Auspicious swooned while planning the ceremonies of enthronement intended to calm the commonalty by demonstrating the untroubled continuity of the Dynasty. Her limbs twitched uncontrollably, while expressions of grief and terror passed across Her exquisite features.

When She awakened, the Empress Grand Dowager summoned the young Empress Dowager, who was the widow of the just-deceased Kuang Hsü Emperor; the Co-Regent; and the Imperial Council to Her bedside. The voice that had guided the Dynasty for almost a full cycle of sixty years conveyed Her final instructions. Her formal Valedictory Decree was hastily drafted by Her Secretariat. Her emendations impressed upon future generations the manifest truth that She had initially been forced to assume the Regency in order to preserve the Dynasty. She further recalled Her intention of promulgating a Constitution and Her decree that all traffic in opium must cease after eleven years.

Two hours before the Holy Mother ascended the Dragon, we begged Her to bestow upon us Her final commands as the Rites prescribe. She replied forcefully: "Never again allow any woman to hold supreme

219

power in the State. The practice is against the house-laws of Our Dynasty and should be strictly forbidden."

At three in the afternoon of November 15, the Holy Mother straightened Her limbs and turned Her face to the south in accordance with the Sacred Rites. The watchers by Her bedside saw Her spirit fly from Her mouth and ascend unto Heaven.

Hilary Metcalfe laid the spy's report down and chuckled disconcertingly.

"I don't see the humor," Harry Sekloong protested. "It's a wicked tale. The decadence, the corruption, the agonies—they may amuse Europeans. But I'm Chinese enough to . . ."

"Sorry, Harry," Metcalfe said. "But the eunuch omitted one detail. Dr. Morrison reported to *The Times* that the Empress Dowager's very last words were the injunction: 'Take great care to prevent eunuchs meddling in affairs of state.' "

"So she did kill him, the old she-devil." Sir Jonathan ignored Hilary Metcalfe's macabre amusement. "I suspected—we all suspected—but no one was sure. That tale Dr. Morrison *didn't* report."

"What's this magical Tibetan root?" Metcalfe asked. "Devilish, nasty, a drug so deadly its fumes kill within hours?"

"Not to worry, Hilary," Sir Jonathan advised. "No one'll ever know just what drug Tzu Hsi used to kill her nephew—who was, perhaps, her son."

"Gentlemen!" Mary's tone expressed her own horror at the spy's tale. "I hate to intrude on your male love of gossip. But, I'd like to know, what does this all mean for us and the future?"

"We can now plan definitely. The Manchu Dynasty *must* come apart in the next few years. No constitution will be promulgated to appease those reformers who're still monarchists. Even they must, therefore, support the republicans. Revolution's inevitable, and the republicans are the strongest, best-organized rebels. The Manchu Dynasty must fall. Barring miracles, Confucian monarchy itself *must* perish."

Sir Jonathan paused, shocked by his own implacable logic.

"Two unashamed thieves now rule China, the young Empress Dowager and Prince Chun, the Regent, supported by the infinitely corrupt eunuchs. That pair are as stupid as they're greedy. They manipulate an infant Emperor, who's probably degenerate, he's so inbred. The Court's split into a hundred factions. The jackals are fighting for fair shares of the carcass. The government's tottering, ineffectual, and indecisive. So much for the Great Pure Dynasty. Strike it from the books."

"And the House of Sekloong?" Harry interposed. "How do you answer Mary's question, Father?"

"I'll say after Hilary says what it means to Hong Kong."

"If you insist, I'll state the obvious. Hong Kong and Shanghai'll become much more important. For a long time, the treaty-ports'll be the only points of political or economic stability. It won't be all peaches and cream —hard cheese too. We'll have to cope with thousands, tens of thousands, fleeing war and pestilence, famine and floods, looting and rapine."

"You're Cassandra today," Mary observed.

"But I trust you won't disbelieve me. Our old complacent ways must change radically. We won't face a suspicious, xenophobic anachronism of an Imperial Dynasty, but a disorderly mob of petty princelings or men-on-horseback. Near chaos will first hamper trade, sharply reduce profits for all but the canniest. But long-term prospects are virtually unlimited. China will want European manufactures. Not only consumer goods, but capital goods—machinery and vehicles, dams and railroads."

"And what," Sir Jonathan prodded, "do we do?"

"That's your pidgin, Jonathan. Remember our compact: I make the wild projections; you make the practical plans."

Mary and Harry exchanged glances. They had speculated on the precise relationship between the two men: the scholarly Englishman devoted almost exclusively, it

221

appeared, to the study of Chinese civilization; and the thrusting Eurasian who was passionately committed to China, but even more passionately committed to his own ambitions.

"Just this time, Hilary," Sir Jonathan pressed, "what would you do?"

"Pick a horse or train a horse," Metcalfe advised, "and bet on it. Put your bundle on the front-runner, but lay off the risk on a few others. Front-runners can break a leg or stumble."

"Expressed with less than your usual polish, Hilary," Mary twitted him, "and less than your usual forthrightness. What do you mean?"

"Simple, my dear. Bet on the politician or general with the best chance. That's Dr. Sun Yat-sen. But keep in with the others."

"And what, precisely, Father," Mary persisted, "do we do?"

"You're a hard taskmistress," Sir Jonathan protested. "But I'll be specific. Take one commodity as a test—take opium, the foundation of Hong Kong."

"But the trade's dying," Harry objected. "More restrictions every year, more resistance, and a dwindling flow—thank God."

"Dwindling, yes. But very robust for an incurable case. A year ago opium brought in five and a half million pounds sterling—almost ten percent of the Colony's trade. Harry, it's still big, much as you'd like to see it stop."

"But it's dying. You know what's happening. Four years ago, the Manchus promised to stamp out the traffic in ten years, and two years ago they issued a formal decree. Last year, London promised to cut imports by ten percent a year for ten years if the Chinese did the same. That leaves only ten years. And only five months ago London told the Governor to close Hong Kong's opium divans. He can't stall much longer by pleading loss of tax revenues. Opium's on its way out."

"But there's still money in it, isn't there?"

"Yes," Harry acknowledged grudgingly, "for those who want money that badly."

"Derwent's does," Metcalfe said softly. "After all, it's traditional."

"Traditional!" Harry snorted. "Derwent's sacred opium tradition, spinning money by any means, no matter how many million lives are ruined."

Mary groped for the right words to forestall a clash between father and son. She, too, had learned to hate the opium traffic—not abstractly as Harry hated the sticky black drug because it debased and weakened China, but most personally. She had seen the effects too often: rickshaw coolies so emaciated their muscles shrank beneath their parchment skins because they couldn't buy both sufficient food and the "black rice" that made their existence endurable; twelve-year-old girls sold to procurers to pay for their fathers' addiction; pinpoint pupils in the shallow pebble eyes of seventeen-year-old youths whose wealthy parents indulged their every wish, even opium. Yet the greater part of Sir Jonathan's fortune came from serving Derwent, Hayes and Company, the *hong* that had, above all others, grown bloated on opium profits. In his hatred of opium, Harry was tearing at one of the chief strands of his father's life.

"I'm sorry, Father." Harry himself broke the tension, abashed but firm. "That's how I feel. Opium's very bad business—for both merchant and customer."

Sir Jonathan carefully selected a golden-brown panatella from the humidor before murmuring: "I agree with you, my boy."

Mary stifled a gasp. She was accustomed to the white-haired autocrat's delight in producing surprises with a subtle flourish like a modest conjurer. But, this time, he had truly astonished her. How could he blandly endorse Harry's impassioned denunciation of the opium trade that had made half his fortune? She would have expected a cynical well-reasoned defense or, at least, a world-weary evasion.

"I agree completely," Sir Jonathan added when his cigar was well alight. "But there was little I could do about it before now. The first thing was to establish myself. It looks different to you who were born to position

223

and comfort. For the natural son of a mad Irish adventurer, the first, the *only* essential was to establish himself. And there was only one sure way—opium. Anyway, Harry, you've never refused the tainted dollars."

"I know, Father!" Harry, too, was startled. "Maybe I should have. By the time I realized, it was late. But, now . . ."

"I wasn't baiting you, boy." Sir Jonathan's raised hand commanded silence. "Hear me out. God knows, I've argued the toss with Dick Wheatley and that dried-up old trout, Rachel. Both swear opium's a blessing second only to Christianity—a gift bestowed upon the wretched heathen. At least I've never been a hypocrite."

"But," Harry insisted, "you didn't hang back."

"I didn't. Whether you approve or not, the old rationale's true: If I hadn't, someone else would've. I couldn't stop the traffic single-handed. Besides, I had to make my mark, and it was the only way, the only *possible* way. Perhaps, too, I didn't realize until it was too late."

Sir Jonathan's long fingers meticulously tapped the ash from his panatella, but his voice rose a tone. The momentary loss of self-control was as uncharacteristic as his deigning to justify himself to his son.

"And now what, Father?" Harry asked.

"I awaited that one. Now, it's different. Wheatley wants to go on to the bitter end. Jardine's want to go on. So do Swire and all the little fish. They want to squeeze the last copper penny out of the traffic. You know they've joined to form the Hong Kong Opium Corporation. They'll peddle the poison drug as long as there's a single customer left in China—or a single peasant planting poppies in India, Burma, or Persia. Opium won't be outlawed in Hong Kong. Not for years, if ever."

"And you, Jonathan?" Hilary Metcalfe eased his question around the mouthpiece of his pipe. "What now?"

"I could use the same old argument. If I don't, others
224

will, so why shouldn't I take my cut? But it's different now. The trade's dying, trickling away, as Harry says. Every *tael* I ship, every blasted ounce, swells that trickle and postpones the day the traffic ends. Then, by the bye, worse things'll appear—morphine, cocaine. I can't worry about them now. But I *must* worry about opium. It touches my self-respect—and my profits."

"Profits, Father?" Mary could restrain herself no longer. "If the traffic's dying, where's the profit, except in going on to the bitter end? You've taught me the big profits are the pennies that turn into dollars."

"And you, Mary, have taught me your motto: *If you're doing something foolish, go the whole hog.* Maybe it's foolish to reckon that we can profit from hamstringing the opium traffic. But I think not. Everything comes together nicely—what we'd like to do, what we should do, and what we'll profit from."

"How?" Metcalfe was blunt.

"We can make firm our repute with the men who'll be the new masters of China. There are ways to cut the traffic down, for the good of our souls, for the sake of our name. To establish ourselves solidly with the republican rebels, and to shove a damned big spoke into Dick Wheatley's wheel for the good of—"

"—us all." Hilary Metcalfe completed the sentence. "But how, precisely, Jonathan? Have you thought it through?"

"I've begun." Sir Jonathan was evasive. "We'll talk when I've got further. Meantime, a thought to show my idealistic son I'm still the same old devil. There's one other great benefit. Getting out of opium will force us into new enterprises—for the good of our pocketbooks."

"How do you mean?" Mary pressed.

"Those who cling to opium will go under," the magnate answered. "Not the big *hongs*—Derwent's, Jardine's, Swire—but the smaller *hongs* with limited resources. If they don't get out, they'll perish. Having lived by the pipe, they'll die by the pipe. Their capital and their talents are limited, and both are committed to the traffic that must dwindle.

"But those who get out now must devote their energy and their capital to new enterprises. No one offers assurance policies to the new, middle-class Chinese in the treaty-ports. And cotton, all kinds of textiles. Why should China always buy from Lancashire? Railroads. We're already involved in a middling way, and railroads must grow. The petroleum trade. Paraffin's already widely used for heating, cooking, and lighting. More ships are burning oil. . . ."

"Petrol for motorcars and lorries is still only a trickle," Mary interrupted. "It should certainly swell."

"Transport, motor-transport." Harry was the unabashed visionary. "Motor-lorries and omnibuses carrying goods and passengers all over China. Entire fleets flying our gold-and-blue pennant, the Flying Dragon Line! Cheap, reliable transport will change the face of China. China'll become a modern country, the flow of commerce its life-blood."

"First build your roads, Harry," Metcalfe advised. "It's only ten years since Parliament required a man with a red flag to walk in front of every motor-vehicle in order to warn pedestrians and horses. Your idea's exciting—but railroads come first. They're proven."

"There are cart-tracks all over China." Harry was bewitched by his own vision. "And remnants of the great post-roads the Mongols built six hundred years ago." He gesticulated broadly as if conjuring up his phantom Armadas.

"Motor-transport's the answer. Motor-roads are easier to build than railroads, less capital and less effort. I can see our flotillas penetrating to remote villages and connecting market towns to big cities—all under the Winged Dragon."

"And, Admiral, leaving a trail of broken wheels and fractured what do y'call 'ems—gears," Mary laughed. "That happens every time you or Charles takes out the new Daimler."

"Those troubles'll be cured," Harry insisted. "We must be in the forefront."

"Why not flying-machines, then?" she mocked.

226

"Those American brothers, the Wrights, their kite with a motor flew—when was it?"

"About Christmas of '03," Harry said.

"Yes, and Berliot crossed the Channel last year. Why not fleets of flying-machines flaunting the Winged Dragon? All they need is a flat place to land. No heavy capital investment, no roads—not like motor-lorries and omnibuses."

"Well, why not?" Harry rejoined, stubbornly ignoring Mary's gentle teasing. "That too—flying-machines, too. But only land transport can change China. Flying-machines will never carry heavy cargoes or more than a few passengers. But motor vehicles will shift massive loads, transport farmers and their produce ten, twenty, fifty miles to market towns, transfer spinning and weaving plants into the interior, and bring their manufactures out—move everything from coal to pigs."

"Perhaps close to the cities to start," Mary conceded. "But who'll train thousands to drive and repair those mechanical monsters? And what about costs, my dear? Who knows what the contraptions'll cost to run?"

"We can sort out details later," Harry replied airily. "Now we need the will. Consortia can provide capital. The big landowners could come in."

"And smash their own power?" Metcalfe interjected.

"Let's think of details, Hong Kong to start." Mary was determinedly practical. "I'll be half-convinced the first time one of your Puffing Dragons delivers lobsters, shrimps, and crabs taken from the sea off the New Territories that morning for me to serve at a luncheon party on The Peak."

"Enough," Sir Jonathan laughed. "Let's consider immediate things, enterprises within our reach. Think of expanded mining, smelting iron and steel. Why not bicycles or spring-mounted, pneumatic-tired wheels for ox-carts and donkey-carts—products we can make now? Or improved hoes and plows, in time harvesters and reapers? The market's not unlimited. But it's big —very, very big."

"Even thermos-bottles and paraffin-stoves." Mary's

practical enthusiasm was engaged. "They'd change everyone's life, those small products."

"And arms." Harry's visionary zeal swelled. "China needs modern arms, not the obsolete rubbish Krupp, Schneider-Creusot, and Vickers are dumping. Rifles, machine guns, and mortars, artillery and warships, first for the revolution and then for defense. China must build her own armaments, not remain dependent on outsiders."

"You'll need money." Metcalfe dourly pricked the bubble. "Money to plant and grow, money to lose on the inevitable failures."

"*We'll* need money, Hilary," Sir Jonathan said. "I assume you're with us."

"Of course I am, Jonathan—in principle. But I want your fledglings' visions reduced to dollars and cents. Then my few dollars are at your disposal."

"For my part, Hilary, I value your counsel above all, though your dollars're welcome. As for money, governments, even poor governments, have resources private merchants can't dream of. And governments can borrow. Borrowing wisely, they insure their sovereignty, rather than selling themselves as the Manchus have done. And governments need financiers to advise them and to arrange loans, disinterested financiers."

"I see, Jonathan," Metcalfe said, "that you're planning to own the next government of China."

"Not own it, serve it. When you deal with an honest government, profits are smaller. But I'd rather one percent of fifty million than ten percent of five million that suddenly vanishes."

"Business must expand." Harry's enthusiasm rekindled itself. "And we're in at the start. Think of the power, power to do what foreigners have promised China, but never delivered. Power to remake a nation for the good of all."

"And, my young cockerel, power to make our own position impregnable," Sir Jonathan added. "The House of Sekloong the greatest firm in Asia, and very strong elsewhere. I'm sending Charles to Europe and America next month to renew connections and set up small offices in London and New York. Where is he tonight, by the bye?"

"Oh, he's out," Mary said noncommittally. "He had someone to see."

"Out?" Sir Jonathan raised his eyebrows. "Someone?"

"He's solid." Mary loyally evaded the implied accusation. "He'd scoff at our notions. But what better emissary to impress the bankers with our stable worth?"

"And Mary and myself?" Harry asked. "What are your plans?"

"Mary remains in Hong Kong," Sir Jonathan announced with magisterial calm. "I need her here. For you, my boy, a very special mission. But it'll keep until tomorrow."

January 5–7, 1909

THE new moon was an abandoned lifeboat awash in scudding clouds. Its beams penetrated the hollows of the paddyfields, and the rice-stubble glowed palely. The next wave of clouds overbore the moon, and the earth was dark. The deserted margin of sand where the ocean met the continent was a whitened scar on the spectral early morning landscape. The smoky ghosts of dead cooking-fires drifted across the paddyfields from the stone-built hovels shining like silver-gray skulls five miles distant. The lingering stench of human excrement strewn on the young rice six months earlier tainted the winter wind that swept the skeletons of fallen leaves toward the South China Sea.

A restless dog lamented the lost moon from the slumbering hamlet called Wong Family Village, and his whining alarmed the watchers in the hillocks overlooking the white-capped inlet. Though the watchers and their long-barreled rifles were concealed in the spiky grass, they glanced apprehensively over their shoulders. Any movement on the land boded ill for their mission and their lives. All men were their enemies that night.

Reassured by the dormant landscape, the watchers again turned their gaze on the bay called Haimen, the Gate of the Sea. Though it was only twenty miles south of the thriving port of Swatow by land and one hundred ninety miles by sea from Hong Kong, the march of commerce had bypassed Haimen. Aside from the cockleshell sampans of the local fishermen, Haimen received only deep-sea fishermen in distress and long, dark-sailed smuggling junks. Winter had frozen the bay into quiescence.

Harry Sekloong peered impatiently at his gold pocket-watch. The radium-painted numerals glowed as faint as the phosphorescence on the waves, and the hands were a single bar of pale-green luminescence. It was six minutes past one, still thirty-eight minutes to wait for the flashes from the sea.

Beneath his plaited-bamboo hat, Harry's eyes searched the shadowed horizon. The only movement within the great semi-circle where water and sky met was the angry leaping of the sea. No man-made object broke its featureless symmetry; no flicker of light pierced its gloom. When the new moon sank beneath waves of clouds, he could not even see the six forty-foot shrimp-boats lying in the dune-screened cove a hundred yards away. When the moon lethargically surfaced, only the swaying of high-raked masts against the clouds revealed the boats' location.

Shifting to relieve his cramped legs, Harry slipped the watch into his pocket. Like the 126 men concealed in the scrub-grass around him, he wore the rusty-black tunic and trousers of the poor of Kwangtung Province. But he could not disguise his height.

Harry had landed just after the early dusk cloaked the water and the hills. Salt-caked and sore after three days spent beating two hundred miles against the southwest monsoon from Bias Bay, he had been delighted to alight even on that inhospitable coast. Each carrying its detachment of armed men from a different port, five other junks had slipped into the cove at intervals. The last put into the Gate of the Sea at midnight from Foochow, 285 miles north.

The absence of more than one craft would imperil the mission. But their captains sailed under strict orders not to use the Daimler-Benz automobile engines mounted in their holds on hand-hewn teak bearers. Resorting to the engines while on passage could betray the operation to the junks of the Imperial Chinese Government or, worse, to the steam-launches of the China Maritime Customs and the British Royal Navy's anti-piracy patrols. Most Chinese captains could be induced by a golden "expression of thanks," *cumshaw,* to disregard the strange spectacle of junks under power. The European captains of the Customs' launches were more wily, but just as incorruptible as the English sub-lieutenants commanding the Royal Naval craft.

The shrimp-junks had sailed by night from their different homeports, where they normally fished with long nets for the bottom-dwelling crustaceans. They were the fastest sailing-craft on the South China Coast, fine-built to hasten their perishable catch to market. The engines had been fitted in an improvised boat-yard in Bias Bay, no-man's waters northeast of Hong Kong. The Manchus' vessels prudently avoided Bias Bay, preferring to accept the *cumshaw* of the pirates, whose domain it was, rather than fight them. The combined forces of the Maritime Customs and the Royal Navy could not winkle those pirates from their lair.

Harry was reasonably content with the execution of his plans. Only one junk had failed to rendezvous at the Gate of the Sea, and it might yet appear to reinforce the force by twenty men. He had allowed for one straggler. Unfortunately, the missing boat, sailing from the anti-Manchu nest of Kaohsiung in southern Taiwan, carried the man called Mr. Woo, the delegate of Dr. Sun'Yat-sen's Tung-meng Hui, the United League. Mr. Woo's absence left tactical command to Elder Brother Lee, an old pirate chieftain, whose honored title derived from his rank of Incense Master in the Secret Society called the League of Elder Brothers.

Harry was himself present primarily as an affirmation of the Sekloongs' commitment to the operation they had planned and financed. But Sir Jonathan had instructed him not to show himself once the clash began. The House of Sekloong could outface the inevitable rumors that it had sponsored the action, but could be gravely injured if Harry were positively identified. Yet Mr. Woo's absence made him the senior representative of the republican revolutionaries who were united with the Secret Societies and the pirates by common hostility to the Manchus. If he hung back in the absence of Mr. Woo, the Sekloongs would lose much credit.

Harry pondered his decision. Strict obedience to his father's instructions would imperil the operation and largely negate its benefits to the House of Sekloong. If he led the vanguard and was seen, he could imperil the existence of the House of Sekloong. He pushed back his bamboo hat and rubbed his forehead in perplexity.

"Soon now, Mr. Sek, very soon." A staccato Cantonese whisper broke into his thoughts.

"I pray so, Elder Brother Lee," he answered. *"Taishan* must come over the horizon in the next ten minutes. Her captain wants daylight no more than we. But it's a very long night."

"Patience, Young Lord," the throaty voice counseled. "When you've been in the trade as long as I, you'll know it's mostly waiting."

"Perhaps, Elder Brother. Lacking your experience, I am prey to impatience."

Harry eased the heavy Scott-Webley revolver holstered under his tunic, and rivulets of sand trickled down the hillock. The barking of dogs and the aggrieved crowing of cocks roused before the dawn signaled that men were astir in Wong Family Village. Their bustle was no less alarming for being expected. From that moment onward, the operation was at risk. The commando was trapped between the turbulent sea and heavily armed force sallying from the village.

If they waited too long for the *Taishan* to appear, they would be attacked from the interior. If they embarked too soon, the sight of their six dark craft could startle the *Taishan* into flight. Even their engines could not then overtake the six-hundred-ton paddle-steamer.

The green hands of his watch read 1:45, and Harry

swore under his breath. The *Taishan* sailed to a rigid schedule. If she did not make her landfall within ten minutes, the transshipment would be postponed for twenty-four hours—and his plan would collapse. Licking his dry lips, he leaned toward the dark shape of Elder Brother Lee.

The men must embark, risking discovery, rather than allow themselves to be trapped with their backs to the sea. The detachment from Wong Family Village was moving closer, its progress signaled by the creaking of harnesses, the squealing of axles and the rattle of rifle barrels. Voices swore aloud in the harsh Swatow dialect, for the enemy felt himself secure in his own territory.

Harry's whisper to the imperturbable old pirate was cut off by a horny hand closing on his biceps.

"Look!" Elder Brother Lee commanded hoarsely. "Look at the horizon!"

A yellow light flared above the whitecaps. Once, twice, thrice, and the sea was dark again. But he could see a darker shape breasting the waves where the signal had flashed and the white bow-wave curving back from the hard-driven *Taishan*, running without lights.

Elder Brother Lee shrieked like a gull, and the hillside sprouted men. Black shapes tumbled down to the shore, slithering on the coarse grass to clamber over the teak-sides of the narrow junks. Wooden blocks banged, ropes snapped, and bat-wing sails creaked up the raked masts, blotting out the sky. The moon vanished in a torrent of clouds.

Harry's boat came alive when its anchor was untethered. As the slim craft took the first shock of the waves crashing beyond the sheltered cove, his eyes searched the surrounding darkness. Six lighters lay like stranded whales in the outgoing tide, where his men had scuttled them. Since the lighters would not put to sea that night, their rear was secure against attack. Harry's junk gave way to clear the furthest lighter. A half-naked form was spread-eagled on the foredeck.

"Only one guard," Elder Brother Lee said contemptuously. "We only had to slit one throat."

233

Harry's stomach clenched, and bile rose bitter in his throat. He blamed the fish stench and the narrow-gutted junk's wild pitching, alternating with cork-screw gyrations when the quartering waves slammed against the prow. Once beyond the promontory's shelter, the junk lay over on her side, and white water swirled in the leeward scuppers. The heeling motion eased when the southwest monsoon blowing beam on bellied out the bamboo-battened sails.

"The engine?" Elder Brother Lee shouted in eagerness above the wind's falsetto screaming through the shrouds. "Start engines now?"

"Wait for signal," Harry shouted into his ear. "Must not alarm *Taishan*."

For thirty minutes the frail junk pounded through storm-waves, and her timbers groaned. A monstrous wave lifted the junk thirty feet on its crest. The junk skidded down into the trough, and the next wave towered above the wildly swaying mainmast. Righting itself, the junk bobbed in the maelstrom like a cork.

Clutching the foremast, Harry searched for the loom of the *Taishan* in the enveloping darkness. The wind-driven spume that stung his hands and face obscured his vision. Elder Brother Lee beside him was unconcerned.

"Fast time," he shouted. "Helmsman good."

A golden flare arched into the night above the black bulk of the paddle-steamer. A second followed, and the flares hung in the sky for thirty seconds before plummeting into the sea. Red pinpoints flared like angry fireflies in the *Taishan*'s battered superstructure.

"They're firing," Elder Brother Wong shouted. "Not smooth as hoped. Must make speed. Engine now?"

Harry nodded and the older man scuttled along the wave-swept deck toward the high poop. A red lantern cast faint radiance into the night. The clatter of gears and the coughing of pistons from the junk's hold were just audible above the shrieking storm. The wind snatched a cloud of gray-white smoke from the stern, shredding it like a puff-ball. Gears grated and the ex-

234

haust popped as tyro engineers struggled with the balky motor.

The engine settled into a pounding roar after three minutes. It raced wildly when the waves lifted the screw out of the water and Harry feared it would break loose from its mounting.

All *Taishan's* lights flared bright to make a beacon for the junks. They were no more than a mile from the paddle-steamer, less than ten minutes sailing at their mad pace. His watch showed that just fifty-two minutes had elapsed since they weighed anchor.

The *Taishan* slowed, butting her blunt bows into the wind, and a searchlight swept the sea to guide the junks alongside. Ropes snaked from the decks, and the rebels swarmed aboard. Elder Brother Wong shouted orders at two men with a heavy, canvas-wrapped package slung between them.

Harry snatched at a dangling rope-ladder. With his foot on the first rung, he paused. The wind snatched him off the deck. He clung desperately to the water-soaked ropes which writhed in the air as the *Taishan* rolled on the swell.

His decision had made itself, since it was the only possible choice. He could not hang back and let his allies bear the full risk. The *Taishan's* crew had resisted, and might still fight. The emissary of the House of Sekloong could not cower in the junk's cabin while the buccaneers and the revolutionaries climbed through the darkness toward unknown hazards.

The tarry ladder twisted in the wind despite his one hundred and eighty pounds. He was flung against the ship's side, and rusty rivets tore through his clothes, leaving bloody welts. He fought upward inch by inch, until a convulsive effort carried him over the teak-capped bulwarks to lie gasping like a landed fish on the coal-stained deck.

Incongruous in a sailor's white smock, the lean body of the Shanghai intellectual he knew as Mr. Woo loomed over him. The apparition flashed white teeth and spoke in cultivated Mandarin.

"I must apologize, Mr. Sek, for not notifying you. We decided at the last moment that I should sail as a member of the crew. My men hold the officers at pistol-point on the bridge. Deckhands and engine-room gang are under hatches.".

"The cargo?" Harry panted. "What of the cargo?"

"Ten tons of first-grade Bengal opium, worth more than fifty thousand pounds. The year's big shipment, and they were desperate to land it unseen by Customs. There'll be no opium in most of south China for many, many months."

"That's wonderful!" Harry replied. "And the unloading?"

"Your men know their places," Mr. Woo answered. "Look, they're beginning."

Black-clad figures wrestled aside the heavy timbers that secured the hatch-covers. Others climbed the rickety ladder to the bridge, where the British captain, first-mate and engineer were under guard. The decklights flickered, tantalizing the smugglers stranded on the beach beside their scuttled lighters.

"Everything under control?" Harry asked nervously.

"Everything is going as planned. All under con . . ."

The white figure bent gracefully from the waist, and Harry heard a single shot above the wailing wind. Mr. Woo fell to his knees, his forehead touching the deck in a formal kow-tow.

A torrent of fire from the bridge hosed the black figures on the ladder. They toppled from the perch. Two cartwheeled into the sea, their despairing shrieks piercing the wind's screaming. Three crashed to the deck and lay still. The rest were an unmoving heap at the foot of the bridge-ladder.

"The officers," Elder Brother Lee shouted, drawing Harry into the doorway of the deckhouse, "they've broken loose. Those damned coolies couldn't keep three men under control."

"What now?" Harry cried. "How do we get them off the bridge?"

Elder Brother Lee did not reply. He was struggling

to open the butterfly-nuts that secured the iron-door behind them. Harry threw his weight on the hasp, and the door swung open on the saloon. The officers' last meal was smeared across the table bolted to the deck, the plates smashed on the worn green linoleum. A steward wearing a grimy white jacket raised his hands above his head.

"The lights?" Elder Brother Lee demanded. "Where are they?"

The steward pointed to the switch-box on the far bulkhead. The old pirate's gnarled hand flipped the master-switch, and the *Taishan* was again cloaked in black.

Elder Brother Lee edged into the gloom on his stomach. He crawled to the bulky package his men had left in the scuppers. Pushing it before him, he signaled to Harry to follow. Single shots sounded from the bridge.

"They want to keep our heads down," Elder Brother Lee shouted. "We'll oblige—cheerfully."

The painful crab-crawl along the scuppers with the package seemed interminable, though it took no more than five minutes. Forward of the bridge, a hatch offered shelter. The old pirate ignored the body sprawled on the hatch-cover, but Harry tasted copper bile when a limp hand brushed his cheek.

The pirate knife slit the canvas-wrapped package to reveal a brass jingal shimmering in the half-light. Oblivious to the shots from the bridge, Elder Brother Lee extracted an oilcloth packet from his waistband. He measured out black-powder and inserted a fuse in the touch-hole.

"Now give me a hand," he directed.

Harry's skin crawled, and his head drew into his shoulders. He steeled himself to help the old pirate manhandle the miniature cannon onto the hatch. Bullets plowed the timbers around them, but Elder Brother Lee imperturbably sighted the weapon. Finally satisfied, he extracted a wooden match from the oilcloth packet, stuck it on the jingal's rough breech, and lit the fuse. The match's flare drew a volley of shots.

Thunder crashed around Harry's head, flinging him

to the deck. Red fire erupting from the muzzle blinded him. The jingal hurled stones, broken bottles, nails, scrap-iron, and six-inch bolts at the open bridge.

"The old ways are still the best ways," Elder Brother Lee observed contentedly. "We'll wait a minute or two."

Striking a second match, he drew no fire, but lit the hand-rolled cigarette that had magically appeared between his lips. He fluttered the canvas wrapping, and the bridge remained silent. The only sounds were the wailing of the wind and the crashing of the waves.

"Come," he said, rising. "It's all right."

Clambering over the still, black forms at the ladder's foot, they climbed to the bridge. Elder Brother Lee contemptuously flung open the steel grill that had not protected the British officers and stepped into the wooden enclosure.

The bridge-house was a torn shambles. The engine-telegraph was buckled, and the teak steering-wheel drooped on its iron pylon. Ripped charts were plastered on the bulwarks, the sheet depicting Haimen Bay impaled by a rusty nail. Two white-clad shapes that had been men were crumpled on the deck boards. The nearer, cut almost in half at the waist, spilled yellow intestines on the polished teak. The further body lay headless, though otherwise untouched, in a puddle of blood. Blond hair and gray brain-matter spattered the bulwarks. A third figure rested on its back as if sleeping, but a six-inch bolt protruded from its chest. Harry retched at the stench of blood and feces. The older man clapped him on the shoulder.

"First time's always the worst." He grinned as the lights came on again to illuminate the horror. "But you're blooded now—well blooded."

An English voice rose in loud protest over the wind's roar. Two revolutionaries emerged from the chart-house, hustling a frightened young man between them. The trousers of his cheap tweed suit were stained yellow by urine.

"My Lord," he expostulated in pidgin. "What for you silly fellows do this thing? You know big gunships belong English king come makee boom-boom makee dead all you bloody fellows."

Deeply unimpressed, his guards pushed him forward. They were apprehensively proud, like young terriers that drag a dead rat into the parlor wondering whether they'll be praised or berated. Harry stepped into the shadowed corner of the bridge, but the prisoner had already seen him.

"Thank God!" The young Englishman was volubly relieved "Harry Sekloong, by God. What the devil are you doing here? By God, it's good to see you. Tell those fellows . . ."

Harry stared unspeaking. The Englishman's voice trailed away, and his eyes started in renewed fear.

"Harry! For God's sake, Harry Sekloong! You remember me. Peakton, George Peakton of Derwent's. They shipped me as supercargo to see the stuff safely ashore. Surely you remember me?"

Harry drew his revolver from its holster. Unthinking, he thumbed back the hammer and leveled the weapon with both hands. Unspeaking, he shot the young Englishman through the right eye and mechanically reholstered the revolver.

While the body was still crumpling, Harry leaned over the side of the bridge-house and vomited onto the deck below. Heaving paroxyms shook him, and sweat bathed his body in the chill night.

Later, he dimly remembered watching the black-clad figures shift the cargo into the junks, piling up the brass-bound opium-chests until the craft sank dangerously low in the water. Long after the junks left the *Taishan* adrift, he finally fell into dream-tortured sleep in the dank cabin.

The next morning he awoke to find the gale subsided and gentle waves sparkling in the sunlight. The convoy raced southward, borne by the following wind toward Bias Bay. Harry sat on the foredeck, his back braced against the mast. His teeth chattered, and shudders shook him. He saw the half-formed features of George Peakton superimposed on the white clouds that drifted like tufts of wool against the blue vault of the sky.

The nineteen-year-old English youth had traveled far from the grimy corridors of his third-rate public school to die in the charnelhouse of the old *Taishan* during a shrieking gale on the South China Sea. He had done no more than follow his superiors' instructions to sail on the old paddle-steamer that carried a cargo of misery and degradation for tens of thousands of unknown Chinese. In their youth his superiors had begun to amass fortunes by landing similar shipments on the same coast. Peakton could not have known that the times had changed. No more could he have known that he had sentenced himself to death by appealing to the one man he recognized amid the slaughter. It was not his fault. It was no one's fault that he had spoken the wrong words in the wrong place at the wrong time.

Harry concluded somberly that he himself had had no choice. George Peakton had to die, because he had committed a fatal mistake. He had obstructed the way of history; and he had placed the Sekloongs in danger of trial for piracy by learning of Harry Sekloong's part in the hijacking. Harry gazed with loathing at palms still stained by the black powder of the revolver, and thrust his hands into his pockets to hide them. No such gesture could expunge his guilt. The murder was necessary. It was not excusable.

Steering well east of shipping channels, the shrimp-junks met no other vessels on the broad South China Sea as they raced toward sanctuary in Bias Bay. When late afternoon shadows darkened the whitecaps, a puff of smoke drifted on the horizon to the southwest. As the minutes passed, the closing course of the unseen craft was marked by a trail of wind-blown smoke.

Harry Sekloong braced himself against the foremast shrouds, lifted his powerful Zeiss binoculars, and struggled to focus on the distant smoke. He finally centered the feathered smoke-banner in the binoculars' bright disc and slowly brought them down to glimpse an elongated funnel. Against the funnel's vermillion side pranced the golden winged dragon on a royal-blue field. The smoke signaled the hard-pounding approach of *Regina,* his father's eighty-five-foot steam-launch.

Regina butted into the waves. White water foamed around her sharp cruiser-bows and broke on her fore-deck. Her white superstructure and gold-striped blue awnings shone in the pale sunshine. The binoculars revealed Sir Jonathan Sekloong, immaculate in blue blazer and white flannel trousers, braced straddle-legged on the open bridge. Beside him stood a square figure in the high-frogged blue-gabardine tunic of a prosperous Chinese merchant. Beneath a full head of hair parted in European style, the tanned round face displayed a long, straggling mustache. He did not wear the braided pigtail, the queue the Manchus had imposed upon their Chinese subjects as an outward mark of their subservience.

Regina drew abeam the junk, her bow pointing into the waves, her bulk sheltering the junk from the gusting wind. The shrimp-boat came alongside *Regina*, sails flapping. Ropes tumbled from the launch onto the junk's stained decks.

Harry took formal leave of Elder Brother Lee, who replied briskly, "Forget it now. You did what you had to do. We'll make a sea-rover of you yet."

The rope-ladder from *Regina* was braced by wooden treads and kept from the launch's side by teak props. After his perilous climb to the *Taishan*'s deck, it was like boarding an ocean-liner on a stable gangplank. Sir Jonathan and his companion waited at the rail.

"*Shen-ma tou nung-hao-la ma?*" he asked in Mandarin. "Everything go off all right?"

"No real problems, Father. The cargo is all aboard."

"That's splendid," Sir Jonathan said. "Mr. Hwang, this is my son. I present you to Mr. Hwang Hsing."

The militant editor Hwang Hsing was second only to Dr. Sun Yat-sen in the revolutionary United League. He paused before clambering down the ladder to the heaving deck of the shrimp-boat to say, "*Hao! Hao! Fei-chang hao!*"

"Good! Good! An outstanding job!" The accolade rang in Harry's ears. Hwang Hsing was the field commander of the revolution in China. Dr. Sun was chiefly occupied abroad, raising money among the overseas

Chinese for the revolution and seeking the support of foreign governments.

When Hwang Hsing's feet touched the scarred deck-planks of the junk, the sailors cast off the ropes that bound their craft to *Regina*. The convoy curved in a broad arc to the southwest, while *Regina* turned due south toward Hong Kong.

In the paneled saloon, Harry lolled in the embrace of a red-leather easy-chair, relaxed for the first time since sailing from Bias Bay five days earlier. He sipped a pink gin and contemplated the thick-carpeted saloon with its gold-mounted decanters, its attentive steward, and its two-hundred-year-old scroll-painting of Tien Mu Hou, the Goddess of the Sea. He was home again.

"Well, Harry," his father asked, "any problems at all?"

"No, Father, not really. Only one thing . . ."

Sir Jonathan listened silently to Harry's account of the battle and the death of George Peakton.

"I regret you had to, but it was the only way," he finally commented. "No joy, was it? But you couldn't let him live to report your presence. There could have been a trial, disgrace, bankruptcy. Forget it now, boy."

"I'll try, Father." Harry could not quite shift the burden to his father's willing shoulders. "But it was the devil. Not just the fight, but Peakton!"

"I know, son. A revolution isn't exactly a garden party. You did what you had to do."

"I hope so. And now they'll make a bonfire that'll spread across all China—a funeral-pyre for King Opium."

"Harry," Sir Jonathan said softly, "they won't burn the opium."

"What? Not burn it? I thought . . ."

"I know, but I can't force hotheaded revolutionaries and old-fashioned brigands to burn the opium. Besides, I wouldn't if I could."

"What's to become of it, then?" Harry demanded, setting his glass down so hard the pink liquid slopped on the rosewood table. "It's a betrayal."

"Careful with the drink, Harry," Sir Jonathan advised equably. "Your mother wouldn't like the finish stained. However, I assure you it's *not* betrayal. Far from it."

"What's to become of the opium?" Harry's voice was tense. "Is this just another way to fill the coffers of the noble House of Sekloong? Did young Peakton die to make you richer?"

"By no means. The cargo'll be transshipped to ocean-going junks. Their destination is Vinh in Indo-China."

"And there, what? More chicanery?"

"Harry, that'll do!" Sir Jonathan snapped. "Hear me out. Remember we embarked fifty chests of our own on *Taishan* to camouflage our intentions. And we won't get a penny from the sale."

"How not? Who profits?"

"A syndicate of French officers is buying the opium —with the genial approval of the thieving Governor-General of Indo-China. Some will end up in France. Most will be peddled to the Tonkinese and Annamese. Not to our people, not to Chinese."

"And in return?"

"A substantial quantity of gold. The revolution needs greater funds than Dr. Sun can raise in the Chinese communities of America, Canada, and Southeast Asia. Equally important, arms will move across the Indo-China border into Yunnan and Kwangsi Provinces— field-pieces, rifles, and mortars. The revolution must be armed."

"I don't like it," Harry protested, only slightly molli-fied. "I don't like it at all. We're exporting misery and suffering."

"Fair enough. You may be right. But what would you suggest? Can you make a revolution with inspira-tional tracts and passive resistance?"

"Maybe not. But victimizing another people and en-riching corrupt Frenchmen. It stinks like week-old fish."

"Harry, our first concern is the Chinese people. We're not anointed to save the whole world. Our first concern is China and our second . . ."

243

"The House of Sekloong, no doubt. What does this charade do for your sacred *hong?*"

"Harry, don't bait me. I understand your indignation, but don't take it out on me. A little trust might not come amiss."

"I'm sorry, Father. I'm tired. But my question stands. What of the House of Sekloong?"

"I'll answer in the same spirit. We've diverted a large quantity of opium from China, and we've struck a major blow at the China Opium Corporation. My esteemed step-father Dick Wheatley's been badly hurt. In time, he'll know who struck the blow. But he'll never be able to prove it."

"I can't argue with that. But . . ."

"Nor can you argue with the general result. The opium traffic'll dwindle further. Costs'll go up as fear of hijacking forces merchants to hire more guards. Smuggling will become harder. Even the Imperial authorities will act a little more forcefully—in the time left to them."

"And the House of Sekloong, Father? I don't want to insist, but . . ."

"Since you do insist, I'll spell it out. We've lost a goodish sum. Call it an investment. We've risked your life to consolidate our position with the revolutionaries. Mutual confidence is now sealed in blood, fortunately not your blood. When they triumph, we'll help them rebuild China. The profits, honest profits, won't be small."

"All right, Father," Harry wearily conceded. "I see your point. But I tell you honestly it still goes against my grain."

Sir Jonathan lit a panatella while he pondered his reply. Despite his caution, he thereupon committed the worst mistake he ever made in dealing with his hotheaded, idealistic second son. The consequences of that error were not to manifest themselves for many years. They would then be catastrophic.

"Harry," Sir Jonathan said slowly, "a revolution consumes blood and gold. The chronicles of progress are written in blood and paid for with much treasure. Your muzzy ideals *must* recognize those realities. Otherwise, Harry, you'll never be able to lead—to command. And Mary knew the plan. She didn't want you to go, naturally enough. But she knew the entire plan, including the disposal of the opium. And, Harry, she approved —after kicking up her heels for a while."

January 29, 1909

THE marble-walled room with the marble bath sunk in its marble floor was called "Mary's Folly," the name bestowed by a bemused Elizabeth Metcalfe. During the year Mary and Charles lived with the elder Sekloongs in The Castle while their own Small House was being completed, Mary had skirmished stubbornly against the wilder fancies of the exquisite "interior decorator" Sir Jonathan imported from England. But she had yielded on her own bathroom, and had subsequently found unexpected pleasure in its extravagance.

Chubby, pale-gold-plaster cherubim frolicked on the cerulean ceiling. The white-veined walls of emerald marble were inset with four gilt-framed mirrors cunningly placed to repeat their reflections endlessly. The round bath with gold, swan-shaped taps was the pale-green of new grass. Light diffused through apple-green glass completed the illusion of a secluded hollow under a cloudless Mediterranean sky.

Mary lay in the marble bath early on the evening of January 29, 1909. Her red-gold hair was caught up on top of her head, which was supported by a small damask pillow. The jasmine scent in the bath water mingled with the sandalwood oil her masseuse had kneaded into her skin. She was totally relaxed, half-dreaming in the fantasy chamber that was her secure refuge from the world.

With detached approval, she contemplated her white legs shimmering incorporeally under the green-tinged water. Her waist was still slender, and her full breasts floated deliciously weightless in the perfumed water.

Quite adequate, she concluded, more than adequate for a matron approaching her twenty-ninth birthday. Even after five children, the firm swell of her abdomen was unmarred by the striations her mother's generation considered the unavoidable wound stripes of motherhood. Dr. Moncriefe, who insisted that she exercise during her pregnancies, had advised Sir Jonathan to find the Shanghai masseuse who still served her. Each day, they performed the gentle, intense exercises the Europeans called "soft shadow-boxing" and the Chinese called *Tai Chi Chüan*—"Fists of the Ultimate." She was always wryly amused when she recalled that the fearsome Boxers had used the same exercises to prepare for battle.

Mary Sekloong sighed languorously. Her hand found the green-silk bell-rope and, after a moment's hesitation, summoned her amah. The door concealed behind the far mirror opened, and Ah Fung sidled into the steamy bath chamber. She unfolded a six-foot-square bath-towel from its heated rack.

Mary rose, scented water dripping from her rounded hips, and ascended the three marble steps from the sunken bath into the towel's warm embrace. While Ah Fung patted her dry, her mood shifted from its demi-dream of mindless pleasure. She smiled at her own fancies, in which the Small House was like the dollhouse with the removable façade her daughters adored. Family and servants were bustling about their separate business in the different rooms, invisible to one another, but revealed to the curious eyes of the gargantuan beholder of Mary's imagining.

In the basement, a swarm of servants was chopping food, stirring saucepans, and polishing silver in the glow of massive cast-iron stoves. A formal dinner was to be served to twenty-four that evening to bid farewell to the master of the household, who sailed in the morning for a year's stay in Europe on the business of the House of Sekloong. The scene in the kitchen would be familiar to any privileged Edwardian child, although the maids' flushed faces framed Chinese eyes and they exchanged coarse jests in strident Cantonese.

In the drawing-room, the butler was just closing the
246

blue-silk drapes embroidered with golden winged drag-ons. After he had laid out the wines, spirits, and cor-dials in the pantry, his stately tread would carry him to the red-velvet dining room to inspect the table setting of Georgian silver. Ah Sam, the former pirate with the amiably ferocious grin, had been transformed into the simulacrum of a dignified English butler—except for his incorrigible habit of dropping pungent comments into family conversations. Her father's former Number One Boy had assumed his new role as if his earlier life were no more than a rehearsal for attending the wife of the heir of the House of Sekloong and, incidentally, the heir himself.

In the nursery, the older children were having supper with reasonable propriety, though Jonathan, just seven, protested volubly at "eating with the baby girls." Guin-evere and Charlotte, six and five years old, already gave themselves the airs of young ladies. Mary reserved an hour each day to frolic with the two small red-haired girls and gravely discuss their party wardrobes of satins, silks, and tulles. Nonetheless, she feared that the amahs, who resented her interference, were spoiling the "Little Ladies." Anticipating the girls' every possible wish, the servants' constant attentions further encouraged them to make peremptory demands.

The small boys, Thomas, just past four, and James, three, were quite different from each other, but none-theless, inseparable. They were playing with their tin soldiers, having already finished supper in their own nursery. Yawning broadly, Thomas was quite ready to retire obediently to his miniature bed. The younger James was protesting that it was much too early for him to climb into his crib, which was palisaded with carved bars. But he would finally allow himself to be tucked in by his Uncle Harry, who told excitingly frightening tales of pirates, soldiers, and princes.

In his own bathroom, the master of the house was shaving with a shining Sheffield steel razor. Floridly handsome at thirty-two, Charles regularly took his plea-sure in beds other than his wife's. Even his concubine, the Swatow girl who had borne him two daughters, was neglected as he sought new sensations with ingenious courtesans. Still, he was discreet, while Mary had reached a plateau of toleration, sustained primarily by his conviction that she was "cold." His vanity compelled him to the self-vindicating conclusion that Mary's unreasonable fear of pregnancy had destroyed the sensual passion she formerly displayed. The same vanity rendered him incapable of either realizing that she actually shrank from him or of suspecting that she too might have found consolation elsewhere. Charles firmly believed that Mary devoted her energies to the family enterprises in order to compensate for the joys of the nuptial bed she had renounced.

Mary herself reveled in the freedom and the fripperies sanctioned by the Edwardians after the stuffy solemnity of the Victorian Age. The new fashions were more amusing, more daring, and slightly less constricting than the multitude of stiff petticoats and the whaleboned corsets that had confined her a decade earlier. Deeply cut *décolletés* revealed that a lady possessed two softly molded breasts, rather than a single formidable shelf of a bosom, while low-cut slippers with high heels allowed glimpses of ankles in silk stockings amid softly swirling petticoats. It was more "fun"—that old word just revived—to be a woman than it had been a decade earlier. Mary delighted in putting off her sober daytime self to become a pampered feminine being, rather than an indispensable cog in the intricate machinery of the House of Sekloong.

Wearing only a thin silk wrapper, Mary sat before her mirrored dressing table. She was still glowing from the bath, and the warmth of the small cast-iron fireplace was comforting. Frowning in concentration, she dusted her face with a swansdown powder-puff and touched her lips with rouge from a round enamel box that had once served Manchu Court ladies like those painted on its lid. Only in the past three years had ladies again begun to enhance their attractions with cosmetics, under Victoria the mark of the actress or the harlot. Mary still felt a wicked thrill when she "painted" her face, though the Colony had accepted the new mode without demur. Chinese ladies had never re-linquished the ancient feminine prerogative; and Hong Kong's customs were much influenced by its enormous neighbor, despite its pretence of preserving the purity of English manners.

The coal fire was making her drowsy. She spoke softly to the little amah, who was brushing her hair. Diverted from that comfortingly monotonous task, Ah Fung opened the mullioned casement window a crack. She shivered ostentatiously and glanced reproachfully at her mistress. Everyone knew the dank night-air on The Peak abounded with evil humors, but *Tai-tai,* so sensible in most matters, insisted on opening windows.

Mary ignored Ah Fung's pantomimed disapproval and threw off her silk wrapper. When she raised her arms so that the amah could slip her ivory-silk shift over her head, her breasts rose proudly. On the bed was laid out the "under-paraphernalia," as she called it, of formal female attire: the corset with light whaleboning; the sheer pink silk stockings; three petticoats, the outer a delicate rose; and the shamefully flimsy knickers of cream satin.

The little amah held out the corset, but Mary gestured her aside. Anxious to look her best, she wanted to inspect again the evening-gown hanging on the cupboard door. The exclusive design by Worth of Paris had cost her a round sum.

From Worth's pattern Madame Rachelle had produced an airy confection that should draw every male eye—and kindle envy in every female eye. The cream-satin skirt flared from the high waist, while the green-and-mauve embroidered bands extending from the bustline to the hem outlined her figure. The bodice, scooped to reveal the upper swell of her breasts, was supported by two bands embroidered with the same green-and-mauve pattern.

Reassured, Mary told Ah Fung that she was prepared for their mutual ordeal. The amah sighed and slipped the corset around her. It was blessedly lighter than either the formidable stays of her youth or the corsets *de rigueur* only last year to create the S shape favored by King Edward's favorite, Lily Langtry. No longer need she submit to the exquisite torture of a bosom relentlessly thrust forward and a derriere protruding behind. The new modified-S silhouette, which distorted nature's handiwork only slightly, left her breasts free under the gauzy shift. Mary clung to the bedpost, and her amah pulled on the long corset laces.

A peremptory knock sounded. In the same instant, the door opened, and Charles entered wearing a quilted blue dressing-gown. His color was high, and his eyes sparkled. Mary waved the amah out of the room. The corset fell to the carpet, and she stepped out of the confining ring. Realizing that she was shielded only by the semi-transparent shift that barely covered her hips, she groped for her wrapper.

"Why bother, Mary?" His words were slurred. "You're charming that way."

"Now, Charles," she sparred. "We do have guests coming, you know. And you could wait an instant after you knock."

"No need, my dear. You'd hardly be up to anything embarrassing, would you? You never are."

"What do you mean?" she countered, tying the sash of her wrapper.

"Just that you lead such a blameless life. You're infatuated only with those damned, fat, thick, square ledgers—too blameless, really. So I blame myself."

"Charles, that's silly. What do you really mean?"

"You won't be sorry to see me go, will you? Give you more time to plot with the old man and Metcalfe, more time to dream up mad political schemes and make poor Harry carry the can."

"Charles, that's not true. You've been wanting to go to Europe. Besides, I've promised to join you in the autumn."

"You don't understand. I said I blamed myself."

Mary realized that he was maudlin drunk, much further gone than she had originally judged from his flushed face and liquid eyes.

"What happened to the girl I married?" Charles demanded. "Lady in the drawing-room and tigress in bed. Must be my fault—who else's?"

"It's no one's fault," she temporized. "Besides, I thought you were happy with . . ."

"With the Swatow concubine and my little bits of fluff, you mean? A man's entitled to more children. But I must've failed you. Otherwise, why get yourself so involved with the damned business? It's not right, not at all."

Mary was alarmed. Charles inebriated was not a new problem. But Charles self-reproaching rather than self-justifying was beyond her experience and, perhaps, her ability to cope.

"That's not fair," she stalled. "The business does fascinate me. But I'll be glad to get away this autumn and to see Europe again—with you."

That much was wholly true, she reflected, seating herself on the edge of the chaise longue. She longed to escape the oppressive Hong Kong heat, broken only briefly by the equally depressing chill winter. She was, further, appalled by the callousness of the Chinese toward each other and by the compulsive money-grubbing of the foreign community. Europe beckoned alluringly.

"Do sit down and stop glowering, Charles."

"All right, you'll come when it suits you." His tone was aggressive. "But it'll be a long time alone for me."

"I'm sure," she replied with a trace of malice, "that you'll manage to find consolations."

He ignored her taunt. "Besides, God knows what new deviltry you and the old man'll get up to. Sometimes I think I'm the only sane one in the family."

"Perhaps, Charles," she placated him. "You know I'm sad to see you go. But we agreed it was best . . ."

"Best for who? The old man and your schemes? Without me holding you back, next thing you'll be building railroads to Tibet!"

Mary smiled defensively. Charles had come too close to the truth deliberately kept from him. Dr. Sun Yat-sen was obsessed with the vision of a railroad that would run more than 1,000 miles west from Wuhan in Central China to Chengtu in Szechuan Province and thence to Lhasa in Tibet, almost 1,500 miles further through the world's highest mountains. Hilary Metcalfe and Harry Sekloong were bemused by Dr. Sun's grand design, while Sir Jonathan discussed the project seriously with the republican leader's emissaries. If Sun Yat-sen proposed building a rocket to the moon, she suspected her father-in-law would pretend earnest interest. Sometimes, she felt she was living in Cloud-Cuckoo-Land and all the Sekloong splendor would vanish abruptly one morning. The Chinese, who boasted of their hard-headed practicality, were given to wild fancies. Worse, they often attempted to transform those visions into reality.

"Surely not a railway to Tibet, Charles," she parried. "Not right now, anyway."

"I suppose not," he agreed glumly. "You're not as daft as that. But almost anything else. And you keep it from me. I just do the work, give the firm a little solid respectability so you lot can spin your crazy schemes."

"Charles, you can't blame *me*. Why not talk to your father? He's the *lo-ban*, the boss."

"Who the devil can talk to the old man?" Charles exploded. "I can't, haven't since I was twelve. And I *do* blame you."

"I won't take that," she snapped. "I've tried to be a good wife to you, tried not to interfere, but . . ."

"But, but—always but. If you acted like a normal woman, found your pleasures at home with the children —if you did, things'd be different."

"If you behaved like a normal husband, not a rutting he-goat, things might be different."

"But I do." He was genuinely surprised. "I *do* behave normally. A little pleasure outside the house, that's only normal. Everybody does. It was my duty to take a concubine and get more children. And I've taken only *one* concubine. It's perfectly normal."

"Normal, perhaps—to you Sekloongs. Not to civilized people. How would you feel if I . . ."

Mary flung up her arms in disgust, though she knew

she was on dangerous ground. Her loosely knotted sash slipped, and the wrapper opened to reveal her glowing body, veiled only by the shift.

Charles pulled her up from the chaise longue. His arm around her waist thwarted her efforts to retie the sash.

"No, Charles, no!" she protested. "Not *now!* The guests'll be here in a minute. And it's the wrong time."

"Wrong time be damned!" He slipped the wrapper over her shoulders. "There's still *one* thing I can do you can't!"

"Charles, please!" Her words were faintly ludicrous to her own ears. "Charles, mind my hair."

She had forgotten his strength. Holding her powerless, he broke the straps of her shift. The filmy undergarment slipped to the floor, leaving her naked. She stiffened in resistance, but he lifted her effortlessly and carried her to the bed.

Despite herself, she responded to his hands on her thighs and his lips at her breast. He was by no means abhorrent to her, though she hated this forcible approach, as if she were a street-girl. Determined to remain passive, she responded involuntarily when he entered her. But, she promised herself, she would not forgive him this violence—not, at least, for a long time.

May 13, 1909–May 31, 1909

"WELCOME, Motherly and Auspicious. Your humblest subject welcomes you to your domain."

Harry bowed theatrically low and opened the door to Mary's minuscule office, which was still known as the Junior Clerks' Room. The desk and chair were battered by long use, and the chief sign of her occupancy was an orange double hibiscus in a 160-year-old vase painted with spindly crickets and plump butterflies. He lifted the veil from her narrow-brimmed straw hat and, dodging a menacing ostrich plume, kissed her.

"As lovely as ever," he sighed. "More lovely than even poets imagine, oh Motherly and Auspicious."

"I'm not quite old enough for an Empress Dowager," she laughed. "Moderate your transports!"

"If I but could! The gallant knight commands our presence, most delectable mistress of my heart, upon whom no man can look unmoved—especially me. Is that better?"

"Much better," she replied. "But what does His Majesty's trusty and well-beloved knight want today?"

"Don't know, but be careful. He's in high good humor, roaring ferocious good humor. Maybe we're buying Buckingham Palace. Perhaps St. Peter's is up for sale."

"You really don't know why he's so pleased?"

"I'm not sure. Of course, he's still burbling like a tea kettle over *your* news, and his spies write that Charles is doing well. Solid London bankers are bowled over when a proper British gentleman appears in black coat and striped trousers, instead of the wily, pigtailed Oriental they expect. So Charles gets what he wants."

"I'm so glad, Harry. It's what Charles needs, a success on his own. No wonder Father's delighted."

"His joy's not undiluted. He's torn between paternal pride and profound misgivings about the younger generation. You'd think Charles was twelve years old. But that's not all."

"What else? Have we discovered a goldmine?"

"I'm afraid not, though the Canton–Kowloon Railroad'll be finished next month, and there's gold in those rails. Otherwise, I don't know. But let's let him tell us."

Pierced for ventilation by louvers just below the fourteen-foot-high ceiling, the walls of the narrow corridor were drab as befitted the frugal dignity of commerce. Business was, after all, a serious business. But Sir Jonathan had added his personal touch. The walls were not hung with the customary sepulchral portraits of the Royal Family and half-forgotten princes of commerce. Instead, bright paintings on glass advertised the charms of Shanghai courtesans and the stars of Shaohsing Opera troupes.

Sir Jonathan's corner office, austere compared to the library in The Castle, was itself palatial compared to the mazes where his clerks toiled. Only the black upright telephone distinguished the room from the study of a Confucian scholar. It was dominated by a long desktop set on ebony pedestals, which were inlaid with mother-of-pearl. Behind his high-backed chair hung twin scrolls inscribed with the bold writing of Kang Yu-wei, the master of modern calligraphers. Kang Yu-wei was also the intellectual mentor of the Reform Movement that, having signally failed to transform the Manchu Dynasty into a progressive, constitutional monarchy in 1898, reluctantly supported the republican revolutionaries in 1909. "All under Heaven ordered for the benefit of all the people," the right-hand scroll promised, in the terse, classical language of the *Book of Rites*, which had, early in the first millennium before the Christian era, already described and lamented China's long-past mythical Golden Age. The left-hand scroll exhorted in the words of the same canonical work: "It is not meet to leave wealth unproductive as if buried in the ground."

Sir Jonathan, this once, wore a cream-colored pongee lounge suit with high-set lapels and a flowing red-damask four-in-hand tie under a stiff wing collar. His narrow head and aquiline features completed the illusion; it seemed that a European gentleman was awaiting the Chinese scholar to whom the study belonged. But Sir Jonathan was very much at home behind a copy of *The China Mail*.

"Come in, come in," he called. " 'Twould be a lovely morning, even if the Chinese weren't finally getting down to completing their stretch of the Canton–Kowloon Railroad. I want to give you some news from the old *China Mail*."

The Irish lilt was pronounced. His panatella, an unusual indulgence in the morning, described an expansive arc as he spoke.

"Harry's little adventure is coming up roses. Reading between the lines, but not too far between them, I've learned that it was old Dick Wheatley who ordered the

255

hijacking of the *Taishan*—that rascal Dick Wheatley."

"Richard Wheatley, they say?" Mary echoed incredulously.

"Yes, my esteemed step-father, presumably to corner the market. The newspaper johnnies *don't* have to make sense as long as they draw readers. If they lose their childlike faith or learn to distinguish between reality and falsehood, they lose their jobs. So we learn from their broad hints that Dick Wheatley conspired with pirates to seize a ship carrying his own cargo."

"Why, in God's name?" Harry asked. "How can anyone believe that?"

"It's so ridiculous, it's believable," his father replied. "The explanation runs so: Twenty-six Hong Kong opium divans were closed down two months ago. The rest'll be padlocked by year's end. No one can now legally export big smoke to any place that forbids its import. So the opium traders are uneasy."

"Of course they are," Mary said. "But that doesn't explain why Dick Wheatley should turn pirate in his old age."

"He's always been a pirate, but that's another story. Anyway, the writer hints my esteemed step-father wanted to corner the remaining supply. Then he'd smuggle to prohibited areas."

"That's ridiculous," Harry said. "The traders now face a glut, not a shortage."

"True, but newspaper logic makes a world all its own. Better still, the House of Sekloong is reportedly incensed at losing its portion of the cargo, and relations between Sekloong and Wheatley are very bad."

"That's true enough," Mary commented, "even if the reason is upside down."

"A moment, my dear. There's better to come, a large and gritty grain of truth. The *Mail* says flatly, no beating around the bush, that the piracy was organized for Wheatley by Sam Chivers, our perennial Deputy Colonial Secretary. Just listen: 'It is well known in commercial and legal circles that S. Chivers is in league with all the pirates of the China coast.' *All*, mind you, *all!* Exaggerated, but not much."

"How delightful," Mary smiled. "There'll be a lovely libel suit."

"But," Sir Jonathan said, "we hold only a few percent of the *Mail*. Our liability's trifling."

"How much did it cost you," Harry asked, "to fob this fantasy onto the editor?"

"Not a brass farthing. He hadn't a jot of an idea where it came from, but was overjoyed to print it. He's been itching for revenge since Chivers and Wheatley got him expelled from the Hong Kong Club for habitual drunkenness. From the Hong Kong Club for drunkenness! Unbelievable!"

"Father," Mary asked, "should we root in mud this way? Mud can stick."

"Don't be silly, darling," Harry interjected. "Of course, it's worth it. This goes beyond the gentlemen's agreement among thieving *hongs*. The scandal'll split the business community. Our honorable associates will scuttle to line up against Chivers and Wheatley. Better, *we're* the injured party, and the traffic will dwindle more. Congratulations, Father."

"I thought it wasn't a bad move." Sir Jonathan smiled away his daughter-in-law's scruples and complacently accepted his son's praise.

Overruled, Mary did not object again. She could not really quarrel with striking at the opium traffic and benefiting the House of Sekloong, even if she could not quite rejoice in the means employed. Much crueller stratagems were normal business practice on the China Coast. Perhaps her distaste sprang from her condition, for her concern was, once again, turning inward. The new life growing within her daily absorbed more of her psychic energy hardly four months after she had yielded to Charles at the wrong time. Though her sixth pregnancy was still concealed by flaring skirts, she had confided in Lady Lucinda.

"And, Mary, Charles wrote me of his joy over the new child," the Old Gentleman added. "Wants to name it Philip or Philippa after your father."

"So he's written me," she acknowledged. "We'll see."

Harry glowered. Her lover was acting like a betrayed husband because she was carrying a child by her lawful husband. But Harry was too good-humored to sulk for long. Sir Jonathan proffered just the right words to soothe his wounded pride.

"Any rate, we needn't think for a while about Harry's marrying. Plenty of heirs already."

"Is there anything else, Father?" Mary asked. "I have some things to attend to."

"Nothing in particular. Remember, I want the whole family, including children, to turn out for my installation as chairman of the Tung Wah Hospitals. We must follow the proper rites, even if the honor will cost much time and many dollars."

"Charity doesn't come cheap," Mary observed dryly. "Nor do your plots."

"I don't mind the money. What worries me is knocking some sense into the directors' heads. They won't let a Western-style doctor in. I've got two young fellows, local boys with advanced training in England. They're eager to help. But the directors won't play. They say patients want herbal medicines and acupuncture. The old ways were good enough for grandpa and grandma."

"Everyone knows," Harry declaimed, "that Western doctors cut up Chinese patients, maim their bodies, their ancestors' sacred legacy. Then the foreign doctors sell Chinese eyes and brains to alchemists to make magical medicines."

"Why take on the chairmanship?" Mary asked. "It sounds like a lot of trouble and a waste of time."

"Because," Sir Jonathan replied, "it's necessary. Hong Kong's our base. Some things I must do for Hong Kong, even if they're much trouble. Anyway, I might do some good."

"So, if the drought would only end, your cup of joy would overflow," Mary said. "You know, if we don't get rain soon, there'll be no water for drinking or the rice-fields. Vegetable prices're already soaring."

"All prices," Harry added. "Most people don't know rising rents are as much to blame, though the drought makes everything worse. Did you hear the Buddhists are praying for rain, a ten-day nonstop prayer?"

"Look on the bright side," Sir Jonathan advised. "The rats are coming out."

"That's hardly the bright side!" Mary was severe.

"It is for some people," Sir Jonathan riposted. "The rats are coming out because food is getting short. Some coolies are making a nice living from the bounty of two cents a rat-tail. There's dark talk of tails smuggled from Canton. No way to tell a Hong Kong rat-tail from a Canton rat-tail, and no bounty in Canton."

Mary rose. She normally enjoyed Sir Jonathan in his satirical vein, but their customary morning conference was deteriorating into the masculine equivalent of backfence gossip. Besides, she wanted to check the latest invoices of silk shipments. The telephone's shrill bell halted her at the door.

Sir Jonathan spoke briefly in staccato Cantonese. When he replaced the bell-shaped receiver in its forked bracket, his face was momentarily grave.

"That was Tung Wah Hospitals. They report twice the normal number of fever cases for this time of year. Just admitted a new lot. Probably just springtime fever a little worse than usual. Not to worry."

Hong Kong's 440,000 Chinese and 12,000 foreign inhabitants were not easily dismayed by fear of epidemics in the early summer of 1909. There would have been no Hong Kong if the pioneers of both races—who, seventy-odd years earlier, settled the island that Lord Palmerston, Britain's Foreign Secretary, dismissed as "a barren and pestilential rock"—had not stoically endured intermittent decimation. Hong Kong would not have grown if their successors had valued survival above profits. Even at the beginning of the twentieth century, when epidemiology and bacteriology were making immense strides, the typical Hong Kong dweller simply ignored the threat of disease.

Besides, malaria, which Sir Jonathan called by the Colony's customary euphemism, "springtime fever," was rarely fatal. Fevers and chills usually racked victims for three to four days, debilitating, but not killing. The Europeans treated those symptoms with quinine and gin; the Chinese preferred measured doses of opium, their specific against most bodily ills.

Cholera, "blackwater fever," was more virulent, its course swift and usually fatal. Western doctors prescribed rest and fluids, while Chinese doctors drew upon the race's three-thousand-year-old pharmacopeia for remedies that ranged from snake's gall and powdered bat's liver to cooling herbs.

The center of European habitation had early shifted to the less pestilential Mid-Levels and The Peak from the marshland that was called Happy Valley as a propitiary invocation because of its many cemeteries. Thereafter, the incidence of cholera in the foreign community declined sharply. Nonetheless, marble headstones in Happy Valley recorded the reverent acceptance of the blackwater death by men and women in their twenties —as well as the ascent of innocent infant souls. Confined by their poverty to the lowlands, the poor Chinese who made up the bulk of the population died by the hundreds and were buried in mass graves. When the blackwater fever raged, merchant and naval ships canceled all shoreleave, while ten to twenty soldiers dropped on parade each day. Themselves virtually immune, the *taipans* on The Peak bore the deaths of European juniors and Chinese coolies with pious equanimity. The Chinese, the *taipans* consoled themselves, accepted their fates with stoic resignation.

One disease, however, terrified all Hong Kong's inhabitants. The Europeans called it the Black Death, and the Chinese *Ta Wen*, the Great Heat, or the "forty-eight-hour disease," because its implacable course from the first symptoms to death with a fever of 107° was so swift.

Plague had been endemic since the beginning. Though there had been no major outbreak since 1894, the Great Heat normally carried off more than a thousand persons a year. The bounty on rat-tails was the Government's half-hearted concession to the new theory that rats carried the disease, although the Chief Medical Officer of Health scoffed at that theory. "It's more likely that rats catch plague from human beings than vice versa," he asserted. "Should we put a bounty on human heads to protect the poor rats?"

Even the Europeans considered the plague an unalterable act of God and therefore did not cavil at the learned doctor's opinion. After the great epidemic of 1894, sanitary laws had for the first time been imposed upon the skeptical Colony, but their harsh provisions were self-defeating. The Sanitary Board was reluctant to order the razing of premises suspected of harboring plague. Those buildings were, after all, property, and Hong Kong's moral code was based upon the inviolable sacredness of private property. The law courts safeguarded property by dispensing fierce justice: two hundred strokes with heavy bamboo canes for petty theft and hanging for grand larceny. Upon those infrequent occasions when punishment was actually imposed for violating the sanitary laws, a fine of HK$50 neither deterred blatant offenders nor encouraged the law-abiding.

"The business of Hong Kong is making money, not coddling Celestials or half-baked medical theorizing." Thus spoke Samuel Chivers, Deputy Colonial Secretary for sixteen years, who had first landed in Hong Kong as a boatswain's mate deserting a broad-beamed East Indiaman. The plutocrats of the Hong Kong Club toasted his further exhortation: "The faint-hearted can clear out. I'll put my trust in God and two bottles of claret a day."

Some Britons did not share Sam Chivers's robust faith in the Lord and the grape. Two hospitals cared for European civilians, and the red-brick British Military Hospital had been built on Bowen Road in the 1870s after the generals belatedly recognized that it was more economical to preserve the lives of seasoned soldiers than to train recruits. The Chinese-financed Tung Wah Society, which ran schools and hospitals, eschewed the demonstrably dubious benefits of Western medicine for the ancient Chinese therapy that was demonstrably

261

efficacious—except, of course, when the Will of Heaven decreed otherwise.

European doctors and missionaries railed against the "rank superstition" of traditional Chinese diagnoses and remedies. They laughed at Chinese doctors' restricting their examinations to taking "the five pulses" of fully clothed female patients who indicated the sites of their pain on carved ivory figurines more remarkable for anatomical restraint than anatomical accuracy. With morbid glee, they retold the story of nineteen-year-old Ah Poe, one of the first five Chinese student-nurses enrolled under the formidable Mrs. MacDonald, sometime matron of Charing Cross Hospital. The young lady had withdrawn, saying "I can't be happy in a place where people are always dying." Mrs. MacDonald had tartly countered: "Poor Ah Poe will never be happy. Where can she find a place where people do *not* die?"

Despite such raillery, Hilary Metcalfe noted, Tung Wah had a much better recovery rate than the European hospitals, particularly for plague patients. He bluffly informed the British medical fraternity that the traditional Chinese pharmacopeia was not only the world's oldest, but still its most extensive. Herbal doctors and acupuncturists, he added, had for three millennia maintained the Chinese race in rude health, as attested by its vigorous proliferation. Moreover, Tung Wah treated fifty times as many patients as did the three European hospitals.

The first warning was sounded by Tung Wah on May 16, 1909. Three days earlier Sir Jonathan had observed comfortably that Hong Kong was in for nothing worse than a slight increase in the number of normal "springtime fever" cases after Tung Wah reported admission of thirty-one patients in one morning.

On the first day, those patients displayed the classic symptoms of malaria: fevers, chills, acute headaches, dizziness, and dehydration from constant vomiting and diarrhea. On the second day, the staff was alarmed by two portents: forty-two new patients with the same symptoms were admitted; and a young doctor found globular swellings in the left groin and the right armpit of a delirious coolie.

The doctor was equipped with the cumulative wisdom of his professional ancestors. Their meticulous annals recorded not only the Great Plague that killed thirteen million throughout China in 1380 and the epidemic that swept Eurasia and forced Attila the Hun to retreat from Italy in A.D. 452. Outbreaks of almost equal virulence had been recorded as early as the third century B.C. and as recently as 1866. But the Chinese doctors ventured no definite diagnosis until the third day, when sixty-eight patients were admitted. The wards were already so crowded that new patients lay on straw mats in the aisles between long rows of wooden bed platforms.

The coolie died on the evening of the third day, mercifully carried off by respiratory arrest. In addition to the buboes in his groin and armpit, Tung Wah's Chief Medical Superintendent noted with alarm the dusky-blue tinge of his skin. After examining some twenty patients with similar symptoms, the Superintendent concluded that he was dealing with a probable epidemic of the Great Heat Disease. Distrusting the newly installed telephone, he dispatched by messenger to Sir Jonathan a note brushed in fine calligraphy on rice-paper and couched in impeccable classical Chinese. But Sir Jonathan himself employed the telephone to relay the information to the Colonial Secretariat.

Acting Colonial Secretary Samuel Chivers was conferring with his solicitors. He had with difficulty been persuaded to lodge a suit for libel against the editor of *The China Mail*, rather than carry out his threat upon first reading the report of his alliance with *all* the pirates of the South China Sea: "I'll give that damned inky wretch a damned fine hiding with my riding crop."

The effective prime minister of the Colony, since his superior, the Colonial Secretary, was on leave, Chivers was more than normally irascible. He fueled his righteous anger by increasing his customary intake of two bottles of claret a day to five bottles supplemented with tumblers of neat brandy.

Replacing the telephone's hand set, he snorted his contempt for the diagnoses of "chink witch-doctors." He was not concerned about "some damned funny disease among the Celestials, probably from their disgusting food and habits." Besides, no European had been afflicted. He swore he'd be damned if he'd run to His Excellency the Governor with "vague, crazy rumors started by a bunch of half-baked chink quacks and passed on by that half-breed rascal Sekloong." Sam Chivers dismissed the danger from his muddled consciousness with the words: "I tell you there's no plague. That horse won't run."

That pronouncement was the most spectacular misjudgment of a career almost as notable for sweeping errors as for grandiose peculation. His cronies at the Hong Kong Club were soon to change his nickname from "Two-Bottle Sam" to "No-Horse Sam." The new nickname was later to force him to leave the Colony, though he might otherwise have weathered even his most spectacular error. After pursuing the hapless editor through the Hong Kong Courts, Sam Chivers was finally to take his case to the Privy Council in London, which awarded him derisory damages of one penny. In a memorable *obiter dictum,* one learned Law Lord remarked: "The horse to which the appellant referred, the pestilence, was anything but a nonstarter. In the event, it galloped as rapidly and as devastatingly as its precursor among the mounts of the Four Horsemen of the Apocalypse."

It did. By May 30, some two weeks after Tung Wah's first warning, Governor Sir Frederick Lugard was compelled to disregard Sam Chivers's complacent counsel. Eight hundred and twelve cases had already been reported, 463 fatal, and even the Chief Medical Officer of Health acknowledged that the figures "erred on the low side." Though fourteen Eurasians and two Europeans were infected, the Chinese were the chief sufferers, and the Chinese were notoriously reluctant to entrust their kinsmen to any hospital, even Tung Wah.

Most invalids, they felt, entered hospital to die, not to recover. They were equally reluctant to report deaths at home, since they feared that intrusive Sanitary Law Inspectors would order their houses fumigated or even destroyed.

The Governor convened an emergency meeting of senior civil servants and community leaders on May 31. He already feared that the epidemic might prove as virulent as the pestilence of 1894 when 100,000 died in Canton and almost half that number in Hong Kong itself. Since the forceful Sir Frederick Lugard had served extensively in Africa, he firmly believed that the superstitious natives would always seek to deceive him. Although similarity between the primitive tribes of West Africa and the heirs of the world's oldest civilization was obscure to less forthrightly vigorous minds, Sir Frederick was, in this case, quite right. Several hundred additional cases, more than half fatal, had been concealed.

Among those summoned to the green-curtained conference room of Government House were the relatively subdued Acting Colonial Secretary Sam Chivers; the Commander, British Forces; the Chief Inspector of Police; the Chief Medical Officer of Health; and the Financial Secretary. The last represented the administration's primary concern, the Crown Colony's commercial well-being. Maintaining public order was the second-most concern, while public health was third in priority.

Sir Frederick had also summoned Richard Wheatley, who spoke for the business community as *taipan* of the chief *hong*, and Sir Jonathan Sekloong, Chairman of the Tung Wah Society. Since the problem lay with the Chinese, the Governor had also invited two younger men: Robert Hotung, assistant comprador of Jardine, Matheson; and Mosing Way, vice-chairman of the East Asiatic Bank. Both spoke English well.

Two other participants so enraged No-Horse Sam Chivers that his ruddy complexion flushed choleric purple. The first was Dr. George Parker, a twenty-four-old American who was making a name in Shanghai for his research into tropical diseases. He espoused the much

265

derided theory that the plague bacillus, *Pasteurella pestis,* identified simultaneously fifteen years earlier by a Japanese and a Swiss scientist, was spread by rats. No-Horse Sam was apoplectic when his bloodshot eyes fell upon Mary Sekloong, demure in a high-necked gray-pongee dress.

Mary had been invited because she was Honorary Secretary of the Ladies' Benevolent Society, founded two decades earlier to "succor deserving, unfortunate Europeans and Eurasians." Though she had no idea what she could contribute, the Governor's aide-de-camp had been pressing. Sir Frederick was convinced that females were particularly qualified by nature to cope with illness, and he had been warned that the Chinese females would prove particularly troublesome. Mary Sekloong was virtually unique, not merely in speaking both English and Cantonese, but in possessing entrée into both European and Chinese circles.

"Mrs. Sekloong and Gentlemen." Sir Frederick's peremptory Sandhurst accent was strained through his extravagant mustaches. "We appear to have a problem on our hands. I'd welcome suggestions."

He allowed the swelling voices to compete for a full minute before himself asking pointed questions. Not a patient man, he was, nonetheless, particularly attentive to the Financial Secretary and to Dr. George Parker.

Volubly supported by Richard Wheatley, the Financial Secretary argued against proclaiming an emergency.

"It could ruin business," he summed up. "Remember what happened in '94. Your Excellency, we must, whatever the cost, *not* declare Hong Kong an infected port. If we warn off shipping, our trade will suffer a blow from which it may not recover for years."

"See what we can do, Financial Secretary." Sir Frederick was brusque in his contempt for money-grubbing civilians. "See what we can do. But what happens to your trade if people start dying by the thousands? Not quite good for business, eh?"

The Governor was surprisingly courteous to Dr. Parker, though the casual young American omitted the formal respect the British tendered to the King's personal representative.

"Rats, you say, Dr. Parker?" he asked. "But how do the rats convey this what-d'you-call-it to humans?"

"Bacillus *Pasteurella pestis,* Governor," Dr. Parker replied in a soft Virginia drawl, "isolated by Kitazato and Yersin in 1894. My microscope's found it in all blood specimens from the victims."

"That's interesting, Dr. Parker," the Governor rejoined. "Great scientific interest, I'm sure. I've got the highest respect for you scientific johnnies. But how do the rats carry this bacillus of yours? Does it fly through the air?"

"We're not sure, Governor," Parker answered, "though some scientists believe it's the fleas on the rats."

"Well, what do we do then?" Sir Frederick asked rhetorically. "Get rid of the rats, I suppose."

"And cleanse the infected premises, Your Excellency." The Chief Medical Officer spoke for the first time, having judged it impolitic to refute the American's ludicrous theory of a rat-borne plague when the Governor apparently accepted it.

"Not with fire and the sword, eh?" Sir Frederick asked jocularly. "Wouldn't do, would it? Not a military operation, after all."

"Fumigation with toxic gases is usual," Dr. Parker suggested. "But we can't be sure. Badly infested places should be burnt."

"You'll need the sword, then, Your Excellency," Sir Jonathan Sekloong advised. "The Chinese won't cooperate unless they're forced to. They won't let your inspectors into their homes—certainly not into the women's quarters."

"So, it must be fire and the sword, Sir Jonathan?"

"No, sir. The threat of force should be enough. And Tung Wah should treat all Chinese patients. The people's suspicion of Western doctors could otherwise lead to violent resistance."

"See what we can do about that, Sir Jonathan," the Governor said. "But we can't be too tender. 'Twould destroy confidence if we relied chiefly on your group of . . . though mind you, I've the highest respect. I'll count on you to help persuade 'em. Perhaps the charming Mrs. Sekloong will mobilize her ladies to care for the dispossessed. But she's to stay away from the plague areas."

"It may be necessary, Your Excellency." Mary was intimidated despite herself by the male assemblage.

"No, that's flat." Sir Frederick cut her off. "You're to keep clear of the infected areas. Well, gentlemen, that's it. Inspect 'em, find the hidden cases, turn 'em out, and burn the houses, if necessary."

He directed his hard stare at the Commander, British Forces, and the Chief Inspector of Police.

"General, the troops'll go in, if necessary. Chief Inspector, the police'll maintain civil order and back up the troops."

"Further instructions, Sir?" asked the aide-de-camp.

"I want detailed recommendations from all departments. Medical Department to survey emergency facilities. Marine Department to report on capacity to move civilians, if necessary. Agriculture and Fisheries to assess food supplies. Wheatley, Sekloong, Way, and Hotung, we may need additional funds. And, of course, our commerce must be maintained."

Sir Frederick Lugard then brusquely restated his strategy: "That's it, then. Turn 'em out and burn 'em down!"

June 10, 1909–September 11, 1909

JOSS-STICKS smoldered in red-and-gold shrines before the shop-houses whose steplike roofs marked Bonham Road's steep ascent. The air was behazed over ramshackle stalls that purveyed goods ranging from black cloth tunics and thick-soled cloth shoes through rice, meat, and vegetables to earthenware cooking pots and credible copies of three-hundred-year-old vases manufactured two weeks earlier. The rising tendrils of smoke bore the musky scent of incense Heavenward. Behind the padlocked gates of their mansions on neighboring Seymour Road, the wealthy burned groves of votive candles and joss-sticks in enamel altar furniture. The poor offered incense and prayers to garish lithographs of the God of Plague.

All Hong Kong was terrified by the sudden onset of the Forty-eight-Hour Disease, but the crowded Western District above the Canton Steamer Wharf swirled in mass panic. Rich or poor, almost every household had already been visited by the God of Plague, and death itself had already stricken every fourth family. Men, women, and children scurried through the streets as frantic as ants threatened by a brush fire, though less rational than those insects. Elderly women hobbling on bound feet to the illusory shelter of overcrowded tenements collided with coolies fleeing toward the harbor with all their possessions tied up in cloth bundles. Old gentlemen gathered together as if their pooled wisdom could turn aside the scourge of Heaven, but the impromptu parliaments disintegrated as abruptly as they assembled. Conferring gravely one moment, the groups of elders were splintered by terror the next.

A procession of Buddhist monks in yellow vestments trudged through the swirling mass. Eyes downcast, the shaven-headed votaries chanted monotonous sutras in corrupt Sanskrit none understood. A file of gray-robed Taoist priests debouched from an alley, their clashing cymbals, tinkling bells, and wooden clappers further inflaming the throng's terror. Pleading for mercy to the same vengeful Heaven, the rival holy men ignored each other.

Long hair matted, eyes glowing in his black-grimed face, an emaciated beggar capered down the cobblestone road. His teeth flashed in a tigerish grin, and his tattered, filth-encrusted cloak swirled to the rhythm of his wild jig. The throng initially divided before the solitary dancer. But first two, then five, and soon tens followed the madman, and hundreds of respectable artisans were dancing in hectic gaiety.

Mary Sekloong shuddered at the manic quadrille and

269

clutched the arm of her brother-in-law who was her lover. His lips close to her ear, Harry Sekloong shouted: "Whither thou goest—but this is no place for you."

"And for you, Harry? I couldn't let you come alone."

Mary sensed a pattern in the crowd's apparently aimless milling. Some were retreating behind the walls of dwellings that had for years sheltered them from typhoons, marauders, and tax collectors. Though their homes harbored mortal peril, they instinctively sought those familiar refuges from a hostile world. Laden with their portable possessions, others were pressing downhill toward the docks. The scheduled steamers were still departing for Canton one hundred and five miles away, their superstructures black with terrified human beings. Gold and silver coins tarnished by years of hoarding were pressed on the captains of trading-junks that did not cast off until their heavy-laden decks were only inches above the choppy green water.

Fleeing was as senseless as retreating behind walls, since Canton, the metropolis of South China, was as severely afflicted as Hong Kong. Dr. George Parker suspected that the pestilence had been introduced into the Colony by rats leaving the lighters that carried rice from Canton. Nonetheless, the Chinese fled unthinking to the Motherland.

The throngs drew aside from six stocky British infantrymen in scarlet tunics, who tramped up the steep street. Men whispered that the "red-backed foreign devils" carried the Forty-eight-Hour Death in their cartridge pouches. Mothers hid their infants under their jackets. They knew that foreign doctors would scoop out their babies' eyes to make magical potions that would protect the "western people" from the God of Plague. Some men warned that the hairy barbarian warriors had come to loot the few treasures of the oppressed Chinese and to snatch away Chinese corpses to manufacture other potions.

The infantrymen's scarlet tunics glowed like gouts of blood among the drably attired Chinese. An officious subaltern had ordered his men into parade uniform to render them more imposing, but had actually succeeded in rendering them more frightening. Mary saw with relief that the soldiers' Lee-Enfield rifles were slung. Some officer had been foresighted enough to prohibit their carrying their weapons at the menacing port-arms. But the soldiers feared the Chinese as much as they feared the plague or the Chinese feared them. Pervasive fear made the atmosphere explosive, despite the heavy, damp heat.

Two infantrymen poked their rifles into open rice sacks, which spilled their granular white contents onto the pavement before a clapboard stall. Mary shuddered, and her fingernails dug into Harry's arm. Six sleek brown rats as large as rabbits scampered from the open stall. Their long whiskers were cocked arrogantly, and their obscenely hairless tails trailed on the grime-encrusted cobblestones. A single shot fired at the rats shocked the panicky throng into frozen immobility. A mustached corporal struck up the smoking rifle with an oath. The two Sekloongs watched in dismay as the corporal methodically struck eight Bryant and May matches and tossed them into the stall. Ignoring the angry owner's protests, a private prodded the cursing man with his rifle.

Orange flames from the dry boards shot fifteen feet into the still air, and a fusillade reverberated as successive segments of the bamboo poles supporting the flimsy structure exploded. Blue kerosene flames soared high, and greasy smoke settled upon the throng.

The soldiers set eight stalls afire, and streams of rats poured into the street. Women shrieked as the crowd battled in frenzy to draw clear of the rats. Smoke-stung eyes streamed tears, and the bright afternoon sun was blotted out by gray smoke-clouds. Bonham Road was transformed into a Brueghel scene: terror, fire, rats, and smoke maddened the keening throng.

Huddled in a doorway, Mary tasted the copper flavor of terror.

"But the rats . . ." she exclaimed. "They're escaping."

"Can't shoot them," Harry answered heavily. "Can't shoot them without hitting the people."

Urchins wielding poles and clubs darted into the gray-brown mass of rats that flowed like a living river toward the harbor. The rats squealed in agony, and the cobblestones were littered with mangled carcasses, bright-red blood and yellow-green guts spilling from matted fur. Some injured rats dragged themselves forward, while others tore at their own wounds. But the stream flowed on relentlessly. The rats were themselves too terrified to stand and rend their maimed fellows.

"Let's go, Mary," Harry urged. "Nothing we can do here."

"Hey, Missus, Mister," a ruddy-faced sergeant demanded. "You speak the lingo? I'm ordered into the big houses. And they're locked tight as drums."

"What're you looking for?" Harry asked.

"Damned if I know, Sah," the sergeant answered. "Sick 'uns, I suppose, and rats, they say. Don't need no more rats. Never saw so many rats in all my born days."

A sallow boy with a pinched face sidled up to Harry and tugged at his sleeve.

"Oi, Sin-sang, lay-ah, lay-ah. Wang Dai-yen uh-kay yau ho-daw bing yen," he whined. "Say, Mister, come along, come along. Lots of sick people in Big Man Wang's house."

"How do you know, son?" Harry asked.

"I work for Big Man Wang. For ten cents and a bowl of cold rice a day. But eighteen hours every day: 'Ah Dzai do this, fetch that, carry this.' Big Man Wang's a monster. He ran away to Canton, and *Tai-tai*'s dying. He doesn't hold with doctors. They cost too much."

"What's all the jabber, Mister?" the sergeant demanded.

"The lad says he knows a house with many sick and dying," Harry responded. "His master wouldn't have a doctor in."

"Well, that's my orders. Tell him to show us where, Sah."

The urchin led them down a lane so narrow they
272

were forced to walk two abreast while their shoulders brushed the high brick walls on either side. He stopped before wrought-iron gates with two Chinese characters scrolled above them: *"Wang Lü—Wang Residence."* Corrugated-iron sheets behind the grillwork guarded the compound's privacy, and festoons of heavy chain clasped by three ponderous padlocks secured the gates. A bellrope dangled on the brick wall.

Only distant tolling responded to the sergeant's repeated tugging. The gates remained blank and unmoving. At the sergeant's nod, two privates attacked the gates with rifle butts. The wrought-iron buckled, but did not break.

"Stand back," the sergeant ordered, unslinging his rifle.

Holding the muzzle two inches from a padlock three times the size of a fist, he fired. The shots reverberated in the narrow brick-walled alley, and acrid cordite mingled with the kerosene-saturated smoke. After three shots the padlock disintegrated in a shower of bright metal.

"O'Hara," the sergeant said, mopping his sweaty face. "Next one's yours."

A snub-nosed private wearing a look of perpetual good humor stepped forward. He fired five shots before the remaining padlocks fell apart, allowing the soldiers to unravel the tangled chains. The gates swung open under the repeated blows of rifle butts, but no sound within responded to the din without.

Inside the twisted gates, an ornamental pool surrounded by bright porcelain flower-pots dominated a shaded courtyard. Seven giant goldfish floated, white bellies upward, on the cloudy surface. Beyond, tile-roofed pavilions ascended a terraced hillside, which was bright with azaleas in flower.

"Don't go in." Harry grasped Mary's arm. "It's no place for you."

"Perhaps I can help," she insisted. "The boy said there were women inside."

Harry followed her into the antechamber of the mansion. The conventional furnishings were typical of a wealthy merchant's reception hall: a blackwood table inlaid with mother-of-pearl patterns, chairs with painted porcelain plaques set into their high backs, hanging scrolls with black-brushed couplets extolling familial solidarity and filial piety.

A young man in a silk long-gown sprawled across the table, sightless eyes glaring in his blue-tinged face. A puddle of bilious yellow-green matter on the tiled floor swarmed with iridescent blow-flies. The air was heavy with a sickly-sweet stench compounded of vomit, feces, urine, rotting rice, and the feral reek of rats.

Mary retched, but followed the soldiers despite Harry's restraining hand. The phlegmatic riflemen strode through the maze of rooms and courtyards in awed silence. The mansion would normally have resounded with the cacophony of Cantonese jests and quarrels, but the only sound was the high-pitched bark of a prize Pekinese. The dog's golden-brown hair swept the filth-splattered floor. His bright eyes and nervous movements showed vigorous health. O'Hara stopped to pat the Pekinese. The dog snapped, and O'Hara snatched his hand away with an oath. His heavy boot lashed at the small animal. Mary stifled a protest, struck by the horror of the dog's angry defense of his blasted household.

The intruders penetrated to the innermost courtyard after five minutes. The women's quarters were protected by a round moon-gate, its massive wooden doors studded with brass nailheads. The wooden beam that barred the doors lay on the ground, and the doors stood ajar.

A wrinkled crone in black trousers and white tunic hobbled into the courtyard. She was almost bald; the gray hair above the intelligent walnut face had been pulled back into a tight knot for more than half a century.

"*Tai-tai, ngo ho . . .*" she said in Cantonese, oblivious to Mary's un-Chinese features. "Madam, I am so glad someone has come. The master fled to Canton three days ago, taking the servants, the children, and his concubines. My mistress, the chief wife, lies ill within, and I dared not go out to seek help. I am Ah Ying. I have been her amah since she was an infant."

A slender Chinese woman in her early forties lay on a high blackwood bed in the dark-curtained chamber. Her pale skin was taut over her high cheekbones, and her eyes glittered with fever. Ah Ying had tended her mistress lovingly, though she, too, could have fled. The light coverlet was freshly washed, and a damp cloth lay on the lady's forehead. She gazed at them blankly, and a delirious gabble welled from her cracked lips.

"Get her out to hospital." The sergeant's voice was low in the presence of imminent death. "That's my orders. Then the medical johnnies can decide. Fumigate the place or burn it."

Surprisingly gentle, he tucked the coverlet around the wasted figure. Ah Ying sprang at him, protesting fiercely.

"Say the lady'll get good care."

Harry added his own hollow assurances that the foreign doctors would cure the mistress Ah Ying had possessively served all her life. The maidservant hobbled about the bedchamber packing toilet articles and garments into a small red-leather case.

Mary glanced around the shaded bedchamber, unable to look upon either the doomed lady or the old amah's wracking grief. She stiffened in shock, and her legs trembled. A still figure in white tunic and black trousers lay curled on the floor in the far corner. The plump, dimpled hands showed that the girl had died young. Three sleek rats rooted in the raw, red flesh that had been her face. A gray film veiled Mary's eyes, and her head whirled. She felt Harry's arms around her.

A somber procession wound through the narrow alley. The sergeant carried Ah Ying's mistress, and the weeping amah soothed her lady with soft endearments. The privates were silent, and their feet dragged. Harry supported Mary, though she protested that she could walk by herself. Moving as slowly as a funeral cortege, they returned to Bonham Road.

The street was a kaleidoscope of violent motion and deafening uproar. Scarlet knots of soldiers wanly backed by khaki-clad Chinese policemen in white sun-helmets fended off a screaming crowd, which swung bamboo poles and hurled filthy ordure. A brick struck a young lieutenant on the temple, and he fell to the cobblestones. His angry sergeant ordered his men to load and aim. A captain countermanded the order just as the rifles were leveled. The scattered scarlet figures slowly drew together, clearing a way through the hysterical mob with rifle butts.

The half-company, fifty-three strong, retreated down Wing Lock Street toward broad Des Voeux Road. Cobblestones, pots, filth, and shouted imprecations pursued them.

"Murderers. Mother-rapers. Red-coat foreign devils. Whore's spawn. Thieves and killers. Bring black death and steal our bodies. Turtle-egg bastards who steal our women. Rape your mothers."

Dr. Moncriefe ordered Mary to bed within the security of Sekloong Manor on the pest-free Peak. When she protested that she had merely felt giddy, he cut her off acerbically.

" 'Twas no ladylike swoon, young woman," he said. "You fainted dead away—and with good reason too. That was a daft thing to do in your state. I've no time to waste with you. There are dying people out there. You'll stay in bed and not trouble me."

Lassitude overcame Mary. Her objections were half-hearted, as was her insistence upon returning to the offices of J. Sekloong and Sons, which had become the center of relief activities. She felt she must help the victims, but she was revolted by the misery concentrated in the foothills and narrow plains 1,500 feet below.

She could understand the mindless anger of the bewildered, ignorant crowd at the soldiers sent to succor them. She knew why the superstitious Chinese had stoned the "red-backed foreign devils," whom they believed spread the plague and abducted the sick. But the enraged, blood-engorged faces, their open mouths shouting obscenities, alternated in her dreams with the macabre tableau in the bedchamber of the Wang mansion. Revulsion overcame reason, and she despaired of such a wilfully perverse people. She even shrank from the smiling solicitude of her own amahs. Only the fierce tenderness of Ah Sam could ameliorate her revulsion from all Chinese, and she regarded even Ah Sam with occasional suspicion.

By late June, Mary began to move around the Small House, but she tired easily and was glad to return to her bed. Her will was so enfeebled that she hardly protested when Sir Jonathan decreed that her children must retreat with Lady Lucinda to plague-free Shanghai.

"You'd go too," he said. "But Moncriefe won't hear of your being moved. Damned if I know what's the matter with a healthy young girl like you. He mumbles about shocks to the nervous system."

"I'll be back in the office in a week," Mary insisted with a brief flash of spirit.

"We'll see," Sir Jonathan placated her. "But I want you to stay out of this. It's becoming very unpleasant."

To her own surprise, she made good her promise. By the first week of July, she was again traveling by Peak Tram to the dingy offices in St. George's Building. Dr. Moncriefe had reluctantly assented.

"She'll do herself more harm fretting at home," he had conceded. "She can go back if she doesn't overdo it."

The pestilence raged unabated. During one tragic twenty-four-hour period, 168 corpses were counted. On "normal" days, the death carts collected fifty to sixty corpses. Mary was appalled by the devastation that had occurred during her own illness. It was no exaggeration, but a simple statement of fact: Hong Kong was dying, the pulse of the civic organism slowing to a weak tremor intermittently convulsed by feverish spasms.

In May 1909, the Crown Colony of some 450,000 had been a major commercial center, a vigorous community where Chinese and Europeans lived and worked together in proximate harmony only occasionally disturbed by the flaring of underlying tensions. By August

1909, the stream of commerce was dwindling to a meager trickle, and the two races regarded each other with suspicion that almost daily erupted into violent clashes.

After twelve soldiers died of plague and three more of injuries inflicted by rioters, the Commander, British Forces, informed the Governor that he could provide only volunteers for the house-to-house searches which aroused the Chinese to frenzy—and no more than one hundred of those volunteers a day. The number of volunteers regularly exceeded the general's figure three-fold or four-fold, but neither soldiers nor medical officers could arrest the Black Death. Modern Western medicine, which the Chinese considered a conspiracy to mutilate their sacrosanct bodies, was even less effective than millennia-old Chinese medicine, which the Europeans considered black superstition.

The strains overthrew the precarious balance of trust between two antithetic races and cultures. A semblance of mutual confidence might have been preserved if the Government had yielded to Sir Jonathan's pleas that the Tung Wah Hospitals care for all Chinese victims. Sir Jonathan himself esteemed Tung Wah's treatment hardly more than the vain efforts of the small corps of Western doctors, but he feared that Chinese distrust of foreign medicine would turn into hatred of all foreigners. Yet Sir Frederick Lugard rejected his requests. All his advisers, including the young American doctor, George Chapman Parker, warned that the plague would become even more virulent if Tung Wah were allotted the primary responsibility. The intricate web of shared responsibility and minimal trust that had bound the races was rent.

Only the rats thrived. The few nocturnal pedestrians saw packs of sleek rodents, some so obese they waddled. Despite intermittent slaughters, their numbers increased. Large packs scampered from one unguarded warehouse to the next, gorging themselves on rice and wheat.

Early in August, the "war of the placards" shattered whatever tenuous mutual confidence still linked Chinese subjects and British administrators. The inflammatory posters first appeared in Canton, their fulsome language and elegant calligraphy proving that they were composed by the die-hard "literati," aspirant officials who had been deprived of hope of preferment by the rapid alterations within the ancient Imperial System stimulated by Western incursions. The slogans inveighed against the inhuman practices of Western doctors who, according to the posters, cut up Chinese bodies to manufacture medicines and stole the precious jewels often found within Chinese skulls. Those doctors further extracted the eyes of living Chinese infants and amputated the penises of young men to brew long-life elixirs that commanded high prices in Europe. Similar placards blossomed in Hong Kong, mysteriously renewing themselves each time they were torn down.

Their effect was catastrophic. The new alarms paralyzed whatever normal life still endured in the Colony. Schools, homes, workshops, shops, and offices were emptied by a mass exodus to Canton and Shanghai. Most firms shut down, and European managers joined their families in safe retreats like Weihaiwei and Peitaiho in North China. Deprived of their Chinese staff, the *hongs* virtually ceased functioning.

The Colonial Government reacted with a mindless reflex to the Chinese "betrayal." A total of more than 2,000 buildings were burned, and an additional 25,000 homeless families swelled the exodus. When large "disaster areas" were cordoned off, their inhabitants, too, sought to leave Hong Kong. But the Government would, quite inexplicably, permit no more than fifteen junk loads to depart, and the disaffected police dissipated their energies trying in vain to apprehend the "snake ships" that smuggled out those refugees who could scrape up extortionate fares. Guardships patrolled the harbor. But they could neither stem the exodus nor protect even the improvised pest houses on the waterfront from the mobs.

The Government ordered "a war of extermination" against the rats, threatening to demolish one out of every five structures in the Colony. Yet the rats multiplied, and the Black Death pursued its inexorable course. Food prices soared, as ships avoided the pestilence-stricken Colony. The essential compradors of the foreign *hongs* withdrew. Since their compatriots were not allowed to depart at will, they would no longer serve the foreigners. Infuriated mobs stormed food stores and warehouses, but other consumer goods could not be sold even at a loss. The pulse of the social and economic organism called Hong Kong beat so feebly it was barely perceptible.

The offices of J. Sekloong and Sons remained open, though the exodus reduced the staff by half and the chief business was striving to sustain the chaotic Tung Wah Hospitals. But the walled compound called Sekloong Manor remained a sheltered enclave. Only three cases of plague appeared among two-hundred-odd dependents and servants, perhaps because the Sekloongs fought a relentless battle against the rats with Dr. George Parker's advice.

When September began and the vainglorious sunshine was still unrelieved by rain, the rodents had almost vanished from the Manor. On September 10, 1909, Ah Sam proudly told Mary that not a single rat had been killed during the preceding twenty-four hours —because none could be found. Many servants had fled during the terrible days of July and August. Supported by two aged gardeners, by Mary's personal maid, by the scowling baby-amah Ah Lam, and by Sir Jonathan's cook, Ah Sam was the pillar of the establishment.

By September 10, the Colony's death toll had fallen to two or three a day. Chinese or European, the survivors allowed themselves to hope—as the crew hopes when the winds begin to subside after their ship has been battered by gales for many days.

The next day, September 11, was the culmination of the terrible summer of 1909 for the Sekloongs. Sir Jonathan ordered his sedan chair early to carry him to a meeting of the Governing Board of the Tung Wah Hospitals. After the pestilence began to recede, his chair bearers had reappeared to explain that they had departed without notice in order to attend family funerals in their ancestral villages on the West River outside the market town of Sekloong. Sir Jonathan gravely heard their involved tales out. To express doubt would have stolen the coolies' face.

Besides, he required their services, and he had good reason to believe that the worst had passed. He was, nonetheless, appalled by a report just received from the Chief Medical Officer of Health. The cumulative toll was 15,463 known dead. But Sir Jonathan knew the plague was abating, and he had prepared a proposal he believed the Board would accept.

At eleven on the morning of September 11, 1909, Sir Jonathan returned on foot to St. George's Building. A wound in his forehead seeped blood, and he carried his left arm awkwardly. Harry hurried out to find Dr. Moncriefe.

"Hit by stones," Sir Jonathan told Mary. "My chair was overturned, and the coolies ran away."

His account was halting, for the pain of a torn shoulder ligament subdued even his spirit. His report of the death toll had been greeted by the Tung Wah directors with muted moans, but without antagonism. His proposal had called up a storm of protests. Staid old gentlemen rose screaming when he suggested that Tung Wah employ two English-trained Chinese doctors. Such renegades, they shouted, would be spies for the hated British witch-doctors who had allowed thousands of Chinese to die for their own sinister reasons. The board-meeting dissolved in anger. A mob gathered outside the Tung Wah Hospitals stoned Sir Jonathan after overturning his sedan chair and forcing his bearers to flee. Abashed by its deeds, the crowd then dispersed.

As she helped her father-in-law to a sofa, Mary felt pain lance her abdomen, swollen in the seventh month of pregnancy. She collapsed on the floor. When Harry returned with Dr. Moncriefe, two patients required his care.

At the wheel of the big Daimler, Harry slowly drove Mary and Sir Jonathan up Peak Road to the first sedan-chair stage. Relays of chairs carried them to The Peak. As they passed under the dragon arch, barrages of thunder rolled and rain fell in opaque sheets. The drought had ended. Within two days, the plague, too, vanished as swiftly and mysteriously as it had descended.

Summoned by cablegram, Charles arrived from London four weeks later by fast steamer. He had suggested returning on hearing the first reports of the epidemic, and had repeated his cabled pleas almost weekly. But Sir Jonathan withheld permission, and Charles would not in this case defy his father, who was, after all, on the scene. Although she knew she was being irrational, Mary could not forgive his absence.

Charles found a household and a community in a state of shock after the long siege. Trade was bad—and would not improve for some time. Only the opium traffic had flourished, providing solace for tens of thousands amid universal terror. The resources of the House of Sekloong had been depleted by lavish contributions to relief funds. Sir Jonathan's prestige among the Chinese had sunk as dramatically as it had risen among the Europeans. Exhausted by his injuries and his labors, Sir Jonathan was, nonetheless, cheerful. He was confident that his reputation would rebound, since some Chinese associates were already proffering flowery apologies. Sir Jonathan faced the arduous task of rebuilding with confidence that inspired his sons.

But Mary was sunk in depression. Having lost a perfectly formed girl-child, she was overwhelmed by a sense of deprivation. She shrank from the attentions of the servants who had deserted her in peril. Even when Ah Sam, that pillar of constancy, entered her room she felt irrational antipathy. Despite his loyalty, he was Chinese—and she feared all Chinese. She had seen them abandon their own dying; she had seen them attack British soldiers who came to help them. The Chinese had savaged Sir Jonathan, who had poured out his strength and his treasure to succor them. They had driven her to exhaustion—and they had murdered her girl-child.

The family kept knowledge of a further catastrophe from her for two weeks. But her repeated inquiries finally forced Charles to tell her that Hilary Metcalfe had been trampled by a mob he was trying to persuade to vacate its houses peacefully. He had died the next day. Elizabeth Metcalfe, stricken beyond reason, had closed the house on Wyndham Street and sailed for England a week later.

Mary was desolate. The Chinese had become abhorrent to her. They were no better than vicious tigers, indeed worse, for tigers would not abandon their mates and cubs to the hunter. The Chinese were ravening hyenas, which knew no law but self-preservation. Aware that her emotions defied logic, she nonetheless felt trapped on a vile little island amid a people she detested and feared.

Part Four

Mary and Jonathan

December 6, 1911–June 10, 1916

December 6, 1911

"BUT, hark, Madam, to the Immortal Bard. The Sweet Swan of Avon said it long ago: 'There is a tide in the affairs of men, which, taken at the flood, leads on to fortune.'"

Mary was mildly amused. But the resonant bass tones declaiming from Shakespeare's *Julius Caesar* raised the hair on Harry's neck, and he shivered. The flexible actor's voice dropped to a rumble.

"We shall not be found wanting. The Manchu Dynasty has been overthrown by revolution. We shall not procrastinate to test our barque. We shall embark upon the flood-tide and sail to splendid triumph. We know, as the Bard hymned of those who miss that tide: 'Omitted, all the voyage of their life is bound in shallows and in miseries.'"

The small company assembled in the library of The Castle was as much bemused by the speaker himself as by his heroic sentiments. He delivered the rolling phrases with immense gusto and dramatic timing—in a cockney accent marked by the guttural sibilants and tortured diphthongs of a music-hall Jew.

"But, General Cohen," Mary objected. "Shakespeare also wrote: 'There's a divinity that shapes our ends, rough-hew them how we will.' Don't you fear overconfidence?"

"No, Madam, no, a thousand times no," the extraordinary voice replied. "The poet himself further said: 'Men at some time are masters of their fates: The fault, dear Brutus, is not in our stars, but in ourselves, that we are underlings.'"

The General's appearance was as extraordinary as his manner. His broad shoulders strained the seams of his green-tweed jacket, and his heavily muscled thighs rippled beneath his blue-flannel drain-pipe trousers. A battered prizefighter's face, its nose flattened and its ruddy cheeks thickened, rose from the red-and-white

287

cowboy's bandanna knotted around his columnar throat, and his domed skull was covered with black curls. When he leaned back, his jacket opened to reveal two Colt .44-caliber revolvers in tooled-leather holsters.

"I see why you're called Two-Gun Cohen," Sir Jonathan observed dryly. "But why do you serve Dr. Sun Yat-sen?"

"Yes, General," Charles Sekloong added. "You're not the most likely fighter for the Chinese revolution."

"At your service, Madam, Sir Jonathan, Gentlemen." The massive head bowed, inviting them to partake of his vision. "And always at the service of His Excellency Dr. Sun Yat-sen, soon the first president of the Republic of China."

"It does seem odd," Mary probed. "How did you, of all people, come together with Dr. Sun?"

"Morris Abraham Cohen, once sergeant major in the Royal Marines, sometime interpreter of Cantonese to the law courts of Alberta, and now brevet lieutenant general in the Army of the Republic of China. That's my tale, 'bounded in a nutshell,' as it were."

The exuberant personality momentarily dimmed even Sir Jonathan's steely glitter. The newly commissioned General quaffed a half-pint of beer from a silver tankard before resuming. As he himself acknowledged, Morris Abraham Cohen swam in the attention of his audience with "as much unassuming joy as ever Leviathan tossed his streaming bulk through the high and salty waves."

"Gratitude, Madam, gratitude has brought me here. As the deathless Bard declared, 'I hate ingratitude more in a man than lying, vainness, babbling, drunkenness.' His Excellency Dr. Sun Yat-sen found me in Canada while seeking funds from his compatriots to liberate their Motherland from the Manchu yoke. I was employing my slight knowledge of Cantonese to assist unfortunate Chinese caught in the toils of the law. Dr. Sun made me his bodyguard. Now he's made me a general in the army he'll build to defend the new Republic of China. He owns my eternal gratitude—and you will not find *him* ungrateful."

The four Sekloongs heard him out. When he cared to exercise it, Sir Jonathan actually possessed the remarkable patience foreign folk wisdom attributed to his Chinese ancestors—as well as his Irish forebears' love of a good tale and a bravura character. Mary and Charles were intrigued by the young Jew, who was like an irresistible force of nature. Harry's spirit was exalted by the outsider's devotion to the cause he had himself served for years.

"Gratitude, Madam and Gentlemen," the adventurer resumed, "and a certain wholesome desire for revenge. Retribution, if you will. The Chinese people have suffered under foreigners' oppression at home and abroad. The Hebrews, my own people, have also suffered much —and someday we too shall reclaim our homeland. Meanwhile I serve justice."

"Justice, General Cohen?" Mary asked.

"Justice, Madam, hard justice for the evil-doers of this sorrowful world. I have seen much injustice, having had much to do with the coolies who built the great railroads that bind the American continent with bands of shining steel. Some came of their own will, but many others were grievously coerced. Their suffering was inhuman. You may recall the infamous Dutch ship *Banca*. She lay off Macao for a month at the height of the equatorial summer with three hundred and fifty coolies under hatches, while her owners haggled with the shipwrights over costs of repairs. The two hundred or so coolies who survived disease one day burst out of confinement. The crewmen barricaded themselves on the quarter-deck and laid down a veritable hail of lead. Fire broke out, swiftly reaching the magazine. The explosion killed all but eighty coolies."

Sir Jonathan remained silent. He saw no reason to confide to their flamboyant visitor that he himself had been involved in the coolie trade as a young man—or that he had subsequently fought to suppress the traffic in indentured workmen, which differed from the old African slave trade primarily in the presumed consent of its human merchandise.

"I don't see the connection between the coolie traffic and the revolution." Charles was genuinely puzzled.

"Perhaps I can best explain in the words of another. I have here Ah Choong's account to an Alberta court when he was had up for threatening his foreman with a cleaver."

Cohen extracted a much folded slip of onion-skin paper from his wallet and smoothed it on his knee with spatulate fingers.

I was a 20-year-old native of Sunning [he read] when I came to Macao to seek employment in the year 1890. A cousin lodged me in a foreigner's house. I never knew his name. Two days later, the foreigner took me to a coolie barracoon, where many men waited for ships all packed together as we cram market chickens into wicker-baskets. I was brought before a Portuguese officer in a green-and-gold uniform, and his interpreter told me I must go to Peru to work for four dollars a month. If I refused, I would be sent to a chain-gang for six years and then to the dungeons.

Unwilling, I put my mark to a paper covered with Chinese and European printing. I could read neither. A seal was affixed—and I was given eight silver dollars, two suits of clothes, a padded jacket, and a pair of cloth shoes. With others, I was then marched to a ship manned by foreigners. We lay on the bare boards without even a grass mat. After we sailed, I was very sick. We had neither water nor fresh air, for the hatches were sealed tight.

After two hours I smelled fire, and smoke poured into the hold. We all cried out in fear, and an old man said we would all die. When the hatches were removed, we all rushed for the ladder. Many fell to their deaths. My own feet slipped, but two young coolies pulled me to the deck. Half-suffocated by the terrible struggle, I saw that the ship was wrapped in flames. An instant later, the masts fell.

I found myself in the sea—I know not how. A round spar floated by, and I seized it though it was half aflame, for I could not swim well. After some hours, the spar bore me to a small island, and I felt I was saved.

Three others had drifted to the same islet. We all gave thanks to the gods for our salvation when we spied a small foreign boat rowed by Europeans. But they ignored our cries and swiftly drew away.

My companions despaired at this final sign of Heaven's displeasure. One old man lay down to die. Before pressing his lips together and swearing he would speak no more till he stood before the Magistrates of Heaven, he told us he had voluntarily taken passage to Peru to seek out his eldest son who had been indentured twelve years earlier. The son had married a native woman, who gave him six children. The old man had only learned of his son's fate and his grandchildren's existence two months earlier when a Chinese trader brought him a tattered letter written by a public scribe.

We others thought the old man's despair foolish. The islet, though small, was firm rock—and we saw the sails of fishing junks in the distance. But the incoming tide swept over the rock, washing away my companions in misfortune one by one. I clung to the last projecting pinnacle till the tide swept me into the waves.

Then a miracle occurred. A chicken-coop from the sunken ship drifted by, its feathered denizens drowned and limp, and I clambered onto the tossing platform. After several hours, a fishing junk from Hong Kong trailed its nets alongside. Since I still had the eight silver dollars tied to my waistband, the fisherman gave me passage to Hong Kong. Five other unfortunates clinging to bits of the wreck the fishermen abandoned, for they had no silver.

Sir Jonathan gave his attention to lighting a fresh panatella. Charles yawned behind his brandy snifter, his thoughts drifting to the letter he was drafting to the Rothschilds regarding railway financing. Himself totally committed to Dr. Sun Yat-sen, Harry felt automatic indignation.

Mary was at once puzzled and irritated by the rambling account. The Europeans' actions were reprehensible, but they were rapacious adventurers far removed from normal moral restraints. The behavior of the Chinese, she felt, was characteristic of a race overwhelmingly concerned with profit. His own cousin had sold Ah Choong into serfdom, while the Chinese fishermen had rescued only those castaways who could pay.

291

But she no longer allowed herself to grieve over the cruelty Chinese practiced against other Chinese.

"A sad tale, General Cohen," she said. "Perhaps my wits are muddled by your eloquence, but I can't see what it proves."

"Consider it a moral homily, my dear Madam," the burly bodyguard replied equably. "This same Ah Choong was subsequently employed by your esteemed father-in-law and, later, given passage to Canada as a reward for faithful service. The first time I heard the name Sekloong was from Ah Choong's lips."

"I think I remember the fellow," Sir Jonathan said, embarrassed.

"He remembers you, Sir, with great affection and gratitude. But the lady asks how his tale relates to our present endeavors. The Manchus, whom we have over-thrown, connived in the coolie traffic—despite their public disapproval. The Europeans exploited the poor folk abominably—aided by corrupt officials who should have been their suffering compatriots' natural protec-tors. And avaricious profit-seekers first imperiled Ah Choong and later succored him, while condemning his penniless fellow castaways to death."

"Some capitalists contributed heavily to the revolu-tion," Charles objected. "I still don't see how Ah Choong's tale ties in with the revolution."

"We shall destroy all such evils!" Cohen's bass voice boomed, and his fist struck his knee in violent indignation. "Dr. Sun has not striven these long years merely to change one set of *Imperial* rascals for another set of *republican* rascals. His program is comprehen-sive. He will drive the money-changers from the tem-ple, while honoring the upright merchant and the far-seeing entrepreneur. He will make China a great, proud, and noble nation."

"I'm reassured, General!" Sir Jonathan did not con-ceal his patrician distaste of the adventurer's bombast. "But you haven't told us why you're so eager to help China?"

"Because, Sir, I detest injustice—and I love great en-terprises. Because the lost tribes of Israel made their way to China millennia ago. If one ancient people is re-deemed from injustice, then another ancient people, my own people, shall also find redemption!"

The young Jew's declaration of faith rang in the si-lence. Charles retreated into his duties as the eldest son of the house. He refilled Cohen's tankard, replenished his wife's brandy-and-soda, and splashed dollops of brandy into balloon glasses for his father, his brother, and himself.

Charles, Mary reflected, was outwardly becoming more British every day, for he was acutely uncomforta-ble with any display of emotion. Neither the wild Irish strain in the Sekloong blood nor the Chinese delight in histrionics affected his public demeanor. His father was different. Fires burned behind Sir Jonathan's courtly façade, occasionally flaring high. Though both were passionate men who showed the world calm faces, nei-ther Sir Jonathan nor Charles was imaginative, not as poets or revolutionaries are imaginative. Their over-leaping ambitions were guided by cold-blooded calcula-tion.

Mary feared that their cool shrewdness was frosting her own heart, though she was repelled by their quasi-religious devotion to the House of Sekloong. Professing Roman Catholics, they nonetheless paid homage to the clan like high-priests serving a jealous, demanding deity. Her revulsion had increased with the successive years. She sometimes despaired, feeling herself no longer an individual human being, nor even a wife and mother, but a reluctant high-priestess—or, perhaps, a sanctified temple prostitute—of the Sekloongs' cult of Mammon.

Only Harry was gradually renouncing that cult and stealthily detaching himself from the clan. The Celtic and the Sinitic passions ran strong in him, though cam-ouflaged by his habitual irreverence. At thirty-two, he had finally marked out his personal goal. His purpose had crystallized during the stormy night when he at-tacked the opium-smuggling steamer *Taishan*. The ab-stract, bloodless intrigues of the counting-house did not stir him as had staking his life against the waves and bullets. He was intoxicated by the cause Two-Gun Cohen so grandiloquently described: the salvation of a nation and a people—his own nation and his own people—that had been exploited and oppressed for centuries. Mary knew in sorrow that Harry was all but lost to herself as well. He was giving himself wholly to Dr. Sun Yat-sen's revolution, which had just overthrown a 267-year-old dynasty and shattered a millennia-old civilization.

Ah Sam's knock broke both her unhappy reverie and the awkward silence that lay upon the four men. When the old pirate swung open the teak doors, she saw that he had cut off his queue, the long plait his countrymen had worn since the Manchu conquest. His act was portentous. When that staunch conservative, Ah Sam, cast off the symbol of loyalty to the Great Pure Dynasty, the republicans had all but won the hearts of the Chinese people.

Ah Sam showed an oddly matched pair into the library. A stocky Chinese with grizzled mustaches in a square peasant's face entered first. He wore a broadcloth frock-coat, and a heavy gold chain hung across his double-breasted waistcoat. Mary recognized him as much from his commanding air as from his photographs: Sun Yat-sen, Doctor of Medicine of the University of Hong Kong, for decades the Manchus' most dangerous enemy and, if General Cohen judged right, soon to be the first president of the Republic of China.

The revolutionary's companion was his antithesis, a high-bred patrician. The second man's figure was slender, and he stooped as if he spent his days hunched over old manuscripts. Dr. Sun's tread was heavy, and his features were blunt. His companion's step was light, and his narrow face was dominated by a high-arched nose. His waistcoat was embroidered with flamboyant yellow roses, and his deepset brown eyes shone with intelligence. When he spoke, his fine white hands gesticulated like butterflies hovering in a subtle aerial ballet.

Though Judah Haleevie lived in Shanghai, Mary had met him several times. A valued business associate of Sir Jonathan, like the Sekloongs he straddled two

294

worlds. With a few other Iraqi-Jewish families like the Sassoons and the Kadoories, the Haleevies had built the modern metropolis of Shanghai from a somnolent fishing port on the muddy delta of the Yangtze River. The Haleevies could command large sums from the Rothschilds, the Salomons, and the Warburgs. The Middle Eastern Jews were bound to their German co-religionists not primarily by their faith or by common interests, but by mutual dedication to building a Jewish homeland in Palestine.

Judah was known for his philanthropies, though he did not seek personal renown. The man they called the Hebrew Mandarin was an anomaly among the harddrinking, anti-intellectual China Coast merchants—not only because of his biblical scholarship, but because of his curious family life. Blessed with seven sons and one daughter, Sarah, who was the pampered youngest of his brood at the age of six, he had adopted seven Eurasian orphans, all girls.

"They'll make fine brides for my boys," he would explain defensively. But Sir Jonathan observed, with a touch of envy, that Judah Haleevie was indulging the patriarchal propensity that was as pronounced among the Jews as it was among the Chinese.

"Well, Sir Jonathan, my old friend, I think we can all be happy tonight," Dr. Sun said exuberantly in English. The American intonation overlaying his sibilant Hong Kong accent recalled his high-school education in Hawaii.

"Let us hope so, Dr. Sun," Sir Jonathan replied ceremoniously. "May I present my son Charles and his wife Mary? My useless younger son, Harry, you know."

"Delighted, Madam, Mr. Sekloong. Your brother's told me a lot about you."

Judah Haleevie's formal manner recalled his distant Spanish ancestors. His heavy-lidded eyes lingered on Mary's open features, appraising her red-gold hair and her figure in a yellow-silk, high-waisted dress. He nodded to Two-Gun Cohen like an old acquaintance. Actually, they had met for the first time the previous day, and the scholarly Jewish merchant-prince had little in common with the bombastic Jewish adventurer.

"As you know, Jonathan," Haleevie observed quietly, "Dr. Sun shares your passion for railroads. We've been drawing long lines on the wall map."

"Your railroads . . . *our* railroads . . . will unite China." Dr. Sun Yat-sen spoke with the practiced orator's authority. "From Manchuria to Tibet we will spin a web of steel across the nation. China will no longer be a sheet of sand, but a granite pillar bound by steel hoops. China will also be a living organism, ever changing, ever moving. The railroads will be the arteries through which the nourishing life-blood flows. Harry's fleets of motor-lorries will be the capillaries feeding every cell, no matter how remote!"

"*Your* railroads, Dr. Sun," Judah Haleevie interposed, "not *our* railroads."

"Well," the statesman laughed, "ours and yours—in the beginning at least. We'll need much financial help, though the railroads must belong to the Chinese people."

"Agreed," Sir Jonathan nodded. "And a fair return for the financiers."

"A fair return," Sun Yat-sen answered. "Not exorbitant."

"If you don't feed the goose," Sir Jonathan said tartly, "it won't lay eggs—golden or not."

"A remarkable coincidence," Judah Haleevie interposed diplomatically. "Railroads loom large in your plans, but resistance to railroads brought you to power."

"Not coincidence, my friend," Dr. Sun replied, "but providence. The entire Yangtze Valley from Szechwan to Shanghai rose in revolt because the railroad consortium assembled by the Manchus meant unbreakable foreign domination for many years—perhaps indefinitely. *Our* railroads will be different. Financing from abroad, but Chinese control."

"Were you," Mary asked, "surprised by your quick triumph?"

"No, not in a larger sense," Sun answered. "We

knew the Manchus must fall. We were surprised by the minor incidents that toppled them. Scattered anti-railroad riots in the southwest and an explosion—a very small explosion—in Wuhan. The revolutionaries in Wuhan exercised more enthusiasm than skill in handling dynamite. When the Manchus ordered their army to suppress them, the troops revolted. So many officers were listed on our secret rolls. If the Manchus had found the lists, they would have been slaughtered."

"And, then," Mary persisted, "everything went as you wished?"

"I was sorry when the Manchu garrisons were slaughtered. They weren't soldiers any longer, just fat, pampered pensioners. Then the whole structure collapsed. The Ta Ching Chao looked like an immense impregnable fortress. For years, we had hurled ourselves at the towering walls, sometimes gaining a foothold. We were always thrown back, though we knew the structure was rotten with internal decay. Then, suddenly, that small accidental explosion—and the fortress tumbled like a house of cards."

"But, Sir," Harry interjected, "if it weren't for Viceroy Yüan Shih-kai, you wouldn't be going to Nanking to preside over the National Assembly."

"True, Harry," Sun said. "We couldn't be sure the Great Viceroy would betray the Dynasty to the revolution in 1911 just because he betrayed the reformers to the Dynasty in 1898. His masterly inactivity was an unexpected, decisive boon—and he'll demand his reward. Unfortunately, we must still temporize with the self-serving vestiges of the old regime like Yüan Shih-kai. But their time will be short. We'll build a new China from the best of East and West—after purging the corruption of two thousand years of Confucian government. Our task is great, but we will execute it as swiftly as the Ching Dynasty collapsed."

Mary suppressed a smile and retired into her own thoughts. She was quite certain that Dr. Sun Yat-sen could not attain a tithe of his goals even in a century. His promise to remake the inert mass of China "as swiftly as the Ching Dynasty collapsed" was not merely visionary. It was abysmal nonsense. The essential character of the Chinese would prevent any sweeping transformation. Hong Kong itself demonstrated the impossibility of mitigating the ingrained selfishness of the average Chinese or altering his total disregard for all other human beings. Despite their snobbery, their cliques, and their avarice, the British were efficient and selfless by comparison with the Chinese. But they had failed to affect the fundamental nature of the Chinese.

"Hong Kong's an ideal sociological laboratory." Hilary Metcalfe had confided his near despair during the plague year, 1909, only months before his death under the feet of a Chinese mob. "Small and isolated, if imperfectly controlled. British behavior's been foul, but we're selfless angels compared to the Chinese ruling class. Our efforts to create a new society blending East and West were, at least, well meant. But the upshot? Look around you. The Chinese transformed us—it was quite a feat. The Chinese further corrupted men you'd think couldn't be more corrupt, men born with no more moral sense than that *cheechuk*."

He gestured toward the ceiling, where a two-inch-long, translucent lizard darted its tongue at a black ant.

"The only bond was avarice. A number of Europeans and a few Chinese tried to communicate across the immense barrier of divergent cultures. Even language we couldn't teach. Hong Kong English—it's not a language, but a damned ineffective jargon. Only thing worse is Hong Kong Chinese as spoken by British Colonial Officers. Yet some people think the Chinese can transform themselves. Rubbish!"

At the time, Mary was shocked by his vehemence. She had not yet fully comprehended the vulpine character of the race, the overwhelming rapacity that impelled one Chinese to prey upon his compatriots, or the miasmic superstition that mired progress. Her subsequent experiences had supported Hilary Metcalfe's dire judgment. Since a well-ordered society was impossible in Hong Kong, it was inconceivable in China. The deluded idealist Dr. Sun could not see his own people clearly. He was blinded by his own enthusiasm, by his protracted absences from China, and by his foreign education.

Sir Jonathan believed in China's future, almost in defiance of his own cool assessment of men and events. It was his one blind spot, for his judgment of China was shaped far more by his impulsive heart than by his calculating brain. But his personal investments were dispersed in Europe and America, as well as Asia. That disposition demonstrated the skepticism regarding the future of the China he loved he would not express in words.

The autocrat had, moreover, not objected to Mary's proposal that her eldest child, his grandson Jonathan, be educated in England. At his insistence, all the children were tutored in Mandarin and calligraphy by an elderly scholar, a distant cousin whom they affectionately called Uncle Kwok when they were not teasing him. But Sir Jonathan's fervent Chinese patriotism had yielded to his hard practical sense when Charles and Mary consulted him regarding young Jonathan's education.

"He's old enough—nine, almost too old to begin the trials of an English boarding-school. But it's necessary, and he can spruce up his Chinese later. Of course, it must be a Catholic school."

"No question about that, Father," Charles replied.

Mary was almost as startled by Sir Jonathan's insistence upon a Catholic school as by his easy concession of the good Chinese education Jonnie could not, in any event, obtain in Hong Kong. Would Sir Jonathan, she wondered, have been quite so compliant if the entire Chinese educational system were not in flux and an English education were not essential to success in commerce? She herself still shrank from delivering her firstborn into the hands of black-clad priests. After a decade of marriage to a Catholic, she was still haunted by the irrational fear of the Church of Rome inculcated by her Nonconformist upbringing.

"And, Father," Charles added, "it must be the Jesuits. They did well by you and me."

The decision that had wrung Mary's heart for months

299

was taken in minutes. She had agonized over parting with Jonathan, though she knew she must. However satisfactory for most Hong Kong Chinese and Eurasians St. Stephen's College might be, the school would not do for a Sekloong of the third generation—and certainly not for *her* son. If Jonathan were not to be a typical Hong Kong man, a deracinated dweller in an isolated cultural-village, he must go to England to school.

Mary's vivid memories drew an invisible curtain between herself and the five men's discussion of Dr. Sun's grandiose plans. After an absence of eleven years returning to England to put Jonnie into school had been a memorable—and unexpectedly decisive—experience.

The splendid spring and summer of 1911, the first full year of the reign of George V, was historically unique. Even at the moment, intelligent men and women were consciously aware that they were living through an epoch-making change in Britain's life. The fiery Welshman David Lloyd George was demolishing the structure of privilege that had been England. A cowed House of Lords was stripped of its power of veto, and the golden days of the landed gentry were numbered; the income tax, blocked for so long, was enacted, and the era of immense private fortunes began to close; new laws granted trade unions the right to organize, and a new class grasped at the levers of power. Those events were so portentous that many informed contemporaries clearly saw the matrix of their lives altering.

However, only a few Britons foresaw the great catastrophe that impended, the first total war to convulse Europe, the first great war since the Battle of Waterloo had shattered Napoleon's cosmic visions in 1815. A century of buoyant optimism amid bounding progress was to close on the blood-sodden fields of Flanders only three years later. But only sour pessimists expressed their forebodings that their civilization was hurtling toward destruction. They were derided by the solid citizenry. The Royal Navy was supreme, and the pound sterling was lithically solid. Gay holiday crowds, the men flaunting boater-hats, the women trailing kimono-like sleeves, whistled "Lily of Laguna" on the promenades at Brighton, and hemlines crept upward to reveal trim ankles in sheer silk stockings. Popular optimism was as glorious as the unbroken sunshine.

For the second—and last—time in her adult life, Mary Sekloong was oblivious to great public affairs. After flurried preparations that, Charles grumbled, "wouldn't disgrace the embarkation of an expeditionary force," she had sailed for Southampton in March 1911 on the Peninsular and Oriental liner *Monarch*. The thirty-one-day voyage contrasted sharply with her fifty days aboard *Orion* in 1900. She was attended only by her personal amah, who looked after herself and Jonnie. But the Sekloong name commanded assiduous service from both Chinese stewards and British officers; she traveled like a crown-princess.

After her regal journey, England was at first a disappointment. Though she soon entered an enchanted realm she had never known, the unseen magician who ordered her affairs was capricious. Bleak boredom alternated with moments of delight at the half-forgotten land that had bred her. At her brother Thomas's new house near Hampstead Heath, Bandmaster John Philip Osgood, finally forgiving her marriage, doted on his daughter and the grandson he was seeing for the first time. Her father was as gruffly matter-of-fact at fifty-seven as he had been at forty-seven. But his eyes glowed when, thinking himself unobserved, he watched Jonnie frolic with his young cousins. Her brother, transformed into an ambitious solicitor, was embarrassingly attentive. His admonitory cable inveighing against her marriage was deeply regretted—or so he would have had her believe, for the passing of a decade had made the Sekloongs' wealth an acknowledged force in the City of London, the financial capital of the world. Thomas told her baldly that his brother-in-law required the services of a lawyer who was a member of the family and was, therefore, both totally trustworthy and wholly committed to the Sekloongs' interest. Mary politely parried his unsubtle advances.

She was inundated with invitations after she took a small country house, which was staffed by only three servants, at Esher in Surrey, twenty-five miles south of London. She had left England a nobody. She returned the wife of the heir-presumptive to an expanding commercial empire and herself, *they* whispered—the omniscient, omnipresent, anonymous *they*—a major power in that empire in her own right. They beseeched her presence at dinners, theater parties, receptions, and balls. Only in July did she have a moment free to examine herself and her England. With the London season at its end, the old Edwardians who had become the new Georgians retreated to Scotland or Ireland for the shooting; traveled to France, Germany, or Switzerland to revive their overburdened livers at spas; or embarked in their yachts on long Mediterranean cruises. Their era was closing fast, but, blissfully unaware, the overprivileged sported in its golden twilight.

Equally unaware that the unchallenged supremacy of the English ruling class was ending, Mary instinctively put a certain distance between herself and that ruling class, which courted her as diligently as it had once negligently ignored her. Instead, she gravitated to the Haleevies' cousins, the Sassoons, who, established in ducal splendor in Sussex, were pressingly hospitable. Although they had, as the young Baronet Sir Siegfried said, "become more English than the real English," the Sassoons no more wished to forget their ties to the Far East than they wished to alter the proud, Semitic arch of their noses. Mary realized that she felt more comfortable with the Sassoons than with her own family because they shared with her not only knowledge of the Asia she had briefly fled, but the attitudes of that other world. She hesitantly recognized another tie: The Sassoons possessed the great wealth to whose pleasures she had become habituated.

At a house party at Guilford she met again Lord Peter Comyn French. Still unmarried, he was almost uncannily unchanged from the languid young captain she had known eleven years earlier. To her surprise, he greeted her as an intimate and paid court to her like a cavalier. She discovered that Peter, who shared her experience of both Hong Kong and England, was almost as satisfactory a confidant as Harry Sekloong had been before he was seduced by the twin lures of danger and politics. Mary was, quite consciously, rediscovering England. She candidly acknowledged to herself that she was pleased to make that voyage of discovery in the company of a scion of the aristocracy. His acute comments revealed an England she had never really known.

Lord Peter wore the crown and star of a lieutenant colonel when he occasionally took himself off to his military duties, but seemed to possess almost unlimited leisure. Commanding the duty battalion of the Coldstream Guards, he spent more time at her house in Esher than in London. His presence was, Mary assured herself, quite proper. Besides a puritanical Irish butler and her own suspicious amah, they were always chaperoned by other house-guests, usually two respectable married couples. Peter was unassertive, yet constantly attentive and remarkably sensitive to her moods. She could lower her defenses and enjoy their innocent flirtation. Under his guidance she sought new roots that might sustain her in exile in Hong Kong or, perhaps, nurture her should she return to England, an expedient she still considered.

Jonnie accepted his new uncle unreservedly. Peter displayed inexhaustible patience with the nine-year-old and bestowed upon him an equally inexhaustible largesse of gold sovereigns or small gifts like the pearl-handled penknife that made Mary shiver with apprehension whenever she saw its blade glittering in Jonnie's small hand. By the end of the summer, it seemed only natural that Lord Peter French should help her move to the Ritz, where they left the little amah to watch over Mary's belongings like a vengeful Buddha. As a matter of course, Peter entrained with them at Euston Station for Preston in Lancashire to enter Jonnie in St. Mary's Hall, the preparatory institution for Stonyhurst College, Britain's premier Jesuit public school.

Jonnie darted from side to side of the open landau in

excitement when the matched grays trotted through the white gates and between the two shining man-made lakes to the stone castle. Stonyhurst was, the Jesuits noted, the largest building in England, the refuge where Oliver Cromwell had spent the night before the decisive battle of Preston in August 1648.

"Old Noll must spin in his grave every time he remembers that Stonyhurst's a citadel of the Scarlet Woman of Rome," Peter laughed.

The landau turned sharply to the left before the stone lions that guarded the entrance to the main hall, and they were borne through leafy groves to the smaller gray bulk of St. Mary's Hall. Small boys wearing short trousers and black blazers scampered about the lawns, greeting each other with shrill cries. Some newcomers hung back, but Jonnie was out of the landau before it stopped. While Mary chatted with the headmaster, finding his black cassock with the flying Jesuit sleeves they called wings oddly reassuring, Jonnie disappeared into the throng. He had already left her, apparently unperturbed by the prospect of a separation that would endure for at least two years. Only after she had seen the room he was to share with six other small boys did he reveal his awareness of her feelings.

"Don't cry, Mother," he urged. "I'll be fine, though I'll miss you and Uncle Harry and Grandpa—and Daddy, of course."

She did cry when the landau bore them through the white iron gates. Peter's arm about her shoulders comforted her, though, she told herself, any masculine arm would have done as well. Still, it seemed only natural, almost foreordained that he should take her hand on the red-carpeted, marble staircase at the Ritz. She was surprised chiefly by his gentleness when he closed the door behind them and took her in his arms. He led her to the broad bed as if that, too, were the most natural thing in the world.

Theirs was a quiet passion, generating more of warmth than flame. They experienced no wild ecstasies during the five days before her ship sailed, but knew comforting gratitude for mutual needs fulfilled. Though he hinted that she could if she wished remain with him, presumably in marriage, she instinctively turned the talk before he could make a formal declaration. Peter seemed to understand and pressed her no farther, while Mary only half-understood that she had taken another critical decision.

When the interlude ended, not only an idyll, but an era closed for Mary. When she stood on the boat-deck of the *Olympus* at Southhampton Dock, her eyes were wet, but she shed no tears. The foreshortened figure of Peter French waved from the pier, and her handkerchief fluttered in grave dismissal.

Mary had never felt quite so alone in all her life. She would never again see Jonnie, her first-born, as a vulnerable, engaging small boy. Harry was already lost to her, seduced by Dr. Sun Yat-sen's revolution. Peter she had rediscovered only to leave him. She was eager to hug the girls, Guinevere and Charlotte, and the younger boys, Thomas and James. Charles and Sir Jonathan were fixed if flickering beacons in a Hong Kong she despised, yet yearned to see again. Above all, she knew eerily, she would never again live in England.

"Mary!" Charles's voice broke into her reverie. "Mary, our guests are leaving."

She shook herself into full awareness. The men were filing out the double-doors, Dr. Sun Yat-sen and Judah Haleevie followed by Sir Jonathan, Harry, and Two-Gun Cohen.

"The very best of luck to you, Sir," Charles called to Sun Yat-sen.

Sir Jonathan muttered, barely audible: "He'll need it. We all will."

June 2, 1914

THE sun rising over the jade-green South China Sea lit the outlying Chinese-held islets and kindled those British outposts, the Ninepins, Waglan, and Poktoi Islands.

Its rays burnished the pyramidal Peak with gold. Half-light suffused The Peak's shadowed northwestern slopes, and the City of Victoria lay in a pool of darkness. Across the bay, where heavy-lidded boatmen steered their purple-sailed lighters, the Kowloon Peninsula was a shining silver spearhead. The jagged hill ranges that guarded the troubled Chinese nation slept like gray dragons beneath the roseate sky.

Sir Jonathan Sekloong slipped from his high ebony bed and padded barefoot to his wife's adjoining bedroom. Satisfied that Lady Lucinda's smooth face, supported by a blue porcelain pillow, bore its accustomed half-smile of unconscious contentment, he gently closed the door before kneeling on the embroidered rail of the carved-walnut prie-dieu that had once served Isabella of Spain to recite two Pater Nosters. After five minutes of silent prayer, he intoned two Ave Marias and was ready to attend to the day's business.

An hour later, at 7:06 A.M. on June 2, 1914, he stepped from the green-painted Peak Tram and noted with complacent approval that his sedan chair was waiting. Four arrogant coolies in his blue-and-gold livery ignored the throng that flowed around the chair like the sea split by a rock. Royal-blue enamel plaques on their breasts flaunted the golden Sekloong winged dragon, and the panels of the sedan chair displayed the same motif. When their master was seated, the bearers swung uphill. They trotted along Upper Albert Road, where rigid sentries in scarlet coats guarded Government House, before plunging into the Chinese-inhabited labyrinth that clung to the steep slopes above Queen's Road. Halfway down a narrow lane, they stopped before a red-painted door.

The door opened, and an elderly manservant clasped his hands in obeisance. Filigree-iron balconies looked down on a miniature courtyard paved with russet tiles, where mauve-and-red jardinieres flaunting multicolored zinnias alternated with blue-and-white jardinieres holding miniature orange trees.

A slender young woman knelt in the courtyard, her red-and-green robe spread like a circular fan around her. Gold-embroidered sandals peeped from the hem of her robe, and her glossy black hair was caught in a chignon. Her wide-set eyes shone with pleasure above the high cheekbones of her camellia-soft face. Three small girls kneeled behind her, each a miniature replica of her mother. She was twenty-three, her daughters seven, five, and three years old.

"Pao-chu, chin-ai-ti, shen-ma tou hau ma?" Sir Jonathan spoke in the soft northern dialect. "Precious Pearl, my dear. All is well with you?"

"Yes, My Lord, we thank you. All is well."

The solemnity of the three diminutive ladies dissolved into giggles. The Pearl Concubine looked at them reproachfully, but surrendered to their gaiety. Her own laughter was silver wind-bells tinkling on a pagoda's unswept eaves.

"They are overjoyed to see their father, though they forgot the proper formulas of respect," she said. "And I tried so hard to get it right this time."

Sir Jonathan happily cast off the formality the Rites enjoin on the master when he visits his concubine and her family. He raised Precious Pearl to her feet and embraced her, gently rubbing his cheek against hers. Released from their mother's silken discipline, the girls swarmed upon his tall figure. Their arms clasped him, and inquisitive hands explored the pockets of his frock-coat. Sir Jonathan kissed his daughters and murmured into three small, warm ears.

"I must leave you now, Pearl." He pressed into her hands a red envelope crackling with new banknotes. "But I shall return for a longer stay one evening this week."

Her face shadowed by disappointment, the Pearl Concubine bowed submissively and murmured the formula of farewell. Her daughters' treble tones gravely echoed her words.

Sir Jonathan smiled in contentment as he opened the small iron gate half-hidden in the corner of the courtyard. Precious Pearl and their daughters were possessions that entailed little responsibility. Since they were but females and only tangentially part of the clan, he need not train them either to bear the burdens or to enhance the glory of the House of Sekloong. At most, he might gain marginal advantages through his daughters' marriages. Otherwise, they were to him a source of pure pleasure blessedly detached from his ambitions.

His private pleasure was not a secret pleasure. Lady Lucinda never spoke of the Pearl Concubine—no more than she spoke of the Jade Concubine whom Sir Jonathan had pensioned off. But she sent Pearl's daughters lavish presents at Christmas and Chinese New Year, and on every other occasion when her own children and grandchildren received gifts. That generosity was her duty and her privilege as the First Wife. Both the Chinese and the British communities knew of Pearl's secluded existence. Hong Kong law legitimized both polygamy and concubinage as respected Chinese traditions. Even Sir Jonathan's confessor, a tolerant Jesuit, did not press him, but observed: "A blind eye's essential to a priest, essential as his theology."

Sir Jonathan was less easy about his next call, though it was as respectably customary in his milieu. Father Collins laughed openly at the "black, heathen superstition," and he felt the bite in the gentle Irish laughter.

Musing on his own inconsistency, he climbed rickety wooden stairs hung on a ramshackle brick building. When a pock-marked youth opened the weathered door, Sir Jonathan blinked at the abrupt transition from the morning sunlight to the somber chamber dimly lit by revolving oiled-paper lanterns on which green dragons endlessly chased their own tails. A gilt Buddha brooded on a low altar-table, half-obscured by the smoke of incense sticks and votive candles in vermillion-and-gold holders. Behind an ebony table inlaid with mother-of-pearl sat an emaciated figure wearing a Taoist monk's gray robes. His eyes were concealed by smoked glasses.

"Good morning, Lord!" he murmured in the dialect of Sekloong Town.

"Good morning, Seer," Sir Jonathan answered in the same dialect. "Is all well with the Silver Seventh Brother? And how are the auguries?"

"All is well," the blind man answered, "thanks to Your Lordship's benevolence. As for the auguries, I fear they are mixed. They require further explication."

"Then get on with it!" Sir Jonathan snapped colloquially. "Don't grow moss on your buttocks."

The name "Silver Seventh Brother" recalled the Taoist mythology's Eight Immortals of the Hills and enhanced a profitable trade in prophecies and counsel. The soothsayer's clients—hard-headed businessmen, as well as staid matrons and tremulous virgins—were further impressed by his blindness. They believed that his inability to see illusory external shapes facilitated his comprehension of the invisible inner workings of fate.

Though Silver Seventh's clients were many, he was above all the creature of Sir Jonathan, who had discovered him in Sekloong and brought him to Hong Kong. Though he derided the soothsayer's powers, the master of the House of Sekloong consulted the seer whenever he felt himself threatened or planned a new enterprise. Silver Seventh therefore knew more about the affairs of the House than anyone except Sir Jonathan, who could no more distrust the soothsayer than he could distrust those other useful articles—his abacus, his desk, and his writing brush. Like any tool, Silver Seventh lay in the palm of his patron's hand. But that patron periodically reinforced his servant's loyalty by recalling his dependence.

"I don't have all day to waste on your gibberish," Sir Jonathan added irritably.

"I have recast your horoscope with great care, Lord," the unperturbed soothsayer replied. "It will take a while longer to read the full Will of Heaven through the prescribed rites. But I must warn you. Your horoscope warns that you are menaced—and vulnerable."

"That's no great revelation, Seer," the merchant-prince rejoined with contemptuous candor. "Anyone who reads newspapers can guess I must soon quit Derwent, Hayes—or be crushed by my esteemed stepfather, the *taipan* Way-teh-lee."

"I do not rely upon newspapers, Lord," Silver Seventh answered. "I cannot read them—and I do not bother having them read to me."

Sir Jonathan knew the fortune-teller was lying. The pock-marked youth who was Silver Seventh's attendant had learned to sift the news for nuggets his master could transform into gold, fool's gold from the credulous. The blind soothsayer found half the revelations he offered his lesser clients in the dozen-odd Chinese-language "mosquito papers" that retailed scurrilous gossip. But Sir Jonathan disdained to challenge the lie. He was not concerned with the man's character, but with his undeniable occult gifts. Besides, all soothsayers were rascals; it was the nature of the breed.

"I read the future behind its veils, not the newspapers," Silver Seventh insisted. "Today, Lord, your horoscope warns that the foundations of your house are unstable. They will crack if you do not act properly. The dragon now flees the moon across the skies, but must soon turn to struggle against the orb's morbid light."

"That mumbo-jumbo's good enough for women and coolies," Sir Jonathan snapped. "*I* pay you for specifics. Render to me that to which I am entitled."

"As the Lord wishes! I can only tell you that a close member of your esteemed family is threatened personally. More I cannot say until I have read the Trigrams and consulted the sacred Tortoise Shell."

"Please do so, Venerable Sage." Sir Jonathan's sarcasm verged on the savage. "Do so with dispatch."

Silver Seventh bent to his instruments, his lips moving in silent concentration. He let a handful of five-inch-long bamboo-wands fall from a carved-lacquer cylinder onto the table-top. His scurrying hands gathered up the wands and restored them to the cylinder until only three remained. He repeated the procedure eight times before pushing up his dark glasses and rubbing his milky-gray eyes with the backs of his hands.

Sir Jonathan sat tensely impatient and disdainful during the ritual, but did not interrupt. His own lean figure in formal frock-coat and striped trousers was utterly foreign to the contrived Oriental mysteries of Silver Seventh's sanctuary. His silver-gray hair was parted in the European style, and his hazel eyes glinted through the smoke of his panatella, which he had lit, stubbed out irritably, and, most uncharacteristically, relit. However, one immemorial racial gesture, the nervous jiggling of his left knee, revealed his Chinese blood. Whatever else they might be, the Chinese, above all the volatile Cantonese, were not the inscrutable Orientals of Western folk belief.

Sensing his patron's impatience, the soothsayer deliberately prolonged the ritual. Six times, he let three ancient coins drop onto the inlaid table-top from a time-polished tortoise shell and assessed their fall with sensitive fingertips. Frowning in puzzled concentration, he repeated the ritual before finally laying his hands on the table to display inch-long, black-rimmed fingernails.

"I can now be more specific, Lord," he said, "much more specific."

His patron tossed away his half-smoked panatella, careless where it fell. He knew that Silver Seventh learned more from his clients than he told them, for their questions were unavoidably self-revealing. When the hyperrational Western strain in Sir Jonathan's character recoiled from the age-old Chinese superstition, he invariably told himself that he utilized Silver Seventh's talents as an intelligence agent, rather than an initiate of the occult. Though the soothsayer was also useful for flying the kites of rumor, his greatest value was his almost uncanny knowledge of the secrets and the sentiments of the Chinese community.

"Some men still grumble against you, Lord," Silver Seventh continued, "because of the events of the plague year. They are jealous of My Lord's eminence and wealth, favor in the eyes of the bearded English King, *Jaw-jee.* Evil men, especially *one* evil man . . . I see an aged foreigner . . . are exploiting that envy."

"That, you fool, is a revelation?"

"Be patient with your inept servant, Lord. I shall be more specific, but I must speak the hidden truths in the

311

order they have been revealed to me. Otherwise, I could shatter the pattern—and perhaps cause great harm."

"Go on, then."

"The aged foreigner bids his Chinese henchman whip up anger against you. I am not sure—yes, I can see. Strangely, I see a sheaf of wheat."

"You're a pious mountebank. You know well that it's old Wheatley." Laughing, Sir Jonathan pronounced the name in English. "I congratulate you on your command of the foreigners' tongue. But what does he plan this time? What do you hear?"

"I have, Lord, it is true, learned a little English. But I do not understand the symbolism." Silver Seventh bowed his head modestly. "However, Way-teh-lee is angering the Chinese community against you.

"It is evil, his henchmen declare, that the Tung Wah Hospitals now employ three Western-trained doctors. Besides, was it not you and your interfering white daughter-in-law—I honor the Lady wife of your son greatly, but it is they who speak so, you understand, Lord. Is it not so, they ask in whispers, that you two interfered, collaborated with the British, and helped bring the death of the Great Heat upon the poor and helpless Chinese for your own profit? So they speak, Lord."

"And, Venerable Seer, do your auguries tell you precisely how this man plans to injure me? What can you tell me beyond empty warnings?"

"The Yin principle of the Orient, the wisdom of your honored forefathers of the house of Kwok, is in conflict with the Yang principle of the Occident, which is also present in your nature. You are torn between the passive, patient Eastern way and the thrusting, aggressive Western way."

"That, too, is no revelation, Master of the Occult!"

"Your enemies intend to exploit that conflict in your own nature. They will harry you—until, in disgust and anger, you impetuously take one disastrous path or the other. You may retire, they calculate, retire to a life of scholarship, withdrawing from the world of strife as

312

have so many great men of China. Alternately, you may meet them head-on like a hotheaded Westerner—and destroy yourself by your own vigorous anger."

"That makes sense," Sir Jonathan mused aloud. "Old Dick can't force me out as comprador. But the wily devil wants the stage clear for his precious son Iain. So he goads me . . . tries to provoke me by withholding my mother's legacy he says he's just found. The few bits of jewelry and the battered old Buddhist rosary only I would treasure."

"And, may I venture to remind you, Lord, the signs say that he is stirring up the Chinese community."

"Yes! If he can discredit me, the directors will want me out. A comprador who has lost the trust of the Chinese is as little use as a eunuch's penis, only good for pissing. If I lose the Derwent power-base before I'm ready . . ."

"Further, Lord," the soothsayer interjected, "he seeks to discredit you with the British. There will be charges . . . I see only dimly . . . charges of financial manipulation and selling the country, the country of the English."

"Treason!" Sir Jonathan exploded. "Treason to the British after all I've done to reconcile the Colonial Government with China, after my service on the New Territories' lease and my contributions to the Boer War. It sounds fantastic. But the damned English will stop at nothing. My father, O'Flaherty, warned me."

"There is more, Lord. A member of your family is in danger, great personal danger. This Way-teh-lee intends to use your love of that one to break you."

Sir Jonathan rose, his normal imperturbability restored in an instant. He laid a red envelope on the table, and Silver Seventh Brother bowed his head in acknowledgment.

"I am grateful, Lord, for your bounty."

"Continue to be grateful," his patron instructed him. "Remember you are an earthen jug under my feet. If my heel touches you, you will be dust. If you hear any-

313

thing more—anything at all—send word to me immediately."

"It shall be as you say—should Providence reveal more to me."

"Bugger Providence! Find out all you can—immediately. Shake your sticks and rattle your coins. More important, draw in all your informants and send out all your spies. Spare no pressure. I *must* have more detail within the next two days."

"It shall be as you say, Lord." The still figure with the shrouded eyes repeated the obsequious formula without mockery.

The thick teak door of Sir Jonathan Sekloong's private office remained closed all that day. His seemingly ageless, apparently sexless, and utterly devoted Portuguese secretary, Rosita Remedios, literally obeyed his orders to admit no one. Each time she brought him another ponderous ledger or bulging file, she locked the door behind her. When Charles stopped by for his customary midmorning chat, she informed him that his father might be disturbed "only for an overwhelming catastrophe." She added: "He instructed that you were not to permit any such catastrophe to occur today, Mr. Charles."

Jonathan Sekloong did not wholly credit Silver Seventh's occult powers, not without reservations. But his respect for the blind soothsayer's insights and sources impelled him to a comprehensive stock-taking that was, in any event, overdue. For ten hours, refreshed only by numerous cups of green tea and twenty-two panatellas, Sir Jonathan assessed his past record, his present position, and his future propects.

He had come an immeasurable distance from the wiry eight-year-old who earned his first dollars as a runner for the coolie barracoons of Macao before his scandalized grandfather, the great Kwok Lee-chin, placed him in the care of the Jesuits. He had laboriously overcome the intense prejudice both British and Chinese felt for an aggressive half-caste, the by-blow of an Irish adventurer upon a romantic Chinese girl of good family. "You're a chee-chee bastard," he remembered his father's saying in part-remorseful, part-pitying mockery just before Liam Francis O'Flaherty gaily set off to die at the first siege of Peking in 1860, "a poor little bastard—without a prayer, without a hope." Yet he had made his own way by suppressing both the soft emotionalism and the wild adventurousness his parents had shared, the traits that had produced himself.

If he wished, he could continue until he died—replete with years, honors, and riches—as the faithful servant of Derwent, Hayes and Company, the invaluable comprador who could never be his own man. But he had not been born to serve others, no matter how bountiful their rewards. He would not be another fat, pompous "tame Chinese," bound to the service of the arrogant foreigners by the meaningless title they'd put before his name. Sir Jonathan indeed! He was Sekloong, *the* Sekloong, and he would be wholly his own man. No more than he had bowed his head to the haughty Mandarins of the old Dynasty or to the swaggering generals who had usurped their power would he humble himself to the foreigners. The be-damned-to-you-all arrogance he had inherited from his father was controlled. It was not quashed.

Since wealth was the only road to power on the China Coast, he had early determined to make himself richer than the most rapacious foreign merchant-adventurers. He had already almost succeeded. Yet his position, he saw wearily but clearly through the smoke of his eighteenth cigar, was precarious. He had come to a crossroads of total peril. He could fight, or he could temporize. He had no third choice, though he could not yet see the end of either road, whether it led to triumph or disaster.

His affairs, the purpose of his life, teetered in the balance, and his liabilities were outweighed only by his prospects. Three factors, distinct though linked, were forcing him to stake all on glory or eclipse: the Wheatleys' long-nurtured antagonism, which was becoming virulent; his own character, which alternated between the cautious, canny accumulation of wealth and reckless casts of the dice; finally—and most damaging—the decline of his friend and protégé Dr. Sun Yat-sen.

The last factor was the more irritating because it was not his own doing. Dr. Sun's stubborn unrealism had not merely deprived the man himself of power and China of his talents. His uncompromising idealism had deprived his financial adviser Jonathan Sekloong of a dominant position as the honest broker between China and the West. Dr. Sun's maladroitness had further deprived Jonathan Sekloong of the services of his son Harry, either in the firm or as his representative in the councils of the two-year-old Republic of China. The House of Sekloong was still powerful in the realm of commerce and in the half-world of the Secret Societies, but lacked even the semblance of major influence within the formal structure of the government of China.

Rapid, retrogressive alteration of that structure had provoked Dr. Sun's abnegation of all power. Elected provisional president of the Republic of China on December 25, 1911, he had resigned on April 1, 1912, in favor of the former Imperial Viceroy Yüan Shih-kai, whose deliberate procrastination had originally allowed the revolution to spread, while his subsequent failure to deploy the Imperial troops under his command had allowed the revolution to triumph. Dr. Sun hoped to reconcile the antagonistic elements in the new government by placating the conservatives, who considered Yüan Shih-kai their man. Misguided by modesty, Dr. Sun had accepted the powerless Ministry of Railways and dissipated his energy on grandiose plans for a nation-wide network of railroads that could not become reality for another century.

By early 1913, with Dr. Sun's progressives sidetracked, Yüan Shih-kai had openly revealed his immense ambition, as blatant as it was archaic. He was determined to be the Founding Emperor of a new Confucian Dynasty, and his first move was, quite logically, to suppress Dr. Sun's fiercely republican Nationalist Party, the Kuomintang. By late 1913, the Kuomintang had withdrawn from the virtually powerless National Assembly, and Sun Yat-sen had fled to Tokyo, accompanied by Harry Sekloong and other loyalists. The Japanese freely offered refuge to all disaffected Chinese from extreme rightists to extreme leftists, not because they honored the principle of asylum, but to encourage political and economic disruption that would render China helpless to resist the conquest they already planned.

In May 1914, Dr. Sun prepared to move to Shanghai, where foreign rule ironically provided an open forum for political activity by Chinese patriots on Chinese soil. Harry Sekloong, wholly devoted to the republican cause, would follow Sun Yat-sen wherever he chose to go or was forced to flee. Besides, Harry had just married Mayling How, the daughter of a poor Shanghai editor, whose weekly was Dr. Sun's public voice. He informed the Sekloongs of his marriage by telegram. That implicit expression of disregard for the clan and for his filial obligations was accompanied by explicit expression of his continuing devotion to both. His father was enraged at Harry's fecklessness, though he knew that his son was, at least in part, armoring himself against the passion he still felt for Mary and thus serving the family's deepest interests. Hong Kong gossip was already asking why Harry had not married and speculating on the attachment between himself and his brother's wife; Harry knew that public revelation of their protracted liaison would shatter the family and destroy its reputation. But Sir Jonathan could neither acknowledge his second son's complex motivations nor admit that his own uncharacteristic laxness had permitted the menace to arise. He assessed his own position against the background of a useless political alliance and his son's—no other word would serve—desertion.

First on his balance sheet were dubieties and debits. As comprador for Derwent, Hayes and Company he enjoyed great prestige in the Chinese community, as well as real power whose depth even his suspicious stepfather Richard Wheatley could not fathom. He was a director of twenty-one firms, including insurance and shipping companies, railroads and importers, mines and mills. But most of those directorships had originally been offered because, as Derwent's comprador, he exercised great influence among the Chinese. His railroad investments were dormant, except for his substantial share in the Canton–Kowloon Railway. Even that Sino-British enterprise could become a political whirligig, torn from his grasp by the changing winds of power, just as his interest in the proposed Yangtze Valley Railway had been lost when Dr. Sun went into exile.

Next on the balance sheet were his assets. Since his personal fortune was conservatively invested in Europe and America, he would remain a very rich man whatever happened in China or Hong Kong. He enjoyed a virtual monopoly of the South China sugar trade from Shanghai to Canton and as far as Ichang, the gate to the Yangtze River gorges. Though nominally an agent for international companies, he held a commanding personal position in the growing trade in petroleum products—still chiefly kerosene, though the demand for lubricating oil and motor fuel was expanding rapidly. His landholdings in Shanghai, Macao, and Hong Kong were much more extensive than even Charles and Mary knew. He had bought overcrowded tenements cheaply during the slump of 1910, and he was raising rents so slowly that no one protested. The large tracts in the New Territories he had acquired by acting as go-between in Sino-British negotiations over the lease of that 370-square-mile tract still lay fallow economically. Utilized in part to raise rice and vegetables or to breed poultry and pigs, they represented potential power, rather than a force in being. Finally, his firm alliance with Judah Haleevie and the Rothschilds would give him much depth and many reserves if he were forced to confront the Wheatleys.

Sir Jonathan pushed aside the barricades of files and ledgers that surrounded him. What was the new catchword? Yes, net worth. What, he wondered, was his net worth? Impatiently he dismissed a question as meaningless as it was modish. His personal fortune could support the clan in comfort for two or three generations, though he could only estimate its value to the nearest £100,000. But he could not realize those long-term investments without major losses. They might be thrown into the battle in desperation, as a general might mobilize his sappers, cooks, bandsmen, and clerks to defend his threatened headquarters. They were not available for a broad assault, the decisive offensive battle.

For the next six months, Sir Jonathan concluded, he must stave off the Wheatleys' attacks. Taking the offensive might be the best defense, and he would not hesitate to use violence—judiciously and surreptitiously. For the next six months, at least, he must remain comprador of Derwent, Hayes and Company, since he could not survive the humiliation of being forced out before that time. By the same token, he must be prepared to break with Derwent, Hayes thereafter—if it were absolutely necessary. But it would be better to play out the charade as long as possible.

Should he feel compelled to resign, it must be clearly seen that he had left of his own will. A roaring public fight would, he concluded, then best insure that Derwent's rather than Sefkloong's was humiliated by his departure. He could provoke a quarrel over principle, hardly difficult considering the Wheatleys' intricate chicanery. He could thus win the respectful sympathy of both the foreign and the Chinese business communities. The former because his cause was just; the latter because he had publicly humiliated the despised *guai-lo,* the devil people. But, all in all, it would be better to stay with the *hong,* if necessary in a state of armed truce, while he consolidated his own realm.

Sir Jonathan methodically tore up sheets of paper covered with his neat calculations before ringing for Miss Remedios and instructing her to order the Daimler. There was one other matter. His wife Lucinda, his daughter-in-law Mary, his daughter Matilda, and his grandchildren must be removed from the line of fire. Peitaiho on the Gulf of Chihli would be an idea bolt-hole. His commercial and Secret Society connections in the north were extensive. Since it was normal for women and children to go north to escape the grueling Hong Kong summer, their departure would not reveal that he was sending his noncombatants to safety while mobilizing his combatants against the Wheatleys. Charles he would keep by him, for he required a trustworthy adjutant.

But, Sir Jonathan concluded wearily, those final dispositions could wait a few days. Tonight he would relax with his favorite concubine, Precious Pearl, and their delightful daughters. It did not occur to him to remove them from the line of fire. If they were injured, he would grieve, but the clan, the House of Sekloong, would not suffer. They *were* his own, but they were *not* his hostages to fortune.

June 5, 1914–August 8, 1914

I WANT to buy wooltops and graycloth in job lots," Mary Sekloong declared, "And boots, military boots and work boots."

"Your department, my dear," her father-in-law answered abstractedly. "Did you discuss it with Charles before he went off to Shanghai?"

"I didn't—and I don't terribly care to. I mean very large quantities, by the thousand gross—all available goods. And I'd advise you to buy all the tungsten and coal you can."

Sir Jonathan cocked a thin, gray eyebrow. His daughter-in-law was in a strange mood. Foregoing the badinage and gossip that normally preceded their consultations, she had put forward extreme proposals that were virtually demands. He had not seen her so assertive since her bitter confrontation with Charles nine years earlier. Yet she had appeared reasonably happy during the past three years. If she wept at losing Harry, she wept in private. He had himself constantly reminded her that Harry must in time leave her to marry, and his second son, her lover, had been more often absent from Hong Kong than present since the Revolution of 1911. She had apparently accepted his sudden marriage with resignation, rather than bitterness. Herself increasingly caught up by the affairs of the House of

Sekloong, she had undoubtedly recognized the danger to the House in their liaison's continuing. Her partial reconciliation with Charles, capped by the birth of another son, named after his father, in late 1912, seemed to have restored her to mild contentment.

"But why, my dear?" Sir Jonathan asked, putting aside his musing on her tangled emotions to consider the straightforward commercial question. "Why such enormous quantities?"

"There'll be war in Europe before autumn. I've had a letter from Peter French, who's a full colonel at the War Office now. He's certain all Europe will be at war within six months."

"Your old friend Lord Peter!" Sir Jonathan's eyebrow rose higher. "You accept his judgment as gospel? I always thought he was an aristocratic fop."

"He's changed since you knew him," Mary answered shortly. "Other people have changed too. Charles, for one."

"I thought," Sir Jonathan gingerly probed the unavoidable emotional question, "all was well between Charles and you."

"Well enough, I suppose, but hardly satisfactory. Even little Charles, he doesn't need me, not with all the doting servants. Nor do the others. Jonnie'll soon be home for a while, but . . ."

Mary paused in perplexity. She did not herself comprehend the springs of her own discontent. How could she convey her fretful bewilderment to the autocrat who dominated their lives?

"Yes, but what?" he prompted. "Do tell me, Mary."

"I suppose I'm bored, and I feel trapped in Hong Kong. It's small and dull and snobbish. I'm accepted— up to a point—because of your name. But I'm only tolerated by both the white and Chinese communities. I'm a kind of licensed leper, an outcaste, an untouchable, once the formalities are discharged. And sometimes . . . I'm sorry, Father . . . sometimes I don't like the Chinese very much."

"As bad as that?"

"I'm afraid so. Aside from you and the children,

there's no one left I really care strongly about. Harry's gone. Hilary Metcalfe's gone too. I have no real women friends. The children? Because of their amahs they don't truly need me. I hardly know them. And I feel I'm stifling."

"But you have all the freedom in the world."

"Freedom in Hong Kong, not the world. Like a trustee in jail."

Sir Jonathan deliberately positioned his panatella in the massive malachite ashtray. Only his lifted eyebrow showed his astonishment.

"At least you're fascinated by the business."

"The business *is* fascinating, but it's not enough." Mary sighed. "Life's too orderly. Too flat. I'm almost thirty-four. And I can see only the same gray existence until I die."

"Oh, come now." Sir Jonathan smiled uncomprehendingly. "Things can't be all that bad. You're just tired."

"I'm sorry." Mary smiled to ward off tears and spoke curtly. "Can we go back to business? I'm convinced we should buy heavily before prices soar."

"If you wish, I suppose so," Sir Jonathan responded, satisfied that her mood had passed. "But there may be some difficulties."

"We're not short of liquid cash," Mary persisted. "Besides, the House of Sekloong can raise nearly a million on your signature alone. If you doubt my judgment, I'll buy as much as I can on my own. I assume our agreement holds, that I can dispose of my accumulated percentages as I wish."

"It's not so much doubting your judgment, my dear, though I'd naturally like to discuss your proposals. You won't have to speculate on your private account. It's substantial. As I recall, about £45,000, though that won't go far considering your grand ideas. But the firm itself could be short of funds in the next few months."

"Why?" Mary's alarm at Sir Jonathan's warning diverted her from her own bored discontent. "Last time we talked the reserves were very healthy."

"True. But we can't overextend ourselves when we may need all our reserves to defend ourselves."

"Defend ourselves? From what? Who'd dare attack us now, Father? We've never been more solid."

"My esteemed step-father's up to his old tricks."

"But that's not new," Mary objected. "And you're always more than a match for Old Dick and that hot-handed son of his, Iain."

"The Wheatleys' hostility isn't new. Their tactics are."

"What could they possibly . . ."

"The usual slander, poisonous whispers. Worse than before, but I can manage. Any serious charge they trump up must smear themselves. After all, I'm their comprador. But I've heard from various sources about a new plot. It's ingenious—and very dangerous."

"Not the old opium lark, surely. The Shanghai trade's still legal, even if Hong Kong has cut back. Anyway, we're out of it. Or are we?"

Sir Jonathan smiled at the indignant figure in the ankle-length hobble-skirt of fawn serge set off by a long-sleeved basque, her only ornament a small gold-dragon pin. Though she loved clothes, Mary wore simple costumes in the office as if to neutralize her gender.

"Yes, we're out of the trade," he answered. "Have no fear. This is different, so ingenious I can't believe Dick and Iain Wheatley thought it up themselves."

Sir Jonathan stubbed out his panatella and beheaded another with his gold pocket guillotine. It was the first time Mary had seen him smoke one cigar immediately after another. When the slim golden-brown tube was tipped with red coal, he spoke again.

"Everyone knows the honorable President of the Republic of China, that old rascal Yüan Shih-kai, wants to make himself Emperor, establish the Great Constitutional Dynasty. He needs a large sum, about two million *taels* of gold to pay and arm his troops, to bribe his rivals."

Mary calculated automatically. Two million *taels* was 2.66 million ounces of gold, about £11 million.

"But he's pawned everything pawnable," she argued, "and the Customs revenues are pledged for the next ten years. Where can he possibly get that much money?"

"From us, it appears, though I'd be pressed to raise a quarter of a million *taels* in gold."

"From us? How possibly? Why?"

"So it's to appear. The Wheatleys are making up the stake. And they've let it be known the gold is really for me. They're simply helping a faithful servant pull himself out of a hole."

"I see. Load you with an imaginary debt. No one'll believe your denials. And involving you with Yüan Shih-kai. Your Chinese friends will be livid, and your foreign associates will be convinced you're heading for bankruptcy."

"That's the scheme."

"But," Mary objected, "Dick Wheatley'd never part with a hundredth of that sum without cast-iron security —and Yüan Shih-kai has no realizable assets."

"The Wheatleys, being the Wheatleys, will get solid collateral, far more than the value of the loan. But it won't be cast-iron. Quite the contrary."

"What do you mean, Father?"

"The Imperial Household Treasures, the personal possessions accumulated by emperor after emperor through dynasty after dynasty, are kept in the Imperial City in Peking. As you know, the little Emperor Hsüan Tung keeps his title, though he's lost his throne and all power. Only China could be a republic with an Emperor. And his treasures, the National Treasures, are priceless. Ancient bronzes, jewels, porcelains, paintings, jades, gold and silver ornaments, ceremonial vessels, and funerary figures . . . I could go on for hours."

Sir Jonathan knocked white ash from his panatella.

"Theoretically, that immense wealth is the Emperor's personal property. Legally it belongs to the nation and can't be sold off by either the Emperor or President Yüan Shih-kai. But it will be alienated. The Wheatleys' collateral will be £15 to £20 million worth of Imperial Treasures."

"But," Mary asked, "how can Yüan Shih-kai possibly—"

"Quite easily. The treasures will be moving openly. Some pieces will go to London for display. China needs friends, and what better way to make friends than through displaying her ancient culture? The shipment'll move through Tientsin."

"And there?"

"The Wheatleys' collateral—small in bulk, immense in value, and camouflaged by the public shipment to London—will be deposited secretly with the Gazetted Bank of Gibraltar and Asia. In short, in the Wheatleys' vaults in the foreign concession of Tientsin beyond the reach of Chinese law. This humble director of the Gazetted Bank will, by an oversight, not be informed of the transaction."

"And the gold itself? How precisely will we be victimized? I'm muddled by this business."

"Not business," Sir Jonathan snapped, "but grand larceny. That much you grasp. Since you're muddled, I'll try to explain as simply as I can, even if I repeat myself: First, Yüan Shih-kai, who's certainly no republican, wants to reestablish the Empire, with himself as Emperor. He needs large sums to make his *coup d'état*. Second, the British Foreign Office doesn't want a Chinese Republic either and backs Yüan's ambitions. London's chosen the Wheatleys as the conduit to funnel the gold to Yüan, having conceived the plot and arranged details through the British Secret Service. Third, the Wheatleys' illegal collateral will be the Imperial Treasures. And, finally, the Wheatleys—whether they succeed or fail in the scheme—plan to ruin me by leaking rumors that it's Sekloong, not Derwent's, illegally providing gold, avariciously grabbing the National Treasures, and brazenly manipulating internal Chinese politics."

"That's clearer," Mary said. "But the mechanics are still obscure."

"Somewhat obscure to me, too. But, as I understand it, the bullion shipment'll be camouflaged by the pretext of moving China's meager gold reserves for safety. That way, Yüan'll have his gold, the Foreign Office'll have a new Chinese Empire, and the Wheatleys'll have the National Treasure—as well as dominant influence in the new Imperial Court."

"Why can't you blow the gaff, expose them?"

"Anything I say will count against me. I'd look like a criminal, caught in the act and trying to shift the guilt. I'd be pilloried by both Chinese and Europeans. Jonathan Sekloong, thief of China's priceless national heritage, receiver of stolen goods, a common fence, a clumsy gold manipulator—a plotter against the Republic for profit."

"And the upshot?" Mary asked. "What happens to us?"

"We're bankrupted when all our creditors call their loans. We're pressed to repay two million *taels* we never borrowed and to restore the Imperial Treasures we never held. The Wheatleys then take over my holdings at ten cents on the dollar and use our assets to repay the loan. It's beautifully Machiavellian."

"But can't we fight?" Mary flared. "Knowing so much already, surely you can thwart them."

"I do have some notions." Sir Jonathan mused. "And I'll have to develop them. We have time. Moving that much gold will take some time."

"And what can *I* do?" Mary asked.

"You can take a holiday at Peitaiho."

"Peitaiho, Father? For Heaven's sake, why Peitaiho? You can't mean it. My place is here."

"Because Peitaiho is just one hundred ten miles from Tientsin where the bullion exchange must take place. I need you on the scene. It's perfectly normal, your taking the family north for the summer. The Wheatleys mustn't guess what we know—or even suspect."

"How much of what you've told me," Mary asked suspiciously, "is actual knowledge and how much guesswork?"

"Let's say that I pieced it together. Many details I still don't know. But I must have you at Peitaiho, just

326

near enough to Tientsin to be useful, just far enough to avoid suspicion."

"Are you using me as a decoy?"

"Of course, Mary, that too," he acknowledged. "And you must leave within a week. The *Foosing* sails on the twelfth of June."

"Well, if you really believe I can be most useful there," Mary conceded. "And we should get the children away."

"Of course. The House of Sekloong must live in its heirs—and the Wheatleys have used assassins."

"All right, then," she agreed. "Your logic overwhelms me."

"There's a side advantage."

"What's that?"

"You've said you were bored, your life deadly dull. A change of scene and company could do you good. There'll be danger, too, but you'll be well guarded, very well guarded."

"There are so many things I must do, clothes for the children and myself, so many things. I must get started."

"Do that, by all means."

Sir Jonathan rose to kiss Mary's cheek and closed the door behind her. He was content with his morning's work, though he had improvised grandly to fill out the tale. He was removing his most valuable property, Mary and the children, from his enemies' reach in preparation for his own counterattack. Perhaps, he mused, the only way to avoid contrived charges of treason and grand larceny for despoiling the Imperial Treasures was to engage in grand larceny.

"Man," the Chief Engineer of the S.S. *Foosing* said to the First Officer, "that lot're not just sailing on this wee tub. They're taking over like Bias Bay pirates."

Mary laughed and flashed the officers of the 2,100-ton coaster a smile that brought them to her side, eagerly profferring assistance. The sardonic Scotsman was not far off the mark. The Sekloongs and their entourage clambered up the gangway from the fifty-eight-foot steam pinnace *Lucinda,* amid confusion that would have been excessive for the embarkation of a squadron of irregular cavalry and its camp followers. More than a hundred pieces of heavy baggage, including a baby grand piano, were already stowed in the hold. Though thirty-five cases of wine and eighty-six crates of food, ranging from tinned tongue, *pâté de foie,* and caviar to Cantonese dried vegetables and prepared sauces not available in the barbarian North, had been loaded, the servants were still carrying aboard an uncountable variety of boxes, cloth-wrapped bundles, woven-straw cases, and leather valises. The children's four small pet dogs, three kittens, and a white rabbit contributed their barking and shrill mewing to the din. Six Alsatian guard dogs bayed menacingly.

She had persuaded the children that they should not bring the three faithful donkeys that carried them to the Peak Tram Terminus on fine days. She had assured them that there would be donkeys and, even better, ponies at Peitaiho. She hoped fervently that she was right. Otherwise, the children's pining for their own donkeys would mar the entire summer.

Lady Lucinda stood beside Mary. At fifty-eight, she was still physically vigorous, but forty years as the pampered and intimidated wife of Sir Jonathan had so subdued her that she was hardly more useful than the children. She did, at least, quiet them with dried sour plums from her capacious handbag when they bickered. Mary's drab sister-in-law, Matilda, just turned twenty-one, tried to help control the throng. But, like her mother, she was pathetically uncertain, having been alternately coddled and cowed by her autocratic father. Still, Matilda's help was better than none at all. The servants were already clutching their stomachs and turning pale green, though the *Foosing* still rocked gently at anchor in the shelter of sun-drenched Hong Kong harbor.

Only the apparently ageless Ah Sam was comfortable on the teak decks, actually invigorated by returning to the environment of his early adventures. He barked orders at the children and under-servants, who all obeyed him promptly even as they muddled Mary's soft-spoken instructions.

Smiling at the ship's officers' astonishment, she calculated rapidly. Including the servants, the Sekloong party totaled forty. Among the adults were Lady Lucinda, Matilda, and Mary, while her children numbered six in all. The eldest was Jonnie, almost thirteen, just returned from preparatory school at St. Mary's Hall, and puffed with the self-importance of a young man who would that autumn enter the Lower Grammar class of Stonyhurst College. The youngest was the toddler Charles, already so gravely articulate that the others called him "The Mandarin." Between were the girls, Guinevere, eleven, and Charlotte, ten; and the boys, Thomas, nine, and James, seven. Three aged Kwok cousins, two ladies and a frail old gentleman, whose exact relationship and reasons for accompanying them were obscure, completed the intimate family party sailing for a modest summer holiday.

Even after fourteen years' exposure to the grandiose Sekloong style, Mary was startled by the size of the accompanying entourage. The "division tail" her father would call it, she remembered with a rush of amused affection for the aging Bandmaster. She could almost hear his sour complaint about "jumped-up chinks giving themselves airs."

By chance, the number of those below the salt—or the soy-sauce—matched the number of those above. Fifteen servants, headed by Ah Sam, would look after the fifteen gentry. Finally, Sir Jonathan's inevitable surprise: ten scarred toughs in workmen's clothing, who held the Alsatians on heavy chains. These Secret Society Braves would guard the ship against pirates and protect the family during the long summer under the loom of the Great Wall.

Sir Jonathan had taken the ship's entire accommodation, asserting his prerogative as a director of the line. They were nevertheless fearfully crowded. The Captain had given up his own cabin to Lady Lucinda and Mary, who crammed in young Charles and his baby-amah.

The others—Matilda, the children, the aged relations, the governess, and the tutors—were jammed into the passenger accommodations, overflowing into the officers' cabins. The Chief Engineer and the First Officer were to sling hammocks on deck, while a cargo hold was cleared for the crew, whose own quarters had been taken over by the Sekloong servants and guards.

Mary wished again that the *Foosing* carried a physician. However, young Dr. George Chapman Parker had promised to join the ship at Shanghai and to spend most of the summer at Peitaiho.

"Oh, the deuce with it," she said aloud, drawing a shocked glance from her jejeune sister-in-law.

Mary was determined to enjoy the eight-day voyage before encountering the perils of the North. She consciously relaxed, willing herself not to worry about the smaller children's falling overboard, but to trust to the vigilance of the amahs.

The ship's siren screamed, and the anchor chain clanked. From the deck of *Lucinda,* Sir Jonathan and Charles waved their straw hats. The pinnace bobbed beside the *Foosing* long after they had left the harbor through narrow Lyemun Gap. Only when *Foosing* passed the Ninepins and turned her bows toward the open sea, did *Lucinda* toot six times and swing around in a shower of spray to show her neatly rounded stern.

Disembarking at Peitaiho was not quite the ordeal embarking at Hong Kong had been, largely because Dr. George Chapman Parker's masculine authority subdued the unruly children and the fluttering servants. The lean, thirty-year-old Virginian had acquired even greater assurance than he displayed during the plague of 1909 as his pioneering studies in tropical medicine won wider recognition. But he badly needed a holiday from his exhausting efforts to instill elementary concern for public health measures into the Chinese and foreign inhabitants of Shanghai. Most of the Chinese struggled too desperately for economic survival to bother about hygiene, while their rich compatriots and the self-indulgent foreigners unconsciously considered their wealth the surest protection against epidemics. Despite the lines of strain around his wide mouth, George Parker's manner was still breezy. His deep blue eyes and light blond hair made his sharp, intelligent features attractive. But the plentitude, almost embarrassment, of chaperones surrounding Mary and Matilda wholly satisfied the proprieties.

They were housed, all forty-one of them, in a Confucian Temple "on loan" from the town elders, who owed Sir Jonathan many favors. Confronted with primitive brick stoves and water hauled from wells, Mary resigned her responsibilities to the servants' ingenuity under Ah Sam's direction. Somehow, they were all fed —and well fed. Somehow, they all were provided with beds and essential mosquito nets. Since she could not find her way through the maze of courtyards, reception rooms, red-pillared altar chambers, bedrooms, store rooms, and out-buildings, Mary cast off all household cares, finding herself idle for the first time in years. For two weeks, she simply relaxed, reading desultorily and painting in ink. The rhythm of their days was determined by their meals and the morning and afternoon swims.

She reveled in the recuperation her contemporaries called "taking a breather to ginger up," and a later generation was to describe with equal ambiguity as "unwinding and recharging your batteries." Besides, social life was brisk in the seaside town where diplomats, missionaries, and foreign traders passed their summers. In Hong Kong she was received with strained tolerance because the Sekloong name commanded such respect; but her reception in Peitaiho was delightfully spontaneous and unconstrained.

At once exotic and familiar within their aura of great wealth, the Sekloongs intrigued the British diplomats who clustered on the headland called Legation Point. Through their introductions Mary soon knew the entire foreign community, which was eager for new faces and new conversation. All were frankly curious regarding the English girl who had married into the clan of the Eurasian merchant-prince. Moreover, her father-in-law's knighthood was taken at its face value, rather than as a bauble Hong Kong's Colonial Government had bestowed to placate the natives. She was, she realized, becoming a queen bee of Peitaiho society—and it was not unpleasant.

In the unbuttoned atmosphere, she reverted happily to her youthful disregard of artificial conventions. She romped with the children in the gentle surf, wearing a bathing costume that was daringly brief. She joined them on the biddable Shanshi donkeys which abounded in Peitaiho. For the first time she felt she was beginning to know her own children.

Jonnie was fascinated by politics, the great events of not only China and Britain but the entire troubled world. When she answered his incessant inquiries, Mary was surprised by the knowledge she had acquired unaware. But his questions on theology defeated her, and she dispatched him to the retreat house maintained by the Roman Catholic Diocese of Peking. Indulgent after their long separation, she ignored most of the high-spirited escapades that were his natural reaction to three years of strict Jesuit discipline.

He "just nicked" a box of cigars and six bottles of wine for a party with his new friends, but Mary felt his agonizing hangover was punishment enough. He frayed a fishing net in sheer mischief, and the cords parted to lose the catch. Mary recompensed the fishermen and told Jonnie that she could not forgive him for imperiling the livelihood of the poor. She smiled to herself when he teased his pompous English tutor, and she found more amusing than disturbing his "borrowing" ten donkeys for a nocturnal expedition.

Only the incident that was celebrated in the small annals of quiet Peitaiho as the "Gun-Powder Plot" provoked her wrath—and that only fleetingly. The self-important British Minister, Sir Alistair Lermotte, was injured only in his dignity when the black-powder extracted from hundreds of firecrackers exploded outside his study window. Like herself, Jonnie went the whole hog when he did something foolish.

The girls were less troublesome and less diverting, though Guinevere and Charlotte were already quite different persons. Guinevere was the perfect little house-wife-to-be, sometimes, Mary felt, too docile. She would sit for hours over her embroidery or at the baby grand that was itself already famous in Peitaiho as a concrete symbol of Sekloong lavishness. Guinevere did join her hoydenish younger sister Charlotte in swimming to the diving-raft anchored two hundred yards off shore. Mary fretted about their recklessness, but was reassured by both Ah Sam and young Dr. Parker. The children, they pointed out, were never out of sight of her own or someone else's servants, while a boat manned by local fishermen lay halfway between the raft and the shore. Charlotte, Mary feared, would later be a problem; she was already too eager for masculine attention. But, for the moment, Charlotte was a manageable handful.

The little boys lost themselves in the simple recreations of the holiday resort. Normally isolated from the Chinese masses of Hong Kong by their lonely eminence on The Peak, they discovered with delight that the Mandarin their grandfather had insisted they learn was, after their quick ears had adjusted to the local dialect, intelligible to fishermen, shopkeepers, and artisans. They drifted happy and undiscriminating among the street urchins and the foreign children from Tientsin and Peking.

Thomas and James were alike in neither temperament nor appearance. The elder was a throwback to his Kwok ancestors, small, dark, and, Mary feared, both secretive and envious. The younger each day grew more like the strapping, forthright man he called "Uncle Harry." They quarreled noisily, but stood side by side against the street urchins and schemed with one mind to evade their tutors. The pair were at an awkward age. They had outgrown their stiflingly overattentive amahs, but were not quite old enough for personal manservants.

Both Thomas and James were fascinated by the platoon of the East Yorkshire Regiment that was Sir Alistair's ceremonial guard and by the leather-faced U.S. Horse Marines on leave from their posts at the American Legation. When all other coveys drew blank, the two boys could be found squatting on the sand with the hard-bitten Marine gunnery sergeant or the ferocious sergeant major of the East Yorks. Mary was more amused than shocked when they sang bawdy versions of the "Marine Hymn" or "Soldiers of the Queen," using words she pretended not to understand. After two weeks, Thomas and James declared their firm intention of becoming soldiers when they grew up. She did not pass on that resolution in her chatty letters to their father and grandfather, who would have been truly shocked. Both believed implicitly in the wisdom of the Chinese maxim: *From good iron, one does not make nails! Of good men, one does not make soldiers.*

Even little Charles asserted his independence at twenty months by demanding that he not be called Charlie, but Young Charles or Master Charles. The grinning servants gleefully complied with his treble instructions. They also called him *Shao Yeh,* "Little Lord," or *Hsiao Kuan,* "Small Mandarin." Precociously peremptory, Charles was always loving, more loving than her other children. Mary was alternately enchanted and bewildered by the self-confident infant who taught himself the alphabet by sitting quietly in the corner when the tutors instructed the elder children. She was astonished one day to find him tracing Chinese characters in the sand with a twig.

In remote Peitaiho she had only one cause for worry. Her husband and her father-in-law wrote regularly, but the mails were slow; and their letters did not allude to their countercampaign against the Wheatleys. Mary fretted, though she knew that discretion was essential. She felt she had been deliberately removed from the center of events, despite Sir Jonathan's argument that he needed her near Tientsin, where the exchange of gold for the Imperial Treasures was scheduled to take place. In reality, Peitaiho was almost as isolated from Tientsin, 110 miles away, as it was from Hong Kong, 1,500 miles away.

Her chief source of information was the eccentric *Peking and Tientsin Times,* edited by the equally eccentric Putnam Weale. In early July, he published alarming reports of unrest in Central Europe. But she had to look hard to find those snippets among fulsome social notes and labored analyses of byzantinely complex Chinese politics—as rival generals the newspaper called warlords fought each other, and President Yüan Shih-kai maneuvered to make himself Emperor.

Almost every issue carried a dispatch headlined: AN-OTHER BANDIT OUTRAGE. The fabric of Chinese civilization had not been restored, but had been more deeply rent by removing the corrupt Manchus. The new political structure was so rickety it appeared that China either had no government at all or a dozen contending governments. Smug in its insular security, the foreign community interpreted such reports as confirmation of the inability of the Chinese either to rule themselves or to maintain minimal civil order. Reading those dispatches with strained attention, Mary was dismayed by the rise of provincial despots who alternately strove for foreign support and denounced the West's extra-legal privileges in China.

On July 22, 1914, the *North China Daily News* abandoned its normal reserve to proclaim in a bold block type headline across three columns: GREAT BANDIT OUTRAGE: HANKOW—PEKING LIMITED DERAILED, BULLION FEARED STOLEN.

It is reported from Chengchow in dispatches lately reaching us [The article reported.] that bandits halted the crack Hankow—Peking Limited on the relatively unpopulated stretch between Hsinyang and Suiping on the nineteenth day of the present month.

The engineer espied a log barricade across the tracks and applied the emergency brakes. However, the train's momentum carried it into the barricade. The locomotive, the tender, and the leading passenger-waggon were derailed. Fortunately, personal injuries were slight. Two Europeans suffered lacerations, and the Chinese fireman was killed when his head struck a projecting lever.

Passengers were terrified when a band of more than 100 armed men attacked the three special goods-waggons that had been attached to the last carriage just before the departure of the Limited. The out-numbered guards fired only a few shots before fleeing. The bandits broke into the goods-waggons and made off with a large number of stout wooden boxes.

Reports from knowledgeable sources, though unconfirmed, indicate that those boxes contained bullion. Our own Economic Correspondent has noted persistent rumours that the gold reserves of the Republic were to be transferred to a new place of safekeeping. However, it is not known whether the gold reserves were indeed in the looted goods-waggon. But our Economic Correspondent understands . . .

The report tailed off into a farrago of speculation, and Mary threw the paper down in frustration. The allusion to a transfer of the Republic's gold reserves had alerted her, since the Wheatleys planned to transport their enormous loan to President Yüan Shih-kai under that pretext. Searching subsequent editions, she found no further mention of the incident.

"Who knows," George Parker remarked, "whether the news was suppressed—or whether it's just the *Tientsin and Peking Times*'s casual approach to our times."

After a few weeks Mary began to chafe at the simple pleasures of isolated Peitaiho. The restless enthusiasm of her youth reasserted itself after its protracted suppression by domestic and business responsibilities, and she longed for a change in the pleasant monotony. She would be delighted to do something mildly foolish with her whole heart—if she could find some such diversion in the smug enclave of foreign privilege on the edge of a troubled nation.

The expedition George Parker proposed was hardly foolish. He suggested an excursion to Hsienfenghow, ninety-five miles northwest in the shadow of the Great Wall. Mary's interest in Chinese civilization had reawakened, largely because the big-boned, slow-spoken, and courteous Northerners were more congenial than the slight, nervous, and contentious Cantonese. She longed to see the town built on the ruins of an old feudal capital.

They set out in three broad-wheeled Peking Carts, each unsprung wooden platform on wooden wheels pulled by two stocky ponies and a patient donkey harnessed abreast. Its only luxury was a canvas hood that could be raised to protect the travelers against the sun and the rain. In addition to the cartmen, four servants, and three guards, they had originally planned to take only Matilda Sekloong as a chaperone. But Jonnie insisted upon the eldest son's right to accompany them and Guinevere surprised them by demanding the same right as the eldest daughter. Her schoolgirl crush on "Uncle George" made her uncharacteristically assertive. Mary yielded, pleased at having her two elder children virtually to herself.

For two days, the little caravan rolled along deep-rutted roads incised by millennia of turning wheels into the soft yellow soil of the flat North China plain. Unlubricated wooden axles squealed an undulating marching song, and the cartmen swore goodhumoredly at the animals. They occasionally passed sparsely inhabited villages beside golden millet fields reeking of night-soil. North China was almost deserted by comparison with the hectic, overpopulated South, and they saw more white-washed, womb-shaped tombs than packed-earth dwellings. But the travelers found new pleasure in each other's company. Amiable and intelligent, George Parker controlled the servants without effort. Free of the bickering younger children, Jonnie and Gwinnie chatted intelligently. They were gravely aware of their new privileges and responsibilities.

When they halted at dusk on the third day, the servants lit small fires before erecting one tent for Mary, Matilda, and Guinevere and another for George Parker and Jonnie. The northern twilight was engulfed by the tides of blackness flowing across the vast inverted bowl of the sky. The moon was an incandescent sliver, and the stars were brilliant arc lights in the clear air, undefiled by smoke from huddled domestic hearths. But the valley was dark, and the flickering cooking-fires silhouetted the figures squatting around their yellow flames. High cheekbones shone under dark pools of eyesockets, and wooden chopsticks hovered over iron grills in disembodied hands to sweep up strips of mutton mixed with leeks, fragrant coriander, sesame oil, and soy-sauce. In the outer darkness, the ponies whinnied nervously.

"Just like the nomads on the steppes two thousand years ago," young Jonnie thrilled, biting into a sesame bun stuffed with mutton.

"So it is, Jonnie, except we're so much safer and healthier." George Parker could never resist a didactic tribute to progress. "If we were nomads, we'd be afraid of attacks from other tribes. You'd lead the caravan because your mother and I would already be very old. Without modern medicine, you know . . ."

"Yes, Uncle George," Jonnie agreed tolerantly. "I see."

"That's so interesting, Uncle George," Guinevere flirted. "Can you tell us more?"

"Well," the American answered, "you see, in the days when the nomads roamed North China and Siberia, they had no doctors, only medicine men who were called shamans. They tried to cure people of disease by expelling evil spirits."

"Father McAllen," Jonnie interjected, "says people can still be possessed by the Devil—but not often."

"Perhaps that's right," Parker conceded. "But, as I was saying, today we are conquering disease. And no one would want to attack us."

A pony whinnied, and the donkeys brayed hoarsely. George Parker cocked his ear to the sounds of the night. Only the soughing of the wind disturbed the still darkness beyond their fires.

Mary nodded, lulled by the soft chatter of the servants and an overwhelming sensation of ease. She had eaten too much lamb and drunk too much warm yellow rice wine. She nodded again, half-asleep.

A whiplash cracked, startling her into full wakefulness. She rose to her feet and reached toward the children.

"A shot," Dr. Parker said, throwing himself to the hard ground. "Everybody down."

338

Dazzled by the firelight, the guards fired their rifles blindly into the darkness. The whiplash cracked again, and a cartman fell. A fusillade of rocks scattered the fires and struck down a guard.

The soft, enclosing darkness that had lulled them into a sense of security was transformed into a vast, brooding menace. Immemorial China stalked the intruders from outside the minuscule circle of light cast by the embers of their cooking-fires. Hoarse shouts volleyed back and forth between their invisible assailants, and a tinny bugle pealed. Resentful of the foreigners' complacent ease, the voices shrieked half-comprehensible threats.

"*Sha! Sha yang kuei-tze!*" The high-pitched command shrilled across the valley. "Kill! Kill the foreign devils!"

"*Wang-ba tan! Tu-fei!*" A guard shouted, emboldened by the abrupt lull in the attack. "Sons of turtle-bitches! Thugs!"

"Kill the running-dogs of the foreigners!" The enveloping darkness responded.

Dim figures on squat ponies circled the embers, firing their rifles into the air. The aggressive guard aimed carefully, and one figure toppled from its saddle. But the mounted men were drawing their cordon tight around the isolated travelers, and other men on foot were approaching closer. When two men burst into the circle of dim light, the guards clubbed them with their rifles.

Mary frantically drew the children to her, but Jonnie wriggled free in excitement. Almost as tall as she, he was determined to play a man's role. She grappled with her son's wiry strength, trying to pull him down. A black figure brandishing a rifle appeared in the embers' light. The butt struck her head. Mary's hands opened, and her limp fingers released her son.

Later, when she tried to remember, she dimly recalled an interminable journey in the jolting Peking Cart. Later, she dimly recalled jouncing across a roadless plain cradled in Matilda's arms. Her first clear memory was the terror she felt when she opened her eyes to see George Parker's distorted face hovering amid woolly grayness. She feared her sight was impaired, but a greater terror swept aside that first fear.

"The children?" she asked. "Are they all right?"

"The kids are fine, Mary," Parker soothed her. "But you have severe concussion. You must rest, otherwise . . ."

Reassured, she sank gratefully into oblivion. Later, she was told that she had hovered on the edge of unconsciousness for eight days, sustained by Matilda, who spooned thin millet gruel into her mouth. Later, she was told that she had suffered a hairline skull fracture from the blow. But her own memories were as hazy and distorted as a bad dream.

She knew flashes of lucidity. She clearly remembered waking when Dr. Parker's stubby fingers changed the dressing on her wound.

"It'll be all right, Mary," he said. "We've been taken by bandits, common bandits. They're talking about ransom. They must let us go. I think they're a bit frightened by what they've done."

During another moment of fitful consciousness, she saw Matilda's plain, tear-stained face. Guinevere and Jonnie stood behind their aunt.

"Are you all right, Mummy?" her daughter asked. "Are you feeling better?"

"Uncle George says you'll be fine," Jonnie told her with masculine assurance. "Crikey! What an adventure! Bandits holding us in a cave for ransom. If I were bigger, I'd . . ."

Even Jonnie's ebullience yielded to fear on the fifth day after their capture when two angry brigands stalked stiff-legged into the cave. The smaller, wearing a tattered red tunic that had obviously been taken from the body of some British sergeant long dead, fingered the hilt of his sword. The half-moon-shaped blade, three feet long and a foot broad, gleamed from repeated polishing. It was the only clean thing about the angry brigand chief, whose clawed fingernails were rimmed with filth. The burly subchief beside him was dressed in the faded blue-cotton jacket and trousers of the North China peasant. A constellation of blackheads surrounded his broad nose, and his coarse hair was grimy. He wore a heavy bandolier slung across his chest, and he swung his battered submachine gun in malicious menace.

"It's finished!" The chieftain spat out his words like venom. "All finished! If there's no reply tomorrow, we send them your ears."

Matilda strained to comprehend the heavy Shantung brogue and began translating in response to George Parker's gesture. But the brigand silenced her.

"No reply in three days," he stormed, "and we send them heads, your heads."

After the chief permitted Matilda to translate, Parker pondered his reply.

"Tell him," the American finally said, "not to be afraid."

Though Matilda looked at him astonished, Parker overbore her fears.

"I know what I'm doing," he asserted. "Go ahead."

While Gwinnie gazed adoringly at the young doctor, Matilda haltingly repeated his words in Mandarin.

"Afraid?" She interpreted the chieftain's answering tirade. "He says *we* should be afraid, not him. He has nothing to be afraid of. We're in his power—and he can kill us easily as stamping on cockroaches, dirty foreign cockroaches."

"Tell him," Parker replied, "that we understand why he is afraid, why he is blustering. No one, no sane Chinese harms the Sekloongs, and he is obviously a man of intelligence. We know he has been misled."

The chieftain replied briefly, and Matilda's voice quavered as she translated: "If that's true, he says, then . . . then the best thing he can do is kill us and bury us all right now. No one could ever know. . . ."

"I've written as he asked, to the most appropriate man, to Harry, Sek Sai-loong," Parker said. "The ransom will come soon. If he treats us well, with courtesy, we will understand it is not his fault, that he was misled. If he threatens further or harms us, no power can save

341

him from the vengeance of the Sekloongs. The Societies, the Green and Red Bands, will hunt him to the furthest corner of Mongolia, even to Turkestan or Tibet."

"He asks: 'Can you guarantee the ransom?'" Matilda passed on the reply.

"Of course. Just as I can guarantee his fate if he mistreats us. But the Sekloongs will forgive him, since he is only a tool—if he treats us with courtesy."

George Parker's hectoring was effective, though similar scenes were played almost daily. His pretence of calm confidence subdued the brigand leader, who was indeed fearful of the consequences of the kidnapping. It had seemed a simple affair when it was originally proposed to him by emissaries from the capital. Even he did not know whom he served, though the emissaries had hinted that the Universal Ruler in Peking himself approved the punishment of the arrogant foreigners. Worse, he had not known that the seemingly insignificant foreigners were connections of the Sekloongs until after he had seized them.

At dusk on the ninth day, Mary returned to full consciousness. A small fire burned near the mouth of the cave, and she lay bundled in quilts on a tarpaulin spread over millet straw. George Parker beamed with professional satisfaction, and Guinevere seized her mother's hands with fierce affection. Matilda smiled tremulously, and Jonnie jumped up and down, bubbling with long-suppressed words.

"Mummy, you know what, Mummy? Today . . ."

"Your mother needs her rest," George Parker admonished. "I'll tell her quickly. Mary, the ransom's promised. Tomorrow—or the next day—we'll be free. I'll give you a sedative now."

Mary was ravenous when she awoke the next morning. She insisted on feeding herself from the earthen pot of millet gruel. Matilda yielded, as Matilda always yielded, and afterward produced a pocket mirror. Shocked at the grimy, wild-eyed visage that stared back at her amid a turban of stained bandages, Mary set to work with a damp cloth to repair the worst ravages.

"They've come," Jonnie shouted from the mouth of the cave. "They've come. I can see. . . . It's Uncle Harry and a big foreigner with six guards on ponies."

Harry Sekloong erupted into the cave. He swept up his niece and nephew without breaking stride and kneeled beside their mother. When he kissed Mary's cheek, she felt her tears welling. Behind Harry padded the ponderously comforting figure of Two-Gun Cohen, his broad face beaming.

"At your service, Madam," he boomed. "Rescues rapidly and painlessly performed. No charge, courtesy of the Gazetted Bank of Gibraltar and Asia."

"Are you all right, Mary?" Harry whispered. "Mary, my dear!"

"Fit as a flea." She smiled to reassure him, and pain scythed her temples. "Fit as two fleas—and crawling with fleas."

"That's my girl!"

If only I were, she thought bleakly for an instant. But relief swept aside her momentary grief. She heard the Two-Gun General's rumbling voice. His words puzzled her, perhaps because she was half-dazed.

". . . and a fine addition to our war chest," he seemed to say.

September 28, 1914

MARY Sekloong's perception of the next month was fogged by pain. She was bedridden when European civilization began its systematic self-immolation in August 1914. The armies of the Great Powers marched after the assassination in Sarajevo of Archduke Franz Ferdinand, heir to the crowns of the Austro-Hungarian Empire, ignited the war that was to destroy the world created by nineteenth-century optimism, dynamism, and imperialism. No human mind could yet conceive the awful consequences of the Great War, but the Sekloongs were well prepared for the immediate commercial opportunities. Despite his preoccupation with the

Wheatleys' threat, Sir Jonathan had acted upon Mary's advice to purchase large quantities of raw materials and basic commodities. Yet the lingering optimism of the golden era just ending was so pervasive that Jonnie was sent back to Stonyhurst with hardly a thought of the dangers he might face on the journey or in England. The Hong Kong business community, equally complacent, saw no need to alter its accustomed style of life. Everyone knew the war that had begun in August would be over by Christmas.

By mid-September Mary felt strong enough to press Sir Jonathan for an explanation of why her party had been kidnapped and how the ransom had been paid. He was evasive, pleading the press of business and admonishing her that she must rest free of care until she was fully recovered. Though she gathered from Charles's casual remarks that the Sekloongs were on excellent terms with His Majesty's Government, while the Wheatleys were in disfavor, she had to restrain her curiosity until the Old Gentleman was quite ready to speak. He finally chose to do so on September 28, the first day she was well enough to attend a family dinner at The Castle to celebrate both her own recovery and Harry's fleeting visit to Hong Kong. Giving the family champagne in the library, Sir Jonathan offered the information she had sought earlier.

"We, the Allies and China, will finally defeat our enemies," he observed. "But it will be a long war. However, I want now to give Mary her share of the profits already earned as a result of her advice. We've acted most honorably, and we've profited thereby."

Mary accepted a check as large as a page from an old family Bible. Startled by the barbaric display, she folded the thick paper and tucked it into her silver-mesh evening purse. Her finicky genteel mother had instilled the convention: One never so much as glanced at the amount of remuneration in the donor's presence. Besides, she always left accountings to Sir Jonathan. The sum, she was confident, would buy her a necklace, a sumptuous present for Charles, and a few baubles for the children.

"Have a look," Sir Jonathan urged.

Mary overcame her reluctance and stiffened in astonishment: *Pay to Mary Philippa Osgood Sekloong—* £116,327/6s./11d. The single sheet of paper made her independently wealthy.

"But, Father," she protested, "it's too much, much too much. I never dreamed . . ."

"Actually, Mary, it's too little," Sir Jonathan interjected. "The finder's fee I'd normally pay for information and the profits from your personal trading account total 151,378 pounds, 3 shillings, and 8 pence."

"He's cheated you, old girl," Charles guffawed. "He's holding out, let me see, 35,055 pounds, 6 shillings, and 10 pence."

"Correct, Charles," Sir Jonathan said. "Whatever your failings, your reckoning's excellent. By the way, it's for Mary's individual use, not your joint account."

"So I gather," Charles laughed. "But, Mary, he wants you to ask why the deduction."

"Yes, Father," she responded mechanically, still shocked by the sum, "why the deduction?"

"I deducted your share of the ransom, 35,000 pounds, plus out-of-pocket expenses totaling 53 pounds, 6 shillings, and 10 pence. You'll note I've debited you with only one fifth the ransom."

"My share of the ransom, I see," she echoed unthinking, then flared: "Shouldn't you deduct Jonnie and Gwinnie's share? What about George Parker?"

"No need," Sir Jonathan answered softly. "Charles pays for his children—and Dr. Parker was looking after you, my valued business associate. His ransom's a legitimate charge on the firm."

"Then," Mary persisted, "why must I pay my part?"

"Because you're an independent trader, doing business on your own account. Besides, it was your rashness, your foolishness that got you all captured. You were responsible for the family. I'd put you in charge. Therefore, you pay for yourself—until you learn how to make others pay for you."

Mary's resentment was diluted by amusement. The sting in the tail of a princely payment was characteristic of the Old Gentleman's business philosophy, as was the meticulously precise figure. He was normally scrupulously fair; he could be excessively punctilious when it suited his purposes; he occasionally shaded reckonings in his own favor, though always honestly; and he insisted to the last farthing upon receiving all sums due him. She acknowledged the force of his argument and took the moral.

"You never told us, Father," Matilda ventured, "how you paid our ransom. The Wheatleys must've had us kidnapped. But what then?"

Sir Jonathan deliberately chose a panatella, decapitated it with his gold cigar-cutter, and lit it before speaking.

"All right, I'll begin and let Harry sum up. Of course the Wheatleys were behind it, and others even more powerful. Otherwise, no brigand would've dared kidnap a Sekloong. The Wheatleys were desperate after their gold shipment somehow disappeared. They thought they could recoup by putting immense pressure on me. Jonnie, Charles's heir, and Mary, my invaluable aide —they were taken as hostages. I was to be compelled to end my interference with their plot—the plot blessed by His Majesty's Foreign Office—to make President Yüan Shih-kai Emperor. Yüan's men, agents of the *Tsung-tung,* the Universal Ruler in Peking, actually put the brigands up to the kidnapping."

"The story, Father," Matilda reminded him.

"My part was simple. They asked a ransom of 60,000 *taels,* say 350,000 pounds. But the Wheatleys themselves ended up footing half the bill. That's the story."

"Don't be provoking," Mary pressed. "That's an accounting, not an explanation."

"Harry?" Sir Jonathan nodded to his younger son.

"I can't be quite as brief. You all know the Wheatleys'd arranged to lend two million *taels,* about 11 million pounds, to Yüan Shih-kai, their collateral the Imperial Treasures. The Sekloongs were supposed to take the blame, and the Republic of China was to be the real victim. The House of Sekloong would be damned for trafficking in stolen goods; the republicans would be crushed by a new Imperial Dynasty."

"Get on with it, Harry," Charles chided. "We all know that. But even I don't know just what happened next."

"I obey, Elder Brother," Harry mocked. "It's really simple. Before Yüan Shih-kai turned over the Treasures, half the gold, a million *taels,* was to be delivered to Peking. Curiously, it never got there."

Harry inserted a cigarette into a stubby ivory holder and sipped his champagne. Gauging the moment precisely, he resumed just an instant before Charles would have erupted in impatience.

"You may've read that the Hankow–Peking Limited was robbed by bandits on July nineteenth. Those were no bandits. They were soldiers of the revolution, Dr. Sun Yat-sen's Nationalist revolution. We merely reclaimed part of the loot the Wheatleys've stolen from China over the years."

"That simple, Harry?" Mary taunted.

"Well, not quite," he grinned. "Our men could only take about half the bullion, say 18.5 tons worth about £2.8 million. Cohen and I had a thousand men in the hills. It came to about 80 pounds a man. The rest we buried."

"And the ransom?" Mary asked. "The figures don't tally."

"Dr. Sun insisted the House of Sekloong should be rewarded for information that led to recovery of stolen property—and for preserving the National Treasures. He insisted on paying half the ransom, though I urged him to forget my personal interest."

"You, of course," Mary laughed, "had nothing to do with rescuing us."

"Well, I did take leave to see you safe. Charles couldn't get away from Shanghai. He worked with Judah Haleevie to pinpoint the bullion shipment and later in clearing our gold. Two-Gun Cohen insisted on coming along. But let Father finish. The rest is really his story."

Sir Jonathan's magisterial manner combined the absolute authority of the two most authoritarian beings on earth, a senior Mandarin and an Anglo-Irish earl.

"The final accounting was clear. Item: The Wheatleys retained 1 million *taels,* an unavoidable concession. Item: We paid 30,000 *taels* of the ransom and Dr. Sun's Nationalists the other half. That was equitable. Item: I've debited Mary for one fifth the total, perhaps excessive, but she had to learn the lesson."

"And the Wheatleys?" Mary asked.

"Losing some five and a half million sterling was a crippling blow, almost a fatal blow. And the word went round—with our help. Yüan Shih-kai lost all confidence in the Wheatleys when they didn't deliver the gold. Other Chinese were infuriated by the plot after we told them, very discreetly. London was infuriated at the Wheatleys' and Yüan Shih-kai's clumsiness. That ended the Foreign Office's flirtation with the former Viceroy who wanted to be Emperor. The practical British politicians washed their hands of the Wheatleys and gave their confidence to the loyal Sekloongs."

"It gave us an in with the War Office," Mary suggested, "helped our sales, didn't it?"

"Quite," Sir Jonathan answered crisply. "Besides, I couldn't really explain to Derwent's Chinese customers why the *hong* was interfering in Chinese politics—and, worse, intervening ineptly. Fortunately, the humble comprador had to talk only with Derwent's *Chinese* associates. The Wheatleys had to explain to both His Majesty's Government and their British associates—but couldn't."

"So everyone profited," Mary mused.

"Except," Harry amended maliciously, "so-called President Yüan, the bandits, who met with a mortal misfortune, and the Wheatleys."

June 8, 1916–June 18, 1916

THE Ballroom of Hong Kong's Government House was a serene enclave of archaic ceremony in a world at war on the forenoon of Thursday, June 8, 1916. The glaring tropical sunlight filtered through woven-grass blinds shone on the oiled leaves of potted palms, each leaf polished separately by the servants. Crystal chandeliers tinkled in the faint breeze above rows of red-velvet chairs. The ritual pomp displayed the total self-confidence still felt by an era that was obliterating itself on the battlefields of Europe. The bejeweled ladies in pastel morning dresses and the bemedaled gentlemen in frock-coats or full-dress uniforms betrayed no awareness that thousands of young men were at the moment dying in the man-made purgatory around the fortresses of Verdun in northeastern France half a world away.

Before the pitched battle that had begun in February finally ended in October, almost a million soldiers in khaki and field-gray would have perished on blood-sodden fields pounded into a morass of mud by high explosives. General Philippe Pétain would have made his name a synonym for stubborn integrity by ordering, "They shall not pass!"—the same Philippe Pétain who was to besmirch his name by collaborating with France's conquerors a quarter of a century later. General Erich von Falkenhayn would have dissipated his reputation as a master strategist, and the Imperial German Armies would have receded from their high-water mark of conquest. The generals' pawns, the instruments of their grisly craft, were an entire generation of Europeans that marched with flags flying and bands playing to its destruction.

Far from the calm security of His Britannic Majesty's Crown Colony, men impaled on barbed-wire cried out in vain appeal; other men were torn apart by shells in an uncomprehending instant; and horses screaming in agony were entangled in the slimy snares of their own intestines. The heavens' fitful thunder occasionally overwhelmed the ceaseless thunder of the guns, and the rains of summer fell on the louse-infested troops. Explosions cast up geysers of mud seeded with the shattered bones and battered steel helmets of those who had died earlier. The Allied Forces were advancing gloriously, crawling on their lacerated bellies across the fouled earth. The Central Powers would attack time and time again before both sides finally halted in utter exhaustion of spirit and body six months later.

The Armageddon that was demolishing a civilization did not stir the Ballroom where portraits of King George V and Queen Mary gazed benevolently upon the overdressed audience. The Colony's elite were gathered for the presentation of honors bestowed by the Crown. Several unescorted ladies, who would have walked barefoot across broken glass rather than fail to appear, demonstrated that a number of the Colony's young men were serving their Sovereign in uniform abroad. Otherwise Hong Kong was utterly untouched. The conflict was so remote it might have been fought on another planet.

The distant holocaust did, however, preoccupy some members of the complacent assembly. Demure in a tiered skirt of gray silk and a matching jacket with wide military lapels, Mary Philippa Osgood Sekloong strove to restrain her wandering thoughts while keeping an anxious eye on her scrubbed and polished brood. Guinevere and Charlotte preened in light-pink dresses, while James and Thomas squirmed in starched collars and flannel jackets. Fourteen-year-old Jonnie was lying in his narrow bed at Stonyhurst dreaming of cricket in the brief Lancashire summer and the College's Combined Cadet Force, while Charles, not quite four, was too young to attend. Their mother remembered that it had all begun for her sixteen years earlier in the same Ballroom, but her thoughts were irresistibly drawn to the carnage in France.

Her father, John Philip Osgood, had died of a heart attack at Paschendaele in 1915. His lifelong quest for a commission having finally succeeded, he was, at sixty-one, a captain (temporary/acting) in the Royal Wessex Fusiliers. The steadfast admirer who was briefly her lover, Lord Peter Comyn French, had been among the first to go. A shell splinter had pierced the brain of the newly promoted Brigadier General in Flanders in 1914. Even her brother Thomas was serving in

France. Though an insignificant lieutenant of the Territorial Forces, he had characteristically contrived assignment as an intelligence officer on the staff of Field Marshal Sir John French.

Seated beside his wife, Charles Sekloong was also thinking of France. He twisted his heavy torso against the unaccustomed constriction of his bandbox-new khaki uniform, crossed by a gleaming Sam Browne belt, and a major's gold crowns glittered on his epaulets. His younger brother Harry was austere in a gray, high-necked tunic, the Sun Yat-sen suit that was the hallmark of the Kuomintang, the Nationalist Party. He regarded his elder brother quizzically. Harry rendered allegiance not to the British Crown, but to his idol, Generalissimo Sun Yat-sen of the new Revolutionary Alliance, who was soon to become President Sun Yat-sen of the Provisional (and precarious) Republic of China with its capital at Canton.

The war in distant Europe did not concern Harry Sekloong. He was dedicated to reclaiming power in North and Central China from the warlords who had cast the country into anarchic civil war by usurping the authority of the legitimately elected Dr. Sun Yat-sen. He could not know that it would take more than a decade to achieve that purpose; he could not imagine that the Nationalists' triumph would initiate two decades of even more vicious strife.

All the men still living who had touched Mary's life deeply were assembled in Government House that June morning. The Victoria Cross on John Williams's breast, simply inscribed FOR VALOUR, drew greater attention than the crossed swords and pip of a major general on his epaulets. He had arrived earlier that week as head of a military purchasing mission, and she had not yet spoken with him. But the Major General was to attend the Sekloong banquet that night, as was Dr. George Chapman Parker, who sat behind her, casual and neutral in a cream-linen American suit.

Mary gathered her wandering thoughts and took her mother-in-law's hand. Lady Lucinda was immense in a most unsuitable mauve-and-pink confection, and her massive diamond bracelet was more brilliant than the crystal chandeliers.

The Governor stood stiff on the red-carpeted dais in the splendid discomfort of his white dress uniform. His sweat-slippery fingers eased his gold-scrolled choker collar. Sir Francis May's ruddy-cheeked aide-de-camp stood behind him, holding a velvet-lined box in which lay a six-barred bronze cross on a saxon-blue, scarlet-striped silk ribbon.

"Sir Jonathan Sekloong, Knight Bachelor," the aide intoned. "Please present yourself."

Jonathan Sekloong ascended the red-carpeted steps and bowed fractionally. Despite his simple long-gown of blue silk, his silver-gray hair and pointed beard endowed him with authority.

"Sir Jonathan Sekloong," the Governor read, "it has pleased His Imperial and Royal Majesty, George V, of the United Kingdom of Great Britain and Ireland, King, Emperor of India, Defender of the Faith, and Sovereign of the British Orders of Knighthood to admit you in the grade of Knight Commander to membership in the Most Distinguished Order of St. Michael and St. George.

"This honor is conferred in recognition of your extraordinary services in advancing the prosperity of His Majesty's Crown Colony of Hong Kong by your indefatigable endeavors in the realms of commerce and philanthropy, and, further, by your great services in promoting amicable relations between the Colony and the Republic of China, and particularly in recognition of your unceasing endeavors in providing for the supply of the implements and necessities of war to His Majesty's forces now engaged in mortal conflict with the enemies of the Crown."

Sir Jonathan inclined his head, and Sir Francis May slipped the silken collar of a Knight Commander of St. Michael and St. George around his neck. The heavy cross entangled itself for a moment in Sir Jonathan's beard.

"The devil!" the Governor murmured.

Applause welled from the senior officials and *taipans* in the front rows. Richard Wheatley, bent with age, slapped his palms together perfunctorily once. Mary concealed her amusement behind her fan before resuming her vigorous clapping.

"That damned Sekloong!" Dick Wheatley's stage whisper was clearly audible. "First Knight Bachelor, now K.C.M.G.—'Kindly Call Me God.' First Chinese to get that gong. Don't know *what* we're coming to."

The Sekloongs exchanged glances. The disastrous loan to Yüan Shih-kai had deprived Richard Wheatley of the knighthood he would otherwise have received as *taipan* of the Colony's chief *hong*.

Hong Kong tradition, that unstable amalgam of Chinese and British folkways, required the House of Sekloong to give an ostentatious banquet to celebrate the honor. Sir Jonathan had pretended reluctance, though Mary knew he would have dared bankruptcy to observe the convention—if the sacrifice had been even remotely necessary. In the same spirit, he flicked the heavy cross with his forefinger and contemptuously recited the engraved motto: "AUSPICIUM MELLIORUM AEVI. 'Portent of a Better Age,' indeed! We'll be lucky if it's worth another £1,000 a year."

Nevertheless, the young Sekloongs knew that he was possessively proud of the honor. The first Chinese to build on the sacrosanct Peak had become the first Chinese to receive the K.C.M.G. Yet they were not able to completely understand his motivation. Was it simply his fierce competitiveness? Was it satisfaction at forcing the Hong Kong Establishment to bestow the unprecedented honor with a pretence of good grace? Both those feelings were undoubtedly strong. But did he not also feel pride in recognition by the British Crown he had, in his own way, served well?

The new insignia shone beneath his wing-collar above the Order of the Phoenix conferred by Dr. Sun Yat-sen when the family gathered in the library of The Castle. A hundred or so honored guests had been asked to join them for drinks before going by sedan chair to the Peak Hotel, which the House of Sekloong had pre-empted for the formal Chinese banquet. Even The Castle could not accommodate the 2,000 who would sit down to dinner.

"I see, Father," Harry remarked irreverently, "that you're still perverse. White tie, boiled shirt, all the foreign trimmings for the Chinese banquet, but a long-gown for the British ceremony this morning."

Inured to his younger son's raillery, Sir Jonathan raised his crystal champagne glass in a toast.

"We have much to celebrate tonight. This small honor to myself and the greater prosperity recent circumstances have brought us. We also have much to regret. As you know, Charles sails in three days' time for England and, I imagine, later France. God grant him a safe return!"

The Sekloongs raised their glasses, and Sir Jonathan continued: "Harry will return to serving Dr. Sun Yat-sen and the Republic. God grant their arms victory!"

Again the toast passed, and Sir Jonathan raised his glass for the third time.

"My sons are not deserting me. Each follows his conscience. I rejoice that they do, despite my fears for their safety. However, they are not leaving me wholly unhelped in using my small abilities to provide for the family."

Anticipating his words, Mary composed her features in appropriate modesty. But she fingered the massive gold-and-jade necklace she had capriciously worn to recall the past to John Williams.

"The ladies!" Sir Jonathan said. "God bless them. Lucinda, my constant companion! Without her, I would face the world alone. Matilda, my precious daughter, always a great comfort. And Mary, also a comfort, and my strong right arm in the business of the House."

The Sekloongs again raised their crystal goblets. Drinking to herself in the Chinese manner, Mary looked over the rim at the wily Old Gentleman. Alone, indeed! The Pearl Concubine, who was pregnant again, the Jade Concubine, though retired, and other complaisant ladies were delighted to comfort Sir Jonathan most thoroughly whenever he chose. But they were his concern, not hers, and he was still speaking with unwonted formality.

"Just one last toast: the Republic of China. As you know, President Yüan Shih-kai died two days ago in Peking, after his plots to make himself Emperor collapsed. The road to power's now clear for Dr. Sun. He'll need good fortune."

"I drink to that cheerfully," Harry responded. "Not to Viceroy Yüan's death, but to the collapse of all efforts to restore the Empire. To the Republic of China."

"The guests, Jonathan," Lady Lucinda prompted after they had sipped the champagne. "They'll be arriving in a minute. Shouldn't we . . ."

"By all means, my dear. Let us greet our guests."

At 7:35 P.M. on June 8, 1916, the descending sun was just touching the jagged hills behind Kowloon. The guests were punctual, their deviation from Hong Kong's habitual tardiness acknowledging the occasion's unique importance. Before moving to the Peak Hotel for the largest banquet the Colony had ever known, the chosen hundred came to toast the newly created Knight Commander. Sedan chairs painted in their owners' livery swayed through the golden-tiled arch under the winged dragon that guarded the House of Sekloong. The sweating coolies "trotted with the inborn arrogance of thoroughbred horses," as a Chinese essayist had described their proper gait four centuries earlier.

The Governor's chair, marked by a gold crown, was first. Since protocol prescribed that the King's personal representative should arrive after the other guests had gathered, the unique compliment was unmistakable. Sir Francis May, tall and fiercely mustached, extended a scarred hand. Beaming with blatant hypocrisy, Richard Wheatley followed the Honorable Rachel Wheatley. He was tissue-paper thin at seventy-nine, silver-frail as an ascetic bishop. His wife was painfully emaciated, and her skin was so taut she appeared all prehensile nose.

Since Derwent, Hayes was unquestionably the Number One *hong,* the Wheatleys' precedence was unchallengeable. The chair coolies of the *taipans* of Jardine, Matheson contended for second place with the coolies of Butterfield, Swire. They were followed by their compradors, Robert Hotung of Jardine's, who was to receive his own knighthood a few years later, and Y. K. Mok of Butterfield. Mosing Way of the East Asiatic Bank came next. Like the Colony itself, all those men had been tainted—and enriched—by the opium trade. Like Sir Jonathan himself, Robert Hotung and Mosing Way had gained much credit among enlightened Chinese and Europeans by disengaging early and by fighting to stop the traffic. None could have known that opium, outlawed in China in the mid-nineteenth century, would not be banned by Hong Kong law until 1946.

Successive sedan chairs discharged their eminent passengers without regard to formal precedence: the Colonial Secretary and the Chief Justice; Sir Shouson and Lady Chow; and the Parsees, Mr. and Mrs. H. N. Mody, alighted before The Castle. The Commander, British Forces swung through the winged-dragon gate in a gold-and-vermillion chair, followed by Major General John Williams, V.C. Bemused by British pomp, Dr. George Chapman Parker, wearing a white dinner jacket, stepped from a red public sedan chair.

The stream flowed on. Two royal-blue chairs flaunting the winged Sekloong dragon discharged Sydney and Gregory Sek, who had come from Shanghai. Two years apart in age, Sir Jonathan's sons by his first wife were pudgy twin penguins in tight tailcoats, unprepossessing by any standards, Chinese or Western. Their mother, Lillian, had been the daughter of a minor Ningpo merchant by a Cantonese peasant girl first brought into his family home as an eight-year-old *mui-tsai,* an indentured servant.

The Seks' presence was faintly disquieting. Then plain Mr. Sek Howan, Jonathan had espoused their mother in a traditional Chinese ceremony in 1873. He had married Lady Lucinda in the Church in 1875, five years before Lillian died in his stead under the daggers of Secret Society assassins hired by his business rivals. Though polygamy was unexceptionable, the normally imperturbable Sir Jonathan felt uncomfortable in the brothers' presence. They forcefully recalled the tawdry days when he was clawing his way toward affluence and respectability.

Judah Haleevie had also come from Shanghai, accompanied by his eleven-year-old daughter Sarah. Mary offered a special smile of welcome to the financier and his dark-eyed daughter. She waved when General Morris Abraham Cohen squeezed his bulk out of a public sedan chair. She felt great affection for the ill-matched pair, the Hebrew Mandarin and the Two-Gun General.

She saw with half an eye that Guinevere had thrown her arms around "Uncle George" Parker, while twelve-year-old Charlotte was flirting with Manfei, the eighteen-year-old son of Mosing Way. Thomas and James were converging on the Two-Gun General, demanding another highly colored installment of his adventures. All small boys, she knew, were fascinated by the romance of soldiering, but her two seemed incapable of thinking about anything else.

The man who had briefly been her own soldier was sweeping down upon her. She remembered the John Williams of sixteen years ago, the big, hearty athlete. Dismayed, she saw that he was no longer simply burly, but had become immense, bulging his short mess-jacket and red-striped trousers like the rubber-tire Michelin man. His powerful muscles had turned to fat, and broken blood vessels blotched his puffy cheeks. Although he was not yet forty, his corpulence made him appear twenty years older.

"Mary!" He advanced with open arms. "Mary, dearest!"

Heads turned at the salutation. She offered her cheek as his arms closed around her, but he kissed her full on the lips. His breath was heavy with gin.

She heard shocked clucking from the Chinese ladies and scandalized whispers from the Europeans. Behind his silver tray of champagne glasses, Ah Sam was impassively disapproving. His frozen smile weighed and condemned the man he had remembered fondly as Miss Mary's friend.

"My dear John," Mary said coolly, "how are you? I hear you've done great things since I last saw you. It's been so long, I can hardly recall . . ."

"I see you're wearing my necklace, Mary darling!"

He did not lower his voice, though he stood only a few inches away, breathing gin into her upturned face.

"Oh?" Mary strove for composure. "I'd forgotten."

"Come off it. You couldn't forget where those bloody great chunks of jade came from."

His heavy forefinger flicked the miniature of the Victoria Cross on his lapel.

"Of course, it's a pretty bauble," she answered. "My husband's a connoisseur of jade. He often admires the necklace—and wonders which Imperial princess it belonged to."

John Williams grinned, unabashed by the snub. The cold perspiration of anger prickled on Mary's back. She wanted to snatch off the necklace and hurl it in his face. Instead, she affected polite interest in his activities.

"Congratulations. I see you're now a major general. What brings you to Hong Kong?"

"I'll be about for a while. Big purchasing mission, you know. But *cumshaw,* too. I'm sure we can do business, much business under the right conditions—all the right conditions."

His heavy eyelid winked, and his muscle-knotted forehead crinkled. The proposition could not have been cruder; while better men were dying in France, he was boldly proposing in public that the House of Sekloong bribe him to award it contracts.

"*All* the right conditions," he repeated, parading his confidence that she would fall into his arms and his bed.

"Perhaps, John," she answered. "My father-in-law strives to serve the war effort to the utmost. But, now, you must excuse me while I play the hostess."

She evaded his extended arm and turned away to murmur trivialities to a startled Mosing Way.

She had longed to slap John's grinning face. Yet she

358

knew she would be forced to smile at the Major General again, while evading his advances and praying his visit would be short. Business was, after all, business. The chief business of the House of Sekloong at that moment was with His Majesty's War Office, represented by Major General John Williams V.C., who had been transformed from an engaging youth into an obese lout.

The Royal Mail Steamer *Triton* of the Peninsular and Oriental Line sailed for Southampton at 4 P.M. on Sunday, June 11, 1916, from her anchorage off Blake Pier. Her passenger list included Major (temporary) Charles Sekloong and six war-service second lieutenants. The directors of the big *hongs* had deemed it necessary to offer an additional contribution to His Majesty's Forces, since young British manhood had been brutally scythed by the war. Pressed by those *hongs,* the civil servants in London still maintained that the best service they could render was maintaining the Empire's trade. Nonetheless, a gesture was desirable, as long as it was not overdone. Each *hong* had contributed one subaltern, chosen by lot from dozens of volunteers. In June 1916, fifty-odd lieutenants were dying and more than one hundred and fifty were wounded each week in France. But the *hongs* had, after all, not started the conflict that swelled their profits.

R.M.S. *Triton* was a famous passage-maker, and the P & O guaranteed that she would reach Southampton in twenty-eight days, "barring acts of God and the misfortunes of war." She would not encounter acute danger until she passed through the Straits of Gibraltar into the Atlantic to dare the prowling submarines of the Imperial German Navy. The light cruiser *Emden* had slipped into the Indian Ocean in August 1914 to join the armored cruisers *Scharnhorst, Gneisenau* and *Nürnberg,* which had escaped from the German naval base at Tsingtao in North China under Vice-Admiral Graf von Spee. *Emden* was sunk on November 9, 1914, by the cruiser *Sydney* of the Royal Australian Navy. On December 8, von Spee's squadron had been brought to

359

bay and destroyed off the Falkland Islands in the South Atlantic. In Far Eastern and Indian waters, *Triton* faced only the remote peril of commerce raiders disguised as innocent merchantmen.

Nonetheless, it was a wartime sailing. Though the portholes of Charles Sekloong's spacious cabin were open to catch the afternoon breeze, their glass was painted black. Awareness of possible danger to *Triton* and those who sailed in her heightened the mixed gaiety and sorrow both travelers and those left behind customarily felt whenever the Blue Peter fluttered aloft and the ship's siren shrieked periodic warnings that the anchors would soon be coming up. Alone with Charles in his cabin, for a few moments free of the throngs of children, relations, and friends, Mary Sekloong clung to the husband toward whom she thought she had become comfortably indifferent years earlier.

"You *will* see Jonnie if you possibly can," she reminded him for the fourth time. "Just as soon as you reach England, won't you, Charles?"

"Of course, my dear," he reassured her. "As soon as I can. He must be training hard in the cadet force. Bet he won't mind showing off the old man's uniform."

"You *will* see him?" Mary repeated her plea. "You *will* make an effort? If this war goes on, he . . ."

"Don't worry about that, my dear." Charles was surprised by his sudden sense of deprivation at leaving her. "It'll be over long before he . . ."

"And, Charles, I . . ." Mary's voice faltered, finally halting.

"Yes, my dear?"

"Charles," she blurted. "I *do* love you, Charles."

His familiar features, their impression blurred by long familiarity, assumed again the lean contours and the youthful intensity that had first attracted her. His hazel eyes, she saw, were damp.

"You know," he replied slowly, abashed by his own emotion, "Mary, darling, I haven't been the best husband. But I do love you too."

He kissed her with unaccustomed tenderness, and Mary felt the ardent response she had thought his touch had lost the power to evoke. She tightened her arms around his neck and let herself float in rediscovered passion.

The moment of renewal was brief. Thomas and James erupted into the cabin, demanding that their father rejoin the party in the saloon. It was neither wholly love nor hero worship; they wanted to show off his new uniform to their unfortunate cousins and friends whose fathers wore familiar, drab lounge suits. Tugging at his hands, the boys drew Charles away. Mary followed slowly.

She had, she realized, misassessed not only Charles, but others as well. Lord Peter, whom she originally thought a callous, lighthearted rake, had before his death revealed himself as the best of the men she knew. She recalled with shame that she had rejected John Williams in part because she judged his prospects poor. He had prospered, but the clean-limbed hero she had known had been corrupted by avarice and drink. Harry? She would not think about Harry at all.

But Charles remained her own, and she prayed silently that he would return unharmed. She had, she finally realized, married Charles not primarily for his prospects, but for himself. The Sekloongs' wealth had undeniably influenced her decision, as had the lure of the exotic, but she knew she had married Charles for himself first. She swore they would truly make a new beginning when he returned. After all, she was almost thirty-six, and it was time to settle down.

Mary was not allowed to brood on either her regrets or her new resolution. Her cavaliers set out to divert her. "Mary's Four Musketeers," Sir Jonathan called them: heavy-bodied Morris Cohen, the Two-Gun General; hotheaded Harry Sekloong, his lighthearted banter belying his patriotic dedication; patrician Judah Haleevie, the most astute financial brain in Asia; and boyish Dr. George Parker, caught up in her entourage for reasons he did not quite comprehend. Early Monday morning, the four carried her off to Shatin in the New Territories.

The old Daimler had been replaced by an open Rolls-Royce with folding windshields, front and back, four spare wheels on the running-boards, and eight places for passengers. The Rolls could barely fit in the barge that carried it across Kowloon Bay. The battered Model T Ford Harry had driven down from Canton looked like a mechanical dwarf beside the royal-blue limousine with the inevitable winged dragon rampant on its side panels.

Guinevere and Charlotte were missing school to come along. With instinctive female solidarity, they were obtrusively, lovingly, almost irritatingly protective of their mother after watching their father sail away. Their three-year-old youngest brother was bundled between them in the Rolls, since his sisters believed little Charles would take Mary's mind off big Charles. Thomas and James behaved as if the excursion had been mounted for their sole pleasure. They cried out shrill demands, which their Uncle Harry at the wheel of the Ford cheerfully ignored. His own purposes, camouflaged by the family outing, were even more important than the rare pleasure of spending a day with Mary and their son, James.

The motorcars attracted stares as they rolled between the spreading trees that shaded broad Nathan Road. Motor-vehicles were rarely seen on the flat plain dotted with occasional buildings, and the rickshaw-pullers were as startled as the carthorses and water buffaloes. Casting out puffs of black smoke and heralded by the clattering of gears, they passed the Walled City of Kowloon. That legally anomalous enclave, preserved under nominal Chinese sovereignty by treaty, was a bolthole for criminals and Secret Society Braves. The British preferred not to send their police into its labyrinthine alleys, and no effective Chinese government existed to maintain order.

Crossing Boundary Street into the New Territories, they entered the age-old Chinese countryside. Plump ducks lifted incurious eyes at the snorting conveyances, and startled chickens scuttled clucking into tile-roofed farmhouses. Their bellies brushing the ground, sway-

362

backed sows led squealing piglets to succulent garbage-heaps. Thick-ruffed chow dogs barked imprecations at the rattling wagons that trailed a fearful stench, unlike the familiar aroma of pungent night-soil. Hakka women were foreshortened mushrooms under the wide, crownless circles of straw hung with black-cloth strips they wore to protect their complexions from the implacable sun. The women waded through flooded fields, stooping laboriously to transplant pale-green rice shoots. Plodding behind wooden plows drawn by patient water buffaloes, their men furrowed the fields.

The dirt road wound along the east coast of the New Territories, occasionally skirting the water's edge, more often clinging to the lip of precipices overlooking distant green islets. Though the party stopped once for a picnic lunch and three times to repair punctured tires, the motorcars made excellent time. Only three hours after crossing Hong Kong Harbor, the Rolls and the Ford triumphantly halted at Shatin, thirty-one miles away.

The boys were abashed when their arrival went unnoticed, though only two other motorcars, an Auburn and a Mercedes, stood amid the crowd that rimmed a red-earth field at the foot of the pine-covered hills. Farmers squatted on the damp ground beside peddlers who fried bright-red chunks of offal and plump brown bean-curd cakes on their portable stoves. European ladies in horse-drawn phaetons held organdy parasols over their heads, and Chinese gentlemen in cotton long-gowns directed the sodden air at their perspiring faces with painted fans. Even the ragged urchins barely glanced at the Sekloong motorcars. The throng's attention was focused on an ungainly contrivance of wire, bamboo, and cloth perched at the far end of the field—an immense kite with double wings and an elongated wooden ship's screw mounted on the engine at its prow.

The boys' pride was restored when Harry led them across the field to the airplane. They saw a small, wiry man in a close-fitting leather helmet nervously wielding a monkey wrench. Figure-eight goggles peered blindly from his forehead like an additional pair of eyes. His beady eyes were alert, and his nose was a thin beak above a hair-line mustache. Harry introduced him as Lieutenant Eddie McCormick.

"She's an Avro 504, boys," he explained in an American drawl, "eighty horsepower Gnome engine, range two hundred fifty miles, and maximum speed eighty-two miles per hour."

"You mean, Mister . . . Lieutenant," Thomas demanded, "you're going to fly that fast? Right here and now?"

"That's right, Sonny. Just as soon as I get this danged magneto fixed."

"And where to, Lieutenant?" James asked.

"Oh, just around and around for now, Sonny."

"Shall we let the Lieutenant get on with his job?" Harry suggested.

The boys swaggered across the hard-packed red earth. With the hauteur of superior beings, they ignored the surrounding urchins gaping at them.

"Uncle Harry," Thomas asked, "is he only a lieutenant? Daddy's a major. What kind of a lieutenant is he?"

"The American Army, he says," Harry replied shortly.

As if their arrival were a signal, Eddie McCormick tightened two bolts, tossed the wrench to his Chinese mechanic, and climbed into the cramped cockpit. Pulling his goggles down, he called out: "Contact!" The crowd stared as the mechanic spun the wooden propeller.

The airplane did not move, and the mechanic spun the propeller again. Three times the propeller described a half circle before stopping with a jerk. The fourth time, puffs of black smoke erupted from the engine's sausage-link exhaust pipes, and the propeller whirled amid a volley of explosions.

"There he goes," Harry cried.

The propeller's revolutions stopped abruptly, and the engine's noise died. The sweat-drenched mechanic again tugged at the propeller. The engine caught, and the propeller settled into a continuous, buzzing revolution flatulent with greasy smoke puffs. Accelerating rapidly, the Avro rolled across the field. Harry's breath caught when the machine dipped into a rut. But the airplane righted itself and lurched into the cloud-flecked sky, the string of firecrackers tied to its tail skid popping merrily.

"He's up!" the boys shrieked. "He's up!"

"So he is," Harry said. "There never was any doubt . . ."

Judah Haleevie glanced quizzically at his friend, but did not speak. The airplane circled the field six times before settling to earth again like a clumsy seagull alighting on the crest of a wave. It struck the same rut, and the tail dropped heavily.

"That's the show, gentlemen," Harry announced. "That's it. I'll have a word with Eddie McCormick before we go."

During the drive back, James and Thomas rained questions on Harry. After answering patiently for an hour, he threw up his hands when James demanded: "But why does it fly, Uncle Harry?"

"I'll explain later, when I've got a piece of paper," he answered. "We'll need a diagram."

When the boys subsided, Harry said softly to Two-Gun Cohen: "Cracked a tail plane and a landing-carriage strut. Another postponement."

A week later, Eddie McCormick became "the first man to conquer a city singlehanded," as he later boasted. A crude bomb strapped between its landing wheels, the Avro lumbered through the summer sky toward Canton ninety miles away. His target was the headquarters of General Mok Wing-sun, one of the ambitious local potentates the Chinese called *tu-chün*, "warlords," who had turned against President Sun Yat-sen. McCormick released the bomb by slashing the rope with his sheath-knife. Although the explosion merely shook the ground five hundred yards from his villa, General Mok decamped and Sun Yat-sen returned in triumph to Canton. It was a great victory at the time, though the city was to be lost and regained repeatedly. A decade was to pass before the Nationalist armies streamed out of Canton to unify China in alliance with the Communist Party, which had not yet come into existence in 1916.

The successful bombing raid was marred on the return flight. Eddie McCormick ran out of fuel and crash-landed in a flooded rice-field. He climbed out of the Avro, redolent of liquid night-soil. The American spat explosively and grinned at the incredulous Cantonese farmers.

"I guess Harry Sekloong'll just have to buy himself another air force. The Avro's a write-off, and I'm going back to the States. When you force-land in Iowa, the worst that can happen is a few broken bones and a dusting of horse-manure."

The miracle of flight was no more than a fleeting catspaw across the ruffled surface of Mary Sekloong's mind on the morning of Saturday, June 17, 1916, five days after Eddie McCormick's first triumphant ascent into the skies of Asia and four days before his one-man attack on Canton. She was not concerned with the coming triumph of airpower, as represented by the frail contraption the local Chinese had dubbed "the foreign, fire-breathing, flying-dragon with the wooden snout." Her concerns were wholly personal.

She lay late abed, exhausted by the continuing festivities that celebrated Sir Jonathan's elevation, exacerbated by the unexpected wrench of Charles's departure and the bone-shaking drive to Shatin. Besides, she felt a cold coming on. She had learned to respect the stubborn ailment the doctors called "summer grippe" and attributed to the damp heat. She suspected that they understood neither the illness nor its cause, but she had already suffered its protracted discomfort too often to flout their advice to drink large quantities of fluids while resting in a darkened room.

This particular Saturday was a good day to take to her bed. The last race-meeting of the season was scheduled for the early afternoon. She had no wish to endure the ritual attended by every notable in the Colony, as well as throngs of wager-mad Chinese. Besides, Major

General John Williams V.C. would certainly be in the Governor's box. In her exhausted state, she simply could not face his heavy innuendoes and sly leers.

Since Lady Lucinda detested the races and her daughters solicitously chose to stay with Mary, the Sekloong race party was made up of three generations of males. In a holiday mood, Sir Jonathan, Harry, Thomas, and James swung off in sedan chairs to ride the clanking Peak Tram to its lower terminus, where the Rolls waited.

Mary's Number One Boy Ah Sam had effaced himself early that morning to walk down to Happy Valley, where he hailed a rickshaw to carry him the last half-mile in state. He loved horses, and he shared his compatriots' passion for gambling. Ah Sam looked forward to spending the afternoon crammed against the railing, laying small bets, sipping tea, and nibbling delicacies sold by strolling hawkers.

Ignoring the glaring sun and the press of hundreds of sweating bodies, Ah Sam gossiped with his cronies and waited for the notables' arrival. Despite his tolerant contempt for most of the men and women he so often served, he enjoyed their pomp. The Governor and Lady May ascended to their box, which was draped with clouds of bunting, fifteen minutes before the trumpets announced the first race. Richard and the Honorable Rachel Wheatley had just taken their places in Derwent's box. The white-uniformed Chinese ushers greeted them with no less deference than the Queen's personal representative—perhaps a shade more. Respect was due to their years, their frailty, and their wealth.

The bend of the track blocked Ah Sam's view of the Sekloong box, which was further obscured by the grass-matting canopies spread above the grandstand on bamboo poles to shade the gentry from the blazing sun he resignedly endured. But he knew the entire family would attend the climactic race-meeting of the season. Protocol required their presence; the gala assembly was a quasi-sacerdotal rite, a mass obeisance to the God of Fortune. Racing was the closest thing to a common reli-

367

gion Hong Kong possessed, the only devotion shared by Chinese and Europeans, by rich and poor.

Inching at five miles an hour through moving thickets of carriages, rickshaws, sedan chairs, and pedestrians, the Sekloong Rolls boiled over in the 93° heat. Disgusted, Sir Jonathan told the chauffeur to allow the engine to cool. Since no other conveyance was available and walking was unthinkable, they would have to wait. Sir Jonathan and Harry, though not the eager boys, resigned themselves to arriving after the first race. Fortunately, their own horse, Golden Dragon, was running in the third, and they would not miss that race.

While the Sekloongs fretted in the stalled Rolls, Ah Sam cast his critical eye over the horses parading around the paddock. Though hardened by exposure to the grueling Hong Kong climate, the ponies showed their distress at the drenching humidity. Their flanks shone with sweat, and their eyes rolled white with nervous fatigue.

"Gam-tin mng ying-goi po-ma," Ah Sam magisterially told his friend, Robert Hotung's Number One Boy. "They shouldn't be running today. Everyone knows it's too late in the year and too hot. But try to tell anything to those *fan guai-tau!"* The epithet, "foreign devil-heads," rolled off his tongue without malice. That was what one called foreigners, just as one addressed them as Missy or Master.

Despite his misgivings, Ah Sam put a dollar on Number Seven. That was invariably his first bet, since he esteemed the talents of the soothsayer Silver Seventh Brother more highly than Sir Jonathan would admit to doing. Ah Sam grinned when the ponies pounded past the turn, lathered with white foam and laboring under the weight of the gentlemen jockeys. Number Seven, a rough-coated beast with a mean eye, was leading. The jockey in the scarlet-and-chartreuse silks of the Wheatleys was using his whip with sadistic urgency. On the inside, Number Three, carrying the blue-and-purple silks of Mosing Way, was closing the gap. The herd pounded past Ah Sam and out of sight around the bend.

He waited in a fury of expectation until the numbers went up on the signboard: 7, 3, 1.

Ah Sam turned to clap his friend on the back, but his heavy hand stopped in midair. In the corner of his eye he saw a red flare in the shadows under the mat-shed canopies. The next instant, a piercing cry arose from the sweating crowd jammed against the fence.

"Faw-jook! Faw-jook!" the spectators shrilled. "Fire! Fire!"

An urgent echo rolled back from the stands: *"Gow meng! Gow meng!* Save life! Save life!"

The crowds boiled into violent, mindless motion like a beehive threatened by smoke. Most spectators in the grandstand fought toward the rear exits, though a few enterprising spirits vaulted over the railing onto the field. The close-packed throng around the rail hurled itself with a single will toward the safety of the open center field. Policemen wearing white sun-helmets pushed through the fleeing spectators to the Governor's Box, while a handful of young Chinese and European men fought to clear the narrow aisles.

Ah Sam stood irresolute, his solid bulk unmoving under the impact of the screaming throng. The next instant, loyalty ingrained by sixteen years' service overcame his instinct to flee. His conscious choice required no more than twenty seconds. He hurled himself into the panic-stricken crowd like a swimmer breasting a torrent that was becoming a raging flood.

His head low, Ah Sam thrust against the fear-maddened crowd. His powerful legs worked like pistons, and his heavy hands clawed through the fleeing mass of humanity. He saw orange flames envelop the mat shed and charged like an enraged bull.

"Ma-lee Siu-jieh, wo lay-la! Ma-lee Siu-jieh, wo lay-la!" He proclaimed his single primary loyalty. "Miss Mary, I'm coming! Miss Mary, I'm coming!"

Ah Sam's momentum carried him to the railing of the grandstand, and the flames' fiery breath scorched his eyebrows. A tall European in a white suit elbowed him aside, and he stumbled. Off-balance when the next wave struck, he fell to the ground.

He was struggling to rise, still shouting, "I'm coming, Miss Mary, I'm coming!" when a policeman's thick-soled boot struck his temple. He was only half-conscious when the throng trampled him. Each successive blow forced an anguished gasp from his drawn lips and slowly pummeled the life from his body. Finally, he lay still.

Thomas and James returned late in the afternoon to report the conflagration to their mother. Mary sighed in shamed relief when they told her that all the Sekloongs were safe. Sir Jonathan and Harry had remained to direct the emergency measures at Tung Wah Hospitals. All the injured were brought to Tung Wah, which was near the racetrack, all racial distinctions, for once, ignored. Equal in death, the corpses were laid out in the adjoining Yee Szeh Mortuary.

Mary dressed distractedly, anxious to descend to Happy Valley to help at Tung Wah. But a united front of amahs convinced her that she could offer little help and might actually be a hindrance. Pacing the veranda in her voile robe, she waited for Sir Jonathan and Harry's return. She could not even busy herself seeing that a hot meal would welcome them, for the servants were already preparing quantities of food. Even Ah Sam's absence did not impair the household's efficient, raucous operation. Early in the evening, when she noted absently that he had not returned, Mary assumed that he, too, had gone to the hospital to help. Ah Sam usually did what he thought best and asked permission afterward.

The men returned shortly before midnight. Both were hollow-eyed with fatigue, and their clothes reeked of smoke. Sipping a brandy-and-soda, Harry spoke tonelessly.

"It's hellish! Last count we had was forty-three dead and more than a hundred seriously injured. God knows how many we missed."

"Who are they?" Mary was selfishly secure in the knowledge that all her household was safe.

"They found the Wheatleys, Rachel and Dick, sitting stock upright in their box in the grandstand," Harry answered. "They weren't touched by the fire, not even suffocated by the smoke. Shock, the doctors said. But, by God, the old rascal was tough. Miracle he lived this long the way he drank. Old S. Y. Lo was burned to death . . . a horrible sight. Otherwise, clerks, servants. No one you'd know, except . . ."

"Except?" Mary was chilled by apprehension.

"Two others you know, Mary," Sir Jonathan replied reluctantly. "John Williams. Six men carried him out still breathing, but he died in the ward. Heart attack or stroke. And, Mary . . . Ah Sam . . . your Ah Sam. They found him trampled underfoot, quite dead. It must have been quick, since . . ."

"Don't tell me any more," she commanded. "Not just now."

At two in the morning, Mary Sekloong sat alone in a cane chair on the veranda outside her bedroom while the household slept. Dry-eyed, she looked down into Happy Valley, where moving lanterns flickered like restless ghosts as the Fire Brigade turned over the debris.

Revulsion against the man John Williams had become initially dulled the shock of his death. But, alone in the night, she remembered the eager young lieutenant and grieved in silence for the swift passing of all youth and beauty. Not for what he was, but for what he had been—and for what she had been.

All were gone, the men for whom she had cared before marrying Charles: Hilary Metcalfe, Lord Peter French, her father, and now John Williams. Except for her distant brother, death had severed all living ties with the young woman she had been before she entered the House of Sekloong.

Her thoughts turned reluctantly to Ah Sam, and she wearily rubbed her eyes. Her fingertips came away wet with unshed tears for that rocklike man. Ferocious in aspect and cheerfully disrespectful when his judgment of her interests clashed with her own, the former pirate turned irreverent servant had, she realized, been a pillar of her existence.

Then Mary wept in fearful loneliness. Abandoned to grief, she wept in the silent night, sobbing desperately and inconsolably.

Part Five

Thomas and James

March 2, 1924–December 15, 1927

March 2, 1924

THE daffodil-yellow hull—one hundred and six feet from the cap of bowsprit to carved poop-rail—slid down the greased ways into the green water. Standing on the bunting-draped platform where the prow had rested a minute earlier, Charles and Mary Sekloong laughed together. Splattered with foam from the jereboam of champagne she had swung to christen the schooner *Regina Pacis,* they were momentarily deafened by the ten-foot-long strings of firecrackers that hung from the eaves of the boatsheds and trailed on red ribbons from the sharp cut-water. Amid the billowing clouds of smoke, they shared their joy.

Charles shifted the gold pommel of his malacca walking-stick to his left hand and took his wife's hand with his right. Mildly surprised by her husband's public display of affection, rather than astonished as she would have been ten years earlier, Mary pressed his fingers. They were leaner and, perhaps, less powerful than they had been a decade earlier, but they fitted better between her own.

Charles Sekloong had not had what the British, with heavy understatement, called "a good war." The conflict had neither brought him martial glory nor drawn heavily upon his courage and endurance. The Great War had, nonetheless, changed him substantially. In the early spring of 1924, he was a more impressive and self-possessed figure than the new-minted major who had sailed on *Triton* for Southampton in the summer of 1916. His figure, then tending toward corpulence, was slimmer, though he was still a heavy broadsword beside his rapierlike father. Steel gray at the temples, his hair was thinning, but the sleeked-back mode of the day made his high forehead imposing. No longer dimmed by flesh-cushioned sockets, his hazel eyes looked forthrightly at the world. At forty-seven, Charles Sekloong had finally become an adult, with a grown man's self-assurance and compassion.

Mary did not know precisely what had changed her husband during his absence of more than two years. The new Charles suited her, and she was wise enough not to probe the deeper reasons for his transformation.

Perhaps it was no more than the awareness of his own powers and the power his wealth commanded—an awareness that had blossomed when, for the first time in his life, he had not walked in his father's shadow. He had emerged from the war a full colonel wearing the pink-and-gray ribbon of an Officer of the Most Excellent Order of the British Empire and the tricolor of the French Croix de Guerre, as well as the Chinese Order of the Phoenix. For almost a year after arriving in London in July 1916, he had been attached to the Ministry of Armaments, an assignment fitted to his talents, if not his inclinations. He had negotiated war loans from abroad, his success facilitated by the Sekloong connections in the United States. His services were invaluable; they were not glorious.

After China declared war in August 1917, he was released from the condition he self-deprecatingly described as "my bondage to J. P. Morgan." The United States had entered the conflict in April 1917, and London no longer needed to woo private consortia to fill her war chest. Already promoted lieutenant colonel, Charles was sent to France in September 1917. That posting finally brought him within sound of guns and insured his promotion to full colonel. The rank was necessary to his function as liaison officer to the 60,000 troops China hastily sent to Europe. Those raw levies were not employed as infantrymen, but as labor battalions. Charles became, as his brother Harry laughed, "field marshal of the coolie hordes." He was one of the few field-grade British officers who spoke their languages, and they gave him their trust because of his name.

Charles had finally overcome sensitivity about his inglorious war service, but preferred not to talk about the wound that left him dependent on a walking-stick. Neither German infantrymen nor German artillerymen had inflicted that wound. A berserk coolie, screaming in the incomprehensible Foochow dialect, had rushed at him with a pick-ax. Fighting drunk on unfamiliar Calvados, the coolie had not halted when Charles coolly shot him in the shoulder with his pistol. But Charles could not shoot to kill. The pick-ax had hewn into his thigh, and splintered bone protruded through torn flesh. Finally conquering the ensuing gangrene, the surgeons were pleased to leave him with no more than a bad limp. They had discussed amputation to save his life.

Mary sympathized with his disinclination to talk about an incident that verged on farce. But the memory returned unbidden at the moment of his great triumph. The launching of *Regina Pacis* was Charles's formal declaration of independence, a ceremony celebrating his belated coming of age. The schooner was bigger, more luxurious, and heavier-engined than any craft his father had built. Charles wanted to call her *Mary*, as Sir Jonathan had named *Orchidia* after his mother and *Lucinda* after his wife. But Mary had rejected the compliment and his countersuggestion of *Guinlotte*.

"Then I'll call her for Our Lady," Charles decided.

The golden winged-dragon burgee would fly at her main trunk, but Charles had irritably rejected Harry's jesting suggestion that he have the dragon embroidered on the square-sail that would cross *Regina Pacis*'s foremast when the wind was on her quarter. The emblem was essentially his father's, and Charles was determined that *Regina Pacis* would be his ship. He was still annoyed by Mary's refusal to allow him to name the schooner after her or their daughters.

Adamantly opposed to the vulgarity of calling the craft *Mary*, she was appalled by the preciosity of a name compounded of her daughters' names. *Guinlotte*, indeed! It reminded her of villas in Surbiton called *Jametta* for James and Henrietta, or the gimcrack cabin cruisers of new-rich stockbrokers named *Milbert* for Millicent and Albert. Hypersensitive at twenty-one and twenty, the girls would have been excruciatingly embarrassed. They already presented problems enough to her, while facing problems enough of their own.

Although her self-reproach was mitigated by the practical difficulties the war had interposed, she still regretted yielding to Charles and Sir Jonathan's insistence that Guinevere and Charlotte need not go to England for schooling. Mary felt she should have insisted that they attend the Convent of the Sacred Heart at Roehampton. Instead they had been enrolled at St. Paul's, which was adequate for the daughters of middle-class Eurasians, aspiring Portuguese, ambitious Chinese, and those British who could not manage schooling in England. St. Paul's was not adequate for her daughters.

Assessing his granddaughters with a fond, but critical eye, Sir Jonathan had discerned no promise of their mother's vigorous talents. Girls like Guinevere and Charlotte, the autocrat had declared, need at most learn reading, writing, reckoning, and the household arts. Well dowered, they would marry well, and their husbands would look after them. The Old Gentleman did not like "clever" women, although he relied upon Mary's judgment. Intelligent, educated women affronted his traditional Chinese conviction that respectable females should confine their activities to the kitchen, the drawing-room, the nursery, and the bedroom.

Mary could not really contest Sir Jonathan's judgment of the girls' potential, though she was infuriated by his arrogantly dismissing all women as inferiors—"all but the few astonishing exceptions like yourself and my wonderful mother." But remaining in Hong Kong had put a stamp upon her daughters' personalities. It was, Mary saw with growing dismay, almost a stigma. Despite her own efforts, they were slightly cheechee, neither quite Chinese nor quite British in accent and attitude. Archetypically Hong Kong women, they floated uneasily between two worlds, Eurasians in manner and spirit, as well as blood.

Their eldest brother, Jonnie, was utterly self-confident. Nine years at Stonyhurst had nurtured an impregnable conviction of superiority and an accent so effortlessly posh it sometimes moved Mary to quickly suppressed laughter. He had talked like a Lancashire plowboy until the astonishing transformation worked by the final year the Jesuits idiosyncratically called Poetry. When unwary sprigs of the Hong Kong British Establishment snubbed young Jonathan Sekloong, he looked down his nose, drawled a few contemptuous syllables, and left them in speechless chagrin.

His sisters, who had known only Hong Kong, were pathetically unsure of themselves. Their grandfather's wealth and his title attracted envious comments and required their presence at interminably boring formal functions. But they were not invited to the parties by the Colony's younger set. Mary and Charles had outgrown their resentment at their exclusion from the Hong Kong Club, the Colony's European holy of holies. Their daughters agonized over their exclusion from the livelier Cricket and Yacht Clubs. Guinevere withdrew into her passion for housewifery, while the irrepressible Charlotte concealed her unhappiness in hectic parties with the freer St. Paul's girls and their brothers. The madcap spirit of the 1920s had touched even remote Hong Kong. Young Eurasians, Portuguese, and even Chinese shocked their elders by drinking nauseating American concoctions called cocktails, dancing entwined to saccharine songs like "Dardanella" and "There's a Rainbow Round My Shoulder"—and prattling about sex and complexes. Freed of the constricting underclothing that had confined their mothers, girls wore skirts above their knees and rolled, flesh-colored stockings. Youths were grotesque in tight-waisted jackets and flaring trousers. The Jazz Age was creeping over the Colony, but the old social barriers still stood firm against the tides of self-conscious emancipation.

The quarter of a century since her arrival in Hong Kong had moved with dizzying speed, Mary reflected when she and Charles evaded the clouds of well-wishers to leave the boat-yard in the new Rolls-Royce landau, isolated from the driver by thick glass. The motorcar's steady upward progress from Aberdeen was itself a sign of the new age. A road had been cut through to The

Peak just a few months earlier, and the inconvenient progression from Peak Tram to sedan chair to Sekloong Manor was no longer necessary. Electricity, a rare luxury in the early 1900s, was commonplace, and ceiling fans had replaced creaking punkahs. Some punkah-pullers joined the ranks of the sweating coolies who still carried up to The Peak provisions and ice shipped in sawdust from North China. But the coolies, too, were becoming redundant. Patent iceboxes and the occasional, still expensive refrigerator kept food fresh for days, while angular motor-vans with wooden-spoke wheels carried perishable goods almost as cheaply and much faster than could coolies. The new unemployed grumbled, for even the ubiquitous messenger-coolie was being replaced by the telephone. A fixture in business offices, the instrument was becoming commonplace in the homes of the well-to-do.

Goaded by his son Harry, who made flying visits to the Colony, Sir Jonathan was deeply concerned about rising discontent among the working class. Since the mercantile Colony was virtually devoid of industry, it was not as troubled as China, where the miners of An-shan in Manchuria and the railway workers of Chengchow in Honan had struck for better pay and safer working conditions. The pioneering strikes were organized by the "Bolsheviks" of the three-year-old Communist Party of China. The worst the Colony itself had suffered was, however, a brief seamen's strike in 1922. In Hong Kong, as in China, menial tasks still offered employment to those forced to work for a pittance. The Sekloongs themselves employed more than two hundred servants and gardeners.

Nonetheless, the age was moving so fast that even Sir Jonathan could not look to the future confident in his judgments. Neither he nor Charles could wholly control Thomas and James, who were just nineteen and seventeen. Aided by the Great War's disruption, they had escaped following Jonnie at Stonyhurst, and they were indifferent students at Wah Yan, the Jesuit school on Kennedy Road. Openly scornful of both commerce and scholarship, they were at the moment fascinated by the

380

new magic called wireless. They hunched over spider-web devices of wire and crystal, rejoicing when they "brought in" a static-splintered transmission from Manila, Singapore, or Shanghai. The heterodyne tube had already been perfected by the American Lee de Forrest, and the boys were constructing a wireless set they swore would "bring in London clear as a bell." They were, above all, intrigued by the military potential of wireless, which equipped some ships on the Royal Navy's China Station.

Inspired by Harry's enthusiasm, they were also fascinated by the military capability airplanes had demonstrated during the Great War. The German Dornier Company had just begun serial production of its passenger-carrying flying-boat, the *Whale,* while the Italian pilot Francesco de Pinedo was preparing to fly a 35,000-mile round trip from Rome to Tokyo by way of Australia in his *Gennariello.* Visionaries already spoke of a regular flying-boat service that would reduce the voyage from Hong Kong to London to an unbelievable seven days. Though practical businessmen were justly skeptical of that prospect, they lived in a wholly different world from the era of gaslights, sedan chairs, coolie transport, and swaying punkahs Mary Philippa Osgood had entered on landing at Hong Kong less than twenty-five years earlier.

Family solidarity had been the cornerstone of Chinese society, and, at the least, the coping-stone of European society in 1900. But that rock was cracking in 1924, as the negligent attitudes of Thomas and James demonstrated. All the children had, however, attended the launching of *Regina Pacis.* The girls saw visions of gay parties on the schooner's broad decks, while Jonnie and young Charles would not have dreamed of disappointing their father. Though discerning little military utility in the anachronistic schooner, Thomas and James delighted in its splendor. But the children had scattered to their own friends, instead of returning to Sekloong Manor for the family party that would, a few years earlier, have sealed the occasion. Harry and his wife Mayling had promised to call, but

381

only Mary and Charles rode in the leather-cushioned comfort of the black Rolls—and Mary suddenly felt herself ancient at forty-three.

Charles interrupted her musing, his normal lilt intensified by excitement. She realized that they were still holding hands like young lovers—or like a prematurely aged Darby and Joan.

"Well, old girl," he bubbled, "she's a beautiful thing, isn't she? More than a hundred feet . . . designed by Laurent Giles . . . mahogany strip-planked . . . and a Sulzbach diesel of 250 horsepower from Bremen. The Huns still build well, blast them. Not many wives get presents like that."

"I'm grateful, Charles," she laughed. "But the children call *Regina* 'Daddy's new toy.' "

"My new toy, indeed!" Mild indignation edged his lilt. "Nonsense! You know it's *your* present. I can't wait to sail for Honolulu."

"Nor I, Charles. It's a lovely present."

"We can leave right after the wedding. Only two months now before . . ."

Mary stiffened in resentment, and her hand stiffened in her husband's. But he burbled on.

"Charlotte'll be the first to go. Makes you feel a bit old. But we'll give her a big send-off. I've been thinking that . . ."

"Charles," Mary interrupted. "I'd rather not discuss it now. Charlotte's a wanton little fool, and as for Manfei . . ."

"But, my dear, you never said a word."

"Not a word? If I'd shouted from the housetops, I couldn't have made my feelings plainer. You know perfectly well I don't want this marriage. But let's not talk about it now. Let's just enjoy this day."

"Damned if I will!" Charles's temper flared beneath his new equanimity. "We'll talk it out right now. Charlotte's in love with young Manfei Way, and he's suitable, most suitable. The old man agrees it'll be a great alliance. Bring the Way interests and the Sekloong interests even closer together. You like Mosing, and his son's a fine boy."

"Yes, Charles, I know," she replied. "Eminently suitable, even if he's not a Catholic—though that doesn't bother me, only you. Wealthy, intelligent, well-mannered, and well-educated. Dunross College isn't in the same class as Stonyhurst. More like a training school for the Wheatleys' bright young recruits, but it's all right. I rather like Manfei too. Yes, eminently suitable."

"Then, why do you object? Charl's certainly old enough. You were. What's bothering you, Mary?"

"Old enough at twenty? I'm not so sure. But that's not it."

"Then what *is* it?"

"If you must know," she exploded, "it's very simple: he's Chinese!"

"Chinese?" Charles was stunned. "How can you feel that way? *I'm* mostly Chinese. Why, your own children . . ."

"Don't be dense, Charles. You know exactly what I mean. He's Chinese, with all the old Chinese arrogance under the veneer of British education. I dread my daughter's suffering what *I* endured in the early years of marriage."

"Suffering *what?*" Charles was on edge. "Just *what,* Mary?"

"His philandering. And he *will* philander because it's his God-given right as a Chinese man. She'll be treated like a pampered pet, not a person. And she'll be trapped in pompous, stuffy Hong Kong. She *won't* take it for long. I know my own daughter!"

"I never knew it." Charles spoke with bitter anger. "I never knew you were anti-Chinese."

"That's rubbish. I'm not anti-Chinese. But I don't want Charlotte to suffer the same humiliations, the same slights, the same sneers I've put up with. If they lived in London, then perhaps . . . but Hong Kong, this Hong Kong! No."

"Manfei's a good boy. Don't forget Hong Kong's been good to you. China, too. Now that . . ."

"Now that you've settled down, you mean," she smiled wryly. "Charles, it doesn't have anything to do with us, with our marriage. But I've lost too much to China."

"Too much?" Unfeigned bewilderment contended with his rising anger. "What do you mean?"

"Our life's been racked by China. The girl-child still-born after the plague. I wanted another girl. Now, Thomas and James want to go to that frightful military academy at Whampoa Harry's so keen on."

"And Harry?" Jealous anger overcame Charles's discretion. "You've lost Harry to China, too?"

"Harry never belonged to me, you know." She lied equably, confident that he did not know the truth or wish to know. "Though *you*, of course . . . your adventures. The Swatow girl—and the others."

He lowered his eyes beneath her level stare.

"No," she continued, "it's China itself. I want my children to live civilized lives. Not provincial Hong Kong, not the gory, clawing horror of China."

"It's their heritage. *You* insisted that they learn Chinese. I simply don't understand."

"China, Charles, China! There's no hope for China. Misery will spread. The killing will be worse. There'll never be peace. The children are giving themselves to a chimera, decades of turmoil. And they'll always be wogs . . . chee-chee Eurasians . . . to the British in Asia. They do have another heritage elsewhere, as do you . . . and I."

"I'm not so keen on China," he conceded without rancor. "Maybe you've got a point. But, Mary, you puzzle me, always have, though God knows I try to understand you. But, I tell you, *this* marriage will take place."

"Perhaps, Charles, perhaps." She smiled, unable to rise to anger. "So many perhapses in our lives, aren't there? But I tell you . . . I promise you with no perhapses I'll fight this marriage tooth and claw."

The day that had begun with the triumphant launching of *Regina Pacis* tried Charles Sekloong's patience to the utmost—and beyond. Harry and Mayling were waiting in the drawing-room of the Small House, and he knew the women detested each other. Mayling was a lacquered Shanghai doll, the archetype of the frivolous, parasitical Chinese woman Mary despised. Her features were glossily immobile, since she feared that displaying emotion would mar their smooth perfection with lines. She looked as if she devoted four hours each day to her excessive make-up, her glassily coiffed hair, her pointed fingernails shiny with vermilion varnish, and her clinging *cheongsams* with discreet sideslits—as indeed she did. Mary was convinced that Harry had deliberately chosen a woman who was her own antithesis when he impulsively decided he must marry to cut himself off from her and end the danger their liaison posed to the clan.

Though more tolerant than his wife of feminine vanity, Charles recognized the pursed mouth, the calculating eyes, and the false smile. All those outward signs of self-absorption he had seen among the gilded courtesans he frequented before the Great War. Had he not known that Mayling's father was a respectable editor, he would have suspected that Harry had found her among the nightclub hostesses of Shanghai's Bubbling Well Road. Even less than Mary could he understand why the fastidious, irreverent Harry Sekloong had married a frivolous woman who did not even pretend interest in the political struggles that were his own life work. Her doll-like fragility and self-indulgent idleness were repellent. But Mayling's demeanor exuded complacent self-satisfaction; she had totally justified herself by giving Harry a son, Chieh-hsiang (also called Jason), now eleven years old.

Still, Mayling was essentially passive, an irritant rather than a disruption. She was proficient only in the crackling Shanghai dialect. Her Mandarin and her Cantonese were rudimentary, while her English was virtually nonexistent. Mayling's linguistic deficiencies and her narcissism effectively prevented her interjecting herself into family discussions. Besides, she was normally preoccupied with patting her hair into place, repairing her make-up, and smoothing the wrinkles in her *cheongsam*. Her obsession with her own person effectively excluded all other human beings.

Mary and Mayling greeted each other with contempt revealed by tight smiles and extravagant inquiries after each other's children. Harry himself was brimming with enthusiasm, with news, and with demands.

"Well, Charles," he drawled, inserting a cigarette into his stubby ivory holder, "I congratulate you. You've beaten the old man in ostentation."

"The boat's for Mary, you know," Charles replied defensively. "I promised her we'd take six months off and sail wherever she wants. Hawaii, Tahiti, Bali—who knows? Besides, we have to keep up a position."

"Just what position? Exploiting the people?"

"Harry, that's not fair." Mary slipped into the familiar role of buffer between the brothers. "Building *Regina* has employed dozens of your precious common people. With the slump, they'd otherwise be idle. Regardless of our position, we do employ many people."

"It's not a defense, Mary," her brother-in-law answered. "But I haven't come to argue."

"What for, then?" Charles asked with unwonted asperity.

"Why, to give the Sekloongs an opportunity to demonstrate their generosity toward my precious common people."

"How?" Charles rejoined. "What is it now?"

"Now, Charles, that's no way to talk for the man who owns the grandest yacht between Honolulu and Monaco, is it?"

"Maybe it is, speaking to the new ally of the Bolsheviks," Charles flushed. "Your own people are hardly better than the Bolsheviks. Your living treasure Chiang Kai-shek is really a Bolshevik. Even Dr. Sun . . . I wonder about Dr. Sun. Nobody *made* him join the Soviets and turn the Kuomintang, your great Nationalist Party, into a Chinese version of the Soviet Communist Party."

Harry sat tensely on the edge of his chair, and Charles bristled.

"Gentlemen!" Mary interrupted. "Or should I say 'boys'? Must you fight the battle between capitalism and Bolshevism in my drawing-room?"

The brothers were momentarily abashed. The elder retreated into his duties as host, turning to the drinks cabinet. The younger accepted the rebuke with his habitual nonchalance and smiled in apology. His wife looked up suspiciously, her antennae stirred by the demonstration of Mary's influence over the two men who loved her. Reassured by the social calm, she resumed stroking her hips to smooth her wrinkled *cheongsam*.

"But, Harry, what's the point?" Charles persisted. "I can't understand your alliance with the Communists. Can't be good for business. So far, you've just made greater turmoil. While you Nationalists play with the Bolsheviks, practically every province is ruled by a warlord who squeezes the merchants and the people. It's a bigger mess than old Viceroy Yüan Shih-kai made."

"We'll change that," Harry said mollifyingly. "That's the point, to unify China and create a new order. Order's good for business. But politics is a messy business."

"You know," Mary recalled, "Napoleon said something about that. I can't quite recall, though."

" 'China is a sleeping giant,' " Harry suggested. " 'Beware, for it will shake the earth when it wakes.' Something like that."

"That's not it, not what I'm thinking of. It'll come to me. Yes, I've got it. Napoleon advised playwrights to base their dramas on politics. He said roughly: 'It is, after all, politics that leads to catastrophes without any formal crimes being committed.' "

"That cuts to the heart," Harry acknowledged. "It may even be true. But we Nationalists are trying to head off catastrophes."

"What do you want now?" Charles demanded suspiciously. "More money for your Bolshevik friends?"

"Not precisely, Charles. I want to draw my share of accumulated profits, and yes, to ask for a little more. I need to buy airplanes: twelve Handley-Page V/1500 bombers and another twelve Sopwith Camels. Then we'll sweep the warlords from China in two years."

"Why don't you ask your Soviet friends?"

"They've got no airplanes. Anyway, we don't want to get too close to Moscow, though no other country'll help us. Even the Communists, the Chinese Communists, would take only a token subsidy from Moscow when they set up their Party in 1921. That bushy-haired young fellow Mao Tse-tung . . . he's working directly with us now, and he's very strong on keeping a distance from Moscow. He's a Communist all right, but a Chinese first. Not even the Chinese Communists want a Soviet-dominated China."

"And," Charles grudgingly completed the thought, "if you can't get aid elsewhere, the Russians'll move in?"

"Seems obvious, doesn't it? Look at the foreigners still nibbling at China, particularly the Japs. If we don't win, foreigners, probably the Japs, will dominate China. And where'll your precious business be then? Or, if the Soviets dominate China, what then? Just look at the record."

"What about the record?" Charles stalled.

"Oh, come, Charles," Mary protested, "you know what he calls the record as well as Harry does. But I myself can't see how anyone can change China, *really* change her.'"

"No, Mary," her husband answered stolidly, "I don't necessarily know the record. You think China's future is hopeless. That doesn't mean it is. Let Harry have his say."

Harry flashed her a grateful glance before resuming. She had adeptly maneuvered Charles into a receptive attitude by her own show of recalcitrance.

"You know that only two things kept the Jap dwarfs from eating up China like *sukiyaki*: China went to war in 1917; and the students rioted in Peking on May 4, 1919," Harry resumed. "If we hadn't declared war on the Central Powers, the Japs would've taken over half the country in the name of the Allies. They'd already grabbed the German concession at Tsingtao. And if the students hadn't rioted in 1919, the warlord government in Peking would've signed away China's sovereignty by accepting Tokyo's Twenty-one Demands. God knows, the ministers had been paid enough, bribed lavishly by the Japs."

"Just a minute," Mary interjected. "I'm all in a muddle. I never really understood what happened after Viceroy Yüan Shih-kai died."

"To put it simply," Harry answered, "think of two opposed groups: the power-people and the word-people. All the warlords coming after Yüan Shih-kai are power-people, including the so-called President in Peking now. Their ideas didn't change when the Empire fell. All they want is power and spoils.

"Now, the word-people were also as disunited till recently. But they have a clear purpose. They're dedicated to making China a united, modern country, where no one's oppressed and everyone can live in peace and prosperity."

"Why do you call them the word-people?" Mary asked.

"Because they all believe in a power beyond naked force, the power of words, and the ideals the words stand for. That's really the old Chinese way. Confucius was a word-man, not a power-man, and the Confucian Dynasties believed in justice beyond might. But the Confucian way couldn't deal with the other power-people, the foreigners with their guns."

"And then?" Mary prompted. "This *is* a new way of explaining things."

"In 1917 the word-people began getting together. The words of Confucius were still the only ideal China possessed. But his words were outmoded, useless. So they set out to change the word. Instead of the classical style of writing, which took decades to learn, they wanted everyone to write in *pai-hua,* 'plain language.' That meant writing as we talk Chinese, so that everyone could understand. Some of the word-people wanted liberal Western representative government. 'Science and democracy' was their battle cry. Others said representative democracy couldn't work in China. They wanted to change everything, and they adopted the word of Karl Marx—particularly after the Marxists won in Russia."

"Mary's not simple-minded, Harry," the elder brother protested. "Don't tell us a child's story."

"All right, Charles. I'll be more specific."

Harry recalled that Peking University was the center of the New Language and Literature Movement. In 1917, Professor Hu Shih, a liberal democrat with an American Ph.D., published an article calling for a new written language in the magazine, *The New Youth*. The editor was the Dean of Letters, Chen Tu-hsiu, who had studied in France.

"I remember bits and pieces," Mary said. "But we were busy with other things in 1917. How did all this academic excitement affect the real world?"

"The Europeans and the Americans fixed that," Harry laughed. "Fixed themselves too. After the Great War, Chinese idealists thought Woodrow Wilson's Fourteen Points meant justice for China, too. But the Versailles Conference let the Japanese keep the territory and privileges they stole during the war—and bound China to honor the secret agreement to accept Tokyo's Twenty-one Demands. On May 4, 1919, the students of Peking University rioted and forced the warlord government to renege on those Twenty-one Demands. Honoring them would have made China virtually a Japanese province.

"But the students went further. They rejected Western liberal democracy and turned to authoritarian solutions. Dean of Letters Chen Tu-hsiu founded the Communist Party in 1921. Soon afterward, Dr. Sun Yat-sen himself turned to the Soviets. In January 1924, this year, the Kuomintang, his Nationalist Party, agreed to unite with the Communists. Agreed on other things, too. Mainly that we must build our own armies. That's the only way to destroy the power of the warlords and their backers, the European and American capitalists."

"As a capitalist," Charles said stiffly, "I'm not impressed. We all cheered the May Fourth Movement, but where did it lead? To creating the Communist

Party. You Nationalists haven't touched the warlords yet. You're talking, talking, but never fighting. Harry, it won't work. Mary may be right. Maybe China is hopeless and we should be looking for other fields."

"How can *you* talk that way?" Harry exploded. "China made you fabulously wealthy. Anyway, we're not out to destroy capitalism or capitalists—just the foreign capitalists and their Chinese running-dogs who support the warlords. The only hope for an independent China is the new alliance of the Nationalists and the Communists, who're both Chinese patriots. We'll use the Communists—and then cast them aside like a squeezed lemon."

"Look out they don't squeeze you first." Mary's mouth puckered. "Besides, who can eat lemons?"

"One for you," Charles laughed. "Mary's beating you at your own game. All those fancy words. But have another drink and tell us just what you want."

"I must raise a half million pounds sterling. The old man still has faith in Dr. Sun. He's agreed that my share of accumulated profits, naturally less management costs, plus recompense for liaison services comes to about £250,000."

"The same old Sekloong, isn't he?" Mary smiled. "To the penny, I'll wager. I'm sure the figure ends with something like sixteen shillings and ten pence, the last penny rounded in his favor."

"You're right." Harry was briefly diverted. "I was worried about him after Mother died. But I don't see any change."

"Oh, he misses her," Mary said. "It's not six months yet. He misses her, but won't admit it. He's still angry at her for daring to leave him, for giving up at sixty-seven, when he's now seventy-one and going strong as ever."

"Strong as ever with the ladies," Charles added, "though Mary may not approve."

"Mary approves heartily," she interjected. "He's not hurting anyone—and he can certainly provide for any children. But he misses Lady Lucinda—whatever he says or does."

"And Matilda?" Harry asked. "I haven't seen her yet."

"Still the good gray mouse," Charles answered. "She seemed happy enough looking after the old man, but there's a German fellow dancing around her. Named Biederstein, Hans Biederstein. Mary thinks they'll marry."

"I'm certain she will," Mary added. "Matilda wants to escape and Hans seems a strong man, so . . ."

"We'll see," Charles interjected. "But you were saying, Harry."

"So that's roughly a quarter of a million, my share. I need the same again. A loan or contribution—or a combination?"

"Why come to us?" Charles asked. "The old man makes those decisions. Of course, we might put in a little money of our own, but he's the boss."

"Not this time, Charles. He says he won't help unless you and Mary agree. Says he's getting on."

"Nonsense," Mary laughed. "He just wants to lay off the responsibility. He knows better than anyone that power and trade, politics and dollars march hand in hand. If he's agreed, I don't see how we could object."

"Might put in a little on our own, too," Charles repeated. "Can't do any harm keeping in with your people. You'll remember where the money came from?"

"How could I ever forget? You'll remind me all the time."

"We'll talk it over, Mary and I. We can work out details later. I want to talk to the old man."

"We'll be going, then. Dinner with Mayling's blasted cousins." Harry paused at the heavy double doors.

"Mary," he said lightly, "I might want to borrow Thomas and James for a while."

"For a while? What do you mean, Harry? 'Borrow them'?"

"We can talk about it later. Don't worry. I'm not kidnapping them. Just borrowing them for a while."

June 7, 1924–June 9, 1924

ALL the ridiculous traditions had been observed, every trivial convention honored seven times over, Mary told herself as she dressed in irritation after lunch on Saturday, June 7, 1924. Reading the warning signs in her mistress's gestures and brusque orders, Ah Fung, the little amah whose appearance had hardly changed in twenty years, walked softly. The red-gold of her mistress's hair had been only slightly dimmed by the passage of the years, though it was discreetly "touched up" at her daughters' insistence. Tai-tai was not pleased, Ah Fung knew, and she took care not to provoke an explosion of anger. She was anxious to be done so that she could blacken her own glossy braid and put on her best flowered tunic for the wedding.

"All the stupid traditions," Mary repeated aloud, "not a single stupidity omitted."

A June wedding, of course. A nuptial high mass in the flying-buttressed Cathedral banked with chrysanthemums from Japan, orchids from Malaya, lilies from Taiwan, and gladiolae from Shanghai, all shipped in ice by fast steamer. Veritable squadrons of monsignori in purple robes surrounding the red-robed Bishop, who would perform the ceremony. Charlotte, a conventional bride-to-be, was conventionally swinging between apprehension and exultation; only two hours earlier she had agreed with joy and then rejected amid tears her mother's renewed reminder that they could still call off the wedding. That foolhardy suggestion was Mary's last desperate card, though she really knew that the preparations had already gone too far. Wedding presents arriving from Shanghai, Tokyo, Canton, New York, London, and Paris overflowed not only the spacious mansion called the Small House, but almost overflowed the Great Hall of The Castle. There was even a magnificent Georgian silver tea service from her own brother Thomas, still seeking a larger share of the Sekloongs' legal business to hasten his progress from the back-benches of the House of Commons to a ministerial appointment.

Nothing had been omitted, no conceivable vulgarity or ostentation from the trousseau that frothed over three rooms to the eight-karat blue-white diamond set in jade that was the engagement ring. Charlotte's would be the most lavish wedding Hong Kong had seen since her own marriage more than twenty-three years earlier. Hundreds would crowd the church, and thousands would attend the reception. The nuptial pair were to leave the reception to embark on the twenty-one-day voyage to San Francisco, whence they would travel by private railway car across the United States, after two months finally reaching London to spend six months in Europe. The uniting of two great houses was an occasion of state, though the Sekloongs were decidedly senior to the Ways. The pomp of Charlotte's wedding had, therefore, been meticulously choreographed; it would almost equal, but not outshine the splendid ceremony in which the crown-prince Charles Sekloong had taken his bride.

And that bride, now the mother of the bride? Fiercely amused, Mary realized that the mother of the bride was behaving almost precisely as convention dictated. She swore she would not dissolve into public tears in the Cathedral as tradition further dictated. But she was edgy and nervous, wrung by doubts, and deeply unhappy. Charlotte had enraged Mary with the stubbornness inherited from her mother and her iron-willed grandfather. That wilfulness, coupled with her father's quiet strength, allowed her to listen dutifully to her mother's warnings for two months—and adamantly reject them. That morning's scene had been no more than a repetition of the same stormy battles.

"Look, Mother," Charlotte had finally said, removing the cold compress from her reddened eyes, "I may be doing a very foolish thing, but it's my life. I know I'll be a good wife to Manfei and a good mother too."

Mary had finally abandoned the fight. An eleventh-hour victory would, in any event, be worse than defeat. Even Mary quailed at the scandal that would follow if Charlotte withdrew on the day of her wedding. But Mary remained convinced that her daughter was marrying the wrong man and, barely twenty years old, certainly at the wrong time.

Yet there almost seemed to be a cunning conspiracy to deprive her of all her children at one swoop. Guinevere, who had always tagged behind her strong-willed younger sister, was following Charlotte's lead again. Amid her concern with Charlotte, Mary had abstractedly noted that Guinevere was not happy. She sat for long periods in silence, staring into the distance with her needlework forgotten in her lap, as if wrestling with a decision. Mary had ascribed her elder daughter's distraction to concern for Charlotte that reflected their mother's freely expressed misgivings. Guinevere normally worried more about others than herself. The older girl was, Mary felt, naturally unhappy at losing her lifelong companion to a stranger. Besides, even unselfish Gwinnie must be disturbed by her sister's marrying while she herself, fourteen months older, was still unpledged. Mary had resolved to reassure Guinevere after the excitement of the wedding.

Her complacent explanations of her elder daughter's moodiness had been exploded only the previous night. While the amahs fussed over Charlotte's trousseau, Guinevere drew Mary aside.

"I'd like a little talk, Mother," she said.

"Of course, my dear." Mary was pleased to escape the cloying scene. "Is something wrong?"

"No, Mother, nothing's wrong. Quite the contrary."

Having withdrawn from the lacy and flowery fantasies that heaped Charlotte's bedroom and her adjoining sitting-room, mother and daughter sat in the morning-room overlooking the rear terrace and the long sweep of the gardens.

"Well, Gwinnie my dear, what is it that's so urgent? I know I've been neglecting you, but we'll have lots of time to talk when this madness is finished."

"Mother, Charl's getting married tomorrow. It'll be a beautiful ceremony."

"I'm not senile yet," Mary snapped. "Even if your sister's determined to make me a grandmother before my time. I could hardly be unaware of those two plain facts, could I?"

"No, Mother, of course not, though Charl's the same age you were when you married Daddy." The normally hypersensitive Guinevere did not react to her mother's testy reply, although she automatically championed her sister. "I just wanted to tell you that I don't want a grand wedding."

"If that's all, I can promise you won't. You can please yourself."

"Oh, thank you, Mother," Guinevere said. "I knew you'd understand. I'm so happy."

"I still have some influence over my own household and my own children, I hope." Angry at her younger daughter's defiance, Mary responded to her elder daughter's words but not to their meaning. "When the time comes, there'll be as little fuss as you want."

"I'm so pleased, Mother. You are a dear. Then you don't mind?"

"Mind?" Mary demanded, only half aware that she was talking at cross-purposes with the usually direct, uncomplicated Guinevere. "Mind what?"

"You don't mind that George and I want a small wedding. Just Father Collins to preside, and only the immediate family. Even if Grandfather and Daddy . . ."

"No, of course not, dear."

Mary smoothed her skirt over her hips as she rose. The flimsy material would ride up, and skirts were disgracefully, almost uncomfortably short—even though the girls teased her for refusing to show her kneecaps. She relapsed into the chair as the meaning of Guinevere's words finally struck her.

"George?" she demanded. "George and you? George who? What *are* you talking about?"

"Mother, I can't keep on calling him Uncle George or Dr. George. Not after we decided. You do see?"

"I only see that talking to you is like shouting through a sheet of glass. Either I'm an idiot or you are. Will you please tell me . . ."

"Yes, Mother, of course. I thought you knew, would have seen. George Parker wants to marry me, and I love him, and I think he's wonderful and so kind, but strong, and I said yes."

"Gwinnie, he must be twenty years older than you."

"Eighteen years, Mother, actually seventeen years and eleven months. But it doesn't matter. We've discussed it, and it doesn't matter."

"Well, Gwinnie! Well! Well! Well!"

Totally nonplussed, Mary Sekloong retreated behind the barricade of parental authority.

"So you and George Parker have it all worked out. I suppose I should be glad to hear that. It spares your father and me so much trouble. To you the difference in age may seem a trifle. But George is a mature man, not a silly young girl. He should know better. He's almost forty, and you're not yet twenty-two. Have you thought? You'll be forty when he's sixty. You could be left a widow at fifty. You do plan to marry in the Church? You can't go back, you know. Have you told your father?"

"No, Mother, I wanted to tell you first." Quiet, obedient Guinevere was wholly in command, the steely Sekloong strain showing itself in her for the first time. "Yes, Mother, we have thought it out. We've discussed the age difference many times. George was . . . still is a little reluctant. He wants only what's best for me. But I know, Mother, I know with all my heart that he's best for me. If I don't marry George, I won't ever marry anyone else, and I'll regret it all my life."

"Are you asking my permission?" Mary was astonished by the strength of her daughter's will. "Or are you just telling me? I suppose you want our blessing, your father's and mine?"

"Yes, Mother dear, of course we do. I'm asking you, begging you with all my heart."

"And if we say no? What then?"

"I'll be very sad."

"Sad—and what then?"

"I don't know, Mother, really I don't. We don't want to defy you."

Mary gazed at Guinevere's calm, candid features as if seeing her for the first time. The petite, red-haired girl was absolutely determined, while shrewdly evading a direct confrontation. How could she have known her child for more than twenty-one years, yet not known her at all?

"Where," she asked mechanically, "will you live?"

"We thought Shanghai for a year or so. George can't leave his work yet. But he wants to go back to America. He really belongs there, and it'll be better for me. In Shanghai, he says, I'll always be different . . . be cruelly snubbed as a Eurasian. In America they may not notice. Anyway, it won't be as bad."

"It's a long way from home," Mary stalled.

"We know—and we're sorry. But you'll visit, and we'll visit. George says we must decide—either to settle here or put down roots in America."

"Except for the age difference, Gwinnie," Mary conceded, "you could do much worse. George Parker's a good man. And I agree with him about Shanghai."

"I know, Mother," Guinevere smiled. "We discussed that too."

"Well, let me think about it," Mary temporized. "I'll speak to your father, but *you* must tell your grandfather."

"Thank you, Mother. You're a dear. I *knew* we could count on you."

Guinevere smothered her mother with a hug. Weary of fighting her daughters, Mary knew she would finally give her blessing to the match.

"I haven't said yes," she nonetheless cautioned. "Just we'll see, just maybe. But what about money?"

"George says he doesn't want any money. Not because he doesn't respect you and Father. He just doesn't want anyone to think he's marrying me for money."

"Very high-minded," Mary observed dryly. "Particularly since his own father's by no means impoverished.

A banker, isn't he? We'll see about that. You can hardly come to him in your shift."

Mary was never to be able to remember Charlotte's wedding clearly. She retained only a confused impression of incense, chanting, and massed flowers whose heavy fragrance and many hues overwhelmed her senses. The shocks that preceded and followed the ceremony remained clearer in her memory than the marriage she had been forced to accept—and to view through a mist of the tears she had sworn she would not shed.

Shortly after Guinevere left her in the morning-room, Charles had returned home. Obsessed with her own news, Mary barely noticed his troubled frown.

"Parker? George Parker?" Charles was taken aback when she told him of her conversation with their elder daughter. "Nice chap, but this *is* a surprise. Never thought Gwinnie was sly. Anyway, I always thought George was more your admirer than Gwinnie's."

"How do you feel about it, Charles? I'm afraid she'll insist whatever we say, and I'm tired of fighting. But how do you feel?"

"Damn it, how can I know what I think when I haven't had a chance to think? You only told me twenty seconds ago."

"I'm sorry, my dear," she replied with unwonted humility. "I suppose it was a shock."

"Truly a shock. At this rate, we'll soon have no children left. But I suppose you approve. After all, he's *not* Chinese."

"Charles, I've said I was sorry about that. I can't say more. I don't necessarily approve just because he's not Chinese. And there's the age difference, the distance if they live in America."

"Also, he's not Eurasian." Charles would not lightly relinquish his righteous grievance. "That's on the credit side, too."

"Charles, I love you and you're Eurasian. I could hardly dislike Eurasians—my own children, by my own choice. But I hate what the world does to Eurasians,

399

what you've suffered and I've suffered—myself and for you."

"All right, my dear. That was unfair."

He kissed the top of her head in a rare gesture of tenderness. Gratefully, she reached up and stroked his cheek.

"Look here, Mary. We've got other problems. Harry's turned up for the wedding, and . . ."

"But why shouldn't he?"

"Of course, he should be here. But he's told me what he meant by 'borrowing' Thomas and James. I think he was afraid to tell you."

"Borrowing? I'd almost forgotten. I thought it was just another of Harry's wild fancies. What *does* he mean?"

"They both want to play soldiers, attend the Whampoa Military Academy. Harry's all for it. I'm so damned angry it's hard to tell you."

"But I thought that—or something like that—was what you wanted." Mary could not restrain her own bitterness. "After all, it *is* Chinese."

"Dammit, Mary. I won't bicker with you, not now about this. I don't want my sons to be soldiers, Chinese or not. Good iron doesn't make nails, you know, and good men don't make soldiers. I'm not so devoted to China. That's Harry's line and the old man's, not mine. Can't we discuss this without . . ."

"I'm sorry, Charles," she said with honest contrition for the second time in three minutes. "I can't think what's got into me tonight. You'd think *I* was the nervous bride."

"What do you think of Harry's latest craziness?"

"Very little, I confess. What's that song? 'I Didn't Raise My Son To Be A Soldier'?"

"Don't dither, Mary. I know it's a shock, but this is serious. Damned serious. Of course, the boys are all for it."

"Suppose we refuse?"

"We could. But what good would that do? I'm afraid they'd just go. They're too old. And my lunatic brother would smuggle them to Canton with great pleasure. Besides, I don't want to split the family further."

"Charles, can we really do anything?" Mary realized that she could not oppose Harry's plans for his own son, while Thomas would, as usual, follow his younger brother. "They've both been mad about soldiering since they were small."

"We could try. Send them away to school in England."

"Do you really think so, Charles?"

"No, I suppose not. Not really. We can't lock them up. And I can't stand any more family fights."

"I've been afraid of this," Mary mused. "James is becoming as hot a political firebrand as Harry. And Thomas won't be separated from James."

"It may be just as well, though . . ." Charles said hesitantly.

"How can you say that? If we can't persuade them, can't stop them, that's one thing. But we must try, we must talk to them. How can you say it's just as well?"

"I wasn't going to tell you, Mary. Thought it wasn't necessary. But the old man's furious with James and almost as angry with Thomas. Might be good to get them away for a while."

"Why?" she asked. "The boys and Father don't see each other that much."

"That's right," Charles rumbled in embarrassment. "But it's *who* James has been seeing. That's the trouble."

"I'm sorry, I don't understand."

"Well, it's not easy to tell you, my dear. But James, it seems, is running wild. A woman."

"At seventeen?" She was mildly disturbed, but not surprised. "Why should your father mind? How could *he* object? James is a chip off the old block. *Both* old blocks."

"Because of one particular girl. You don't keep up with the old man's adventures, do you?"

"Certainly not! I don't care to and couldn't if I did."

401

"It seems there's one particular young lady. The old man took up with her six months ago, and now James has got himself involved with her."

"Foolish girl should know she can't have the best of both worlds. That's not James's fault."

"The old man doesn't take to it that kindly."

"He'll cool down," she replied with composure. "He always does. But what of Thomas?"

"Oh, he just tags along. Thomas Tag-along, he is. Not that girl, of course, but others. But when I left him, the old man was saying: 'Let them go. Let them go to Whampoa. Maybe it'll do them some good. Their parents obviously can't control them.' It's not very nice."

"He won't pull the temple down on our heads because of adolescent misbehavior, will he?"

"No, I suppose not, of course not. But he can make himself damned unpleasant."

"I know that. But I'll have a word with him just as soon as this wedding, this alliance you and he want so badly, is over."

"And the boys?" Charles asked. "What about Whampoa?"

"All we can do is have a word with them when the marriage hysteria's over."

Two days after Charlotte's wedding, Mary sat in another church for an utterly different ceremony. The new electric fans suspended from the blue-stippled wooden beams of St. John's Anglican Cathedral whirred uneasily over two plain pine coffins. The sparse ranks of mourners were varied: a few local Portuguese; a group of itinerant British, American, and Australian reporters from the *China Mail;* and a sprinkling of lower-middle-class Eurasians. Mary's attendance was a conscious penance, for she hated funerals with superstitious, unreasoning dread. Young Charles, loving, sensitive, and remarkably erudite at eleven, had insisted upon accompanying her.

Within one coffin lay a young American named Harold Hobson who had been chief sub-editor of the *China Mail*. Within the other was the body of his fiancée, a

Eurasian girl called June Shaw who, Mary suspected, was Sir Jonathan's unacknowledged granddaughter. She had, therefore, felt that some member of the family should be present, and she had ordered the car without informing Charles. As the Anglican priest in his pleated white alb droned through a brief, repellently sterile service, she recalled the conversation that had brought her to the Cathedral.

Michael Ford, a middle-aged Irishman everyone called Henry, was acting-editor of the *China Mail*. He was one of her unlikely friends whom the children called "Mother's waifs." She found his pawky humor amusing and his conversation, ranging from Shakespeare to cricket, more interesting than the gossip about social and commercial machinations she heard too often. Henry Ford had appeared unannounced and unexpected at the Small House about tea time the Sunday after the wedding. Although he obviously did not need another drink, Mary had ordered him a whiskey-and-soda.

"I've come, Mary Macushla, to tell you a curious tale." His words were slurred. "Would you like to hear it? A fairy tale that's nothing to do with the real world you live in?"

She smiled and waited.

"Once upon a time, there were two princesses called Shaw, May and June Shaw. Not really princesses, but young, poor Hong Kong Eurasian girls. Perhaps you know of them?"

She nodded, for she had heard the persistent rumors regarding their ancestry.

"May Shaw, the older one, married a Yank. He wasn't much of anything in our grand little community, just a chap trying to get by. Worked as a clerk for Gilman's. No real future. You know Hong Kong. But for May anything white in trousers was a way upward—a way to break out of the pigeonhole where our tolerant, generous Colonial Society filed her. I warn you, this isn't really a fairy tale. It's a tragic farce—funny, pathetic, and sad, like the lives of most Eurasians on the China Coast.

"May, like her sister June, was very sensitive. Didn't like thinking about their mixed blood. Very sensitive. No one knows exactly what happened, perhaps just a word someone dropped. But May took it as a slur on her mixed blood, slurped down a bottle of Lysol, and died in Queen Mary Hospital.

"A year or so later, her sister June, good-looking colleen, became the inamorata, soon fiancée of Harold Hobson, my chief sub. One of Hob's assignments was writing headlines for the Dorothy Dix column, that Yankee advice-to-the-lovelorn syrup. And one morning, the day before yesterday morning, Hob gets a call from Queen Mary Hospital. The same thing, Lysol.

"He was shattered, but he figured out what'd happened. 'Twas all the fault of that Dorothy Dix woman. Hob'd read a puff in her column for blood-tests before marriage. Foolishly mentioned it in passing to his Miss June Shaw—and she brooded. She didn't know what a Wassermann test was . . . begging your pardon, Macushla. She thought it was to test her mixed blood and that Hob was throwing her over. The Lord knows, she was sensitive enough about her mixed blood. So June, too, took the Lysol way out. Hob put the telephone down and just sat there stunned. Then he asked would we run a short obituary. I said sure and loaned him ten dollars. After visiting the Hospital, he bought a bottle of whiskey and took it to his room at the European YMCA in Kowloon. Wrote some letters, finished the bottle, then jumped from the roof, six stories up. End of my fairy tale, Mary."

Although the story was a baroque blend of farce and tragedy, Mary decided she must attend the funeral. The macabre tale of June Shaw epitomized those unfortunate Eurasian girls who were sustained by neither position nor wealth; they were moved by desperate longing to escape the narrow world without hope in which the prejudice of both Chinese and Europeans confined them.

Mary sat dry-eyed through the impersonal service. When she and young Charles emerged into the blinding sunlight afterward, she felt her gesture had been meaningless. Her youngest son put his hand into her own and led her toward the St. George's Building. Without speaking, he fished in his pocket for coins as they passed the row of beggars on Battery Path. Accustomed to the Little Mandarin's thoughtful silences, she was immersed in her own thoughts.

"Mother, we did right to come," he finally said with the precocious insight that still surprised her. "It was proper that someone from the family should be there."

She wanted to protest, to deny his knowledge of June Shaw's parentage. But she kept silent, allowing him to continue.

"Mother, we owe a lot to many people, don't we? And we don't always pay our debts, do we? Sometimes I think the whole Sekloong family, except you, is so busy worrying about itself and its place and its possessions that we never worry about anybody else."

Mary smiled wanly. She could not at that moment refute his observation.

"Mother," young Charles said, "I don't want to be that way. If there were only you and I—perhaps Father and the girls—it might be different. But there's *too* much family, *too* much money, *too* much pomp and pretence. Mother, I want to go to Stonyhurst. And perhaps I'll become a priest."

May 31, 1925–July 9, 1926

THE scrolled neon sign flickered violet on the vermilion pillars flanking the entrance of the Alhambra Night Club and dyed the doorman's gray-caracul shapka a sickly mauve. The six-foot-three former major in the Czar's Own Preobazensky Guards, who had fought the Bolsheviks to the hopeless end with Admiral Kolchak in Siberia, wore the full-dress regalia of a Don Cossack. Bandoliers crossed his chest; a curved saber hung at his side; and soft-leather boots encased his calves. He contemplated the rabble on Bubbling Well Road with supreme disdain, even his waxed mustaches curling scornfully. A patrol of Chinese policemen pushed through the throngs, their British sergeant's commands demonstrating that foreign law governed the Chinese city.

A semi-circle of rickshawmen, pimps, touts, hawkers, and beggars jostled each other just beyond the doorman's reach. They shouted in a half-dozen languages at the men emerging from the Alhambra's portals. The patrons, Chinese, Europeans, and Eurasians, were all sleekly well dressed. One woman dared the raucous cordon. The semi-circle parted respectfully when a Packard limousine discharged a · heavily painted Chinese opera star. Her powdered white cheeks and sequined *cheongsam* showed that she was hastening to a rendezvous with her protector.

The chill Shanghai night was damp and penetrating. Sheltered by a corrugated cardboard windbreak, a figure in gray rags lay on the grimy pavement. Jonathan Osgood Sekloong glanced idly at the beggar and saw with revulsion that an emaciated baby sucked one shriveled breast. Groping in his pocket for a silver Mex dollar, worth about four shillings, he looked away from the mother's pock-marked face. She obviously hoped that the generosity of the International Settlement would help her evade her imminent rendezvous with death. Jonnie dropped the silver dollar into the battered enamel basin at her black-soled feet.

But he had not come to the most exciting city in the Orient to dwell on the misery beneath its hectic gaiety. Though he had other business as well, his business that night was to enjoy himself.

Just six months past his twenty-third birthday in May 1925, Jonnie prided himself on his capacity for drink. Alternatively stern and tolerant, the Jesuits of Stonyhurst had not only polished his accent and honed his mind, but had also taught him to carry his liquor. Yet he was already glowing with the Hennessy brandy he had consumed during dinner at the Sunya Restaurant. His glass was never empty, for his middle-aged half-uncles, Gregory and Sydney Sek, had constantly proposed new toasts. His raffish uncles had also insisted on visiting the Alhambra, the current favorite among dozens of nightclubs where White Russian refugees danced and drank with the clientele for a small fee. Most of the distressed "countesses" and "baronesses" offered more intimate services for a slightly higher price. Scrabbling for survival, all dreamed of security with the desperate yearning of the dispossessed. Jonnie had required little persuading to visit the Alhambra, though his business was with the financier Judah Haleevie and his inclinations turned toward Haleevie's vivacious twenty-year-old daughter, Sarah.

A revolving globe of a thousand mirrors hung from the ceiling. Its many-colored rays pierced the dimness to play on bored hostesses in low-cut evening-gowns and five sweating Filipino musicians in frilled flamenco shirts, who pumped out their syncopated rendition of "Valencia." An obsequious headwaiter led them through the smoke-wreathed din that astonished Jonnie. British Hong Kong took its pleasures more staidly or, at least, more discreetly.

Once seated on the red-velvet banquette, his uncles demanded champagne and hostesses in the same breath. Unaware of the whispered comments and stealthy glances that greeted their entrance, Jonnie stared at the doily-sized dancefloor.

A six-foot python writhed around a dancer whose golden hair cascaded over her shoulders and bosom. Her harem-dancer's diaphanous pantaloons revealed minute black-lace panties, and her breasts were free under an open bolero. She caressed the drowsy snake provocatively. Her mouth gaped slackly wet in simulated passion, and her cornflower-blue eyes were half-closed above broad Slavic cheekbones. She slithered to the floor, and her hands guided the snake's head between her outspread thighs. As the python attained the lacy triangle, the spotlight dimmed. The audience shouted obscene protests into the blackness in French, English, and Shanghai dialect.

The entrance hall bustled with new patrons, eight burly Chinese wearing blue workmen's jackets, who were obviously out of place amid the perfumed, self-conscious decadence of the Alhambra. They elbowed hostesses, waiters, and patrons, peering at their faces in the beams of small flashlights.

Jonnie turned to Sydney in mute inquiry, but his uncle's hand clasped his arm to counsel silence. The other patrons betrayed neither surprise nor even awareness when two of the intruders stationed themselves beside the service doors; two more stood sentry at the entrance; and the remainder dispersed through the nightclub.

A slender Chinese wearing a black-silk tunic secured by looped frogs entered between another pair of bodyguards. The sleek headwaiter bowed so low his head almost touched the floor. Mincing backward as if for royalty, he showed the slight figure toward a front table where two additional bodyguards stood alert, their hands resting on the butts of revolvers revealed by their loose tunics. The new arrival paused and inclined his head to the Seks. His features were reptilian, and his slitted eyes shone like flat black beads.

"Well met, Elder Brother," he said in the sibilant Shanghai dialect. "I trust you are well."

Gregory and Sydney Sek replied in the same elaborately courteous manner, but Sydney's hand on Jonnie's arm urgently deterred his question. When the ostentatiously sinister figure moved beyond earshot, Sydney, the elder Sek, spoke to his nephew.

"Tu Yueh-shen, a most important man," he breathed in English.

"Who is he?" Jonnie demanded. "Why all the fuss?"

"All that fancy education didn't do so much good, did it?" Sydney Sek spoke in slurred treaty-port English seeded with second-hand American slang.

"Afraid not, Uncle Syd," Jonnie acknowledged cheerfully in his Stonyhurst drawl. "But who is the chap?"

"The most powerful man on the China Coast. Didn't the old man or Charlie tell you about Tu Yueh-shen?"

"Afraid not. Grandfather's bringing me along slowly. He says I'm a dunderhead, and he's afraid to cram too much into my brain. But, more important, who's that dancer? Is she . . . ah . . . available for light conversation?"

Gregory Sek guffawed appreciatively and snapped his fingers at a rat-faced waiter. After issuing rapid instructions in sizzling Shanghai dialect, he spoke softly to his nephew.

"All fixed. She'll turn up when she's dressed. But you *must* know Green Dragon Tu."

"Let me tell him, Greg," the older brother interrupted. "Tu Yueh-shen's Grand High Dragon of the Green Band. You know the Societies, don't you, kid?"

Jonnie nodded. However sheltered, no native of Hong Kong was unaware of the powerful Secret Societies. The Green and Red Bands were, however, much more powerful in Shanghai, where vice, crime, and, occasionally, even virtue were far less inhibited than they were in the Crown Colony.

"His big card's opium, ten times as profitable now it's illegal. But his hand's in everything—gold, girls, gambling, protection, even a dozen legal businesses. He can put ten thousand Braves into the streets by winking an eye. So who's gonna argue with him? The Police Commissioner comes running when Tu Yueh-shen calls. That Bolshevik fellow, Harry's buddy Chiang Kai-shek, is his sworn blood-brother. Green Dragon Tu's a big man, but you saw he respects us." `

"And we? Are we still in opium, Uncle Syd?"

"No chance, kid. The old man won't touch the stuff with a barge pole. Anyway, Dragon Tu's got it all sewed up."

"This town's different from sleepy old Hong Kong, ain't it, young feller?" Sydney's mock-American bonhomie was overwhelming.

"Perhaps," Jonnie replied defensively, a touch of his father's occasional pomposity suffusing features that were a fined-down replica of his father's. "But not that different. Just more open. British colonial rule requires a decent pretence of morality."

"Where are the dames?" Gregory asked impatiently. "There's plenty more where they come from if they can't get their fannies over here quick."

"Yeah, there's plenty of Russian stuff," Sydney laughed. "Most of 'em princesses or countesses, they say. But they're all eager, young feller, real eager. They'll do anything—and I do mean anything—for a passport. More marriages've broken up since the Russky ladies came to town than in a hundred years before. Just play 'em along, and don't get committed. They're hungry."

Jonnie nodded with the solemn sagacity of semi-inebriation. His half-uncles' crude affability accorded with his own mood. He thought of the snake-dancer, and his blood raced. The rat-faced waiter whispered in Sydney's ear while refilling their glasses.

"Getting themselves dolled up," the older Sek said. "Be here in a coupla minutes. Meanwhile, let me finish filling you in. Last few years, thousands of Russkis've turned up in Shanghai. The dames make out okay, the young ones. The guys, that's another story. They take any job they can get from doorman to taxidriver. So help me, I've even seen Russkis pulling rickshaws."

"But good fighters," Gregory added judiciously. "Don't sell 'em short. Funniest damn thing happened the other day. All this warlord pressure's making the Settlement's Commissioners nervy. So they organized their own Russky battalion. Who comes along but Old General Chang? Thinks he owns Shanghai just because he's boss of Kiangsu Province. He sends his own Russky battalion forward, so we send out our Russkis. Damned if they don't look at each other and turn around and chase away Old Chang's Chinese troops. Now we've got two Russky battalions."

Jonnie laughed uproariously. The champagne following brandy made the incident hilarious.

"And all those warships with the big guns," he chortled. "No fear here."

"Yeah, kid, we're pretty safe in old Shanghai," Sydney guffawed. "The rest of China can tear itself apart. Big warlords marching back and forth in every province, big fake battles, big squeeze. Why that screwball Harry had to get himself so mixed in I don't see. But Shanghai's okay. No danger. *Ding gwah-gwah!*"

"Here come the dames," Gregory interjected. "Jonnie, this one's on me. Don't put your hand in your pocket. Make better use of it."

The girls were young and fresh-faced, by no means the hard-eyed professional ladies of the evening Jonnie had expected. Two were vividly dark, while the snake-dancer's long hair was so fair it shone silver. In their short-skirted, low-waisted dresses with swaying silken fringes, they might have been his sisters' friends. His fleeting pang of conscience was overcome by the blond dancer's appeal. Her make-up was subdued, and her air of refinement accentuated her sensuality.

"I am Titanya Kerelenkova." Her accent was charming. "One calls me Tanya."

"Yeah, princess," Sydney interjected before his nephew could speak, "and this is John Stone."

"And Mister Stone, are you English?"

"Quite," Jonnie fell in with his uncle's deception. "John Stone, Esquire."

The Sek brothers were already fondling the brunettes, but mutual timidity separated Jonnie and the shy blond girl who had minutes earlier performed the explicit *danse de ventre*. Tanya sipped her champagne and smiled broadly.

"But it is real!" she said with surprise. "And . . . how do you say it? . . . lovishly *sec*."

"Of course it's real," Jonnie said indignantly. "What do you think I am?"

"I do not know, do I? But I meet very strange mens . . ."

"Well, I'm not strange. Not at all."

Tanya placed her white hand on his thigh, and he covered it with his own.

A shout across the dancefloor broke their self-absorption. A tall young man with fair hair swayed drunkenly before the table where the Green Dragon, Tu Yueh-shen, sat. Two bodyguards closed upon him.

"Damned cheat . . . took me for every penny." Tears runneled the foreigner's flushed cheeks. "Your crooked roulette wheel . . . loaded dice. Every penny."

The foreigner lunged at the unruffled gang leader. A knife flashed, and he staggered. As his assailant fell, Tu Yueh-shen shifted a highly polished black shoe. When the bodyguards dragged the bleeding form away, the fair head trailed on the crimson carpet.

"Christ!" Sydney Sek exclaimed. "Let's get out of here before the cops . . ."

"Self-defense, Syd," his brother observed equably. "No worry. Clear self-defense. But he must've been a *big* loser."

"Let's get out anyway," Sydney urged. "They've gotta call the cops, and I don't wanna get stuck here. Let's go!"

The former major of Imperial Russian Cavalry still guarded the Alhambra's portals, and the dank night was still illuminated by the neon sign. In the sickly violet light, the beggar lay stiff and cold. Her infant clung to her cold breast, and Jonnie's silver dollar had vanished from the enamel basin.

"Reserved a room for you at the Majestic." Sydney bustled Jonnie and the dancer into a taxi. "Name of Stone. Enjoy yourself. And remember, not a penny to the dame. It's on me."

Jonnie woke to a throbbing champagne hangover. Beside him, Tanya's face was childlike in sleep. She had been surprisingly tender, though her imaginative virtuosity had astonished him. She had led him to a plane of experience utterly different from his fumbling with sweaty Lancashire village girls or the passive acquiescence of pallid Hong Kong flower girls. He was totally drained and absolutely content.

He padded barefoot across the thick-piled cream rug to the vestibule where the *North China Daily News* had been slipped under the door. He turned the pages silently to avoid awakening Tanya, for he owed her much more than his uncle could possibly pay.

He found no report of the knifing in the Alhambra. A short item told a tangled tale: Chinese students demonstrating against "exploitation of the workers" by Japanese textile-mill owners and against the suppression of striking workers by Japanese and British troops "had compelled" a Sikh police detachment led by an English lieutenant to fire upon them on Nanking Road. Eleven students had been killed and a greater number wounded.

Tanya called: "Jonnie! What is it you are doing?"

She was sitting up, her arms open and the roseate nipples of her full breasts erect. He sauntered across the room feigning nonchalance he certainly did not feel.

"*Bolshoi . . . harusho*," Tanya murmured. "What a magnificent . . . how do you say it? . . . lusty young one."

Jonnie dropped the newspaper and forgot the world to immure himself in her beckoning arms.

The elder Jonathan Sekloong had been awake for several hours in the Kwok Family Mansion in the Western District of Canton when his grandson plunged again into the full-blooded pleasures he had discovered with Titanya Kerelenkova. Sir Jonathan had in 1912 bought his grandfather's walled compound a few hundred yards from Shameen Island where the European factors were confined to their factories before the First Opium War of 1839. The new Republican Government, prodded by his son Harry, had allowed him to cut the legal tangle created by the claims of his numerous legitimate cousins—and to thwart the Wheatleys' claim through his own mother. A possessive passion had driven him to reclaim his heritage by rebuilding the tumbledown stone mansion, though he deprecated the project as "a sentimental gesture, no more."

Wearing a cotton robe, Sir Jonathan sat in a straight ebony chair with marble back. In the damp heat of morning rivulets of perspiration dripped down his lean chest, but his rigidly disciplined spirit was untouched by physical discomfort. Shaded by upcurled eaves above broad verandas, the spacious bedchamber where his own mother had been born in 1833 was furnished exactly as it had been by his grandfather Kwok Lee-chin. The ebony altar-table and the scrolls extolling filial piety and frugality as mankind's chief virtues were depicted in George Chinnery's pencil sketches of the Kwok Family Mansion dated 1837. The essential bribes, legal fees, reconstruction, and refurnishing had cost Sir Jonathan some £28,000 when the pound sterling was worth almost five American dollars and men considered themselves not merely comfortable, but modestly wealthy on an annual income of £1,000.

"Sentiment comes high, and I don't often indulge it," he had replied defensively when Mary twitted him about the unproductive investment. "But I can afford this sentimental gesture."

Another Sekloong investment was half-concealed by the marquee-like mosquito net that draped the raised bedstead. A slim golden foot and the strawberry-tipped swell of a single breast peeped from the bedclothes. Sentiment had not dictated his acquisition of eighteen-year-old Yuk-lan, "Jade Lotus," who had originally been purchased at the age of eleven by a retired courtesan for training in the amatory arts. Her maidenhead had cost Sir Jonathan £1,000, but he considered the cost well justified. Jade Lotus was a necessary comfort, a proper business expense. Though he felt himself no less vigorous at seventy-one than he had been ten years earlier, her erotic skills reawakened his ardor while her warmth was comforting during the dank winter. By serving his body's needs, Jade Lotus helped relieve the tensions induced by his complex business affairs. Besides, the old Chinese belief that a young bedmate kept a man youthful was by no means unfounded.

Sir Jonathan removed the eggshell lid of his blue-and-white porcelain teacup and sipped the steaming amber liquid. Despite the muggy, 89° heat of Canton, he had no patience with the younger generation's passion for iced drinks. A cup of green mountain tea infused with white ginseng, the mandrake root from Korea, was more cooling and more invigorating. He sighed, and his hazel eyes stared unseeing at the half-revealed figure in the canopied bed. The flimsy-paper file of the Reuter News Agency, delivered by special messenger a half-hour earlier, lay untouched on the ebony side table. Preoccupied, he merely brushed the crackling sheaf with his fingertips.

His own affairs, like the affairs of China herself, were confused—at once promising and threatening. It might have been different if Sun Yat-sen had not resigned the presidency in 1912, and, the next year, broken with the National Government in Peking to form his own Provisional Government. It would certainly have been different had Dr. Sun succeeded in his mission to the Northern Warlord Clique undertaken on the last day of the previous year, 1924. But Sun Yat-sen had failed to "save the country in cooperation with the warlords," as he had confidently predicted. Instead, Tuan Chi-jui, the presumed ally of the Nationalists, and Chang Tso-lin, the master of Manchuria, had together proclaimed a new "National Government" that excluded the Nationalists. Worse, Feng Yü-hsiang, the volatile Christian General who baptized his troops with firehoses and flirted indiscriminately with reactionaries, Nationalists, and Communists, had withdrawn from Peking to sulk in his stronghold at Kalgan beneath the Great Wall, where he still threatened the capital ninety miles away.

Feng Yü-hsiang's defection and the duplicity of the Chang Tso-lin–Tuan Chi-jui alliance negated Dr. Sun's efforts. A Chinese solution to China's problems became impossible. By applying to the Soviet Union for the arms, technical assistance and funds the West would not provide Dr. Sun had already virtually destroyed hopes of China's being united under a liberal regime that would encourage commerce. In return for aligning himself with the Russians, transforming his Kuomintang into an authoritarian party, and taking the fledgling Communist Party into the Kuomintang as Moscow wished, he had received few material benefits, not even the airplane corps of which Harry Sekloong dreamed. The Western powers would not sell aircraft to the Kuomintang, while the Soviets could not. The new infantry battalions and artillery batteries training at Canton and the elite officer corps being created by the Whampoa Military Academy might, in time, bring the

Kuomintang to power. But not, Sir Jonathan feared, as an independent, nationalistic Chinese government.

Calamitously, Dr. Sun had died in Peking on March 12, 1925, two and a half months earlier. Sir Jonathan's grief was still fresh, and it was as much personal as political. Toward the end, he had felt little confidence in Sun Yat-sen's ability to lead China out of chaos. Almost fifteen years, half a generation, had passed since the Revolution of October 1911, but all Dr. Sun's endeavors had exacerbated, it seemed, suffering and disorder. For a weak, corrupt monarchy China had substituted a congeries of rapacious, cruel warlords. Besides, Sun Yat-sen had virtually sold the nation to the Bolsheviks, his foolhardy action hardly justified by the Western powers' maneuvers to keep China splintered so that they could dominate and exploit the nation. Nonetheless, the stomach cancer's rapid spread had shaken Sir Jonathan profoundly. Sun Yat-sen was his friend as well as his ally, and it was not pleasant to see a friend die at only fifty-nine.

Dr. Sun's death had inflicted a new wound on a bleeding nation. Already split into right and left wings, the Kuomintang was riven by new personal rivalries. Harry Sekloong's mentor, Wang Ching-wei, had hovered over the bed in the hospital of the American-supported Peking Union Medical College, elbowing aside the dying man's second wife and his son by his first marriage. Wang Ching-wei claimed to be the legitimate successor of Dr. Sun, but the Japanese-educated Chiang Kai-shek, Commandant of the Whampoa Academy, was also contending for supreme power. The pro-Soviet clique, too, was growing stronger, virtually hallowed by the impetuous Dr. Sun's remarks at Kobe en route to his rendezvous with death in Peking: "Russia symbolizes a live-and-let-live policy. Other powers aim at dominating the so-called weak nations. We Asiatics must emancipate Asia and the down-trodden states of Europe and America from European and American oppression. Japan and China must join hands and harmoniously lead the Asiatics to fight for a greater Asiaticism, thus expediting world-peace."

Sir Jonathan frowned, remembering those muddled, ill-chosen words. He required no second sight to see that they would provoke major conflicts in the years to come. But he put aside his forebodings for the distant future to assess what Dr. Sun had really left. Little, in truth, besides a faction-ridden Nationalist Party and his Political Testament. Already canonical, that Testament offered another inflammatory exhortation: "For forty years I have devoted myself to the cause of the people's revolution with but one end in view, the elevation of China to a position of freedom and equality among the nations. . . . To attain this goal we must bring about a thorough awakening of our own people and ally ourselves in a common struggle with those people of the world who treat us on a basis of equality. The Revolution is not yet completed!"

The ginseng tea Sir Jonathan sipped was flavored with bitter memories. Just a week earlier, the Central Executive Committee of the Kuomintang had repudiated all hopes of reconciliation with the National Government in Peking and had dedicated itself to cooperation with the Soviet Union. That decision was too much. He was a patriotic Chinese who had spent millions for China, but he was also committed to free commerce and to amity with the West. China's salvation could not come from cooperating with—or toadying to—either Moscow or Tokyo.

His slender fingers lifted the Reuter file. He began reading idly, but stiffened as his eyes scanned the second item:

BULLETIN . . . BULLETIN . . . BULLETIN

SHANGHAI, MAY 30 (REUTER)—STUDENTS AND STRIKING WORKERS JAPANESE-OWNED EIWA COTTON MILLS TODAY CLASHED INTERNATIONAL SETTLEMENT POLICE.

UNDER COMMAND BRITISH LIEUTENANT J. EVERSON, INDIAN POLICEMEN OPENED FIRE. PRELIMINARY REPORTS 12 STRIKERS KILLED, 32 INJURED. SOME INFORMED SOURCES REPORT MOST OF SLAIN NOT WORKERS BUT STUDENTS.

The file included no follow-up, but the bulletin told Sir Jonathan all he needed—and more than he wished

—to know. Unlike his twenty-three-year-old grandson, who was dozing in the arms of Titanya Kerelenkova at the Majestic Hotel in Shanghai, he understood the over-whelming significance of the incident in a single appalling insight. The rising waves of anti-foreign hatred were breaking on the rock of Western obduracy. Greater and gorier clashes—demonstrations, riots, and confrontations—were certain to follow. The productive, if avaricious, business community in which he had worked all his life would inevitably be aligned with the Western powers and the warlords against the radical Kuomintang backed by the Soviet Bolsheviks. The personal dilemma was insoluble. Sir Jonathan suddenly felt aged. Even Jade Lotus, just stirring behind the diaphanous mosquito net, could not at that moment make him feel younger.

He yearned for the presence of his son Charles and his daughter-in-law Mary. That yearning, he reassured himself fretfully, did not stem from declining self-confidence. At his time of life, a man was entitled to the moral support of his children, the only human beings he could trust without reservation. But Charles and Mary were cruising leisurely through the South Seas aboard *Regina Pacis*. To his astonishment, their brief messages indicated that they were delighting in a second honeymoon after almost twenty-five years of marriage. Having left Hong Kong five months earlier, they were not planning to return until late July.

Retreating before the rising tide, Sir Jonathan embarked on the steam pinnace *Lucinda* for Hong Kong the following day. Jade Lotus remained in Canton to amuse herself—wantonly he feared, but discreetly he hoped. Sekloong Manor was not only his monument, but his strong fortress; Hong Kong was the firm base for his defensive strategy against the forces of anarchy.

His grandson Jonnie in Shanghai was unaware of those forces. He was enchanted by the polyglot metropolis on the mudflats of the Yangtze, where Western enterprise and Chinese labor had reared towering buildings on the riverside Bund. The city's attractions were diverse. Tutored by his half-uncles, Gregory and Sydney Sek, he was fascinated by the Sekloong enterprises' intricate connections with sources of power that ranged from the assertively respectable Hong Kong and Shanghai Baking Corporation to the racket-plagued Secret Society–dominated docks through which flowed the trade that nourished the brawling metropolis.

Jonnie Sekloong was the most fortunate and the most perplexed young man in the cheerfully sinful port. He had simultaneously discovered two passions: pure love and pure sexuality. His passions centered on two quite different young women. Reluctantly blessed by the family, his romantic yearnings were fixed on Sarah, the twenty-year-old daughter of his grandfather's associate Judah Haleevie. Her dark vivacity personified the perfect damsel, the fairy princess in a bright tower of whom Jonnie had dreamed at Stonyhurst. While his heart was given to the virgin Sarah, his body was possessed by the earthily inventive Tanya Kerelenkova.

The resilient insensitivity of youth contrived to reconcile the contradictions between the two women and the divergent roles he played—with Sarah by day and with Tanya by night. Jonnie's self-indulgence was not deterred by the tough-minded common sense he had inherited from his mother and his grandfather. At his desk in the offices of J. Sekloong and Sons in Sassoon House on the Bund, he occasionally wondered what his mother would say if she learned of his dual life.

Jonnie's younger brothers Thomas, twenty, and James, eighteen, were belatedly accepting the stern control he had escaped. At the Whampoa Military Academy, they were for the first time subject to strict discipline. Unlike Jonnie, they were not isolated from the political tides that were sweeping over China, the tides their grandfather feared. But their own responses diverged sharply.

"I came to Whampoa to soldier," Thomas complained, "not to listen to ranting Bolshevik agitators."

Less than a year after entering the joint Nationalist-Communist officer training school, Thomas had already fixed upon the lodestar he was to follow all his life. His ideal was a thirty-seven-year-old former Shanghai stockbroker who had returned to the career of arms for which he had trained at the Tokyo Military Academy. A follower of Dr. Sun Yat-sen for almost two decades, Chiang Kai-shek had been appointed Commandant of the Whampoa Academy and Commander-in-Chief of the National Revolutionary Army because he was the most experienced among the few trained officers in the Nationalists' ranks. He had visited the Soviet Union early in 1924 to seal the Kuomintang's alliance with the Communists and had been appointed an honorary member of the Executive Committee of the Communist International, a distinction whose significance was unclear even to himself. The Kuomintang's chief soldier was a Confucianist by conviction, soon to be a Methodist by conversion, and an unwavering opponent of his Party's pro-Soviet left wing by instinct. Between military maneuvers and political intrigues, he was courting Mayling Soong, the sister of Dr. Sun's window and the youngest daughter of one of the richest and most strongly Western-oriented men in China, Yale graduate and Methodist Charlie Soong.

Both Chiang Kai-shek's ideological inclination and his candid ambition evoked Thomas Sekloong's admiration. Above all else, the cadet was awed by the military achievements of the dashing figure in the well-cut uniform. Chiang's detractors scoffed at his spit-and-polish mentality and condemned his tortuous political maneuvers. The superstitious, who were still a majority among the self-consciously "modern" cadets, whispered that the Commandant's face in repose resembled a skull. However, Thomas Sekloong, the most traditionally Chinese of Mary's children, had found the warm and stern paternal authority he sought. Charles had unwittingly evaded that role, while Thomas's autocratic grandfather was remote.

The first rift between Thomas and his younger brother James was opened by Thomas's total commitment to Chiang Kai-shek. Though both brothers had irrevocably chosen to serve China as soldiers, James was

420

already moving in another direction. The pronunciations they preferred for their Chinese names demonstrated their differences. Thomas used the Cantonese, calling himself Sek Lai-kwok—his personal name meaning "Build the Nation." James used the Mandarin (or National Language): Shih Ai-kuo—his name meaning "Love the Nation." The radicals who opposed Chiang Kai-shek's gradualism were determined to make the National Language, based on the tongue of Peking, the medium of communication among all Chinese. The welter of dialects, which included Cantonese, was to be eradicated.

Unaware of his true paternity, James was already showing himself his father's son. After the death of Sun Yat-sen, Harry Sekloong had given his loyalty to the man he considered Dr. Sun's legitimate successor. Wang Ching-wei, a fiery activist who had once attempted to assassinate Viceroy Yüan Shih-Kai, was close to the Soviet advisers who were guiding the reorganization of the National Revolutionary Army into a modern military force and the transformation of the Nationalist Party into a semi-totalitarian political force. Harry was Wang Ching-wei's closest adherent amid the internal struggles that were splitting the Kuomintang into left and right. Attempting to bridge the rift between the Nationalists and the Communists, Wang Ching-wei and Harry Sekloong opposed Chiang Kai-shek and his conservative supporters.

Harry maintained his personal friendship with Morris Abraham Cohen, but the Two-Gun General had become politically irrelevant after the death of his beloved leader. Other foreigners had, however, become powerful in the councils of the new revolution.

A taciturn former Czarist officer who called himself General Galen was the Soviets' Chief Military Adviser to Chiang Kai-shek. Mikhail Borodin, representative of the Communist International in China, was a more winning personality. With his American-born wife, who affected peasant blouses and flowing skirts, he had been expelled from the United States in 1916 for political agitation under the name Michael Grusenburg. Jewish like Cohen, Borodin too was charmingly ebullient, and his tall frame was elegant beside the Two-Gun General's ponderous strength. Borodin's open features belied his political subtlety. When its American president invited him to lecture at the Canton Christian College, the heavily mustached Comintern agent declined.

"Communism," he observed bluffly, "is an ideal and a philosophy for which China is far from ready. China is a hundred years behind the times. From skyscrapers to rickshaws—what a contrast!"

Borodin rubbed his hands in delight after the massacre in Shanghai that was already hallowed as the May Thirtieth Incident and remarked to his intimates: "We did not make May Thirtieth. It was made for us!" Some years later, as a disillusioned pensioner editing the journal of the Communist International, he was to observe acidly: "The next time a Chinese general comes to Moscow talking of world revolution, send the Secret Police. The Chinese are only interested in guns."

Yet in June 1925, when the cauldron of Chinese politics began to overflow, the Soviet advisers still appeared to control the flames under that cauldron. Moscow was the prime source of financial assistance to the Nationalist–Communist alliance, as well as its ideological mentor, and the native Communists were at the center of the Kuomintang.

Slim and apparently diffident, twenty-seven-year-old Liu Shao-chi, vice-chairman of the Communist-controlled All China Trade Union Federation, had proved himself by organizing the Shanghai textile workers' strike. He was later to become Chairman of the Chinese People's Republic and, finally, to be purged as an "agent of the Nationalists and the Imperialists." An impetuous thirty-two-year-old, whose Hunan accent was hardly more intelligible than Chiang Kai-shek's slurred Chekiang Mandarin, was a deputy chairman of the Central Executive Committee of the Kuomintang. The irrepressibly self-willed Mao Tse-tung was later to attain almost absolute power as the first Chairman of the Chinese People's Republic and the perennial Chairman of the Chinese Communist Party.

James Sekloong gave his unreserved loyalty to a man who in 1925 ranked higher in that Party than either Liu Shao-chi or Mao Tse-tung. Chou En-lai, just twenty-seven, who was later to be the Premier of the Chinese People's Republic, had recently returned from several years of study in France, Germany, and the Soviet Union. Having organized the Chinese Communist Party's first branches abroad, he was Moscow's favorite protégé. A true cosmopolitan, who delighted in his command of French, Chou En-lai wore his uniform with the elegance of a Parisian boulevardier.

Though he was Chief Political Commissar of the Whampoa Academy, Chou's uniform appeared identical to the cadets'. But the Sekloongs saw that the khaki cloth was finer, the cut more skilful, and the Sam Browne belt more pliable. Though General Chou wore the peaked garrison cap prescribed for the cadets, his riding-boots came from Kow Hoo, Shanghai's most expensive boot-maker. He did not affect the straw sandals the cadets sometimes wore to demonstrate their solidarity with raggle-taggle peasants who were the privates and noncommissioned officers of the Revolutionary Party.

His own uniforms, like his brother's, having been made by their father's tailor, James fiercely defended his idol against the zealots who dismissed him as a "bourgeois fop." Like the Sekloongs, the Political Commissar was a scion of privilege. His father had been a rising Mandarin under the Manchus and, after the revolution in 1911, a wealthy businessman. Though Chou En-lai was in revolt against both Confucian and bourgeois China, he could neither conceal nor alter the impress of his ancestry: his slender, whipcord figure; his personal fastidiousness; his fine features dominated by large, wide-set eyes; and his inherent assumption that his orders would be obeyed without question. James Sekloong, the grandson of a Eurasian free-booter, was already half-converted to the egalitarian Marxist creed preached by Chou En-lai. But he felt himself inferior to that paladin of the Communist Party—almost as much because of his humbler origins as because of his ideological immaturity.

Despite their burgeoning political differences, Thomas and James remained inseparable. They slept beside each other on wooden planks covered by thin straw mats; they drilled together on the muddy parade-ground; and they shared the same crude bench in their improvised classrooms. The brothers were further united by intense indignation when General Chou En-lai lectured on the Current Situation and Its Opportunities early on June 23, 1925.

The rough stone building was cooled by neither electric fans nor punkahs. The humid air was stirred occasionally by a lethargic breeze that carried the acrid reek of drying fish and the fecal stench of privies overhanging the river. Stretching drowsily, Thomas saw that green mold spangled the distempered ceiling.

"Comrades!" The taut figure in the fitted uniform spoke the word like a command, rather than a greeting. "Comrades! We stand at a decisive fork in the history of China and humanity. A revolutionary high-tide is rising through the nation. The spontaneous indignation of the working class under the leadership of the Communist Party—and, of course, our allies of the Nationalist Party—is rising to a tidal wave that will sweep away all existing institutions.

"Comrades! We must rapidly prepare for the critical moment when the powerful armed forces we are building will act decisively. We will smash the exploiting landlords, the rapacious capitalists, the bloodsucking warlords—and their foreign masters. The struggle to liberate the people of China is indistinguishable in essence from the struggle against the European and American imperialists who support, manipulate, enrich, and, also, exploit their Chinese puppets. Only the great Soviet Union, alone among the nations of the world, has demonstrated its sympathy for our just cause by providing generous material assistance and invaluable political guidance. Only the Soviet Union is the life-long, unswerving friend of the Chinese people. We are fighters in the worldwide liberation movement with the Soviet Union at its head."

General Chou En-lai flicked drops of sweat from his long upper lip with a starched white handkerchief and sipped tea from a handleless porcelain cup.

"In the long run, the working class under the guidance of the Communist Party must, inevitably, take power over China and transform our nation into a modern Socialist state. But that time is still far off. For the moment we are all—Nationalists and Communists alike —wholeheartedly engaged in a life-and-death struggle to destroy the native exploiting class and its foreign overlords. Comrades! You will soon be fighting in the vanguard of that struggle. The exploiting class will not leave the stage of history of its own accord when its role is finished. It must be driven from the stage of history by force. You are the spearhead of that force.

"But you must never forget that force, armed force, is no more than the expression of the will of the masses. A single politically conscious peasant or worker-soldier motivated by righteous hatred is worth a platoon of warlord mercenaries. A hearty welcome by the people of a liberated village is worth a regiment; a popular uprising led by the working class in a city is worth a division. You must cultivate the techniques of political warfare—agitation, propaganda, education, and loving kindness to the *lao pai-hsing,* the common people who are the ultimate source of all power, all strength, and all virtue. The *lao pai-hsing* must be guided to full political consciousness."

"Comrade Chou!"

A thin youth with a beaky rose to put his question. James knew him as a member of the Young Socialist League, the training corps for the Communist Party, and an outstanding cadet, though he was only seventeen. Lin Piao was the son of a bankrupt cotton-mill owner from Central China who earned a meager living as a purser on the riverboats of the China Merchant Steam Navigation Company that plied the Yangtze. He was later to be a Marshal of the Chinese People's Liberation Army; the moving force of violent civil disorder that almost destroyed the Chinese People's Republic; the heir-designate to Chairman Mao—and, finally, a charred corpse in the wreckage of a transport aircraft on the steppes of Mongolia after vainly attempting to assassinate Chairman Mao Tse-tung and seize power by a *coup d'état*. At least, such was the story of Lin Piao's treachery Chou En-lai told the world. At that moment, almost four decades before the dénouement of their relationship, Chou En-lai strained to hear Lin Piao's question. The ambitious youth's harsh voice rose over distant, hoarse shouts.

"Comrade Chou!" Lin Piao asked ingratiatingly. "Are we not already close to the stage of final victory? The proletariat are rising in Shanghai, in Canton, and in my native Wuhan, where they toil in textile plants and steel mills. One strong blow could sweep away the rotten structure of the old society and give power to the people, could it not?"

"Not yet, Comrade Lin, not yet," the Political Commissar replied. "Lenin teaches we must be patient as well as determined. These strikes, the wave of protest, will have great effects. But our organization is not complete—militarily or politically. A long struggle lies ahead."

The distant shouting grew louder, distracting the cadets. Even the obsequiously attentive Lin Piao glanced toward the windows. A civilian in black worker's clothing slipped through the creaking wooden door and spoke to General Chou in an undertone.

"Comrades!" the Political Commissar declared brusquely. "Comrade Liu Shao-chi sends to tell us that the workers are marching on the Anglo-French island of Shameen. Shall we see just how high the tide has risen? Perhaps Comrade Lin is right. Perhaps not."

Even more than Shanghai, Shameen, James Sekloong knew, was a foreign creation, a wholly alien speck in the midst of Chinese territory. It was a largely man-made island, expanded to its present dimensions, a half mile long and an eighth of a mile wide, in the mid-nineteenth century when British and French engineers methodically dumped fill onto the mudflats on the edge of the river. Connected to the mainland by a concrete causeway less than one hundred feet long, Shameen had been sacked by an angry Chinese mob protesting foreign domination in September 1883. The Sekloong brothers had been taught only two days earlier about Shameen's creation, its foreign control, and the patriotic rising it had already experienced.

Stepping over whining beggars and avoiding scabrous pi-dogs as he hastened through the fetid streets, James wondered if history would repeat itself. The cadets' uniforms cleared a passage through the screaming crowds. Gnarled hands reached out to pat their shoulders and rough voices called out: *"Ho! Ho!* Good! Good!"

The causeway, which was sheltered by a peaked roof, debouched from the tree-shaded island onto a small plaza thronged with workers, fishermen, and farmers carrying placards aloft on long poles. At the far end of the causeway, British and French soldiers in khaki lay behind sandbags, while two erect sentries stood ceremonial guard over the Chinese territory ruled by foreigners.

Chou En-lai waved a pale hand, and his cadets halted obediently on the edge of the crowd. James saw that young men in workers' clothing moved purposefully among the demonstrators. Despite their garb, their smooth faces and officious manner identified them as intellectuals. Those young men leading the chanting, James realized, were Comrade Liu Shao-chi's agitators.

"British imperialist dogs, get out! Leave China! We demand apologies and reparations. Revenge our martyred Shanghai compatriots!"

A tall fisherman in tattered black tunic tossed high a vertical banner reading, ALL CHINESE PATRIOTS DEMONSTRATE!

The sentries ostentatiously cocked their rifles. Behind the sandbags, other rifle bolts clicked. For an instant, the plaza was silent.

"Kill the foreign devil-heads!" a bespectacled young agitator cried hoarsely. "Take back China's soil!"

The crowd surged forward, but halted involuntarily

as the feet of the first rank touched the stones of the causeway. The agitators shouted and hurled themselves forward. Flourishing clubs, cleavers, cargo hooks, and sharp-pointed bamboo spears, the crowd rolled toward the sandbag barricade.

A volley of rifle shots crashed across the shouting. The foreign soldiers had fired over the heads of their assailants.

The shocked mob recoiled momentarily, then rolled forward again, a river battering against the frail sandbag levee. The smooth-faced agitators were screaming: "Forward! Forward! Defy the barbarians' weapons."

As the human wave broke on the barricades, rifle fire rattled continuously. After no more than two minutes, the mob began to withdraw. Bleeding bodies lay crumpled on the causeway, and an old woman sprawled on the stones of the plaza was trampled by the retreating mob. General Chou spoke softly, as if to himself.

"Not, perhaps, Comrade Lin Piao's revolutionary high-tide. But a beginning—a definite beginning."

Chou En-lai withdrew his cadets. It was no part of his policy to sacrifice them in street battles. The expensively trained cadets were too precious to risk in demonstrations. Liu Shao-chi's expendable agitators were, in any event, much more effective in whipping up the hysteria that would provide the revolution with the martyrs it urgently required.

The siege of Shameen continued. The charging mob was scythed by the foreign rifles until the soldiers were sickened by the slaughter. Shortly after nightfall, the All China Federation of Trade Unions announced that fifty-two patriots had been killed and hundreds had been gravely injured. The actual numbers were unverifiable at the time and were to remain unverifiable. Nor had the mob taken Shameen. But that failure mattered no more than the true casualty toll. They had kindled another link in the chain of fires that was burning across China to inflame the masses and ignite the soldiers of the Revolutionary Army.

William Hayward Driver nodded over his dog-eared

copy of *The War of the Worlds*. Even the magic prose of H. G. Wells could not dispel his drowsiness in the close radioroom of *Regina Pacis*. The earphones around his neck offered no diversion but the crackle of static, and it was the third time he had read the novel.

Bill Driver did not regret sailing aboard the yacht, though his employers, the Marconi Corporation, had warned him the duty might be monotonous after the lively Dollar Liners to which he was accustomed. The undemanding routine had allowed him to reread all his intellectual idols: Wells, Jack London, Upton Sinclair, G. B. Shaw, Henry George, and John Reed, the angry prophets of cataclysmic technological and social change. Besides, he had been surprised at finding Mrs. Sekloong not condescendingly "gracious," but an intelligent, if challenging, audience for his own theories. He could not quite say the same for her husband or *Regina*'s scathingly anti-intellectual Australian captain.

It had been revealing for a poor boy from Schenectady to see how the very rich lived. The contempt for those parasites instilled by his machinist father, a convinced anarchist and a founding member of the militant International Workers of the World, had been slightly diluted by the experience. He had grudgingly recognized that Mrs. Sekloong could prove as formidable an adversary as she had been a sympathetic friend, while her husband was hardly the brainless wastrel living on inherited wealth his father's doctrine described. Nonetheless, Bill Driver was glad the cruise was drawing to an end. It was time to move on.

"CR3A . . . CR3A . . . CR3A." The staccato Morse of the yacht's call sign crackled in his earphones. *"Regina Pacis,* calling *Regina Pacis."*

Bill Driver deliberately inserted a slip of paper between the pages to mark his place and centered a note pad on his folding desk before touching the sending key. They would, he assumed, be transmitting more stock-market quotations or boring commercial news, as they had almost every evening of the past six months.

"CR3A . . . CR3A," he tapped out on the bronze key. "Receiving you. Who is calling?"

"CR3A . . . CR3A." The dots and dashes sounded in his ears. "Yacht *Regina Pacis*. I have an urgent message for you. Do you read me?"

"I read you clearly, five by five. Ready to copy. Please proceed."

"CR3A, CR3A, this is Hong Kong Wireless. Message follows: Charles—Return immediately repeat immediately. Proceed with all haste repeat all haste. Do not repeat not delay. Signature J. Sekloong. Acknowledge."

Five minutes after Bill Driver delivered the message, the 250-horsepower Sulzbach diesel's throbbing vibrated through *Regina Pacis*. The yacht heeled sharply as the crew shook out the reefs in the courses, raised the topsails, and snapped staysails aloft between her masts. A white bow-wave creamed into foam. At twelve knots, *Regina Pacis* would push her prow into the green waters of Hong Kong Harbor within fifty hours, instead of the leisurely week Charles and Mary had believed would conclude their long cruise.

They agreed not to ask the Old Gentleman to expand his peremptory message. He would presumably have said more if he wished; the speed of wireless communications was paid for in part by their public nature. Charles surmised that his aging father was finally feeling—and acknowledging—the need for his eldest son's counsel and support. He further suspected that his father was worried by widespread rioting in China's major cities, as well as Hong Kong itself. Mary did not take issue with him, though she was skeptical of his explanation. The Old Gentleman had, after all, yielded to impulse in the past. His urgent command could have been inspired by an inauspicious reading from the aged soothsayer, Silver Seventh Brother, or by a desire that they should admire a particularly fine Ming porcelain piece newly acquired. The old autocrat was growing more imperious and capricious with age.

Both Charles and Mary concealed their private apprehensions, reassuring each other that Sir Jonathan would certainly have been more explicit if the matter were grave. Mary thought instinctively of illness or injury to one of the children. Charles imagined a major business setback, perhaps a disastrous clash with the Wheatleys. But those fears faded amid the lingering euphoria of their island-hopping cruise. When *Regina Pacis* dropped her sails off Stonecutter's Island and motored toward Blake Pier at ten on the morning of June 27, 1925, Mary and Charles were relatively relaxed. Though the green hills and terraced houses of the port surrounded them, they were still far away in spirit.

The thrill of homecoming Mary felt despite herself was inexplicably clouded when she contemplated the familiar harbor. She involuntarily recalled her first arrival a quarter of a century earlier. The panorama was little changed, though the groves of masts had given way to steamships' stubby funnels and pastoral Kowloon was becoming tenemented. But something, she felt instinctively, was amiss. Hong Kong's air of lassitude was not attributable solely to the damp heat that enfolded her like a sodden blanket, though her white sportsdress was light cotton and all her clothing weighed no more than an eighth of the summer-serge dress and the voluminous undergarments that had burdened her in 1900. The difference between the Hong Kong *Regina Pacis* had left almost seven months earlier and the Hong Kong to which she had just returned was elusive.

"Mary, something's wrong!" Charles, too, was troubled. "But damned if I can see just what."

He gazed at The Peak, emerald green with the summer rains, and saw the boxy Peak Tram crawling up the heights. The colonnaded buildings along the Praya in downtown Victoria stood unaltered. Beyond them, he saw khaki ranks of soldiers wheeling on the Murray Parade-ground. All appeared normal, but his nagging unease persisted.

"Somehow, Charles, it looks like the plague year," Mary ventured. "It's *too* quiet."

"That's it, dear. Not something new, but something missing. Look, not a lighter's moving in the harbor. Not a single ship's loading or unloading."

"And where are the rickshaws? I can see only a few motorcars. And where are the morning crowds?"

"Something's damned wrong! The old man wasn't just blowing the wind!"

Sir Jonathan himself waited on the rough planking of Blake Pier when *Regina Pacis* made her deliberate approach. He lifted his walking-stick in salute and resumed his nervous pacing as the heavy warps snaked ashore. The two-inch manila cables were hauled onto the pier's bollards by sailors in the Sekloong livery of striped blue-and-gold shirts, rather than longshoremen in rusty black. The black Rolls-Royce Phantom II, with its enormous locomotive headlights and license plate HK 7, stood foursquare and familiar on the Pier. But Mary looked in vain for the uniformed driver. A rush of joy momentarily obscured her apprehension when her eldest son, Jonnie, stepped out of the Rolls. Debonair in cream linen, he waved vigorously.

In his lustrous light-blue-cotton long-gown, Sir Jonathan was as erect and dignified as she remembered him. But his behavior was uncharacteristic. Not waiting for his son and daughter-in-law to descend to the Pier, he hurried up the gangplank while the sailors were still setting it up. His grandson took long strides to keep up with the septuagenarian.

Sir Jonathan kissed Mary perfunctorily and laid his arm on Charles's shoulders for an instant. Jonnie greeted her with an exuberant bear-hug. Though his grandfather was abstracted, her normally reserved son was ebullient. He swung her into the air before greeting his father with a hard handshake and a half-embrace. Mary wondered that Jonnie, instilled with English restraint, should be so demonstrative while his grandfather was withdrawn.

"Leave the baggage," Sir Jonathan commanded. "Leave everything for the servants. I want to get back to the Manor."

The streets were oppressively quiet, the normal throngs of clerks, hawkers, messengers, rickshawmen, and coolies absent. But an effervescent Jonnie whipped the Rolls around the curves to The Peak. His grandfather grunted irritably, and he slowed momentarily. Mary caught her breath when her eldest son, turning in the driver's seat to grin at his passengers, almost ran the motorcar over a precipice.

"Jonnie, do be careful." she admonished. "We haven't survived the Cannibal Islands to be killed in Hong Kong."

"Right you are, Mother." Jonnie did not slacken his speed. "No danger at all, I assure you. You're safe with the best driver on the China Coast, maybe the entire world."

"What's wrong with the boy?" Charles asked indulgently. "Touch of the sun?"

"He's in love." Sir Jonathan's gravity lightened for a moment. "Or so he tells me."

"Now, that *is* interesting," Mary said. "Who is it, Jonnie?"

"Well . . . ah . . . it's a long story, Mother. Hard to say."

"You mean you love everyone, the entire human race?" Charles's irony was heavy. "Isn't your love fixed on one person, female I presume?"

"That's more like it, definitely female." Jonnie turned to grin at them again, swerving at the last instant to avoid an oncoming lorry.

"And who, may I ask . . ." Mary laughed.

"Till the sands of the desert grow cold, and the infinite numbers are told," he crooned, "God gave thee to me—to have and to hold."

"Let the boy be." A smile quirked the corners of Sir Jonathan's mouth. "You'll hear soon enough. God knows, I've heard nothing else since I called him back from Shanghai. However, there are more important matters."

He leaned forward to crank up the glass panel that separated the passengers from the driver. Unabashed, Jonnie sang on merrily.

"I called you back," Sir Jonathan resumed, "because I'm worried about what's building up."

"The demonstrations?" Charles asked.

"The demonstrations—and worse to come, much worse."

"We've had demonstrations before, Father," Mary remarked, "and the Chinese situation's no worse—though, naturally, no better—than it's always been. Why worse to come?"

"You saw the streets practically empty, didn't you? Where are the longshoremen? For that matter, where's my driver, Ah Wai? It's a strike, a general strike, and it's just beginning. They'll close Hong Kong down before they're through."

"The rioting in China's anti-foreign, anti-British," Charles objected. "It can't really hurt the Sekloongs. After all, we're Chinese."

"When it suits you," Mary observed dryly. "Don't be so obtuse, Charles. We're not really Chinese, for one thing. And, if we are, we're still running-dogs of the foreign imperialists to the revolutionaries."

"Not quite that bad," Sir Jonathan interjected. "The name Sekloong still counts for a lot. We still have a big credit with the Nationalists, and Harry's a power again. His man Wang Ching-wei's certain to become President of the Provisional Government when they finally choose Sun Yat-sen's successor in just a few days."

"Then what's the worry?" Mary asked.

"The Bolsheviks," Sir Jonathan replied. "They're calling a general strike throughout Kwangtung Province —and especially Hong Kong—because of what they're calling the 'Shameen Massacre.' The strike will spread, and we'll be hurt badly by the shock waves."

"Can't we use it?" Mary suggested. "If our competitors are struck, and we . . ."

"No one's immune, Mary," the Old Gentleman replied. "A general strike's like the plague, sparing no one. When they close down Hong Kong's commerce, we'll all suffer. And God knows how bad the rioting will become or when it'll end. That's why I called you back. I need you both here."

Sir Jonathan's admission that he needed Charles and her was the gravest portent to Mary. Granted he was

434

getting older. But, for the first time since Charles had roused the wrath of the Green Band in 1905, the Old Gentleman had acknowledged that he was neither omniscient nor self-sufficient. Both China and the world were changing so fast that even the supremely self-confident Sir Jonathan was deeply perturbed. He spoke of his anxieties only once more before they drove under the great winged-dragon arch toward The Castle to review the reports from his network of informants.

"We've passed through many changes," he mused. "China, Asia, and the West—all are totally different from what they were a quarter of a century ago. This time the coming changes—political, economic, and social—will not simply mean the end of one era and the beginning of a new one. It will be a completely new epoch we won't recognize. *Tien Kai, Ti Chen!* 'The heavens are opening, and the earth is splitting!' "

Nothing could have revealed Sir Jonathan's profound sense of loss and apprehension more than his invoking the old Chinese warning of disaster.

The depression induced by Sir Jonathan's forebodings was, for that evening at least, dispelled by the joy of homecoming. Charlotte and her husband Manfei Way joined them for dinner, and Mary dandled her first grandchild. To Charles's delight, it was a boy. The furry-haired, two-month-old bundle called Mokhing looked like a Chinese doll with chubby red cheeks and glowing dark eyes. When Mary cradled him in her arms, she was reconciled to becoming a grandmother at forty-five. Her scapegrace eldest son heightened her pleasure. His dark hair slicked down, he was a new Jonnie in a tight-waisted jacket and flaring trousers called "Oxford bags." During her seven-month absence he had been transformed from a sober-sided young English gentleman into that new creature the Americans called a "sheik." She almost expected him to produce a ukulele and croon "The Japanese Sandman." Instead, he drew her into the chintz-bright morning-room overlooking the garden, which was hung with firefly lanterns.

"I wish to speak with Mother alone," he declared, firmly closing the door on the rest of the family.

"Now, Jonnie, what's the mystery?" Mary asked, seating herself in the familiar easy-chair and tugging at her short skirt.

"No mystery, Mother." The blarney fell easily from his lips, and his voice took on the Sekloong lilt. "Just that I'm in love with the most smashing, beautiful, charming girl in the world—next to you, of course!"

"May I ask who she is, this paragon?"

"She's Sarah, Sarah Haleevie."

"Little Sarah? Who would've suspected?"

"You're twitting me. Don't tell me you knew?"

"Let us say I suspected."

The glow in Jonnie's hazel eyes faded. Like a small boy, he was crestfallen at being deprived of his surprise. But his smile soon flashed again, and he whooped in joy.

"If you guessed, I imagine there'll be no trouble. Uncle Judah says he's all for it."

"Does he? And your grandfather? Is he delighted, too?"

"Not quite. Mumbled the same line. What about a nice *Chinese* girl? But his heart wasn't in it. Later, he conceded Sarah was *kuo-te-chü,* 'can pass okay,' and Judah Haleevie's a great man. So, if you and Father . . ."

"Not so fast, Jonnie. You know she's Jewish, don't you?"

"I never thought you were prejudiced, Mother?" he said defensively.

"I am, you know. I've got many prejudices you don't know about. But anti-Semitism's not one of them. I was thinking about the children."

"Oh, Sarah's agreed. They'll be baptized Catholics, though she won't think of converting herself. And I'd never press her."

"I'm not concerned about that, Jonnie. I didn't convert either, though my religious feelings aren't as strong as the Haleevies'. But there's bound to be tension over the children."

"There won't be, Mother, I assure you. When two people love each other . . ."

"I rejoice at the wisdom of your youth, but please don't read me a lecture on love. Life doesn't always work out as we plan. I don't want Sarah to be resentful later."

"Oh, we've thought of that. Discussed it. She makes only two conditions. Any children must be given instruction in their Jewish heritage, and, she says, learn about their Chinese heritage as well."

"A sensible girl," Mary said. "So all is arranged except for your parents' blessing, is it?"

"You do approve, Mother," he pressed, "don't you?"

"Yes, I suppose so. We're getting to be a very mixed lot, aren't we, Jonnie?"

"Bless you, Mother, bless you!" He dropped a kiss on her cheek. "I knew you'd understand."

"All right. Now go and tell your father. And apologize for telling me first."

Jonnie bounded out of the morning-room. When the door slammed behind him, Mary leaned back against the flowered slipcover. She had known from the beginning that she was "mixed up with a damned strange lot," as her father had said. Recalling her affection for Judah Haleevie and Two-Gun Cohen, she reflected somewhat guiltily that she much preferred the vivacious Sarah as a daughter-in-law to the dull Manfei Way as a son-in-law, and she wondered idly how Jonnie would tell Charles.

The encounter between father and son was initially smoother than Jonnie's talk with his mother. Tolerant and relaxed, Charles Sekloong heard the news with pleasure. His dynastic sense had been troubled by the single state of the heir-presumptive to the House of Sekloong.

"Told your mother first, did you?" he remarked without rancor. "Well, I suppose marriage is women's business."

"But what do you think, Father?" Jonnie pressed.

"It's a good match, good for business, too. She won't get much, though. Not with seven brothers. But making the Haleevie connection closer won't do us any harm. Like the girl, do you?"

"Father, she's super. Lovely, a good sport, and smart as a whip. We talk the same language, too."

" 'Twould be surprising if you didn't. She's not a Hottentot or an Eskimo, after all. But what about your children? They'll be Catholics, of course."

"It's all right, Father. We've agreed on that. And Grandfather finally said he'd talk to the Bishop, work out any problems with the Church."

"I'm surprised at old Judah," Charles mused. "I wouldn't expect him to take kindly to . . ."

"There was some discussion, a fair amount of palaver," Jonnie admitted. "But he says it'll be all right. Uncle Judah says the children can be Catholics, but they'll still be Jewish too. Says a Jewish mother makes them Jewish."

"Well that's his business, just as long as they're brought up as Catholics. So everything's settled, is it?"

"Actually, Father, not quite." Jonnie studiously regarded the dark paneling of the study. "Not everything. There *is* one slight complication."

"What's that? Old Judah making conditions? Money? He's an old fox, you know."

"It's nothing to do with Uncle Judah, Father. Neither he nor Sarah knows about the . . . ah . . . complication. If they did, it would ruin everything."

"A girl, is it?" Charles understood instantly.

"You're right, Father. A girl, a Russian girl I met in Shanghai."

"You haven't told your mother, have you?"

"Lord no!"

"Don't. She won't like it. But what's the trouble?"

"Actually, Father, the Russian girl . . . Tanya. Well, I'm afraid. That is . . ."

"Spit it out, boy. Pregnant, is she?"

"I'm afraid so, Father."

"You're a damned young fool." Charles suppressed a smile. "But what's to be done?"

"She's poor, desperately poor, though she comes of a
438

good family. Earns her living as a dancer, but very soon now she won't be able to."

"They all come of 'good families.' You'll find *that* out. Never met one who didn't."

"Yes, Father."

"What's the problem then, money?" Charles resumed. "She's not demanding you make her an honest woman?"

"She hasn't yet, although I did think about it. But it's impossible. It would be impossible even if it weren't for Sarah. She'd never fit in, and she knows it. But she wants to keep the baby."

"All right, my boy. Something can be arranged. She'll have to leave the China Coast, of course, and she'll need enough to see her through. A settlement, maybe."

"Whatever you think. I just don't want Tanya and the child to be in want."

"That's fairly simple. It won't be the first Sekloong love-child. You know the money'll come out of your account?"

"Fair enough, Father. I'm very grateful."

Charles motioned his son to fill their brandy snifters.

"As I said, it's not the first time. Maybe it won't be the last . . ."

"Actually, Father, I assure you. That's all behind me now that I've found Sarah."

"I hope so, though we'll see. Better not to, though. Checkbooks can't solve all problems. Be careful and, whatever else, never, never tell your mother or Sarah."

Sir Jonathan still resented the restraint his granddaughter Guinevere's wedding had imposed on his penchant for lavish hospitality. Guinevere was his favorite granddaughter, not only because of her gentleness, but because she personified the traditional Chinese feminine virtues. She was soft-spoken, self-effacing, devoted to domesticity, and attentive to her elders. Her doting grandfather had, however, never quite forgiven her for insisting upon a family wedding followed by a reception for no more than two hundred guests when she married

Dr. George Chapman Parker in September 1924. Unassuming modesty might suit Guinevere, but it was not the Sekloong way. He still complained, only half jesting, that his business associates had suspected the fortunes of the House were declining when Sir Jonathan Sekloong married off his eldest granddaughter under "drably middle-class circumstances."

Sekloong weddings, like Sekloong hospitality, were legendary. Charlotte's marriage to Manfei Way had been nicely calculated to be only slightly less pretentious than her mother and father's. More than a thousand guests had been invited, and the flood of wedding presents had provided Hong Kong with material for gossip that lasted for months. Feeling himself belittled by Guinevere's subsequent modesty, Sir Jonathan was determined to recoup when Jonnie, the heir-presumptive, married Sarah Haleevie.

Three thousand were to attend Jonnie's reception, and fifteen hundred were asked to the banquet afterward. The Old Gentleman was confident that the volume and splendor of the wedding presents would make the largesse showered upon Charlotte seem no more than a provincial viceroy's hoard compared to the Imperial Treasury. His own chief gift was the Second Small House, the replica of Mary and Charles's mansion originally built for Harry, who had never occupied it. Sir Jonathan furnished it with a selection from his choicest treasures, and matched Bentley sports coupés for the bride and groom stood in the garages. His confidence was justified. All his associates rendered fitting tribute to the House of Sekloong's joy, though they ranged from great European financiers through China Coast merchants who had made new fortunes in the post-war boom to Secret Society chieftains who preferred not to discuss the gambling, gold-smuggling, prostitution, drug traffic, and strongarm men that provided their wealth. Like the new breed of thrusting populist politicians, with whom they were allied, the presence of the Secret Society chieftains might be distasteful. But it was necessary.

The marriage of Sarah Rebecca Haleevie to Jonathan Osgood Sekloong on the afternoon of November 16, 1924, was the most memorable wedding Hong Kong had seen. For all the wrong reasons. Though the gifts had exceeded Sir Jonathan's expectations, none of their donors from abroad was present. The bride glowed like a star ruby in her Alençon lace gown, but the expected phalanxes of her relations and friends from Shanghai were absent.

The formations of riot police outside the Roman Catholic Cathedral on Caine Road outnumbered the guests at the ceremony. When they emerged from the Cathedral, those guests were assailed by jeering. Banner-waving demonstrators pressed against the police cordon, shouting slogans in Cantonese and broken English.

"British murderers, quit Hong Kong! China for the Chinese! Death to the Chinese running-dogs! Death to the dog-legs who serve the British!"

The newly married couple's Rolls-Royce was driven by a young English clerk of Derwent, Hayes. The colored streamers flying from the fenders and radiator-emblems of the motorcade fluttered through streets empty except for screaming demonstrators. Larger crowds besieged the long, ocher Repulse Bay Hotel to which the reception had been shifted because access for guests and provisions to Sekloong Manor was difficult. The waiters nervously handing round the champagne and caviar were the Hotel's senior staff, supplemented by Sekloong servants, since the junior staff had vanished. Misled by his pride, Sir Jonathan Sekloong had badly misjudged the temper of Hong Kong.

A scant half-dozen bandsmen of the Argyle and Sutherland Highlanders, flaunting their scarlet and green kilts, played in the Repulse Bay Hotel's Ballroom to honor the gallant knight who was the groom's grandfather and the groom's father, whom the two subalterns the Regiment could spare to attend the reception punctiliously called "Colonel." Like the police, the soldiers were heavily engaged elsewhere on more pressing, non-ceremonial duties.

Though sporadic clashes had affrighted Hong Kong

for several months, the chief threat the security forces fought was not violence, but paralysis. The general strike ordered by the Communist-led and Nationalist-supported All-China Federation of Trade Unions was alarmingly effective. When Charles and Mary returned in June, most employees were still at their posts. By September, most had yielded to either indignant propaganda or direct threats. Factories, shops, offices, and warehouses were virtually deserted. As it had during 1909, the plague year, the city's pulse dwindled to a slow, irregular beat. European volunteer and "loyal" Chinese, supported by the military, maintained essential services like water, electricity, and transport to prevent the pulse's stopping.

The Sekloongs were no more immune than they had been in 1909, perhaps less immune. The political scourge, while almost as virulent as the Black Death, was less discriminating. In early June, Sir Jonathan's erratic driver, Ah Wai, had vanished to visit his "dying mother" in distant Kweichow Province, and by October only a few stubborn retainers remained in Sekloong Manor. Some were just too old to care; others were more frightened of leaving the only secure home they knew than the radicals' retaliation; a few, like Mary's amah Ah Fung, consciously chose to maintain decade-long loyalties. The caretaker staff in the Sekloong offices and godowns dwindled under increasing pressure. Those who defied the agitators' verbal persuasion were offered more convincing arguments. A single beating usually sufficed.

The most powerful force was renascent patriotism. For the first time, the Chinese workingman felt that his own actions could directly affect his country's fate—and his own. For the first time, instinctive subservience to authority, British or Chinese, was gravely shaken. For the first time, a larger cause than their families' well-being moved the masses of Kwangtung Province and Hong Kong.

The workers deserted the Colony as much because it had become a place of ill omen as because of the agitators' exhortations. Women with infants nodding on their backs in scarlet-cotton slings fought to climb the gangplanks of steamers to Canton, where the strike affected only British and French firms. Some found it even less pleasant to starve for one's country than to fight for it and returned to their jobs by bribing the vigilantes at the Canton docks and railway station. A number of those renegades were captured by the Strike Committees. The driver Ah Wai, who sought to return after finding his mountain village intolerably frugal and dull, was among those summarily condemned. Alongside three other "pro-British traitors" he was tied to a stake in the hot sun on the Canton Wharves. After two days without food or water, the wiry old man died.

The Sekloongs had drawn up a comprehensive plan to limit the strike's effect on their interests. Based on the assumptions of another era, that strategy failed. It was like fighting a noxious, incorporeal cloud. For the first time, the Sekloongs were moving against great historical tides, not with them. The systematic mass agitation carried out by Liu Shao-chi under the direction of Mikhail Borodin and Chou En-lai had ignited a true popular rising for the first time in twentieth-century China. For the first time, Sir Jonathan's instinctive understanding of the hidden sources of power misled him. He was confronted with a phenomenon beyond his experience: not a spontaneous, superstitious uprising crudely encouraged, as had been the Boxers', by political dilettantes, but a mass movement orchestrated by trained professionals. The Communists had learned not merely to fan smoldering popular resentment into flame, but to sustain—and direct—the conflagration.

The Sekloongs could, however, survive almost unscathed if the strike were not prolonged indefinitely—or they could withdraw. Even after six months, their vast resources still provided a virtually impregnable defense in depth. Since political upheaval was the single constant on the China Coast, Sir Jonathan had invested substantially in land and enterprises in Europe and the United States. But retreat to another continent was unthinkable. The Hong Kong–Shanghai sector was the bastion of his fortunes, and his heart was given to China. Besides, the House of Sekloong was more successful than its British competitors in channeling a trickle of necessities through its godowns. Ocean-going shipping bypassed Hong Kong after longshoremen refused to handle cargo. But the junks that carried the Colony's meager exports to other ports for transshipment to foreign vessels returned with imported goods. All South China was not united against the British, and the independent junk-masters took their profits where they found them.

Nonetheless, hostility between Chinese and British erupted in constant clashes in the Colony. Both communities were self-righteously indignant. The British railed over brandy-and-sodas at the "ingratitude" of a people they had given employment; the Chinese denounced the arrogance of their Colonial overlords. The Sekloongs were torn by antagonistic loyalties. After his sour disappointment with Dr. Sun and the Nationalists, Sir Jonathan's cautious liberalism had progressively eroded. The normal conservatism of age was intensified by disillusionment and by his fear of the new tides; yet he still considered himself Chinese rather than British. Mary instinctively sympathized with the poor Chinese; her lower-middle-class background overcame a quarter century of privilege and her latent anti-Chinese feeling. Charles—that quintessential man of commercial Hong Kong—fumed alternately at the British and the Chinese whose squabbling was disrupting his home. But the Sekloongs, unlike many European businessmen, would not desert the city torn by conflict between rulers and subjects.

Sir Jonathan was more depressed by the moribund Colony each time he rode to the hushed offices of J. Sekloong and Sons. His ebullient self-confidence dwindled visibly. But his imperious temper flared when his "step-brother" Iain Wheatley came to him on behalf of the British Chamber of Commerce. Nor was his anger allayed by Iain's fellow emissary, his "senior Chinese secretary," Charlotte's husband, Manfei Way, whom the Old Gentleman had learned to distrust.

Formally flanked by Charles and Mary, Sir Jonathan received Iain and Manfei with cold courtesy. He offered straight-backed blackwood chairs to the heavy-set fifty-year-old *taipan* and the slight, twenty-eight-year-old Manfei. It was a family confrontation, and within the family Sir Jonathan was unquestionably senior to both his step-brother-by-extension Iain Wheatley and his grandson-in-law, Manfei Way.

"We will not stand on ceremony." The Old Gentleman omitted the traditional tea of hospitality and the normal preliminary pleasantries. "Why have you come to me?"

"We are honored, Sir." Manfei formulated the prescribed Chinese courtesies in English. "Both your humble grandson-in-law and your younger brother are honored at your receiving us."

"Let me speak, Manfei," Iain Wheatley interrupted. "It's more my pidgin."

"Let's have it, Iain," Charles said neutrally. "No point in beating around the bush."

"Sir Jonathan," Iain resumed, "the Chamber's had long discussions. We're convinced Hong Kong will go under, we'll all go to the wall unless this strike is broken."

"How?" the Old Gentleman asked.

"Indian labor. If we bring in twenty thousand South Indian coolies, the Chinese will go back to work. They don't want their rice-bowls smashed forever. The Chamber feels your cooperation is essential."

Charles crossed his legs, leaned back in his chair, and raised his eyes to the plaster moldings on the ceiling. Mary framed a protest, but thought better of it. The Old Gentleman was on his feet, leaning over the pair. He spoke slowly in ice-rimed tones.

"Gentlemen, my cooperation *may* be essential, but it will *not* be offered. Under *no* circumstances will I join you or endorse this move. If you go ahead, I shall close down the firm of J. Sekloong and Sons, announce my sympathy for . . ."

"Grandfather-in-law," Manfei interrupted ingratiatingly, "we are proposing only a temporary measure to bring the Bolsheviks into line."

". . . my total sympathy for the strikers." Sir Jonathan ignored Charlotte's husband. "I shall urge them to expand the strike. The Tung Wah Hospitals will cease even their present emergency services. No junks will carry any cargoes at all to Hong Kong. I'll see Hong Kong perish before it becomes a battleground between the Chinese and the British supported by Indians."

"Sir Jonathan, perhaps, we've not made ourselves clear," Iain Wheatley said placatingly. "We propose chiefly a threat. Once a few thousand Indians arrive, the strike will die a natural death. Don't you see that . . ."

"Is there anything else, Gentlemen?" Sir Jonathan asked. "I have other business."

When the door closed, Mary regarded the Old Gentleman with respect approaching awe. At seventy-two, his fires still burned high.

"Can't say I disagree," Charles observed. "But you know this makes an open breach with the Wheatleys and the British Chamber of Commerce?"

"So be it," said Sir Jonathan.

The General Strike did peter out as hunger forced workers to return to their resentful employers. Hong Kong's commercial paralysis finally ended in June 1926, a year after its onset, when the Nationalist–Communist alliance that had organized the General Strike was itself being torn apart by its own conflicting purposes. The renewed rift between the British and the Chinese was, however, not to close until December 8, 1941, when the two communities united in futile resistance to Japanese invaders.

The three Sekloongs who supported the strike did not see its effects upon their home. From September 1925 to June 1926 neither Harry nor Thomas and James could visit Hong Kong, since the British authorities did not welcome firebrands from Canton. They were, further, caught up in the bitter clashes that split the Nationalist–Communist alliance and splintered both political parties.

Harry Sekloong had rejoiced when his leader Wang Ching-wei became President of the National Government proclaimed in Canton on July 1, 1925. But President Wang Ching-wei and General Chiang Kai-shek were again fighting each other. The General's frustrated ambitions were not assuaged by command of the National Revolutionary Army. Harry Sekloong was further alienated from the former stockbroker when Chiang Kai-shek began to purge the Kuomintang of the Communists against the wishes of President Wang Ching-wei.

Thomas and James were already virtually committed, the older brother following Chiang Kai-shek, the younger Chou En-lai. But the tenuous Nationalist–Communist alliance was formally preserved, and the brothers were not compelled to confront each other. They were instead given the opportunity to practice the profession of arms that had entranced them since boyhood. In November 1925, the fledgling Revolutionary Army marched into eastern Kwangtung Province to win its first victories over a local warlord. Though still cadets, Thomas and James commanded platoons in those Eastern Expeditions and delighted in their first experience of combat, which was almost bloodless. Marshals' batons—at least, generals' stars—glittered in their imaginations. In the pleasant subtropical autumn the reality of war had proved as glorious as their youthful dreams.

On July 9, 1926, Lieutenants Thomas and James Sekloong marshaled their platoons in the Fourth Division of the National Revolutionary Army. Their company commander was Lin Piao. The youth who had known all the answers in General Chou En-lai's political study courses was promoted captain by the underground Communist apparatus within the Revolutionary Army because he was already a secret member of the Communist Party. The officers carried Mauser pistols, and the soldiers were armed with Lee-Enfield rifles. All ranks wore foreign-style khaki uniforms: high-collared

447

tunics, knee-breeches, white puttees, and peaked garrison caps. The Fourth Division was the first military unit in Chinese history that marched to battle in leather boots. Under the command of General Chiang Kai-shek, the Northern Expedition that would sweep the warlords from power and establish a unified Chinese national government for the first time in two centuries departed from Canton with banners flying and trumpets blaring.

April 11, 1927–December 15, 1927

"A TRAVELING carnival, a troop of opera-players touring from festival to festival—that's what we are!" Lieutenant Thomas Sekloong had complained so often in the same words that his brother James automatically completed the litany: "To fight the enemy we mobilized men and assembled horses like the heroes of the *Romance of the Three Kingdoms*. But the enemy just fades away. We never fight battles, only celebrate bloodless victories!"

James suppressed his laughter to point the moral once again: "Just as Comrades Chou and Borodin predicted. This, respected second elder brother, is *political* warfare. The less we fight, the better. Bloodless victories because the *lao pai-hsing*, the masses, support us!"

Encamped outside Shanghai on April 11, 1927, the young officers of the Ironsides Fourth Division were jubilant in victory. Recalling the campaigns that had wrested half China from the warlords in nine months' time, the brothers were bidding each other farewell with excitement more fitting to raw recruits than the hard-bitten veterans they considered themselves. Just promoted captain, Thomas had been reassigned to the staff of Commander-in-Chief Chiang Kai-shek.

The General had halted his triumphant National Revolutionary Army outside China's largest city while he negotiated with the foreign-ruled Concessions and with leading Chinese citizens. Political Commissar Chou

En-lai and his Workers' Militia had seized the native city, and Shanghai virtually belonged to the alliance.

After withdrawing when he found himself deprived of all effective power by Chiang Kai-shek, President Wang Ching-wei had on April 1, 1927, ten days earlier, returned from self-imposed exile to resume his office and to endeavor, once again, to cooperate with his strong-willed military commander. The brothers were cheered by that reconciliation and delighted by their reunion with their Uncle Harry, who had returned to China with the President. They warmed their hands over the campfire and reminisced about the spectacular successes of the Northern Expedition.

In truth meeting no more opposition than an itinerant carnival, the 92,000-man Revolutionary Army had marched through a welcoming countryside. The soldiers could have carried tea instead of cartridges in their bandoliers or flaunted chrysanthemums in their rifles. Their progress was a romp rather than a campaign until they began skirmishing with the stubborn troops of the warlord General Sun Chuan-fang on the borders of Kiangsi Province in mid-September 1926. The first two months of the campaign had proceeded as smoothly as a training exercise from the field-manuals prepared by the Revolutionary Army's Communist-controlled Political Sections, who preached the new art of Polwar/Agitprop —Political Warfare/Agitation and Propaganda.

The army had behaved remarkably well. Their enemies, the ragged soldiers of the unstable warlord coalition, raped and looted, alienating those peasants who had not fled. But even the Kwangsi Province warlord Li Tsung-jen's Eighteenth Division, stiffened by Whampoa Academy officers, generally abstained from marauding. The troops were encouraged to refrain from the depredation practiced for millennia by Chinese armies because they were actually paid at fairly regular intervals. Less generous with gold than advice, Moscow, nonetheless, provided funds to the forces Joseph Stalin believed would conquer China for him. Intelligently self-interested Chinese patriots like the House of Sekloong also contributed to the revolutionaries' war chest, as did a

449

few far-seeing foreign firms. The enlisted men of the victorious, adequately fed National Army could, therefore, be kept from scourging the countryside. Even those officers who were neither Communists nor Whampoa Academy graduates stole very little.

The farmers' ingrained fear of men in uniform was transformed, initially into incredulous wonder at that restraint and subsequently into timorous hope. Perhaps, this once, their self-appointed liberators might honor their promises to give the peasants freedom and land. The farmers did not really understand the word *dzu-yu*, "freedom," which literally meant "self-decision"; they skeptically awaited the distribution of land deeds. But they were, at least, not stripped of their meager possessions.

The army was preceded not only by armed patrols, but by Propaganda Units that incited the oppressed farmers to rise against their landlords. Women were the most effective Agitpropagandists. Singers, dancers, and actresses performed on improvised stages in village squares. The plots of millennia-old traditional dramas were adapted to convey their political message: The National Revolutionary Army would free the *lao pai-hsing* from centuries of exploitation. Their "oppressed sisters" responded passionately, the patient Chinese women, protected by fewer legal safeguards than the plodding water buffaloes, who held families and communities together by their stubborn courage and unremitting labor. The Women's Liberation Movement demanded: "Destroy all the mechanisms used by the male-centered society to oppress and exploit women— traditional morality, economic power, and armed might!" Inspired by the resentment of generations, the peasant women were militant converts who prodded their menfolk into serving the Revolutionary Army as recruits, couriers, and informants.

The Sekloong brothers were surprised by the effectiveness of the Agitprop Teams. They were making a journey of agonizing discovery; the very texture of the countryside and the society they saw for the first time was a shattering revelation. By giving their allegiance to the abstraction called China, they had sworn to emancipate and unify a nation they did not know. Brought up in the splendid isolation of Hong Kong and the foreign-ruled treaty-ports, they had been almost as ignorant of the primitive hinterlands as were the purse- and race-proud European *taipans*. The interior of China was as foreign as Patagonia to most of the young Whampoa Academy graduates, who were the sons of the pampered urban bourgeoisie. The cosmopolitan metropolises receded from their consciousness as they marched north through immemorial peasant China and backward through the centuries.

In the smoky cave dwellings of mountainous Kiangsi Province, the youthful idealists saw mothers and fathers who tended a single pig or a donkey with devotion they could not give their rickety, scabby children if any were to survive. Entire families—twenty human beings spanning three generations—were crammed into hovels of packed earth that disintegrated under the rains. The "big house" of a landlord dominated almost every village. The peasants wore patched rags, supplemented their coarse rice with wild grasses, and considered themselves blessed by the God of Fortune if they ate a sliver of pork, half an egg, or a few shreds of chicken at the Lunar New Year. Some "big houses" were peasants' hovels only slightly enlarged, but others were mansions amid groves of pines and bamboos. The landlords who lived in those houses wore wool or silk and daily fed upon fowl, meat, and fish. Since no other authority existed, they exercised the powers of magistrates and mayors—and enriched themselves further by money-lending. Not all were the callous exploiters depicted by the Revolutionary Army's propagandists. Some assumed the gentry's traditional responsibility for the *lao pai-hsing*—assisting the poor by maintaining schools and dispensing alms. But the decay of Confucian morality and the anarchy that followed the Manchus' collapse had left the gentry with a single over-riding moral imperative: the welfare of their own families.

Like James, Thomas was shocked by the blatant jux-taposition of poverty and comfort. Unlike James, he was impressed neither by the wickedness nor the state of the landlords. The country was so impoverished that even the rich landlords were poor by his standards; most lived no better than the Sekloongs' servants. Moreover, he respected the divinely ordained hierarchy among men. He shared his idol General Chiang Kai-shek's Confucian conviction that the proper ordering of mankind required strict distinctions between superiors and inferiors. No more than the General was the mat-ter-of-fact Thomas moved by abstract moral indigna-tion, though both recognized that the peasantry's lot must improve if China were to become a powerful, modern country.

Thomas was, however, shocked when he discovered that no peasants and only a few landlords used the word *Chung-kuo*, literally, "The Central Kingdom," which meant China. They called themselves not *Chung-kuo jen*, Chinese, but *Tang jen* or *Han jen*, "men of Tang" or "men of Han," the two greatest Im-perial Dynasties. Nationalism, the first of Dr. Sun Yat-sen's Three People's Principles, was central to Thomas's personal creed. He was outraged to find that the *lao pai-hsing* knew neither China nor, certainly, the concept of nationhood.

James, for his part, had inherited—or acquired by proximity—his father Harry's idealism, as well as his irreverence. The younger brother discovered in anger the virtually immeasurable and perhaps unbridgeable gap between his own accustomed manner of life and that of the peasant masses. Popular welfare, the second of Dr. Sun's Three Principles, stood foremost in his personal creed. But China, he learned, was so vast, so diverse, and so abysmally poor that he sometimes de-spaired of ameliorating the people's brutish poverty. Unknown to his brother, James already was a member of the Socialist Youth League and a candidate member of the Communist Party. Ordered by his cell leader to reveal neither those affiliations nor his personal feel-ings, he concealed his moral indignation behind raillery.

But his precarious self-discipline failed spectacularly upon one occasion.

A week before the carnival ended in bloody skirmishing against the warlord Sun Chuan-fang, the company was billeted in the market town of Hsinkan, one hundred and three miles south of Nanchang. The ever-smiling local magnate, who was called Squire Lee, asked the officers to dinner. Despite his personal reservations, Company Commander Lin Piao accepted the invitation. The Chinese Communist Party still followed Moscow's explicit instructions: "Cooperate with the Nationalists to win victory for the national bourgeois revolution before rising against the Nationalists to make a proletarian revolution." Since Squire Lee was unquestionably a "national bourgeois," virtually untainted by association with the "foreign-imperialist capitalists," Lin Piao was bound to seek his cooperation. Squire Lee would have entertained the Emperor of Hell and his attendant demons if they controlled Hsinkan. Neither Captain Lin Piao nor Squire Lee had any reason to fear the explosive temperament behind the laughing face of Lieutenant James Sekloong. Even Thomas could not have anticipated his brother's violent response to the Shell Company's red scallop-shell posted on Squire Lee's gate.

Nonetheless, Lin Piao's eyebrows knotted above his deep-sunk eyes. He was tensely uncomfortable in the scroll-hung dining room of the landlord whom he knew to be his true enemy. But the other young officers appeared relaxed, and pewter teapots poured out Shaohsing rice wine to stimulate their gaiety. They fell upon the lavish cold hors d'oeuvres with gusto: thousand-year-old eggs, their gleaming jade centers nested in translucent green and garnished with shaved red peppers; thin-sliced pork doused in a garlic-pepper-soy-and-coriander sauce after the manner of Chengtu; shredded chicken breasts in sesame paste and vinegar; tiny fresh-water shrimp in wine; pickled goose; and cubes of subtly seasoned Shanghai-style ham. The servants obsequiously placed the next courses on the round briar-wood table: a tureen of costly sharks' fins and crab; tender minced squab accompanied by tissue-thin wheaten pancakes; plump frogs' legs crisp-fried in a delicate batter; and eel seethed with garlic.

To James's pampered taste the food was no more than passable. But he indignantly contrasted Squire Lee's fare with the few shreds of wild greens made palatable by coarse salt that accompanied the minuscule bowls of broken rice the poor farmers had shared with his platoon that morning. He tossed down successive thimble-cups of warm yellow rice wine, fueling his morose anger. His fellow officers, he noted scornfully, refuted like trained parrots their host's obligatory disparagement of the elaborate courses.

While lean watch-dogs snapped at the discarded scraps, the servants bore in the next round of dishes: birds' nest soup from Borneo with quail eggs; tidbits of tenderloin simmered with lotus stalks; mushrooms stuffed with spiced pork; scallops and fresh abalone blended with pungent vegetables; the honey-braised ham of neighboring Hunan Province in steamed white buns; whole chickens wrapped in lotus leaves before they were baked in the fragrant sediment from wine jars; ducks smoked over tea-leaf and camphorwood fires; and the great Golden Fish from the Tungting Lake steamed whole in wine.

"It is nothing!" Squire Lee expressed the false humility required by traditional Chinese courtesy. "I apologize deeply for these badly prepared scraps. They are unfit for the Young Lords who honor my poor hovel with their bright presence."

"You do us too much honor, Sir." Thomas responded automatically. "Your banquet is superb. Far beyond our poor merits, it is so abundant it dazzles us."

"And besots us," James muttered. "We gorge like landlord exploiters, we soldiers of the people."

Thomas was alarmed by the dark flush that suffused his brother's face, and Lin Piao glanced sharply at his subordinate. If Squire Lee, sweating as he shoveled his food into his greasy mouth with ivory chopsticks, had heard James's surly comment, he gave no sign.

"I am particularly honored that I may claim connections with two of the Young Lords." His smile was unctuous. "The Shell sign at the entrance to my hovel shows I am the unworthy agent of the princely merchant Mr. Sek Howan, the great Sekloong."

Even Thomas winced at the abject flattery, and James flushed crimson when he heard the word *kwan-hsi*, connections. Half China's sorrows arose from *kwan-hsi*, the personal connections that dominated all other social, economic, and moral forces. His political instructors had taught him that *kwan-hsi* was a web of corrupt privilege sustaining the evil, exploitive, old society.

"Kwan-hsi," he growled. "You mother-raper. Bugger your *kwan-hsi*. I have *no* connection with bloodsuckers."

The officers' laughter ceased abruptly. Captain Lin Piao hastened to repair the social lapse, though he agreed with James. The son of the impoverished bourgeoisie had been drilled in the elaborate traditional courtesies before breaking with his family at the age of fifteen to join the Young Socialist League. Besides, the Communist Party had instructed him to placate the "national bourgeoisie"—until the time came for their liquidation.

"We do not, Elder Brother Lee, talk of *kwan-hsi*," Lin Piao explained. "We are concerned with justice, not connections, justice for *all* the people of China."

"I am old, too old and too ignorant." Apologies cascaded from Squire Lee's flaccid lips. "I do not know the proper new forms. I beg you to pardon me, Young Lords."

"How much do you pay for a catty of fire-oil, Mr. Lee?" James tossed back his twenty-second cup of yellow rice wine. "And how much do you charge?"

"It is difficult to calculate, honored Lieutenant," Squire Lee evaded the question. "Many factors contribute to the cost—overhead, shipping, insurance, transportation. When your noble National Revolutionary Army creates a new government, I will sell fire-oil for their lamps much cheaper to the noble farmers."

James knew that Squire Lee had never before that

instant spoken of "noble farmers." *Kwei nung-min*, noble farmers, his mother's! Fat Squire Lee would normally call peasants *yung-jen*, "serfs."

"I'll tell you then," James said. "After all expenses, you make three hundred percent clear profit."

"I assure you, young sir, your figures err."

"You lie," James spat. "You're not only a bloodsucker, but a liar without shame or honor."

"And your noble house?" The merchant's normally autocratic temper asserted itself. "Your own so noble house? What profit do you make? Twice mine—and grind me if I'm a week late in settling. You're the bloodsuckers masquerading as the masses' saving stars. You Sekloongs are the running-dogs of the foreign devils. You've only joined ranks with the National Army to protect your own damned connections, your own *kwan-hsi!*"

James swept the dishes to the floor. He leaped onto the table, his mud-spattered boots grinding broken porcelain into the polished briar-wood. One hand gripped Squire Lee's throat; the other groped for his sheathed bayonet. He shook off his slighter brother's restraining grip, and his bayonet flashed free.

Squire Lee's face was sickly puce, and his soft hands clawed at the fingers gripping his throat. James's bayonet transfixed the merchant's plump thigh. Lin Piao snapped an order, and his lieutenants pulled the two apart. The Captain bent solicitously over the writhing merchant to search for the femoral artery amid the spurting blood. But a sour half-smile twisted the red lips shadowed by the heavy stubble on his sallow cheeks. He could, he knew, be reasonably certain of the loyalty of at least one member of his clandestine Communist cell. Lin Piao drew James Sekloong aside after shepherding his abashed subalterns from the landlord's house.

"That turtle's egg doesn't matter much," he said mildly. "An enemy anyway, he's now a confirmed enemy. This night's work could restore our name with the peasants. They wonder why we promise to liberate them—and then swill wine with their oppressors."

"Sir," James said earnestly, "I regret that . . ."

"Oh, you'll regret it. No doubt about it. You'll be publicly reprimanded for violence to a civilian."

"I deserve that." The chastened James wiped his bayonet. "I won't break discipline again."

"You certainly won't. But your real punishment's up to the Party Committee. You'll probably lose your candidate membership—at the least."

"But, Company Commander," James objected. "Squire Lee is the enemy, the class enemy we fight. How could the Party Committee . . ."

"Because, Platoon Commander, you disobeyed orders, barefacedly broke discipline. The Party's collective wisdom is greater than yours or mine, greater even than the Secretary-General's. If the Party commanded us to march on Peking to restore Pu Yi, the so-called Emperor Hsüan Tung, to his throne, we would march."

"But, Company Commander, I . . ."

"No arguments, Platoon Commander. Without discipline, we matter no more that the senile brigands of the Secret Societies. A good Communist must surrender his will to the Party, surrender his personal feelings—and his family pride. Above all, a good Communist obeys. Otherwise, he's as much use to the revolution as a heap of dog turds."

James withdrew into silence while his self-esteem recovered from the humiliating public reprimand and he awaited the decision of the Party Committee. His brother officers were inconsequentially gay as strolling players in the glorious October sunshine until they came to Nanchang. The city's high walls had dominated mountainous northern Kiangsi for centuries, commanding the age-old invasion route to the central Yangtze Valley and the North—the road to Shanghai, Nanking, and the old Imperial Capital of Peking. Warlord Sun Chuan-fang was, therefore, as determined to hold strategic Nanchang as the Revolutionary Army was to take the city. The National Revolutionary Army met a resolute enemy in a set-piece, conventional battle for the first time—and recoiled. Political warfare was unavailing against troops unmoved by nationalistic propaganda. Sun Chuan-fang hurled more than 150,000 men into the battle, and the Whampoa officers learned for the first time that war was cruel.

Captain Lin Piao had won the honor of serving as the point company, and the unit's losses were heavy. The young officers were shaken by their discovery that "national revolutionary warfare" was not always a triumphant parade in the sunlight. Thomas Sekloong admitted only to himself that he was frightened by the enemy's artillery and appalled by the hand-to-hand skirmishes. James could not admit even to himself that he was afraid, for he was determined to repair his breach of discipline by his courage. He led his platoon in a frontal charge against the twenty-two tile-roofed houses of the village that blocked their road to Nanchang.

The mud walls exploded with machine-gun and mortar fire that struck down eighteen of his forty men. James did not take cover, but ordered his dazed survivors forward. The astonished defenders broke and ran before troops who would neither fall nor go to the ground. The Nationalists slaughtered their dazed enemies with bayonets and half-moon-shaped machetes. Delighting in his victory, James did not count his own losses or see the gory shambles of the village. His own bayonet dripped red, and gray brain-tissue clung to the butt of his Mauser pistol. His eyes exultantly bloodshot, he rejoiced at having redeemed himself when Lin Piao led up the main body. He had been ordered to take the village, and he had obeyed.

Captain Lin surveyed the village square, where twenty-three gray-uniformed warlord soldiers lay contorted in death. The dogs were already tearing at the corpses, ripping away their cotton jackets to get at the sweet flesh underneath.

"You obeyed orders, Platoon Commander," Lin Piao observed. "Obeyed to a fault. Wouldn't it have been better to go around and take them on the flank? The point is to kill the enemy—*not* your own men."

"I'll remember, Comrade . . . ah . . . Company Commander." James did not resent the gentle reprimand. "It seems I learn the hard way."

"As long as you learn, Comrade," Lin Piao said softly. "That's the important thing."

The generals learned more slowly than did Lieutenant James Sekloong, though their normal failing was not rashness, but excessive caution. Cock-a-hoop over the cheap victories preceding the battle of Nanchang and mesmerized by the doctrine of "total political warfare" preached by Mikhail Borodin, Chou En-lai, and General Galen, the divisional commander ignored the injunction of Sun Tze, China's master strategist of the fifth century B.C.: "Always allow the enemy a way out! Always leave him an avenue of escape." The enveloping advance of the Nationalist Revolutionary Army left General Sun Chuan-fang no way out—and he fought desperately for Nanchang.

The warlord's soldiers ignored the appeals that had induced other warlord units to desert: "Come join us, fellow Chinese patriots, in unifying the country!" Companies and battalions would have deserted to the Revolutionary Army *en masse* if they had been offered gold. But the revolutionaries' coffers were empty, unlike those of General Sun, who understood that mercenaries must be paid. Having taken Sun Chuan-fang's gold, his troops fought with a ferocity that astonished the Political Commissars.

Nonetheless, the Revolutionary Army's noose of men and steel tightened around Nanchang. The climactic battle began on November 1, 1927, and the city fell just a week later. His power smashed, Sun Chuan-fang fled northward with his gold and his concubines, abandoning the soldiers who had refused to desert him. When they counted the losses, the Nationalist commanders were shaken. The warlord forces had suffered more than 90,000 dead and wounded. The generals did not reveal their own losses, but every man had seen his comrades fall in ranks around him. Some of his fellow officers nodded subdued agreement when Thomas Sekloong said quietly: "Our purpose, I thought, was to unify China—not to kill Chinese."

Many of the ardent young officers, however, shared James Sekloong's exultation in victory, though not all agreed with his retort: "We'll kill many more Chinese. We must so that the people can take power."

If Commander-in-Chief Chiang Kai-shek shared his subordinates' dismay, he displayed no outward sign of regret at the slaughter. His purpose, too, was fixed—to unify China under the rule of the enlightened bourgeoisie, the modern, responsible men of property James despised. Chiang appeared close to his goal in early 1927 after the fall of Nanchang gave him military control of the Yangtze Valley and the entire South, more than half China. But he was hampered by political conflicts within the Nationalist Party that were even more disruptive of his purpose than the increasing tension between the Nationalists and the Communists.

Though President Wang Ching-wei was still abroad, the Nationalist Government moved to Wuhan, the industrial heart of China, in January 1927. It was dominated by the left wing of the Kuomintang, which included many overtly pro-Soviet figures, and its *éminence grise* was Mikhail Borodin, the Communist International's delegate to China. The left wing airily dismissed the threat of Russian domination Sir Jonathan Sekloong had warned against three years earlier.

But Chiang Kai-shek flatly rejected Borodin's advice that, instead of advancing, he consolidate the areas already under Nationalist control with Communist assistance. As the warlords retreated north in disarray, the Revolutionary Army took Nanking. Chiang's exultant troops looted the riverside city's foreign concessions and set fire to the oil tanks of the Esso Petroleum Company. Panic-driven foreigners scrambled over the walls of their compounds to seek refuge on the gunboats of the U.S. and Royal Navies that lay at anchor in the Yangtze.

The looting ceased when those gunboats shelled the Nationalist troops. But General Chiang had taken Nanking, and he meant to keep Nanking, the ancient Southern Capital, the symbol of legitimate rule second only to Peking, the Northern Capital. He had simultaneously acquired a name in the foreign press as a "blood-thirsty Bolshevik"—at just the moment he was rapidly moving toward a decisive break with his Communist allies in Shanghai, the actual wellspring of power in modern China.

The great port, which Chou En-lai's Workers' Militia had seized on March 22, 1927, two days before Nanking fell, was central to Chiang Kai-shek's strategy. He who controlled Shanghai controlled the economy and communications of the Yangtze Basin, which dominated all Central China. The city could also provide financial support for the right-wing Nationalists, who distrusted Moscow's largesse. Chiang's resolve to exploit those alternate sources of power was hardened by a warlord police raid on the Soviet Consulate in Peking on April 6. Seized documents outlined Moscow's plans to destroy the Kuomintang after the joint Nationalist–Communist victory and take all power over China through the Chinese Communist Party. Chiang Kai-shek made his final plans as his army marked time outside Shanghai and the Sekloong brothers said their boisterous farewells.

Jonnie Sekloong would have recognized the reptilian head and obsidian eyes of the sleek figure who slipped from his Packard into General Chiang Kai-shek's headquarters through the evening of April 11, 1927. But Thomas Sekloong, completing his first full week as aide-de-camp to the Commander-in-Chief, saw just another of the Shanghai men with whom his chief had been conferring. Some he had known by reputation, while others had greeted him warmly. Judah Haleevie had called twice, and General Chiang had glowed with satisfaction after their protracted talks. The visitors included foreign businessmen and foreign officials of the Shanghai Municipal Council; Chinese bankers and merchants; and the Japanese Consul-General. But Thomas could not place the man who called himself Mr. Wong, and he was alarmed by the visitor's four bodyguards in blue workers' clothing. The Green Dragon, Tu Yueh-shen, magnate of the opium traffic and commander of ten thousand Secret Society Braves, was conferring with his sworn blood-brother Chiang Kai-shek.

Thomas glanced surreptitiously at his shoulder straps, where the three gold bars of a captain shone. A shower of promotions had fallen on their unit. Lin Piao, promoted to major, commanded the battalion, while the newly minted Captain James Sekloong took over the company. General Chiang Kai-shek had chosen Thomas as aide-de-camp not only to strengthen his ties with the Sekloong empire, but to provide himself with a wholly trustworthy emissary who had entrée to both foreign and Chinese commercial circles. The General, who had watched his cadets with obsessive care, felt that Thomas Sekloong was his man to the death. He repaid that devotion with confidence as complete as his innate suspiciousness permitted.

From his desk in the anteroom of the General's office, Thomas's dark eyes unwaveringly watched Mr. Wong's four bodyguards, who slurped their tea and spat out sunflower-seed shells. Thomas sat erect, his hand near the buzzer-button that would summon the ready squad of the General's elite guard that was always within earshot. It was his function to be always alert, though Mr. Wong and General Chiang were obviously close friends. The reserved General had actually clasped his visitor's hand with both his own. The allies apparently trusted each other, but "not too much," as the strategist Sun Tze had advised.

When a bell summoned him, Thomas took up his notebook and knocked quietly. Wall maps studded with colored pins had replaced the scrolls that had marked the faded blue walls with darker strips; two green-cased field telephones, their thick cables trailing across the stained carpet and out the shuttered windows, stood on the ebony writing table instead of the classical scholar's paraphernalia of inkstones and brushes. The study was a microcosm of changing China: the ugly, utilitarian appurtenances of modern warfare had replaced the artifacts of the ancient civilization. Only one scroll remained: a crimson magnificence of peonies in the foreground framed a shadowed hillside where a tiger, half-hidden in the deep grass, stalked a pair of browsing stags.

"Commander-in-Chief!" Thomas saluted before expressing his concern. "I have discourteously left Mr. Wong's associates alone in the anteroom."

"Don't worry, Captain." His infrequent smile warmed the General's spare features. "Mr. Wong and I are old friends. His . . . ah . . . associates will not be offended."

The sleek adder's head nodded to acknowledge the compliment. Relaxed in the ebony chair, Mr. Wong was as self-assured as the General himself.

"Tom, *wo peng-yu.*" The affectionate diminutive in English was as incongruous amid the General's accented Mandarin as his calling his youngest aide "my friend." "You speak Cantonese, of course?"

"Yes, Sir! I await your orders."

"And you comprehend the barbarous Kwangsi tongue? It is similar? Most of our allies of the Eighteenth Division speak no other."

"Yes, Sir!" Thomas was uncertain whether he was confirming his ability to speak the Cantonese-derived dialect of the troops from Kwangtung's neighboring province or agreeing that it was a barbarous tongue.

"Hao! Hao!" The General beamed. "Fine! Fine! You're appointed liaison officer between my old friend here and General Pai Tsung-hsi of the Eighteenth Division. My friend's name is not Wong. He is Tu Yueh-shen, a great patriot and my blood-brother."

Thomas bit back his surprise. He knew that the opium smuggler Tu Yueh-shen, master of the Secret Societies that were the extra-legal government of Shanghai, was the emperor of the underworld of the world's most blatantly wicked city. What business could there be between China's most rapacious gangster and his austere Commander-in-Chief, who hated opium and frowned upon both tobacco and wine?

"Your young friend is startled, Chung-cheng." The Green Dragon casually used the General's familiar name.

"Perhaps I should explain." Chiang Kai-shek looked quizzically at Thomas.

"I await your orders, Commander-in-Chief." Thomas repeated the formula.

"My old friend is a much maligned man, *Tom*." Again that English diminutive. "He and I have striven together in secret to advance the revolution, but he is denounced as a brigand. He is actually a great patriot. Has not his Green League resisted both the Manchus and the foreigners for decades? He is now convinced, as I am, that we must crush the Communists before they destroy the national revolution."

The reserve impressed upon Chiang Kai-shek's personality by his Confucian training made him appear withdrawn and arbitrary in public meetings. But his low-keyed, laconic style was persuasive when his audience was small and his normal stiff authority yielded to relaxed paternalism.

"The great menace in the world today is not imperialism." General Chiang's voice rose in pitch as he heated his anger over the fire of his indignation. "It is Communism—an international conspiracy determined to rule the entire world. Our own . . . the Chinese Communists are only tools of that conspiracy. Communism is far more dangerous than imperialism, already in its dying throes."

Chiang used the anti-imperialist rhetoric of his enemies, the Communists, without embarrassment. The Marxist-Leninist concepts were fundamentally altered as they passed through the filter of his mind. His Confucian mentality, lightly overlaid with Western ideas, spontaneously transformed the Communist cant into his own original concepts.

"We must, therefore, purify both the Kuomintang and the Revolutionary Army. We must purge ourselves of the Communist virus and those infected by that virus, the so-called left wing of the Kuomintang. A monolithic party like ours cannot tolerate contending factions. The glory of China is the unity of the Chinese people and their leaders. As it has always been, so must it be today."

Grown wealthy and powerful by exploiting the same Chinese people, Tu Yueh-shen nodded his complacent agreement. Behind the façade of the model staff officer, Captain Thomas Sekloong experienced a moment of doubt. The chronicles of China, as he knew them, were a record of disunity: constant power struggles, unremitting intrigues, and wily stratagems on the part of princes and generals who totally disregarded the interests of the common people. But the flow of his commander's words, so logically marshaled, swept away his momentary disbelief. The General, after all, knew more of China than he himself could ever know.

"We have," Chiang Kai-shek went on, his voice dropping confidentially, "organized a Settlement Committee. Its responsibility is to sweep the Communists from the Party, the Army, and the Government. Our first task is to cleanse Shanghai. Until I hold Shanghai, I shall possess no base from which to complete the revolution, as Dr. Sun Yat-sen commanded in his last testament. Blood-brother Tu's loyal Braves will make the initial move—and the Eighteenth Division will mop up. For the moment we make common cause with the foreigners of the imperialist commercial community, since our common enemy is the Communists. The foreigners have promised the financial support I require. In our own time, we shall deal with the imperialists and sweep foreign rule from China."

Buoyed by the torrent of his own rhetoric, the General was apparently prepared to continue indefinitely. Tu Yueh-shen glanced at his watch.

"It is eleven o'clock, Chung-cheng," he said.

"Ah, yes! Well, another time . . . but you must understand my thinking totally, *Tom*, my friend. Another time I shall tell you of my plans to fulfill China's destiny."

"Orders, Sir?" Thomas asked.

"You will convey my instructions to General Pai Tsung-hsi. The Eighteenth Division is ready to move. Then you will place yourself at the disposal of Blood-brother Tu. His men will strike first."

Thomas Sekloong shivered in the predawn chill of April 12, 1927. It was just past 4:00 A.M., and all the

General's dispositions were complete. Wearing a civilian raincoat over his uniform, his peaked garrison cap concealed, the Captain waited for the action to begin. He and his orderly, who was similarly attired, were hidden in an alley between a noodle shop and a shoe store. In silence they watched the pale dawn creep across the dingy brick building of the Shanghai General Federation of Trades Unions, which a hand-lettered banner identified as: HEADQUARTERS OF THE SHANGHAI WORKERS' MILITIA FORCE. The assertion was uncharacteristically modest. At that moment, the nondescript structure was the seat of the provisional government of the largest city in the Orient. Under General Chou Enlai's direction, the Communist unions ruled the Chinese quarters of the city they had seized from the warlords three weeks earlier. The authority of their patrols was unchallenged, though the irregulars in worn civilian clothing displayed only two symbols of authority: brassards inscribed with the characters *Kung-jen Min-Ping,* "Workers' Militia," and rifles so old and so diverse they might have been looted from a military museum.

A weary four-man detail was entering the Headquarters. The militiamen did not look into the shadows beside the building, which sheltered men dressed like themselves in blue workclothes. Feet dragging, they were returning from patrol at the loneliest hour when the darkness of the night begins to give way to the light of day, the moment when men's spirits and vitality are at their lowest. Their thoughts were fixed on the hard comfort of their wooden pallets within the sanctuary of their headquarters. The split-paneled door began opening to receive them.

The hollow hour was shattered by a submachine gun's hoarse chatter. Bullets flung the leading militiaman against the wooden door, and a chorus of submachine guns chanted his dirge. The other militiamen fell, blasted by new volleys. One crawled toward the door, but died under the heavy boots of the Green Dragon's Braves. Other Secret Society gunmen poured from the surrounding alleys, ignoring the first sporadic shots from the startled Militia Headquarters.

Two blue-clad gangsters pushed through the half-open door before it swung shut. Crammed under the stone lintel, their fellows hammered on the wooden panels with rifle butts. The militiamen were finally alerted, and shots cut down four of the assailants. The gangsters' withdrawal to the cover of surrounding buildings was hastened by ragged volleys. The surprise attack had failed after ninety seconds.

Thomas nodded to his orderly. Ears ringing from the shots and eyes watering from the sting of acrid cordite, they darted to the far end of the alley before discarding their raincoats and donning their peaked garrison caps to insure that they would not be attacked by either gangsters or troops. The initial assault having failed, the regulars were moving in.

The Kwangsi men of the Eighteenth Division were already in position, the vanguard disguised in blue workclothes like their allies. A corner militia post was under attack by a Kwangsi platoon. The workers fired their rifles through the crevices between the sandbags that barricaded the isolated rice shop. Machine-gun fire ripped through their flimsy protection, and the regulars swarmed over the sandbags. Bayonets flashed in the half-light, and despairing shrieks affrighted the pale dawn.

The Kwangsi troops' orders were clear: "Exterminate the enemy!" And they were carrying out their orders with relish. The illiterate farmers of the Eighteenth Division hated the Shanghai workingmen who jeered at their accents and their ignorance. The mystic unity between the "two oppressed classes," the peasants and the workers, discerned by Communist theorists proved illusory when it confronted the realities of instinctive antagonism between city and countryside and ancient hostility between North and South.

Though Militia Headquarters held out stubbornly, the dawn attack swept all else before it. As Thomas returned to General Chiang's command post, he passed struggling knots of militiamen and gangsters. The rattle of their shots was echoed by distant volleys elsewhere. The regulars swore in high good humor as they methodically hunted Workers' Militiamen through the crooked alleys.

An unarmed militiaman, red brassard on his arm, scurried toward the two soldiers of the National Revolutionary Army. His broad face split by a shriek, he threw himself at their feet.

"Chiu Ming! Chiu Ming!" he pleaded. "Help me! Save me!"

A young, fox-faced lieutenant of the Eighteenth panted at the worker's heels, his Mauser pistol smoking.

"Seize him," Thomas commanded, and his orderly gripped the worker's arm.

"Wo-ti pu-lo, Chung wei," Thomas snapped. "My prisoner, Lieutenant."

The Kwangsi man stared at Thomas dully. Steadying the heavy Mauser with both hands, he deliberately raised the weapon to shoulder height. His finger squeezed the trigger, and a red cavity opened in the militiaman's temple. The angry orderly unholstered his pistol. Thomas hesitated as his subordinate raised the weapon, but finally knocked the pistol down and turned his back on the lieutenant. Unspeaking, he strode away while the Kwangsi officer ground his boot-heel into the militiaman's sightless eyes.

At the General's command post, messengers were coming and going in an atmosphere of controlled hysteria. After reporting to the Chief-of-Staff, Thomas slipped back into his proper role with conscious relief. Collating the couriers' dispatches and telephoned reports, he crossed one red-ringed militia strongpoint after another off the detailed wall map of Shanghai with black strokes. He consciously suppressed his revulsion, though the half-formulated thought persisted beneath the surface of his awareness: "Not only are Chinese killing Chinese! The National Revolutionary Army is slaughtering its own allies!" He reassured himself that the General knew far better than he what measures were necessary for the nation's good. But he realized that, no matter how long he soldiered, he would never become inured to the violent death that was the relentless counterpoint of his chosen career. Yet he had chosen freely, just as he had freely given his loyalty to his General. He would, he affirmed to himself, never waver.

By late afternoon, Thomas Sekloong was numb with exhaustion. Though he had not slept for thirty-eight hours, he would not leave his post until Militia Headquarters capitulated. Chiang Kai-shek had rejected his staff-colonels' advice to bring up artillery or, at least, trench-mortars. It was not his purpose, he declared, to raze Shanghai, but only to destroy the Communist virus that infected the city. Thomas's admiration for Chiang Kai-shek renewed itself. No more than himself did his General delight in slaughter; he was merely executing an essential task with the minimum force necessary.

At 5:34 P.M. the field telephone's irregular, handcranked ringing irritably demanded attention, and Thomas automatically lifted the receiver.

"Wai! Wai! Tsung-ssu-ling-yüan ti pan-kung-shih," he shouted. "Hello! Hello! Commander-in-Chief's office."

"Wai! Wai!" The clacking Kwangsi accent was further distorted by the telephone's static. "Major Lee . . . Major Lee, Eighteenth Division. I have . . . honor to . . . to report . . . Communist bandits' headquarters . . . fallen. Two hundred . . . dead . . . fifty captives including . . ."

The line crackled, and Thomas shouted: "Say again. Say again. You . . . are . . . not . . . clear. Say again last sentence."

"Wai! Wai!" The handset reported. "Two hundred dead . . . fifty, I say again, fifty bandit captives. We have captured . . . leader of . . . Chou En-lai. I say again, Chou En-lai."

When Thomas reported the Commissar's capture, the General's deep-set eyes glowed. The battle was over and the chief enemy secured; the revolution could resume its proper course. The General also felt justified personal gratification. He was not excessively fond of the twenty-nine-year-old Communist who had infringed upon his authority at the Whampoa Academy.

"Have *Comrade* Chou," the General directed with heavy irony, "brought here immediately."

Thomas nodded when Chiang Kai-shek added: "Now, old *Tom*, will you sleep a little? You should be satisfied."

Two hours later, a heavy hand shook Thomas and his canvas cot trembled.

"Shang-wei Hsien-sheng . . ." his orderly said. "Captain, Sir, the General wants you."

A pale major wearing the insignia of the Eighteenth Division stood at attention before the General's desk, surrounded by staff officers. Chiang Kai-shek's bony features were drawn tight, and he spoke with slow fury.

"Where, I ask again, is the bandit chieftain Chou En-lai?"

The major's lips were white with fear, and his heavy Kwangsi brogue was barely intelligible. Thomas concentrated intensely in order to interpret his reply.

"We were proceeding with the captive as ordered. I was hailed by a captain wearing General Headquarters' insignia. He led a full platoon, and I had under my command only a six-man escort. He came, he said, from His Excellency the General to take possession of the captive Chou En-lai. I told him I'd been ordered to deliver the captive to Headquarters. New orders, the captain said. The General was impatient . . . must see the captive immediately. I protested again, and his men unslung their rifles. Since he wore the proper Headquarters insignia, I yielded the captive."

"No further reports of *Comrade* Chou?" the General asked.

The staff officers' silence was eloquent.

"The worst of the lot's escaped," the General snapped. "There'll be evil consequences from that few minutes' work."

Chiang Kai-shek's wiry hands snapped a writing brush. His face unmoving, he methodically shredded the bamboo cylinder before looking up again.

"Describe the captain!" he commanded.

"A tall man with curly hair and strange, light eyes that seemed green when he argued with me. He looked something like a foreigner, but he spoke perfect Cantonese. I regret, General . . ."

Chiang glanced up from the debris on his desk and ordered softly: "Take this fool outside and shoot him. His story's either a deliberate lie—or he's too stupid to serve me."

Queasy with apprehension, Thomas summoned the ready squad. He sighed in relief when he heard two shots a few minutes after the soldiers had half-carried the terrified Kwangsi man away. The major was obviously an incompetent who deserved his fate—and he could never repeat his damning tale.

Not until the next evening could Thomas leave his post to look for his brother James's unit. He found them packing their equipment.

"We're moving out again," James explained. "Special duty in Nanchang."

His tone neutrally flat, Thomas repeated the major's description of the captain who had seized Chou En-lai.

"A strange tale," James commented casually. "Damned fool of a major, but what can you expect of a Kwangsi man?"

"And the captain," Thomas mused. "I wonder who he could be."

"Likely some Communist in disguise. Don't ask me. We were on alert right here all day. Battalion Commander Lin Piao four times requested permission to enter the city and assist in the extermination. But Division Headquarters refused. I seem to have missed all the action."

Thomas had no further opportunity to question his brother. James's company vanished with Lin Piao's battalion into the maelstrom set whirling by Chiang Kai-shek's decision to purge the Communists. The bloody "liquidation" of the Communists proceeded systematically, not only in Shanghai, but in such widely separated centers as Nanking, Hangchow, Foochow, and Canton. Nationalist troops and police, guided by universally hated *teh-wu*, "special duty" secret agents, broke up Communist cells, shot down suspects, disarmed Workers' Militiamen, and closed down Communist-controlled trade unions. Blood and fire were destroying the "Red infestation."

Resistance was negligible and ineffective, for the purblind Chinese Communist Party sought still to obey Joseph Stalin's orders to cooperate with the Nationalists. Delighting in the two-fold irony, Chiang Kai-shek, himself still an honorary member of the Central Committee of the Communist International, insisted that he had no quarrel with Stalin, with the Comintern, or with the Soviet Union. His sole purpose was to prevent China's Communists from sabotaging the national revolution.

Himself locked in a struggle for supreme power with Leon Trotsky, who denounced the Stalinist strategy in China, Joseph Stalin was grandly unconcerned with the fate of the Chinese Communist Party. His chosen instrument for attaining domination over China was, in any event, not that small Party, but, despite its inherent weakness, that left-wing Nationalist Government at Wuhan under President Wang Ching-wei. Stalin's monstrous blunder in sacrificing his Chinese comrades was compounded by those naive Communists. Despite Chiang Kai-shek's ruthless persecution and Wang Ching-wei's obvious ineffectiveness, they slavishly strove to comply with Moscow's instructions to work with the left-wing Kuomintang. In any event, they saw no other possible course.

Only one contender in the triangular power struggle was effective in early summer of 1927, the right-wing Nationalist Government just established at Nanking. His confidence and his resources bolstered by his alliance with the Shanghai commercial community, Chiang Kai-shek appeared on the verge of making himself the undisputed master of China. It seemed he need only negotiate with those warlords who would negotiate and crush those warlords who would not negotiate. He was actually amused when, on April 17, the left-wing Wuhan Government formally relieved him of command of the National Revolutionary Army and expelled him from the Nationalist Party.

"Wang Ching-wei's running true to form," he observed to Thomas. "He's always confused words with realities. Now he's freed me to form my own government. I imagine your uncle protested. But what could he do? Wang's a puppet of the Communists."

"Yes, Sir!" Thomas encouraged his leader's confidences. The political and military situation was so confused it was almost impossible to comprehend. Each day's reports appeared to contradict the previous day's. Yet the General, adroitly maneuvering to consolidate his power and unify China, obviously saw the entire picture clearly.

"Ah, *Tom*," Chiang added, "it's as complicated as a fortune-teller's predictions. But one thing's obvious: Whoever keeps his head clear and his armies intact will inherit the Mandate of Heaven. By the way, when did you last read the *San-kuo Chih Yen-yi*, the *Romance of the Three Kingdoms?*"

Thomas was disappointed and baffled when the General thereupon ended the discussion by opening a bulky file on his desk. If Chiang Kai-shek could contribute no more to his enlightenment than an oblique reference to China's most popular folk novel of intrigue, treachery, and war, how could he hope to comprehend the events unfolding around him? He wished fleetingly he were back in the field. Tactical problems were much more easily solved than grand political-strategic riddles.

Thomas suddenly saw that the General had indeed given him the key: *China remained China despite the invasion of Western technology and Western ideology.* The *Three Kingdoms* told the tale of triangular contention for power in a China splintered by the collapse of the great Han Dynasty in the third century A.D., and the parallel with the present situation was obvious. The General had also referred to the Mandate of Heaven that legitimized all Chinese governments. Not only the *lao pai-hsing,* but the rival politicians believed that successive dynasties were created by Heaven's express decree. The century of famines, floods, pestilence, droughts, and rebellion preceding the fall of the Ching Dynasty had conclusively demonstrated the Manchus' loss of the Mandate of Heaven. Chiang Kai-shek's victory would prove that he had legitimately inherited that Mandate.

Other similarities with the past were as striking. Even the intrusion of greedy barbarians armed with novel weapons was an ancient and often-repeated threat to the Central Realms. Why else had China's First Emperor built the Great Wall to protect the north in the third century B.C., or the Ming Dynasty sent fleets south to counter sea-borne intruders in the fifteenth century A.D.?

One great difference would, however, prove decisive this time. Since Chinese were themselves using the technology and tactics of the West, China would not again be over-run by rapacious foreigners. Thomas feared no repetition of the catastrophic defeats that had brought the Mongol Kublai Khan to the Dragon Throne in 1280 and permitted the Manchu Nurhachi to establish the long-lived Ching Dynasty in 1644. The Communists were the vanguard of a new barbarian invasion from north of the Great Wall by the Russians. In enlightened 1927, the Mandate of Heaven would, however, pass to a Chinese leader, and that leader would be Chiang Kai-shek.

General Chiang Kai-shek confidently moved northward, while President Wang Ching-wei was irresolute. He had entrapped himself by reassuming the Presidency. He could neither command the Communist-officered troops who were the core of his army nor control the Communist-influenced officials who were the framework of his tottering administration. He made a desperate cast on April 18, the same day Chiang Kai-shek proclaimed his own right-wing National Government in Nanking. Again allied with the Christian General Feng Yü-hsiang, President Wang Ching-wei accepted the pressing advice of the Comintern's representative, Mikhail Borodin, to launch his own Northern Expedition. After he had taken Peking, he planned an Eastern Expedition to crush Chiang Kai-shek's Nanking Government.

The incongruous alliance of Social Democrats, Communists, and the Christian Warlord advanced into Honan Province, which lay just south of Hopei Province where the glittering prize, Peking itself, was situated. The old Northern Capital was the ultimate objective of all the contenders for power. Both the Chinese people and the foreign powers assumed that he who held Peking legitimately ruled China, and both still tendered formal recognition to the crumbling warlord government in the Northern Capital. Nonetheless, the conquest of Honan and its vital railroad plexus at Chengchow, only four hundred and seventy-five miles south of Peking, proved a political disaster for Wang Ching-wei. The new satrap of Honan, the ambitious Christian General Feng Yü-hsiang, insisted that Peking would fall only to an allied expeditionary force composed of his own forces and the reunited armies of the reconciled Wuhan and Nanking Nationalist Governments. On June 2, Chiang Kai-shek had taken Hsüchow, four hundred and fifty miles from Peking, and the road to the north was also open to him.

Mikhail Borodin and the Chinese Communists rejected the Christian General's strategy. They denounced his proposal as "not a joint attack upon the Peking warlords, but a joint extermination of the Chinese Communist Party." When President Wang Ching-wei in Wuhan therefore demurred at undertaking a joint Northern Expedition with Chiang Kai-shek in Nanking, the Christian General, realistically expecting no further aid from Moscow, renounced his alliance with Wuhan. His new price for reconciliation was Wang Ching-wei's expelling the Communists from his government—and Mikhail Borodin from China.

While the rivals maneuvered, a time bomb was ticking in the desk drawer of M. N. Roy, a Bengali dispatched to Wuhan by the Communist International to assist Borodin. Joseph Stalin had sent Roy a telegram ordering the Comintern representatives and the Chinese Communists to recast their strategy. The Bengali was appalled by Stalin's instructions, which were, in any event, impossible of fulfillment. Even attempting to carry them out would, he knew, infuriate President
475

Wang Ching-wei. Obeying Stalin would destroy all the Communists' hopes in China, and Borodin had in disgust disavowed all responsibility. After pondering for a week, the Bengali finally acted—foolishly and self-destructively. "In order to show my complete trust and confidence," as he said, Roy gave a copy of Stalin's telegram to Wang Ching-wei—and effectively destroyed the alliance of the left-Kuomintang and the Communists.

The President was as brilliant as he was erratic. Yet he had never quite grasped the essential fact that armed force was the key to power. His fingers irritably stroked the hand-written copy of Stalin's telegram when Harry Sekloong entered his office on the morning of June 6, 1927.

"Have a look at this, *lao-hsiang*," the President said.

The intimate salutation, *lao-hsiang*, "old fellow," surprised Harry no more than his chief's manner. They had so long shared both defeat and triumph that the son of the Sekloong dynasty and the nervous political firebrand reacted almost with a single will. But Harry was astonished when he read the text, turgid with Marxist rhetoric. His soft whistling as he reread the telegram irritated his volatile chief.

"Na chiu shih-la, Lao-pan!" Harry said. "That does it, Chief! Stalin wants to take us over, lock, stock, barrel—and troops."

"We can't go along, can we?" Wang Ching-wei feared an affirmative almost as much as a negative reply. "He wants to squeeze us dry."

"Can a dog read Confucius?" Harry characteristically masked his own dismay with the old peasant saw. "Just look at what they want! How can we possibly let the Communists organize their own independent army and militia? How could we conceivably help them take over the Kuomintang, *our* party? Their own land reform, for God's sake! Giving our blessing to Communist courts that would execute our own friends! And that's only the half of the Russian bastard's demands."

"What *can* we do, old fellow?" Wang Ching-wei appealed.

"Do? Why nothing. The Communists have their orders. Let them try to carry them out. I can't see why we should sharpen a knife and hand it to them to cut our throats."

"Doing nothing means we lose Soviet support. What then?"

"I don't really know. We've tried for years to organize our own army, but always failed. No guns of our own means no power."

"I suppose," Wang Ching-wei reflected, "I could talk to that son of a turtle-bitch Chiang Kai-shek again. That buffoon, the Christian General, still insists he can heal the breach—if we get rid of the Communists."

"No harm in trying, though it won't work. I'll be packing my bags again. Hong Kong's too hot this time of year. Perhaps Paris or London?"

Harry's pessimism was wholly justified, though slightly premature. More than six months were to elapse before he was forced to set out on his travels again in company with an embittered, vengeful Wang Ching-wei. Nonetheless, the isolated Wuhan Government was virtually powerless in mid-July 1927, and Chiang Kai-shek would not even negotiate with Wang's left-wing Kuomintang. A disgusted Mikhail Borodin was motoring across the Gobi Desert toward Moscow, after having told the Chinese Communists to withdraw from the Wuhan Government while remaining members of the Nationalist Party, which was equivocal advice at best. President Wang Ching-wei vacillated, first exhorting the same Chinese Communists to obey his orders as loyal members of the disintegrating left-wing Kuomintang and, two days later, expelling the same Communists from the Wuhan Government, the Kuomintang, and the few military units he still controlled. It was, as James Sekloong observed, "like being expelled from a cemetery."

Abandoned by all their friends and mentors, the Chinese Communists, of necessity, went their own way. They formally—and pointlessly—proclaimed their own provisional government of the Republic of China in Kiukiang, eighty miles north of the stronghold of Nan-

chang, whose capture in November 1926 had precipitated the totally destructive crisis. The demoralized
native Communists were merely rearranging the stage
furniture for the next act of their own particular tragedy,
any realistic hope of their attaining even a share of
power having been blasted by Joseph Stalin's clumsiness and Wang Ching-wei's indecisiveness. As if determined to immolate themselves they next threw their
few intact military units at China's cities.

Major Lin Piao briefed his officers on the evening of
July 31, 1927. They were tense and impatient, for the
battalion had seen little action since April, when it was
relegated to the backwater of Nanchang.

General Chiang Kai-shek's apparent lack of interest
in discovering who had snatched Chou En-lai from his
grasp was actually a politic expedient. Relieved by the
hapless Kwangsi major's execution, the devoted
Thomas had for once underrated his Commander-in-
Chief's astuteness and tenacity. Already suspicious of
Lin Piao, the General had surmised that the captain
with the light eyes who freed Chou En-lai was James
Sekloong. But he wanted no quarrel with the Sekloongs
who, with their foreign and Chinese associates, were
providing him with essential financial support. He had
therefore sent the battalion into safe-keeping to garrison the walled city of Nanchang and help train the
cadets of the Nanchang Branch of the Whampoa Academy. Even Chiang was, however, not omniscient. He
did not know that the school's Commandant, Chu Teh,
a warlord turned patriot, was also a secret Communist.

James lingered when the other officers dispersed. Despite official denunciation, *kwan-hsi*, connections, were
still the essential mortar that bound the clandestine
Communist organization. James had enjoyed a special
relationship with his battalion commander since his rescue of Chou En-lai.

"Comrade Lin," he asked, however reluctantly determined to use that *kwan-hsi*, "is this move necessary?
Do you think it wise?"

Lin Piao's dark brows drew together in the scowl
478

that rebuked any subordinate who questioned his will. A tight smile illuminated his sallow face in the next instant, for James Sekloong's family connections made him important to the cause. Lin Piao had also learned to avoid personal confrontation when his rough-edged charm might prevail.

"Necessary, Comrade?" he drawled. "Necessary? The question is not pertinent. We have our orders."

"But we can't possibly win," James persisted. "We'll merely throw away our advantages. Even if we do succeed, it can only last a few days."

"The Party Center has spoken, Comrade. Do you question their wisdom?"

"But, Comrade Battalion Commander," James insisted doggedly, "we are on the scene—and they're not. How can impractical intellectuals judge the military situation?"

"And if we do not obey, Comrade? What then? A Party without discipline, I've told you a hundred times, is no more than a heap of dog turds."

"I understand, Comrade, but a hundred tactics and a thousand stratagems are still untried." James unconsciously dropped into the Communists' stylized rhetoric, which was an unstable compound of classical quotations and Marxist jargon. "A frontal assault is unwise."

"You are either a Communist or a running-dog of the imperialist, capitalist exploiters," Lin Piao snapped. "You either obey the orders of the Party Center or . . ."

His commander's reiterated indirect threat had already passed from James's mind as he lay unsleeping on his grass mat on the floor of the Buddhist temple that sheltered his company. He respected Battalion Commander Lin Piao, but he no longer feared him. A man incapable of making his own decisions was not truly formidable. The twenty-year-old James refused to surrender his will to the enfeebled Central Committee of a blundering Communist Party that had withdrawn his candidate-membership after his attack on the landlord-usurer Squire Lee—and restored it after he rescued Chou En-lai in Shanghai. How, he wondered, could Lin Piao render unquestioning obedience to such doddering fools?

The still night was humid. The odor of unwashed bodies mingled with garlic fumes exhaled through rotting teeth by the snoring men around him. Neither the heat nor the stench disturbed James; he was resigned to the one and accustomed to the other. But he was not resigned to the action planned for the morning. Lin Piao's exhortations had neither intimidated nor impressed him; he was determined to make his own decisions. Since Shanghai, James had given his considerable leisure to analyzing his country's predicament—and his own. He could slip away that night and alert the Nanchang Garrison Commander or he could blindly obey the Party's orders. He knew he had come to a decisive fork in his life, but he still did not know which road he would take.

Taking the left fork could mean outlawing himself indefinitely among men who floundered in the political morass. The commanding presence, incisive logic, and bright courage of a single Chou En-lai could not counterbalance the blatant ineptitude of the Party Center. James was impressed by the personal force of the Party's most prominent dissident, but he had little faith in the practical judgment of the monomaniacal Mao Tse-tung who was obsessed with the fancied revolutionary potential of the peasants. He further acknowledged that even the bumbling Party Center did at least see its goal clear—a united China, strong and self-sufficient, where all men and women lived in dignity. But could that vision ever become reality? Was the remote possibility of its realization worth passing decades as a hunted outlaw?

All his experience before his introduction to Marxism at the Whampoa Academy impelled James to the center road. Although his Uncle Harry and Wang Ching-wei proceeded with unerring instinct from disaster to disaster, they were at least free men trapped in an impossible predicament. They had not become automata like Lin Piao, who obeyed mechanically and demanded the same reflex obedience of his subordinates. Besides, there *was* the family, and he owed the family loyalty, perhaps a greater loyalty than he owed the Communists' illusory and probably unattainable vision. If he rose from his grass mat and gave the alarm, he would serve the House of Sekloong well and become a hero to the center and the right. He would, however, insure a great career for himself by betraying the peasant and worker soldiers who lay sleeping around him. He would condemn them to the certainty of execution, rather than the possibility of death in battle they faced gladly because—false modesty could not obscure the reality—because he led them.

Still pondering his dilemma, James Sekloong slid into deep slumber at two in the morning. When he was awakened at six, his decision had been taken—almost in spite of himself. The throat-rasping hawking and guttural spitting of his soldiers confirmed that decision. His loyalty, he realized, was pledged to the ninety-seven men with whom he had served for fourteen months and whom he had commanded for four months. Abstract visions like perfect social justice in the Marxists' earthly paradise-to-come or a strong, independent, respected China could not assert the primary claim upon his own life. Nor could the profits of the House of Sekloong.

His allegiance was already given to Ox Woo, the plowboy from Kweichow who, at the siege of Nanchang, had shot a warlord private just before the private's raised bayonet plunged into his lieutenant's chest; to Ferret Yang, the gutter fighter from Swatow who sustained the company by his endless stock of dirty jokes and his uncanny ability to forage food in the barest countryside; to his First Sergeant, Old Baldy Chang, their only veteran professional soldier, who had become a dedicated Communist under his company commander's tutelage. His was, James concluded as he checked his Mauser before turning out his company, by no means an ignoble loyalty. It was certainly no less noble than the ambitious Lin Piao's unquestioning obedience to the Communist Central Committee or his brother Thomas's slavish devotion to General Chiang Kai-shek. Besides, Uncle Harry would approve of his decision. Harry Sekloong, too, had given up a life of ease and pleasure because of his concern for the *lao pai-hsing*, the common people.

James whistled cheerfully as he inspected the company. Squinting down a filthy rifle barrel, he realized that the tune was *"Gaudeamus Igitur,"* an unconscious echo of music appreciation courses in Hong Kong under the Jesuits. But why not? He was young, and there was reason to rejoice. He tossed the weapon back, remarking that it would blow up in Ferret Yang's face if he could not trouble himself to run an oil-soaked wad through the barrel. James contemplated his tattered rapscallions with affectionate distaste before rasping in his high-pitched, parade-ground voice: "Move out!"

With the shuffling gait of men still more at ease in grass sandals than leather boots, the company debouched between the red gate posts of the Buddhist temple into a muddy lane. The scuffling of many feet —some bare, some sandaled, and some leather-shod— was the true anthem of the Revolution. The second company joined them at the junction of the lane, and the third fell in behind them. At the head of the column, Lin Piao issued no new orders. His officers already knew their asignments, and it was too late to tinker with the plan. They were committed.

Irregular volleys sounded from the stone-faced three-story building with the dun-tiled roof that housed the offices of the Nanchang government and garrison. When the Communist column moved cautiously into the city's central square, James saw that the cadets had anticipated them. Though lacking the spit-and-polish smartness of the officer candidates at the main school in Canton, the 1,200 cadets at Nanchang were already an effective fighting force. Commandant Chu Teh, the broad-faced, thick-set archetype of a Yunnan Province peasant even to his shuffling gait, gave his orders with no more excitement than a farmer sowing the spring rice. The first fierce volleys from the defenders were already dwindling to scattered single shots as Lin Piao's battalion went into action.

The August First Rising, which was to be commemorated as the birth of the Communist People's Liberation Army, won total victory within hours. The Nationalist Governor surrendered, and his troops joined the insurgents. For the first time, Communist regulars had seized a city by armed force. For the first time, they held a firm revolutionary base. The new revolution—no longer national bourgeois, but Socialist and Communist—had begun spectacularly, and the soldiers rejoiced. Irrevocably committed to the Communist cause, James Sek-loong rejoiced with his illiterate followers. His doubts and skepticism had dissipated; he *knew* he had made the right choice.

James's renewed confidence survived the shock of Major Lin Piao's quiet announcement at the officers' morning conference on the third day after General Chu Teh had proclaimed the Communist Provisional Revolutionary Government of China.

"Comrades," the Battalion Commander directed, "we move into the countryside this afternoon. The reactionary forces converging on Nanchang are too powerful to resist. It would be folly to sacrifice our victory by fighting them and risking defeat."

"Then we surrender our victory, instead?" a shocked lieutenant objected.

"No, Comrade!" The undertone of hysteria normally apparent in Lin Piao's voice shrilled. "We consolidate our victory. Our deeds these past days have laid the foundation for our ultimate victory. How foolish to toss that precious pearl away like yesterday's burnt rice by hazarding defeat. The glorious conquest of Nanchang will inspire and inflame the masses. Soon, very soon, we will win total victory—when all China is aflame with the hatred of a politically conscious proletariat."

Rejoining their units, the officers issued their orders for the withdrawal. Some were subdued, those who yearned in their new-found confidence to fight the encroaching Nationalist forces. Others, having learned revolutionary patience, consoled themselves with Lin

483

Piao's promise of ultimate victory. The pragmatic common soldiers were glum.

"A great victory!" James heard his First Sergeant, Old Baldy Chang, grumble. "A great victory, screw their mothers! Some victory! We take a city and then surrender it. You can't win if you don't hold the ground."

The troops dispersed. Some units followed General Chu Teh and his cadets into the hills of northern Kwangtung Province. Lin Piao's battalion marched toward Swatow on the coast of Kwangtung Province, three hundred and forty miles northeast of Hong Kong, to seize that undefended port and proclaim a People's Commune that endured a few weeks. In the hills of Hunan, Mao Tse-tung led his beloved peasants in the Autumn Harvest Uprising and was sent reeling in flight by two companies of local militia. The Central Committee of the Communist Party was purged and the Secretary-General himself removed as a "Trotskyite traitor." A new group took command, Chou En-lai prominent among them. But it all amounted, James Sekloong reflected during the retreat from Swatow, to "no more than a heap of dog turds," in Lin Piao's favorite phrase. The Communist movement was in total disarray, its remaining troops scattered in a half-dozen encircled pockets and its leadership splintered.

The Nationalists' simultaneous discomfiture was little consolation to James, who feared he had indeed traded his expectations of life for an illusion. Both the left wing and the right wing of the Kuomintang were reeling under the blows of their resurgent warlord enemies. Hsüchow, the high-water mark of Chiang Kai-shek's Northern Expedition, was already lost, and the united warlords drove southward to threaten Shanghai and Nanking in mid-August. Faced with a mutiny by his generals, Chiang resigned "to remove dissension" and dashed off to Japan to woo Mayling Soong, Madame Sun Yat-sen's youngest sister. Bereft of almost all military strength, President Wang Ching-wei fled to Canton, which he formally designated the capital of his tottering, virtually powerless regime. Harry Sekloong observed with bitter humor that they could have saved themselves much trouble and travel. Wang and he were back where they had begun with Sun Yat-sen more than a decade earlier, while a rump National Government of conservatives sat in Nanking, and Peking remained in the warlords' hands.

With China once again reduced to anarchy, the shrewd Chiang Kai-shek returned to Shanghai with his new bride, Mayling Soong, to again claim supreme political and military authority over the demoralized Nationalists. Having embraced the Soongs' Methodism, the man branded a "Bolshevik bandit" after the Nanking conflagration in March had by late November won enthusiastic foreign support as the champion of law, order, and private enterprise. When Wang Ching-wei embarked for Shanghai to negotiate with Chiang Kai-shek, Harry Sekloong remained in Canton to preside over their simulacrum of a National Government. The final act of the gory tragedy into which the year 1927 had been transformed for the Chinese Communists by their own ineptitude and Moscow's conflicting orders was played in that southern metropolis.

Sir Jonathan Sekloong had lost little of his capacity for indignation, though he was seventy-four years old in late 1927. Ever since the virtual collapse of the Nationalist forces in mid-August he had lived in a fever of discontent. He was, nonetheless, mildly gratified when the Kuomintang's left wing and his son Harry finally split with the Communists, finally following the lead of Chiang Kai-shek, whom the Old Gentleman despised with the unrelenting contempt of one *arriviste* for another. Despite that contempt, he continued his discreet subsidies to the General, who, he felt, was the only man who might impose some order on China's chaos. His sons Sydney and Gregory Sek assiduously courted Green Dragon Tu Yueh-shen, Chiang Kai-shek's "blood-brother." Sir Jonathan was determined to extract whatever advantage he could from the spectacular disorder that seethed behind the calm façades of the foreign-ruled treaty-ports.

"The family is scattered all over China," he observed to Mary and Charles on November 30, 1927. "Harry's in Canton, but can't come near us. Thomas is back in Shanghai with that clever gangster Chiang Kai-shek. As for James, God knows where he is! I must know what they're all about."

Mary was deeply worried about James, who had vanished from their ken after the Swatow Commune's collapse in September. But she remained silent, lest she provoke a new anti-Communist tirade from the increasingly choleric Old Gentleman by expressing her fears for her favorite son. Charles replied quickly in order to forestall another of his wife's biting comments on China and the Chinese.

"Jonnie can lend you a hand here. Suppose I go up to Canton and talk to Harry?"

Sir Jonathan had, as usual, elicited the response he desired. He characteristically amended Charles's suggestion.

"By all means, and take Mary with you," he answered. "The servants in Canton want shaking up. I'll manage with Jonnie. He's finally displaying some glimmerings of business sense. Anyway, things are slack. Thank God this disastrous year's almost over."

Mary Sekloong's spirits rose when she and Charles boarded the Canton steamer two days later. She had felt herself virtually a prisoner in Hong Kong while the armies wheeled and counterwheeled like the Duke of York in the nursery rhyme who marched up the hill with 10,000 men and then marched right down again. She had tried to guard her tongue, for Sir Jonathan had grown hypersensitive to any allusion to the inability of the Chinese to either govern themselves or refrain from betraying each other. He had also grown more credulous, as if seeking in the supernatural realm the certainties that suddenly evaded him in the material world. His heartfelt thanks that 1927 was drawing to a close, she knew, echoed the promise of the old soothsayer, Silver Seventh Brother, that 1928 would be a good year, a very good year for both the Sekloongs and China. It would be the Year of the Dragon, auspicious for all, but particularly auspicious for the clan whose emblem was the winged dragon. Though she scoffed at Silver Seventh, Mary, too, hoped for a favorable turn of fortune. And Christmas was coming, and it was good to escape Hong Kong, even briefly.

Austerely elegant in his high-collared Sun Yat-sen tunic, Harry met them at the Canton Wharves. The throngs parted before the three-spoked star on the radiator of the Mercedes-Benz, virtually his badge of office as President Wang Ching-wei's counselor. He, too, was in high spirits, and he confidently predicted that Wang Ching-wei would very soon attain a working agreement with Chiang Kai-shek to reunite the Nationalists.

"And then we'll sweep the chessboard clear," he added. "Chiang just wants to play soldiers. After we take Peking, he'll be happy with the geegaws—the uniforms, gold braid, decorations, and parades. We'll get on with building China. There's also an excellent chance of reconciliation with the Communists."

"I hope so." Mary did not wish to mar their reunion with sour skepticism.

Charles allowed himself a tight smile. Thomas's artless letters praising his General were revealing. Charles felt with Mary that only supreme power, free of all restraints, would satisfy Chiang Kai-shek. But he, too, wished to avoid a political argument that could become acrimonious.

"I hope you're right about Chiang, Harry," he said while the Mercedes maneuvered through the narrow passage between the gate posts of the Kwok Family Mansion. "And I hope your confidence in the Communists proves justified."

"After all, they're still good Chinese, the Communists," Harry laughed. "They're your people and mine. They'll be all right."

Mary glanced sharply at her brother-in-law, remembering the mocking irreverence and the clear-sighted rejection of illusory cant that had first drawn her to Harry. He had changed fundamentally. It appeared that politics, like journalism, demanded a special kind of hard-shelled, humorless naiveté of its practitioners.

The wrought-iron gates closed behind the Mercedes, and the three Sekloongs were enclosed by the ancestral womb, the tiled courtyard of the Kwok Family Mansion. The servants were lined up to greet them, sixteen in all from the immaculate Number One Boy to three ragged gardeners. The entrance hall sparkled with new paint and polished woodwork. Someone, she saw, had already shaken up the staff.

"I think it's not bad, Mary." Harry reacted to her unspoken thought. "Though it's been a bachelor household since Mayling took Jason to Shanghai last month. Time for the boy to spend some time with his grandparents."

Delighted at being spared Harry's vapid wife, Mary wanted only a hot bath to complete her contentment at playing truant from Hong Kong. The riverboat always left her feeling grittily unattractive; she wanted to wash away the grime of the voyage before having her hair done by the skilful Ah Fung and restoring her make-up. At forty-seven she supposed she should be beyond such vanity, but she reveled in the undistracted attentions of the two men who meant most to her—and to whom she was determined to remain the most important and the most attractive woman in the world.

A tall man in a gray tunic stepped from behind the inlaid Coromandel screen that masked the moon-gate leading to the family quarters. The tight-curled hair, the mocking smile, and the laughing hazel eyes were achingly familiar. For an uncanny instant, she felt she was again meeting the young Harry Sekloong.

Powerful arms closed around her, and her son James exclaimed: "Mother! Mother! What a joy to see you!"

Mary felt overwhelming relief. James was obviously safe and quite sound, though a new maturity had etched itself upon his features in the eighteen months since she had last seen him.

James embraced Charles in an unusual display of affection and said softly in Cantonese: "Respected Father, I rejoice at our reunion."

A fleeting frown clouded Harry's brow. Mary knew that he had kept their compact not to tell James of his true parentage, though the temptation must have been great.

"James," she said, "James, my very dear, my favorite rascal. How did you come here? You are well? You must tell me all about . . ."

"So many questions, Mother," James replied with new authority. "Later we can talk. First, may I present my respected teacher?"

A slender man with glowing black eyes set in a lean face stood before the Coromandel screen. He bowed with the boneless grace of a Chinese opera star.

"Mr. and Mrs. Sekloong," Harry made the introduction in Mandarin, "my beloved sister-in-law Mary and my honored elder brother Charles. General Chou En-lai, who is staying with us."

"Enchanté, Madame, M'sieu," Chou En-lai responded in heavily accented French before continuing in Mandarin: "I am honored to meet the parents of my young pupil, the eldest brother and sister-in-law of my protector."

"Protector?" Charles was startled, but quickly remembered his duty as the host, the senior Sekloong. "We are, of course, honored by your presence. May I, belatedly, also welcome you to our home?"

"General Chou is too kind." Harry laughed, and his natural gaiety dispelled his professional politician's self-importance. "I'm hardly his protector. But, for the moment, both he and James are better off behind these high walls."

"How much longer, Uncle Harry?" James asked.

"A few weeks at most. Once the President and the Generalissimo have come to terms, there'll be no problems. Patriotic Communists are Chinese first. We'll all be working together again soon."

Mary wondered again at Harry's optimism, so different from the laughing cynicism of his youth. He, too, had become a believer like her son James and the suave General Chou En-lai. If they still believed so earnestly in China's future, she could not intrude her own disillusionment. Besides, they would undoubtedly dismiss a woman's opinion with courteous inattention. The tight ring of Chinese masculine superiority was closing around her once again. But she responded against her will to Chou En-lai's charm, and she fell in love again with her troublesome third son.

Chou En-lai and James did not quit the shelter of the Kwok Family Mansion. Harry's black Mercedes bore him off early each morning, and he returned late at night, still pursued by messengers bearing telegrams. As the days passed, his high spirits visibly declined. His jests about family matters and his high optimism regarding the negotiations in Shanghai were forced. Mary and Charles called at the offices of J. Sekloong and Sons, but business was slow. Besides, the atmosphere in the litter-strewn streets was electrically disquieting. Despite the dank, cold weather, workmen gathered on streetcorners to sneer at the police and the soldiers. Even the antique splendors of the reconstructed Kwok Family Mansion behind the high, glass-shard-studded walls was besmirched by the creeping unease. A young German called Heinz Neumann regularly slipped through the small garden gate to confer with Chou En-lai. He invariably arrived after midnight, and James interpreted his fluent, ungrammatical English. The presence of the Comintern's representative within the walls of the fortress Sir Jonathan had built against the world was palpably menacing.

On December 11, 1927, Chou En-lai and James Sekloong left the Mansion for the first time. When Mary awoke at seven, the Number One Boy told her that they had been gone for several hours. Puzzled but not worried, Harry drove through the gates in his Mercedes at 8:30. Half an hour later, he returned on foot.

"Something's up," he said soberly. "But damned if I know what. Barricades across the roads, and I had to abandon the car. We're cut off, and I don't know why."

Harry repeatedly tried to telephone his office, but evoked only the repeated surly reply from an unfamiliar operator: "I cannot connect you."

Mary glanced at her watch when clashing cymbals, pounding drums, and booming gongs sounded in the normally quiet back street at 10:43. The harsh chanting of male voices rose above the discordant din. They sang "The Internationale," and the words were even more menacing in clacking Cantonese: "Arise ye prisoners of starvation, Arise ye workers of the earth . . . The International Soviet shall be the human race!"

A crackling loudspeaker directed: "Remain in your homes. All will be well. Today, we have established the Canton People's Commune. The workers rule. The people rule. The glorious moment has come!"

The Sekloongs waited, totally insulated from the seething city by the walled compound. Mary was oppressed by their isolation and by worry about James. Charles was sustained by his conviction of Sekloong invincibility. Harry wandered distracted through the courtyards, starting at each sound from outside. But no message came to the counselor of the President of the Republic of China until a loud hammering on the garden door startled them at two in the afternoon.

Harry and Charles opened the gate themselves. James stood outside grinning like a schoolboy in uniform. Behind him was mustered a ragged formation of six workmen awkwardly carrying rifles and wearing the red brassards of the Workers' Militia.

"I've come to fix things," he said incoherently. "You'll all be safe."

"What is it, boy?" Charles demanded. "Fix what? What the devil's up?"

"Calmly, James, calmly," Harry cautioned. "Explain yourself."

"We've seized the city, we Communists. We've established a Commune, a People's Commune. General Chou sent me to post an official notice that this house is under the protection of the Commune."

"Damned decent of him," Charles exploded. "But why? So he can kill us later?"

"You can't hold Canton, you know," Harry said quietly.

"Perhaps not, Uncle. I can tell you General Chou is *not* delighted. He counseled against this rising. But Heinz Neumann insisted, and he speaks for the Comin-

491

tern. The insurrection will succeed, Neumann insists. Moscow has ordained it."

James did not return to the Kwok Family Mansion for three days, and the telephone remained sullenly silent. But Harry's network of agents began to function again. Fewer than five thousand armed militiamen, stiffened by a cadre of no more than five hundred Communist soldiers, could not control all egress and ingress to the city of 850,000. The first reports Harry received dismayed him: The Communists were systematically slaughtering their enemies, the bourgeoisie. The next reports were almost as daunting: Nationalist troops were marching on Canton to avenge those executions, and there would be more slaughter.

"It'll be over soon," Harry declared after a protracted session with a shadowy informant late in the evening of December 14, 1927. "Three corps are closing on the city. The Ironsides Division is only sixteen miles away."

"About time, too," Charles said.

"Damn those fool Communists." Harry added bitterly. "This so-called Commune is the end. They've sown the seeds of bitterness deep. China will eat the fruit of sorrow for years."

"And James?" Mary's obsessive fear for her son excluded all other concerns. "What will become of him?"

"We must get him out," said Charles. "But how?"

After his shocked inaction during the preceding three days, Harry was once again the vigorous activist. His self-confidence had rebounded when he learned that his allies were marching to his relief.

"How, indeed?" he repeated. "It can be done, but not easily. Though my signature should . . . but first we must talk to the young idiot."

Again wearing the Sun Yat-sen tunic that was the Nationalists' symbol, rather than military uniform, James slipped through the garden gate at two in the morning.

"You sent for me, Father?" His diffidence, which contrasted with Harry's renewed confidence, demonstrated his realization that the Communists' last adventure was doomed.

"Yes, James," Charles answered. "You've got to get out of Canton. Otherwise, there'll be nothing for you but a bullet—or jail, if you're lucky."

"Mei fa-tze," James sighed resignedly. "Not a hope."

"You're giving up, James, are you?" Mary goaded him. "I never thought . . ."

"What's the use, Mother? Besides, I can't leave without General Chou."

"Damn General Chou!" Charles snapped. "He got you into this mess. A strange way of repaying our hospitality."

"But he kept us safe while others were shot or their houses were sacked," Mary reminded her husband. "We *are* in his debt. What's to be done, Harry?"

"Will Chou come with us?" Harry asked.

"Ta dzen-ma pan?" James shrugged. "What else can he do? Why should he be a martyr to a revolt he opposed?"

"I want you both here at six this morning," Harry commanded. "Not an instant later. The Canton–Kowloon Railway's too dangerous. But the first steamer sails at 8:45."

"How can you possibly get us out?" James responded. "The piers will be heavily guarded."

"Just do as I say," Harry answered. "Six in the morning."

When James had left, Harry told his sister-in-law peremptorily: "You and Charles must leave now, though it would be safer to wait a few days. It's the only hope for James."

At 7:35 on the morning of December 15, 1927, Harry Sekloong's black Mercedes emerged from the Kwok Family Mansion. The luggage rack was piled with Mary and Charles's trunks, and their owners lounged in the spacious rear seat. Restored to his authority, the Counselor to President Wang Ching-wei sat beside them. Two servants in worn black suits covered by bulky overcoats were crammed beside the driver. One was a burly youth with an incongruous black fedora shading his face, the other a slender twenty-nine-year-old whose features were concealed by a woolen muffler drawn high against the morning chill.

The road to the docks took them through the center of the tormented city, past Admiralty House and the Wireless Masts that were the primary objectives of the relieving Nationalist forces and the last stronghold of the defeated Communists. The first roadblock the Mercedes encountered was manned by troops of the Ironsides Fourth Division. The lieutenant in command scrutinized the documents the chauffeur offered before stepping back and saluting Harry Sekloong. He glanced in curiously at the menservants who were huddled into their overcoats. There was no reason for him to suspect that one had been an upperclassman and the other the Communist chairman of the Political Studies Department when he himself entered the Whampoa Military Academy.

Mary relaxed her grip on her husband's hand. After the Mercedes had moved another fifty yards forward, her nails dug into his palm. Three foreigners hung from a scarlet flame-of-the-forest tree. Their faces were livid purple, and their feet twitched in the air. Placards pinned to their chests identified them in black characters as SOVIET IMPERIALIST SPIES.

Beside the road, mutilated corpses were heaped upon each other. A grinning head lolled in grisly imitation of life. The corpse's throat had been cut so savagely that only the backbone and a strip of skin joined the head to the body. A calloused hand, outflung as if imploring mercy, was bloodlessly waxen. From a bayonet thrust in the back of the topmost corpse fluttered a red brassard that identified the Workers' Militia who had only yesterday been the masters of Canton. KUNG-JEN MIN-PING, it read—literally, WORKERS' PEOPLE'S-SOLDIER. Some hand had crossed out the character *min*, meaning "people," and written *chu*, "pig," so that the brassard read: WORKERS' PIG-SOLDIER.

Beside the gates to the docks fifteen militiamen

slumped in sullen hopelessness against a corrugated iron wall. A machine-gun squad of the Fourth Division jeered at the Communist workers.

"Pigs and dogs' legs! Pig-soldiers! Where are your great leaders now? Sister-rapers! Mother-sellers! Brother-buggers! Screw your mothers!"

Mary closed her eyes, but the machine gun's cruel chatter imprinted the slaughter on her mind's eye.

Yet the customs officers were attentive, and the party was bowed onto the deck of the *Fatshan*. The servants shouted curses at the baggage coolies until the luggage was stowed to their satisfaction. They then reported to their master and mistress.

"They'll pay for this!" James muttered. "They'll pay and pay—in blood."

"All China will pay," Chou En-lai said wearily. "All China will pay—in torrents of blood. *Mei-yu pieh-ti pan-fa!* There is no other way."

Part Six

━━━━━━━━━━━━━━━━━━━━━━━━━━━━━━━

James and Harry

July 7, 1937–December 9, 1944

THE pine groves of the Western Hills glowed emerald in the long summer twilight, and the old capital took its fitful ease on the ochre plain irregularly patterned with pale-green fields of ripening millet. The air was so still that the sweet-acrid tang of charcoal-fires clung to the red-and-gray-tiled roofs of the city called Peiping. The Nationalists had changed its name to "Northern Peace" after they finally took the city in 1928 and moved the government to Nanking, the "Southern Capital." But the conservative natives still called the city Peking, the "Northern Capital." The tired peace of the serpentine alleys called *hu-tungs* was occasionally disturbed by the swishing of a passing bicycle, the whining of a restless dog, or the cries of an itinerant hawker. The heat wave had just broken, and the exhausted citizens relaxed in the brief respite from the parched North China summer on the evening of Sunday, July 7, 1937.

The city was instinctively egalitarian, arrogant only in its assertion of cultural preeminence. Manual laborers and university students sat side by side at the time-rubbed tables of the eating shop called *Lao Chiao Wang,* the "Old Dumpling King." The wooden walls were polished by oil-saturated steam that had for two centuries risen from cooking pots bubbling over the brick stove behind the cracked glass windows. Familiarly attentive as the staff of a private club, waiters in grimy white jackets squirmed through the maze of close-packed tables, bearing aloft heaped platters of dumplings, both the crisp-fried *kuo-tieh* and steamed white *chiao-tze.* The patrons avidly devoured the envelopes of translucent dough plump with minced pork and vegetables.

If culinary skill was a chief ornament of Chinese civilization, James Sekloong reflected, his people's chief vice was gluttony. That universal passion defied explanation by his Marxist doctrine. It was common to all

499

social classes, as was the city's distinctive burr, which marked the speech of all from rickshaw men to professors. Perhaps twentieth-century Chinese were food-besotted because they, like their ancestors, had so often known gut-griping hunger. Perhaps, though, the gourmet passion was bred into Peiping's citizens, as it was in the Viennese his sister Charlotte had met on the world tour that was her honeymoon. Peiping was in so many ways like the Vienna she had lovingly described. Both cities were utterly devoted to their cafés and their unique cultures; both cities were bemused by the vanished glories of imperial capitals that had endured so many sieges. Both Peiping and Vienna sustained themselves with those memories, for both had been reduced from centers of continental power to impotent political symbols.

James dismissed those pointless speculations, abashed by his lapse from strict intellectual discipline. He and his shorter, paler companion on the rickety bench both wore workmen's tattered blue clothing, and both were tautly alert. They dipped their *chiao-tze* into a blend of soy-sauce, clear vinegar, and sesame oil; they listened intently to their neighbors' rough badinage. The students' and workers' accents were indistinguishable, as was their hearty pleasure in the dumplings. But the laborers bantered personal gossip and broad sexual jests, while the students muttered angrily at the implacable encroachment of the "Japanese dwarves" and anxiously discussed the fledgling alliance between the Kuomintang of Generalissimo Chiang Kai-shek and the Communist Party of Secretary-General Mao Tse-tung.

After a decade of mutual slaughter, China's chief political and military forces were again joining together to resist the invasion mounted by Tokyo. The Imperial Japanese Army had exploited China's disunity to separate Manchuria in the northeast from the Motherland and to establish the puppet regime called Manchukuo, the Land of the Manchus, under the last Ching Emperor, Hsüan Tung. They had subsequently "maintained" their treaty rights in Shanghai and routed the

Chinese defenders. All of eastern Hopei Province with its center at Peiping had been declared a demilitarized zone by the League of Nations, which, in theory, enforced the withdrawal of both Chinese and Japanese troops. In practice, the agreement rendered both Peiping and Tientsin defenseless, for the Japanese claimed the right to exercise their troops around Peiping under the terms of the Boxer Protocols imposed after the Allied Forces had relieved the siege of the Legation Quarter in 1900. Moreover, the Japanese *Kempeitai,* who were military police, intelligence operatives, and *agents provocateurs* in one, methodically subverted Chinese society.

Though naked Japanese aggression had finally compelled the Nationalists and the Communists to talk to each other again, the seeds of hatred sown in 1927 were still bearing their bitter fruit. After that disastrous year, the Communists had established scattered Soviet Areas under their rule, the largest in Kiangsi Province near Nanchang dominated by the bushy-haired agitator Mao Tse-tung, who was obsessed with raising a peasant revolt. Repeated Nationalist Extermination Campaigns had by 1934 driven the Communists to embark upon their eight-thousand-mile Long March to Shensi Province in the northwest. Only 16,000 of the 100,000 men, women and children who began the Long March reached that sparsely populated refuge. Mao Tse-tung had emerged as their chief leader, while Chou En-lai, ever flexible, served Mao Tse-tung as chairman of the new Soviet Area's Military Affairs Commission and his chief emissary to the Nationalists.

Raised to the Political Bureau that ruled the Chinese Communist Party, the labor leader Liu Shao-chi was the Commissioner for the White Areas, responsible for covert activities in the territories under Nationalist or Japanese control. His mission had been defined by Mao Tse-tung's secret directive: "Our fixed policy should be seventy percent expansion of our own power, twenty percent coping with the Kuomintang, and ten percent resisting Japan."

Like James Sekloong, whom he knew as Shih Ai-kuo, Commissioner Liu Shao-chi eavesdropped in silence and marveled at the resilience of the people of Peking. He unconsciously used the city's former name, as did the workmen and students. Through changes of name and regimes, the men and women of the city appeared unchangeable. Slow to rise to anger or to fear, their talent was to endure. Unlike the volatile students, the workmen resignedly accepted the presence of the new invaders whom they were powerless to resist. Despite some success among the students, James and his superior chafed at the slow progress of their seventy-eight-strong Agitprop group among the working masses. Even the students' indignation was diluted by the centuries-old conviction that, whatever dangers threatened or calamities occurred, Peking would remain Peking.

James wondered if he, himself, was not being infected by the stolid Northerners' complacency. He yearned for action. Though "underground work" was essential, it could not compare with commanding his own regiment during the Long March, when his decisions had meant life or death for hundreds. Besides, the police, who were infiltrated by the *Kempeitai,* harried the Communist agents in their own heavy-footed Northern fashion. Far more dangerous were the *teh-wu,* the "special duty" secret police of Chiang Kai-shek's Central Government, and their allies, the neo-Fascist Blue Shirts of the Nationalists' extreme right wing. Their pursuit was relentless, although both Mao Tse-tung and Chou En-lai were at that moment negotiating with the Nationalists at Lushan in Kiangsi Province. Telling himself that he, too, would nonetheless survive, James wiped his mouth on his sleeve and tossed a few coppers on the table.

"A reckoning of twenty-five coppers and wine money of five!" The waiter's bellow signaled the departure of the two Communist agents. "Twenty-five and a munificent five. We thank the generous gentlemen, the open-handed lords."

"A bourgeois hangover, no doubt, Comrade." Comrade Shao-chi's thin lips curled in a wry smile. "I suppose it reinforces the slave mentality, this crying out of the tip. But, I confess, I find it charming."

"I like it." James involuntarily contrasted the humane Commissioner's relaxed tolerance with the hectoring dogmatism of his former commander Lin Piao. "But I suppose it will have to go."

"Tipping, certainly," Liu Shao-chi agreed. "But not all the old ways and manners. Changing *everything* would make China un-Chinese. Throwing out the soup stock but keeping the same bones—changing the forms but not the substance—would be worse."

James smiled at his chief's use of the old classical maxim that was itself gastronomical, reflecting his people's chief passion. A strange conversation for two hunted "Communist bandits" making for a secret midnight meeting of their five chief lieutenants in a warehouse in the old Tartar City. Yet Comrade Shao-chi was like that. He was as uncompromisingly dedicated to the cause of the self-righteous zealots of the Party Control Commission, who were the Communists' own Secret Police. But the man who staked his life for his principles every moment of every day and night leavened the revolutionary struggle with welcome humor. James used the word *yu-mo* in his thoughts. It was funny that there was no native Chinese word for humor, but only the transliteration from English. Funnier still that there was a perfectly good Chinese word for funny, though, perhaps, significant that *ke-hsiao* literally meant "laughable." Although humor was an alien concept, Commissioner Liu truly possessed humor as well as compassion. Those qualities had won him a unique distinction among commissars whose nicknames were often derisory, like Eaglebeak for the hooked-nosed Lin Piao or Rubber Doll for the indestructibly compromising Chou En-lai. He was with much affection called simply Comrade Shao-chi.

The regular tramp of boots affronted the still night, and the pair blended into the shadows of the eaves overhanging the narrow *hu-tung*. Embraced by the darkness, they were virtually invisible in their dark clothing.

503

The police patrol passed unseeing. The constables carried their rifles carelessly by the slings, and the ill-fitting tunic of the sergeant in command brushed James's hand. The heavy tread of the constables' boots and the rattle of their rifle slings receded down the twisting *hutung*. Their cloth slippers silent in the heaped yellow dust, the Communist agents moved cautiously away.

Comrade Shao-chi squeezed his subordinate's arm. The tramping boots were returning along the alley. James cocked his head and, a moment later, laughed mirthlessly.

"It's rifle fire," he whispered. "Some distance away."

"Are you sure?" The civilian deferred to the soldier's experience. "Sounds like another patrol."

"No!" James answered decisively. "Rifle and machine-gun fire."

"The Japanese, no doubt. Drunk again and shooting for joy. Some joy!"

"No, not that," James insisted. "They're regular volleys. A fire-fight somewhere to the southwest."

"Ah, well," Comrade Shao-chi smiled, "the more confusion, the better for us."

The volleys were an unremitting drum-fire above the ornate arches of the *Lukouchiao* nine miles away. That structure, crowned with rows of guardian lions, was called Marco Polo Bridge after the Venetian who had come to Peking in the thirteenth century when the city, called Kambalac, was the capital of the Mongol Empire of Kublai Khan. The bridge carried the road across the broad Yungting River to the gates of the walled town of Wanping. As they had so frequently, Chinese and Japanese troops were once again clashing. The Chinese garrison defending Wanping returned the Japanese fire from the balustraded, forty-foot-thick wall. But the incident was destined to be different from other incidents.

On the balmy Sunday night, the Imperial Japanese Army had ordered a "reconnaissance in force." Private Yoshimoto Eijiro of the Guards Regiment had not returned to his barracks that evening. The Japanese captain commanding was officially charged only to find Private Yoshimoto, but his infantry company had been strengthened with three field-guns. The Imperial General Staff was determined to demonstrate Japan's power to the feckless, insolent Chinese. Lieutenant General Katsuki Kiyochi had received his orders directly from the militant new Cabinet that took office on June 5, 1937. No longer would the Japanese exercise patient restraint while the Chinese sought to heal the split between the Communists and Nationalists—and impertinently defied Japan's might.

The Emperor's infantrymen hammered on the gates with rifle butts, and the field-guns trundled into position.

"Oi, ni! . . . Kai-kai . . . Wo-men lai . . . kan-kan . . . Yi ko Jih-pen ping . . . mei-yu-la." A lieutenant screamed in pidgin Chinese at the uncomprehending sentry. "Hey, you. . . . Open . . . open. We come . . . look look. . . One piece Japanese soldier . . . have not got."

The bewildered Chinese private summoned his sergeant, who regarded the formidable Japanese array and called his lieutenant. The alarm ranged upward through the ranks, and ten minutes later the sleepy Chinese captain commanding the Wanping garrison listened to the Japanese lieutenant's half-intelligible expostulations. When their meaning finally emerged from the gabble of broken Chinese, the Nationalist captain tried to temporize.

"We'll have a look for your man just as soon as it's daylight," he offered. "I'm sure he's not here, but no one could find him in the dark anyway."

"Dzai shuo!" The Japanese lieutenant demanded, "Say again."

His temper rising, the Chinese captain shouted in pidgin Mandarin: "We look-look your soldier when come light. I know he no can be here, but anyway in dark no can find."

"Sudeni! Sudeni! Haieranakereba narain!" the Japanese captain snapped at his lieutenant. "Immediately! Immediately! We must enter!"

Obediently, the Japanese lieutenant repeated to the

dark figures on the wall: "Right now! Right now! We must come look-look. We demand . . . demand!"

"Wait till daylight." The Chinese captain's reply was equally decisive. "Then we'll search. Japanese troops may not enter Wanping."

"So be it," the Japanese captain snapped, having found his *causus belli*. His samurai sword slapping against his side, he strode into the night. His lieutenant followed, trailed by five privates carrying long Nambu rifles. The points of light twinkling from their fixed bayonets slowly receded into the enveloping gloom and were extinguished.

"Faced the dwarf bastards down this time," the Chinese captain told his officers. "Just a little firmness —and they give way."

A row of fireflies winked red in the darkness. Half a second later, the high-pitched rattle of Nambu rifles resounded against the brick wall, and the Chinese officers threw themselves down behind the parapet. A machine gun coughed in asthmatic spasms.

"Return fire," the Chinese commander shouted. "Return fire at will."

The Chinese aimed their rifles and machine guns at the winking red lights that betrayed the Japanese position. Though the troops exchanged fire for more than two hours, neither side suffered notably. The Chinese were protected by the town wall and the Japanese by the darkness. But both sides fired their volleys jubilantly. The Chinese rejoiced at finally standing up to the arrogant intruders, while the Japanese were determined to teach their opponents the folly of defying their invincible arms.

Shortly after 3:30 on the morning of July 8, 1937, the Japanese commander's tenuous patience broke. He spoke a few words, and the crump of field-guns rumbled over the crackle of small-arms fire. Within Wanping, the defenders' morale plummeted from exultation to despair. Tile roofs collapsed amid fountains of dust; terrified women shrieked; and the old town walls trembled with each explosion.

Since Chinese small arms were impotent against Japanese artillery, the Japanese marched triumphantly into the town a half-hour later. They did not find Private Yoshimoto, who had crept into his barracks just before midnight, when the engagement began. They did, however, create the pretext for further "punitive operations" to deter further Chinese armed defiance. Japanese reinforcements swarmed out of occupied Manchuria, accompanied by the tanks, heavy artillery, and motorized transport the Chinese lacked. Japanese warplanes circled virtually unchallenged over Peiping and the Western Hills. The second Sino-Japanese War had begun.

The first Chinese counterstrategy was criss-crossing Peiping's streets with trenches—not in anticipation of a last-ditch stand, but to hamper any sortie by Japanese troops from the Legation Quarter. When a detachment of cavalrymen rode out of that enclave, the Chinese opened fire, wounding one soldier and forcing the others to retire. Flush with their easy victory, the Nationalists closed in on the cavalrymen. They were more disappointed than dismayed to find that they had repelled the U.S. Horse Marines who had guarded the American Legation since the Boxer Rising.

No further action took place within Peiping. Instead, Japanese troops captured railway junctions to encircle the city before slaughtering a battalion of the Thirty-seventh Division at Nanyüan, fifteen miles away. The commanding general of the Chinese XXIX Army Corps withdrew from the city on July 26, 1937. Rather than fight a hopeless battle and risk destruction of the ancient capital's architectural and artistic treasures, the Chinese surrendered Peiping to the Japanese without resistance.

Two days later Tientsin fell. With its chief port in Japanese hands, North China was indefensible. The few remaining Chinese who still advocated compromise were shouted down. After a forty-two-year truce, roiled by armed clashes and diplomatic confrontations, China and Japan were again formally at war. Few of the Western statesmen and journalists who deprecated the outbreak of hostilities realized that World War II had just begun on the plains of North China. The leaders of both Chinese factions, Nationalists and Communists alike, prepared for a protracted war of attrition, which, they were confident, would eventually end with Japanese exhaustion or with Japanese defeat by Western intervention.

Colonel James Sekloong and Commissioner Liu Shao-chi were indistinguishable amid the few blue-clad spectators who, blank-faced and silent, watched the triumphant entry of the imperial Japanese Army into Peiping on August 8, 1937. Their underground apparatus had been expanded to more than three hundred by the influx of ardent students after the belated formal Nationalist–Communist agreement to unite against the Japanese. Their immediate objective was rallying the people of North China to subvert Japanese military rule. Their long-term objective, as defined by Mao Tse-tung, was unchanged: to increase their own strength and to infiltrate every layer of society, particularly governmental organs and essential services like water and electricity, in order to facilitate the ultimate Communist conquest of China.

"It's come at last," Comrade Shao-chi mused. "The final era of imperialistic wars Lenin foresaw. The capitalists will destroy each other—and the masses will pick up the pieces. Within a decade, the masses will rule China."

"Under the leadership of the Communist Party, of course, Comrade!"

James reassured himself by reaffirming the dogma that had sustained the Communists through the bleak decade following the terrible year 1927. The professional soldier, who had fought against the overwhelming Nationalist Extermination Campaigns, was less optimistic than his civilian chief as to the "inevitable outcome" of the new struggle against even greater odds. A worm of doubt still gnawed at his faith in the Marxist-Leninist doctrines to which he had pledged his life. He knew that serving the just revolutionary cause was the only possible occupation for a patriot. Yet he wondered if the sages Karl Marx and V. I. Lenin had adequately allowed for the irrepressible human factor. He had seen his comrades contend for personal power within the Communist hierarchy as ferociously as they fought their Nationalist enemies. Even a dedicated Communist was, James knew, not a secular saint, but a human being. Though they strove for the masses' welfare and for a strong China, too many good Communists were obsessed with attaining and using power—often through betrayal or assassination. Moscow, the holy city of Marxism-Leninism, was itself no different. During the months he spent there with Chou En-lai after their escape from Canton, James had found that even the leaders of the Comintern struggled unceasingly against each other for power and position.

"We shall prevail, of course," James repeated.

"Of course," Comrade Shao-chi replied negligently. "Who else is there?"

His chief's absolute confidence was irritating, since James suspected that Liu Shao-chi, too, was attempting to reassure himself. James was, moreover, worried about his wife, Lu Ping, the half-educated daughter of a bankrupt small-holder whom he had married in the Kiangsi Soviet Area in 1929 without informing his parents.

Ai-jen, "loved person," was the Party's new term, though James thought of Ping as *chi-tze,* "wife." Their "revolutionary relationship" was, however, more responsive to the Party's demands than to their personal needs. Lu Ping seemed untroubled by their prolonged separations. Even in bed, when they could whisper unheard, she expressed no particular concern at their own infrequent meetings or her own separation from their young son. Though he had renounced Catholicism upon joining the Party, James yearned for a normal, monogamous family life. Unlike Liu Shao-chi, he could neither take casual mistresses nor divorce one wife to marry another as personal desire and political expediency directed. The Party encouraged sexual flexibility, though it did not absolutely require such demonstrations of a good Communist's liberation from "bourgeois inhibitions." But Lu Ping had given her body and her spirit wholly to the Communist Party that had rescued her from the servitude of an arranged marriage to a small landholder. She sometimes seemed to rejoice in their disrupted private life as further proof of her revolutionary dedication, and sometimes, he feared, she slept with other male comrades to prove her "revolutionary emancipation."

James deliberately swept his mind clear of personal concerns. Self-discipline was essential to a field officer when hundreds of lives hung on his decisions. Locking away his private fears was equally essential to survival in the half-world of the underground movement. A moment's abstraction could lead to a fatal error, the minor indiscretion that would unmask him to the Japanese or the Nationalists. When Comrade Shao-chi and he entered the eating shop called the Old Dumpling King, James's mind was totally concentrated on their coming meeting with their eight cell leaders.

The eating shop was a convenient rendezvous, since men came and went as they pleased for an obvious purpose. The meeting on July 7, the night of the Marco Polo Bridge Incident, had been scheduled for a warehouse in the old Tartar City to avoid establishing a regular routine the police might mark. However, Comrade Shao-chi had judged the Old Dumpling King safe again on August 8 as the Japanese marched into Peiping and massed for a new assault on Shanghai.

The conspirators slipped into the atmosphere redolent of spices and cooking oil singly or in pairs. Some lingered over their *chiao-tze* before vanishing into the loft above the shop. Others hurried through the grimy backdoor toward the noisome latrine in the backyard. An hour passed before all ten men had climbed the rickety outside stairway to the loft, leaving two student lookouts at the table at the foot of the interior stairway.

The conspirators' features were obscured by the darkness in the loft. Despite the 80° heat, some also pulled scarves over their faces. Comrade Shao-chi preferred discomfort to rashness and further insisted that all his agents use false names. James was known as Old

Tang, and he called his leader Mr. Wu. If any one were arrested, he could not reveal the other conspirators' identity under torture.

"You've all seen the latest directive," the pale Commissioner said. "The Anti-Japanese War has begun, and we are joining the Kuomintang in a United Front. Today we'll go over each group's assignment."

A slight, bespectacled youth gestured for attention. James knew the Peking University student he had himself recruited and given the incongruous Party-name *Hsiao Hu,* Small Tiger.

"Can we trust the Nationalists, Mr. Wu?" the student asked. "Won't they turn on us after we've beaten off the Japanese dwarves?"

"Of course we can't trust the Nationalists," Comrade Shao-chi replied. "Can they trust us? But we must work with them—for the moment."

"And, Small Tiger," James added sardonically, "don't worry too much about what happens *after* our victory. There'll be lots of time to worry later, unless the dwarves withdraw. And that's as likely as a hen's crowing."

"I must stress one point," Comrade Shao-chi added. "Our ultimate objective is unchanged. We *will* destroy the Nationalists. We *will* liberate the Chinese people. The masses *will* rule under the guidance of the Communist Party and the leadership of the proletariat. For the moment, we fight the Japanese to overthrow the Nationalist exploiters."

"I understand," Small Tiger acknowledged. "Your instructions, Mr. Wu?"

"The general line is: expansion, infiltration, intelligence gathering, and disruption—in that order. We must prepare for the struggle against the Kuomintang by strengthening ourselves and struggling against the Japanese. Your group, Small Tiger, will collaborate with the dwarves, serving them as interpreters, informants, technicians, clerks, and . . ."

"Collaborate!" The student-leader protested vehemently. "I'd rather be a guerrilla in the hills than collaborate."

"I said collaborate." Comrade Shao-chi's low voice was implacable. "Infiltration is a primary mission. Your group will first infiltrate and subsequently execute specific instructions as received. You have sworn to obey the Party's orders—and the Party has determined that your proper role is pretended collaboration."

James mopped his perspiring face with a hand towel to conceal a smile. He had suggested Small Tiger's assignment—and anticipated his protests. The veteran colonel was amused by his mental picture of the weedy young student scrambling over the hills carrying a rifle he could not use among hardy peasant guerrillas who would walk him into the ground within hours.

"Each man will serve to the utmost of his ability according to his qualifications," Comrade Shao-chi continued inexorably. "Old Tang will remain my deputy, while organizing and commanding sapper squads. He is best qualified to carry out principled terrorism and assassination. Small Tiger's group will . . ."

The clatter of breaking dishes and voices raised in shrill dispute rose through the cracks between the floor boards. As arranged, the loud quarrel between the lookouts warned of a raid. Comrade Shao-chi broke off in midsentence, and the conspirators poured down the rickety outside stairway as heavy boots clattered on the interior stairs. After waiting twelve seconds, James was the fifth man through the door. Clambering over the backyard wall, he glanced back. Four cell leaders were at his heels, but Small Tiger was kicking in the grip of a stout Peiping policeman. A squat Japanese *Kempeitai* sergeant was raising his pistol. Small Tiger, James reflected wryly, had begun his collaboration earlier than planned. He could be invaluable if he followed his instructions and yielded—after convincing resistance—to the *Kempeitai*'s demands that he become *their* double agent.

The *Kempei*'s pistol cracked. A gust tugged at James's left shoulder as he tumbled over the wall. Racing for the maze of *hu-tungs,* he clapped his hand to his shoulder. His palm was red and sticky. The bullet's impact had numbed his nerves, and he felt no pain. He automatically followed the escape route mapped in his mind. Communist Colonel James Sekloong's personal war against the invaders had begun—with first blood to the Japanese.

Nationalist General Thomas Sekloong barely noted the formal Japanese occupation of Peiping. The High Command had already written off the city, and he was overwhelmed by the volume of papers passing across his desk. Following the XXIX Army Corps' withdrawal from Peiping, Generalissimo Chiang Kai-shek's Military Secretariat was obsessed with the impending threat to Shanghai, the Orient's largest city.

After their rapid victory in North China, the exultant Imperial General Staff in Tokyo confidently predicted that all China would be conquered in three months' time. The Japanese were convinced that the Nanking Government would be incapable of coherent resistance when it was deprived of financial sustenance and its trade was choked by the loss of the cosmopolitan port on the mudflats of the Yangtze River. The conquest of Shanghai would shatter the Nationalists and force the Generalissimo to accept Tokyo's stringent terms for peace.

Most Japanese officers were wildly ebullient. The pendulum that governed the psychological life of their manic-depressive nation was swinging high. But some staff officers reexamined their projection that their "lightning-storm attack" would sweep across China within three months. Negotiations between Communists and Nationalists to implement their prior agreement in principle to form an Anti-Japanese United Front were inching toward success. If the contending Chinese parties actually stopped fighting each other, Tokyo feared its "lightning storm" would be delayed—and sparse Japanese resources were already overcommitted. Recognizing that it could not sustain a protracted campaign on the vast Chinese mainland, the Japanese command ordered a swift, decisive stroke. The preemptive attack on Shanghai would not only paralyze the Nationalists. It would undermine the Nationalist–Communist rapprochement and insure that the enemy remained divided.

The same urgency dominated Thomas Sekloong's thoughts as he studied the map of the Japanese build-up around Shanghai at 8:15 on the morning of August 17, 1937. He was scheduled to brief the Generalissimo in fifteen minutes. At thirty-two, Thomas was trim in a high-collared khaki tunic crossed by a gleaming Sam Browne belt, and the two gold stars of a major general (junior grade) shone on his shoulder straps.

He owed his rapid advancement to both the Generalissimo's personal preferment and the Sekloongs' influence. Promotion in the National Army depended more upon connections, the traditional Confucian *kwan-hsi,* than upon ability or achievement. Thomas was wholly Chiang Kai-shek's man, one of the "modern officers" the Generalissimo had promoted rapidly because of their personal loyalty to himself. Most were Whampoa graduates, the elite core of the armies the Generalissimo was building to grind down the Communists and the remaining warlords, the grand design he had been forced to postpone by the Japanese assault. Their unquestioning allegiance made those officers at least as vital to their commander as his three elite divisions, which were still trained by German advisers although the Nationalists were fighting Adolf Hitler's allies, the Japanese.

His southern General further valued the young Major General because he was a southerner. Thomas's Cantonese origins were apparent in his dark, intent features, which hinted of his European blood only in the slight arch of his nose and the brown tinge of his thinning hair. As Deputy Military Secretary to the Generalissimo, he was the exemplar of the new China his chief envisioned. Alert, disciplined, and trained in Western techniques, he nonetheless retained the Confucian virtues of absolute loyalty and obedience to his superiors. Even his devout Catholicism worked in his favor, for the Generalissimo, himself a Methodist convert, was deeply impressed by the moral force Christianity bestowed upon its adherents. Yet Thomas Sekloong was in reality no more than a single brick in a fragile façade made up of a few thousand Western-oriented officers and bureaucrats and buttressed by, at most, a half-dozen effective infantry divisions. Behind that facade lay the immemorial China, conservative in its thinking, traditional in its customs, divided by regional feeling, and grandly disunited. If the Japanese cracked the façade, they could dominate and exploit the inchoate mass of China.

At 8:26, Thomas again checked his papers and the wall map of the Shanghai area where cabalistic signs indited by junior officers showed the disposition of friendly and enemy forces. Just fifteen seconds before the stroke of 8:30, he rose and stood stiffly to attention. The door opened, and the Generalissimo entered alone.

"Sit down, *Tom*. Sit down." Chiang Kai-shek smiled, and the skin drew taut over his high cheekbones. His black-brush mustache fluttered on his long upper lip as he sank into the green-plush easy-chair. Thomas Sekloong saw that the General was in good humor and decided to reinforce that mood before conveying information that might irritate his chief. He had learned the courtier's art of pleasing by offering good news with a flourish before communicating bad news in subdued tones.

"Good morning, Your Excellency," he said. "Shall I deal with the Shanghai front first?"

"*Hao! Hao!*" the Generalissimo replied with his habitual formula. "Good! Good!"

"The Eighty-seventh and Eighty-eighth Divisions are holding firm—here, here, and here." The pointer in Thomas's hand hovered over the wall map, alighting momentarily on the blue shading indicating the Chinese positions. "The Japanese are pushing—here and here. No action larger than platoon size. Intelligence feels the Japanese were surprised by the determination of our first resistance. They are not moving with their customary dash and aggressiveness. They apparently expected Shanghai to be as easy to crack as Peiping."

"Hao! Hao!" the Generalissimo repeated. "Good! Good! I planned that. What else significant in the military picture?"

"It's little changed, Sir." Thomas ventured onto shaky ground. "As you anticipated, the dwarves are bringing in ground reinforcements. In addition, two cruisers and six destroyers of their China Fleet are steaming toward Shanghai. Their bomber bases display unusual activity. Intelligence feels they're building up their air strength and will soon bomb Shanghai. But the bombers must make long flights over our territory from their northern air fields. No precise figures on air yet."

"As I anticipated, *Tom*," the Generalissimo mused. "An order of the day to the Eighty-seventh and the Eighty-eighth: Tell them I am proud of their valor— and I count upon them to fight to the death."

"Sir, Operations recommends that we alert the Divisions' Commanding Generals to implement Plan Phoenix within the next two weeks."

"Phoenix? You mean withdrawal?" Chiang snapped. "We will *not* withdraw. The Eighty-seventh and the Eighty-eighth *must* hold."

"The Generals understand, Your Excellency," Thomas persisted, his tone deliberately neutral. "But Operations warns that our position is untenable in the long run and fears we could lose both divisions. Your pardon, Sir. I have been asked to recall to the Generalissimo that those divisions are the core of our loyal Central Government forces."

"They will hold until *I* say otherwise." Chiang Kai-shek's lips compressed resolutely. "Hold until *I* give leave to withdraw. If they retreat after token resistance, I cannot unify the country behind me—and the dwarves will be even more dangerous, drunk with their easy victories. You understand, *Tom*, I *must* hazard those units. They are expendable."

"Yes, Sir. I shall draft the signal for your approval." Thomas paused in perplexity and rubbed the bridge of his nose; he was caught between his near adulation for his chief's genius and the training that required him to inform the Generalissimo fully. "I must also tell you that the German advisers recommend preparation for withdrawal. The Cabinet has also expressed anxiety."

"*I* command, *I*—not the Germans or the Cabinet!"

Chiang Kai-shek's cheeks mottled with rage, and Thomas braced for an explosion of wrath. But the Generalissimo's rage subsided as abruptly as it had risen.

"I command," he said meditatively, "and I shall do so until we triumph—or I am removed. No more resignations, you understand. I shall not resign again. If the politicians turn against me, this time they must throw me out. Only I can save China."

"Yes, Sir," Thomas replied cautiously. "And the Communists? What are we to say to them?"

"Why," Chiang smiled broadly, "we'll accept their terms—in the spirit in which they're offered. Let them believe, if they're foolish enough, that we're foolish enough to believe them. Do you think for an instant they'll do as they say? Will they *really* put their armed forces under my command and subordinate their Soviet Government to the National Government?"

"No, Sir," Thomas replied. "But why, then, public collaboration with the Communists?"

"Because I have no choice. Because they have no choice. We are fighting the Japanese, but the prize is control of China. The people demand resistance to the Japanese. We must show that we can fight better than the Communists."

"And afterward, Sir?"

"Not afterward, but *now* we must maintain our vigilance. The troops blockading the Red Areas will resist the Japanese—when they encounter the Japanese. But their primary mission remains unaltered—holding the Communist bandits. We must destroy the Communists. The Japanese are a disease of the skin, painful, irritating, and disfiguring, but not mortal. The Communists are a cancer of the bowel, a mortal affliction. We shall let the cancer ripen, then cut it out. When we have destroyed the Communists, the Japanese will be no threat."

For the first time in five years, Harry Sekloong came

to Hong Kong to participate in the family councils. The Sekloongs were preparing for the readjustments required by his father's impending retirement as comprador for Derwent, Hayes and Company. Just past eighty-five in late June 1938, Sir Jonathan was finally relinquishing the compradorship to which he had clung so long. Even creating an independent commercial empire that rivaled the Wheatleys, the Old Gentleman had not wished to see another man occupy the position that had been his for more than fifty years. If his father had been a lesser, weaker man, Harry reflected, he might have been moved primarily by the emotional security represented by the title that had for more than a decade been largely ceremonial. But Sir Jonathan was *the* Sekloong, a major power in his own right. His son finally concluded that he had hesitated to relinquish compradorship for two quite different reasons: malice and patriotism.

"Will the old bastard never die?" Iain Wheatley, himself sixty-five years old, had exclaimed over a last unneeded brandy in the sacrosanct Hong Kong Club six months earlier. The waiter told the barman, who told the doorman, who passed the word to a chauffeur, and Sir Jonathan was informed of the two-tiered insult the next morning.

"Yes, he will die, but not quite yet, my esteemed step-brother," Sir Jonathan had murmured to himself. "Not quite yet."

However, a force stronger than righteous malice had kept Sir Jonathan from giving up his formal connection with the firm his grandfather Kwok Lee-chin had virtually created. As long as he was the comprador, the Wheatleys were constrained. They could not overtly seek to destroy the Sekloong empire, a purpose almost as important to Iain Wheatley as increasing Derwent's swollen profits. Neither could Iain cement his alliance with Mitsubishi, which was chief among the great Japanese conglomerates called *zaibatsu*, though Derwent's branches in China and Southeast Asia were already cooperating closely with the Japanese. Iain Wheatley had picked his winner in the Sino-Japanese War. He was waiting only for Sir Jonathan's departure to place all his resources behind the Japanese war effort. It was, after all, only good business.

"But, Father," Mary argued, "by retiring now, you can veto—or even force—Iain's choice of your successor. If you wait too long, he'll be free to pick his own man—and there'll be no check whatsoever on his alliance with Mitsubishi."

Sir Jonathan had yielded in principle, but had delayed his formal resignation for three months. Mary surmised that leaving Derwent's was, in his eyes, a symbolic surrender to death, the foe that stalked him during his sleepless nights.

"He doesn't fear death," Charles replied. "He's ready for death, and he knows he'll be reunited with Mother. Despite all the concubines over all the years, he always loved her best. And he's not used to giving in. Besides, even his death must serve his own purposes. He'll die when *he* decides to die."

Harry smiled appreciatively at Charles's perception of their father's motivation. The Old Gentleman had become a living symbol of stubborn, undefeatable China. He would, indeed, go when he was quite ready, and he might not be ready until China had overcome this latest and most dangerous menace—the Japanese. But the Old Gentleman's resolute will would be tested to the utmost by that endurance contest. Harry's own certainties had been shaken by the torments of the decade from 1927 to 1937 and by the anguish of the past year, but he was sure of one thing. It would be a long war, an agonizingly long and destructive war unless an act of God ended the conflict.

"The Japanese have done something very foolish this time," Mary contended. "The more strenuously they pursue their foolishness, the worse off they'll be."

Harry looked appraisingly at his sister-in-law. At fifty-seven, Mary Philippa Osgood Sekloong was not merely what the gallant Edwardians would have described, with respect for past glories and admiration for their preservation, as a "damned handsome woman." Always beautiful in his eyes, although she had never

519

been conventionally pretty, she had become more beautiful. Her violet eyes had grown softer as experience taught her compassion. Her red-gold hair still glowed as brilliantly, perhaps aided by discreet artifice. Despite her many years in the debilitating subtropical climate, her skin was still fair and virtually unlined. The few strokes time had drawn upon the canvas of her face accentuated her strongly molded cheekbones and jawline. Behind her beauty lay the assured self-confidence of a woman who had learned not merely to command herself, as well as others, but had made herself mistress of an alien world.

Mary still stirred him physically and emotionally as his wife Mayling had never done, and he was almost equally drawn by her intellectual powers. He acknowledged that she was at least his intellectual equal and, perhaps, his superior. Mary's strong-minded perception was stiffened by her pragmatic North Country common sense, while he knew himself a dreamer reluctantly compelled to play the man of action.

Nevertheless, he could not share her facile confidence regarding the Japanese threat. Her attitude reflected the detached optimism of the treaty-ports, where the foreigners who called themselves Old China Hands contemplated the nation through plate-glass that shut out both the tumult and the stench of the conflict. For more than thirty years a participant, Harry knew the sour-sweet reek of corruption and fear, the agonizing shrieks of strife and terror as no spectator could. Emotionally exhausted, he was on the verge of despair. Even should the Chinese ultimately triumph, he recognized that a nation already torn by a century of civil wars would be decimated by another decade of foreign war. His imagination could not conceive of scenes more grisly or more pathetic than those he had already seen, but his analytical intelligence warned him that greater tragedies must inevitably occur.

One of the worst wounds had been self-inflicted. Desperate in early June 1938, the Nationalists had cut the dikes restraining the Yellow River, which was called without hyperbole China's Sorrow. Two hundred thousand had drowned when more than thirty thousand square miles were inundated. Eight million had been rendered homeless, their homes, livestock, and meager possessions swept away. The prelude to that fearful and unsuccessful attempt to stem the Japanese tide by a counterflood of raging waters had been almost as scarifying. Harry and his chief Wang Ching-wei, once again at odds with Chiang Kai-shek in the intrigues of the Kuomintang, had watched the inexorable tragedy, powerless to affect its course.

After a three-month siege, Shanghai had fallen in mid-November 1937, and the Japanese had immediately driven northwest toward Nanking. Each time the Germans relayed new peace proposals from Tokyo, Wang Ching-wei, once more prominent in the councils of the Kuomintang, had urged their acceptance. Since neither he nor Harry could discern any prospect of a Chinese victory, they preferred to negotiate regarding those harsh conditions. They were even prepared to surrender a portion of China's sovereignty, rather than continue a conflict that must inflict fearful suffering; destroy China's armies; bring her to her knees—and render her incapable of negotiating at all. The warhawks in the Generalissimo's entourage had played on Chiang Kai-shek's irresolution to prevent any positive act—of either acceptance or rejection. The Communists had also firmly opposed peace talks, since a long war of attrition would weaken the Nationalists and strengthen their own forces for the ultimate conquest of China. To demonstrate that Chinese could defeat Japanese, Mao Tse-tung diverted some of his units from the confrontation with the Nationalists. At Pinghsing Pass in northern Shansi Province in late 1937, General Lin Piao ambushed a full Japanese brigade to give the Chinese their first clear victory and arouse hopes of greater victories.

Suddenly it was too late for anything but war. The Japanese had themselves destroyed any prospect of negotiation, and China was doomed to fight alone, deprived of German assistance, while the Western powers sold Japan oil and steel, the indispensable sinews of modern warfare.

On December 12, 1937, the Imperial Army took Nanking, and the mixed Japanese–Korean force indulged for three days in a mass orgy, which was disingenuously described by one Tokyo apologist as "a few regrettable, but fortunately minor transgressions occasioned by the soldiers' justified high spirits." No such devil's festival of slaughter, rapine, and devastation had actually occurred since the Middle Ages. With calculated cruelty more atrocious than spontaneous medieval brutality, Japanese officers ignored their code of chivalry, which they called *bushido*, the "way of the warrior." Their soldiers wreaked vengeance upon the people of China's capital for the hardships, the hazards, and the loneliness of war. During three days of unrestrained looting, the drunken Imperial troops killed more than a hundred thousand civilians. No female older than six was too tender to avoid repeated rape, and none under seventy was too grizzled for violation. Soldiers and male civilians were impaled upon Japanese bayonets, thankful for the release of death after hours of brutal torture.

Fleeing in one of the last motor-vehicles to leave the burning city, Harry Sekloong coughed in the searing acrid smoke of the flaming oil tanks. Tears streamed down his begrimed cheeks from his inflamed eyes, and his automobile swerved to avoid disemboweled corpses. On the southern bank of the Yangtze, James Sekloong's guerrilla unit peered incredulously at the gray pall over the Southern Capital. Like his father, James wept—and swore himself to revenge.

Later, after the war when they learned of the deliberate atrocity, the Japanese people were appalled at the deeds of their sons, fathers, and husbands. And other peoples still cared. The relative innocence of mankind in 1937 was demonstrated by world-wide revulsion against the Rape of Nanking. In later years, the "Nanking Incident" was to appear no more than simple barbarism—after the Germans' methodical extermination of more than ten million Europeans, after the American nuclear holocausts consumed Hiroshima and Nagasaki. But in 1937 the horrors of Nanking shocked the world and hardened the Chinese will to fight. Peace was no longer possible on any terms.

Although the Generalissimo shifted his capital to Chungking, he himself remained in Wuhan, the strategic and industrial plexus of Central China, to direct the continuing resistance. Chiang Kai-shek encouraged the Chinese people to migrate *en masse* to the security of the Szechwan Basin in the far southwest behind jagged mountain ranges pierced only by precipitous passes and the gorges of the Yangtze. Tens of millions responded. Entire schools, universities, factories, and even towns trekked thousands of miles into the interior by foot, bicycle, ox cart, ramshackle bus or truck, and manhauled junk. Half China was on the move, and all China would fight.

Determined to occupy all Eastern China, the Japanese pressed on. From Nanking to the south and Peking to the north their columns converged on Hsüchow, three hundred and twenty miles northwest of Shanghai, and the Chinese held heroically as they had held at Shanghai. In early April 1938 Nationalist troops routed 30,000 Japanese near Hsüchow, and all China rejoiced. The victory was far greater than Lin Piao's triumph at Pinghsing Pass, but it was a fleeting victory. In mid-May the Chinese evacuated Hsüchow. The Generalissimo had chosen to preserve his strength rather than sacrifice tens of thousands of his best troops in a hopeless fight. Finally in early June 1938 the dikes restraining the rising Yellow River were breached.

Harry Sekloong was drawn irresistibly to the deluge. Secure in an army motorboat, he felt himself a despicable voyeur as the swirling waters, heavy with yellow silt, surged over the millet sprouts. The soldiers of his crew pulled thirty-eight men and women into the small boat. Many peasants had refused to believe the authorities' hasty warning, and many more had received no warning. Drowned pigs and dogs were swept under the boat's blunt bows, and eight bullocks thrashed past, their pleading eyes rolling in round, red-rimmed sockets. The bullocks' pitiful lowing receded, then ceased when a new surge of flood-waters overwhelmed them. Thatched roofs smashed against the boat's planks, and the craft rocked violently, almost overturning. Wooden houses drifted past with families clinging to their sides. A screaming youth desperately struck out for the boat, and the coxswain altered course to avoid him. One more body would swamp the craft. Not only more intelligent but tougher than their animals, the farmers were the last to perish. When the boat finally turned toward the distant land, its diesel engine sputtering black smoke, some twenty corpses were already bobbing in its wake.

Harry Sekloong suspected the bitter truth when he flew into Hong Kong in late June 1938: The mortal sacrifice was to delay the Japanese for no more than a few months. At first, the self-satisfaction of the placid Crown Colony was, therefore, violently abhorrent to him. After a few days, he sank into the cushioned comfort of Sekloong Manor, gratefully accepting the assiduous attention of the servants. When he could, he refused to think about his sons. He had learned circuitously that James was a Communist underground agent in the Japanese-occupied areas, while twenty-six-year-old Jason, a captain in the Nationalist artillery, was stationed at Wuhan, the strategic heart of Central China that was obviously the next Japanese objective. His wife Mayling had established herself in the safety of the French Concession of Shanghai, where she occupied herself with gossip and self-adornment.

Harry Sekloong attended the banquets and receptions attendant upon his father's retirement with no more zest than an automaton. He could muster little interest in discussions of the future of the Sekloong empire at a moment when China was in mortal peril. His chief interest was in collecting funds for the war effort. But even that activity was semi-automatic, for he had lost almost all confidence in China's ability to withstand the Japanese onslaught. At fifty-eight, Harry had spent more than half his life in the arduous service of the

Chinese revolution. He had wheedled and schemed and killed, hoping always that the next year would see the fruition of his dreams. Instead he had witnessed internal strife and mass suffering greater than any inflicted by the Manchus. He was reluctantly becoming convinced that the revolution would never be completed. Having lost his own resilience, Harry felt that China had lost hers.

He saw little point in disputing Mary's unfounded optimism and none in imposing his forebodings on Sir Jonathan. Totally confident, his father had unhesitatingly contributed an additional £1 million to the Nationalist war chest. The Old Gentleman's inability to despair had sustained his progress from a twelve-year-old runner for a Macao coolie barracoon to the absolute ruler of a vast commercial empire. The disillusioned Harry attributed his own exhaustion to the nation, while his indomitable father could no more conceive of China's falling to her enemies than he himself could give in to fate.

But the Old Gentleman was still capable of scorn and anger. Sir Jonathan raged contemptuously when in August 1938 Reuter reported that British Prime Minister Neville Chamberlain had "attained peace with honor" by agreeing to the Nazis' occupation of Czechoslovakia's German-speaking Sudetenland. Still reposing great faith in Britain, he had believed that Chamberlain would either face Adolf Hitler down or go to war. Either action would have helped China—the one by cutting Japan's European ally down to size, the other by bringing on a general war in which Britain and France were compelled to ally themselves with China. Despite that disappointment, Sir Jonathan's confidence in England was still strong when, on September 18, 1938, he embarked on Charles's yacht, *Regina Pacis,* for a long cruise through the Pacific Islands to celebrate his reluctant retirement from Derwent, Hayes and Company.

"It's my last chance, boys!" He addressed his middle-aged sons as if they were still youths. "Within a year, at most two, all Asia will be in flames. A total war is coming, a world-wide war. It will make the Great

War seem like a skirmish between two bands of brigands, but it *will* save China."

"The old man's getting senile," Harry told Charles and Mary while, with Jonnie and his wife Sarah, they watched the *Regina Pacis* spread her white sails after chugging away from Blake Pier. "The British, the Americans, the Germans—they're all helping the Japs one way or another. Fat chance of their coming to China's assistance."

"I've known the old man to be wrong," Charles replied. "But never that far wrong. Just wait and see."

"Of course there'll be war, Uncle Harry." Jonnie, just commissioned a lieutenant in the Hong Kong Volunteer Defense Force, offered an incisive refutation. "War in Europe, as well as Asia. The European powers and America can't let the Japanese use China as a base to conquer the raw materials and markets of Southeast Asia. Besides, Hitler's sure to go too far."

"Out of the mouths of babes." Harry mocked his thirty-six-year-old nephew's upper-class accent and British certainty. "Didn't they teach you logic at Stonyhurst? No nation will help China unless it's forced to—and the Japanese are too clever to force them."

"Were they too clever to bomb Shanghai and rape Nanking?" Sarah Haleevie Sekloong asked quietly. "Was Hitler too clever to alert the world by his persecution of the Jews? They all make mistakes. All tyrants do—and then . . ."

Harry's despair was too deep to be ameliorated by either generation's optimism. Neither his father's instinctive confidence nor his nephew and niece's cogent reasoning could move him. Although he was bringing back almost £5 million for the Nationalists' war chest, his mood was somber on October 5, 1938, when he boarded a DC-2 of the China National Aircraft Corporation at Kaitak for the long hedge-hopping flight to Chungking, eight hundred miles distant over mountain ranges and river gorges. Nor did the atmosphere of the wartime capital in the early winter of 1938–1939 allay his settled depression. The vastly overcrowded, squalid city hung from cliffs above the confluence of the Yangtze and the Chialing Rivers. The perpetual fog seeped into his bones and chilled his spirit. Mildly annoyed at his wife's refusal to join him, he was deeply distressed by the virtual powerlessness of his leader. Wang Ching-wei, trusted by neither side, had been shelved with a ceremonial title by the new Nationalist–Communist alliance. His remaining influence was largely moral, but the Communists were winning over the intellectuals who had followed Wang Ching-wei as the legitimate political heir of Sun Yat-sen.

Besides, the news was bad. The Generalissimo was determined to hold Wuhan, since loss of that industrial center would deliver all Central and Eastern China to the Japanese. But twelve Japanese divisions were closing in. Though the Chinese fought well, they were inexorably pushed back—and Harry's son Jason commanded a field-artillery battery athwart the approaches to Wuhan. The only consolation for patriots was the slow pace of the Japanese advance, despite their overwhelming air superiority. The Nationalists finally possessed the nucleus of the air force Harry had envisioned decades earlier, but their few planes were too old and their few pilots too ill-trained to oppose fleets of Japanese bombers.

Harry Sekloong was cast into the furthest depths of despair, the nadir of his life, on December 3, 1938. A formal note from the National Defense Mobilization Board coldly expressed official regrets at the "death in action of Captain Shih Chieh-hsiang." Harry wept in his bedroom, wept as he had not wept since fleeing from the rape of Nanking. Undemanding Jason had never possessed the spirit of James, the son his father could never claim. But his younger son had been amiable, loving, and obedient—perhaps too obedient. He had amiably agreed that he would, as his father desired, serve the revolution by becoming a professional soldier. Jason's own inclination, Harry suspected, was toward literary scholarship, but he had never questioned his father's wishes. Harry's grief was intensified by merciless self-reproach. He had, he realized, contrived his son Jason's death.

Harry Sekloong could speak of his sorrows only with Wang Ching-wei. But his leader was unable to offer him consolation. Instead, Wang reluctantly dealt Harry another paralyzing blow. Jason, he had learned, had not been killed in action, but had been executed by the Generalissimo's direct order. He was charged with abandoning his guns under Japanese attack, Wang said, though he had actually received orders to evacuate his position.

"Chiang Kai-shek had to save the face of *his* general, the man who gave the order," Harry's mentor explained. "Your son was the sacrificial goat—largely, I fear, because he was *your* son."

Harry was stunned by the callous, self-serving brutality of the faithless Generalissimo. He instinctively grasped the enormity Wang Ching-wei hesitated to put into words. Jason's selection for execution over many other officers was undoubtedly due to his parentage. By executing Harry Sekloong's son, the court-martial had struck not only at his father, but at his father's leader, Wang Ching-wei, who was the Generalissimo's chief rival. Harry Sekloong's own actions, his lifelong dedication to China, had truly killed his son.

"Do you want to talk now?" Wang Ching-wei asked. "He was a good boy."

"Brooding won't bring him back," Harry answered with deliberate calm. "What business do we have?"

"Prince Konoye's Six Principles of November third," Wang said. "I've been thinking about them. I believe they could be a basis for peace."

"I'm ready for *anything* that'll bring peace," Harry replied. "I'm tired . . . bone-weary of killing. It's been going on forever, it seems. Why should men die for the tyrant Chiang? Chinese must stop dying for nothing!"

Harry Sekloong knew as well as Wang Ching-wei the Japanese Prime Minister's proposals for a "New Order for East Asia" that would create an "Asia for the Asiatics." The concept was attractive, and he himself could give greater faith to Premier Konoye, who had a personal interest in ending the fighting and the drain upon Japan's resources, than he could to Generalissimo Chiang, who had a personal interest in prolonging the war in order to enhance his personal power. Konoye had suggested that China and Japan end their war: for the purposes of jointly seeking peace and amity throughout Asia; defending themselves against Communism; and initiating close economic cooperation. The Japanese foresaw not only stability and a renaissance of Asiatic culture, but the eventual expulsion of foreign influences from Asia.

"You remember," Wang Ching-wei persisted, "Dr. Sun Yat-sen said in 1924 that peace in Asia *must* be based upon Sino-Japanese cooperation, that Japan's new strength gave hope to *all* Asiatics for freedom from Western domination. I'd like to test Konoye's new proposal, but I find little support here. Nonetheless, I'd like to test it."

"Nothing could be worse than our present situation," Harry shrugged. "Why not?"

The late afternoon of March 7, 1939, was cold and rainy in Japanese-occupied Nanking, the seat of the newly established Provisional Government of the Republic of China. The gray weather intensified the bleak joylessness of the man who occupied the ornate office of Prime Minister of that powerless government. Nonetheless, Harry Sekloong, having made his choice, was laboring to close the breach between Japanese and Chinese. While his chief Wang Ching-wei, President-designate of the formal regime still in the egg of time, negotiated with the Japanese and spoke to public meetings, Harry struggled with the administrative tasks of creating an effective government. He was not happy, but he was busy, and his wife Mayling, temporarily wrenched from her self-absorption by Jason's death, had joined him in the mansion overlooking the Yangtze in Nanking's fashionable Northwest District near the I Chiang Gate. Harry found the Japanese often overbearing and frequently intractable, but he bridled his resentment in order to preserve outward amity. His internal fire was, in any event, permanently banked.

The goal of peace for China and unity for Asia seemed to Harry a scant few inches closer to attainment —if that. Despite his skepticism, he still felt strongly that any course that offered China even a remote chance of peace was preferable to war. Though he knew his father would disapprove of his actions, he was, nonetheless, disturbed at having had no word from the family in Hong Kong since December 18, 1937, when he and Wang Ching-wei boarded an airplane in Chungking. Their announced destination was Kumming, capital of Yunnan Province in the deep southwest, but their pilot pointed the Fokker Trimotor's nose toward Hanoi, the capital of French Indo-China, which was dominated by Tokyo. As Wang Ching-wei wished, they had set out to test Japanese intentions.

Four days later, Prime Minister Prince Konoye announced in Tokyo that Japan would destroy the "usurper" Nationalist Government of Chiang Kai-shek and "adjust Sino-Japanese relations" in cooperation with the "legitimate, new regime" of Wang Ching-wei, the rightful heir of Dr. Sun Yat-sen. Japan "demonstrated her sincerity" by renouncing all territorial claims on China and promising to return to Chinese rule all her concessions and leased territories, as well as relinquishing all extraterritorial privileges for Japanese citizens. The Nanking Provisional Government in turn supported the united front against Communism, exemplified by the Anti-Comintern Pact that linked Tokyo, Berlin, and Rome. True economic cooperation between China and Japan as "equal partners" was guaranteed by Japan's promise not to seek monopoly rights in China. The words of the program rang splendidly.

By March, Harry saw that, as he had feared, drafting a great design was far easier than implementing it. But he persisted after the Generalissimo flatly rejected peace talks and expelled both Wang Ching-wei and himself from the Kuomintang. He had no choice but to initial agreements that recognized Japan's puppet state of Manchukuo under the last Manchu Emperor Hsüan

Tung; allowed Japan to station troops in China to oppose Communism; granted Japan broad privileges to exploit China's raw materials; and appointed Japanese "advisers" to China educational institutions. The reality contradicted Prince Konoye's promises in virtually every respect. At least, Harry felt, he could negotiate, giving much and gaining a little, rather than fighting unwinnable battles at an enormous cost in Chinese lives.

If not content, he was resigned as he signed the last of the documents his secretary had laid on his desk. For the first time, he was actually exercising power. The silence from Hong Kong demonstrated his father's disapproval of his collaborating with the Japanese. But Harry was following the fatal advice Sir Jonathan had tendered on that bright morning in the South China Sea twenty-nine years earlier just after the hijacking of the opium-smuggling paddle-steamer *Taishan*. Politics was not for the finicky or the faint-hearted, as the Old Gentleman had said. Harry accepted opprobrium among the Chinese and insolence from the Japanese to strive for peace.

"Call my wife," he told his male secretary, "and remind her we're having General Katsuki Kiyochi to dinner tonight. I'm leaving now."

Four policemen saluted as he left the monumental Government Building.

His black Packard limousine waited at the foot of the stone steps. An open truck carrying a half-dozen workmen in paint-stained blue clothing rattled across the forecourt. Harry noted and dismissed its noisy progress, recalling that the Provisional Government's offices were still being renovated.

His driver opened the door, and Harry paused to look back at the building where the blue-and-white Chinese flag flew beside Japan's red-and-white rising sun. His wry contemplation of those two symbols of flawed sovereignty was interrupted by a metallic clash. The workmen's truck had inexplicably swerved and grazed the limousine's fender. The truck driver threw up his hands in dismay and descended to offer his formal apologies. He was followed by the six workmen.

531

"Your Excellency," the driver said, "I am abjectly sorry. I have erred deeply, but the steering is worn."

Harry impatiently dismissed the apologies. Though the driver's voice and bearing were vaguely familiar, the provisional Prime Minister was concerned with more important matters than a smashed fender or a truck driver's fears. The driver came closer, still expostulating. When he was shielded from the policemen's gaze by the limousine's open door, he drew a Beretta pistol whose muzzle was elongated by a tubular silencer.

The pistol cracked three times. Harry felt each bullet's impact, marveling that the shots were quieter than the tapping of a woman's high heels. He fell to the grimy cobbles, and, looking up at his executioner, he saw his own face as it had been twenty-five years earlier.

"For China!" Colonel James Sekloong said tonelessly. "For China's sake, traitors must die!"

"But . . ." Harry rasped. "But . . . James . . . James, my own . . ."

James fired again. The impact pushed Harry Sekloong to the verge of death. But he clung desperately to life. There was so much to explain—and to justify. James knew neither his true father nor his father's reasons for collaborating. It was supremely important that he should understand.

"James . . . James, you don't know, you don't understand. James, my own . . ."

The Prime Minister's voice dwindled to a gabble of unintelligible syllables. Neither bitter nor resentful, but sadly welcoming death, Harry Sekloong died trying to justify his life to one of the two human beings he had deeply loved—his own son, his own executioner.

August 24, 1939–June 10, 1940

THE shell from the six-pounder arched high into the cloud-flecked sky over Sekkong in the New Territories.

Through his Zeiss binoculars, Lieutenant Jonathan Osgood Sekloong marked the impact two miles distant. The earth erupted in a fountain of red mud, and six khaki-uniformed figures dropped.

"Three points lower," Jonnie ordered. "Traverse left four points."

Stripped to the waist in the 95 percent humidity, the sweating, beer-bellied gun crew fumbled another shell into the breach. The Hong Kong Volunteer Defense Force, chiefly Europeans and Eurasians with a leavening of Chinese, had taken the field in full force. Despite the artillery fire, the enemy ranks were encircling their positions and attacking their flanks.

"They'd be all over you," Charles Sekloong laughed when the second shell fell short. "With you fellows shooting like that, my God, it'd be over before it began. I remember once in France . . ."

"Pater, this isn't France," Jonnie deliberately exaggerated his Stonyhurst drawl. "It's only poor old Hong Kong, and my chaps haven't fired more than ten rounds in their lives."

"That's obvious," Charles smiled. "They'd better pull themselves together."

Gray-haired and self-assured in the uniform of a full colonel bedecked with two rows of medal ribbons, Charles Sekloong flourished his walking-stick like a field marshal's baton. Although he was a staff observer, the veteran of battles more than two decades past was gripped by a sense of urgency alien to the younger civilian-soldiers. On August 24, 1939, they lightheartedly went through the maneuvers ordered by the newly established Hong Kong Defense Headquarters, which was itself dubious regarding the exercise's necessity. The Japanese held major strategic pockets through East China; having taken Canton ten months earlier, the Imperial Army had stationed its sentries along the twenty-two-mile-long border between the New Territories and Kwangtung Province. But Hong Kong felt itself still secure on the rim of the cauldron. British Hong Kong *knew* the Japanese would never defy the might of the British Empire and the Royal Navy by attacking the Crown Colony.

"It's a waste of time, Jonnie," his Sergeant Major confided. "Our chaps'll never learn to shoot straight, and the Japanese'll never attack."

Jonnie grinned at the informality. The Sergeant Major was a junior director of Derwent's and his favorite tennis partner. At thirty-seven, Jonnie was himself still breezily informal, though his height, his aquiline nose, and his wide hazel eyes gave him an air of command hardly justified by the three casual years in the Stonyhurst Cadet Force that had won him his commission.

"Probably not, Bill," he said. "Anyway, let's pack it up for today. We're down to three rounds, and I've got to get back. Will you take over?"

Father and son mounted Jonnie's massive fire-engine-red 450K Mercedes roadster for a fast run through the open New Territories on the only Hong Kong roads where he could use even half the car's brute power. The twelve-cylinder model, designed to prove the supremacy of Adolf Hitler's super-race on the motor-racing circuit, had been in production less than a year, each vehicle painstakingly hand-built by proud master-craftsmen in Stüttgart. Jonnie had secured his 450K at an inflated price through unabashed pressure. Agonizing over the persecution of her fellow Jews in Germany, his wife Sarah refused to ride in the vehicle she called "the blood-red monster." She had earlier tried to dissuade him from buying the 450K.

"Look," he'd argued, "the Reichsmarks were blocked anyway. You could say I'm depriving the Nazis of the foreign exchange they'd otherwise get for the beast. Anyway, the German Jews aren't really your people. That kefuffle is just a fight between different kinds of Germans. Besides, the German Jews certainly aren't my people."

"Jonnie," Sarah had replied, "they may not be yours, but they *are* my people. Britain must fight the Nazis sooner or later. Then the Germans will be *your* enemies too."

"No bloody fear," he'd laughed. "I see now that Chamberlain can handle the little paper-hanger. You had me panicked last year, you and the Old Gentleman. The danger, if any, is from Japan."

Knowing the argument futile, Sarah had pressed her full lips together in silent dissent. It was the only major disagreement they had had in fourteen years of a marriage cushioned by secure wealth, blessed by two children, and sustained by mutual trust that was breached by only one omission.

Jonnie had never told Sarah of his son by Tanya Kerelenkova, who lived in Sydney married to an Australian barrister. Jonnie knew that the boy, called Jonathan Stone Roberts after his adoption by Tanya's husband, was fair-haired and hazel-eyed. He was called "Chink" by his schoolmates, just as Jonnie himself had been called "Chink" at Stonyhurst, because of the almost imperceptible tilt of his eyes—though none suspected his son's Chinese blood.

Tanya and Jonathan were his secret—his only secret. A man was entitled to one secret from his wife, particularly when it was for her own good. Besides, his present behavior was so blameless that his father, remembering his own philandering, occasionally raised an astonished eyebrow. "But," Jonnie told himself, "rank has its responsibilities." In the same spirit, he murmured ritually, "Rank has its privileges." Then he stepped into the 450K and left his section the dirty work of disassembling the field-piece for its return to the gun park.

Remembering the long, dizzying ride by sedan chair in his youth, Jonnie slewed the heavy roadster through winding, narrow Peak Road to Sekloong Manor. He stamped on the brakes before each curve, then tramped heavily on the accelerator to pull the two-ton 450K through the turn.

"You'll probably kill a poor coolie one of these days," Charles muttered darkly. "You'll surely kill yourself."

Nonetheless, the older man also reveled in the rush of wind past the red roadster. Regarding the panorama beneath them, Charles felt that neither Hong Kong nor he himself had altered materially since he'd maneuvered the black Rolls-Royce through the same curves when the road opened in 1924. Coolies still trotted up and down hill on their daily errands, and the green expanse of the foreshore was marred by only a few new structures. Most of the crenellated buildings along the waterfront were exactly as they had been in 1900 almost four decades earlier. The Hong Kong Club still stood in aloof state, looking across a grassy mall at Prince's Building. Beyond, St. George's Building was the domain of the Sekloongs, who were still barred from membership in the all-European Hong Kong Club. But time had mellowed Charles's resentment of the exclusion. Besides, in the wider world outside Hong Kong, the Sekloongs were not merely accepted, but were courted for their wealth and power. Charles Sekloong touched the crown and two stars on his shoulder strap. At sixty-three, he was well content with his life.

The 450K's wheels rolled under the winged-dragon arch, side-slipped on the circular driveway, and threw up a spatter of gravel as Jonnie braked the roadster to a skidding halt before the brass-bound teak doors of The Castle.

"I'll drop you here, Father, if you want to see Grandfather," Jonnie said. "I must get back. Sarah was fussing about Albert's sore throat. You'd think he was six months old, not six years. With Henry at boarding school, he's her only chick, and she does make a fuss. Thank God *I* didn't have a Jewish mother!"

"Your mother always took excellent care of you," Charles said stiffly. "Why I remember . . ."

Sarah Haleevie Sekloong's emergence from the open doors interrupted her father-in-law's reminiscences. Her dark vivacity was set off by a simply cut cream-linen summer dress tied at the waist with a rainbow-striped scarf; the hem, four inches below her knees, set off her finely molded calves. She offered her lips to Jonnie before speaking.

"You're both wanted. The Old Gentleman wants to talk with all of us."

"I thought the old boy was fully occupied with his new lady friend," Charles laughed. "Please God, I'm half as hale at eighty-six."

Sarah smiled at her father-in-law's reference to the relationship between the aged Eurasian knight and the lush sixteen-year-old Polynesian girl who had returned with him from Tahiti on *Regina Pacis* the preceding year. Opal, he called her, the dark jewel. She was obviously hot-blooded, though by Polynesian standards slightly past her prime. Above all, Mary and Sarah were delighted by the Old Gentleman's revitalization. Nurtured by Opal's constant attentions, he was once again peppery and decisive.

Mary waited in the circular entrance hall. The marble floor cast back a shimmering, blurred reflection of her blue georgette dress embroidered with tiny golden winged dragons. The whirling ceiling fans stirred the still air and ruffled her hair. But the inescapable humidity was as oppressive on the cooler Peak as in the valley.

Charles Sekloong glanced warily at his wife. He ascribed her mercurial moods to "post-menopausal depression," the glib diagnosis of the portly English physician who had replaced Dr. Moncriefe. It did not occur to him that Harry's assassination distressed her more deeply than the other members of the family.

Mary Sekloong still grieved profoundly and silently for the man she had loved above all others. Emotionally detached from China, she had not condemned Harry's defection to the Japanese. She had understood his reasons and had sympathized with his vain hopes of making peace. She could no more express those sentiments to the Sekloongs than she could admit her embittered resentment of the Chinese, resentment sharply intensified by Harry's murder. It did not really matter who had killed her lover, the Communists or the Nationalists. Both were Chinese, and she had come to despise the Chinese race.

"Good evening, Gentlemen. Did you have a good time playing Boy Scouts?" she teased.

"Mary, dammit! It's no joke," Charles exploded, then smiled when he realized his wife was baiting him.

"Sorry, Charles," Mary apologized. "I know it's no joke. Certainly the gallant knight thinks it no joke. He wants to see us all in the study. And he's up in the air."

"Not again," Jonnie groaned. "What now? Everyone would be much happier if he'd just tend to his venery —and let the three of us run the firm."

"Jonnie!" Mary automatically rebuked her thirty-seven-year-old eldest son. "How can you talk so about your grandfather?"

"It's true, isn't it, Mother?"

"Well," she smiled, "let's say it isn't wholly untrue."

Wearing a blue-cotton long-gown, Sir Jonathan Sekloong was seated in his favorite red-leather chair beside the granite fireplace banked with flowers. His white beard bristled with vitality while his hazel eyes scrutinized his descendants. His son and grandson barely glanced at the vigorous patriarch. The figure standing behind his chair drew their eyes irresistibly.

Despite her youth, Opal was totally self-confident. Almost six feet tall, her sturdy body was voluptuous in a scarlet muumuu patterned with frangipani flowers. The jasmine lei around her columnar neck set off her generously carved features, transforming her into a South Seas temple sculpture come to life. She was proudly aware of her sexuality, since the Polynesians, unlike some civilizations in theory more advanced, honored both women and the act of sex. She felt it no stigma, but a cause for pride, that the aged multimillionaire had bought her from the French planter with whom she was living when *Regina Pacis* sailed into Tahiti atoll. He was not only kind, but tolerant of her discreet forays in search of more robust love-making than he could offer. In return, she gave him total devotion.

"Well, the balloon's going up." Sir Jonathan delighted in keeping up with the latest slang. "Hitler and Stalin have signed a nonaggression pact."

"And I hoped the vermin would kill each other," Sarah said bitterly.

"So did we all, my love," Jonnie agreed. "But, Grandfather, what difference does it make?"

"It means war!" Charles offered. "His greatest enemy is neutralized. The little clown Hitler can strike where he wishes."

"Don't forget Stalin," Sir Jonathan reminded them. "His ambition is unlimited."

"Oh, Father, you've always made too much of the Bolshevik menace," Mary interjected. "They didn't do well in China . . . haven't after fifteen years. They're not that great a threat to your money-bags."

Sir Jonathan lifted his hand, and Opal placed a panatella between his slender fingers. He had been obsessed with the Communists since Harry's assassination. Despite the great rewards he offered, his network of informants had not discovered the assassin's identity. Yet he was certain the Communists had ordered the killing, and his previous distaste for them had become pathological hatred.

"War with who?" Jonnie asked. "I've been so busy drilling for a war that may never come, I'm out of touch."

"With Poland," Sir Jonathan replied. "Hitler's been threatening the Poles for months . . . trumping up excuses for invasion. Now he can divide Poland with Stalin."

"Britain and France *must* come in," Sarah breathed. "Hitler will be defeated—and the Jews will be saved."

"I'm not so sure," Mary advised. "The Poles can't hold long, and England is miserably unprepared."

"I think England will fight," Sir Jonathan said. "But what of the effect on China . . . and on ourselves?"

"I haven't thought it out," Mary confessed.

"Damn it, Mary," Charles exploded. "He's right—again. How can the Nationalists and the Communists cooperate now, really cooperate?"

"What do you mean, Father?" Jonnie asked while Sir Jonathan nodded approval of Charles's reasoning. "How does a pact between two European bandits change the anti-Japanese struggle?"

"Mao Tse-tung and his Communists owe primary loyalty to Moscow, not to China," Charles explained. "Berlin and Tokyo were already allies. Now Moscow and Berlin are practically allies. The enemy of my enemy is my enemy, and the friend of my friend is my friend. The new friends of the Nazis, who are old friends of the Japanese, are the Russians, who are the best friends of the Chinese Communists. So our Communists and the Japanese could become friends."

"Not that bad, surely," Mary objected. "The Communists would lose almost all popular support if they turned around and helped the Japanese."

"You're half right, Mary," Sir Jonathan said. "It won't go that far. But far enough: Mao Tse-tung's already told his men to give ten percent of their efforts to fighting the Japanese and the rest to expanding their power and fighting the Nationalists. Ten percent will now become five or two percent."

"You mean the United Front will break up?" asked Jonnie.

"Not immediately, not formally," his grandfather answered dryly. "But the Communists and the Nationalists will fight each other tooth and claw. Perhaps they'll fight the Japanese in their spare time."

"The Nationalists won't do a deal with the Japanese, will they?" Mary asked. "The Generalissimo and Hitler have been friends of a sort for years."

"No, not that," Sir Jonathan answered thoughtfully. "Sun Tze, the great strategist, advised princes to make alliances with the distant enemy against the nearby enemy. But both the Japanese and the Communists are nearby. The Generalissimo may be tempted to deal with the Japs, but he can't. He'd lose control over his people. He's not chairman of the board. Just executive secretary—and there is no chairman."

"Besides," Charles added, "Wang Ching-wei's preempted that line and . . ."

"And much good it's done him," Jonnie filled in bitterly. "Just Uncle Harry's murder."

The study was still with the silence of mourning for

half a minute. The Sekloongs did not often talk about Harry.

"If fighting between Mao Tse-tung and Chiang Kai-shek becomes so fierce," Mary finally broke in, "they'll have no soldiers to fight the Japs."

"And, both sides, both Communists and Nationalists, will fight a holding battle," Charles summed up. "They'll wait for their own allies to win and then carry them to total power in China. The Generalissimo's thinking that way. He's sending Thomas to raise money and support in Paris and London."

"Good job for Uncle Tom," Jonnie said. "But what about us? I know Mother insisted we buy up commodities in 1914. The same drill this time?"

"God forbid," Sir Jonathan answered. "Anything but that. No commodities to buy in China and no way to ship them. This time we invest in America—sell oil and tin to America. These may be the last days of the British Raj. Enjoy them while you can. But invest in America."

"And the Wheatleys and their pals, the Mitsubishi?" Jonnie was amused by the motion-picture-disseminated fad for American slang. "Do we blow the whistle on them?"

"We'll see just what," Sir Jonathan directed. "But we won't, ah, do nothing."

Mary recognized the glint in the Old Gentleman's eyes. Clear the decks for action, she thought. She knew the Old Gentleman's plans to smash his former employers. They had not only discussed strategy, but had sent detailed instructions to their agents, associates, and friends throughout Asia.

The Japanese were ubiquitous. Everywhere in Asia, except unoccupied China, Japanese businessmen, technicians, and craftsmen diligently plied their peaceful trades. In the city of Angeles on the island of Luzon in the Philippines near Clark Field, the chief American air-base in the Far East, streets of Japanese shops offered cheap services and goods ranging from hairdressing through electrical appliances to farm implements. In the hamlet of San Mateo, eighteen miles away, the general store was run by the amiable Suzuki Tadao, who had married a Filipina fifteen years earlier and embraced her Catholicism. In Manila, the *zaibatsu*—the five big conglomerates of Japanese commerce and industry—maintained offices four times as large as those of American firms and staffs ten times larger.

"All our correspondence with the home office must be in Japanese," the managing director of Mitsui explained blandly. "We need larger staffs, Japanese staffs. Japanese is a very difficult language."

The same pattern was apparent in independent Thailand; in British Burma, Malaya, and Singapore; in the Dutch East Indies; and in French Indo-China. Harbor dredgers skilfully practiced their craft, as did plantation managers, masseurs, mining engineers, and curio dealers. Half held commissions in the Japanese Army or Navy, while an additional 40 percent were civilian agents of the Japanese Intelligence Service. Some 10 percent were legitimate businessmen who served Nippon's economy first and its imperial ambitions second.

Almost as ubiquitous were the offices of Derwent, Hayes and Company, called in Chinese *Teh Wan,* which meant "Virtue Universal." The bitter Chinese jested that *Teh Wan* really meant "Grab Everything." The cynical pun, based on a slight shift in intonation, was inspired by Iain Wheatley's flexible business ethics. Derwent's did not, however, lower itself to retail trade —unless the quick profits were irresistible. But its shipping lines, tea plantations, departmental stores, jute factories, rubber plantations, construction companies, tin mines, and general trading firms were a dynamic network centered on Hong Kong.

Natural affinity attracted Derwent's and Mitsubishi. Though itself immense, the Japanese firm did not disdain the petty retail dealing Derwent's spurned. But Iain Wheatley and his hand-raised company of gentlemen merchants were accepted in Government Houses and Chancelleries closed to the Japanese. Sir Jonathan had initially watched the development of cooperation between the two giant enterprises with only slight misgivings, for it was a natural commercial alliance. But his informants had been relaying disturbing news ever since the Japanese incursion into Manchuria in 1931 signaled Tokyo's ambition to conquer all Asia. Derwent's services to Mitsubishi verged, originally, upon the unethical; subsequently, upon the illegal; and, most recently, upon espionage. Only Iain Wheatley knew the full extent of the social introductions, the political influence, and the commercial intelligence with which Derwent's provided Mitsubishi "for a reasonable commission." Mary, Charles, and Jonnie constantly heard of specific deals that shocked even their sensibilities, long calloused by intimate acquaintance with the infinitely flexible business ethics of the China Coast.

Sir Jonathan was the master of all the ramifications. The Sekloongs' own network was smaller and less obtrusive than either Mitsubishi's or Derwent's, but it was more cohesive and homogeneous. Their gold winged-dragon emblem was displayed on twenty-odd freighters and sixteen branch offices throughout Asia. Nine million overseas Chinese, who controlled the retail trade of Southeast Asia, were bound to the Sekloongs by both racial sympathy and the House's intelligently magnanimous business practices. The patriarch, Sir Jonathan, was not only a generous philanthropist, but a spectacular *Chinese* success in a business milieu dominated by foreigners. Besides, Mitsubishi or Derwent's allowed a Chinese shopkeeper in Semarang on Java no more than 8 percent profit on textiles, while J. Sekloong and Sons permitted him 12 percent. Self-interest, coupled with patriotic sentiments, therefore provided Sir Jonathan with a network of associates, informants, and collaborators that dwarfed the resources of both the Japanese *zaibatsu* and the Hong Kong British *hongs*.

The widely dispersed overseas Chinese had already demonstrated that they could bring the commercial life of Southeast Asia to a standstill *if* they acted in concert.

A *hartal*—a total shutdown of overseas Chinese business accompanied by a general strike of Chinese workers—was, however, a dangerous weapon. It could paralyze normal life, but it could also provoke vicious pogroms against the Chinese themselves as it had in the past.

On August 25, 1939, Sir Jonathan sent out messages to all the chief Chinese merchants of Southeast Asia. In coded telegrams, chatty letters, and by word of mouth, the Sekloongs informed their countrymen that Derwent, Hayes and Company was collaborating with the Japanese invaders of the Motherland not only by providing commercial assistance, but also by furnishing military and political intelligence to the enemy.

An epidemic of minor difficulties beset the Universally Virtuous *hong*. Salesmen in Malaya were met with bland protestations that reorders were impossible because business was so bad. Normal bill collections were snarled in the East Indies, while bank drafts were mysteriously delayed or defaced. Chinese money-lenders in the Philippines abruptly called their loans to customers of the Virtuous *hong*. Shipments went astray in Burma, and freighters plying the Indian Ocean suffered inexplicable breakdowns in engine rooms manned by Chinese stokers. Rumors cascaded throughout Asia, multifarious in their multiplicity and ingenuity: "Derwent's is approaching bankruptcy. . . . Iain Wheatley has promised to raise $200 million for the Japanese for armaments. . . . Derwent's ships are transporting Japanese troops disguised as coolies."

Within five days, Derwent's directors, assembled for a routine board-meeting, were presented with sheafs of alarming reports. However, no clear pattern was discernible. Unfortunate coincidence appeared to have contrived that difficulties, each itself minor, all came at once. The *hong's* Managing Director Iain Wheatley shrugged his heavy shoulders and reassured his directors. The Universally Virtuous *hong,* he said, had survived many grave threats in its long history, and the present difficulties were no more than a bad patch. Besides, the firm was solid. Its financial reserves were great, and the impending war in Europe would offer new opportunities for profit.

On August 31, 1939, Sir Jonathan Sekloong leisurely drew on a panatella pierced by the attentive Opal. The Old Gentleman sat back in his red-leather chair, smiled benignly—and waited.

The battlefields of China were quiet, though minor harassment, like that James Sekloong's guerrillas mounted, irritated the Japanese. The vast expanse and the primitive communications of China, rather than Chinese fighting men, sapped Japanese strength. A virtual truce prevailed in the undeclared war, leaving Nationalists and Communists free to direct their most punishing assaults against each other under the tattered cloak of their United Anti-Japanese Front. China had become a sideshow of the international circus.

Politicians and journalists turned from the confusing Far Eastern imbroglio to concentrate upon the border between the National Socialist Greater German Reich of Chancellor Adolf Hitler and the demi-fascist Republic of Poland. Having forestalled any Soviet reaction by the Russo-German nonaggression pact that secretly promised Joseph Stalin his share of the spoils, Adolf Hitler sent German infantrymen rolling in Mercedes trucks across the table-flat Polish plain on the night of September 1, 1939. German bombers swept low over Warsaw, and, most ominously, columns of German *Panzerwagen*—dark-green battletanks marked with black crosses—thrust deep into the heartland of Poland. *Blitzkrieg*, "lightning war," was dismembering the Polish Republic, as it would later dismember Western Europe.

Germany did not declare war. Responsibility for formally proclaiming the greatest conflict in human history devolved upon the wan British Prime Minister Neville Chamberlain, who had a year earlier confidently promised "peace in our time." On September 3, 1939, Chamberlain told the British people that they were at war with Germany. Britain had kept her promise to come to Poland's assistance.

The wiry young man standing on the cobblestones of the Place Pigalle outside the Moulin Rouge was oblivious to the speculative glances of the heavily perfumed women in tawdry finery hurrying to their evening's work in the bars and nightclubs of Montmartre. A black overcoat, its heavy collar buttoned around his throat, protected him from the chill winds of December 2, 1939. But his head was bare, his black homburg swinging negligently in his gray-gloved hand. He was deaf to the bellowed enticements of the doorman of the Moulin Rouge, who attempted to compensate by volume for the wartime blackout's extinguishing the nightclub's revolving red-neon windmill. His short-cropped glossy brown hair was shot with reddish undertones, and his hazel eyes were fixed on the dusk-blurred silhouette of the Church of the Sacre Coeur.

Charles Philips Sekloong marveled that the grotesque confusion of spires, domes, and cupolas, familiar from dozens of bad paintings, could move him so profoundly. Aesthetically, the Church of the Sacre Coeur was so monstrous that the baroque Castle in Sekloong Manor appeared harmonious in comparison. But the soaring edifice was dedicated *Ad Maiorem Dei Gloriam,* "to the greater glory of God," and its fantastic tracery against the graying sky was a proud reaffirmation of man's faith in his Creator. The prostitutes, pimps, strongarm men, and musicians of the *quartier,* those practitioners of the varied, sordid skills that catered to the base appetites of naive tourists, needed the consolation of Holy Church at least as much as did the stolid bourgeoisie who inhabited most of Paris.

Charles glanced at his wristwatch. It was still a few minutes before the 5:30 rendezvous his brother Thomas had appointed in that incongruous location. He clapped his hat foursquare on his head, uncomfortable at the unfamiliar constriction, and pulled his coat-collar higher around his throat. Since the Place Pigalle was no fit place for a priest to loiter, he preferred not to advertise his calling by displaying his Roman collar. Besides, he was still self-conscious about the narrow strip of red silk that identified him as a monsignor. It was, he had protested to his superior, ridiculous to elevate him at the age of twenty-eight, only four years after ordination. The old Archbishop had reprimanded him for "false humility" when he argued that he was better suited to a pastoral mission, a humble post as a curate, rather than the diplomatic assignment to which he was ordered.

"My son, you have taken vows of obedience," the aged prelate had admonished Charles. "You will go where you can best serve Mother Church—as decided by your superiors. These are troubled times for the Church. You must, above all, obey."

"I shall, of course, obey," Charles replied. "But is it absolutely essential to make me a monsignor? There are so many others more worthy who would rejoice in the honor. I entered the priesthood to atone in part for the excessive material blessings the Lord bestowed upon the Sekloongs, not to seek advancement."

"It is no more fitting for you to question the Lord's allotment of worldly goods than to question the decisions of His Church," the Archbishop reproved Charles. "You will be attaché to the Papal Nunciature in Paris, as a monsignor, and you will obey. Without discipline, the Church would be no more than a mass of moldering buildings."

"But, Father." Charles still objected, and the Archbishop frowned. "Why am I chosen?"

"We require a representative who is neutral, yet can move with ease in the diplomatic milieu. You are, in the eyes of most men you will meet, a neutral Oriental. Yet you possess the requisite languages and close ties with England through Stonyhurst."

"I shall obey, Father," Charles affirmed reluctantly, though his heart remained heavy with doubts.

Afterward, he had prayed that he might accept with grace the assignment that would have delighted so many of his colleagues. To Charles it was a burden, for he had hoped to return to the interior of China to serve the suffering Chinese people. He longed to hear the lowing of water buffaloes and hearty jests in rough Cantonese, rather than the irritable honking of Citroën motorcars and the nervous flow of liquid French. He had been home only twice in the fifteen years since he entered Stonyhurst, once after leaving the school, the second time for his ordination by the Bishop of Hong Kong. Monsignor Charles Philips Sekloong, the newest member of Paris's *Corps Diplomatique,* was as homesick as a schoolboy. Even if his cloth had not debarred him from many of the pleasures of Paris, he would have found no joy in the City of Light.

Charles was virtually unique in his sense of deprivation. Although the fabled lights of Paris were dimmed as a precaution against German air raids, the city's fabled gaiety was even more frenetic than it had been in peacetime. Adolf Hitler had been quiescent since completing his conquest of Poland at the end of September. The only serious fighting in Europe was taking place in frozen Finland, where Stalin was attempting to compel the Finns to subservience. But Helsinki was far from Paris, almost as far, it seemed, as Chungking. Secure behind the deep concrete bunkers of the Maginot Line, which was manned by the finest army in the world, the Parisians called their bloodless confrontation with the Germans *la guerre drôle,* "the phony war." Men dying elsewhere were not their concern.

The remote danger symbolized by men in uniform and the imperfect blackout merely spiced the pleasures of the Parisians. The wealthy, the celebrated, and the bearers of ancient names flocked to dinner parties, receptions, and glittering balls. Their sexual behavior was as unrestrained as their public revels. Nero, Charles reflected sourly, must have dined and danced and postured like the pampered French plutocrats *before* Rome burned.

"Ah-dazi! Ho giu mei gien. Nei cheung-dai-la. Ho mng ho?" A light touch on his shoulder broke Monsignor Charles's abstraction, and a familiar voice spoke in Cantonese. "Little brother! It's been a long time. You've grown, I see. How've you been?"

"Lo-yee, ho giu. Tai giu-ah!" he replied in the language of their childhood. "Second older brother, very long. Too long indeed!"

Thomas Sekloong, eight years older and four inches shorter than his youngest brother whom they had called the Little Mandarin, was debonair in a double-breasted dinner jacket with wide, corded lapels and a pinched waist. His velvet-collared overcoat hung open to reveal the perfect butterfly of his black bow-tie and the gleaming front of his starched shirt. Command had stamped his dark features with authority, but he smiled at his brother's frank scrutiny.

"You didn't expect me in uniform, did you?" he asked. "I'm conspicuous enough already. This phony war—it's hard to tell who's on whose side."

"Tell me everything." The questions cascaded from the younger brother's lips. "How are Mother and Father? Still grace in dissension? And the Old Gentleman? Still the iron hand in the steel glove?"

"The iron hand and the restless penis, you mean!" Thomas replied coarsely.

"And Charlotte? I haven't seen her yet. Are Gwinnie and George Parker coming to Paris? They wrote they might, and . . ."

"Hold on, youngster," the general told the priest. "We can't stand around swapping family confidences in the middle of Pigalle. The Jap dwarves are having me followed. But I know a place."

The Lapin Agile, the "Nimble Rabbit," on the narrow alley halfway up the hill had not changed since Maurice Utrillo painted it in 1897. The black door beneath the lath-crossed plaster façade opened at Thomas's knock, and they entered a virtual rabbit warren of low-beamed, dark rooms. Six in the evening was still very early, but wartime Paris took its pleasures when it could—whenever it could. The medieval rooms were already half filled: with soldiers and their girls; with students self-consciously defiant in worn civilian clothing; and with *petit bourgeois,* the women elegant in inexpensive dresses, the men stiffly uncomfortable in their best blue suits. Wearing a loose red shirt that vaguely recalled a medieval jerkin, the waiter did not solicit their order, but placed on the rough wood table two globular glasses of brandy garnished with maraschino cherries. The chorus of a song Monsignor Charles did not recognize resounded from the next room. As far as he could make out, it related the remarkable feats of a marchioness with eighty hunters.

"I assure you, Little Brother, it's a perfectly respectable place," Thomas said. "You may even see another Roman collar or two. And the songs, mostly old folk songs, they're not that bawdy."

"I've heard worse," the priest said dryly. "But, if you're satisfied that you're concealed in this throng, start talking. Don't keep me waiting any longer."

"Well, I doubt that any of these types speaks Cantonese," the general conceded in that remarkable language, alternately as formal as a court ritual and as earthily crude as a Billingsgate fishmonger. "Our respected parents are well. They live in great outward harmony. Father's slowed up a little, not like the Old Gentleman. And Mother's will is as strong as ever, when she cares to press. Jonnie and Sarah? Well, it looks like true love—and he's practically running the business, day to day, that is. But the old man's still full of piss and vinegar. The gallant knight's got a new concubine, a Polynesian girl he calls Opal, and . . ."

"So I've heard," Charles interrupted. "What about James?"

"James? Him?" Nationalist Major General Thomas Sekloong frowned when he spoke of his brother, the Communist colonel. "James is crawling around in the mud and night-soil somewhere. I haven't seen him in years. But I hear—that's all, just hear, you understand —he's working in the Japanese-occupied areas. Against the Japanese, he'd say, but undermining the legal government for the Communist bandits, I'd say."

"I see," the priest said meditatively. "And his wife and son?"

"God knows," Thomas shrugged. "Probably plotting to blow up the Imperial City. Little Red Devils, they call those Communist-bandit spawn—and they *are*."

"Then tell me about Gwinnie and George. Still in New York, I know, but they wrote they might come to Paris this winter."

"No bloody fear. I saw them three weeks ago. They're real Americans, all of them—Gwinnie, George, and the two kids. Junior's eleven. At least nobody ever called you Junior. And Blanche is ten. Typical spoiled American kids. The Doctor's a big noise in tropical medicine, as you know. But a real American. The State Department warned them not to come. The war, you know, the danger. *What* war? If they want to see war they should come to China. Christ, I haven't even had a chance to look for a girl to marry. But, no, they won't be coming."

"And Charlotte? Have you seen her yet? I know Mother's worried about her."

"With damned good reason. I'm no puritan, you know, but Charlotte! She's still beautiful—more beautiful, but . . ."

"Tell me!"

Dropping his heavily jocular manner, Thomas described his eldest sister's life in succinct, sharp sentences. He paused once to apologize: "Sorry for raking up ancient history, but you've been away so long I don't know how much you've heard."

Charlotte, he recalled, had left Hong Kong in 1931 after her first husband, Manfei Way, was found strangled in their garage. The murder was never solved, but it was definitely the work of the Triad Secret Societies. No one was quite certain as to motive, although Manfei had become an embarrassment to his allies, the Wheatleys. Besides, Sir Jonathan had nurtured a bitter hatred for his treacherous grandson-in-law.

"Verdict not proven, then?" The young priest was deliberately unshockable.

His brother shrugged agreement and continued his account of their sister's peregrinations. Charlotte had left her son Mokhing in the care of his grandparents, the Mosing Ways. Determined to get away from Hong Kong, she had settled first in London. She found the British stiff, unwelcoming, and patronizing about her chee-chee accent. She'd felt, she said, "chilled," despite English respect for both the family's power and the substantial income her indulgent father allowed her.

On the other hand, Parisian society was avid for exotic personalities, eagerly welcoming Laotian, Vietnamese, and Cambodian "princesses." Charlotte's Oriental appearance became an asset when she moved to Paris, which even forgave her imperfect French. But she learned quickly and soon spoke like a Parisienne with a charming lilt.

"She was a great success almost immediately." Thomas signaled the waiter for another round. "The darling of Parisian society . . . an enchanting new toy. The money didn't do any harm . . . or the Rothschild connection."

An alluring, wealthy widow at twenty-seven, Charlotte established herself as a fashionable hostess. Her *salon* initially attracted the raffish nobility and the more lively men of business. It was not notable for intellectual brilliance. However, many visiting Americans and Britons—businessmen, journalists, and politicians, as well as those merely rich and idle—attended her receptions, where they could "meet the real French," but still speak English. Enticed by the confluence of money and power, aspiring French politicians soon appeared at Charlotte's Wednesday afternoons and vied for invitations to her dinners.

A new Madame de Staël has appeared among us, rhapsodized *Gringoire,* the right-wing weekly. *Madame Charlotte Sekloong Way is as beautiful as Marie Antoinette with flaming hair and piquant features. And she is profound with the ancient wisdom of the Orient.*

"Ancient wisdom of the Orient, bullshit!" Thomas snorted. "The ancient wisdom of the hockey fields of St. Paul's School and a hundred rumble seats."

Charles impatiently gestured for Thomas to continue. The outlines he knew vaguely, but the living, vital details had not penetrated his cloistered existence at Stonyhurst, the Seminary, and the English College in Rome.

One ambitious politician who frequented Charlotte's *hôtel particulier* off the Faubourg St. Honoré was a thirty-two-year-old parliamentary deputy called Raymond d'Alivère, Comte de Samlieu. His Breton family was as notable for its poverty as for its pride and the profusion of heraldic devices on its escutcheon. The two egotists, Charlotte and Raymond, recognized kindred spirits in each other. More important, their needs were complementary. Each could provide what the other needed: for Raymond, funds to further his career; for Charlotte, a title and a man to occupy her bed. In mid-1932, Charlotte Sekloong Way became the Comtesse de Samlieu in a splendid wedding at Notre Dame, and in late-1933, she gave birth to a daughter, who was christened Alaine Marie-Claude Raymonde d'Alivère.

Even in her ruffled cradle, Alaine was beautiful. She was not a red, wrinkled morsel of humanity, but a perfectly formed, miniature adult. As she grew older, her beauty grew more radiant. Her long blond hair glowed with copper undertones, and her soft blue eyes were minutely but intriguingly tilted. Her matte-white skin, too, she owed to her mother's genes. Even her temperament appeared idyllic, sweetly docile yet spiced with mischievous self-will. She concealed her fury when her mother's English friends absent-mindedly called her Ellen or Americans chucked her under the chin and called her Ally.

Content with his bargain, Raymond neglected his favorite mistress. He adored his daughter, and he confidently expected that Charlotte would soon present him with a male heir. With logical French practicality, he had ascertained that her family was prolific as well as wealthy before proposing marriage to this creature from another world. But Charlotte was immersed in herself and desired no further experience of motherhood. Her self-love turned her against her own children. She had unconcernedly left Mokhing in Hong

Kong, when Mary reluctantly agreed that it was better for the boy to remain in the Colony, rather than join his peripatetic mother in Europe. After her marriage, Charlotte had not suggested that Mokhing join her, since he might be an embarrassment to Raymond. The young Alaine was a plaything, a beautiful doll to show her friends. But Charlotte's pride in Alaine did not generate tenderness.

Raymond noted her disinterest in their daughter with concern. Charlotte's attitude was as perversely unnatural to a family-obsessed Frenchman as was the marriage settlement's stipulation that, aside from a generous allowance to her husband, she would control her own money. He had reluctantly accepted that unFrench arrangement at the insistence of the Sekloong lawyers in Paris. Though it gave her excessive power, he had been confident that his flighty wife would not use that power.

Still excited by Charlotte's enthusiastic inventiveness in the conjugal bed, the Comte de Samlieu nonetheless tired of the heiress who would provide him with neither sufficient funds nor further children. Besides, her lack of conversation bored him. He discreetly resumed relations with his mistress. Somewhat plain, and a year older than himself, she was a tranquil, clear stream after Charlotte's turbulent, muddy waters—and her conversation was brilliant.

Raymond expected Charlotte to play the conventional role of the neglected wife, amusing herself with fashions and entertaining. He would not object to her seeking masculine consolation, as long as she, too, was discreet. But he could not tolerate her furious rebukes or her public display of her own amours. Charlotte became notorious by flaunting her liaisons in the halfworld where the degenerate hereditary aristocracy met the new semi-criminal aristocracy of power and wealth.

In 1937, the regular use of marijuana and morphine was still a social stigma. The *haute monde* was, however, tolerant of the retired general, rubber millionaire, or colonial governor who returned from Indo-China to smoke a few soothing pipes of opium prepared by a petite Vietnamese mistress. Since that tradition and her Oriental blood obliquely sanctioned Charlotte's indulgence in narcotics, she was not ostracized. Her wealth, her beauty, and her glamour preserved a simulacrum of respectability.

That was quite enough for Charlotte Sekloong Way d'Alivère, Comtesse de Samlieu. Her *salon* flourished, and she was enjoying herself, "as I could not in England, America or, Lord help us, Hong Kong." Her maintaining a precarious façade of respectability was, however, not enough for the Comte de Samlieu. In late-1937, he left her house. He took their daughter Alaine with him, but he was not too proud to collect his generous monthly allowance until Charlotte could secure a civil divorce. With an eye to the future, he initiated the laborious process of obtaining an annulment from the Rota in Rome, chiefly on the grounds that he had been denied his conjugal rights. He further adduced that Charlotte had entered into marriage with mental reservations, demonstrated by her refusal to give him an heir. His advocates darkly, though irrelevantly, questioned the Comtesse's moral capability for a true Catholic marriage, since her faith was flawed and her disobedience to the Church was obvious.

"None of this intrigue and vilification has *gravely* affected Charlotte's position," Thomas summed up. "She's still the darling of a certain group, and that group has power. That's one of the things I want to talk to you about."

"Second Elder Brother," the priest asked softly, "how have her troubles affected Charlotte herself?"

"Damned if I can see any difference!" The general was surprised by the question. "She seems much the same. A little weepy sometimes, but you know women."

"I see," the priest prompted. "And that's all?"

"Well, she did say one thing. Naturally, she wants to see you as soon as possible. But she did say she had a special reason for wanting to see you."

"But no more? Obviously, I want to see her. Shall we go now?"

"A minute, Little Brother. I didn't bring you here

just to swap family gossip. There's something more important."

"More important? What could be more important than Charlotte?"

"I need your help, Little Brother. China needs your help."

"What can I, a humble priest, possibly do, except pray? I assure you I have prayed long and often for China."

"You can do a hell of a lot more. You may not realize it, but you're moving into a position of real power. I want you to use that power for China—and against the Jap dwarves and the Communist bandits. Why do you think I'm here and not in Chungking with the Generalissimo?"

"I never wondered why. I was just delighted to see you."

"It's time to grow up, Little Brother. The Generalissimo trusts me and requires my humble assistance at his side. Yet he's sent me to Europe because we desperately need support—diplomatic pressure, arms, money, and economic sanctions against the dwarves."

"But," the priest protested, "I'm a servant of the Church. As a diplomat of the Holy See, I've forsworn all other loyalties."

"You're Chinese, Little Brother. Don't ever forget it. And China needs your help. I beg—no, I demand your help for China."

"I don't see how I can possibly serve two different masters. But what do you have in mind?"

"Right now I only want you to sound the feelings of the French and British toward China. Toward *our* war, *your* war. The Occidentals tell me what they think I want to hear, just to please me. I must know how they really figure the chances and who they really want to win—us or the dwarves."

"That sounds simple enough. Perhaps too simple, but I'd hate playing the spy."

"Don't be so damned naive," the general exploded. "What's a diplomat but a licensed spy? I'm asking no more than your superiors."

"But they *are* my superiors!"

"And *I* am your elder brother, your superior. The *Generalissimo* is the superior of all patriotic Chinese."

"I must consult my conscience," the priest temporized.

"Then you *will* help us. You'll be asked to do nothing dishonorable, nothing harmful to the Church. How could I ask anything harmful to Holy Church?"

"Give me a better idea, then. But remember I haven't said yes."

"Later, perhaps more active support. Right now, just information. Incidentally, the Old Gentleman's active. He's squeezing Derwent's like a ripe peach, striking back at them for collaborating with the Japanese. Iain Wheatley's screaming like a stuck pig. Derwent's business has dropped by half."

"I'm delighted," Monsignor Charles smiled. Although dedicated to charity and forgiveness, the priest was still a Sekloong, and hatred for the opportunistic Wheatleys had been bred into his bones.

"It's a patriotic duty—and a pleasure, squeezing the Wheatleys. From you, besides information, we may need a word in the right ear, a little discreet pressure."

"I don't see how I could," Charles demurred. "Spying's bad enough, but . . ,"

"Little Brother, I tell you again: *Grow up.* China must have diplomatic support, arms, and money. You must help. Rome certainly doesn't want the Communist bandits to come out on top."

"On that we agree completely, Second Elder Brother."

"All right then," the general over-rode any additional objections. "Let's go see Second Elder Sister."

The small mansion off the Faubourg St. Honoré was a perfect setting for Charlotte, who had, at thirty-six, attained the peak of her attractiveness. The formality of the Louis Quinze furniture was relieved by modern art: a graceful Degas statuette of a washerwoman; a misty Cezanne landscape; an assertive Picasso woman with two blue heads; and a Miró, all swirls and

557

angles in bright primary colors. On the marble mantel-piece of the drawing-room stood a sinuous black-stone Wei Dynasty Bodhisattva, while scrolls in the calligraphy of the Chien Lung Emperor hung beside the fireplace.

Charlotte's stiff yellow-silk skirt flirted around slender ankles set off by small satin pumps, while her hip-length tunic was caught at the waist by a broad green sash. Her chief adornment was a graduated double strand of glowing off-white *fei-tsui* jade with a diamond pendant that nestled in the cleft between her full breasts. Her hazel eyes flashed green when she laughed. His sister, Monsignor Charles reflected, hardly appeared a fallen woman in distress of spirit. The consolations of the material world seemed quite sufficient for her.

"Charlot!" she cried, embracing him. "I shall call you Charlot. Would you rather talk English or French?"

"What's wrong with Chinese?" Thomas growled in Cantonese.

"Tom, don't be tiresome," she answered. "You know my Cantonese is so very rusty. We shall speak English. And how are you, Charlot, my baby brother?"

"Well, Charl, quite well," the priest answered stiffly. "And you?"

"Wonderful." She flung out her arms. "You see how well I am. I have found my métier. I love Paris, and all Paris loves me."

"All *male* Paris, that is!" the General muttered in Cantonese into the priest's ear.

"But my dear," Charlotte said, "I am desolate. I must go out almost immediately. The naughty Tom kept you talking too long."

"Immediately, Charl?" the priest asked.

"I'm afraid so, my Charlot. But I want to see you as soon as we can. My poor baby brother, shut away with all those priests for all these years."

"Come off it, Charl," Thomas said. "It's only us. No need to perform."

"Tom, I am sincere, and I have a wonderful idea. Charlot must come to the grand masquerade tomorrow.

It would be amusing for him to come as he is. Only with a little black mask."

"Hardly," Thomas answered. "You really don't think it's a good idea, do you, Charl?"

"Well," she pouted, "perhaps not. But very soon, then. Charlot, come to dinner day after tomorrow. Just the two of us. We shall not ask Tom. Later, you must come to all my Wednesdays."

"I don't know about the Wednesdays," Charles said in doubt.

"Of course you will," Thomas chided. "It's your job."

"Then, 'til Tuesday night, Charlot. A'voir. And, Tom, you are coming tomorrow, aren't you? I must fly. Give yourselves a whiskey. My house is yours."

Charlotte swept out of the drawing-room in a swirl of yellow silk and red-gold hair, leaving the heavy fragrance of Joy floating on the overheated air. Thomas mixed two whiskey-sodas, laying his hands on the bottles with easy familiarity.

"Doubles, Little Brother?" he asked sardonically. "You look as if you could use a double."

Charles nodded abstractedly. He was bewildered by his sister and deeply concerned. Her hectic gaiety was too intense. It recalled the Old Gentleman's near manic expansiveness when he was troubled. Charlotte had always been lighthearted and gay, almost light-minded, but she had never been so frenetic. His concern was as much professional as it was fraternal. And why, he wondered, had Thomas, who was so anxious for him to move in worldly society, decisively objected to his attending the masquerade that he would, in any event, have avoided as a matter of propriety?

Charlotte's *hôtel particulier* was transformed into a tropical grove by masses of orchids. Their colors ranged from pure white through delicate pink and purple to jet black, and their heavy scent was cloying. An eight-foot-high pagoda of gilded bamboo stood in the passage-way between the drawing-room and the ball-room, for Charlotte was determined to transmute the foggy Paris December into an Oriental spring.

559

Like Chinese musicians, the twelve-piece orchestra wore loose-fitting scarlet tunics tied with black sashes and flaring black trousers. The musicians' features were concealed by black half-masks, as were the features of the servants, who wore similar costumes in blue silk. Charlotte had compounded the confusion of identities by masking the entertainers and attendants as well as the guests. It had also amused her to accommodate a visiting district officer from Nongkhay in Laos. Wearing only a coolie's black trousers and a half-mask, he lay on a red-and-gold divan puffing a long bamboo tube inset with a porcelain bowl to receive the rolled pellets of opium.

Most of the costumes were less imaginative. Bourbon court ladies and Napoleonic officers, pirates and milk-maids rubbed shoulders, breasts, and buttocks on the dancefloor with clowns, Greek goddesses, Roman senators, and Oued Nail dancing girls. A few gentlemen honored their hostess by appearing as Mandarins. A half-dozen Manchu ladies were burdened by heavily embroidered, calf-length silk tunics over wide-legged pantaloons; their hair was hidden beneath jet-black wigs as their ornately enameled faces were behind the half-masks. Charlotte was herself one of those ladies, for she would not reveal herself as the hostess.

The strings struck up a polonaise, and the perspiring throng, heated with champagne and brandy, hurled itself into the dance, but subsided into a gentle fox-trot when the orchestra glissaded into the most popular song of the season, "Tangerine." Some couples gratefully halted their exertions to watch the jugglers, acrobats, and conjurers who wandered through the orchid-hung chambers; others drifted into curtained booths on the enclosed veranda, where they dared each other to unmask.

As three in the morning approached, most revelers had departed. Some dallied in the booths, where bamboo settees with satin palliasses offered both invitation and opportunity, while others retired to the bedrooms. The sallow district officer from Nongkhay was snoring on his pallet, his opium-pipe cradled in his emaciated arms.

Two tall men dominated the remaining eight revelers, who included three Manchu court ladies and a shepherdess. One wore the orders and stars of a marshal of Napoleon, the other the red regimentals of a general of Wellington. Both were flushed with champagne, as were the pirate and the clown who sprawled on Louis Quinze settees. Only flickering candles lit the orchid-hung glade, and the guests, still masked by their hostess's command, were dim in each other's sight.

Stately despite his ludicrous costume, the butler presented a crystal bowl on a silver salver.

"Mesdames et messieurs, le cocaine," he entoned. "In silence, if you please."

The guests plunged minuscule, filigree-silver spoons into the white powder and sniffed the drug. Alternately sipping and inhaling cocaine, they sat in contented silence for half an hour. A delicious, disembodied sensation possessed them.

The butler reappeared carrying a woven-silver basket filled with folded red and blue paper bows.

"Les ballots, mesdames et messieurs," he said gravely. "I am asked to remind you that speech is not permitted."

Each lady selected a rose-red bow, each man a gentian-blue bow. Grave as children obeying the rules of a new game, the ladies and men matched the numbers they had drawn. The couples then withdrew, some to vacant bedrooms, others to the curtained booths. One of the Manchu ladies had drawn the Napoleonic marshal, the other Wellington's general.

The first pair decorously entered the dim booth in the far corner of the veranda. When the curtains closed, the Manchu lady was in the marshal's arms, murmuring *"Mon cher, je t'aime, mon cher!"*

The masked man returned her kisses in silence, while his hands roamed over her body. She pressed closer, and her heavy tunic parted. Impatiently, she untwined the confining sash, and cast off the heavy silk tunic to stand nude to the waist. The man cupped her breasts in his hands for a minute before pulling her down to the settee. She wore only a diaphanous *cache-sexe* beneath the pantaloons his eager hands removed. The next instant, she was naked except for her half-mask and wig. His fingers strayed along her thighs, and his lips brushed her nipples.

The man had discarded his gold-encrusted tunic. While he caressed his partner's shadowy figure, her eager hand fumbled with his belt-buckle.

"*Les sabots, les sabots,*" she whispered, her husky voice unrecognizable. "The boots, the boots."

Pulling off his trousers and jackboots, the man offered himself to the woman's hands. He was four inches shorter without the built-up boots.

"My God!" she gasped. "Who are you? Who in the name of God? I fixed the ballots. My God, you're *not* Randall. Who *are* you, then?"

Abashed at the strange turn the game had taken, the man sensed with rising horror that he knew his partner's identity. Her quick hands clawed his mask, and she stood gaping in revulsion.

"Thomas!" she screamed. "Thomas! My God, what are we doing?"

Thomas Sekloong stood mute before his sister's anguished surprise.

"Get out! Get out!" she shrieked hysterically. "I never want to see you again! We must never see each other again!"

Thomas Sekloong fled from the booth and from his sister's house, abandoning both the uniform tunic and the built-up boots. He was numbed by the obscenity they had almost committed.

Charlotte Sekloong Way d'Alivère, Comtesse de Samlieu, wrapped the Manchu tunic around herself and scurried to her bedroom. Beyond sensation, she collapsed screaming onto the broad bed. Her Bohemianism shattered by the incestuous foreplay, she was horrified. She wept with the hopeless abandon of a small girl, and a terrible jealousy mingled with her grief. She herself had unwittingly arranged for her lover, the

American actor Randall Martin, to make love to another woman by confusing the paper bows so carefully arranged. Even after exhaustion finally bore her into sleep, her slender figure was still shaken by wracking spasms.

The Comtesse de Samlieu did not dine with her youngest brother Charles the next night. He was turned away at the door. She kept to her bedroom for a week, refusing to speak even to her doctor, who was summoned by the servants. The bewildered physician treated her inexplicable condition as best as he could. He kept her heavily sedated and told the curious servants that she was suffering from a "severe virus fever." But *tout Paris* whispered that the Comtesse's dissipations had finally destroyed her strength. She was dying, the all-knowing reported. And no surprise, the partisans of the Comte de Samlieu retorted, since only a miracle had prevented its happening much sooner.

Yet the invitations to the Comtesse's annual Christmas reception were not recalled—as the malicious half-hoped and the pleasure-bent half-feared. Just two weeks after the disastrous masked ball, Charlotte Sekloong Way d'Alivère played the hostess with enchanting verve and bubbling gaiety. She had, the four hundred guests whispered, never been so radiant, so vitally alive.

"Thank you for asking, my dear." The same glowing smile answered the genuinely concerned and the maliciously disappointed. "But reports of my imminent death were grossly exaggerated. Just a touch of fever. So good of you to come. And a very Merry Christmas."

Behind her façade of gaiety Charlotte was, she confessed to herself, as nervous as a bride on her wedding night. It was a strange sensation for her and an even stranger analogy. She had already experienced too many mock wedding nights—too many carnal encounters inspired only by restless lust—as well as the two blessed by the Church. But her pulse pounded, and a tide of crimson flowed over her shoulders and cheeks when the big man entered the room. He was well over six feet tall, and his broad shoulders strained his chalk-striped blue suit. Beneath a mane of blond hair, his regular features were boyishly open. Randall Martin was forty-two, but looked no older than thirty. Even if his face had not stared from a hundred thousand billboards, no one could have taken the actor for anything but an American. His ingenuous features were unmarked by time. His face looked not as if he had used it for four decades, but as if he had put it on brand new that evening with his blue suit and red foulard tie.

The motion-picture star greeted Charlotte with the kiss on the cheek that was the equivalent of a handshake in their milieu. She automatically offered him her other cheek to seal the greeting.

"I didn't," he whispered in the dark baritone that had insured his success when the motion-pictures began to talk. "I was, she said, ungentlemanly. Nanette de Courcy will never speak to me again. But I didn't."

"I'm glad," Charlotte whispered, "very glad."

"And you?"

She shook her head, not trusting herself to speak. She was astonished by her pleasure at being able to tell the truth and by her delight in Randall's fidelity.

"Dinner tomorrow night?" The actor drew her aside proprietorially, for all the world knew they were lovers.

"No, Randy, darling, I can't."

Charlotte was amused by the hurt bewilderment that clouded his open features. Straining hard for originality, one critic had written that Randall Martin commanded only three expressions: "frank joy, wild anger, and bewilderment—one more than absolutely necessary." But the women who stormed box offices in three hundred cities were not troubled by his histrionic limitations, while their husbands and boyfriends grudgingly conceded: "This Martin's okay, not a greasy lounge-lizard."

"And why not?" Martin demanded, anger beginning to replace bewilderment.

"The night after is fine, but I have another engagement tomorrow."

"Who is he?"

"My youngest brother Charles. He's the priest you see over there, talking to the British military attaché."

"Your brother's a priest?" Randall Martin's incipient anger relapsed into bewilderment succeeded by white-toothed joy. "We don't know enough about each other, do we? Dinner, definitely, the night after?"

"Yes, darling. Yes. Yes."

Charles and Charlotte dined alone at the unfashionably early hour of 7:30 in the small morning-room rather than the formal dining room. Despite her own confused emotions, she interrogated him closely. The possessive protectiveness she had felt for her baby brother reasserted itself, though she had made no effort to see him during her years in Europe. When she had satisfied her curiosity, she offered the only apology of which she was capable.

"I'm sorry, Charlot," she explained contritely. "I meant to come see you, but something always came up. Life was so exciting, and I was enjoying myself so."

"You say *was*." Charles's prim manner recalled the infant the family had called the Little Mandarin. "Does that mean you're *not* enjoying yourself now?"

"Of course not," she flared defensively. "That was just a way of speaking. Of course I'm enjoying myself. I *love* my life."

"Charlotte?"

"What, Charles?"

"Just . . . Charlotte?"

"Oh, all right," she conceded. "No, it's not fun any more. I feel terribly soiled. That's why I haven't been home. I can't face Mother."

"If you feel that way, Charl, your troubles are half-solved. Have you told your confessor?"

"My *confessor*?" she laughed bitterly. "What confessor? How can I confess my sins—and promise not to sin again?"

"Everything is possible to a contrite heart."

Monsignor Charles sounded stiffly inadequate even to himself. But he persisted, as he had been taught. Any soul in anguish merited his assistance, and this was his

565

sister, his favorite sister. He had always been drawn more closely to madcap Charlotte than to sober Gwinnie.

"Everything is possible with His help," he repeated.

"But not remarriage, Charlot."

"Remarriage, Charl? I heard d'Alivère wanted an annulment so he could remarry. Do you, too?"

"I want it terribly," she said softly. "You see, Charlot, I'm in love, truly in love for the first time."

"The *first* time?" He did not conceal his surprise.

"Yes, I married Manfei because it seemed the thing to do. It pleased Father and the Old Gentleman. Besides, everyone was getting married, all my friends."

"But you fought Mother as if the world would end if you *didn't* marry Manfei."

"Yes, Charlot," she smiled wistfully. "Some things they didn't teach you at the Seminary. I wanted to get away from Mother, probably wanted to spite her. Mothers and daughters, they're natural rivals. She was too strong for me."

The priest sipped his claret in silence. If his teachers had not revealed the labyrinthine mysteries of the female heart to him, they had at least taught him when to be quiet.

"Then, when Manfei died and I came to Europe, to Paris, I guess I married Raymond for security—and the title, too," his sister continued. "But it didn't work, and now we're bound together. I got a civil divorce from Raymond to keep the money from him. But, as you know too well, remarriage within the Church is impossible without annulment. I'm truly in love, but I can never marry Randy properly."

"I *do* know the rules," he said tartly. "But Randall Martin?"

"Yes, Randy. I want to marry him. Properly. In the Church."

"I'm glad, Charl. Love is precious, even when it makes life difficult."

"That sounds beautiful. But it's not true."

"Charlotte, when you married d'Alivère, did you

566

truly mean to love and cherish him as long as you both lived, and to give him children?"

"Of course not, Monsignor," she mocked. "Even Alaine was an accident."

"Then, perhaps, something can be done. Since you did not sincerely enter into a lifelong marriage, wanting children. I must make inquiries."

"You really think so, that I can get an annulment?"

"I can't promise. I'm not a canon lawyer. I'll make inquiries. But it will take time."

"Oh, Charlot, if you could!"

Christmas of 1939 in Europe was a season of gaiety, if not joy. The victorious Germans celebrated with the traditional rock-hard cookies called *Lebküchen* and the sentimental carols the Nazis could not forbid, though *Deutschland über Alles,* the anthem of conquest, and *Das Horst Wessel Lied,* the Nazis' marching song, were sung as often as *Stille Nacht.* The French sated themselves with their traditional Christmas Eve reveillon, absolutely convinced that the Germans would never dare attack the impenetrable Maginot Line. No German bombs had yet fallen on French soil, and his countrymen believed they owed their immunity to Premier Edouard Daladier's stern warning of the terrible retribution that would be wreaked upon Berlin, Hamburg, and Munich. The British consumed their roast goose, sang their Christmas carols, and happily carried on their ancient traditions by decorating their Christmas trees, a practice introduced by the German Prince Albert of Saxe-Coburg, Queen Victoria's consort, less than a century earlier. A few Britons worried about the war at sea, the only active front of the phony war. German submarines were still sinking too many of the merchant ships that carried not only the arms, but the food essential to Britain's survival. Yet the rate of attrition was still in Britain's favor, the tonnage sunk less than new-built or purchased tonnage. Besides, British intelligence reckoned that the Royal Navy was sinking three times the actual number of *Unterseeboo-ten* it actually sank.

The three wartime capitals were all complacent for the same reason. Germans, French, and Britons believed alike that Adolf Hitler was, if not sated, at least satisfied. Cramming themselves with Polish hams and sausages, the Germans told themselves that *der Führer* had, once again, brilliantly proved his political acumen. Britain and France would remain on the defensive, the gesture of declaring war having satisfied their honor and fulfilled their pledge to Poland. The men who knew in Germany predicted peace within months. They did *not* know that Hitler's peace overtures had already been rejected by Daladier and Chamberlain, who, those insiders declared with absolute certainty, could not be foolish enough to refuse a generous settlement. The French and the British were reassured by the lull in the ground fighting. Since the German conquest of Poland the phony war had become a war of words. The belligerents' radio stations bombarded each other with charges and countercharges, with rumors and counterrumors. Along the static front lines, the only troops heavily engaged were those manning the enormous loudspeakers that hurled propaganda across no-man's land. The enemies' themes were identical: "Lay down your arms and go home. You have no hope of prevailing. Why die in an impossible cause?"

While men talked of peace, hoped for peace, and believed in peace in the midst of war, Major General Thomas Sekloong slipped out of Paris in late January 1940. He did not bid farewell to his sister Charlotte, whom he was not to see again until June 1970, except for a chance encounter at a diplomatic reception in London in 1947, when they ignored each other. But he had several long talks with his brother Charles before embarking on the long voyage from Marseilles through the Suez Canal and the Indian Ocean that was to land him in Hong Kong for a two-day visit with his family before he boarded a twin-motored DC-2 for the dangerous, roundabout flight to Chungking. After arrival, his lengthy written report would merely confirm his gloomy cabled dispatches. His mission had failed.

"They can't understand this is a common effort against the same two enemies, Fascism *and* Communism," he had told Charles bitterly two days before his departure. "Plenty of sympathy's available, but not arms, money, or even quiet diplomatic support."

"The Communists seem to be the only ones helping," Charles observed. "I'm told Chungking's received almost a quarter of a billion dollars, American dollars, in Soviet loans. And airplanes, too. Maybe a thousand."

"The Russians are reinsuring themselves," Thomas said. "What I couldn't tell you about those planes and the Soviet advisers. . . . But I won't spoil your day."

"It's a funny war," Charles persisted. "The Russians and the Japs are at bayonet's point. The Russians are practically allies of the Germans. But the Japs *are* the Germans' allies. The Finns should logically be German allies. Yet they're fighting the Russians, while London and Paris talk of helping the Finns."

"I've warned you against logic, youngster," Thomas snapped. "The Allies won't help the Finns any more than they'll help China. Apply logic to this international lunacy, and you'll go mad too."

"Speaking of logic, I have a few tidbits from London."

"Make me unhappier," Thomas said. "Tell me."

"It won't make you happy. As you know, Winston Churchill is a licensed gadfly since he got back the Admiralty. I suppose he's entitled to interfere, but his audacity's breathtaking."

"What now?" Thomas asked with gloomy resignation.

"Churchill's views on Asia. I can put you in the picture. Briefly, he feels that nothing east of Singapore is worth defending. Hong Kong can go under if the Japanese attack. If it comes to it—he's really thinking cosmically—Australia can go under to be liberated later. But Churchill expects Singapore to hold. Singapore and China, he says, can look after themselves against the Japs. Shall I go on?"

"Not unless you have something more concrete. What you've told me is bad enough. It bears out what I've been hearing, explains why Britain and France have given us less than $95 million U.S. There'll be no more, either. How they've resisted Japanese pressure to close the Hanoi–Kunming Railroad and the Burma Road this long I don't know. But they won't much longer. Then, barring a miracle, we'll be isolated—totally isolated, except for a few daredevil flights from Hong Kong and small coasters sneaking into the small East China ports we still control."

"It's hardly a common struggle, is it?" Charles mused.

"It *is*, I tell you. It *is* a common struggle, but our allies, those who *should* be our allies, they're too complacent or too frightened to understand."

"What . . . I know the question's naive, Tom, but what can China do? What can the Gimo do?"

"Do? There's only one thing to do. We'll fight. The Gimo won't give in. We'll fight the Jap dwarves and the Communist bandits. We'll fight!"

China did fight—and the interminable war of attrition on the mainland of Asia continued. Yet both Nationalists and Communists devoted most of their resources to fighting each other. Feuding among themselves and skirmishing with their warlord allies, the Nationalists commanded larger forces and nominally controlled larger areas. The Communists intelligently utilized the aid they received from the Soviet Union. Their cohesion, their shrewd political warfare, and their firm discipline were all dedicated to one unwavering purpose, the eventual conquest of all China.

The mainland of Europe, the seed bed and the bastion of Western civilization, also fought against the two-fold threat from the east. At least, some West Europeans fought, but none effectively. The phony war ended when Hitler preempted Britain's plans to gain control of the Baltic by invading Norway on April 9, 1940. While the British and French were trying to riposte and fighting continued in the Baltic, columns of

Nazi *Panzerwagen* supported by motorized infantry began rolling over Holland and Belgium. Other columns struck at France through the "impassable" Ardennes Forests. The impenetrable Maginot Line was outflanked, its great garrison reduced to spectators. On the same day the German *Blitzkrieg* struck, May 10, 1940, Winston Churchill succeeded Neville Chamberlain as the First Minister of State of His Majesty King George VI.

Between May 10 and June 22, when France formally surrendered, Adolf Hitler was to make himself master of the European continent from the Mediterranean Sea to the Arctic Ocean, from the English Channel to the Bug River, where his troops faced their new friends, the Soviets. The phony war was over. All illusions and all hopes of peace were trampled under the jackboots of the invincible *Wehrmacht,* and the *Wehrmacht* was poised to attack England.

Amid the universal catastrophe, those who could save themselves did so. Charlotte Sekloong Way d'Alivère received a peremptory telegram from Hong Kong in late-May, just after her brother, Monsignor Charles Sekloong, called at the demi-mansion off the Faubourg St. Honoré for the last time. He repeated at length the injunction their parents' telegram expressed briefly: "Flee. Get out while you still can."

Truly concerned about another human being for the first time in her life, Charlotte pleaded on the telephone with Raymond d'Alivère: "Let me take Alaine with me," she begged. "Let me take her to a place where she'll be safe." But the Comte de Samlieu brusquely rejected her pleas. France would not fall, he insisted. And if France did fall, well, he could undoubtedly make his own arrangements with the Germans. The German armies were after all led by men of his own class, even if Hitler himself was a guttersnipe. "And," he reminded her, "you are not to use the title once the annulment is approved."

After listening to the last words Raymond was ever to speak to her, Charlotte prepared to leave France. Air and rail tickets were impossible to obtain, despite the pressure she tried to exert through her influential friends, who were primarily concerned with their own escape. The Comtesse de Samlieu finally left Paris in her boxcarlike red Rolls-Royce. The vehicle's dignity was marred by the valises and trunks tied to its roof, but the winged angel atop the radiator pointed south toward Spain, Portugal, and safety. Beside her, Randall Martin was relaxed with a glass of brandy in his hand and cockily unafraid.

"Look, Charl, it's gonna be all right," he repeated. "We'll get married in Lisbon, and then no sweat. As the wife of an American, you just sail right into the good old U.S.A. You're practically an American, already. Hell, we're Americans, and we're neutral. Leave these people to their own mess. They can't touch us."

December 8, 1941–December 26, 1941

THE frail hands, liver-spotted with age, riffled the pages of the blue-leather-bound ledger, and the strong mouth above the white beard pursed. At seven on the morning of Monday, December 8, 1941, the Old Gentleman had already been awake for two hours. Having said his prayers and eaten a light breakfast, he was basking in the sunshine on the veranda overlooking the sweep of Hong Kong Harbor and the Kowloon Hills that cupped Kaitak Airport. The words his hazel eyes read were a deliberate jumble of elided Chinese, still-remembered Jesuit Latin, and his own English abbreviations. Stamped in gold on the ledger's cover was the winged dragon above the title: PERSONAL DIARY FOR 1941, THE 88TH YEAR OF THE LIFE OF SIR JONATHAN SEKLOONG, KCMG. His body's feebleness had affected neither his domineering will nor his incisive mind, and he automatically translated his code into plain language as he read:

January 20, 1941: That rapscallion James is the center of a storm of trouble again. God preserve me from another such descendant, unfilial and bullheaded—in short, a Communist. He and his treacherous chief Liu Shao-chi are Political Commissar and Deputy Political Commissar of the New Fourth Army. That Communist army is a unit of the National Forces and sworn to obey the orders of the Generalissimo, who is the best fool we have. He ordered them to move northward, away from Shanghai, in late 1940, but they refused. Instead, the New Fourth Army extended its tentacles southward, impeding operations of Nationalist units.

Chungking was very patient, but the Communists, inspired by that unholy pair, James and Liu Shao-chi, kept pushing outward. On January 5 of this year, the Gimo's patience was exhausted. The loyal 40th Division fell on the New Fourth's Headquarters and captured the commanding general. There was a bitter fight, the first major Nationalist–Communist clash since the United Front agreement. But the stealthy red foxes had already withdrawn most of their troops.

On January 17, Central Headquarters ordered the New Fourth disbanded. The Communists simply appointed a new commander and proclaimed a new Soviet Area. So, once again, James Sekloong, who calls himself Major General Shih Ai-kuo, is an outlaw, in revolt against the legitimate government. The ancestors frown in disapproval.

I am surprised that the Communists didn't attack first. They have been harrying the Gimo's tottering coalition everywhere, trying to destroy the Nationalists. Mao Tse-tung's strategy has been obvious since mid-1939, when he established several "independent" Communist governments in the north and northwest—after promising to subordinate himself to the National Government under the Gimo's orders. The split is now open, though neither Nationalists nor Communists want to resume full-scale hostilities against each other.

January 21, 1941: Mary came to see me alone today; she wouldn't even have Opal in the room while we talked. The topic, naturally, James. I sometimes think she loves that child more than all the others together. Of course, he's Harry's son, and Harry was her great passion. She didn't weep. I've never seen Mary weep. Odd, that! But her voice quavered. She didn't mention Harry, never does, and I don't like thinking about that boy. I went wrong badly with Harry. If I'd been harder on him, quashed his nonsensical idealism, things would've turned out differently.

Mary is desperately worried about James, and complained that none of us have seen his children, a ten-year-old son and a one-year-old daughter by that Bolshevik peasant wife of his.

First time I've heard Mary talk so foolishly. Perhaps it's her age. She's getting on, sixty-one this year. She says we must do something about James. Try to get him out of China and back to Hong Kong. She talks about a thirty-four-year-old *paterfamilias* as if he were still a small boy. If we got him out by some miracle, I asked, would he stay long? He's not married to that creature Lu Ping, but to the blasted Communist Party.

Could we not, she asked, at least find out whether he was well and what needs we might supply him with? I told her he was well, I'd had word through the blockade runners. But he wouldn't take anything from us—except arms or funds for his precious New Fourth Army. And I'm not supplying my country's enemies, not at my age.

Could she communicate with him, if nothing else? Surely, I said, let me have your letter. But don't expect an answer. He's Harry's son, I said, what can you expect? Just like his father, he's cut himself off from his family and the legal goverment. Made himself an outlaw.

Naturally, she didn't weep. But she was shaky when she finally left. What else could I do or say? But Opal, eavesdropping as usual, scolded me for being too harsh. And she asked why my own eyes were wet.

January 25, 1941: They celebrated the hundredth anniversary of Hong Kong's formal founding today, and I had to go down to Statue Square and sit like some animated Buddha. Felt like wearing a tweed suit, instead of a long-gown, just to shock them. But I look so damned European in Western clothing, and Opal said they'd just laugh at me.

They could have used a laugh. Dreariest ceremony I've seen in ages. Not much jollity, though they turned out an honor guard from the Middlesex Regiment. Britain with her back to the wall in Europe isn't the Britain that acquired Hong Kong almost absentmindedly when Captain Elliot did as he damned pleased, sailed through the Emperor's war junks, annexed Hong Kong

—and then let Milord Palmerston in London sort out the tangle until they finally made it legal this day a century ago. Lord, a century ago. Just a little over thirteen years before I was born. It's not only Mary who's getting older!

March 6, 1941: Iain Wheatley came crying to me again. You'd think he'd have better things to do at his age, almost sixty-seven. But he's still full of Wheatley malice and cunning. This time he came to plead, though he's done that before too. I was ruining Derwent's, he said—*I*, who made the *hong*, building on my grandfather's work. Wouldn't I call off my boycott? he begged.

My boycott, I asked? I told him I had nothing to do with it. If the overseas Chinese don't want to trade with a firm that's hand-in-glove with the Jap dwarves, what could I do? He swore he had cut his ties with Mitsubishi. (Not true! They're still thick as the thieves they both are!) Then he promised he *would* break off, if only I'd call off the boycott, the sabotage, and the financial pressure.

Told him I wouldn't if I could—and I couldn't. Then, a true Wheatley, he turned nasty. Said he'd break me, drag me down with him. Cut off my credit in London. Call all my loans from the Gazetted Bank and get the Bank of England to look into my currency transactions. A Wheatley cousin is on the Board of Governors.

Laughed and told him to get out. But I called Judah Haleevie and Mosing Way and asked them to cover my flanks. If Wheatley really wants to take on the Rothschilds and Warburgs who're backing me, let him. He'll just destroy himself. For good measure, suggested to the Green Band that they step up pressure on Derwent's people here. A little judicious violence never hurts, but they're not to kill.

Later, Mary came to see me. She was happy because that rascal James had answered her letter. Said only that he was well and hoped to see the family when "conditions permitted." (What "conditions"?) I didn't shoot down her hopes, but told her, instead, of Iain Wheatley's visit. She was all for driving the Wheatleys to the wall, and Charles came in to add his counsel for "all-out war, war to the knife." Both said we'd put up with Wheatleys too long.

Just what I wanted, now that I've got Derwent's in a noose that's drawing tighter every day. I said fine, we'd do it—we'd break them. But I wasn't quite comfortable with the idea. Maybe I've gotten so used to them as enemies, that I'd miss them. Besides, there *is* the family connection, however thin. Old Dick, the lying old scoundrel, *was* my step-father, though precious little help he gave me.

But, I said: Fine, we'd really let loose, and we were impregnable because of the depth of our investments abroad, not to speak of our allies and owning half Wanchai and the New Territories.

Charles was all for it, but Mary got cold feet when we started planning the new campaign. Curious, Charles seems to get stronger all the time. Mary said we'd better think about it. If we drove Derwent's into bankruptcy, many others would go down with them—and we'd be blamed, we'd face the hostility of all the European *hongs*. Moreover, many innocents would suffer—investors, employees, etc. Besides, she said, we wouldn't be absolutely sure of crushing them, and it was foolish to shoot at a king unless you were certain of killing him.

Charles finally agreed it was better just to keep up the pressure, not go for the kill. Mary's arguments convinced both of us. She's an extraordinary woman, almost as tough as the Old Empress Dowager. Besides, I think she felt my own mood, knew I wasn't that keen. Uncanny!

June 2, 1941: I want the women to leave—and take Albert with them. Almost all European women were forced to leave Hong Kong a year ago because of the presumed threat from the Japanese. There's much resentment against those of us whose women have remained. I raised the matter with Mary, Charles, Sarah, and Jonnie. The boys agreed, reluctantly. But the ladies were adamant. They would not leave their men behind to face danger without them. We finally worked out a compromise. Albert, who's only seven, will go either to Charlotte or Gwinnie in America. No point in sending him from the hypothetical danger of an attack on Hong Kong to the real danger of England under bombardment. His older brother Henry is already at Stonyhurst, so that's another matter. Besides, even the Germans wouldn't want to bomb that great pile in the middle of nowhere.

The solution's unsatisfactory, but I've learned I can't oppose the combined wills of Mary and Sarah. Perhaps

I'm getting old after all. Charles and Jonnie were of two minds themselves, though they knew damned well other dangers beside the Japanese hang over us. But they refused to *order* their wives to leave. Partly, I think, because they don't want to leave them, and partly because they're not sure the ladies would obey. Damned modern nonsense, giving women their heads.

Some satisfaction in telling the Governor Mary and Sarah were not subject to the evacuation order because they were technically Chinese. He laughed and changed the subject.

August 5, 1941: We had our first bomb last night— not Japanese, but Triads. A small explosion in the garden, meant to frighten. Iain Wheatley's getting desperate. I've put out the word; relax the pressure on Derwent's slightly. When it comes on again, it'll hurt even more. I've also asked Judah Haleevie to persuade the Rothschilds to renegotiate their loans to Derwent's on slightly better terms. I can buy the paper when I wish—and then, perhaps, close my hand and crush Iain Wheatley. I'll decide later.

December 3, 1941: Last night Sir Robert and Lady Mary Hotung celebrated their Diamond Jubilee. Not bad, married sixty years. Young Robert must be almost as old as I. But I'll outlive him yet. The Gripps at the Hong Kong Hotel was blinding with uniforms, decorations, medals and jewels. All the Hotung ladies wore traditional Chinese dress, not *cheongsams* but nineteenth-century Court costumes. Looked like a Cantonese opera troupe to me, but it pleased them. I wore my cross of a Knight Commander of the Order of St. Michael and St. George. Robert is only a knight bachelor, poor chap. But he's been very helpful in the work of the China Relief Committee and in our unpublicized squeeze on the Wheatleys. A patriot and a good man, even if inclined to ostentatious showiness when he gives a party. Bad taste!

Unconfirmed reports that the Japanese were moving up three divisions to the border. The Volunteers called up, and Jonnie went off to his unit in high spirits. Returned shortly. False alarm. No orders to mobilize. Charles a staff colonel at Defense Command Headquarters, commuting, as he says, to the war that isn't.

Opal came onto the veranda carrying a cup of hot milk.

"Drink this down, Old One," she directed, shivering in the breeze.

Sir Jonathan sipped and waved her away. It was, he concluded, an interesting record of a remarkable year, though some other years had been even more exciting. Nonetheless, it was good to review the record and see how the Family had fared during the year. Reviewing the record also gave him a chance to fill any gaps. He picked up his pen and began writing.

December 8, 1941: I decided in late November to let the Wheatleys survive, now that they're humbled. It would be no credit to my grandfather's memory or my beloved mother's to extinguish the firm he virtually created and she nurtured. Curiously, Mary is now opposed to relenting. We've already hurt the Wheatleys so badly, she argued, their enmity would be a constant danger to us. She wanted me to close my hand. Charles and Jonnie agreed with me; they are Sekloongs by blood and they understand my motives. But I must be careful. Mary may be right.

The British are behaving as usual. That is to say with a combination of calm courage, bovine complacency, and profound stupidity. At least they finally mobilized the Volunteers yesterday, Sunday. My informants tell me the Japanese are moving right up to the border, an entire army corps. On Saturday, December 6, Japanese civilians scurried away to Canton. But that same night at the Peninsula Hotel, the British staged something they called a "Tin Hat Ball." The idea was to finish raising the sum of £160,000 for the bomber squadron Hong Kong has presented to Britain.

A curious gesture when our own air defense is practically nonexistent. Three amphibians, good only for patrolling, and four Wildebeeste torpedo bombers, with no aerial torpedoes available closer than Singapore. The total lack of interceptor aircraft is criminal.

But the fleet, they say, will provide. . . .

"Old One! Old One!" Opal's husky voice broke Sir Jonathan's concentration. "Look! Look! Many airplanes coming to Kaitak. Now we will have enough."

Twelve aircraft droned in formation through the clear skies above the green Kowloon Hills. The foremost swooped down toward the runway at Kaitak Airport, but pulled up a few hundred feet above the ground. Sir Jonathan's sharp eyes saw black, egg-shaped pellets fall from their silver bellies like pregnant guppies releasing their young. Gray pillars of smoke rose from the airport, and an instant later he heard the explosions reverberate. White puffs burst around the formation, but the silver wings flaunting the red sun of the Imperial Japanese Air Force evaded the anti-air-craft fire contemptuously.

The next echelon dived vertically as if determined to impale itself in the ground. No more than a hundred feet above the airport, the warplanes pulled up with wing-straining deceleration, and the big black bombs under their bellies hurtled into the hangars. Smaller pursuit planes repeatedly swept over Kaitak, the crimson flashes of machine-gun fire winking from their wings.

Five minutes later, the raid was over. Thirty-six Japanese warplanes had destroyed the entire British Air Force in the Far East, as well as a clumsy four-motored Pan American Clipper scheduled to take off at 9:30 A.M. for the long island-hopping haul across the Pacific. The Clipper had missed escape by an hour and a half. The attack came just before eight in the morning, some seven hours after Japanese airpower had wiped out the American battleship fleet at Pearl Harbor on the morning of Sunday, December 7, on the other side of the International Dateline. At 4:45 A.M., Military Intelligence monitors in Hong Kong had intercepted coded signals warning Japanese abroad that war with Britain and the United States was imminent. At 6:45 A.M., Hong Kong Garrison Headquarters was informed that Japan had declared war. At 7:00 A.M., Tokyo home radio, heard clearly in Hong Kong, warned the Japanese people that they were at war with the two English-speaking powers. No preparation against air attack was however attempted, and none could have been effective.

Unprepared psychologically, depleted materially, and stripped of airpower, Hong Kong lay open to the three battle-tempered Imperial Army divisions that were massed on the Colony's twenty-two-mile-long border with Japanese-occupied Kwangtung Province. The Japanese expected little ground resistance, and they were confident of sweeping aside that resistance in a few hours, at most a few days. Lieutenant General Sakai Takashi, commanding the task force, ceremonially downed a cup of *sake* with his staff officers and confidently awaited reports from his forward formations. Japanese infantrymen were already moving into British territory at Shataukok on the shore of Mira Bay at the eastern end of the border. Other units were striking across the muddy Shumchon River onto the flat central plain of the New Territories.

That portentous term "the fog of war" is a cliché, a self-vindication—and a fair description. Coined by historians to explain their inability to see a coherent picture of any engagement larger than a clash between two squads, it was adopted by the generals to justify the miasma of confusion that separates commanders from the men fighting in the field. The description is still derisively correct in the age of instantaneous radio and telephonic communications, when the fog of war even more thickly obscures the human male's second favorite activity. Once committed to battle, the commanding officer of the smallest integral combat unit, the infantry company, finds it exceedingly difficult to learn what his own soldiers are doing, much less the enemy's. The general, deploying brigades and divisions, finds it virtually impossible to follow the action over which he presides. Endowed with abundant leisure and keen hindsight, historians produce plausible accounts years later, but those accounts err as often as they are reasonably accurate.

Exceptions to the frustrating rule do however occur. During the first week of the eighteen-day battle for Hong Kong, Charles Sekloong's vision was not obscured by the fog of war. He possessed a unique vantage point at the Headquarters of the Hong Kong Defense Command under Major General C. M. Maltby, an intelligent and gallant soldier thrust into an impossible assignment. Charles wore the red tabs of a staff officer on his lapels and the bronze crown surmounted by two embossed stars of a full colonel on his shoulder straps, but he commanded no troops. Unqualified for that function, he was ideally suited to the duties assigned to him. He spoke most of the languages of the polyglot force, and he knew the terrain intimately. He was, therefore, the chief channel through which tactical reports passed. Charles observed the debacle of British arms with great clarity and mounting despair. But his view of the global strategy in which Hong Kong played only a minor part was befogged by erroneous intelligence reports and by insistently impractical exhortations from London.

As the first Japanese units crossed the border, the first encouraging reports came into Defense Headquarters. Generalissimo Chiang Kai-shek was massing Chinese armies to take Lieutenant General Sakai's forces in the rear and save Hong Kong. Desperately wanting to believe, intelligence officers pointed out sagely that it was vitally important for the Nationalists to keep Hong Kong open as a backdoor to China; otherwise Chungking would be totally isolated. Only a few realists asked where Chiang Kai-shek would find those troops and why he should divert them from his own battles against the Japanese and the Communists.

But even those realists accepted authoritative intelligence regarding the low quality of the Japanese fighting man, while none saw irony in London's command that Hong Kong be held "at all costs." The Japanese, who had not performed spectacularly well against raggle-taggle Chinese formations, were for the first time confronting valorous, well-trained British soldiers. Charles, almost alone, did not believe Hong Kong could be held, and he expressed his doubts only to his father. That tough-minded octagenarian shared his son's doubts, but cautioned Charles to voice them to no one else, not even to Mary, Sarah, or Jonnie.

Yet the first day's action bore out London's optimism. Major George Gray, commanding a company of Punjabi sepoys of Britain's Indian Army, methodically demolished all border installations and withdrew southward in good order. He then laid a classic ambush north of the hamlet called Taipo Market. When the Japanese marched down the road in formation, the sepoys scythed them with rifle and machine-gun fire from the hillsides, killing hundreds. Undaunted, the Japanese pursued the Punjabis to the town of Taipo. Their column was, once again, massacred by the sepoys, who had been reinforced by an armored-car squadron. Elation succeeded the dogged determination Defense Headquarters had mustered at the first assault. Perhaps this once, just this once, the intelligence assessments were correct. The Japanese, it appeared, could not stand up to the disciplined British forces.

Nonetheless, the battalion to which Major George Gray's Punjabis belonged continued to withdraw, as did the two other battalions of the Mainland Brigade defending the New Territories and Kowloon. They were the fifth battalion of the Seventh Rajputs, and a battalion of the Royal Scots, who were proudly known as the First of Foot, since they were the oldest infantry unit on the rolls of the British Army. Confronting overwhelming Japanese numbers and unchallengeable Japanese control of the air, they could only fight a delaying action until they reached their prepared positions at the narrowest point of the New Territories. Those fortifications extended from Shatin, so called for its Sandy Fields, in the east to Gin Drinkers' Bay in the west, a favorite resort of weekend yachtsmen who asserted that the insatiable native mosquitoes were repelled by the smell of gin taken internally. The impregnability of Hong Kong's Maginot Line, inevitably called Gin Drinkers' Line, was distrusted chiefly by the Commanding General C. M. Maltby, who had arrived only a few weeks earlier. Besides, the Japanese were already outflanking Gin Drinkers' Line by landing in Kowloon from a small craft to cut the Mainland Brigade off from Hong Kong Island.

Yet the first day of fighting on December 8 surprised the Japanese by the effectiveness of British resistance and confirmed the low British opinion of the Japanese. December 9 was, however, a British disaster.

Gin Drinkers' Line pivoted on two major fortifications, the Shingmun Redoubt and the Golden Hill, both held by the Royal Scots, the First of Foot. General Sakai had realized a year earlier that pillboxes, trenches, and bunkers of the Redoubt were the key to the British defenses. His assault companies had trained for months on a replica constructed near Canton until their officers boasted: "We could take the place blindfolded."

Noiseless in mitten-like tennis shoes, the assault troops were not blindfolded when they cut the barbed-wire of the Shingmun Redoubt at 10 P.M. on the ninth of December. Snug in their dugouts, the Royal Scots learned they were under attack when hand grenades tumbled down the ventilating shafts. It was death to remain underground; it was death to fight in the open and be cut down by Japanese machine guns. The Royal Scots, the First of Foot, fled south toward Kowloon, earning a new nickname, the Fleet of Foot.

Sustained by the Punjabis and reinforced by a company of Canadian Winnipeg Grenadiers hastily transferred from the Island Brigade, the British sought to close the hole. It was like trying to patch a tire running at high speed. The Japanese streamed around them, and the British forces could not stand. On Thursday, December 11, General Maltby ordered the Mainland Brigade to withdraw to Hong Kong Island. The miniature Dunkirk across a miniature Channel was completed on Saturday, the thirteenth. The intervening days were brightened by astounding valor and besmirched by base cowardice. The Rajput and Punjabi sepoys executed that single most difficult maneuver, disengaging from an attacking enemy and withdrawing in constant contact with that enemy while preserving themselves as an intact fighting force. The Sikhs of the Hong Kong Police Force almost to a man went over to the Japanese. Scattered detachments of Volunteers fought desperately to win time for their women and children to embark on overladen ferries for Hong Kong Island. Bitter in defeat, the Royal Scots maintained just enough cohesion to retreat as a unit.

By December 14, it was over. All Britain's mainland territories, more than three hundred square miles of the New Territories and Kowloon, had fallen to the Japanese in less than a week. Lieutenant General Sakai Takashi staged his veteran Thirty-eighth Division for the attack on twenty-nine-square-mile Hong Kong Island. The British Broadcasting Corporation was still celebrating the invincible valor of that impregnable fortress. The Union Jack was to wave over that fortress for less than two weeks longer.

"The Japs closed out that lease faster than any Tenancy Tribunal," Captain Jonathan Sekloong told his second-in-command, Lieutenant Peter Hardin.

"They've saved the Gimo the trouble," Hardin replied. "When the Nationalists get here, they can take over the New Territories. No need to wait till the lease runs out in '97, Chink."

Jonnie grinned at his old Stonyhurst nickname. The silly jokes and the gut-gripping anticipation were also reminiscent. The same sickly tension he had felt before a hard rugger match against Ampleforth electrified his Fifth Field Artillery Battery, which, on December 15, 1941, was emplaced above the fixed coastal gun defending Lyemun Pass, the eastern inlet to Hong Kong Harbor. Besides, Peter Hardin was privileged, not only his classmate at Stonyhurst, but a second or third cousin on his Sekloong grandmother's side.

"Let the lawyers worry about that one, Peter," Jonnie said. "All we do is hold till the other chinks arrive —the more the better."

"And the faster the better," Hardin answered. "Though we're pretty snug here."

Jonnie remembered his Uncle Harry's tales of Nationalist military ineptitude too well to believe Chinese forces would charge to their rescue like the U.S. Cavalry in an American cowboy film. That hope, however, sustained most of the outnumbered, outgunned garrison, while immediate worries disturbed the commanding officer of the isolated battery.

"Not snug enough, Peter," he said. "Do you really believe those Dinah Lays'll stand a direct hit?"

"Well, Dinah's a pretty durable girl," Peter drawled. "But I'd like to have old Morosby right here with us."

"What's all this cock about Dinah Lay?" asked the Sergeant Major. "Never heard of the lady."

"Pity, Bill." Jonnie spoke with the easy informality of the Volunteers. "She might just kill you."

"Poxed, eh?" the Sergeant Major laughed. "Well, *I'm* all right. Never met the lady, much less rogered her. Speak for yourself, Jonnie."

"You're new to Hong Kong, Bill, or you'd know Dinah Lay's no lady," Peter Hardin interjected. "We're talking about the concrete blocks, our impregnable defense."

"All right, chaps," the Sergeant Major demanded. "What *are* you nattering about."

"Dinah Lay was, still is, the cleverest and most expensive tart in the Colony," Jonnie explained. "She was set up in a palatial Kowloon flat by old Stan Morosby of the Public Works Department. He bought her a flashy Lagonda coupé and hung her with jewels. Stan was a poor boy from Liverpool, and I'm not one to repeat slander, but rumor has it that he found the cash by . . . ah . . . cooperating with the Fook Wong Construction Company. I'm pretty sure the blocks are hollow and the concrete itself mostly sand. So they're called Dinah Lays."

"Well named," the Sergeant Major conceded. "But a hell of a story to tell a man facing battle for King and country. No regard for troop morale, that's the trouble with you temporary officers."

A clear, high voice cut across their badinage, a familiar voice singing "The Lights of Home."

"By God, Deanna Durbin," Peter exclaimed.

"Shut up and listen," said Jonnie. "The Japs are serenading us."

I can see somebody there. The pure soprano wafted

585

across the Harbor. *Tender eyes and silver hair, beneath the lights of home.*

"Damned nice of them," Bill said. "Do you think we could request . . ."

A distant rattle truncated his labored jest. Somewhere over the water to their left rifles were firing.

"Searchlight, Bill!" Jonnie ordered. "Let's see what the devil's going on."

The blue-white arclight probed the darkness. The whitecaps on the green waves broke in glowing spray, and a waterlogged basket drifted across the white circle of light. The circle moved slowly over the waters. The secrets of the night remained shrouded, and unseen soldiers fired their rifles in ragged rhythms. The light inched westward, persistent and vulnerable as a blind man's cane.

Abruptly as if a Kodacolor slide had been inserted into a projector, a large fishing junk under full sail materialized in the white beam. Through his binoculars Jonnie saw Japanese soldiers squatting on the decks, their conical helmets shining dully. The searchlight illuminated a convoy of small sampans trailing the junk. All were laden with Japanese infantrymen who leveled their weapons at the intrusive light. Machine-gun bullets hammered on the concrete blocks, and the three Volunteers ducked.

"We've made them appear like a conjurer's trick," Jonnie said softly. "Now let's see if we can make them disappear."

"Target in sight," the Sergeant Major bellowed. "Fire at will."

The three field-pieces coughed in succession, and water-spouts geysered around the convoy.

"Have to do better than that," Jonnie said conversationally. "Tell them to track."

"Mark your shots," the Sergeant Major bellowed. "Aim, damn it, aim—and fire!"

The second salvo rocked the junk and doused the Japanese with cold seawater, but the vessel sailed on.

"Traverse left one-half point," Jonnie shouted.

"Down one. Hit the little bastards this time. Hit them!"

Water-spouts bracketed the junk, rising on either side of the wildly rocking vessel. The junk rolled like a log in a millrace, and an orange flash spurted from the foredeck. Three bodies rose high in the air to tumble into the sea amid jagged wooden strips.

"You're on now," Jonnie shouted. "Kill them! Kill the little bastards!"

The junk disintegrated under the explosions. One moment it was sailing forward, wounded but intact. The next, it had disappeared, and the water was alive with thrashing infantrymen. Jonnie watched mesmerized as some were pulled down by the weight of their packs, while others struggled with maimed arms and legs to avoid the deadly shower of debris falling from the sky. The foundering men shouted soundlessly, their mouths gaping wide in macabre pantomime. Through his binoculars the agony was, at once, too clear and too removed, as if he were the detached spectator of a stage play. Blood stained the green water with red streams that became pink tendrils and vanished in seconds.

Jonnie let his binoculars hang from their neckstrap and looked at his trembling hands. His stomach turned over, and bile rose bitter in his throat. He marveled briefly that his brothers Thomas and James had chosen, actually chosen, to devote their lives to such scenes. If this was an easy triumph, his men still unscathed, what could defeat be like?

"The sampans," he heard himself shouting. "Get the sampans. Don't let them get away."

Tossed by the explosions and the frantic thrashing of their long stern oars, the sampans were difficult targets for artillery. They bobbed on the roiled waters like unsinkable walnut shells, but the searchlight pursued them implacably.

The Japanese infantrymen crouching behind the sampans' frail sides twitched and jerked like manic puppets. From the trenches of the Royal Rifles of Canada on the left, streams of red tracers arched across the water to sweep the small boats. The enemy infantrymen despairingly attempted to return the fire. One after another long rifle barrel rose, wavered for an instant, and then fell back into the huddled mass.

"Well," Peter Hardin said complacently. "First blood to us. They're not so great, are they, Chink?"

"Damn it, Peter, don't think it'll be that easy," Jonnie snapped. "Remember what happened to Gin Drinkers' Line. They weren't . . ."

The roar of exploding shells erased his rebuke. The earth trembled under the officers, and a gap opened in the concrete-block wall before them. The Dinah Lays shredded like paper, and, Peter later swore, he saw sand trickling in the explosions' flash. The searchlight flicked off, and the salvoes from the Japanese guns across the Harbor ceased. Since their concussion-deafened ears could not hear the shrieks of drowning men, the night seemed silent again.

"Must've cut the light's cables," Jonnie said. "See to it, Peter."

"Yes, Sir," his Lieutenant replied.

But Jonnie was too busy to ponder his classmate's astonishing display of respect.

"The Japs seem satisfied," he told the Sergeant Major. "But I'll want casualties counted and the men under new cover. Tell Peter to resite the searchlight. It's too vulnerable."

The Sergeant Major vanished into the darkness, leaving his Captain to sum up the engagement in his own mind. The Japanese, Jonnie decided, were neither as fierce nor as proficient as he'd feared. They had not pressed home the infantry assault, though they had responded with reasonably effective counterbattery fire. He could not know that Lieutenant General Sakai Takashi, jealously hoarding his crack units, had feinted with second-echelon troops; his purpose was to draw British fire and thus reveal British positions in order to provide against the unlikely event that the detailed British defense dispositions already communicated by his spies had been altered. Nor could Jonnie know that he was to wait through three days of mounting tension and desultory shelling for General Sakai to fling his murderously effective Thirty-eighth Division across the Harbor with orders not to return. The General was then to command the Thirty-eighth to take bridgeheads on the Island—or to die.

The Fifth Battery's nerve-jangling inaction was enlivened by concerts from the Japanese loudspeakers on the Kowloon Peninsula. The artillerymen cheered the ancient but indomitable destroyer H.M.S. *Thracian*, which was supported by four motor torpedo boats when she punished the few junks and sampans that pushed off from the Peninsula. They swore at the intermittent, well-placed salvoes from the enemy artillery. Though the Japanese assault infantry had shown themselves inept, the professional Japanese artillerymen evoked wholehearted, fearful admiration from the Sunday soldiers, the amateur artillerymen of the Fifth Field Artillery Battery of the Hong Kong Volunteer Defense Force.

Jonnie Sekloong was more fortunate than the men under his command, since he was constantly occupied. He had little leisure either to nurture his fear of the coming battle or to console himself with the bamboo telegraph's reports of Chinese relief columns driving toward Hong Kong. He knew, however, that he was afraid, perhaps more frightened than his comrades because life had been so generous to him. He had enjoyed not only great luxury, but an assured place in a milieu he loved. Just being Jonathan Sekloong of *the* Sekloongs in Hong Kong was a blessing he would exchange for no other conceivable position. Alone among his brothers and sisters, he had totally adjusted to his Eurasian heritage. He had felt no need to become more European than the British as had his sisters, no compulsion to immerse himself in their Chinese origins or a universal cause as had his brothers. Above all, there was Sarah, their love a *mitzvah*, a blessing, as she would say. The world, particularly his world, he knew instinctively, would be different after the Allies had won the war. But he desperately wanted to live and see that world.

Jonnie's brief and uncharacteristic introspection was

relieved by the need to resite his searchlights and guns after Japanese shells ripped into their emplacements. Not all the concrete blocks, the Dinah Lays, disintegrated like ripe mushrooms, but so many crumbled that he drove his men to rebuild the breastworks with sandbags and bricks. The Volunteers grumbled that they had not volunteered to act as coolies, but their officers' casual good humor kept them at work. The men of the isolated Fifth Battery greeted the early twilight of December 18, 1941, in good spirits. They had absorbed the worst the Japanese artillery could throw at them— with minor casualties. The assault infantry was obviously inept, and they knew the Chinese Nationalists were coming.

Black smoke from burning oil tanks lay thick on the Harbor, and opaque rain squalls constantly drove across the choppy waters through the dark, moonless night. When the elite 239th Regiment of the Thirty-eighth Infantry Division of the Imperial Japanese Army landed from ferries and lighters that glided silently to the foreshore, the Volunteers had no warning. General Sakai's 7,500 cherished veterans laid down an overwhelming barrage from machine guns, trench-mortars, and rifles. The Battery's defense platoon, detailed by the Royal Rifles of Canada, died in its shallow trenches at 8:35 P.M., having fired only a few shots. The weight of Japanese metal bore them down even before Japanese infantrymen emerged from the darkness, slashing with blackened bayonets clamped to long rifles. Lyemun Fort was then virtually defenseless. The field artillery fired over open sights at enemies who drifted in and out of the murk like the insubstantial figures of a shadow-play.

The Japanese were among the Volunteers, bayonets stabbing at their defenseless bodies. Jonnie fired two shots from his revolver and toppled the faceless figure advancing on him with bared bayonet. He could not fire a third. The revolver was knocked from his hand, his arms were seized, and his hands were roped behind him. His captors, he noted inconsequentially, stank of rancid sweat and pickled radishes.

Sick rage choked him. They had been effortlessly defeated by the "low-quality" Japanese troops. The "impregnable island fortress" was breached, and he was to blame. Then came fear, nauseating fear. Prisoners of the Japanese, he knew, did not live long.

Jonnie Sekloong looked for his men in the light of burning huts and intermittent flares. He counted only eighteen standing erect. Lieutenant Peter Hardin and the Sergeant Major sprawled on earth powdered into dust by the Japanese shelling. The hands of his surviving men were tied behind them, and the Japanese were tossing them back and forth like puppets. When they wearied of their sport, the Imperial infantrymen stabbed viciously with their short bayonets. Engrossed by the horror of the spectacle, Jonnie did not see the blow that felled him. A bayonet pierced his side, and he fell face down. It was all over, he thought, and recited softly: *"Pater noster, qui est in coelis, nomine . . ."* He relinquished his hold on consciousness.

When a split-toed sandshoe turned him on his back, Jonnie lay limp.

"Konokata shimatta . . . shijitta," the Japanese sergeant said. "This one's finished . . . dead."

He turned to the next Volunteer. While the artilleryman's fingers scrabbled imploringly in the dust, the sergeant fired his revolver into the wounded man's left eye. Methodically, the Imperial infantrymen killed all the survivors. Its first mission accomplished, the Japanese platoon formed ranks to advance on its next objective.

Hong Kong Island's main line of defense was breached. Worse, all the remaining British-held fortifications along the shore were untenable, and no other possible defense line was tenable for an extended time. The hilly terrain and tenuous lines of communication effectively divided the Island into isolated sectors no single line of resistance could protect. When improvised British counterattacks bogged down in a mire of blood, the fate of the British Broadcasting Commission's "impregnable fortress" was sealed. Once they had landed at a half-dozen points on the Island's northern shore, the Japanese could not be repelled. When communication between Defense Headquarters and the field broke down, the fog of war descended on Hong Kong Island. Many units were still to fight delaying actions as gallant as they were hopeless. But only seven days were to pass before the last Union Jack was hauled down in formal surrender. The Crown Colony would then have been under British rule for exactly one hundred years and eleven months.

The chimera of Chiang Kai-shek's relief columns still sustained men's hopes when Mary Philippa Osgood Sekloong replaced the telephone receiver early in the afternoon of Sunday, December 21. For the first time since the Japanese landing on the eighteenth she had heard her husband's voice. Unbidden, Francis Bacon's observation rose to the surface of her mind: "He that hath wife and children hath given hostages to fortune." She fervently thanked God that only three of her own hostages to fortune remained in Hong Kong: Charles himself, Jonnie, and Sarah. Her grandson, seven-year-old Albert, had in June been sent off to his aunts Charlotte Martin and Guinevere Parker, delighted at the prospect of spending his schooldays in New York and his holidays in Beverly Hills. Her other children and her grandchildren were scattered from Paris and Lancashire to Chungking and Yenan.

Her gratitude that most of the family had avoided the trap of Hong Kong only briefly postponed the sad responsibility of conveying Charles's inconclusive report to Sarah. Aware that her white smock was stained with blood and soot, she delayed to renew her lipstick. Looking in her hand-mirror, she avoided the gaze of her red-rimmed eyes and hastily glanced away from her haggard face, which for the first time, looked her full sixty-one years. At least her age enhanced her authority at the Tung Wah Hospitals, where all racial barriers had finally collapsed under the Japanese assault. Scots privates with stomach wounds groaned beside Chinese merchants with shattered legs. In a screened-off corner, a captured Japanese colonel lay dying. Shrapnel had ripped away half his face. Some hand had laid the rising-sun flag over his slight form to honor a fallen enemy. Assisting the Chinese doctors and nurses, Sarah and Mary gave what help they could to those patients who might survive—and what consolation they could to the dying.

Mary beckoned her daughter-in-law into the virtually bare drug cupboard, where they could talk privately.

"My dear, the news isn't good," she said. "But we can still hope. Charles says there's been no word of Jonnie's battery since the landing. We just don't know . . ."

"Jonnie's alive," Sarah asserted fiercely. "I'd know otherwise. I'd *know*. A wife's instinct. . . ."

"I wish a mother's instinct were as certain," Mary whispered, half to herself. "But we have work to do."

"Doong-yong gwai lay-la! Yat-bun gwai lay-la!" The shriek seemed to rise from the battered building itself. "The devils of the Orient are coming! The Japanese devils are coming!"

"Under the bed with you," Mary commanded. "The Japanese colonel's bed. The flag will hide you."

Sarah Haleevie Sekloong docilely slipped under the bed and lay very still. They had heard that drunken Japanese soldiers were raping all women, regardless of age. But she knew it would be vain to implore her mother-in-law to join her in hiding. Mary's authority was unchallengeable in the ultimate crisis.

The erect figure in the filthy smock strode toward the entrance hall. Mary no longer saw that the teak floors, normally spotless, were filthy with blood- and mucous-encrusted bandages, discarded uniforms, broken bottles, and empty food tins. Not trusting herself to glance sideward, she swept past six Canadian soldiers lying on pallets, their faces waxen from loss of blood. Unseeing, she breasted the tide of terrified nurses and amahs who were seeking refuge in the recesses of the compound. Mary Sekloong consciously steeled herself for the most dangerous encounter of her life by divesting her mind of all but her immediate purpose—the confrontation with the enemy.

Four Japanese infantrymen—privates or noncommissioned officers, it appeared from their ill-cut uniforms —swayed in the doorway waving bottles of potent *shamshu* spirits and flourishing bayonet-tipped rifles. Three uncannily resembled the stereotyped caricature of the "brutish Japanese"; they were bespectacled, squat, and buck-toothed. The fourth was a slim youth with light skin and the patrician features of a *Noh* mask. Cheeks glowing red with alcohol, he was also the most aggressive.

"We come inside," he demanded in pidgin Mandarin. "We come in . . . want women . . . want drink."

"This is a hospital," Mary said. "Only sick people. No women. No drink."

"Have got nurses," the drunken youth insisted. "Have got wine."

"No!" Cold anger overcame Mary's fear. "All nurses go away. All wine finished, all bottles broken."

The tall youth lifted his rifle with one hand like a javelin, still clutching the *shamshu* bottle in his other. The bayonet tip wavered six inches from Mary's breast.

"You are foolish," she said contemptuously. "You look for what does not exist."

The *shamshu* bottle splintered on the teak floor. The Japanese grasped his rifle with both hands, and the bayonet's stained point was steady only an inch from her breast.

"Out of the way, old woman!" he shouted.

"Tomare!" The brusque command, "Halt!", brought the four soldiers to unsteady attention.

A Japanese lieutenant led a ten-man squad into the entrance hall. Noting the deliberate effort with which he held himself erect, Mary saw that he too had been drinking heavily.

"Who do you think you are?" he asked in excellent English. "How dare you defy His Imperial Majesty's troops?"

"They ask for women and wine," Mary replied. "The nurses have all fled, and there is no wine."

"You lie!" the lieutenant snapped.

"Do come in if you must," Mary invited. "But, first,

may the defeated show you how *they* have behaved?"

"What do you mean, woman?" the lieutenant asked suspiciously.

"If you'll come with me? You alone."

The lieutenant turned and ordered his sullen men to squat on the floor.

"You must understand," he explained patiently. "My men have fought hard. They are entitled to the fruits of victory."

"We do not believe so," she answered evenly. "Just let me show you just one thing."

"You may," the lieutenant conceded. "We are not barbarians, but civilized men. What have you to show me?"

Mary did not reply, but led him through the crowded wards where the wounded stared in fear. She stopped at the bed where the dying Japanese colonel lay under the flag of the Rising Sun.

"This is how *we* treat the vanquished," she said softly, terrified by her knowledge that Sarah lay on the grimy floor concealed by the draped Japanese flag. "I am afraid the colonel will die. But we have cared for him as best we could. And we have honored his bravery."

"*Shitsurei itashimashita.*" The lieutenant bowed low to the dying colonel. "I have erred grievously."

Sobered, he wheeled as if on parade and returned with a stiff-legged gait to the reception hall. His brusque command brought the fourteen enlisted men to their feet.

"I express the gratitude of the Imperial Japanese Army. I have erred grievously," he repeated.

Incredulous, Mary watched the Japanese squad march out of the compound behind the lieutenant. She grasped the door frame to support herself, fearing that, for the second time in her life, she might faint. Shocked relief overwhelmed her, for she had fully expected to die beneath Japanese bayonets. Verified accounts of women raped and men mutilated by the Imperial Army were as prevalent as the illusory reports that the Nationalist relief force had already entered the New Territories.

"They just went away, Mother," Sarah babbled. "They just went away. I can't believe it."

"Nor can I," Mary replied weakly. "I never thought . . ."

"You were magnificent, Mother. I could hardly believe . . ."

"Nor could I. To tell the truth, Sarah," Mary's voice quavered, "it *was* the only thing to do, but it was a foolish thing to do."

"And you did it!" Sarah laughed.

Reminded of her brazen motto, Mary's self-control broke. Simultaneously laughing and crying, near hysteria, mother-in-law and daughter-in-law embraced. Nurses and amahs emerging from their hiding places gazed astonished through their own tears.

"We still have work to do here. But for how long?" Mary painfully resumed her self-control. "They'll be back. And miracles don't happen twice, not in the same place."

Similar fleeting miracles occurred elsewhere on the ravaged Island. Defended by a company of aged warriors, none less than sixty, most in their seventies, the Island's main electricity plant held out for four days. Three of the defenders died of heart attacks before repeated assaults by elite Japanese troops overwhelmed them.

A quartermaster captain and three sergeants locked the steel door of the innermost chamber behind them when the Japanese invaded the concrete passages of their underground magazine. Unable to break the door down, the Japanese fired submachine guns through the steel grill and tossed hand grenades that exploded amid the stacked artillery shells. Finally, the Japanese withdrew in disgust, leaving the four astonished British soldiers unscathed. When they finally emerged into the wintry sunlight, they found their old Dodge sedan undamaged and drove unchallenged to the British position athwart Wongneicheong Gap.

It was that kind of war. Lieutenant General Sakai Takashi, who had promised his superiors he would take Hong Kong in a week, sent vitriolic messages reproaching his field commanders. He too was amazed by the obstinate gallantry of isolated British units after organized resistance had collapsed.

A private miracle was vouchsafed Captain Jonathan Sekloong, who had yielded himself to death reciting the *Pater Noster*. As consciousness slowly returned to him, the sun shone yellow through his closed eyelids. His entire body ached, and his side burned where the bayonet slash had been turned by his ribs. Without moving, he slowly opened his eyes to look upon the corpses of his men lying in the dust with flies buzzing around their wounds. He cautiously twisted his head, but saw no life, hostile or friendly. He gingerly rose to his feet, alone among the dead. Though his left arm hung limp, he was still functioning.

Jonnie took stock of his resources. His water bottle was full, and his musette bag held five packets of hard biscuits. He could not bring himself to search his dead comrades, though he slipped Peter Hardin's revolver from its holster with a murmured prayer. Swept by blinding waves of pain, he improvised a sling for his arm from a leather strap. The worst ordeal still confronted him.

Three construction coolies lay dead among the Volunteers' corpses. Painfully using one hand, Jonnie stripped the largest coolie. Each movement agonizing, he pulled the black tunic and trousers over his tattered uniform. The coolie's clothing was essential camouflage, while, he reasoned muzzily, his uniform would prevent the Japanese shooting him as a spy if he were captured.

But he had no intention of being captured again. Wearing the anonymous black garments and speaking colloquial Cantonese, his features shadowed by a conical woven-bamboo hat, he could pass as a wounded civilian. After discarding his military boots for a coolie's straw sandals, he began the long, circuitous journey along back trails to the fort on the Stanley Peninsula, the last defensible British position.

The Governor of His Britannic Majesty's Crown Colony of Hong Kong turned in exasperation to the Major General commanding the Defense Force.

"Another damned message from London," Sir Mark Young said wearily. "We must hold out to the last man, buy time . . ."

"Time for what?" asked the Major General.

"That is, unfortunately, not clear. Just quantities of Churchillian bumph about honor and glory and the invaluable contribution we can make."

"I'd prefer two effective brigades and a squadron of pursuit planes." The General's clipped Sandhurst accents were ironic.

"Not a prayer, old chap," the Governor answered. "But our orders are clear."

"Damned bombastic fellow's just putting the monkey on our backs," the General sighed. "It'll be our decision . . . ours not his . . . when the time comes. When we either sacrifice even more lives in vain—or surrender."

"But, meanwhile," the Governor persisted, "there is one hope."

"I'm glad you see hope. There's no joy whatsoever, as far as I can see."

"These reports of a Chinese relief column. . . ."

"Nothing official, not a sausage, Your Excellency," the General objected.

"Still, there *could* be something to them. Haven't been out here long enough to judge. But my people, the old hands, tell me the bamboo wireless can be damnably accurate."

"We've had nothing from the Chinese," the General objected.

"That's my point," the Governor answered. "To find out—if we can. Your man Sekloong'd make an ideal liaison officer. All the Chinese know him, and there's no question about his loyalty."

"Worth a try, perhaps," the General conceded. "He's no use here now. Coordinate communications and intelligence, in God's name! He did a fine job, but we seem to have run out of both communications and intelligence."

"Then you concur? You'll detach him to make contact with the Chinese?"

"It's worth a try," the General agreed grudgingly.

Just before dusk on December 22, 1941, a fishing junk sailed out of Taitam Bay, its tattered sails a patchwork of red, brown, and purple against the gray sky. The British-held Stanley Peninsula still dominated the Bay, and the Japanese did not interfere with the fishing fleet. On the eve of victory, the Imperial Army was already worried about freeing Hong Kong's million and a half civilians. On the scale-flecked deck, wiry fishermen were rigging the net booms. But the junk was not bound for the rich fishing grounds to the southwest. Its course was northeast to Haumun one hundred and eighteen miles distant on the Kwangtung coast, a minute foothold the Nationalists still controlled amid the Japanese torrents that had swept over East China.

The heavy rudderpost squealed in its wooden gudgeons as the junk passed the Poktoi Island group and the sea wind filled the sails. In the big stern cabin, where the fishermen and their families lived in comfortable squalor, a middle-aged French lady huddled in her lustrous mink coat. The timbers' creaking and the rudder's squealing reverberated through the cabin like a cello's soundchamber. Her servant deferentially asked whether she was suffering *mal de mer*.

"Rien. Je fais très bien, Monsieur Woo," she replied. "It's nothing. I'll manage, Woo."

The lady, her passport attested, was Madame Marie Draché. Caught in Hong Kong by the Japanese attack, she had extravagantly chartered the junk for $2,000 to escape the vengeance the mad British might still wreak on a loyal citizen of the collaborationist Vichy government before the Japanese forces rescued her from their power. The manservant had protected her since the death of her husband, a regimental commander in

599

Indo-China. He spoke adequate French for a Chinese, and he walked with a limp that favored his left leg.

The elaborate deception was supported by impeccable documentation, including identity cards, false passports stamped with immaculately forged visas, and the Draché family Bible with the names and birthdates of the lady's children and grandchildren recorded on the flyleaf in ink that had faded from light black to rusty gray according to the age of the entries. The documents' preparation had provided a pleasant diversion for the Intelligence Section of the Hong Kong Defense Force Headquarters, whose officers found little other occupation to divert or cheer them. If Mary and Charles Sekloong, who were concealed behind the façade of paper, were captured, they would, presumably, be treated by the Japanese as friendly neutrals. For their part, the Chinese had nothing against the French.

Only the junk's master knew its destination, and he was prepared for his crew's inevitable questions. Why not, he would ask, combine a foray to the neglected northern fishing grounds with the profitable transport of the foolishly apprehensive Frenchwoman? Besides, it was only prudent to avoid Hong Kong during the first confused day of the inevitable Japanese occupation.

Mary and Charles chatted desultorily in French, preserving the distance proper between mistress and servant. But their thoughts dwelt on Hong Kong Island, which was a dark conical mass against the red ball of the setting sun. Sarah had refused to accompany them —to the relief of the Intelligence Section, which did not relish manufacturing an identity for the daughter of a Frenchwoman whose French was rudimentary. Absolutely convinced that Jonnie still lived, Sarah Haleevie Sekloong had chosen to remain and help at the makeshift hospital set up at St. Stephen's School in Stanley. If he were alive and free, she knew, her husband would eventually find his way to Stanley.

"I am Chinese, and shall stay," Sir Jonathan had snorted, refusing even to consider leaving Hong Kong. "You know I'd only be a burden. I'm no longer up to such games. Besides, where else could an old man help

China? I am the father of Sek Sai-loong, the assassinated premier of the pro-peace Nanking Government, the martyr to Sino-Japanese friendship. I'll get on well with the dwarves—and perhaps find, shall I say, opportunities."

Opal had nodded vigorous agreement, having never considered leaving the Old Gentleman. With the remaining servants, they were secure in The Castle on The Peak—as secure as anyone could be in the crumbling Colony. When Mary advised Opal to think of her own safety and her own future, the Polynesian girl's straightforward reply was tinged with surprise at the suggestion.

"The Old One's been good to me. How could I leave him now? Anyway, he bought me. I belong to him."

Awed by Opal's devotion, Mary wondered whether she herself was playing the coward by leaving. The General could command Colonel Charles Se[k]loong but not her. Yet she had to accompany Charles if he were to deceive any stray Japanese patrol-boats. His soft hands and light complexion enabled him to pass as a superior servant, but certainly not as a fisherman. Besides, her place was with her husband, who had been surprisingly tender during the past four years.

"You're *still* a damned attractive woman," Charles had said, hastily adding: "Damned attractive for any age. But I'm glad you let your hair go gray. Makes you look younger."

Other compelling reasons had guided Mary's decision, though she was surprised by her feeling of guilt at deserting beleaguered Hong Kong to a fate that would be shrouded by the confusion of war. She did not know whether Jonnie was alive or dead, while death could claim Sir Jonathan at any time, even without the intercession of the Japanese. *Someone* had to survive to rebuild the Sekloong empire, and Charles would require her assistance.

While Mary brooded on her decision, the junk was making heavy weather against the southwest monsoon. The clumsy vessel tacked repeatedly, covering only two miles northeast for every five miles actually sailed. The corkscrew motion was excruciatingly uncomfortable since the junk was built—to a design unchanged for more than a millennium—to ride over the waves rather than to plow through them. Having thought herself a good sailor, Mary was appalled at being strapped onto the narrow wooden bunk shelf. But Charles, too, was suffering from the erratic motion, Charles who had clung to the shrouds of *Regina Pacis* in a half-gale shouting exultantly at the shrieking winds. The deep-hulled, heavy-keeled schooner was quite different from this Chinese walnut shell.

Even if their mission were to prove foolish rather than essential, they had at least undertaken it. Mary felt a welling of pride at the gallantry of her sixty-five-year-old husband, and she was struck by the realization that he had in recent years grown more like the dashing youth she had married forty years earlier. She was warmed by the realization that Charles loved her deeply, had always loved her as she now loved him, despite their differences. She could not know whether this voyage was the final chapter in their lives or the beginning of a new volume, but their accounts were finally in balance.

The third day at sea dawned clear and tranquil after the dark turmoil of the gale. Only the long swells under the junk's keelson recalled the storms. Mary and Charles gratefully shared the fishermen's rice gruel topped with shavings of salt fish. Veiled half-glances conveyed their relief in their survival and their pleasure in each other. They could not touch except by apparent accident, and they could communicate their affection only in stilted French. Charles had warned her that the junk's master might understand English.

As if raised by the storm's cessation, a plume of smoke feathered the horizon. Within an hour, a sleek Japanese destroyer of the *Chidori* class bore down upon them. The junk-master ignored the signal flags fluttering on her shrouds.

"More foreign devil nonsense," he muttered contemptuously, but he hove to when a shell threw up a water-spout fifty feet from the junk's blunt prow. That language anyone could understand.

The war was still young, and the Imperial Navy, aglow with its victories, was punctiliously carrying out its orders to search all shipping, even junks. Unwilling to risk his bright new paint by pulling alongside the junk, the destroyer's captain sent off a motor-launch under a lieutenant. Four armed sailors swarmed up the junk's side behind the lieutenant.

Mary was terrified by the officer's resemblance to the young private who had threatened her with his bayonet at the hospital in Hong Kong. He too possessed a light skin, and features sculptured like a *Noh* mask.

"Well, old girl," Charles murmured behind his hand, "we'll see what kind of job our counterfeiters did."

"Thank God, the terrible storm is over." She smiled wanly and spoke in stilted French. "It is comforting, too, that the Imperial Japanese Navy guard the seas against pirates."

As she intended, the lieutenant overheard her. His bow gracefully combined the sweeping salutation of a French courtier of the eighteenth century with the deep inclination Japanese etiquette prescribed.

"*À votre service, Madame,*" he said. "*Matsudaira, Lieutenant, Flotte Impériale Japonaise.*"

My God, Charles reflected in dismay, we *would* run up against the one Jap lieutenant who speaks perfect French.

Mary took the lead, expressing voluble delight that the officer spoke her own language. Sprinkling her rusty French with exclamations, she almost laughed at her ludicrous performance, despite her fear. She did laugh in relief when she realized that Lieutenant Matsudaira's French was even worse than her own.

After apologizing profusely for the necessity, the Lieutenant ordered his men to search the junk. The sailors poked long poles into the salted fish, while Madame Draché pathetically told him of her decision to flee Hong Kong before the perfidious British turned upon her. Despite his sympathy, he leafed through her documents and examined her passport meticulously before returning it. With renewed apologies, he insisted upon opening her luggage.

Charles grasped the knife in his sleeve when the officer lifted the lid of the leather valise containing the field radio. But Lieutenant Matsudaira recoiled from the froth of lingerie Mary had strewn on top of the transceiver.

"We need not trouble Madame further," he said. "I am giving the master a certificate of examination. I regret that I cannot offer passage to Madame and her servant. But we are ordered south. *Bon voyage et bonne chance.*"

The boarding party slithered down the rope-ladder into its motor-launch. Braced against the small boat's roll, Lieutenant Matsudaira tendered Mary a stiffly formal salute.

"We've been weighed in the balance and not found wanting," Charles whispered hoarsely. "We now sail under protection, the protection of the Imperial Japanese Navy, no less."

"What would you've done if he found the radio?" she asked. "I saw you finger your knife."

"Damned if I know," Charles admitted cheerfully. "But I suppose I'd have done something."

"Something foolish, no doubt," she smiled.

"Something like that," he agreed. "Something very foolish."

A day later, the junk tacked into the small fishing port called Haumun. It was already too late, a sympathetic Chinese major told them. They had lost their race against the Japanese, and Hong Kong was on the point of surrender. The mythical Chinese relief force did not exist, and Charles's hopeless mission was over.

"What now?" Mary asked. "What now, Colonel?"

"Chungking, I suppose," he replied dolefully. "I should report to someone."

"It will be a long walk," Mary said. "But I'm game."

"Not that bad. There are ways. But first, we're entitled to a few days' rest."

Captain Jonathan Sekloong discovered during his long walk from Lyemun to Stanley that Hong Kong's Chinese population was at odds with itself. Hidden in the bushes above Taitam Gap, he watched a platoon of Japanese infantry guided by two men, one dressed in the black coolie clothing he himself wore, the second plump in the gray-wool tunic of a prosperous merchant. Twice he met small bands of armed Chinese flaunting blue-and-white Nationalist cockades in their sun-helmets, and they fed him. The mansions on Taitam Road, just northeast of Stanley, swarmed with looters bearing off possessions ranging from porcelain chamberpots to gramophones. Jonnie chuckled, for the central mansion, set amid sweeping terraces, belonged to a notorious collaborator who fervently supported Wang Ching-wei's puppet regime.

Captain Jonathan Sekloong won his race against the Japanese, reaching Stanley at the southwesternmost point of the Island on Christmas Eve. As he hobbled on blistered feet down Stanley Road from the northeast, the enemy was advancing from the northwest to isolate the only remaining organized British resistance on the Stanley Peninsula. The three regiments that made the initial landings had been heavily reinforced, and the Japanese were enraged by the dispersed resistance they had encountered. Such uncivilized behavior, officers complained, they expected of barbaric Chinese guerrillas, but it was no way for civilized men to fight a war.

"They should know they're beaten," exclaimed a disgusted Japanese major after his battalion had taken heavy casualties to push two platoons of the Royal Scots off Chunghomwan Peninsula, the western promontory enclosing Stanley Bay. "I don't expect brave men to surrender, but they could commit suicide with dignity."

On Christmas Eve, small units fought in isolation on Hong Kong Island. St. John's Cathedral, half a mile from the northern shore where the Japanese had first landed, was still a British strongpoint, and the Dean presided over the saddest Christmas service in the Colony's memory. At Pokfulam, three miles west, a mixed detachment of the Volunteers and the Middlesex Regiment occupied positions on the hills where the Dairy Farm's milk cows had grazed. In addition, the British still held Matilda Hospital on The Peak, hurling elite Japanese assault troops down the precipitous slopes.

British obduracy and Chinese stubbornness were enough to enrage any rational man, and Lieutenant General Sakai Takashi was by that time not quite rational. Tokyo was pressing him to finish mopping up, while the tall white horse he planned to ride in triumph into Victoria had been curry-combed so often that his Korean grooms snickered behind their hands. Perhaps irrationally, Major General C. M. Maltby, the British commander, ordered a suicidal counterattack to break the Japanese pincers closing on Wanchai Gap, the key road to The Peak. He was resolute, but he was not hopeful.

Jonnie Sekloong wandered into the British defense lines on the Stanley Peninsula at 6:00 P.M. on Christmas Eve. Intermingled without regard to their original units, men of the Rajputs, the Winnipeg Grenadiers, the Royal Navy, and the Volunteers manned positions on the hillock called Stanley Mound. Assessing the bedraggled, bleeding figure that had appeared from the dusk, the major commanding ordered Jonnie to report to the hospital at St. Stephen's School, less than two hundred yards behind the line.

Half-dazed and exhausted, Jonnie stumbled into the charnel-house classrooms. Moving like rusty automata, doctors and nurses tended the wounded and dying. Their stocks of drugs and bandages almost exhausted, they could offer little more than verbal consolation. Forgetting his own relatively minor wounds, Jonnie watched a dark-haired nurse kneel on the slimy floor to hold the hand of a blond private of the Middlesex Regiment. She murmured low-voiced endearments to the dying man, stoically enduring his convulsive grip. The private stiffened and fell back. The nurse remained on her knees for a full minute before rising to brush tears from her eyes.

"Sarah?" Jonnie's voice quavered in wonder. "Sarah, you? Is it you?"

"Jonnie!" she cried. "Jonnie! I knew. . . . They said no, but I knew . . . knew you were alive. I knew you'd come to me."

"So I have," he grinned happily.

"Jonnie! Jonnie!"

"She laughed through her tears, and only then did they embrace.

"I *knew* I'd find you," he whispered. "But . . . sometimes . . . I couldn't *quite* believe it."

"Let's get you cleaned up." Sarah retreated from nearly hysterical relief into brisk efficiency. "You're a mess."

That night they drank warm champagne and lay together in a cubicle on a grass mat where the school's amah had formerly slept. Their passion was quickly spent, for they were both exhausted, almost too exhausted to sleep. They talked quietly until, toward morning, they slept fitfully. After a breakfast of burnt toast and black tea, Jonnie kissed Sarah gently.

"Now, Captain Sekloong goes back to the war." His humor was forced. "After a night of luxurious pleasure between scented silk sheets with his lady. We're a spoiled lot, aren't we?"

"Jonnie, we're both alive. We've survived thus far—and we will survive, whatever happens."

"I have every intention of surviving," he said, turning to leave her. "Subject, of course, to the exigencies of the service."

Christmas Day was a fearful turmoil of attacks and counterattacks. Rifle and machine-gun barrels glowed too hot to touch, and the Japanese dead piled up before the last defenders of British Hong Kong. But they were forced back implacably. The cordon around the hospital in St. Stephen's School broke, and Jonnie was borne along by the pell-mell retreat toward the last redoubt in Stanley Fort. He struggled to break away and find Sarah again, but the Japanese had already surrounded the school.

A Japanese detachment entered the hospital while the front line troops pursued the retreating British. Taking their vengeance for the insolent British resistance, Japanese infantrymen plunged their bayonets into wounded men, stabbing and sawing. The two medical officers who had chosen to remain with the wounded were shot and their bodies viciously mutilated. Seeking to shelter a helpless Volunteer with her body, Sarah was beaten with rifle butts and hurled into the cubicle where she and Jonnie had spent the night. Six British and four Chinese women were crammed into the narrow space. At intervals, a Japanese soldier beckoned to a woman, and, shortly thereafter, her screams shrilled through the corridors.

Sarah was last. She was dragged past the mutilated corpses of three nurses. Covered only by tatters, the bodies lay on the slimy floor before an adjoining cubicle. Conscious perception had mercifully retreated into the recesses of her mind when a drunken Japanese officer tore her dress from neckline to hem. Spread-eagled on the wooden bed, she endured the penetration of seven men before she fainted. Finally, two soldiers pulled her by the heels into the corridor, her head thudding against the floor each time they tugged. They left her beside the slaughtered nurses, not caring whether she was alive or dead.

In Stanley Fort, the last effective unit prepared its feeble defenses. Jonnie Sekloong swore at himself for not having forced Sarah to accompany him. Finally, he despaired, convinced that she was dead.

At 8:15 A.M., the telephone rang. By some miracle still operating, the line carried Christmas greetings from Governor Sir Mark Young, and concluded: ". . . Fight on. Hold on for King and Empire. God bless you all in this our finest hour."

"Let this day be historical in the grand annals of our Empire," Major General Maltby's message declared. "The order of the day is: *Hold Fast!*"

"We'll hold, but what about them other buggers?" an irreverent private of the Middlesex Regiment, rightly called the Die Hards, shouted. "Have the Japs got the word that we're invincible?"

The telephone did not ring again, and the small group awaiting the final assault felt itself wholly isolated. At Defense Headquarters, General Maltby was still receiving sporadic reports. The improvised unit called Z Force reported at 2:15 P.M. that the Japanese had broken through the last emplacements guarding The Peak. After conferring with his staff officers, the General advised the Governor that they must surrender. The last order went out by telephone and runner at 3:15 P.M. on Thursday, Christmas Day of 1941. A vengeful Lieutenant General Sakai instructed the Governor and the Commanding General to cross the Harbor in a leaking walla-walla taxi-launch to offer their formal surrender to him in the Peninsula Hotel.

At St. Stephen's School, a Japanese officer told his prisoners of their good fortune: "My orders were to shoot you if Maltby had not surrendered by four."

The Brigadier commanding Stanley Fort refused to accept instructions to surrender as a legitimate order, and his men fought until the next evening.

It was futile.

A white flag already flew from Government House, over the halls that had once bustled with gay parties, formal receptions, and viceregal ceremony. Other white flags blossomed throughout Victoria. By 6:00 P.M. on December 26, 1941, no Union Jack fluttered over the Crown Colony, where British power had been supreme for more than a century.

The long night of Japanese occupation had fallen. The darkness was not to lift for three years and eight months.

October 20, 1944–December 9, 1944

"RANDALL Martin's in-laws, are they?" The big *Newsweek* correspondent whistled. "You're kidding, Archie. Is there anybody they *don't* know?"

"Dewey," replied the diminutive Scotsman who was the Chungking representative of *The Times*, the august thunderer of Printing House Square. "They are *the* Sekloongs. There are few anybodies who are somebodies they don't know. And they're related to half the money and power in the world. By blood, by marriage, or by wealth."

"How about Uncle Joe Stalin?"

"Not to my knowledge. But they might have a remote cousin on the Soviet Politburo. You know, I assume, that Major General Shih . . . Shih Ai-kuo who tags along behind Chou En-lai . . . is their son, don't you?"

"I'll make a note. I suppose the Gimo's chief aide is also family."

"Actually, he is. Major General Sek Lai-kwok, chief of the Generalissimo's Military Secretariat, is another son."

"I'll never figure out these Chinese names," the American complained, "much less their connections."

"Just a matter of time, old chap," the Scot assured him. "Then you'll be more confused than ever."

"I can hardly wait. You're an encouraging son of a bitch, Archie."

"I try to contribute to the general enlightenment."

The hoarfrost in the courtyard of the mansion crackled under their feet, and the candles in oiled-paper lanterns guttered on the walls in the October breeze. The Japanese bombed Chungking only by day, and a night fog enveloped the city on the cliffs above the meeting of the Chialing and Yangtze Rivers. The compound on Tang Hill was just above the fog line, and the half-moon's diffused rays mingled with the lanterns' erratic gleams.

The two newspapermen's shadows flickered in incongruous partnership on the white-rimmed cobbles. The heavy-bodied American, Dewey Miller, habitually stooped from his six-foot-five-inch height to catch the words of lesser mortals. His tea-brown eyes were pouched, and his cheeks were sagging dewlaps. Miller shambled like an amiable bloodhound, while the Scotsman Archie MacDonald, red-bearded and shaggy-haired, capered like a sharp-witted Lhasa Apso beside him.

"What's this clambake for?" Miller asked.

"Eh?" asked MacDonald. "Oh, I get you, pardner. You mean: What's this bunfight in aid of?"

"Have it your way. But fill me in before we get there."

"Just a dinner for Randall Martin, the eminent cinema star who's abandoned his career to serve his country. You know the Chinese can't let any occasion pass without consuming vast quantities of food and alcohol."

"Don't worry about Martin's sacrifice, Archie. The Navy made him a full commander and told him to shoot and narrate a movie on the war in the Pacific. Pretty good duty, and it won't hurt his career any. Besides, he makes damned sure he doesn't get shot at."

"Dewey, you Americans're like the Chinese—only it's not food. You're mad for publicity, can't do anything without it."

"If you say so, Archie. But what's the real purpose tonight?"

"Not much," the Scotsman replied. "Just another intimate family banquet for a few score that gives everybody much face. Martin leaves tomorrow, you know. He's covered the Chinese war effort in five days—all from the rear."

"Considering the Nationalist war effort, he could have saved himself some time. Done it in two days."

"No, Dewey, I'd allow three. Fair's fair. Therefore, the farewell banquet with us present as recording angels."

"But, these Sekloongs, Colonel and Mrs. Charles Sekloong, what about them?" the American persisted. "And didn't I see a Monsignor Charles Sekloong on the guest list?"

"I told you the Sekloongs were everywhere, even the Vatican. Actually, they might make a piece for you.

The old couple's been here since the spring of '42. Made a daring escape from Hong Kong and a hellish journey overland. The old boy's some vague kind of British liaison officer to the Chinese."

"And the Monsignor?" Miller persisted.

"Attached to the Papal Nuncio's office. He's one of the Curia's very bright boys."

"What about Brigadier General and Mrs. George Chapman Parker? Who're they?"

"Dr. Parker's chief of the American public health mission. His wife Guinevere, *née* Sekloong, is officially on a Red Cross assignment, but really here to look after him. You should know that much."

"I do, as a matter of fact. Also know they won't be here tonight. They're fogged in at Kunming. But he's married to the old couple's daughter?"

"That's right, Dewey. I told you they were well represented."

"One more question, Archie, since we've got to make our entrance. Who's our host?"

"That's a tale in itself. Third Uncle Kang, they call him. No blood connection of the Sekloongs, as far as I know. But there's some vague business connection—on the legitimate side. Not the other side, where the Kang money and power really come from."

"What's the 'other' side?"

"Opium, gold-smuggling, black-marketing—take your choice. The Kangs practically run Chungking. Even the Gimo's here on their sufferance. Third Uncle Kang's the youngest of three brothers who've made ten shady fortunes. He was actually sentenced to be shot for opium-smuggling in Shanghai. But he was reprieved. Otherwise, the Nationalists couldn't have made Chungking their wartime capital. He's also got excellent Communist connections. Chou En-lai's been known to stay with Third Uncle Kang when he's here talking with the Nationalists!"

"Thanks, Archie," Miller said. "That's enough to start with. Should be an interesting party."

"One can hope," MacDonald replied, stepping

through the moon-gate into a garish crimson reception hall warmed by charcoal braziers.

"Her French, they tell me," MacDonald whispered to Miller, "is even better than her English."

"She'd do me, do me fine—in any language or even tongue-tied," the American answered. "What a dame!"

To the right of their aggressively affable host, who was plump in a padded-silk long-gown, sat the most striking Chinese girl the impressionable *Newsweek* correspondent had ever seen. Third Uncle Kang's daughter by his second concubine, she was effortlessly interpreting for her father and assiduously ignoring the rest of the company. Even Randall Martin's professional blond handsomeness, set off by his blue uniform with three gold stripes on each sleeve, did not visibly impress her. Playing on his ineptitude with chopsticks, Martin tried hard to charm the slender girl in the scarlet *cheongsam*. She was, however, coolly aloof, apparently immune to his renowned charm.

Even the actor's hardened self-confidence finally wilted beneath her cool gaze. He turned to the profusion of courses, each hailed by toasts in fiery, medicated *maotai* spirits, as well as Scotch whiskey and French brandy, provided by the black market at $75 a bottle.

Dewey Miller counted thirty-six dishes, though he could remember no more than half as the *tou-pan yü*, fish in a peppery sauce, signaled the banquet's approaching end. The array of delicacies, which would have been remarkable in a prosperous China at peace, was overwhelming in the remote provisional capital of a poverty-stricken nation fighting for its existence.

The *leng-pan*, cold appetizers, had covered the table when the guests entered the dining hall. Surrounding the centerpiece of minced shrimp balls were the subsidiary appetizers: duck-webs in a mustard and coriander sauce; preserved duck's tongues; thinly sliced cold chicken breasts in a sesame-paste and chili sauce; and pickled cucumbers with crisp jellyfish strips. They were the vanguard for crisp-fried ducks accompanied by steamed buns; huge fresh-water prawns in a garlic-pungent red sauce; braised pork and chestnuts; shoots of young Chinese cabbage garnished with slivers of pungent Yunnan ham; crisp shredded beef; chicken tidbits braised with black chilis; diced bean curd with a pork-and-pepper dressing; sharks' fins with a rare, spongelike mushroom; pork and green peppers with a faintly fishlike flavor; mushrooms cupping a subtle meat filling; beef steamed in a paste of spiced rice flour; and fresh-water eels lightly fried in batter. There had been much more that Miller could not recall. Soup tureens of pork and *cha-tsai,* Szechwan's preserved mustard root, preceded the noodles, rice, and steamed buns that concluded the feast. Still, sweet pastries, melons, grapes, and apples tempted those who might still be hungry.

"People are dying down in the old city." Archie MacDonald expressed Dewey Miller's thoughts. "Dying slowly of malnutrition. The troops are hungry, except those getting American rations. And we've just eaten enough to feed a company."

Dewey Miller looked quizzically at the normally reticent Scotsman. The whiskey and the *maotai* had inflamed his usual cool irony. Miller's glance intersected that of Mary Sekloong, who had eaten sparingly while chatting indifferently with her blond son-in-law. Inured to such banquets, she and Charles had paced themselves accordingly, ignoring their host's obligatory urging: "*Ching tsai chih yi-dien, hao peng-yu*—Eat more, my friends. Eat more, my good friends. I have little enough to offer you. But my humble abode is honored by your partaking of my poor fare."

Having formed her own views of Chungking and the Nationalist war effort, Mary was more interested in the newspapermen than the banquet. She had already dismissed her son-in-law as an amiable narcissist, although she was grateful that he had apparently made the restless Charlotte happy—or, at least, content. The short Scotsman from *The Times* was growing heated, and she wondered whether a small spark might not ignite him. She had no high opinion of the small, incestuous foreign press corps which had been herded into a cramped Press Hostel for easier surveillance by the wary Nationalist Information Ministry. Most of the correspondents she had met at diplomatic receptions, or at Communist Delegate Chou En-lai's Wednesday afternoon tea parties, were astonishingly naive beneath their carapaces of professional cynicism. The big American, who grew more silent and alert as he drank, appeared stolid, but the volatile Scotsman might provide an interesting diversion.

"We've eaten enough for a company," MacDonald repeated loudly. "Though, of course, it wouldn't fight."

"Wouldn't fight, Mr. MacDonald?" Mary sprinkled kerosene on the fire of the Scotsman's indignation. "How can you say that about our allies?"

"Madame, with respect, you must be joking, taking the mickey out of me." Archie MacDonald duly exploded. "You know as well as I, better than I, exactly what I mean. A toast, I propose a toast!"

The Scotsman rose unsteadily, leaning on the table for support. He enunciated each word with the wary precision of the practiced drinker, his red beard bobbing an accompaniment.

"A toast, Ladies and Gentlemen, a toast to the brave Chinese armies and their brilliant leader."

The guests automatically raised porcelain cups of *maotai* to their lips to repeat the toast they had drunk so often over the years.

"*Kan-pei!*" The host responded with automatic courtesy. "Drain the cup dry!"

Though his host sipped only a few drops, Archie MacDonald tossed down his tumbler of whiskey and replenished it. Ignoring Dewey Miller's cautionary pressure on his arm, he waved to demand attention.

"Pray silence, Ladies and Gentlemen! I'm no' finished yet. Let us drink to the Generalissimo's four wars. Only a truly great commander could fight on four fronts at once."

Although he was puzzled by his daughter's whispered translation of the anomalous words, Third Uncle Kang again raised his cup. Perceiving that the red-bearded barbarian was still in full spate, he set it down amid the moraine of scraps, bones, and sauce stains.

"The Generalissimo is fighting one war against the Japanese and another against the Communists," Mac-Donald declaimed. "That's two fronts. He's fighting a separate war against his Allies, mainly the Americans, and a fourth against the Chinese people. Not counting his constant struggle with the cliques in the Nationalist camp, that's four wars. Truly a masterly performance!"

The Scotsman again drained his tumbler and absently extended it for another refill. He did not protest when Miller took the tumbler from his hand, but continued to speak with the excessive precision of the heavy drinker who has drunk himself half-sober again.

"And how's he doing, the great strategist? Against the Japanese, not so well . . . not well at all. The Japs've just swept through Central China and the Southeast . . . captured all the airfields the Americans built with so much effort. Another hope gone glimmering. Bad for that other great strategist, General Chennault, the talking-flying tiger. He doesn't get to prove he can defeat the Japanese in China by airpower alone, without ground forces. Why? Because the ground troops he undercut so brilliantly couldn't defend his airfields."

MacDonald shook off Miller's restraining hand.

"But, the fight against the Americans goes well," he continued doggedly. "To the victor belongs the spoils, and the Nationalists've taken hundreds of millions of dollars off the Americans, so they must be the victors. Their victory was completed yesterday, when the Gimo finally got Uncle Joe . . . Old Vinegar Joe Stilwell . . . sacked. A great victory. Now nobody will interfere with the Gimos' cockeyed strategy."

The party sat frozen. Dewey Miller leaned back, resigned to allowing MacDonald to finish his tirade. The little Scotsman could hardly make matters much worse. He was voiding the accumulated bitterness of four years of personal and professional frustration spent watching the Nationalists bumble, lie, cheat—and fight the Japanese only when it was absolutely unavoidable. Archie MacDonald was simply restating the facts twenty foreign correspondents had already reported privately to their skeptical employers.

"Finally, the other two wars. The Gimo's keeping the Chinese people in check. They don't know any better. He's also keeping the Communists in check. But the Communists do know better, and there'll be a day of reckoning. The Communists don't fight the Chinese people, but the Japs. Meanwhile, the Gimo lets the Americans fight the Japs for him—and schemes to get the Americans to fight the Communists for him after they've beaten the Japs. I give you that brilliant strategist and great leader, Generalissimo Chiang Kai-shek!"

Archie MacDonald paused as if expecting applause. Nonplussed by the silence, he sank into his chair and stared owl-eyed at the company. Dewey Miller recovered first. He draped a heavy arm around the Scotsman's shoulders and lifted him from his seat.

"I'm sorry, Ladies and Gentlemen," the American rumbled in embarrassment. "Mr. MacDonald's had a drop too much. I'd best take him home. My apologies."

Mary's high, clear voice broke the silence as the two newspapermen retreated from the banquet like soldiers withdrawing after an indecisive engagement.

"You mustn't be too embarrassed, Mr. Miller," she said. "Such things happen in Chungking. We're all on edge. Perhaps you'd care to bring your friend to tea tomorrow about four. You know where to find me?"

"I'll find you, Ma'am," Miller replied. "And I'll bring Archie—if he can walk."

The following day, Mary Sekloong saw with amusement that the Scotsman could just manage to walk—very gently, as if each footfall might drive his backbone through his skull.

"You had no difficulty in finding us?" she inquired.

"No, Ma'am," Dewey Miller replied. "We just asked.

Everyone knows Mr. Tang is the Sekloong agent in Chungking."

"Poor man. He's been very kind, and we've usurped his little house."

Mary glanced complacently around the reception room of Mr. Tang's second wife's house. After more than two years, she was still wickedly amused by the juxtaposition of traditional calligraphic scrolls and English hunting-prints. The furnishings were not her taste, though they were anything but ostentatious by the normal Sekloong standard. Reasonably comfortable, they nevertheless appeared extravagantly luxurious in a city where university professors and senior officials lived with large families in single rooms under leaking roofs.

The passing decades had almost obliterated Mary's youthful indignation against the rigid social barriers of the late Victorian age and her own relegation to the wrong side of those barriers. The years had hardened her to the humiliating disparities between great wealth and extreme poverty. She had, of necessity, deliberately cultivated the Edwardians' disregard of the plight of the "lower orders"; she had, nonetheless, become ever more keenly aware of their suffering.

Contemplating the reception room, snug with its long curtains and glowing coal fire, she was disturbed primarily because even her authority had been inadequate to remove the unsightly antimacassars from the bulky easy-chairs resurrected from the godown of a long departed British commercial agent. Those graying cobwebs of crocheted thread were, Mr. Tang knew beyond dispute, as essential to the comfort of Europeans as were the chairs themselves.

"I can offer you tea," she said. "Or would Mr. Mac-Donald prefer something with more authority?"

"I'd no' say no to a wee brandy-and-soda."

The Scotsman's sheepish manner and trembling hands contrasted with his normal brisk assertiveness. Mary found it difficult to equate the monumentally hung-over scrap of humanity that sat before her with the Jovian pronouncements that appeared in her airmail edition of *The Times*. Yet his obvious weaknesses were not merely endearing; they were in harmony with the lapses she had discerned in the articles that appeared under the attribution: *From Our Own Correspondent in China.*

Many possessed a special vantage-point between two worlds because, lacking commercial employment for the first time in decades, she had devoted herself to other purposes. She taught the English language and European history to the children of displaced Chinese intellectuals while discreetly drawing on the Sekloong *kwan-hsi* connections to provide adequate food and clothing for her students' families. With their parents' grateful assistance, she had resumed her long-neglected study of Chinese history and culture. Almost against her will, she had also become deeply concerned with immediate Chinese politics. Though she tried to remain no more than an interested spectator, she found the power struggles engrossing—if often revolting.

"Very good of you to ask us," Dewey Miller rumbled. "To take the time when your son-in-law's leaving tonight."

The big American, she saw, was uncomfortable under her sharp scrutiny. A little charm was in order, as Elizabeth Metcalfe would have said. The memory popped unbidden into her mind: Elizabeth and Hilary. That was a long time ago.

"To the contrary," she replied. "I'm honored that two busy gentlemen of the press can find time to take tea with an unimportant old lady. I've read your dispatches with . . ."

"Contagious, isn't it?" Dewey Miller grinned.

"What's contagious, Mr. Miller?" She responded to the warm humor that lit the American's face.

"Why, this Chinese palaver. I've only been in Chungking a short time, but I know we could go on exchanging high-flown compliments, Chinese-style, for another hour."

"And no bad thing," Archie MacDonald muttered,

still chagrined. "Better than my brusque Scots . . . uh . . . forthrightness."

"Mr. MacDonald, no one was shocked last night," Mary interjected. "Startled, perhaps, but not shocked. After all, every Chinese present agreed with you wholeheartedly."

"Then, Ma'am, why don't they do something about it?" Dewey Miller asked disingenuously. He had often found intentional naiveté a useful professional technique to disarm his sources' wariness.

"First, there's little they *can* do," a light male voice replied. "Second, they're all benefiting—almost all. And finally, though I hate to say so, because they're Chinese."

Monsignor Charles Sekloong had padded into the room, wearing Chinese cloth-shoes and a quilted black long-gown that resembled a cassock. The five years since he had emerged from the isolation of the cloister to join the Papal Nunciature in Paris had given him worldly poise. The novice diplomat who waited uneasily for his brother Thomas outside the Moulin Rouge was no longer discernible in the self-assured priest who stopped to kiss his mother's cheek.

The last year in Chungking had inscribed two vertical lines between his heavy eyebrows. He was, however, concerned not for himself, but for the Chinese people. As Thomas predicted in Paris, Monsignor Charles Sekloong had forcefully rediscovered his kinship with the Chinese after a twenty-year separation. Despite his outward serenity, he was deeply troubled. He reproached himself for the sins of pride and sloth because, he was convinced, he could do more for China than he did. Reporting the frightfully confused situation to the Vatican, while assisting a few individuals, was not enough.

Yet even the Sekloongs' power could not alter the fundamental problem, which was geography itself. Civilians were starving and soldiers were malnourished because even the fertile Szechwan Basin could not feed millions of refugees. Supplies from the outside world could take only two routes: the packed-earth Ledo Road, which wound hundreds of miles through mountains and along precipices, or the American airlift from India "over the Hump" of the Himalayas. Their capacity was so severely limited that General Joseph W. Stilwell, the ground commander, and Major General Claire L. Chennault, the air commander, wrangled constantly over priorities for shipments as small as a hundred gallons of aviation gasoline or a dozen heavy machine guns. No capacity could be spared for civilian needs, though, somehow, the black market provided liquor, perfumes, nylons, and caviar at prices not merely exorbitant, but extortionate. The single alternate channel, caravans of mules and horses trudging from Yunnan through Tibet to northern India, was glacially slow. China was effectively isolated, though the Americans could always find an aircraft for a tinsel celebrity like Commander Randall Martin.

"Good afternoon, Gentlemen," the priest added. "I hope you're not suffering as badly as I am. Perhaps some day I'll learn to survive a Chinese banquet unscathed."

"You're overdoing politeness, Father," Dewey Miller smiled. "Archie and I had a skinful, but you were sober as a bishop!"

"You haven't met many bishops, have you, Mr. Miller?" Charles asked. "I just don't show the drink. Lots of practice, you know. All that altar wine."

Miller, a backsliding Baptist, and MacDonald, a Presbyterian turned agnostic, warmed to the priest. His wit had a slighty musty, ecclesiastical flavor. It nonetheless bridged the awful chasm between the two worldly, self-indulgent correspondents and the clergyman who had taken vows of celibacy and obedience.

"Perhaps we priests should train ourselves to celibacy the same way, by exposure," the priest added. "Tibetan lamas steel themselves against temptation by exposure to pornography. To my regret, that method would be heretical. Besides, the temptation might prove irresistible."

621

"I'm sure, Father, you could do anything you chose," MacDonald observed. "But what can we do for you and Mrs. Sekloong?"

"Nothing, Gentlemen," Mary answered. "Nothing in particular, that is. It's just that we were intrigued by Mr. MacDonald's little oration—as was my husband, who regrets that his duties prevent his joining us. We thought a chat might be enjoyable—and, perhaps, useful."

"Don't mind Archie," Miller drawled. "He's a suspicious type. Probably thinks you're out to sell us a line —or the Father wants to convert us."

"Since my son's never tried to convert me, that's unlikely," Mary replied. "And I have no line. The more I learn of China, the more confused I am."

"The beginning of wisdom," MacDonald muttered.

"But, I'd like to put one thought to you," she continued. "Mr. MacDonald, you probably feel apprehensive today. But you know you won't be expelled for your outburst."

"No," Archie agreed, "the Nationalists will just keep on making life hard for the press. But what's the point?"

"I've known General Chou En-lai for many years, though I can't claim him as a friend," Mary answered. "He can have few friends. He's given himself to a cause much more ambitious and demanding than my son's. But we do get along, and I believe I know a little of his mind."

Monsignor Charles recalled the long association behind his mother's light remark. During the brief madness of the Canton Commune in December 1927, Chou En-lai had saved Mary and Charles Sekloong from Communist-led mobs; and, after the Commune fell, they had spirited Chou to safety in Hong Kong. During the intervening years they had met upon a number of occasions, finding themselves drawn together by common pleasure in intellectual disputation. Another bond was Chou En-lai's apparent affection for James Sekloong, who was to accompany the Communists' *de facto* foreign minister when he returned to Chungking within the week to resume his marathon negotiations with the Nationalists.

"I'd like to ask one question, Mr. MacDonald." Mary's violet eyes gleamed. "What would happen if you had delivered yourself of a similar outburst against Mao Tse-tung in Yenan?"

"But it *couldn't* happen." The Scotsman was baffled. "Everything's different in Yenan. Even if I did get that . . . ah . . . inebriated, why would I talk that way? It wouldn't make sense."

"Archie, you know damned well you'd be thrown out on your tail or worse, don't you?" Miller interjected. "Answer the lady's question."

"Perhaps," MacDonald admitted. "Though it's hard enough to get to Yenan. The Nationalist blockade keeps out journalists as well as . . ."

"Not entirely the Nationalists, Mr. MacDonald," the priest said. "How many applications have the Communists rejected as 'inconvenient'? How many correspondents have been allowed in? Have any but the Communists' very good friends been allowed to stay more than a few days?"

"Aye, there's a point," MacDonald conceded. "They're no' mad for the free press. But they're no' corrupt like the Nationalists. No sickening differences between poor and rich. And they are effective. They know what they want, and they go out to get it."

"That *is* the point," Mary said. "They're ruthless and effective, and they know their purposes. The Nationalists are trying to preserve the suffering, tattered Republic of China. The Communists are determined to destroy that structure—and then make their own China. Destruction's always easier than preservation. Mao Tse-tung's primary objective is not the Japanese but the Nationalists. He's said so himself—repeatedly."

"But the Communist guerrilla movement!" Archie MacDonald objected. "It harasses the Japanese and denies them territory."

"To what end, Mr. MacDonald?" Mary insisted. "Do

the Communists fight to defeat the Japanese or to increase their own power? How many *real* battles have they fought against the Japanese?"

"I should've notice of that question coming," MacDonald objected. "But let me see . . ."

He drifted into a reverie, recalling the four years since he had come to Chungking. Until the spring of 1944, there had been much more fighting between Nationalists and Communists than between Chinese and Japanese. Since more than a million men of the Imperial Japanese Army were mired in the vast expanse of China, Tokyo had strategically decided to bypass China for easier conquests in Southeast Asia. A *de facto* armed truce had therefore prevailed until the spring of 1944 when the Imperial Army launched Operation Ichi to take the American airfields in South China and neutralize the growing threat posed by American bombers to Japan's sea-borne supplies and her home islands. Though some Nationalist forces had fought stubborn delaying actions, the Chinese could not contain the assault. In September 1944 the Japanese had captured Liuchow, the last American base. Yet the Chinese redoubt in the Szechwan Basin remained effectively secure behind its enormous barricades of mountains and rivers. Operation Ichi had, further, virtually exhausted the Japanese forces.

During the past four years the Communists had fought few, if any, set-piece battles again the Japanese. When the Imperial Army directly threatened their Soviet Areas, the Communists had stood and fought, but they had not carried the conventional war to the enemy. Sensibly fearing the overwhelming weight of metal hurled by tanks, artillery, and airplanes, the Communists had instead chosen to harass the invaders. Most of their 400,000 regulars were deployed against the half million Nationalist troops that blockaded and probed the chief Soviet Area with its capital at Yenan. Irregulars had of course harried the Japanese, primarily to extend the territory under Communist control and to enlarge the populace under Communist influence. In large areas of East and North China, the Japanese ruled by day and the Communists by night. Mao Tse-tung was asserting Communist authority throughout China by building a mass political base while Chou En-lai diverted the Nationalists and the Americans with verbal legerdemain.

The Nationalists were almost equally culpable, directing their efforts chiefly to containing the Communists and to mulcting the Americans. Worse, the Nationalists were ineffective. The writ of Generalissimo Chiang Kai-shek ran only where Whampoa-officered Central Government troops actually stood. The Generalissimo could neither dictate to local generals, the new warlords, nor inspire them to patriotic sacrifice. He could only cajole and threaten. His worst enemy was neither the Japanese nor the Communists, but the universal insubordination, inefficiency, and corruption that imperiled his tottering power structure.

That structure's collapse, Archie MacDonald reflected, was an imminent danger, and the Communists were throwing their weight against its foundations. On October 10, Chou En-lai had in Chungking issued a bitter statement that was, of course, ignored by the Nationalist-controlled press. But his attack on the Kuomintang was relayed abroad by Chungking's foreign correspondents, while surreptitious copies circulated among Chungking's intellectual community. Public opinion—Chinese and foreign—was Chou En-lai's chief objective.

The Communist spokesman demanded a "truly representative" coalition government. The proposal, Archie MacDonald acknowledged, *appeared* reasonable. It appealed to the naive Americans, who still believed Communists and Nationalists could fight together against the Japanese. But Archie knew that both Chinese parties were girding for the battle that would decide who ruled China after the Americans had defeated Japan elsewhere. He further recognized that any coalition government that included the Communists would destroy Chiang Kai-shek's own shaky coalition.

The mental recapitulation occupied Archie MacDonald for two minutes. Since Britain was only peripherally involved, he could contemplate those indecisive battles and internecine feuds with a certain detachment. Like most correspondents, except the few who sold themselves to either the Nationalists or the Communists, MacDonald strove for objectivity. But no correspondent could live in China and not finally take sides. It was that kind of country—and that kind of war.

"How many Communist battles against the Japanese have you counted, Mr. MacDonald?" The priest's upper-class accent irritated the Scotsman. "Or do you need more time?"

"Very few battles," MacDonald conceded. "And most to defend their own territories. I take your point."

"Regardless, the Communists are effective," Dewey Miller insisted. "And they're not corrupt."

"Not technically, Mr. Miller," Mary observed. "Not pecuniarily. But doesn't the ruthless pursuit of power, for whatever end, however benevolent, also corrupt?"

"That's a moral question," MacDonald objected, "almost a theological question for the good Father. It's not a political question for the working press."

"It *is* political," Monsignor Charles answered. "The Communist leaders have been corrupted by their own dedication. Historically that's not unique. The same thing has happened to Chiang Kai-shek, who believes he's not only China's sole hope, but China itself. He considers his own interests and the nation's interests indivisible. Therefore, his first duty is to retain power—by whatever means. He, too, is corrupt morally *and* politically."

"Moral arguments are a great intellectual exercise, but they're not the gut issue." Dewey Miller's American pragmatism asserted itself. "No matter how you slice it, the Nationalists are a stinking mess of corruption. The Communists aren't. I'm interested in their effectiveness, not their souls."

"Besides, Mao's not an oppressive dictator like Stalin or Hitler," MacDonald said. "He's making a better life for the Chinese people. Why shouldn't he fight for power? He couldn't do worse than the Gimo."

"And they say," Miller added, "that this Communism's just a means to an end. Mao's not a raving Bolshevik."

"Gentlemen, we differ." Mary's excessively reasonable tone, her son knew, concealed acute annoyance. "I know no one as flexible tactically as Chou En-lai. I know no one more rigidly dedicated to his own ends. Have you heard of the *Cheng-feng Yün-tung,* the Movement to Order the Winds?"

"Can't say I have," Miller admitted.

"It began in 1942." Mary's voice was too sweet. "Total intellectual repression and a sweeping purge. The Movement sought to destroy all Mao's personal enemies in the Communist Party and to insure that the survivors all practice utmost orthodoxy. Thought control, Gentlemen, orthodox Marxist-Leninist thought control as repressive and ruthless as any purge Stalin ever ordered. How can you possibly say they're not *real* Communists?"

"Well," Miller conceded, "I hadn't heard about that."

"Mr. MacDonald, may I introduce a personal note?" Mary asked. "I've been revolted by Chungking: American aid funds stolen, arms sold to enemies, intellectuals persecuted, peasants viciously exploited, money the only value. But it's all very Chinese. If you'd lived in China as long as I, you'd know just how typically Chinese. Moral principles compel the Chinese to look after themselves and their families—at whatever cost to the people and the nation."

"Confucian morality," the priest murmured. "But who will look after them if they don't themselves?"

"The Communists'll try," MacDonald said.

"They're Chinese, too." Mary pursued her thought. "They'll use the most extreme means because they seek the most extreme ends. They are determined to create a Heaven on earth, a Marxist Heaven, when merely mitigating this Hell on earth would be a great achievement.

The only thing worse than a cynical, self-serving Chinese is a Chinese dedicated to a noble, impossible goal. Like my acquaintance Chou En-lai, he's twice as ruthless and cruel as the cynic."

"Maybe no worse than other human beings, though you've given me lots to think about." Dewey Miller rose. "But I've got to say I still prefer allies who are decisive and effective. The Nationalists are just no use."

"The Communists deserve a chance, Mrs. Sekloong," Archie MacDonald insisted. "They can't be worse than the Nationalists."

"Good God!" Mary exploded. "I'm not defending the Nationalists. Far from it. All I ask is that you moderate your transports for Chou En-lai and his henchmen. They're not . . ."

"Mother, it's time for you to leave if you're to see Randall at the airport."

"Oh, I'd forgotten. Gentlemen, another day, unless you're bored with an old lady."

"Bored, never, Ma'am," Miller replied gallantly. "But convinced, no. I keep coming back to it: The Communists are efficient and honest."

When Monsignor Charles had seen the correspondents out, he threw back his head and laughed.

"Now will you be good?" he asked. "That's the clear-sighted foreign press for you. You know a clever Chinese can always fool a clever foreigner. And Chou En-lai is very clever."

"A dusk take-off, very tricky," Colonel Charles Sekloong observed. "But the pilots are good, very good."

The Sekloongs had rapidly exhausted the conversational resources of their famous son-in-law. What more was there to say to Commander Randall Martin after sending affectionate greetings and exotic presents to Charlotte and the children?

Young Charles had pleaded important business elsewhere. Although he did not approve of Charlotte's new marriage, which was bigamous in the eyes of the Church, he was no longer the callow young priest who, on religious principles alone, would have shrunk from any association with Randall Martin. He had on this occasion absented himself simply to avoid any more of the actor's fatuous chatter.

Martin snapped at his five-man crew of Navy enlisted men: "You're sure you've got all the film? I don't want a reel turning up missing. We can't do a retake."

"Aye, aye, Sir," answered his weathered chief petty officer. "We don't want to come back again, either."

"Impertinent," Colonel Charles Sekloong muttered.

"We're doing all right, Sir," Martin said. "Just different ways from your people."

"How do they get those water buffalo off the landing strip?" Mary interjected.

"You've seen the drill. Just before take-off, little boys shoo them away. Haven't lost a plane to a buffalo yet," Charles joked.

They did not mention the long-range Zero fighters operating from the newly captured airfield at Liuchow, three hundred and fifty miles to the east. Commander Randall Martin was already dreading the hazardous take-off from Sand Spit Island, which lay in midstream of the Chialing River. The cliffs flanking the gorge forced pilots to make a dangerous approach by weaving down to the short airstrip, and the transports were totally vulnerable to enemy fighters. American and Chinese interceptors would take off if the alarm were sounded by the network of thousands of aircraft spotters scattered across Japanese-occupied territory. But the transports' best protection was landing just before dusk, a quick turn-around, and a high-angle take-off.

A twinkling speck in the east resolved itself into a twin-engined aircraft. Landing lights glared through the haze, and the cockpit windows glittered like a greenhouse. Engines roaring at full power, the C-46 Commando swooped through the gorge and touched down amid clouds of red dust. Propellers whirling in reverse pitch, it halted a hundred feet from the wood-hut terminal. As the door opened, the engines still turned over slowly.

Two jeeps darted toward the idling aircraft. Commander Randall Martin waved from his perch on a stack of camera equipment. Colonel Charles Sekloong saluted in farewell.

The six men and their bulky equipment were embarked within three minutes, and the Commando swung around. While the pilot, almost standing on the brakes, moved the throttles to full power, the same jeeps discharged the incoming passengers at the terminal. Dr. George Chapman Parker, spry at sixty and wearing the single stars of a brigadier general, embraced Mary and shook Charles's hand. Guinevere Sekloong Parker, who was swathed in an outsized field jacket, kissed her mother and father. The family watched the Commando's juddering takeoff along the steel-strip runway.

The pilot glanced alternately at the runway and the speedometer. Perched in the high-angled cockpit, he was blind to the ground fifty feet forward of the aircraft's nose. The Commando raced toward take-off speed . . . sixty miles an hour . . . seventy-five miles an hour . . . ninety-two miles. The pilot eased back his control yoke, and the wheels began to leave the runway. Feeling lift, the pilot whistled in relief and scanned the twilight-hazed gorge ahead.

The watchers on the ground saw what the pilot could not. A gray water buffalo loped onto the landing strip, pursued by a shouting twelve-year-old waving a long switch. The louder the boy shouted, the faster the frightened animal trotted. As the Commando left the ground, the buffalo broke into a frantic trot. A flashing four-bladed propeller tossed the animal forty feet into the air.

The Commando veered off the runway, sheered through a shack, and plowed to a stop in a rice paddy, one wing cocked high. Fearing an explosion, men tumbled from the hatches.

A jeep carrying fire extinguishers raced toward the aircraft. Clutching his medical bag, Dr. Parker clambered into a second jeep. The Commando lay inert like a beached silver whale.

The air crew were clustered a hundred feet from their wrecked aircraft. The pilot, a slim, red-haired captain, tensely puffed a cigarette.

"Goddamn it! Goddamn it!" he repeated. "At least I cut the switches. Goddamn it! What a way to crash. A goddamned cow."

The sailors were a group apart. The chief petty officer knelt beside Commander Randall Martin, who lay unmoving on the ground.

"We hauled him out, Sir," he told Dr. Parker. "But he's out. Hasn't moved or said a word."

George Parker kneeled in the mud of the rice paddy. He flicked his brother-in-law's eyelids open, applied his ear to the actor's chest, and gently palpitated his skull. Finally Parker rose, shaking his head.

"He's gone," the Doctor said. "Broken neck."

"A cow! For Chris'sake!" The chief petty officer pronounced Randall Martin's epitaph. "What a shitty way to die!"

Charlotte Sekloong Way d'Alivère Martin received her parents' delayed radiogram seventy-two hours later, the day before the Navy Department finally informed her of its deep regrets. Her mock-Moorish mansion in Beverly Hills was thereafter a miniature bedlam; telephones shrilling, doorbells chiming, and mail sacks piling up as motion-picture cameras ground for the sensation-seeking masses.

Caught up in preparations for the most ostentatious obsequies Hollywood had ever staged, Charlotte mercifully failed to comprehend fully her loss of the one man who had given her contentment. Those preparations were at least as complex as the staff work preceding an amphibious landing—and notably more efficient. Since patriotism marched in step with self-interest, the funerary pageant was staged by those two master publicity-mongers: the United States Government, through the U.S. Navy, and the motion-picture community, through Metro-Goldwyn-Mayer. Charlotte's febrile spirit rose to the excitement, and only red Seconal capsules could bear her into disturbed sleep.

Dewey Miller received urgent demands for minute details of the crash, the embalming of the most famous body in the world, and its shipment to the United States. To his intense disgust, even Archie MacDonald was instructed to record the actor's last days and death. Randall Martin bestrode the world of popular culture like a brazen colossus, and flags flew at half-mast throughout the Free World.

Tokyo proclaimed a school holiday to celebrate a "great victory." RANDARU MAHTIN'S DEATH DEMOR-ALIZES AMERICA, bannered the daily *Yomuiri*. HARRI-WADO'S GOD OF FILM PERISHES, apothesized the rival *Mainichi*. "Do not weep for 'Randaru,'" the *Fujin Shukan* (*Ladies' Weekly*) counseled millions of stricken housewives and factory girls. "He was not the gallant hero he appeared in his films, but an evil enemy of the God-Emperor. The Goddess Amaterasu-Omi-kami herself struck him down."

Colonel Tsuji Masanobu, the erratic strategist and spy master who had already attained semi-divinity as Japan's "God of Operations," did not deny that the martyred water buffalo had been divinely inspired; nei-ther did his subordinates deny that their network of agents included a twelve-year-old buffalo-boy in Chungking.

Both Sir Jonathan Sekloong in The Castle on The Peak and Captain Jonathan Osgood Sekloong in a pris-oner-of-war labor camp on the Kobe Docks were in-formed by the Japanese the day before Charlotte received her parents' radiogram.

Sir Jonathan received the news with surpassing calm-ness. He, who had never met Randall Martin, was one of the few thousand human beings in the civilized world who had never seen the actor's image flickering on the screen.

In the winter of 1944, *the* Sekloong was, at ninety-two, a living monument to Chinese endurance and courage. The Japanese had, therefore, dealt with him most correctly. Opal presided over a greatly diminished staff of servants, and many of the former splendors of The Castle had vanished. But the household suffered neither the depredations of drunken soldiers nor severe deprivation. The fact that the Sekloong household enjoyed a sufficiency of food was remarkable in a moribund Hong Kong, from which a million of its prewar population of 1.6 million had been removed, either by flight or by death. The Japanese still believed Hong Kong could serve the Imperial Forces in Southeast Asia as a major supply center and workshop—if only the Chinese would work harder and cease their wilful sabotage. Sir Jonathan's active cooperation with the Greater East-Asia Co-Prosperity Sphere could unlock the gates that divided the conquerors from the recalcitrant Chinese community, *if* they could find the key to the Sekloong himself.

The Old Gentleman had met their previous approaches with formal expressions of gratitude and with protestations of unworthiness. He had regretted that his great age rendered him unfit to join the Japanese administration or even lend it his name. But the Japanese knew he was the enemy of the British, particularly Derwent's, the Universally Virtuous *hong;* and they knew that he was the father of Sek Sai-loong, the martyr to Sino-Japanese amity who was commemorated by the shrine the Imperial Army had erected in Nanking. The occupation authorities in Hong King reasoned that Sir Jonathan must feel both bitter resentment against the British and a burning desire for vengeance upon his son's assassins. This time, they were convinced, they could win him to their side.

Sir Jonathan's protégé, Mosing Way, was an enthusiastic collaborator. He entertained every visiting Japanese dignitary and deployed the resources of the Bank of East Asia in the service of the Co-Prosperity Sphere.

"But somehow it doesn't do them much good," the Senior Adviser to the Military Government confided to his old friend. "You know how inefficient we Chinese are. Papers are always getting lost, and it's so difficult to enforce directives. Of course, I do my best."

Mosing Way had assumed the role Sir Jonathan could not play. His effusive pretence of cooperation had already saved more than five hundred lives. The junks he controlled smuggled wanted men out of Hong Kong and landed Chungking's agents, who sabotaged military installations and transmitted information on ship movements. Two or three such agents were normally part of the constantly changing staff of The Castle, for Sir Jonathan planned the elaborate deceptions Mosing Way executed.

The Old Gentleman's bland obduracy deceived the Japanese more effectively than would either active cooperation or surly defiance. Besides, his grandson, Francis, the son of Sydney Sek, was amassing a fortune in Occupation *yen* and, since he was no fool, gold by trading for the Japanese. After reviewing the favorable auguries, Colonel Okamoto Fusanosuke, chief of civil affairs, decided to carry the report of Randall Martin's death to Sir Jonathan personally.

"I regret, Your Excellency, that I am the bearer of ill tidings," he said in good Mandarin. "The husband of your granddaughter Charlotte was killed yesterday in Chungking. A regrettable accident in which the Imperial Forces took no part. Please accept my deepest, most sincere condolences."

"I am honored by your calling upon me and touched deeply by your news," Sir Jonathan replied as formally. "I shall order mourning for the household."

"Now that I am here," Colonel Okamoto persisted, "perhaps we can chat about general affairs?"

"I am always delighted to chat. A useless old man sees too few guests nowadays."

"I have finally secured permission to release your granddaughter-in-law from Stanley Internment Camp," the Colonel added. "Though certain conditions are required. I have fought to have her released for some time, but my superiors must be satisfied. You'll understand of course."

"Of course," echoed Sir Jonathan, who had used the same device many times. It was always more advantageous to present one's self as an agent, rather than a principal, when negotiating. One could ascribe difficulties to recalcitrant principals, while claiming that all concessions were won by one's own efforts.

Colonel Okamoto chatted for two hours before Opal insisted that Sir Jonathan needed rest. The Colonel left The Castle in his Packard staff car content that he was finally wearing away the Old Gentleman's marble obstinacy. He had won no specific concession, and he had been maneuvered into releasing Sarah Haleevie Sekloong from the civilian internment camp at Stanley. Still, Colonel Okamoto reassured himself with the Japanese proverb that she was only a prawn to entice a tuna —and Sir Jonathan was definitely softening.

Sarah was bowed out of camp with expressions of profound regret for the long captivity that had reduced her to eighty-six pounds. She was further assured that, unlike the Germans, the Japanese had the highest regard for the Jews. She was mildly chagrined. Her premature release might be embarrassing after the Japanese defeat, and after all, her vegetables had been flourishing in one of the small plots the prisoners were allowed to help feed themselves.

That measured wry reaction proceeded from the sturdy self-reliance Sarah Haleevie Sekloong had learned during almost three years of captivity. The fabric of her securely privileged life had been shredded by the Japanese conquest, which deprived her of a home and a much-loved husband, whose fate she still did not know. The integrity of her body and her spirit had been shattered by the brutal mass rape. But she had gradually regained her self-esteem by attaining understanding that her body, but not her soul, had been soiled. Surviving in the internment camp had demanded all her resources, as had helping her fellow prisoners, who in turn helped her. She could not, therefore, permit herself to brood on her humiliation. Besides, she was by no means alone; a number of the women in the Stanley Camp had suffered the same brutal treatment. Outwardly once again sprightly, even seemingly frivolous when she was released, Sarah had developed a strength and compassion that would sustain her all her life. She longed only for Jonnie to make her totally whole again.

Although Colonel Okamoto had not again hinted that Jonnie might be released, his brother-in-law's death gave the prisoner-of-war a respite from coolie labor on the Kobe Docks. The camp commandant offered him condolences, his first full meal in six months, and a week off work "to mourn 'Randaru Mahtin' with dignity." It was not his first respite, for the commandant had been alternately wooing and abusing him for two years. Only the solitary confinement he suffered after each spell of privilege preserved Jonnie's credit with his fellow prisoners. Their moral support stiffened his resistance to the alternating cycles of threats and promises, the "hot and cold treatment" the Japanese hoped would win his public support of their grand design for Asia.

Jonnie wore the rags of his cotton uniform beneath a coat cobbled from a worn blanket, and his feet were filth-encrusted in sandals cut from a discarded tire. The damp October cold lanced through his skin to chill his bones. His sparse flesh was no obstacle to the icy thrust; the bones of his arms and legs, like his ribs, were molded in bas-relief under skin drawn taut by starvation. The strawberry sores of beri-beri ached on his tongue, his lips, and his testicles. Only handfuls of grain and food tins pilfered from the ships' cargoes had kept him alive.

To sit in a cushioned chair in the commandant's warm office was a foretaste of Heaven. Only with difficulty could he remember the comforts and banquets of peacetime; his mind had blanked out such memories of the past in order to preserve its balance. To be louse-ridden, foul-smelling, constantly exhausted, and perpetually hungry had come to appear to him the normal condition of man. He looked around the snug office like a stone-age Papuan contemplating the artifacts of civilization for the first time. The English-speaking commandant's low-voiced sympathy and his pressing invitations to eat more baked fish were an irrelevant distraction indistinctly heard.

"All we wish is a few words addressed to the people of Hong Kong in your own voice," the commandant repeated. "No more than that—and I can persuade my superiors to relieve you of all work, transfer you to a hotel. Afterward, who knows? If you assist our righteous cause, anything is possible. . . ."

"I'm sorry, Major," Jonnie replied with patient courtesy. "I must apologize. I'm afraid it's impossible."

Adequate food, warm clothing, a chance to rest—those were the only goals of his existence at the age of forty-two. Those essential comforts could guarantee his surviving the war, an unlikely prospect otherwise. He had dispassionately calculated his hopes of survival as a hard-driven POW at one in three. But he could no more collaborate than he could take the easy road to oblivion, passive suicide by relinquishing his will to live. It required no conscious choice to reject the Major's renewed inducements. Jonnie had thought the problem through two years earlier and then dismissed it from his mind.

His motives, he had further concluded, were wholly selfish. He yearned to return to Sarah and their joyful, privileged life in Hong Kong. Since he *knew* the Allies would win the war, he knew further that he could not return to that life if he should collaborate. It was that simple, though he was troubled by his ignoble motivation.

The Japanese had told him of his cousin Francis Sek's "profoundly righteous cooperation with the new order." But he dismissed Francis as a fool who would suffer for his opportunism. Jonnie could not know that Francis was not only to be forgiven his trespasses by a Colony that could forgive wealth anything; he certainly could not imagine that, his sins forgiven, Francis was later to receive successive honors culminating in a knighthood "for philanthropy and services to the community." Jonnie was convinced that he had taken a wholly practical decision.

"In any event, Captain," the commandant urged,

"you will not refuse a week's relief from duties and better rations."

"No, Major, certainly not!" Jonnie replied without hesitation, since even a week's respite could mean life, rather than death. But he felt impelled to add: "In honesty, I must tell you that it will not affect my attitude."

The commandant's amazement was mingled with admiration. He had, he knew, finally met that supernal being of whom he had read so much—the English Gentleman.

"This one has the true samurai spirit," the Major later told his adjutant over *sake*. "Give him two weeks off labor."

"You go talk with the reactionaries today, Ai-kuo," Chou En-lai instructed his aide. "I'm entertaining the American press."

"Your special instructions, Comrade?" Major General Shih Ai-kuo, christened James Seekloong, asked.

James knew the comprehensive directive for the Communists' discussions with the Nationalists almost as well as did Chou En-lai, who had drafted the documents. He was, nonetheless, impelled to confirm his instructions by the awe he still felt for his brilliant superior after a twenty-year association, although Chou En-lai, at forty-six, was only eight years older than James in late November 1944. They had met as teacher and pupil when Chou En-lai was already one of the three chief men in the Communist Party at the age of twenty-four. The distance between them had narrowed as James rose in the hierarchy, but they could never meet as equals. The Communist hierarchy was just as rigidly stratified by rank and seniority as the neo-Confucian Nationalists it fought.

"Nothing new," Chou laughed. "The same tactics: relate, repeat, reiterate—and agree to nothing. Object to everything and smile. Keep pushing them. They're flustered."

"I imagine, Comrade," James observed dryly, "your efforts with the American press will be more successful than mine with the Nationalists."

"You're being polite, Ai-kuo," Chou chuckled. "But you're right. Incidentally, stay away from the Americans. Let me handle them."

"It's your pleasure, Comrade." James permitted himself the further wry remark. "I'm glad you don't need me to interpret today."

"Now, Ai-kuo, don't be sour. We're moving forward on all fronts. The Americans are convinced that we are 'agrarian reformers,' whatever that may mean, not *real* Communists, that we're dedicated solely to helping the poor farmers. Forget your British prejudices against the Americans. They're our best weapon. We couldn't do without them."

"Useful, Comrade, true." James reflected that only Chou En-lai would allow himself the minutely barbed reference to his mixed ancestry—and only from Chou En-lai would he accept the jibe. "Useful, but not overly intelligent. I find their naive enthusiasm appalling."

"That's their most helpful trait, their juvenile enthusiasm. Even the so-called professionals, the China experts, are delightfully naive! I'll never forget Comrade Mao's face when President Roosevelt's Special Envoy let loose a red Indian war cry." Chou's voice was acid. "But the correspondents are the most useful in convincing the world that we are only peaceful democrats. They'd probably lynch anyone who dared suggest that I had ever killed anything larger than a mosquito."

"Everyone knows your record, Comrade," James replied. "No one could say you'd ever hung back when the objective situation demanded ruthless action. No one could call you a faint-hearted revolutionary who shrinks from revolutionary violence or necessary blood-letting."

"I thank you, Ai-kuo, for your expression of confidence," Chou laughed. "Now, go off and talk with the Nationalists. Talk, talk, talk! The time to fight, fight, fight will come soon enough!"

James's high spirits lingered while he was driven to the conference building to meet with the Nationalist negotiators for another session of the talks both sides considered essentially a necessary pretence to delude the Americans. His preoccupied superior rarely relaxed to engage in banter. Normally reserved with his staff, Chou En-lai saved his overwhelming charm for susceptible foreigners. James chuckled, recalling his chief's scathing tone each time he used the term *Chung-kuo chuan-men,* China experts.

His genial mood evaporated when he entered the gray, tile-roofed building to confront the Nationalist negotiator. Moved by an impulse like Chou En-lai's, Generalissimo Chiang Kai-shek had sent his own military aide. Major General Shih Ai-kuo faced Major General Sek Lai-kwok across the teacups and ashtrays on the scarred table. Despite his contempt for sentiment, James Sekloong felt premonitory unease at dealing directly with his own brother, his enemy, Thomas Sekloong.

The brothers nodded, too tense to exchange the empty, cool courtesies that had opened each intermittent Nationalist–Communist discussion since 1937. Having not seen each other since their hasty farewell at Shanghai in 1927, they were finally meeting as the principal spokesmen for their antagonistic chiefs.

A sense of unreality momentarily overcame James Sekloong; he felt like a spectator of the scene in which he was actually a leading player. This meeting as enemies was not the consummation Thomas and he had envisioned when they played at soldiers on the beaches of Peitaiho, drilled on the parade-ground of the Whampoa Academy, and marched out side by side from Canton on the Northern Expedition. Half-carried away by his memories, James forced himself to attend to his brother's words.

Always more emotional than his younger brother, Thomas resorted to the stylized half-chant of conventional Chinese oratory and a forbiddingly formal manner to mask his own emotions. He was appalled by the direct confrontation with James. When brother faced brother in open enmity, the fabric of society was rent. Like his devout Catholicism, the traditional Confucian ethos required loving solidarity of brothers—and that the younger render respectful obedience to the older. He consciously closed his heart against its own reproaches. He, after all, *was* the elder brother.

"I have been instructed by the National Military Affairs Commission to inform you that the Third Independent Brigade of the Eighth Route Army has moved out of its assigned area, disrupting our defensive dispositions," he said stiffly. "I am instructed to require you to communicate to the commander of the Eighth Route Army, General Chu Teh, the orders of the Military Commission that the Brigade return to its tactical area immediately."

Such a protest was the normal opening gambit of each session. Because the Communists' Red Army had nominally been the Eighth Route Army of the Central Government force's since the Nationalist–Communist agreement of September 1937, the Nationalists almost invariably stressed the Communists' theoretically subordinate position by giving Mao Tse-tung's representative orders they knew he would not obey.

"I have noted your inquiry," James replied automatically. "I shall consult my superiors."

The Communists would acknowledge neither error nor insubordination by responding to the orders of their titular superiors, the Central Government. The Nationalists would, however, not sacrifice face by pushing the issue to an indignant rebuff.

"I have been instructed by the chief-of-staff of the Eighth Route Army to protest." James did not address his brother by name or title. "The Fifty-ninth Division of the Nationalist forces has encroached upon the Shensi–Kansu Border Area. Innocent farmers have been molested and their food supplies looted. Any repetition will be met with force."

"I shall make inquiries," Thomas replied by rote, "as to whether the alleged action ever occurred."

"I am further instructed," James said, "to restate the proposal of the Central Committee of the Communist Party of China and elicit your attitude."

641

The ballet was proceeding precisely as its choreographers had anticipated. It was necessary to talk—primarily for the benefit of the Americans—while each side recruited its strength for the final battle. It was not, however, necessary to listen. Thomas's thoughts strayed as his brother restated the terms proposed only two weeks earlier, but already drained of meaning by repetition.

The price for Yenan's unreserved cooperation with Chungking against the Japanese, James reiterated, was formation of a coalition government made up of the Kuomintang, the Communist Party, and lesser political parties, all guaranteed freedom of action throughout China.

"Your proposal is unacceptable, as you have been informed previously," Thomas said. "I shall again convey to you the conditions the legitimate Central Government of the Republic of China is prepared to offer."

James in turn allowed his thoughts to wander. He saw no reason to listen again to the Nationalists' terms, which offered the Communists token legitimacy, but excluded their essential condition, a coalition National Government. Without a coalition, the Communists would be denied the opportunity they coveted to undermine the Nationalist regime from within.

They won't accept, Chou En-lai had said. *They can't invite the fox into the chicken coop. No more can we surrender our independence and imperil the future liberation of China by subordinating ourselves to them. But we'll keep talking.*

"I must point out that your counterproposal ignores the essential proposal of the Communist Party: a coalition government." James's face flushed. "Your conditions can, therefore, not serve as the basis for further serious negotiations."

Impelled by his volatile temper, James Sekloong had exceeded Chou En-lai's instructions and almost rejected the Nationalists' conditions outright. The meeting should, nonetheless, have ended at that point, as so many previous meetings had ended with coolly polite disagreement. The meeting would have ended thus if Thomas Sekloong had, in turn, not lost control of his temper.

"You will accept *no* proposals, *none*." His voice rose, and red spots flared on his cheekbones. "*No* proposals that do not pave your way to power, will you, Little Brother?"

"We will accept no proposals," James flared, "that mean the unchallenged perpetuation of your neo-Fascist dictatorship."

"Because your Russian masters won't let you," Thomas jibed.

"You speak of masters, you who dare not shit without consulting your American paymasters. You are running-dogs of American imperialism. You serve one imperialist force, the Americans, in order to destroy their rival imperialists, the Japanese."

Their attendant officers were shocked into inaction by the bitter exchange. They sat icy-faced, afraid to intervene in the personal quarrel between their superiors. The blue clouds of tobacco smoke that normally pervaded the room became a fog as the staff officers nervously stubbed out cigarettes and lit new ones while the butts still smoldered. The staff officers were mute when the brothers reverted to the vitriolic Cantonese that was their childhood tongue.

"And you pretend you're fighting the Japanese, when you're really fighting the Chinese," Thomas shouted. "Fighting your own flesh and blood for the Russian hairy bastards!"

"You're trying to strangle us, the way you've always tried," James responded. "Kill Communists, ignore the Japanese, and lick the Americans' bottoms—that's your motto."

"Ass-kissing, bottom-licking!" Thomas exploded. "Who's kissing ass but you? Who's playing with the Americans, masturbating them and offering them your asses to screw? Not us, but you."

"You don't need to," James shouted. "The Americans've already raped your sisters and mothers a hundred times. You're selling China and your own mothers to them. You're the son of a poxed Swatow whore!"

Cantonese invective invariably descended to abusing the antagonist's mother. James's temper had swept him over the threshold of decency. The abashed brothers were silent, and their staff officers bustled them out of the room.

"I hear James and Thomas had a dust-up the other day," Dr. George Chapman Parker remarked, "a real shouting match."

Guinevere Sekloong Parker looked fondly at her white-haired husband and despaired again of ever bringing him to a respectable level of military smartness. The thoroughly unmartial Brigadier General's olive-green tunic was as crumpled and shapeless as his hand-tailored civilian suits had been when he was a specialist in tropical medicine in New York. Guinevere had little else to complain about after twenty years of marriage. Despite her mother's initial misgivings regarding the difference in their ages, George had not only made her happy, but joyful. Trim, red-haired, and unassertive at forty-one, Gwinnie was well content. Her decision to leave the children in order to accompany George on his six-month tour had not been easy, but her husband needed her more than did their independent son and daughter. Fortunately, her sister Charlotte was, to Gwinnie's surprise, competently and affectionately playing foster mother to George, Jr., and Blanche.

"Thomas and James were always fighting," she commented abstractedly. "But no one could ever come between them. We used to call them one devil in two bodies."

"They're two devils in two bodies now, Gwinnie. They're so far apart you could march a regiment between them!"

"Oh, George, if only they could come together. If only the two sides . . ."

"Forget it, my dear," George advised. "It's hopeless.
644

You've seen enough of this mess in the last four months to know your mother's right. The Chinese will never cooperate. They'll fight each other forever."

"I can't take it as calmly as you, George."

"Calmly? Did I take it calmly when I discovered that three-quarters of the anti-toxin I finally wangled out of Washington had disappeared? Only the rich can get medicines. But they're in for a shock. When, not if, but *when* the typhoid epidemic breaks, they'll find they're not immune. The poor they've deprived of immunization will infect them."

"That bad, George?"

"Worse! I'm holding my breath and praying. That's all I can do. They'd steal my old stethoscope if they could. The corruption's unbelievable—and the infighting's worse than the plague in Hong Kong in '09. But, this time, Chinese are fighting Chinese instead of the British. I can only pray we don't have another plague epidemic. It's already virulent in places in Yunnan. So I tell them to kill rats. It's all happened before."

"But your public health conference, George. Certainly, the governors and mayors can . . ."

"Not a hope. They have no power, and the generals won't move. Too busy stealing supplies, collecting pay for phantom soldiers, and counting their rake-off from the black market. God help us, a vial of penicillin that could save a soldier with peritonitis goes to some fat merchant's concubine, who thinks—wrongly, it happens —that it will cure her cold. All Chinese think an injection is magic, if it costs enough. I'm ready to throw in my hand."

"Only a while, now," Gwinnie soothed, "and we'll be going home."

George Parker's despondency made his wife long for the end of his tour of duty. They had returned to China with enthusiastic hopes of preventing the threatening epidemics. After only three months, even the ebullient Dr. Parker had despaired. Her concern for her husband overcame her concern for her native country, and Gwinnie marked the passage of time with black strokes on her calendar. Another fifty-six days would see them safely out of China.

Compassion contended against revulsion when she looked around the crowded, narrow street on the steep hillside. She had been too long in the United States to ignore the misery her mother pretended not to see; the pervasive suffering was intolerable to Gwinnie. Maimed beggars with suppurating ulcers on their stumps held up emaciated children while officers and their ladies strolled past unseeing. Bone-thin private soldiers in patched uniforms jostled plump merchants in silk long-gowns. Green slime coated the broken cobblestones and, it seemed, hung in droplets in the air itself.

Whoo-ee! Whoo-ee! Whoo-ee! The sirens' piercing ululation silenced the crowds' babble.

"Ching-pao! Hung-cha ching-pao!" The ubiquitous policemen in shabby uniforms shouted. "Alarm! Air-raid alarm!"

Gwinnie and George Parker were swept up by the throngs surging into the mouth of an air-raid shelter. The Chinese were proud of those deep tunnels that honeycombed Chungking's cliffs. Most accommodated at least 30,000, and the new tunnel in the East City sheltered 40,000. The Parkers were carried through the wide portals into gloom half-lit by kerosene lanterns. Jostled by the frightened crowd, Gwinnie clutched her husband's arm.

"Shouldn't be long," George assured her. "Our fighters'll drive them off. Pity there's no fog today."

Seated on their coats near the tunnel's mouth, they heard bombs exploding, anti-aircraft batteries chattering, and airplane engines whining. Gwinnie crushed a crawling insect on her neck. Disease-bearing fleas, mites, ticks, and flies infested Chungking. She shuddered and wiped her blood-stained fingers on her handkerchief.

Her husband did not notice her discomfort. His eyes were fixed on the patch of light cast on the packed-earth wall by the flickering lantern hanging from the low ceiling. A rivulet of earth was trickling from the wall. He knew it was not his imagination, for he could see the fissure widen as he watched. A gout of mud fell from the ceiling, and the wooden beams supporting the packed earth groaned on their stout props. A stick of bombs exploded close by, their serried thunder reverberating through the cavern, and Parker saw the props jump. The wooden crossbeams trembled, shifting in their sockets.

"Let's get out!" He grasped Gwinnie's hand. "The tunnel's going. Come on, Gwinnie, quick."

Daylight shone tantalizingly from the exit thirty yards away. Treading carelessly on reclining bodies, George Parker pulled his wife toward safety. A moment later, the entire crowd pushed toward the exit. The Parkers were twenty feet from the tunnel's mouth when the earth shrieked and the tunnel collapsed. An avalanche of mud, beams, and stones bore them down. Guinevere and George Parker died when the viscous soil filled their noses and mouths. Her hand was still clasped tightly in his.

When Gwinnie and George did not appear for lunch, Charles and Mary summoned sedan chairs to carry them to the American medical team's headquarters in the East City. The telephone system was hopeless. The General and Mrs. Parker, a sympathetic lieutenant told them, had set out to attend a public health conference in a compound near the giant new East City Tunnel shortly before the air raid. No, he said, he'd had no word from them, and the sergeant sent to inquire reported that they had not arrived at the conference hall.

For two days, Mary and Charles watched rescue workers digging in the debris to unearth broken bodies. The workmen, who wore cloth masks against the stench rising from the earth, scraped with crude spades and hoes at the impacted mass of rocks and clay.

Mary was dry-eyed in shock, though unshed tears shone in Charles's hazel eyes.

"I feel old," he said dully, "and helpless."

She slipped her arm around his waist. He grasped her shoulder and pulled her close.

"I never thought it would be Gwinnie," she said slowly. "I've been afraid, so afraid for Jonnie, for Thomas, and for James. But Gwinnie shouldn't even have been here. Why Gwinnie?"

Late in the afternoon, four American bulldozers clanked through the narrow streets toward the blocked mouth of the tunnel.

"Now," Mary reassured Charles, "we'll see something happen. The machines'll get them out."

Fifteen minutes later, Charles clasped Mary's arm.

"The bulldozers are closing the tunnel," he faltered. "They're giving up. It's all over."

The keening of the crowds tormented the cold afternoon. Charles and Mary walked slowly down the hillside. His bad leg dragged on the cobbles, and he leaned heavily on his cane. Her vision obscured by a mist of tears, Mary tightened her arm around his waist. He guiding her and she supporting him, they stumbled through streets bubbling with irrepressible life.

"I hear they've demoted three of the officials who built the East City Tunnel." Dewey Miller stamped his cold feet on the steel-plate runway of the Sand Spit. "Real fierce punishment, isn't it?"

"Who knows?" Archie MacDonald's response was unusually bland. "It *could* have been honest error, not graft."

"You don't really believe that, Archie?"

"No, not really, but there's no proof."

"And there never will be," Miller said savagely. "Someone big might get hurt. After all, what's 40,000 lives?"

"You heard about the Parkers?"

"Yeah, Archie. Your Sekloongs are having a hell of a time. All that money doesn't help much, does it?"

"No, Dewey," the Scotsman replied with his normal acerbity, "though it may cushion the worst. But here they come."

Twelve impassive Communist delegates led by Chou En-lai climbed out of their jeeps and walked with self-conscious dignity toward the waiting American C-47. The Communist negotiator could gain no additional propaganda advantage from further repetition and rejection of the same proposals and counterproposals. He was returning to Yenan on December 9, 1944, just three years and one day after the Great War in the Pacific had begun with the Japanese attacks on Pearl Harbor, Hong Kong, and Malaya.

"Do you have a statement for us, Commissioner Chou?" the Associated Press correspondent called out. "When will you be back?"

"*Will* you be back?" shouted the Reuter correspondent.

Wooden-faced in his role of Major General Shih Ai-kuo, James Sekloong turned to the correspondents. He spoke slowly and distinctly in English.

"Commissioner Chou cannot reply to questions. He will return when the Nationalists show they are sincere in their intentions. He cannot predict when that happy event will occur."

"Anything to add?" the Associated Press man persisted. "Then this isn't the end of negotiations?"

"We hope not," James replied. "We earnestly hope not, but the Nationalists must demonstrate their sincerity. That is all."

"Can't you give us a statement?" insisted Reuter.

James conferred briefly with Chou En-lai before replying.

"Secretary-General Mao Tse-tung has pointed out a clear phenomenon. The Nationalists have said to us: 'If you give up your army, we will give you freedom.' If their offer is sincere, then the parties and groups that have no armies should already have enjoyed freedom for some time. But they have no freedom. Because the workers, peasants, students, intellectuals, and national bourgeoisie have no army, they have lost their freedom. We will not walk into the tiger's lair unarmed."

"General Shih, can you tell us . . ."

"Commissioner Chou, just one more picture."

"General, is there no hope of . . ."

The Communist delegates climbed the short aluminum ladder into the C-47. Before the door clanged shut, James turned again to the throng of correspondents.

"Comrade Chou has asked me," he smiled, "to tell you that he hopes to see you all again, soon. But he cannot say when."

The twin engines spat gray smoke, and the C-47 began taxiing.

"You know," Miller said meditatively, "I could swear that big bastard had been crying. He's not that cut up about the talks, is he?"

"Dewey, don't forget it was his sister," MacDonald reminded him. "They're still family—capitalist or Communist."

"I forgot," Miller answered. "Poor bastard. But when'll they be back? Will they be back?"

"Oh, they'll be back. No question, though who knows when? There's still a lot of talking to get through before the fighting starts. Both sides want to keep up the pretence a little longer, at least till the Japs are out of the picture."

"Fighting?" Miller pressed disingenuously. "You're sure they'll fight it out."

"What else?" MacDonald shrugged.

"And who'll win?" Miller persisted. "The Communists or the Nationalists?"

"Come now, Dewey," MacDonald snapped. "Who do *you* think'll win?"

Interlude

June 27, 1970

10:30 P.M. to 12 M.

THE violent assault of Typhoon Linda, passing just thirty miles from the center of the Colony, enveloped The Peak in opaque cascades. The typhoon's myriad claws ripped at hillsides and gashed foundations. The waves in the harbor rose sixteen feet to batter the sea walls, break over those embankments, and flood the plaza of City Hall. An 18,000-ton freighter was torn from its moorings, her massive iron-chain tether snapping like a silk skein. The *Oriental Monarch* was driven inexorably toward the jutting finger of the man-made runway of Kaitak Airport. Her twin screws thrashed impotently against the foam-whipped waters, while her captain clung white-faced to the binnacle, alternately demanding more power from the engine-room and praying in a terrified monotone. In Repulse Bay, blocks of jerry-built "luxury" high-rise flats swayed in the winds. Windows shattered under the gusts; flying flower-pots and porch furniture crashed into living rooms inches deep in water; and two-inch cracks opened in concrete façades. In Wanchai, the wild torrents pouring down from the hillsides into the tenements and shacks swept away automobiles, filling the side streets with yellow mud that flowed like lava.

Ponderous as a 300,000-ton supertanker riding out a gale off the Cape of Good Hope, The Castle was contemptuously secure against the shrieking 110-mile-an-hour winds. Its great stones withstood the fury of Typhoon Linda as they had the battering of scores of earlier mighty tropical storms. Occasionally, when a door opened, the diners heard the creaking of tortured shutters amid the wild wail of the typhoon. In spite of these intrusions, the banquet celebrating Lady Mary's ninetieth birthday spun out its ceremonial length undisturbed.

Sir Jonathan had built his fortress to withstand the

assaults of nature, the malevolence of human enemies, and the erosion of time itself. Lady Mary remembered her first glimpse of Sekloong Manor when Harry, dead these past thirty-one years, showed her the construction site that recalled the building of the eternal pyramids. The Castle would endure. But, she wondered, would the Sekloongs themselves prove as impregnable against the forces that threatened them? Her own generation had passed, and her children's generation was passing. But what of the others, her grandchildren and great-grandchildren? Lady Mary's violet eyes swept around the table, judging the animated faces of her descendants.

Halfway down the arc of the round table, her son James listened with amused disdain to the loud, adulatory questions of his grandnephew, George Chapman Parker III. Inevitably called Chappie, the nineteen-year-old son of American Air Force Major General George Chapman Parker, Jr., was a self-avowed Maoist who had dropped out of Princeton to "fight for the cause." The heir to $4.5 million through his Sekloong mother and his deceased grandfather Dr. George Parker was annoying his Communist granduncle by the same undisciplined zealotry that had for years enraged his re-flexively conservative father and his uncle by marriage, the Under Secretary of State. This once he looked reasonably clean in the faded jeans and open-necked shirt that were his concession to formal attire, though his long hair, caught by a rubber-band in a pony tail, would have benefited from a shampoo.

Lady Mary wrinkled her nose in distaste. Chappie was no favorite of hers. She was mildly offended by his eccentric dress, his immature political opinions, and the grime that normally layered his neck. Her anger was, however, roused by the impenetrable layers of ignorance that sustained his doctrinaire convictions. She herself had studied every word written by Chairman Mao Tse-tung with great attention—and occasional enthusiasm. But her great-grandson was arrogantly uninformed; he had never read the basic texts of the creed he professed. As far as she could ascertain, Chappie believed simply that his adored Chairman wanted to blow up the world—nothing less and nothing more. While awaiting that universal apotheosis, he regularly blew his own mind with LSD.

"Right on, Uncle Comrade!" Chappie's voice was shrill in approbation. "We'll destroy every last mother of the exploiters, even if we leave nothing but a smoking pyre. Right on, Uncle Comrade!"

General Shih Ai-kuo looked infinitely pained. Regretting his earlier outburst, he reflected that he had not been sent to Hong Kong to quarrel with his elder brother, who still worshipped the fallen idol Generalissimo Chiang Kai-shek. But neither had he been sent to listen to adolescent prattle. He caught the eye of Spencer Taylor Smith, whom Lady Mary had seated three places away, and grimaced in mute disgust at their nephew's idiocy. For once in wholehearted agreement with the Deputy Political Commissar of the Chinese People's Liberation Army, the American Under Secretary of State smiled his sympathy.

"Ah, Chappie." General Shih turned back to his grandnephew. "Who are these mothers you wish to destroy? A most unfilial ambition."

"You know what I mean, Uncle Comrade. You know. All those mother-friggers, the guys who screw the people. You know."

"A strange expression." The representative of the Central Committee of the Chinese Communist Party was deliberately obtuse. "I must study the American language."

"Don't take my son as a model, General Shih," Major General George Chapman Parker, Jr., cautioned. "His jargon changes so fast, Sir, even I can't keep up with it."

"Why don't you call me Uncle James, George?" the Communist leader suggested. "Everyone else seems to. But not, if you please, Uncle Comrade."

"No fear of that, Sir . . . Uncle James," Parker answered.

"I might add, General Shih, that our mutual nephew's political opinions change as rapidly as his jargon." The Under Secretary of State was searching for an opening, for a point of human contact with the enemy. His instructions were clear. Unlike China's Premier Chou En-lai, the American policy-maker Henry Kissinger had defined his subordinate's mission precisely.

"I trust, Mr. Secretary, that, ah, Chappie's opinions will mature," the Communist General replied. "On one point, however, he and I are agreed. There can be no compromise with Soviet social-imperialism or American imperialism. Eventually, of course, we shall destroy you as well as the Soviets. But Chappie himself needs to learn much, needs opportunity for serious study."

The Under Secretary groped for a temperate reply, but Chappie's eager response broke in before he could speak.

"Could I, Uncle Comrade, could I? Hot shit! What an opportunity!"

"Could you what, young man? No one is interested in your bodily functions. And, if you wish to use the facilities, you don't require my permission."

"You know what I mean, Uncle Comrade. Hot shit! Could I come to China and see what you've created? What a trip *that* would be! *Could* I, Uncle Comrade?"

"You could presumably apply for a visa, though that is not within my province. But I don't see that such a visit would benefit either the Chinese people or yourself. You need to learn much beforehand. Above all, you need to learn discipline, self-discipline, if you are to serve the people."

"Shit, Uncle Comrade, that's what they all say. Discipline, that's what the older generation—everybody over thirty—keeps preaching at us. Are you putting us on, too, Uncle Comrade? Anyway, how can I learn in *Amerika*? Man, it's a bad scene. Fascism, suppression, racism, exploitive capitalism. The whole rotten bag!"

"You must read the works of Chairman Mao, learn to understand his thoughts thoroughly and penetratingly." General Shih Ai-kuo was enjoying himself. "You must study and learn . . . learn to make revolution by making revolution. We Communists will help as much as we can. But only the American people can liberate the American people."

"That's a hard one, Uncle Comrade."

"I did not say it was easy. As the Chairman teaches: 'A revolution is not an invitation to a tea party.' You must learn to be relentless and uncompromising."

James Sekloong, formally Comrade General Shih Ai-kuo, was mildly aglow with the wine and with his pleasure in baiting the two American officials who were his nephews. His earlier depression dissipated, he smiled when his bodyguard leaned over his shoulder with a long, red-striped envelope. Still smiling, he read the message written in the Premier's own hand and validated with the Premier's personal seal:

> Comrade Ai-kuo:
> I regret to inform you that your wife, Comrade Lu Ping, has been removed from alternate membership in the Central Committee and from the chair of the Woman's Association. She has volunteered to spend two years on the Red Star People's Commune in Mongolia to learn from the people and remold her thoughts in order to draw a clear line between our enemies and our friends, as the Chairman directs. Her chief mistake, the Party Surveillance Commission found, was advocating accommodation with the Soviet social-imperialists. There is, at present, no suspicion that you share her errors. You may act as you see best. Destroy this.

The General's smile did not alter; decades of intra-Party strife had schooled him never to reveal shock or even surprise. But his mind calculated as rapidly—and almost as dispassionately—as a computer ingesting a problem of three-tiered complexity.

That old fox, the Premier, had obviously known of the Party's decision before his own departure from Peking. The message had assuredly traveled on the same airplane that carried him to Hong Kong—with instructions for its delivery at his mother's table. The Premier had been either unable or unwilling to safeguard James's wife from the "ultra-leftists" who were the Premier's own enemies. The high command of the Liberation Army, itself in disarray, had not looked after its own. Despite the Premier's reassurance, James could almost feel the noose tightening around his own neck. Yet the Premier was his chief ally and, finally, his only protector. Characteristically, the Premier's own wishes were not explicitly stated, but they were nonetheless reasonably clear. James knew the Premier feared Muscovite imperialism above all else.

"Do excuse my reading the note," the General apologized. "A trifling matter an overzealous aide thought I should see now."

He lifted his bowl and inhaled a skein of birthday noodles, long noodles for long life. His mother's life had already been long. But his own? He wondered, but the chopsticks in his hand, he observed with grim satisfaction, were quite steady. No tremor betrayed his inner turmoil.

"Your pardon, Comrade," James's bodyguard whispered in his ear. "This additional message just came in on The Castle's Telex. Uncoded and in English."

23156 SKLNG HKG

IMMEDIATE FOR GENERAL SHIH AIKUO:

YOU ARE AUTHORIZED AT YOUR DISCRETION TO COMMUNICATE THE FOLLOWING UNOFFICIALLY TO UNDERSECRETARY SMITH: PATIENCE OF GOVERNMENT OF PEOPLE'S REPUBLIC OF CHINA IS WEARING THIN. WE CAN NOT REPEAT NOT MUCH LONGER STAND IDLY BY AND WATCH OUR COMPATRIOTS ON TAIWAN SUFFER UNDER OPPRESSION OF CHIANG KAISHEK REMNANT CLIQUE. JUST DEMANDS OF CHINESE PEOPLE, DANGER FROM SOVIET SOCIAL-IMPERIALISTS, AND URGENT NEED TO REUNIFY NATIONAL ECONOMY MAY, THEREFORE, REQUIRE THAT WE TAKE MILITARY ACTION TO LIBERATE TAIWAN IF ATTITUDE OF UNITED STATES GOVERNMENT REMAINS OBDURATE. PEOPLE'S REPUBLIC OF

CHINA IS, HOWEVER, ALWAYS PREPARED TO ENTER
UPON NEGOTIATIONS UPON ANY ISSUE IF OTHER SIDE IN
NEGOTIATIONS IS SINCERE.

FOREIGN MINISTRY

His personal fears forgotten, James's first reaction
was coolly professional. It was, he noted, 11:05 P.M. in
Hong Kong, which meant 10:05 P.M. in Peking, where
the Premier would be just beginning his night's work,
and 9 A.M. in Washington, where officials kept more
conventional hours. There was time for both discussion
and exchange of further messages. Though the Telex
was signed by the Foreign Ministry, the Premier's hand
was obvious. Only his subtle authority could have insured that the message be sent uncoded so that the
American monitors would read it immediately. Only the
Premier would have combined a flat threat to attack
Taiwan with a clear indication that the attack could be
averted by serious negotiation. With the United States
apparently bogged down in Vietnam and many American voices demanding closer relations with the People's
Republic, the timing was superb. The prospect of hostilities against Peking would appall Washington, while
the hint that Peking might join in a common front
against Moscow would evoke great interest. But the
message was "unofficial," its delivery left to James's
"discretion." Characteristically, the Premier had committed neither himself nor the Chinese Government.

"What were we discussing?" James laid his chopsticks down and obeyed his new instructions. "Ah, yes!
The Chairman also points out that the revolution has
many twists and turns. The struggle takes many decades, not merely a year or two. Chairman Mao further
teaches us that it is sometimes necessary to cooperate
with one enemy, perhaps temporarily, in order to defeat
the greater enemy."

The Under Secretary stiffened like a bird-dog that
hears a rustle in the underbrush. The Chapmans, father
and son, stared—bewildered by James's abrupt reversal
of his position. The Political Commissar had moved in

less than five minutes from denouncing American imperialism to hinting at Peking-Washington cooperation against Moscow.

"Under proper circumstances such an arrangement could endure for decades," James continued. "The revolution must be as determined as a bulldog, yet as flexible as a serpent."

A pealing bell interrupted James. Old Sir Mosing Way raised a glass of champagne.

"Your Excellencies, Ladies and Gentlemen, beloved kinsmen and kinswomen, may I again claim the privilege of the second oldest among us? I give you Lady Sekloong. Let us drink to her ninety years of wisdom and love."

"Thank you, Mosing, my oldest friend." Lady Mary rose, resting one hand on the table for support. Her light voice gathered strength as she spoke, "My deepest thanks and my love to all of you, to those who have come great distances and to those who have journeyed only a few miles. I am honored by your presence, and I am warmed by your love. Even at ninety, warmth is still more important than honor."

Laughter bounced around the Great Hall. Only the crew-cut young man who hovered behind Spencer Taylor Smith remained unsmiling as he listened intently to his mini-transceiver. He whispered into the ear of the Under Secretary, who pushed his chair away from the table murmuring, "Excuse me. Urgent phone call. Sorry."

James Sekloong smiled to himself. Washington's monitors were even more efficient than he had thought. The Premier's message had obviously already been read by the Americans, who might already be oscillating between fears of armed confrontation over Taiwan and hopes of reconciliation with Peking. The night, he reflected, should prove interesting—and, in the next instant, reproved himself for his frivolousness. The night could well prove critical to his country, and he was directly in the firing line.

"I have, however, not asked you to come so far

merely to warm an old lady who has already outstayed her welcome on this earth," Lady Mary continued. "I wish to put to you one last request. It is not a demand. Some of you, I know, feel I have always been demanding—and nowadays, excessively tenacious of life."

Forced laughter dutifully responded to that sally. *Taipan* Albert Sekloong, at thirty-seven, handsome and lithe as a Thai Buddha, leaned across to remark *sotto voce* to his dashing older brother, Colonel Sir Henry: "The old girl's in great form tonight. But who's she getting at? Me for piling up riches without virtue, or you for playing soldier? What does she want now?"

"She's twitting neither of us, I dare say," the proper Colonel answered. "Some other bee in her bonnet."

Irritated by his brother's studied nonchalance, the man who directed the Sekloong empire smiled at his slender Japanese wife, Kazuko, whose brother Jiro Matsuyama was a rising power in the great Mitsubishi conglomerate. Aside from his devotion to Kazuko and their two small children, Albert's passions were directed entirely to the pursuit of wealth through commerce. Politics bored him.

Lady Mary sipped her champagne. The blue veins stood out on the back of her translucent hand.

"I am not jesting—not wholly," she said. "However, longevity was not my choice, but the Lord's, and He may soon rescind His edict. Neither was the exercise of authority my choice, but Sir Jonathan's command. I have executed my stewardship as best I could. I shall make no apologies. But I did not, as I have already said, ask you here merely to warm an old lady with your love, though I rejoice in that love. Nor do I plan to reprove you."

A brother and sister exchanged relieved glances. Jonathan III, Sir Henry's twenty-year-old son who would one day succeed to the title, had inherited the male Sekloong sexual appetite. Lady Mary had twice bought off paternity suits in secret for Jonathan—as much to spare his widowed grandmother Sarah sorrow as to spare him his father's wrath. His younger sister,

Mary Philippa Sekloong, nineteen, who was called "Little Lady Mary" by the family and the servants, had inherited the classic brunette beauty of their English mother, Hermione Duane, but not Hermione's placid temperament.

Like her namesake, when Little Lady Mary did something foolish, she invariably overdid it. Her escapades with young men—and some older men—raised eyebrows even in the new age of permissiveness. Besides, only her great-grandmother's intercession had prevented her expulsion from Girton College at Oxford after a casual lesbian experiment with two classmates.

"No, not to reprove you," Lady Mary repeated.

"I'll drink to that," Albert proposed the toast, remembering the dark days in the sixties when he had almost bankrupted the firm. "No vain recriminations."

"Not recriminations, but sincere regrets, yes," his uncle, Charles Cardinal Sekloong, amended. "And remembrance, so that we don't repeat our follies."

Lady Mary's violet eyes had noted the exchange of glances between her great-grandchildren. Neither had known their grandfather, her eldest son Jonnie. She remembered her uncomprehending sorrow at Jonnie's meaningless death after having survived prolonged captivity by the Japanese. The Old Gentleman had arranged for Jonnie to be flown home to Hong Kong on August 29, 1945, a few days after the end of the War in the Pacific. The Royal Air Force pilot had never flown into Kaitak, where aircraft then landed with one wing cocked high to avoid the mountains, and then leveled out at the last moment. The wingtip of Jonnie's Dakota had brushed the mountainside, and the transport had cartwheeled into the harbor. Jonnie had died gazing at the home he had not seen for four years.

Mary had raged at blind fate in her great grief. Jonnie, the first fruit of her marriage, claimed a special place in her heart. Jonnie, who was independent, loving, and irresistibly charming. Only later had she been stricken by the realization that his death had deprived the House of Sekloong of its natural heir, the man who by both right and talent should have succeeded Sir Jonathan and Charles.

"Some of you laugh at what you call my motto: *If you're going to do something foolish, go the whole hog!*" The old lady's high-pitched voice cut through her descendants' light mood; the sacrifices and the tragedies must not be in vain. "But some restraint is always necessary, and I fear, we have transgressed certain limits. Bear with me, if you will. I want to talk about the family as it is today.

"It would be hypocritical—worse, stupid—to pretend we are less than we are. False modesty is as destructive as false pride. We are a power in the world—a great power when we all act in concert. We were already very powerful when the Old Gentleman helped Dr. Sun Yat-sen and, later, Chiang Kai-shek to establish the Republic of China and build its economy. Outsiders call us the Sekloong dynasty. But dynasties begin to decline the instant they reach their apogee. Great power and self-indulgence march hand in hand. We have ourselves progressed from selling opium to consuming LSD in five generations."

The bitter laughter was not forced.

"If we do not employ our power and wealth intelligently, all could vanish in another generation," Lady Mary continued. "Our unity will be destroyed and our strength dissipated. But it need not be so. The best way to use our power—and to save ourselves—is by striving to benefit others. I would therefore charge you all with one mission. All of you, my children, my grandchildren, and my great-grandchildren. We cannot accomplish that task alone, but we can assist greatly.

"As you may know, I married Charles Sekloong in the face of Sir Jonathan's doubts and my own father's disapproval. I loved my husband deeply, but I also saw a vision beyond that transcended the two of us. I dreamt that East and West could be united in harmony and in love.

"I still believe in my vision. We Sekloongs are an

663

alloy of two worlds, a wonderful alloy that can be forged into a useful instrument or a deadly weapon. I would have you become a powerful instrument to bring those two worlds together." Lady Mary paused before adding without stress: "You should know that I am dying. I am told the time is close."

A wordless lament sighed through the Great Hall. Lady Mary's head drooped wearily, but she waved away Cardinal Charles's extended hand.

"My father would have said: 'Cancer? Stomach cancer? What d'ye expect? All that foreign muck you et— rats' tails, snakes, puppy dogs, God knows what!' But ninety-odd is not precisely being carried off in the flower of one's youth."

They laughed spontaneously at her macabre jest and her mimicry of Bandmaster John Osgood's broad Yorkshire accent. She knew then that she held them rapt. Having captured her audience like a great actress, she could make them laugh or cry as she wished.

"You may consider these words a last injunction, though I hope you will consider them a last plea. What I ask must be done out of love, not . . ."

Lady Mary paused again, neither from weakness nor for effect, but in surprise. Tears marred the skilful make-up of the one professional actress among them. Lady Mary sometimes thought Alaine d'Alivère a clever minx and sometimes an inspired simpleton. Piquantly beautiful at thirty-eight, Charlotte's daughter Alaine was the reigning queen of the international cinema, despite her advocacy of extreme and presumably unpopular political causes. Yet the obsessively self-centered Alaine was weeping.

"It must be done from love and with all your heart." Lady Mary's voice quavered with strain. "It cannot be done grudgingly. And all of you must assist, though some can be much more effective than others. I shall be most specific in a moment."

Lady Mary sipped her champagne before continuing in firm tones.

"China is in my heart, as China is in your blood. But

China still stands apart from the world almost three quarters of a century after I first dreamt my dream. That was 1900, when foreign troops were ravaging Peking. However, my dream is by no means impossible of fulfillment today. My vision, my deepest hope, is that the Chinese should enter fully into the world—to work and strive in company with other peoples."

The matriarch's voice quavered, and she leaned on the table. But she smiled to reassure Opal and Sarah, who watched her with open concern.

"The Russians are barbarians who would destroy the civilized world, as Peking has learned. Some call the Americans barbarians. I do not, and I am proud of my American grandchildren. Like the Chinese, the Americans overflow with good will and, occasionally, with anger. But they *are* civilized, and they *are* powerful. They are the balance wheel of the world.

"As you know, I have been forced all my life to interest myself in politics, Chinese politics and international politics, though I might have preferred to devote myself exclusively to the family and the firm. Since I could not, I learned a good deal about politics. And I am cheered by the fact that, at this moment, exploratory messages are passing between Peking and Washington."

Most stared uncomprehendingly at Lady Mary; James Sekloong and Spencer Taylor Smith studied their chopsticks.

"I charge you to strive for reconciliation between the Chinese and the Americans." Her voice was again vibrant. "Some of you at this table hold positions of great power—James and Spencer Smith in particular, but also Charles, Avram Barakian, and even Thomas. Those of you who are in positions of influence must endeavor to direct the course of events by your boldness."

The frail figure drooped, and her words were barely audible.

"Only thus can China become a part of the world—and peace be assured. Only thus can the Sekloongs survive—and become stronger. Strong through service, not weak through self-indulgence."

She faltered, half-whispering, "Now may I say again: Thank you all! God bless you all!"

Leaning heavily on its gilt arms, Lady Mary sank into her red-cushioned chair. She seemed smaller, as if the intense strain of expressing her deepest emotions had depleted her physically. Her descendants read in each other's faces the same awe at the matriarch's undiminished will and her enduring concern for the world from which she must soon depart.

General Shih Ai-kuo and Under Secretary Spencer Taylor Smith avoided each other's eyes.

Part Seven

―――――――――――――――――――――――――

The Sekloongs and the Lao Pai-hsing

November 28, 1950–February 22, 1959

November 28, 1950–July 12, 1951

THE spare figure gnarled by great age was cocooned in cashmere shawls against the chill of the crystalline winter afternoon. But the white beard was meticulously trimmed, and the hazel eyes glowed in the wrinkled-parchment face. Those eyes could still flash green in anger, for the mind that animated them was almost as incisively alert as it had been half a century earlier. Though his body, the vessel of his indomitable spirit, had been worn frail by the years, the obsessively superstitious Cantonese of Hong Kong still spoke with awe of the Ancient Dragon in his mountain lair.

On November 28, 1950, some five years after the end of the war in the Pacific and fourteen months following the Communist victory in China, Sir Jonathan Sekloong surveyed his kingdom from the sheltered terrace behind the weathered stone balustrades of The Castle. In the fullness of his ninety-seventh year, he reviewed with gratified detachment the pleasures and sorrows of a life that had spanned some of the most turbulent years in the annals of mankind. He was well prepared to respond to the imminent summons of his Creator, having set all his worldly affairs in order and reaffirmed his faith in the merciful Deity who had been so generous to him. Only one blow could he not yet forgive his God. The heir-presumptive to his kingdom had been called from his side more than five years earlier. Jonnie's widow Sarah had finally resigned herself to the will of her own stern God, but Jonnie's grandfather could not reconcile himself to leaving the realm he had created bereft of a successor to Charles and Mary.

Sir Jonathan's eyes swept the green arc of the harbor where three dark-gray destroyers of the United States Navy swung at their buoys and a blue-gray cruiser of the Royal Navy steamed among a hundred anchored merchantmen. Asia was at war again, and the pulse of the commercially avid Colony was quickening to the opportunities offered by the conflict in Korea. Yet the debris of the last war was still rolling down upon the Colony; its hillsides were garlanded with the scrap-wood-and-corrugated-iron huts of some 700,000 refugees from the Communist conquest of China in 1949. Nevertheless, the Colony was reasserting the vitality that had increased its population from 86,000 in 1860 to 2.5 million by late 1950. Tokyo was just reviving under American military occupation, while Shanghai had fallen into desuetude with the coming of the Communists twenty months earlier. Its chief rivals having been neutralized, Hong Kong was, once again, the commercial capital of the Far East.

It was a nervous capital. For the first time in a century, Hong Kong feared a Chinese invasion. Assertive after the triumphant conquest of all China, a division of the People's Liberation Army was camped behind the last bare hill range that loomed between the Colony and the vastness of the Chinese mainland.

The Old Gentleman lowered his eyes from the panorama to the leather-bound book on his knees. His broad-nibbed pen moved deliberately, the broad serifs of the letters tapering into slender vertical strokes in the manner of Chinese calligraphy. He wrote in English, rather than his own shorthand. This volume, unlike his private diary, was a chronicle he wished his children, grandchildren, and succeeding generations to read. Like the scholar-officials of the Confucian dynasties, he was devoting his old age to literary composition. Beneath the winged dragon embossed in gold-leaf, the blue leather bore the title: *The Recollections of Sir Jonathan Sekloong, Baronet, Knight Commander of the Most Honourable Order of St. Michael and St. George.*

. . . *but, this time, the outcome must be quite different.* He completed the paragraph, blotted the black ink, and closed the book. His hands, honed fine by time, were translucent in the pale sunlight. But they served him competently, trembling only minutely as he pealed the silver bell that stood on the porcelain rice-barrel beside his cane chair.

Opal strolled onto the terrace. He would allow only Opal to serve him, complaining that the new servants were clumsy. Junoesque at twenty-six, the Polynesian wore a silk-padded long-gown and jacket. The damp cold of The Castle chilled her bones and raised goose-flesh on her bronze skin. Her deep breasts swelled under the long-gown, for she was still nursing the boy-child she had borne three months earlier to a father whose identity only she knew.

"Come inside, Old One," she said, toying with the frogs that secured her bodice. "I'll make you warm, and there is much milk."

"No," Sir Jonathan answered peremptorily. "I don't need it today. Just bring me a cigar and whiskey."

"But you need—what you call it—nourishment."

"Do as I say. The whiskey and the cigar are nourishment and pleasure enough for today."

"I can give you greater pleasure," she rejoined, twisting the frogs.

"I want a cigar and my whiskey. Nothing else. I want to live to a hundred, not forever, you know."

Opal returned with a silver salver bearing a crystal goblet of whiskey, a single panatella, a box of kitchen matches, and a gold cigar-cutter. She idly watched the familiar ritual as Sir Jonathan cut the cigar, lit it with a kitchen match, and carefully laid it aside.

"They're expensive," the multimillionaire said fret-fully. "I'm not made of money, you know."

Parsimony was a new trait, an unaware reaction to the insecurity of the turbulent new age. When the cigar was drawing, the Old Gentleman lifted the crystal goblet and sipped the whiskey.

"You've watered it again," he accused her. "Bring me the bottle. I want a proper drink! Best thing for my arteries."

Opal walked through the terrace-doors and slowly descended the stairs. She had watered the whiskey, for she was determined to give him no more than the two ounces the doctor allowed each day. If she tarried long enough, he might be more amenable when she finally returned.

After twenty minutes, she reappeared with a fresh bottle of Glenlivet. The goblet, she saw, was empty, and a spiral of smoke rose from the cigar in the ashtray. Unmindful of her presence, Sir Jonathan was again gazing at the panorama of Hong Kong, the city-state he had conquered and made the fortress-capital of his dynasty.

"Old One," she said. "I've brought the bottle. Are you *sure* you want more?"

He did not reply, and she was reluctant to intrude upon his reverie. However, he did not stir when she placed the bottle on the porcelain rice-barrel.

"Well, you're showing some sense, Old One," she said. "You didn't really want more, did you?"

Sir Jonathan remained silent, and Opal walked across the balcony toward the stone balustrade in order to see his face. Gold-tinged skin taut over high cheekbones, his head rested against the high back of the cane chair. The blue-white cigar-smoke curled into his unseeing hazel eyes.

Opal stood rooted by shock for a full minute. Then the Tahitian dirge for a great chieftain welled from her throat.

After her first searing grief, Mary Philippa Osgood Sekloong counseled herself to accept the inevitable with grace and humility. So long expected and so long dreaded, Sir Jonathan's death should, she felt, occasion almost as much joy as sorrow. He had taken his leave with the same dignity he had shown all his life. His achievements were attested by the sheafs of condolatory telegrams, by the bold headlines that briefly displaced reports of war and revolution, and by the tremors that shook the chancelleries and counting-houses of four continents. He had lived almost as long as he had wished; he had accomplished even more than he had dreamed as a thrusting youth; and he had died surveying the realm that bore his ineradicable impress. Sir Jonathan Sekloong had bowed gracefully to the world and then departed, holding his head high.

But that rationale was cold consolation for the profound deprivation Mary felt. The Old Gentleman had dominated all their lives for half a century. Charles and she had virtually controlled the Sekloongs' affairs for more than a decade, but Sir Jonathan had always been there to offer his cheerful cynicism, his devout faith, and his tough-minded counsel. Still she could not abandon herself to grief over their loss. Her husband needed all her strength, for he was stricken by his father's death.

At seventy-four, Charles Sekloong had finally come into his inheritance. He was *the* Sekloong, the belated distinction truly earned by his gentle resolution and by his commercial acumen, which had both flowered during the past three decades. After so many years in waiting, the second Baronet was *Taipan* to the Chinese associates and "Sir Charles" to the British officials and magnates who called at The Castle. Yet he started when he was addressed by those titles, having lived too long in his father's radiance to assume his new eminence with ease.

Charles was suddenly a very old man. He had been too long heir-apparent to wear the crown comfortably, too long buttressed by the Old Gentleman's ultimate authority to stand by himself. Besides, no new heir-apparent shared his power, his wealth, or his burdens, since his three surviving sons were committed elsewhere. Mary hoped to allay that anxiety by showing Charles in time that Albert, Jonnie's younger son, was the natural and the happy choice. But her first task was to reassure Charles, who tragically felt himself aged— as if his years, rather than his spirit, were the true measure of a man's age. At seventy, she herself did not feel old. Her internal vision, her innate sense of self, placed her somewhere between forty and fifty in the prime of her years.

The demanding preparations for the funeral were,

however, a revitalizing challenge to Charles, who was determined that the ceremonies must pay full homage to his father. Wholly Chinese in his filial piety, he was assisted in planning the obsequies by Sir Mosing Way and their common grandson, Mokhing Way, who was Charlotte's son. The entire clan, Charles believed, would be diminished if it failed to render splendid public obeisance to the Old Gentleman's spirit. Mary suspected that, despite his devout Catholicism, he feared the old Chinese gods would punish the Sekloongs if they were remiss. For the first time she knew beyond doubt that great love had bound her husband and his father, despite their quarrels.

Her own grief for Sir Jonathan and her anxiety for Charles were distracted by her own tasks. Sustained by Sarah and Opal, Mary dealt with the influx of mourners into The Castle.

Two grandsons came first. Lieutenant Henry Osgood Sekloong was flown by the Royal Air Force from Malaya, where his regiment was, for the second year, fighting the undeclared war against Chinese guerrillas whom the British authorities in that territory contemptuously described as "Communist terrorists." As superstitious as the Chinese regarding ritual terminology, the British further called the uprising the "Emergency," rather than a revolution. Major George Chapman Parker, Jr., United States Air Force, who had arrived on a Military Air Transport Service Skymaster, was required to depart immediately after the funeral. Fighting another undeclared war, the euphemistically termed "police action" in Korea, the Americans were hard pressed by the armies Peking had just committed, the so-called "Chinese People's Volunteers."

Bishop Charles Sekloong was *en route* from Rome to officiate at the Requiem High Mass. Charlotte Sekloong Way d'Alivère Martin was to land that afternoon in the personal Super-Constellation of her new admirer, the Armenian shipping and oil magnate Avram Barakian. General Thomas Sekloong had come to Hong Kong that morning aboard a C-46 Curtis Commando of retired Major General Claire Chennault's airline, Civil Air Transport. The Overseas Chinese Affairs Commission of the Central People's Government of the People's Republic of China had offered public condolences. But James Sekloong had not replied to a telegram addressed to General Shih Ai-kuo at the General Headquarters of the People's Liberation Army. His mother feared that he was already serving in Korea with an army that did not grant "compassionate leave," unlike the sentimental Americans.

Jonnie and Sarah's seventeen-year-old son Albert, a student at the Wharton School of Business of the University of Pennsylvania, telephoned to promise he would be present, "Even if I have to carry Pan American's DC-7 on my back." His twenty-one-year-old cousin Blanche, Major George Parker's sister, was on the same flight, recklessly cutting classes in her final year at Bryn Mawr. Charlotte's eighteen-year-old daughter Alaine d'Alivère cabled sympathy to the family from which she had been estranged for a lifetime, but regretted that the production schedule of her first motion-picture made it impossible for her to attend. Paris was still a long way from Hong Kong—much further, it appeared, than London or Philadelphia, though not as far as Peking.

From Taipei, his capital-in-exile on the island of Taiwan, Generalissimo Chiang Kai-shek sent his personal sympathy and his official representative, a deputy chairman of the Kuomintang who landed at Kaitak with Thomas. Morris Abraham Cohen, the Two-Gun General, emerged from the past on the same C-46. As overwhelming as he had been in his first appearance at The Castle in 1911, he gallantly kissed Mary's hand and volubly mourned "the thrice-tragic passing of the most excellent Sir Jonathan." Both William Shakespeare and Alexander Pope lent their words to his florid expressions of grief.

By the morning of the funeral the black-leather volumes on the rosewood table in the circular entrance hall that recorded the signatures of the men and women calling at The Castle had been replaced twice. Among the earliest callers was Sir Alexander Grantham, the Governor of Hong Kong, bearing a message from King George VI. A subdued Iain Wheatley displayed no perceptible satisfaction at "the old bastard's" death. Judah Haleevie had preceded Sir Jonathan, but Sarah's seven brothers turned out in a phalanx. The dozens of Seks who also appeared astonished the family by the multiplicity of their presumed kindred. Rothschilds, Barings, Rockefellers, and Warburgs sent telegrams by their representatives in the Colony. From Singapore, Bangkok, Saigon, Manila, Tokyo, and Jakarta, hundreds of overseas Chinese telegraphed profuse expressions of sorrow. From Europe, Australia, and America, governments offered sympathy.

All Hong Kong mourned its own special loss. Flags drooped at half-mast, and incense burned before Buddhist shrines as well as Catholic altars. The Anglican Bishop presided over a memorial service at St. John's Cathedral, and the Abbot of the Taoist Monastery on Lantao joined his monks in seventy-two hours of continuous prayer. The Crown Colony tendered its supreme gesture of respect when the Jockey Club canceled the Saturday afternoon races at Happy Valley "to demonstrate sorrow and avoid interfering with the cortege." The Commissioner of Police sighed, canceled all leaves, and ordered all his auxiliaries mobilized to control the throngs.

The family was numb with exhaustion when the cortege finally wound circuitously down The Peak by way of Stubbs Road and through Wanchai to the Roman Catholic Cathedral above Victoria. Five open cars heaped with flowers preceded the great white hearse, and eighty-six limousines followed the massively rounded sandalwood coffin visible through the hearse's plate-glass windows. Saffron-robed Buddhist priests chanted among the black-clad throngs on the pavements, and thirty-two white-uniformed bands played the rousing tunes the Chinese had adopted to demonstrate that joy at the departed spirit's reunion with his ancestors in Heaven leavened the selfish grief of the deprived survivors. "Marching Through Georgia," "The British Grenadier," and "Dixie" resounded through the narrow streets of Wanchai.

Street bonfires were surrounded by scarlet altars heaped with roast pigs, baked ducks, and pale chickens; weeping professional mourners dressed in the white robes of sorrow consigned their offerings to the flames. Transmuted into smoke, there ascended to Heaven miniature paper replicas of the earthly necessities—ranging from rickshaws and chamberpots to piglets and servants—the deceased would require on his journey. That gesture affirmed the unbreakable continuity of the eternal generations of the Chinese race. Before the Chin Dynasty substituted life-sized clay statues in the third century B.C., cooking implements, chariots, bullocks, pigs, and living retainers had been buried with great noblemen. The Tang Dynasty had in the seventh century A.D. brought to aesthetic perfection the statuettes of horses, warriors, servants, friends, and pets interred with high-born corpses. Though the modern age was less profligate, the paper-and-wood necessities provided for Sir Jonathan Sekloong's voyage to the other world included facsimile banknotes for HK$20 billion, a thousand motorcars, three hundred mansions, and ten million gold *taels*. His entourage numbered two hundred fifty servants, a hundred bodyguards, and fifty-six concubines.

After those street spectacles, the service was no more than a fragrant blur to Mary and, at the Catholic Cemetery in Happy Valley, she feared she might faint. A pale, expressionless Charles drew her close, and she leaned gratefully on his arm. In the Rolls returning to The Castle, they held hands and did not speak.

Late that evening in the white fastness of the Hong Kong Club, the Old China Hands drank brandy-and-sodas and reminisced about the Old Gentleman. Their scurrilous tales paid left-handed tribute to both Sir Jonathan's sexual prowess and his commercial shrewdness. Iain Wheatley, the seventy-five-year-old *taipan* of the

Universally Virtuous *hong*, sat silent amid the men who were almost his peers.

"Well, Iain, old boy, John Chinaman really put on a show today," the Managing-Director of the Gazetted Bank of Asia and Australia laughed. "I thought the old bastard would never die."

Iain Wheatley rose and pronounced the impromptu epitaph that shocked the British Establishment into silent near-sobriety: "Jonathan Sekloong was a bigger, better bastard than any of you bastards will ever be!"

Five days after the funeral, Opal brought Charles and Mary the blue-leather-bound volume that had lain on Sir Jonathan's knees when he died.

"This must come to you," she said. "The Old One wrote it, he told me, for you."

> Two streams [Mary read aloud] have constantly intermingled, my own career and historical events. My own endeavors, I believe, altered those events, if but minutely. A man of business, a Chinese patriot, was surprised to find that he was also a British patriot.
>
> I shall first recall events from the end of the Second Great War to this date, July 3, 1950. After that War began in 1941, Hong Kong could no longer live in secure isolation from the outside world or the turbulence of China. My family has been caught up by those political maelstroms.
>
> Late last year, the white-sun flag of the Republic of China fluttered down for the last time, replaced by the five golden stars of the so-called People's Republic of China. The change may ultimately benefit the Chinese people, but I am far too old to alter my allegiance. A new dawn is also rising for Hong Kong, kindled by the energy, the talents, and the capital of hundreds of thousands of refugees, the greatest influx in our history.

"It's the recollections I hoped he'd write," Charles exclaimed. "Perhaps we could publish it—if it's not too personal. How far did he get?"

Mary flicked to the final words Sir Jonathan had written minutes before his death.

There can no longer be any question. [She read aloud again.] The Communists have entered Korea in force. China is, once again, at war with the Western world, just as she fought that world in the nineteenth century almost without a break from the First Opium War in 1839 until the Boxers' siege of the Legation Quarter in Peking in 1900. China lost all those wars.

Today, China appears united against the Westerners for the first time. Perhaps the Korean conflict will make men again proud to be Chinese. My "infallible" soothsayer, Silver Seventh Brother, cannot predict the outcome, since he set off eighteen years ago to explore the occult realms in his own person. But this time the outcome *must* be quite different.

"He didn't get very far." Charles was disappointed. "I want to know about the early days. You're the literary one. You read it. I'm off to the club."

Mary raised an interrogative eyebrow.

"Yes, the Hong Kong Club," her husband laughed. "It seems *Sir* Charles and *Lady* Sekloong aren't wogs, but, perhaps, worthy of membership. I don't know whether to accept. But it won't hurt to drop in and toast the Old Gentleman. Want to come along?"

"Certainly not," Mary replied acerbically. "I have no wish to spend my declining years with those drunkards."

Charles chuckled and closed the door. Mary again took up the blue-leather book to read her father-in-law's final judgments on the past half-decade.

Victory in August 1945 was indelibly marred for me by two events.

The impatient Americans dropped two atomic bombs on Japan and revived my fear of a war of extermination between Caucasians and Orientals. I had thought that danger quashed when Asiatics and Westerners took up arms together against Japan's ambitions. But the wanton use of the fearful new weapon when the Japanese were already on their knees may have begun the Great Racial War. The fighting that began a week ago in Korea could be the first engagement of an all-eclipsing war that lasts a generation.

The second event still fills me with vast, inconsolable sorrow. Jonathan Sekloong, my namesake and heir, died in the crash of a transport aircraft. I sometimes think he was the best of the Sekloongs, neither as ruthless as I was compelled to be nor obstructively resentful as were Charles and Harry in their youth. Jonnie could have carried on my work far better than . . . others. . . .

Unshed tears pricked Mary's eyelids. She turned the page, unable to read Sir Jonathan's lament for her eldest son, and she resolved that Charles must not see those words. Already battered by his father's death, his self-confidence could not withstand his father's slighting assessment.

They made me a baronet in June 1946 [she read], the first—probably the last—Chinese baronet, though the Sassoons got the hereditary title decades ago. I'm too old for such tushery, but it should please Charles. He will be Sir Charles when I die, and Mary will be Lady Sekloong. Perhaps now she'll declare a truce in her war against the British Establishment, but I doubt it. Mary can no more stop fighting than I can.

Mary smiled at Sir Jonathan's back-handed praise. No, she reaffirmed her resolve, Charles must not read his father's book.

I told the Governor I couldn't accept the baronetcy unless Mosing Way got a knighthood. "A collaborator?" the Governor objected. "No more a collaborator than I," was my reply. "Mosing saved thousands by pretending to collaborate. To heal the breach between British and Chinese you must get him his knighthood." The Governor finally said: "If you insist, I'll get it through London somehow. I heard you drove a hard bargain." Then we could get on with putting the pieces of Hong Kong together.

I didn't tell the Governor I knew he'd already asked

Whitehall about Mosing's knighthood—and been put off. No point in showing all my cards. Thomas got me that information.

Poor Thomas was stricken when the Generalissimo made him Ambassador to the Court of St. James's. One day he was a lieutenant general and Chiang Kai-shek's chief military secretary. The next, he was a full general and bundled off to London. After twenty years, the brilliant Generalissimo woke one morning to realize that his trusted aide's brother was a Communist. The great man thereupon sent Thomas abroad to "avoid embarrassment."

Thomas was well out of it. He did not see the final stages of the Nationalists' blundering, stupidity, avarice, and malice that destroyed their regime. Ironically, James was moved from Communist headquarters about the same time. Mao Tse-tung, Liu Shao-chi, and Chou En-lai feared another explosion of temper like James's shouting match with Thomas in Chungking in late 1944. They sent him to serve under his former battalion commander Lin Piao in building up the "Manchurian People's Revolutionary Armies." That force was, in the end, to determine the fate of the country.

Lady Sekloong stared into the blackness of the garden. She had not known that James was among the first Communist generals to enter the vital northeastern provinces called Manchuria, which had been heavily industrialized by the Japanese during their fourteen-year-long occupation. Sir Jonathan had not shown all his cards even to his family. How, she wondered, had her impulsive third son felt when his Russian allies turned over Japanese arms to the Chinese Communists, but simultaneously looted Manchuria of industrial equipment worth two billion dollars?

She lit a cigarette and drew the smoke into her lungs with conscious pleasure. Hesitant for years after it had become not merely respectable but normal for ladies to smoke, Mary had finally acquired the habit from the Americans in Chungking. But she felt daring each time she lit one of the six cigarettes she allowed herself each day. She was, after all, a Victorian, and she had never wholly cast off the attitudes of that era. She had grown up during the reign of the great Queen, who epitomized a complacent age that believed mankind had solved all its fundamental problems, that further great change was unlikely, and that whatever change did occur must be beneficial.

Who, she wondered, was more foolish? Was it her own contemporaries, who had believed the future of mankind was fixed by divine providence and that its course lay ever forward? Was it moderns like her son James, who believed assuredly that force could impel mankind onto a new course decreed by "historical necessity" as revealed by "scientific Marxism-Leninism"? Those moderns, too, were totally dedicated to the illusion of progress.

The obvious fact that the Communists and the Nationalists could never be reconciled escaped the well-meaning Americans. [She read Sir Jonathan's precise calligraphy.] American military and economic intervention, exacerbated by naive American diplomacy, prolonged China's agony. The Americans transported half a million Nationalist soldiers to Manchuria, where they were promptly encircled by Lin Piao's Revolutionary Armies. Forty thousand American troops landed in North China to hold cities and railroads for the Nationalists. Hundreds of millions of American dollars were wasted to prop the Nationalists' worthless currency and for aid projects that singularly failed to improve the people's welfare.

The American special envoy, General George Marshall, perhaps a great soldier, was a mediocre statesman who never understood China. With one hand he supported the Nationalists; with the other he undermined the Nationalists by forcing them to talk peace with the Communists.

The Americans did enrich thousands of corrupt officials and provide employment for tens of thousands of drivers, cooks, houseboys, merchants, pimps, bartenders, gangsters, and prostitutes. They also maintained in sumptuous state a multitude of otherwise unemployable American officers and civilians. The dour people of Peking called Marshall's Truce Headquarters the Temple of the Thousand Sleeping Colonels. Bumbling American intervention in China from 1945 to 1948 virtually assured that the United States would come into conflict with the Korean Communists in 1950—and probably fight the Chinese Communists as well.

Mary marveled at the Old Gentleman's prescience. Writing in July 1950, he had foreseen the entry of the "Chinese People's Volunteers" into the Korean War in November of the year. She flipped through his recounting of the complex alteration of battles and negotiations that had been the Second Chinese Civil War of 1946 to 1949. Only a year later, the innumerable conferences, the million-strong armies' maneuvers, the noble sentiments, and the tawdry realities—all seemed as mustily remote as Waterloo.

All that really mattered was the Nationalists' final retreat, which recapitulated in greatly accelerated tempo their withdrawal before the Japanese, who had also marched out of Manchuria. The Communists completed in four years the conquest of all China that had evaded the Japanese from 1931 to 1945. The Communist high-tide swept across the vast land hailed by a war-weary people to whom Mao Tse-tung promised not Communism, but New Democracy under a "coalition" government. The Nationalists had already withdrawn into permanent exile on the island of Taiwan on October 1, 1949, when Mao stood on the red-brick Gate of Heavenly Peace facing south like the Emperors to proclaim the People's Republic of China.

"Today," he had declaimed, "the Chinese people stand erect!"

The future was murky, though the ostensibly coalition government could obviously not endure long. Could, Mary wondered, the cool realism of her old acquaintance Chou En-lai, Premier and Foreign Minister of the Central People's Government, restrain the visionary zealot she had met just once, Chairman Mao Tse-tung of the People's Republic of China?

Even the Chairman's abounding vitality appeared temporarily depleted by more than two decades of struggle since the split between Nationalists and Communists at Shanghai in April 1927. The first measure of the new government bore Chou En-lai's stamp; they had been conciliatory, almost mild. But a second wave of pitiful refugees was telling of the brutal "land reform" that was exterminating the rural bourgeoisie. The Chinese Communists were, moreover, plunging into the Korean conflict, effectively mortgaging their future to the Russians and fixing Sino-American enmity by that intervention. The United Nations' Armies under General Douglas MacArthur were streaming up the Korean Peninsula to threaten Manchuria, China's industrial heartland. Committing the "Chinese People's Volunteers" to the forward defense of Manchuria by engaging MacArthur in Korea was, therefore, strategically sound and perhaps unavoidable. Committing major Chinese forces to Korea was probably necessary, but, she wondered, was it wise?

Lady Mary sighed and lit another cigarette. Drawn to a passage that expressed Sir Jonathan's concern for the family, she was surprised by his candor and amused by his male vanity.

It is good, as Confucius observed, to contemplate the thickets of one's descendants. I sired a large and diverse progeny, nineteen children of my own loins. In turn, Lillian's two sons, Gregory and Sydney, who call themselves Sek, begot a considerable progeny. But my greatest love was given to Lucinda's children: Matilda, Charles, and Harry.

Matilda, who was cowed by the exuberant masculinity of her brothers and her father, gave me only one grandchild after marrying the German pianist called Hans Biederstein in 1923. All my inquiries could only establish that she had "disappeared" during the War, presumably to a concentration camp. Her son Johann is the *guru* (Strange term!) of the Munich "oceanic impressionists" who smear their naked bodies with pigment and roll upon vast canvases.

Harry's line ended with his only son's execution just before he himself was assassinated. I was appalled by Harry's desertion to the Japanese, but I cannot forgive his murderers. They were, I suspect, the Communists.

And Charles—Charles and Mary? Charles has, during the past two decades, almost become the man I always hoped he would be. His maturing was retarded by his wife's strong will—perhaps, too, by myself. But today, their children and grandchildren are the chief line of the House of Sekloong. They might have been more amenable, more biddable and malleable if they had had another mother. But they would certainly have been far less spirited.

Mary smiled and read on.

However, I was counting my children. The Jade Concubine gave me two sons and one daughter; the Ruby Concubine three sons and one daughter. I promised the Pearl Concubine I would not interfere in the lives of her three lovely daughters after I gave them lavish marriage-portions.

For the rest: To my *certain* knowledge five children by good and generous ladies. They are not of the mainstream of the continuing life of the House of Sekloong.

The mainstream is the descendants of Charles and Mary. My view expanding with my resources, I envisioned the House of Sekloong spanning two antipathetic worlds, Asia and the West. Born of both worlds and rooted firmly in both, those descendants would, I believed, heal antagonisms and engender cooperation between those worlds.

Perhaps I erred. Instead of feeling themselves completely at home in either world, may they not feel alienated from both? Have I been too generous with my grandchildren, as I was not with my own children? Mary hinted incessantly that the stern Chinese patriarch was outmoded. Perhaps I yielded too readily. Instead of uniting the two worlds may not my descendants, corrupted by adulation and notoriety, become decadent, Western-oriented cosmopolitans lacking roots in either world? The riches I labored to amass now, in the final twilight of my life, appear to menace the descendants for whom I built my House.

She smiled at the self-willed autocrat's illusion of his own amenability. But her smile faded, and her own eyes looked inward. Charles and she often discussed her own forebodings. He assured her that the stock was sound, and he cautioned against dominating their children as his father had dominated himself.

Wearying of self-revelation, Sir Jonathan had abruptly returned to his second theme. She read again the final paragraph, which expressed his fears for a China once more at war with a united West and ended: *My "infallible" soothsayer, Silver Seventh Brother, cannot predict the outcome, since he set off eighteen years ago to explore the occult realms in his own person. But this time the outcome must be quite different.*

Mary's immediate concern was more personal, the well-being of her own descendants. But the future of China and the fate of the family were inseparably intertwined, as the Old Gentleman had observed. She would herself state the broader issue differently: "The Chinese are self-isolated, and their inherent pride transcends arrogance. Can they ever exist in harmony— much less cooperate—with the Westerners who have repeatedly intruded upon them and humiliated them? Can they possibly live in peace with the outside world?"

The clash of the new political forces that had risen during the past three decades made those questions urgent. Her grandson George Parker might at that moment be meeting her son James and his son Cheng-wu in Korea in battle, just as James had confronted his brother Thomas in China itself. The family's survival was interlocked with the great issues.

Inspired by Sir Jonathan's self-revelation, Mary explored the circumstances that had shaped her own existence. She was ruthlessly candid, since it would be unpardonably foolish to delude herself. Her thoughts were couched in the third person, as if she were objectively reviewing the life of another woman.

Mary Osgood Sekloong felt herself an exile for much of her life. She regarded the Chinese race almost as disdainfully as did other Britons when she was young a half-century ago. Her conviction of superiority, reinforced by proximity, nurtured condescending distaste. She yearned for England and instilled the same yearning in her sons and daughters. China and the Chinese were the backdrop to her riches and privileges; they were not the matrix of her life.

Mary was but half-aware of those feelings until her daughter Charlotte married a Chinese, Manfei Way, in 1924. Before that time, she told herself she was only being mischievous when she encouraged her daughters to nag their father: "Daddy, why can't we go and live in England?" But she fought Charlotte's marriage, and she did not mourn when Manfei was murdered. Only later did she reproach herself that her own irresponsibility had led to Charlotte's becoming a gilded *demi-mondaine* in Paris.

Distressing experiences nurtured Mary Sekloong's fear of the Chinese. Held to ransom in the North and surviving the carnage of the Canton Commune in the South, she learned to despise the Chinese for their cruelty toward each other and for their inability to live together in peace. The corruption, squalor, and misery of Chungking during World War II reinforced her prejudices. Returning to Hong Kong after the war, she learned that many Cantonese had behaved almost as badly as had the brutal Japanese. Her contempt crystallized diamond-hard during the Civil War. She concluded that the Chinese could neither halt their fratricidal warfare nor subordinate their insane pride to the reality of many nation-states. They still believed that China was *Tien-hsia,* "all that lies under Heaven." They remained immutably convinced that the ancient Chinese civilization was infinitely superior to all other civilizations.

Again the capital of an assertive China after the

Communist victory, imperial Peking had reiterated that conviction of unique Chinese superiority. The Communists had adopted the European ideology called Marxism-Leninism—and immediately begun adapting its doctrines to the eternal *Chinese* pattern, just as Confucianism had transformed and ingested Buddhism. No more than the Confucian Mandarins could acknowledge equals among the "outside barbarians" could the Communist Mandarins acknowledge equals among either "foreign friends" or "imperialist enemies."

Believing the Chinese incapable of altering their perception of non-Chinese, Mary was almost as rigidly fixed in her own view of the Chinese. She acknowledged that reality and stubbed out her third cigarette. She had always resisted identification with the Chinese through the family. But she was too old to change. Another visit to Europe or the United States was long overdue. If it were not for Charles's unbreakable attachment to the Colony, she would insist that they quit Hong Kong permanently. Though she could leave neither Charles nor Hong Kong, she knew she wanted to go home. At seventy, the prospect of death was no longer a remote abstraction. She had lived fifty years in China, but she wanted to die in England.

Sir Jonathan had disposed of his property meticulously. Trust funds insured that Sarah and Opal would never want, while Thomas, Charlotte, and James were given 5 percent nonvoting interests in J. Sekloong and Sons. Smaller trusts provided "reasonable competences" for the Old Gentleman's great-grandchildren—"Not so large that they will be tempted to spend their days in idleness!" After bequests to servants and other dependents, all remaining property went to Charles and Mary as joint-legatees controlling J. Sekloong and Sons.

That disposition shocked Hong Kong and distressed Charles, although the stereotypical Chinese woman, the submissive wife whom the traditional idiom described as "the person within the house," had never existed in fact; for centuries Chinese women had controlled large and small business enterprises, either directly or through their husbands and sons. But Sir Jonathan's action was unprecedented. Formally investing a husband *and* wife as co-managing directors of a major *hong,* a worldwide commercial empire, was something new under the bright Hong Kong sun. Charles felt that he had been publicly humiliated and he stormed at the secret codicil to his father's will: *I depend upon my son Charles's prudence and solid direction to insure that his wife Mary's daring is kept within proper limits. I depend upon Mary's acumen and courage to animate Charles's caution.*

Mary knew that she was still impulsive, and she valued Charles's restraining counsel. But she wished Sir Jonathan had refrained from striking that posthumous blow to his son's ego. Though their daily routine of the past five years remained unchanged by their possession of formal as well as actual power, they could no longer appeal to Sir Jonathan's final adjudication. Mary suspected that Charles complained about their joint-stewardship primarily because he felt compelled to play the role of the dominant Chinese male. He was actually, she consoled herself, little more distressed by his father's last instructions than by the Hong Kong Club's ultimate failure to offer him membership.

The Seks' loud dissatisfaction was, however, unfeigned. Harold and William were the twin sons of the opportunistic Sir Francis. As grandsons of Sydney, Sir Jonathan's eldest legitimate son, they considered themselves the senior branch of the family. The Seks were, therefore, enraged at "being fobbed off" with bequests of one million dollars each and further infuriated, rather than placated, by the inviolable trust funds totaling two million dollars created for their seven children. Avarice and envy impelled the brothers, who were only moderately well-to-do by Sekloong standards, to assert their primacy by enlarging their fortunes manyfold.

Their scheme was appealingly simple, for, as William said, "It would be mad not to take advantage of the market." As a dependency of Britain, which had sent troops to Korea, Hong Kong honored the American embargo on providing China with war matériel and banned exports of goods ranging from munitions to shoes. Fighting its first full-scale war against a foreign foe, the People's Republic was eager to buy all the varied items that are the essentials of modern warfare. Peking, as Harold noted gleefully, could not afford to be too particular about either price or quality.

Moving the contraband to China was almost as easy as first importing into Hong Kong goods "for transshipment" to innocuous, if unlikely, destinations such as Djibouti and Santiago. Appropriate bribes to the appropriate British officials through their Chinese subordinates insured that neither customs nor police patrol-boats examined too closely junks and coasters bound for mainland ports. The Sek brothers concentrated upon those commodities that brought the highest returns: truck tires, gasoline, antibiotics, and insulated rubber boots. Their goods shared another trait: they were all flawed. The tires were third-rate retreads; the gasoline was liberally watered; the antibiotics were heavily adulterated; and the rubber boots leaked.

"After all," Harold defended his flaunting the embargo, "it's a blow for free trade, the reason for Hong Kong's being."

"Caveat emptor!" William aired his single Latin tag, graciously translating for the less erudite: "Let the buyer beware!"

The Seks had already increased five-fold their original investments of one million dollars each, and it was necessary to display their new wealth. Harold built a compound overlooking Castle Peak in the New Territories, a complex of mansions, summer houses, and courtyards under sweeping green-tiled roofs; William built a similar demi-palace on The Peak crowned with Ming-yellow tiles. Though justifiably gratified by their astuteness, the Seks were not quite complacent. Since the war presumably had to end some day, they explored new enterprises: gold-smuggling, arms running and the drug traffic. Commercial acuity and political impartiality dictated three fundamental decisions: They would import opium in fishing junks and small coasters, buying immunity from confiscation for the bulky black gum. They would smuggle the compact heroin refined from that opium by scheduled air and sea carriers. Their opium would come from areas in Burma, Thailand, and Laos controlled by remnants of the defeated Nationalists' armies.

"We do not dabble in politics," Harold declared righteously. "We will sell to whoever has the money, and we buy from whoever has the goods."

Mary and Charles laughed contemptuously at that self-justification. The House of Sekloong had forty years earlier withdrawn from the drug traffic—legal or illegal—because Sir Jonathan judged the opium trade immoral and, ultimately, unprofitable. United in antipathy toward the Communists, husband and wife nevertheless agreed that they would trade with the People's Republic—openly and legally. But they would neither supply Peking with contraband nor cheat Peking on quality.

"It's bad politics and bad business," Charles said. "The Communists will be in power for a long time, and we must trade with China."

Mary concurred that Charles's dictum made sound commercial sense. Besides, she no longer cared who tried to rule China, since she believed no one could rule China effectively.

She was, however, deeply concerned with the plight of nearly a million refugees from the Draconian reforms of the Communist regime. Hong Kong had always admitted Chinese freely, and Hong Kong continued to do so—at its own peril. Though formally excluded, "illegal immigrants" were turned back only if apprehended while crossing the border. If the police did not catch a refugee dripping wet after he waded the Shumchon River or swam Deep Bay supported by inflated pigs' bladders, the Colony's Registration of Persons Offices would issue a Hong Kong Identity Card

691

that transformed him into a legal resident. The influx was therefore overloading all the Colony's essential services: housing, schools, hospitals, transport, and employment. Even food supplies and sewage disposal were inadequate. Both the refugees and the authorities desperately needed private assistance.

Mary's contempt for the Chinese nation had never included individuals, and certainly not the victims of that nation's brutal political struggles. But she was determined to see for herself that her contributions actually provided clothing, food, medicines, and schoolbooks, rather than enriching the sleek police officers, plausible bureaucrats, and Secret Society toughs who preyed on the wretched exiles. Speaking the Shanghai dialect, Sarah Haleevie Sekloong was an invaluable companion on Mary's tours of inspection of the facilities provided for the refugees from the metropolis.

The two were returning from Diamond Hill in Kowloon on a late February afternoon in 1951. Their Austin A-40 labored through narrow, dirt lanes palisaded by jerry-built huts flying miniature Nationalist flags. The compact Austin was handier than the great Rolls and, Mary felt, less offensive to the recipients of her alms. The old chauffeur swore at the car, the dank cold, and the pedestrians' stupidity as he turned and backed the Austin to descend the twisting hill lanes. But the ladies were inured to his monologues against the *pak-yee*, the "northern barbarians" who had invaded his home.

The huts built by earlier arrivals who had found casual employment stood on concrete slabs, and their roofs were corrugated-metal sheets. The newer hovels were tragic fantasies of worm-eaten timbers, splintered packing-crates, and rusty iron-sheets. Fifteen or twenty men, women, and children slept in four-tiered bunks in each minuscule hut. Electric cables snaked menacingly through the muddy lanes, ingeniously poaching on the preserves of the China Light and Power Company.

A one-legged former corporal hobbled on a homemade crutch, while his former colonel, still displaying the badges of his rank on his filthy uniform, trudged

692

under a load of twigs for his cooking-fire. Women in garments donated by foreign charities gathered around the communal pumps, their buckets slopping into the muddy lane. The children at their heels looked like manic dwarves: a three-year-old girl wore a torn Mickey Mouse sweatshirt over a ballet skirt, while a six-year-old boy swaggered in a tattered pony-skin jacket that had once been the pride of a young Scarsdale matron.

A scrofulous sow dragged her pregnant belly across the quagmire. Lean dogs blotched with mange yapped at the long, scabrous-yellow legs of scrawny chickens. The stench of unwashed humanity, moldy bedding, rotting rice, and feces fouled the bleak winter day, and the Hong Kong sky was leaden.

Lady Mary huddled inside her seal coat, a luxury she felt by her age excused, though she had intentionally left her mink at home. The lean brown faces regarding the two foreign women displayed neither rancor nor gratitude. They were the incurious faces of battered survivors who were intent only upon enduring longer. Great chunks of North China's ancient squalor, Mary reflected resentfully, had been transported entire to Hong Kong.

She nonetheless marveled at the refugees' tenacity. In order to provide the next generation with the tools of survival and self-improvement, numerous professional men—lawyers, doctors, and engineers—taught in improvised schools. She and Sarah had just visited a middle school supported by Sekloong funds. The ramshackle former distillery also housed the Alliance Research Institute, which was financed largely by the American Central Intelligence Agency. Its staff of university graduates in their twenties maintained a documentary record of the Communist regime and strove to preserve the traditional culture the Communists were destroying to make way for their own modern culture. Those young survivors were determined that their ancient civilization, too, would survive.

The Austin left the squatter camp for the crammed
693

streets of Kowloon, and Lady Mary eagerly pictured the scented, steaming marble bath in the rococo bathroom she had moved to The Castle. Across the broad thoroughfare of Nathan Road, its neon signs just flickering into a cacophony of light, lay the pier of the Jordan Road Ferry that would carry them back to Hong Kong Island. Having done what she had to do, having required herself to look upon the refugees' misery so that she might better alleviate that misery, she felt herself entitled to relax.

Distant thunder rumbled beneath the constant rattle of handcarts, the honking of horns, the clatter of wooden clogs, the loud voices, and the blaring radios.

"What can that sound be?" Sarah asked. "I've never heard anything quite like it."

"Probably nothing," Mary answered wearily. "Just the soft-voiced, velvet-footed Cantonese going about their normal business."

"No, this is different. Like a waterfall. I wonder what it is."

"Well, my dear, we'll soon find out."

The flow of traffic slowed like a stream trapped behind a dam. Their chauffeur swore at the driver of the green Chevrolet in front and inched between two slat-sided trucks, one laden with flayed hog carcasses, the other carrying indignant ducks crammed into globular rattan baskets. The intermittent rumbling became a constant roar. Police whistles shrilled, and sirens screamed.

"Quickly," Sarah directed, "turn around."

"*Mng-dak, Tai-tai,*" the old chauffeur shrugged. "Impossible, Madam."

All traffic had halted just short of Nathan Road, and the Austin was trapped between the trucks. Greasy black smoke billowed through the side street, and gasoline fumes permeated the Austin. The orange glow of flames flared on Nathan Road, illuminating swirling Nationalist and Communist flags.

Knots of struggling men poured down the narrow side street, engulfing the green Chevrolet. Shouting rhythmically, the rioters rocked the Chevrolet back and forth. A gout of flame sprang from the gasoline tank as the car toppled onto its side. His topcoat ablaze, a gray-haired European scrambled awkwardly from the vehicle. The crowd bore him down, and he vanished beneath its feet. His high shrieking was abruptly choked off.

"My God, what have I brought you into?" Mary cried.

"We were warned, but I never thought . . ." Sarah's voice quavered.

"Ai-yah! Ai-yah! Kwok-min-dong . . . Goong-chan-dong . . ." the driver shouted. "Nationalists and Communists . . . fighting."

"I'm so sorry, Sarah," Mary exclaimed. "So sorry I brought you here."

"God will look after us," Sarah assured her.

"Well," Mary said tartly, "He'd better look sharp."

The tide of rioters flowing toward them bore pork and ducks snatched from the trucks. Faces peered through the Austin's closed windows, the same lean brown faces they had seen in the refugee camp now distorted by mad rage. The small car rocked under the blows of hard brown hands, and the rear window shattered into crazed opacity. A burly Nationalist veteran wearing a service cap with the white sunburst on its peak pried at the chauffeur's door with a crowbar.

"Mng hai sai-yen! Mng hai sai-yen! Sekloong gyah. Tai-tai hai Ma-li Foo-yen . . . Sekloong Ma-li Foo-yen." The white-haired chauffeur shouted desperately. "Not Westerners! Not Westerners! The House of Sekloong. The lady is Lady Mary. Lady Mary Sekloong!"

Mary closed her eyes and began reciting the Lord's Prayer. She heard Sarah murmur: *"Shma Yisroel, Adonai eloheinu . . .* Hear, Oh Israel, the Lord is one. . . ."

Each praying in her own way, they awaited the cruel, dark hands. But there was only sudden silence. Mary opened her eyes in astonishment. The soldier was bowing deep and waving the mob away.

"Ching yüan-liang wo-men, Ma-li Fu-jen, Pao-chien! Pao-chien!" He spoke clear Mandarin. "Please forgive us, Lady Mary. Deepest apologies! Profound apologies! We did not know you. We thought you were foreigners."

"The ladies are of the House of Sekloong," he shouted to the crowd. "One is Lady Mary herself. They are not foreigners. They are Sekloongs. They are *our* people. *Our* people."

Mary and Sarah sat in a copse of silence. The crowd parted to let them through.

On the frozen Korean Peninsula, 1,500 miles to the northeast, men were dying under shells and bombs in the same conflict between the Communists and their foes that had imperiled the Sekloong ladies and enriched the Sek brothers. The North Korean invasion of South Korea in late June 1950 had been countered by American troops, fighting under the banner of the United Nations Organization. Driven into the Pusan Perimeter around the South's largest port by August 1950, the U.N. Command had riposted with an audacious landing at Inchon on the peninsula's western coast in mid-September. When the North Koreans crumbled, the U.N. Forces streamed toward the Yalu River, the border between Manchuria and Korea. To counter the apparent threat to Manchuria, the "Chinese People's Volunteers" had entered the war in force in November 1950, and the overwhelmed United Nations' armies fell back.

Neither gallantry nor superior arms could immediately stem the Communist tide. Seoul, the capital of the Republic of Korea, changed hands for the third time in six months when it fell again to the Communists on January 4, 1951. But the multinational United Nations Forces rallied, and troops contributed by twenty-five nations halted the offensive of the numerically superior Chinese and North Koreans. On January 25, 1951, those forces broke out of their defensive positions in the last major offensive mounted by allied Western and

Asian armies against Chinese armies. Much more effective against much stronger opposition than the Boxer Relief Expedition had been in 1900, the allies retook Seoul on March 5, 1951. The Chinese People's Volunteers and the North Koreans abandoned their desperate counteroffensive on May 22. The Communists were back at the Thirty-eighth Parallel, the original boundary between North Korea and South Korea.

The war became a stalemate because the United States declined to commit the additional divisions necessary to clear the Communists from North Korea. Nonetheless, China's defensive intervention created protracted enmity between the new People's Republic of China and the United States of America. Washington canceled its plans to break with Taiwan and offer formal diplomatic recognition to Peking. The U.S. Seventh Fleet patroled the Straits of Taiwan to forestall a Communist attack against the Nationalist-held island. Peking and Washington had become embittered foes.

The United Nations' Forces were, however, still pushing slowly northward, and the Communists were reeling. But the Chinese veterans did not break as had the North Koreans. The XXXIX Army Corps, commanded by Lieutenant General Shih Ai-kuo of the Chinese People's Liberation Army, doggedly contested each pass and village as it retreated over sharp-ridged mountains still sparkling treacherously with snow and ice. The three divisions of Chinese People's Volunteers were James Sekloong's own troops, the units he had commanded from Manchuria to final victory over the Nationalists in South China. He pitched his command post in a hamlet twelve miles north of Chorwon on the central front in mid-June and dispatched his orders to his battered units by radio, telephone, and runners. The XXXIX Army Corps would retreat no further from its strong defensive position in the rock-ribbed mountains.

James Sekloong's exhausted infantrymen awaited the next assault in deep-dug bunkers and great natural caves that protected them from American artillery, American tanks, and American fighter-bombers, which were immune to air attack. The MIG-15s of the Communist Air Forces had already been beaten into submission by American F-86 Sabrejets.

One of the junior political commissars who exhorted the infantrymen of the 382nd Division was Shih Cheng-wu, the nineteen-year-old son of the Army Corps Commander. The Americans, he told his men, lacked the iron will necessary to attack their natural fortifications since they were accustomed to artillery, tanks, and bombers clearing the way for them. Neither shells nor bombs could penetrate the two-hundred-foot-thick rock-and-earth roofs of the caves in which the Division had taken its stand. Neither shells nor bombs could find the narrow, camouflaged entrances. Cheng-wu contemptuously dismissed the nine silver F-84 Thunderjets circling among the sun-lanced clouds.

"The planes are pretty," he said, "but no threat to us."

He paused for effect before asking rhetorically: "How can the soft-living Americans possibly face the hardships we endure? Could they live on cold rice and dried vegetables, haggard for lack of sleep, lousy, and unbathed? Our proletarian resolution *must* prevail."

While Cheng-wu spoke, the commanding officer of the Twenty-eighth Fighter-Bomber Squadron shifted his big body in the cramped cockpit of the Thunderjet emblazoned: *Painless Parker*. Major George Chapman Parker, Jr., half-regretted the macabre play on the misleading slogan of the California dental firm. Nor was he enthusiastic at attacking ground troops defended only by small cannon and machine guns. But his request for transfer to Sabrejet interceptors had been rejected because the battle required seasoned ground-support pilots. Still, on completing his hundredth mission in two weeks' time, he would be posted to Arizona for retraining on Sabres. Meanwhile, his squadron could orbit waiting for a target only another fifteen minutes before depleted fuel tanks forced it to return to the comforts of the airfield designated K-14, its base where American Red Cross girls waited with hot coffee and donuts.

Beneath his wings, no more than one thousand feet from the ground, the propeller-driven spotter plane dodged ground fire. That job he wouldn't have for a spot promotion to full colonel. The risks were enormous, and the spotter couldn't shoot back. George Parker's earphones echoed the chatter between the spotter and the ground observers as they tried to pinpoint the target.

"Mosquito Four, this is Badger Three," the radio crackled. "Can you see the rock formation like a broken arrowhead?"

"Badger Three, this is Mosquito Four. That's a hell of a description. What color?"

"Mosquito Four from Badger Three. Slate-colored with a snow drift where the shaft of the arrow would be. Come lower. Go to five hundred feet."

"Badger Three from Mosquito Four. For Chris' sake, they're not throwing cream-puffs at me. But I'll make a pass. Keep directing me. I won't acknowledge."

"Badger Three to Mosquito Four, Roger. Come to a heading of one-niner-niner and descend. When you see the arrowhead, mark its tip. We've seen sporadic movement there all morning."

The spotter plane descended on the invisible threads of the ground observers' guidance. Concealed anti-aircraft cannon fired streams of shells that burst in dirty-gray puffs. The spotter plane trembled in the sky, but held its course.

"Mosquito Four: That's it. You're on now."

"Mosquito Four marking."

Two rockets streaked from the spotter's wings. Their explosion raised pillars of red smoke at the tip of the arrowhead.

"Top Tooth to first-echelon Molars," George Parker's throat microphone reverberated. "Go in and paste them."

Across the valley, the ground observers watched three Thunderjets swoop on the hillside. The crump of bombs shook the slopes, and snow geysered high.

"Top Tooth to second-echelon Molars. First sticks hundred yards to left. Correct and go in."

The second echelon plummeted, silver fuselages glittering in the late morning sun. The Thunderjets pulled up two hundred yards above the arrowhead, and their bombs raised snow flurries fifty yards short of the target.

Peering out of the cave's slit-entrance, Shih Cheng-wu smiled in satisfaction.

"You see," he shouted. "They can't hit us, just as I said."

George Parker dropped the nose of his Thunderjet, and his wingmen dived in concert precisely thirty-five feet from his wing-tips. The three Thunderjets hurtled toward the hillside at four hundred fifty knots. Ignoring the flak, George Parker bored much closer than his two previous echelons. When the arrowhead, bracketed by red smoke, filled his sights, he triggered the release and rocketed into the sky.

"Another miss!" his first cousin, Shih Cheng-wu, exulted. "Another miss!"

The entire hillside was engulfed by fifty-foot flames when the napalm cannisters ignited. The explosive combustion of jellied gasoline sucked air from the cave. Ten seconds later, Cheng-wu's lungs collapsed in the near vacuum. Twenty seconds later, torrents of fire rolled into the cave and cremated his body.

On June 23, 1951, Soviet Ambassador to the United Nations Jakob Malik conveyed the willingness of the Democratic People's Republic of Korea and the Chinese People's Volunteers to discuss a ceasefire. The armistice talks thus initiated were to continue for more than two years before the United Nations and the Communists signed an agreement that left the opposing forces just about where they had been when the haggling began. Tens of thousands were to die in inconclusive battles for insignificant hills during the protracted haggling in the blasted village between the front lines called Panmunjom, the "Shop with the Wooden Door."

As the first round of talks finally began in mid-July, a

letter postmarked Peking was delivered to Sir Charles Sekloong at his offices in St. George's Building. He fingered the stained envelope, irrationally fearful of its contents. The family had not heard from James in three years.

Charles centered the rice-paper envelope on Sir Jonathan's old desk, still reluctant to open it. His hand reached for the telephone. But he recalled that he could not reach Mary, who had taken Sarah to "have a look at my middle school on Diamond Hill."

He smiled fondly. Mary's attitude had changed radically since the riot. Her resentful contempt for the Chinese race was burned away, though she still derided the stupidity of politicians and bureaucrats—*all* politicians and bureaucrats, Chinese, British, or Patagonian. Struggling with the influx from China, the Hong Kong civil service dreaded the sudden descents of Lady Sekloong to battle for her refugees. The Colonial Secretariat could not ignore her peremptory demands for food, clothing, shelter, education, and medical services. Lady Sekloong spoke at least once a week with His Excellency the Governor, Sir Alexander Grantham, who, the British Establishment felt, was in any event pandering disgracefully to the Chinese populace of Hong Kong.

The entire Secretariat fervently agreed that Lady Sekloong was not merely a nuisance, but a menace. Her eccentricity was not limited to championing refugees. She harried the mutually profitable alliance of land speculators and those bureaucrats responsible for selling Crown Land; and she had the bad taste to be on excellent terms with the foreign correspondents who had congregated in the Colony after the Communists' "Liberation" of China. Fearful that the resurgent Communists' momentum might yet carry them across the indefensible border, the Secretariat dreaded any publicity that drew Peking's attention to the isolated Colony. The balance was delicate when British troops were fighting in Korea and a British administration welcomed refugees to Hong Kong. Besides, seventy-two civil airliners flown out by their Nationalist pilots stood at Kaitak Airport while the courts pondered the conflicting claims of Peking and Taiwan to their ownership. A flurry of newspaper reports on mistreatment—or, for that matter, excessively good treatment—of refugees might yet bring the People's Liberation Army over the Shumchon River. Memories of 1941 were still strong, and the guard battalions had gone north to Korea. The survivors nervously recalled the Japanese conquest and occupation, but Lady Sekloong was implacable.

Sir Charles marveled at his wife's energy, for he felt old and tired. But his inherited stubbornness flouted his doctors' advice to reduce his intake of the food and liquor that fueled his day's work. He was impelled to work even harder by the need to consolidate his control of the firm and to exploit the opportunities created by the war. The doctors also warned against overwork, but Charles at seventy-five remembered his father's long work-days when the Old Gentleman was the same age. Besides, Mary's change of heart was a tonic to him, though she had only once, and then obliquely, referred to her new feelings.

"Charles, my dear," she had said two weeks earlier over coffee and brandy, "I no longer feel isolated, an exile in Hong Kong. It *is* home—for both of us."

He had half-forgotten the letter on his desk. The crumpled envelope barred with thin red stripes was inertly menacing. He finally slit the flap with a silver letter-opener. The flimsy paper bore a few sentences in Chinese:

Respected Parents,

I must report with great sorrow the death of my son Cheng-wu. He was killed by a treacherous air attack while rallying his company to withstand the shameless assaults of American Imperialism against our beloved Socialist Motherland.

I am sure that you will take pride, as I do, in Cheng-wu's falling with resplendent courage on the battlefield in the just cause. The oppressed peoples of the world will unite and destroy the imperialists.

Your obedient son,
Shih Ai-kuo

Sir Charles Sekloong was unaccountably stirred by the death of the grandson he had never seen. Though James still lived, he too was lost to the family, as lost in life as his elder brother Jonathan and his sister Guinevere were in death. It was unseemly, Charles felt, that he himself should survive his son, his daughter, and, now, his grandson. He might any day receive a similar message from the American Department of Defense or the British War Office regarding George Chapman Parker, Jr., or Henry Haleevie Sekloong. It was almost too much to bear, so soon after the wracking sorrow of his father's death. Cheng-wu's death was another warning, a further portent that the House of Sekloong was imperiled.

"A curse," he muttered thickly, "a curse on the family for what I've done. We are being dispersed. . . ."

His fumbling fingers found the bell-push under the desk. Their tips slipped maddeningly on its glossy surface before he could exert sufficient pressure to summon his secretary. His cheeks were empurpled, and pain lanced his temples. A red mist obscured his vision.

"Mary!" he cried when the door opened. "Get me Mary! I must see her immediately."

Why didn't the damned girl understand? Why did she stand there gawping as if she couldn't hear him? Why did she stare so? He summoned all his strength and spoke loudly: "Mary!"

That final effort burst the massive cerebral aneurism. Sir Charles Sekloong died less than a year after his deeply resented and deeply loved father, who had dominated his life.

May 28, 1957–February 22, 1959

"I HAD to come home," Albert Sekloong told his grandmother with unblinking American facetiousness. "I was tired of explaining why I didn't have a handle to my name."

Lady Mary listened with unconcealed pleasure,

though she had cautioned herself against marring her resumed relationship with Jonnie's younger son by appearing proprietorial. She had seen him only for brief visits since he was sent to the United States in 1941 at the age of seven. But she congratulated herself again for having early discerned the promise that was burgeoning in the young man of twenty-three who had returned to Hong Kong five months earlier at Christmas of 1956.

"It wasn't so bad at the Wharton School," he continued. "They were only interested in money. But, all the time I was working on my MBA at Harvard, people kept asking the same dumb questions. 'If your great-grandfather was a Sir and your grandfather, too, if your brother's a Sir, why aren't you Sir Sekloong or Sir Al or Lord Whosis?' I had to come home. In Hong Kong I'm a Sekloong. And that's enough."

"How did they know about your illustrious ancestry?"

"I guess I told them," he admitted. "But, honestly, Grandma, they kept pressing me, like some kind of freak."

Lady Mary hid her smile behind her fan. Albert's youthful arrogance, cloaked by self-mockery, recalled Harry Sekloong, while his instinctive sense of position was reminiscent of those quintessential men of Hong Kong, Charles and Jonnie. Both had felt the Colony owed them deference, which they reciprocated with civic service. Sir Jonathan had instilled in them the Chinese gentry's traditional sense of responsibility for the less fortunate of the village—and their village was all Hong Kong.

"There was a girl from Radcliffe," Albert went on. "Japanese, but really kittenish. Called me Sir Bertie."

Lady Mary enjoyed Albert's disarmingly casual chatter. Like his father, he knew just how to use his charm. But an even quicker mind than Jonnie's animated the dark, regular features that were lit by the hazel Sekloong eyes when he smiled. Her youngest grandson possessed both Sir Jonathan's acute commercial brain and

704

his compulsive competitive drive. As had the Old Gentleman, Albert attacked the citadels of commerce like an ardent knight-errant.

Perhaps the frailty of age led her to see in the young man the traits of those other men she had loved. Instilled with the Sekloong mystique, she had almost overlooked the obvious fact that Albert also inherited the detached acuity of his grandfather Judah Haleevie. Sir Jonathan himself had acknowledged: "Judah owned a better financial brain than mine, though he lacked ruthlessness." Yet Albert's purpose was blatant. He was already pressing her to give him "greater responsibility," which they both knew meant more power. She would, she knew, gradually yield, while retaining her own overriding veto. She also knew he would be trying to elbow her off the throne in a few years—if she lived that long. On May 28, 1957, she was just a month away from her seventy-seventh birthday.

"They call me Lady Mary, which I'm not." She responded to Albert's banter over the title.

"But you *are* Lady Mary," he flattered. "You *couldn't* be anything else."

"Your other great-grandfather, the Bandmaster, would have roared with laughter at hearing me called Lady Mary. He always warned I'd 'coom doon wi' a boomp'!"

"But you haven't, have you?" Albert objected logically. "And neither will the House. Grandma, what about my proposals? We've got to expand fast in electronics and plastics."

"Not yet." Her mind dwelt still on the uncertainty of fate. "But we could still coom doon wi' a boomp. There's too much playing soldier, *grande dame*, and landed squire. Someone has to mind the store."

"Let them play. I'll be the storekeeper. We only need one, you know."

Although she was not quite ready to tell him, Lady Mary had already decided to try Albert by giving him a free hand in his new enterprises. She herself was more interested in solid real estate: new office buildings, blocks of luxury flats, and hotels throughout Southeast Asia as well as Hong Kong. She and Sarah were toying with manufacturing furniture to take advantage of the growing export market for Oriental furnishings. There was, however, no harm in venturing into the new, technological industries, as long as they didn't affect the fundamentals. Albert also wanted to expand their small airline interests, and she was receptive, remembering Harry's enthusiasm for aviation. But she would be quite certain that each new enterprise was solidly grounded before proceeding to the next. The House of Sekloong could bide its time.

Her grandson's enthusiasm was exhilarating to Lady Mary who had, after Charles's death, withdrawn for three years, letting her managers direct a holding operation. The European *taipans* in the Hong Kong Club had observed with mock regret that the House of Sekloong was faltering because it lacked aggressive leadership. What, they asked, could one expect of an old lady?

The old lady had ignored those taunts. She knew that Charles, who had rendered splendid homage to his father, would have wished her to observe deep mourning in the Chinese fashion. Losing Charles after more than fifty years had almost destroyed her; the shock had been more devastating for being unexpected. She had belatedly learned that Hong Kong had become her true home and the Chinese her people. Her own dependence upon Charles had been so integral to her existence that she had not realized its full extent until his death.

Her new collaboration with Albert was as invigorating as a magical elixir. But she had no intention of allowing either Albert or death to nudge her off the throne of the House of Sekloong for some time to come. She was enjoying her return too much.

Lady Mary was also eager to see the new drama played out in China. The effective administration exercised by the People's Republic had reawakened her hopes that the Chinese might finally learn to rule themselves. She could not approve of the Communist Party's

706

doctrinaire ruthlessness, which had inflicted great suffering. She could hope that a China united under a strong government for the first time in more than one hundred fifty years was moving toward stability and—if not prosperity—fair shares for all of its meager resources.

James Sekloong would have been wryly amused by his mother's optimism had they communicated with each other. His own appraisal of China was far less sanguine than that of the woman he considered a hopeless old reactionary. Still, he rarely thought of his family, except as a minor embarrassment. After drawing a curtain of silence between himself and the Sekloongs, James had taken other precautions. When the Shanghai authorities were deciding just which expropriated mansions would best serve as a rehabilitation center for the city's prostitutes, James had suggested his half-uncle Gregory's thirty-six-room villa on the Avenue Joffre in the former French Concession. The Party, he knew, had duly noted his emancipation from bourgeois family ties.

At fifty, he had on June 2, 1957, just been promoted to full general and duty commander of the multiprovincial Peking Military Region and the Peking Garrison. Nonetheless, the man who called himself Shih Ai-kuo was troubled. His insider's view of the state of the People's Republic of China contrasted with his mother's guarded optimism. His mood was bleak when he alighted from his Russian-built Zis staff car at the Eastern Entrance of the monumental Great Hall of the People on the Plaza of the Gate of Heavenly Peace.

The white-gloved honor guard saluted with gleaming rifles tipped by glittering bayonets. The guardsmen were chosen for their stature and their clean-cut handsomeness; their uniforms were so precisely tailored that they looked like oversized tailor's dummies. James's own uniform was a travesty of revolutionary austerity. Five red stars were embroidered on his gold shoulder boards, and his sleeves were bedizened with gold braid. The peaked cap with the enameled red star chafed both his forehead and his sense of propriety. He preferred the sensible, soft cloth cap he had worn before the Military Affairs Commission reorganized the People's Liberation Army two years earlier. Ten People's Marshals were created, his old commander Lin Piao among them; commissioned officers were sharply delineated from noncommissioned personnel; and those officers were dressed in gaudy Russian-style uniforms like actors in a Viennese musical comedy.

Before entering the ornate Great Hall of the People, James Sekloong paused to glance across the hundred-acre Plaza of the Gate of Heavenly Peace. The grape-like clusters of light globes were just flickering on, but one in five remained dark. In the center of the Plaza towered a white-marble obelisk, the Monument to the People's Heroes, which the irreverent secretly called "Chairman Mao's last erection." The Museum of the Chinese Revolution, which marked the eastern edge of the Plaza, was a mirror image of the Hall of the People. The same sweep of stairs rose to a terrace whose squat pillars semed borne down by the heavy, mock-Grecian pediment. The identical new structures dwarfed the four-hundred-year-old red-brick Gate of Heavenly Peace on the Plaza's northern boundary. The grandiose Plaza, which was twice the size of Moscow's Red Square, had been created by six-months' Herculean labors. It was a marble-and-concrete hymn to the Communist revolution—and to seventy-three-year-old Mao Tse-tung, Chairman of both the People's Republic and the Communist Party.

The puritanical James considered the Plaza as intolerably pretentious as his new uniform. While imposing almost unbearable strains on the Sino-Soviet alliance in the name of revolutionary purity the Chairman was outdoing the Soviets in ostentation. His propagandists were, further, lauding the "Era of Mao Tse-tung," just as successive Emperors had called the years of their reigns by their own names. But the Chairman was not content with the monumental display and abject flattery. He was exalting himself above the authors of the

Communist creed—Marx, Engels and Lenin—and the thought of Mao Tse-tung was hailed as "the highest development of mankind's creative genius, the apogee of Marxism-Leninism."

Premier Nikita Sergeivich Khrushchev had excoriated the "cult of personality" when he denounced the dead dictator Joseph Stalin at the XX Congress of the Communist Party of the Soviet Union the previous year. That cult had been reborn in the People's Republic of China. Chairman Mao's overwhelming self-confidence, James feared, was verging upon megalomania, while his wilfulness was contriving a major internal crisis. That crisis, James assumed, was the reason for his being summoned by Premier Chou En-lai and Deputy Chairman Liu Shao-chi, the first, his mentor in Marxism, the second, his chief in the underground and the New Fourth Army.

James realized that he had been standing in thought between the impassive honor guards for several minutes. Revolutionary egalitarianism notwithstanding, it was not seemly for a full general of the People's Liberation Army to linger in silent reverie in the public gaze. His abstraction could encourage unwholesome speculation. He returned the sentries' salute and strode into the two-story-high marble reception chamber of the Hall of the People. He was briskly passed up the chain of aides and secretaries into the presence of the two men who administered China while the Chairman brooded on his visions. They were seated in green-plush armchairs beside a low table on which documents were strewn amid porcelain teacups. Their heads were conspiratorially close, the Premier's grizzled and Comrade Shao-chi's white.

"I am delighted that Comrade General Shih Ai-kuo has finally found it convenient to join us." The Premier's sarcasm was mordant.

"Sit down, Ai-kuo." Comrade Shao-chi waved aside James's apologies. "Join us. We need your counsel."

"The Deputy Chairman and I are discussing certain problems, Comrade General." The Premier's exaggerated courtesy demonstrated that he would not easily re-linquish the bone of his displeasure. "You can assist by giving us your impressions of the major campaigns since Liberation."

James's throat tightened. He knew that both his superiors wished him well, and they had demonstrated their confidence by asking him to join their private councils. He was nonetheless apprehensive. The too casual question was also too simple. A junior political commissar might put that question to young recruits.

"Fully?" He probed cautiously. "It's a long tale."

"As fully as you wish," Chou En-lai directed.

"Comrade Premier," James replied by rote, "there have been five major campaigns since Liberation, and we are now engaged in the sixth. The Land Reform Movement gave the farmers land and liquidated the landlords. The Three-Antis Campaign corrected evils arising within the Party after our victory exposed cadres to new temptations. The Five-Antis Campaign eliminated the urban bourgeoisie and prepared for total nationalization of private enterprise. The Cooperativization Campaign consolidated the farmers' inefficient private holdings in readiness for mechanization of agriculture. The *Su-fan* Movement rooted out erroneous tendencies persisting with the Party after the Three-Antis. The Hundred Flowers Movement is now displaying the Party's confidence—and testing previous campaigns —by inviting the masses to offer frank criticism of our regime."

"Good," the Premier said. "Very good for a middle-school student. General, that's not what I meant. We don't need a recitation from an indoctrination primer. We want the honest opinion of a man close to the Party Center, but not at the center. We require an assessment, not a . . ."

"Ai-kuo, our problem is easy to state, but difficult to resolve," Comrade Shao-chi interrupted. "We are striving to reform the basic character of Chinese society and the thinking of the masses. Are we succeeding?"

"Speak freely, Ai-kuo." The Premier's formal displeasure relented. "We three are quite alone, and no one is listening. I've seen to that."

James calculated his answer while shaking a cigarette from a red packet of the Heavenly Peace Brand. His expression did not betray his hasty calculation: The Premier and Comrade Shao-chi, he knew, would not waste their time contriving an elaborate trap for a man who had served them loyally for decades. Since they knew he was no fool, absolute frankness, he decided, was his only possible response.

"I apologize for my frivolous reply." His voice was level. "But evasiveness is becoming a habit among us. . . ."

"There you are," Comrade Shao-chi told the Premier. "My point entirely."

"And my point, though not stated with my own normal evasiveness." The Premier smiled at his own serpentine humor. "My point, too."

"No, Comrades," James said, "we are *not* succeeding. We are trying very hard, but not really succeeding. We have erred in considering the Chinese people as malleable as potter's clay. We've wasted much energy and sacrificed too many able men merely to change the outward shape of Chinese society. But we have not really changed the people's thinking. They are still reactionary and feudal-minded. Worse, we are no longer loved."

"Your evidence?" the Premier demanded as he had in the classrooms of the Whampoa Academy. "What is the objective basis of your impressions?"

"Not just *my* impressions." James's stomach turned in renewed apprehension. This interview could not possibly work out well; he would either convict himself of erroneous thinking or earn a distasteful assignment by his own words. "Many reports pass across my desk. People are talking freely. Why shouldn't they? The Party has invited them to speak out."

"They wouldn't," Comrade Shao-chi interjected, "if they had any sense."

"Then," James replied, "we should presumably be

pleased that they don't have much sense. The Hundred Flowers Movement at least shows us where we stand."

"And where *do* we stand?" the Premier asked.

"Up to our necks in cow-shit and the stream rising, as the farmers say. A thousand voices have denounced our regime—actually thousands, including every non-Communist Cabinet member and a basketful of professors. But there's much worse than the criticism of bourgeois intellectuals. Have you heard what that girl student at Peking University said? Or the diatribe of the young peasant cadre at the People's University?"

"I thought they'd come up." Comrade Shao-chi leafed through the documents on the table. "I have the reports here if you haven't seen them."

The Premier shook his head.

"Let me read quickly and divert your spear from Ai-kuo," Comrade Shao-chi offered. "Here we are: 'Wang Hsiao-na, twenty-one, student at Peking U. who joined Red Army at thirteen. Addressed fellow students three days ago. Declared she'd been *utterly* mistaken in supporting the Party all her life. Demanded that entire Communist system be rent asunder . . . and then said she was ready to go to jail.''

"Brave girl!" the Premier commented dryly. "She will. And the other?"

"Wu Wei-ming, twenty-two, pure peasant origins, activist at People's University. His remarks merit quoting directly: 'The Party confronts a profoundly dangerous crisis. When pork is totally unavailable and vegetables have gone up six hundred percent in a year, it is hard to fool the masses with the same old lies about living standards' improving beyond belief. Beyond belief, indeed! The people are losing all confidence in the Communist Party. They say things are much worse than under the Nationalists. The Party has divorced itself from the people. Even more important, the masses are divorcing themselves from the Party. The Party will soon collapse. . . . ' "

"Eloquent!" the Premier observed. "But eloquence won't do him much good where he's going."

"And," Comrade Shao-chi insisted, "young Wu's final remarks: 'The Party can, of course, use machine guns to suppress trouble. But it should remember that machine guns are often turned against those who first use them!'"

"We don't have much choice, do we?"

James nodded agreement to the Premier's rhetorical question.

"And the Army? The Peking Command?" Comrade Shao-chi demanded. "Can you vouch for its loyalty?"

"If we act soon, yes," James answered. "Later, not necessarily. If we wait too long, say six months, no, not at all."

"Then we're agreed." The Premier addressed the Deputy Chairman. "Finish off the coalition government. Get rid of the façade. Clamp down hard on the dissidents."

"An external diversion will be essential," Comrade Shao-chi advised. "Otherwise, how can the Chairman reverse his policy?"

"Taiwan again?" James suggested.

"Pointless," the Premier decided. "Who believes we can take Taiwan? Besides, we don't need war with the Americans on top of our troubles with the damned Russkis."

"Quemoy," Comrade Shao-chi suggested. "Quemoy and Matsu are long overdue for liberation."

"Yes, that might work," the Premier mused. "Certainly feasible militarily. So let's think about Quemoy and Matsu. But what will the Americans do?"

"All right, Ai-kuo," Comrade Shao-chi directed. "Better get back to your office. I don't want all Peking gossiping about a long conference. We'll speak to you again soon."

Returning through the marble corridors, the General returned the greetings of scores of officials——and noted that the one thing missing from the Great Hall of the People was the ordinary Chinese people. He reluctantly concurred in his seniors' decision. Action was necessary, and necessity could tolerate no restraint. There

713

could be no mercy for those who tried to turn back the clock of history. But why, he wondered bleakly, was forcible suppression necessary in 1957? Only a year earlier the Party had believed that the masses and the intellectuals were totally dedicated to the revolution.

The top-secret report entitled *Assessment of the Situation of the Communist Bandits, March 1958,* had been prepared by the Intelligence Section of the Ministry of Defense of the Nationalists' Republic of China. Younger, Westernized officials smiled at its ornately archaic style, while older, traditionally minded officials nodded their approbation. But all rejoiced at the objective report of conditions on the Communist-ruled mainland. Peking's decision to crush dissident opinion had provoked resistance among the people and despondency within the Communist Party. Nationalist generals shook off their protracted torpor, and staff officers reviewed their plans to "retake the mainland." The head-on collision between the Chinese people and their Communist rulers could provide the opportunity Generalissimo Chiang Kai-shek's armies awaited.

Ku yin min chih pu kan ming, min hsin, jih li! [The *Assessment* began with a classical quotation.] Because the people cannot tolerate the present Mandate of Heaven their hearts are daily further alienated. As the Americans say, the people's honeymoon with the Communist bandits is over. *Yi chieh yu wei fa, meng huan pao ying.* All the grand promises are finally recognized as illusions, the shadows of bubbles. The Communists babble with eight tongues in seven mouths, while the people gird for vengeance.

General Thomas Sekloong, restored to favor as senior military assistant to President Chiang Kai-shek, scanned the florid report. The *Monthly Assessment* was a hard-headed appraisal, quite unlike the public propaganda intended to delude, first, the people of Taiwan; next, the Nationalists' remaining champions abroad; and, above all, the Congress and the White House of the United States of America, which the Korean War had transformed into Taipei's staunchest friend. Thomas knew that many influential Americans wanted to cut the Nationalists adrift. He searched the *Assessment* for hard evidence of severe difficulties on the Communist-ruled mainland that might halt the erosion of American support.

. . . more than 100 senior generals sent down to the countryside to learn through labor, [Thomas read] including Shih Ai-kuo, "deputy commander" of the bandit Peiping Military Region and Garrison Command. "General" Shih, a henchman of bandits Chou En-lai and Liu Shao-chi, who imposed those measures to bring the so-called Liberation Army under control, returned after only two weeks. But many senior commanders have been absent from their posts for months.

The Hundred Flowers Movement was abruptly reversed last summer (1957). Bandit "Chairman" Mao Tse-tung declared that he had invited free speech in order to entice "counterrevolutionaries and the People's enemies" into revealing themselves. He had, further, encouraged "a myriad flowers to blossom and all schools of thought to speak out in order to distinguish fragrant flowers from poisonous weeds that must be mercilessly rooted out." The renewed Anti-Rightist Campaign (inception: autumn 1957) is now raging. Ten million intellectuals, managers, and technicians have been sent down to the countryside to "learn from the peasants."

The façade of "coalition government" has been dismantled; all power is now openly exercised solely by the bandit Communist Party. The bandit regime is in disarray owing to widespread, virulent opposition. Neither the masses nor the intellectuals now believe in either the Communists' promises or the bandits' ability to rule. Senior bandit leaders are clashing. The situation is becoming increasingly favorable to us.

The "practical faction" of Chou En-lai and Liu Shao-chi is dismayed by the extremist "leftist faction" of Mao Tse-tung. Dissatisfied with slow progress toward "socialism," the "leftist faction" has raised a new battle cry: "Redness Must Command Expertise." Many cadres, the "leftists" charge, are "like radishes, red outside and white inside." True Reds can become Expert, the "leftists" contend, while "bourgeois" experts can never become Red.

A new "campaign" of much greater scope, intensity, and audacity than any previous campaign is, therefore, planned. Its exact nature is unknown, but the extremists are pressing for: totally remolding the society while relentlessly increasing agricultural and industrial production. Since that upheaval will create an acute crisis of internal security, an external diversion may be judged necessary. However, the general situation is highly favorable to our cause.

Projections: We foresee renewed threats against ourselves. Taiwan is invincible, since the bandit air force and navy cannot match our forces—even without the American back-up. Attack on the offshore islands of Quemoy and Matsu is, however, feasible. Since Quemoy is surrounded by Communist-usurped territory it appears vulnerable, and we advise special vigilance by the Quemoy Garrison. Diplomatic problems may also arise. The offshore islands do *not* lie within "the area of Taiwan" guaranteed by the Americans when they forced our evacuation of other offshore islands in 1955.

Recommendations: (A) Exploiting the Communist bandits' internal disarray by: intensifying our propaganda abroad; enticing the Americans into situations where they can be directly involved in combat; and increasing our agent/guerrilla activities on the mainland. (B) Reinforcing the Quemoy and Matsu Garrisons against possible attack. (C) Preparing to move into coastal provinces opposite Taiwan when the opportunity arises.

Thomas Sekloong removed his reading glasses, laid them beside the document, and lit a cigarette from a blue packet with the Nationalists' white-sun superimposed on the golden wings of the Air Force. The "best service," the fly-boys called themselves, aping the bravado of their American instructors. Whatever else, they undoubtedly had the best cigarettes. The General leaned back in his swivel chair and considered the *Assessment*.

In its enthusiasm, the Intelligence Section had exceeded its jurisdiction. It was responsible for collecting and weighing information from the mainland, not for broad policy recommendations. Though the Intelligence Chief naturally stressed information that would please the Generalissimo, his transgression was itself indirect verification of the *Assessment*. General Cheng Kai-ming had not grown old in the Nationalists' labyrinth of bureaucratic intrigue by venturing beyond his jurisdiction to make such positive statements unless he was quite certain of his grounds.

Thomas jotted a few words on his note pad. General Cheng Kai-ming guarded his sources fiercely, since he was convinced that dozens of Communist agents had penetrated the Nationalist Ministry of Defense. Thomas reluctantly decided he must press his senior, the Intelligence Chief, for his sources. This *Assessment* was too critical to pass to the Generalissimo without full substantiation. If General Cheng Kai-ming was right, the major upheavals on the Communist-ruled mainland could provide the opportunity for a successful counterattack the Nationalists had awaited for nine years.

The blacktop square outside the monumental Edwardian building constructed of red-brick by the Japanese when they ruled Taiwan echoed staccato commands. The "President's March" skirled over the stamping of the Honor Guard's boots. Thomas looked out the window to see the seventy-year-old Generalissimo striding jauntily between silver-helmeted soldiers toward his green Cadillac. Chiang Kai-shek acknowledged the Honor Guard's salute with a jerky wave of his hand. Thomas smiled fondly, for affection tinged his awe of his chief.

White-sun flag flapping on its fender staff, the green Cadillac drew into the mist hanging between the low, tile-roofed buildings of Taipei. Smoke from thousands of wood fires mingled with the chill fog that pervaded the dingy city. Thomas wished himself back in Nanking, where the weather was little better, but somehow seemed much better. He suppressed the thought. The overwhelming longing for China that rose unbidden in

717

his own and his colleagues' minds several times each day was potentially dangerous. While sustaining their resolve to reconquer the mainland, it could inspire over-optimistic judgments that might be as fatal as despair. Thomas reminded himself to press General Cheng Kai-ming for substantiation of his *Assessment*.

Looking down on the gray, featureless city, Thomas Sekloong shivered involuntarily. Despite the Nationalists' efforts to create a simulacrum of Shanghai or Nanking, Taipei remained a dull provincial city shaped by fifty years of Japanese occupation. He was eager to leave for his small house on Grass Mountain, where the air was cleaner.

A black Cadillac ascended the ramp to the Ministry. The American flag fluttering from its fender staff reminded Thomas that his day's work was not over after all. He had forgotten his appointment with the American Ambassador and his niece Blanche's husband, Spencer Taylor Smith, Deputy Assistant Secretary of State for the Far East. He grimaced and pressed a bell to summon his orderly. Lavish quantities of scotch and ice were essential when receiving Americans.

He might not, he mused, have forgotten the appointment if he had felt either personal fondness or professional regard for the smug, handsome career diplomat who had married Guinevere's daughter five years earlier. At least the food would be good at the Shin Yi, Taipei's best Szechwan restaurant. He was, Thomas remembered, giving a dinner for Spencer Taylor Smith, the Ambassador, and a number of Chinese and American officers, including the Major General commanding the U.S. Military Assistance Advisory Group. The Ambassador was bluntly amusing, while he had not seen his Whampoa classmate, the deputy commander of the Quemoy Garrison, for several months.

Struck by a vagrant thought, Thomas stared through his orderly, who stood patiently at attention. Yes, it could be useful, *very* useful—if he could persuade Spencer Taylor Smith.

Two mornings later, General Thomas Sekloong shivered on the canvas bucket seat in the unheated cabin of a camouflaged C-46 Commando. His nephew-in-law the Deputy Assistant Secretary was sleepily withdrawn in starch-new green fatigues and an outsized field jacket. The roar of the Pratt-Whitney engines in the uninsulated fuselage made coherent conversation impossible, but at 5:00 A.M. neither was inclined to chat.

Rising behind Taiwan's central mountain spine, the false dawn gilded the aircraft's wings and suffused the fog that cloaked the peaks. They had arrived at Sungshan Airport at 3:00 A.M. for a 3:30 A.M. take-off, and the Air Force had finally gotten the C-46 off the ground at 4:00 A.M. All military pilots apparently suffered from the same constitutional inability to take off on time, just as they all drove their aircraft hard once in the air. But there was reason for haste if the Commando were to deposit them on Quemoy and take off again before dawn. The Nationalist Air Force could not leave a transport on the ground just a mile from Communist artillery batteries.

The Commando banked hard right, and Thomas's ears popped as they lost altitude. He smiled at Spencer Taylor Smith, and his hands mimed the aircraft's motion. He had explained before take-off that they would cover two hundred fifty miles, though the direct route southwest from Taipei to Quemoy was no more than one hundred eighty miles. After flying due south to Taichung on Taiwan's coast, the Commando was turning west while descending to pass over the Pescadores Islets and the Taiwan Straits at two hundred feet. The Nationalist Air Force was contemptuous of the Communists' radar, and faster DC-6s flew agent-drops deep into China, some penetrating as far as Sinkiang Province 2,500 miles away. Prudence nonetheless dictated the cautious predawn approach under the radar screen of the heavily fortified port of Amoy.

"Like a dog's jaws grasping a bone, Amoy surrounds Quemoy," Thomas had concluded his briefing with the obligatory jest. "But the Communists can't swallow it. Quemoy is really a bone in their throat."

The Commando raced the dawn across the Taiwan

719

Straits. The vertical pink rays of the morning sun caught the tail plane's splotched-camouflage paint just as Quemoy shone bleached dun on the green sea ahead. The island was a low splotch against the jagged gray hills of Fukien Province, nowhere higher than one hundred sixty feet, except for the pinnacle of Tai-wushan thrusting its bare granite eight hundred forty feet above the narrow plain.

The Commando dropped so low on final approach that Spencer Taylor Smith, peering through the circular porthole, saw whitecaps clawing for the fuselage. The plane rose to clear the ridge behind the beach and dropped onto a tar-surfaced airstrip stippled with shallow shellholes. The wheels bounced twice before gripping the runway. Smith waited for the plane to halt. But Thomas bustled him toward the door, where the crew chief's blue coveralls were an incongruous blotch of color against the aircraft's battered aluminum shell.

The crew chief threw the door open as the tail wheel settled to earth. His upraised palm signaled them to wait. When the speed dropped to five knots, he motioned them forward. Ten seconds later, he swept his hand toward the door.

"Jump!" Thomas shouted. "Jump and roll!"

The portly diplomat obeyed, though Thomas's pre-flight briefing had intentionally omitted the exit procedure. Smith landed heavily, his legs churning automatically. He stumbled and rolled on his shoulder as Thomas's compact body flashed by.

The door slammed shut, the engines revved, and the propellers flashed in the bright dawn. The pilot wheeled the transport around and began his take-off run. Ninety seconds after its wheels had touched the strip, the Commando was again airborne. As it cleared the ridge, four shell-bursts threw up fountains of sand beside the strip.

"They're firing for effect—psychological effect," Thomas reassured his nephew-in-law. "Primarily to keep us on edge."

Spencer Taylor Smith was shaken and indignant—as his uncle-by-marriage had intended. Though an infantry

720

captain during World War II, he had never encountered the simultaneous hazards of artillery fire and a heavy transport's landing on a short, improvised airstrip. Though his self-esteem was more badly bruised than his shoulder, he concealed his annoyance. Treating the dramatic landing as anything but a slight variation from the normal would place him at a disadvantage. He sensed that Thomas Sekloong was skilfully playing on his nerves, presumably to gain some specific advantage.

Spencer Taylor Smith had welcomed Thomas's suggestion that he visit Quemoy. A deputy assistant secretary could allow himself an escapade that would have been unthinkable if he stood a single step higher in the State Department's hierarchy. It would be useful to have seen Quemoy if, as Thomas predicted, the island became the center of an international storm. He had not felt it necessary to tell Thomas that Washington's intelligence reports also forecast "increased pressure" on Quemoy.

"A bit hairy, that landing, General," the American joked. "What do you lay on for really important visitors?"

"Fairly routine, Spencer," Thomas replied. "And do call me Tom. General is too formal, and Uncle Thomas would make me feel too old."

The riposte pierced the American's guard. We Nationalists, Thomas had implied, are inured to danger, for we face the enemy in the front lines while you sit safe in Washington, juggling with our fate. He had also recalled their family relationship by implicitly claiming and explicitly disclaiming the deference due to his seniority. Thomas had further reminded Smith that the younger man was, at forty-one, precisely midway between the ages of his fifty-three-year-old uncle and his twenty-nine-year-old wife.

Thomas Sekloong was a formidable antagonist, Spencer Taylor Smith concluded with wry admiration as they clambered into a jeep. He had, however, shown one of his cards. The American diplomat knew the Nationalist General wanted to dicker. But he too could play a waiting game.

Although he had been warned that the Nationalists would make his "unofficial" visit a formal occasion, the American stiffened indignantly when he saw the silver-helmeted Honor Guard waiting before the green-camouflaged entrance to Quemoy Garrison Headquarters. Bugles blared and drums rolled as the Commanding General saluted them.

"You must forgive these poor fellows, Spencer," Thomas murmured. "They're terribly isolated, just can't help making a fuss over their rare visitors. And they admire anyone who ventures into the tiger's mouth when he doesn't have to."

"I appreciate that, Tom. But you will remember, won't you? No publicity."

"Of course, Spencer, of course." Thomas was pleased, since his nephew's appeal revealed that he was disconcerted. "As far as the press knows, you're in consultation with the Prime Minister and the Foreign Minister all day."

The briefing in the underground auditorium that seated three hundred was smoothly professional, for the Nationalists had learned the theatrical technique from their American advisors. Even the accent of the trim young major wielding the pointer before the large-scale map was American. Major Liu, Thomas whispered, was a graduate of the General Staff College at Fort Leavenworth.

". . . took refuge on Quemoy . . ." Spencer Taylor Smith, drowsy after his early rising and the exhausting flight, heard scattered phrases of the major's briefing. ". . . we crossed in sampans and on rafts. By the time the Communists were ready to attack . . . all boats destroyed . . . tried row across on doors and logs. We beat off attack. . . . Almost ten years now . . . harassed us . . . but unable take Quemoy. Reveals their weakness . . . nearest Communist position is . . . outpost less than a quarter of a mile away. . . . Quemoy now impregnable. Garrison of fifty thousand . . . in caves and bunkers. . . . Relatively prosperous farmers ignore intermittent shelling. . . . One chief problem . . . supply lines to Taiwan not wholly secure . . . but garrison will fight to death."

The American automatically sifted the kernels of significance from the chaff of rhetoric, but felt uneasily that he had overlooked some vital point. He culled his memory during the long luncheon while responding to toasts in fiery *pai-kar,* the colorless, 120-proof spirits distilled from Quemoy's sorghum. He had not recalled the revealing remark when they left the headquarters bunker to inspect the island.

Quemoy's defenses were as impressive as any American command's. The camouflage nets were skilfully draped to blend with the island's sandy soil and green vegetation. Their jeep was only fifty feet away when Smith saw that a cleft in the sandy hills concealed a battery of 105-howitzers. Armed sentries popped out of the ground like jacks-in-the-box, and entire infantry battalions were alert in deep caves.

Taylor Smith counted no more than four Communist shells an hour, but each shot was unnerving. The Communist batteries were less than a mile distant, while the island was so silent between explosions that he could hear the sweet song of the larks in the young pine groves. He had known fear under the unheralded explosion of incoming artillery shells. Never before that day had he heard an enemy gun fire, listened to the express-train tumble of the projectile, and then heard the crump of the impact. He flinched at each discharge, feeling as if every shell were aimed directly at himself.

"Now I know," he told Thomas, "what it's like to be a tin duck in a shooting gallery."

"A quiet day despite the build-up," the General answered. "The Communists are husbanding their ammunition."

Ascending Taiwushan, Quemoy's sole height, they paused before an obelisk that praised the garrison in the Generalissimo's own calligraphy. From the observation platform, Thomas pointed out the Communist positions with a proprietorial air. Through powerful tripod-mounted binoculars Taylor Smith saw Communist gunners lounging beside their revetments on the Amoy Peninsula that sheltered the largest port between Shanghai and Hong Kong.

"There seems," he baited Thomas, "to be a lot of peaceful coexistence."

"On both sides," the Nationalist General rejoined. "Our artillery could close Amoy to all shipping. But we, too, are restrained."

"Somehow, I don't get the feeling of an impending crisis," the American persisted.

In reply, Thomas beckoned to a staff officer who carried a plastic-encased map on which red-crayoned boxes marked the Communist artillery positions. The staff officer swiveled the binoculars so that the American could see the reality of gun-metal tubes each symbol represented.

"Every one of the batteries you're now seeing has been emplaced during the past three weeks," Thomas said. "They're constantly bringing up ammunition and reinforcements. Aerial observation and agent reports confirm the build-up."

"Then you'd say the present quiet's an illusion?"

"Calm before the storm," Thomas replied. "And we're already outgunned. That's worrying."

"Worrying? I thought you were confident."

"We are confident—except for one factor."

The Deputy Assistant Secretary waited in silence for the General to reveal why he had been enticed to Quemoy.

"This island can hold out indefinitely, even against air attack," Thomas said. "Our Air Force controls the skies. But our Navy's small and, between us, not really first-class. I'm *not* confident we can maintain adequate resupply of ammunition and food."

"Therefore?"

"We need an understanding that the U.S. Navy will insure resupply."

"And risk war with Peking? Hardly likely, Tom."

"Spencer, suppose Quemoy falls into the hands of Peiping." Thomas stressed the Nationalists' old name for Peking, the Communists' renamed capital. "It would be a major American political defeat, in the States as well as abroad. If American promises were shown up, all Asians would lose heart. And many Americans would object strenuously."

"I see your point, but I'm not concerned with domestic politics."

"You can't ignore politics, can you?" Thomas pressed. "Eisenhower would look a proper fool if the Communists took Quemoy because he failed a sworn ally, reneged on promises."

"You know very well that Quemoy is specifically excluded from the Taiwan area whose defense we've guaranteed."

"And would that fine distinction preserve American credibility or American interests? More like Korea. Dean Acheson had specifically excluded Korea from your defense perimeter, and look what happened."

"It's not that simple, though I follow your reasoning." The Deputy Assistant Secretary sacrificed the point like a chess master. "Speaking hypothetically . . . you understand I have no authority to make commitments, even to discuss eventualities officially. But, *hypothetically*, what would you need?"

"No more than an *understanding*, shall we say, that we'd receive American naval support for resupply. Only if absolutely necessary, of course."

"It might be possible," Taylor Smith conceded. "But public opinion cuts two ways in the States. Lots of Americans would scream bloody murder if our Navy actively supported your operations, even if we didn't fire a shot."

"American ships wouldn't have to shoot," Thomas replied. "The Communists wouldn't dare challenge them at this stage. They're not yet ready to take on the U.S. again."

"That's *your* assessment of enemy intentions. It's not hard intelligence, just a self-serving guess."

"Perhaps, but you've undoubtedly made your own assessment and . . ."

"I'll be frank, Tom. Our assessment isn't as optimistic as yours. We think the Communists *might* not react against our ships. But the risk's too high."

"Speaking hypothetically, though, you *might* risk it? Is my understanding correct?"

"You've boxed me in," Taylor Smith laughed. "Quite unofficially, that *could* be Washington's view, if our people agreed that your losing Quemoy would hurt us badly. But we'd need something to placate your opposition at home, the very vocal group of Americans who oppose any aid to your government."

"What's the *quid pro quo* you want from us?"

"A firm commitment, a public declaration that your government renounces the use of force to retake the mainland."

Thomas winced. The American had caught him in his own trap.

"That's impossible," he protested automatically. "You're asking us to renounce our national purpose. We'd rather take our chances."

"If Quemoy falls, your national purpose, reconquering the mainland, would look damned hollow. Anyway, I said renounce *force*. Political means could still be used. You could restate your determination to free the Chinese mainland by political means."

"Power grows from the barrel of the gun," Thomas bitterly quoted Mao Tse-tung.

"No gun, then no power," Smith replied. "No gun emplacements on Quemoy and no power to retake the mainland. It cuts both ways. Look, Tom, we're trying to do the best we can. We're not pressing for withdrawal from Quemoy, but only . . ."

"Impossible, absolutely impossible," Thomas interjected. "We've already withdrawn from too many offshore islands. We can't . . ."

"I know that, and we don't want you to withdraw from Quemoy. Therefore this proposal, hypothetical of course. We're not asking the impossible, just an undertaking not to attack the mainland. Circumstances, of course, could subsequently alter cases. But, without public renunciation of force, you'll have no case at all as far as we're concerned. And Quemoy could then fall."

"I'll have a word, Spencer. Unofficially, of course."

"And I'll have a word, Tom. Hypothetically, of course."

The Chinese and the American chatted inconsequentially while they completed their guided tour, though Thomas was enraged. The Chinese General hated begging scraps from the rich Americans. But the Americans possessed the power, and his Generalissimo desperately needed their power. Thomas lapsed into silence as the jeep carried them back to the airstrip.

Through the subtropical twilight a black speck skimmed the waves of the Taiwan Straits, and the Communist batteries roared a full-throated barrage. As shell-bursts showered sand around the strip, their escort hurried the Chinese General and the American diplomat into a foxhole.

"It doesn't seem so peaceful now, does it?" Thomas shouted. "The plane won't stop. We'll board while it's rolling—slowly, I hope."

Just before the Commando touched down, they climbed into the jeep to race onto the airstrip. The two men jumped to the ground and leaped for the small aluminum ladder dangling from the moving aircraft's open door. The strain wrenched Spencer Taylor Smith's arms, and his hands slipped on the smooth metal. A burly crew chief hauled him aboard. He lay panting on the scarred floor as the Commando rose into the air. A final salvo exploded just behind its mottled tail plane.

"Could you tell the pilot how grateful we are?" the American shouted over the engines' noise after regaining his breath and strapping himself into the bucket seat. "I see it's a different crew, but I suppose the pilot's landed here so often it seems routine."

Thomas Sekloong returned from the flight compartment five minutes later. He grinned enigmatically be-

727

fore shouting. "The pilot appreciates your compliment. He says he was scared, too. Hardly routine! He hadn't been into Quemoy for two years!"

"I know it's overdoing things. Just like this display, but backwards." The Minister of Defense of the People's Republic tapped the giant red star of a People's Marshal on his gold-encrusted shoulder board. "It's a reverse fanfare, muting the trumpets and muffling the drums, placing my Headquarters so far from the city."

"It's a waste of time and petroleum running back and forth to Peking, *Ta Chiang*." James Sekloong automatically used the Minister's nickname, "Great General," the accolade bestowed by Mao Tse-tung himself before relations between the Chairman and his best general became gelid.

"*Chin-tien ta chiang-lai, ming-tien mei chiang-lai!*" The Minister wryly punned on the word *chiang,* meaning both general and future. "Today a big future, tomorrow no future!"

James ignored the bitter pun. Defense Minister Marshal Peng Teh-huai, senior member of the Political Bureau of the Communist Party and former Commander-in-Chief of the Chinese People's Volunteers in Korea, could still jest about his conflict with Chairman Mao in late July 1958. But it was wiser for others not to react, even a full general who was a member of the Party's Central Committee. Suspicious distrust was as thick in Peking as a spring fog on the Yellow River.

"I suppose," James sidestepped, "that putting Headquarters twelve miles out does enhance security."

"*Hu-shuo pa-tao,*" the Minister smiled. "That's nonsense. Any Nationalist spies must be planted here in Headquarters. They wouldn't walk off the streets of Peking to inspect our secret files. It's just making a big show of not making a show. So much of that nowadays."

"Times change," James commented cautiously. "Sometimes so fast I can't keep up. It was simpler when we were in Korea together."

"True enough. I can't keep up either. But I didn't ask you for a philosophical discussion. Though, perhaps, later?"

The question hung in the air. James knew the Minister was recruiting allies for his inevitable confrontation with Chairman Mao Tse-tung. He was to a certain extent in sympathy with Peng Teh-huai's views, while he admired the straightforward Marshal personally and professionally. But James was already committed to Premier Chou En-lai, to Deputy Chairman Liu Shao-chi—and to self-preservation.

"We can talk philosophy another time." The Minister ended the awkward silence. "Meanwhile, I want to check nation-wide dispositions with you."

"At your command, Great General!"

James offered the conventional response and gave silent thanks for his own discretion. No military necessity, not even professional courtesy required the Minister of Defense to consult with the Deputy Commander of the Peking Military Region regarding the nation-wide deployment of the Liberation Army.

"The Army has been assigned an extraordinary mission." The Defense Minister's Hunanese burr thickened in anger. "We've been ordered to attack right, left, and center. But we've also been ordered to attack to the rear."

"The rear, Great General?"

"Yes, the rear. The build-up against Quemoy is completed, and heavy shelling starts next week. But Quemoy is really our strategic rear."

"I don't quite understand." Honest bewilderment over-rode James's caution. "Quemoy *is* the front line, isn't it?"

"Not at all. To isolate the Nationalists and the Americans, we should intensify the conflict in Vietnam and Laos. Quemoy is a risky diversion that could provoke American retaliation."

"And the frontal attacks?" James's curiosity rashly prevailed over his prudence. "You mean troops supporting the Great Leap Forward and the Great People's Communes?"

"Yes, Heaven help us! This is the first time the Liberation Army's been deployed solely to crush popular resistance—and *before* it occurs." The Minister's burr was so thick James strained to understand him. "Rape their mothers! The *lao pai-hsing* will be calling us the People's Suppression Army before this lunacy ends."

"The plans do look ambitious." James deliberately drew out the Minister. "Is that why you're disturbed?"

"Disturbed? I'm not disturbed, I'm appalled. This is total national mobilization for national suicide. Great Leap Forward, screw their mothers! Catch up with Britain industrially in five years and America in fifteen. Build ten million midget blast furnaces to quadruple steel production in a year. Put one hundred million men to work on dams to make deserts and marshes bloom, rape their grandmothers. Use more slave labor than the feudal princes and make the First Emperor look like a benevolent despot. Replace all local administrations with fifty thousand Great People's Communes. Every Commune self-sufficient agriculturally, industrially, culturally, militarily, and commercially. Abolish the family . . . put husbands and wives in separate dormitories and take their children away. Heaven trembles and the earth shakes. Confiscate all privately held land and livestock. Collectivize everything and call the mess a Great People's Commune. The man's mad!"

"But, Great General, it's not just *his* decision." James's instinct for survival compelled him to protest. "The Party Center has approved, and the theoreticians say it's possible. How can we . . ."

"*This* room's not bugged," the Minister interjected contemptuously. "And *I* won't repeat our conversation, whatever *you* do. Some people still dare speak out."

"*I* am no informer." James objected and contritely reverted to the traditional courtesy: "I beg enlightenment."

"It's all a great hoax, like a hawker peddling a universal cure. Poor fellow can't cure his own pox. But guarantees everyone else miracles—all on the cheap."

The Minister spat into the enameled spittoon beside his desk.

"Attain Communism by reforming the spirit of man. Bullshit! Marx said true Communism would take centuries after—mind you, *after*—creating material abundance. But these two-penny conjurers promise true Communism in a couple of years."

"What other course is open?" James chose his words with care.

"We can only back their play, not too strenuously, till it collapses," the Minister conceded. "Then we can pick up the pieces. Be particularly vigilant in Peking. I don't want a mutiny or a *coup d'état.*"

"And the Russians?" James probed. "Where do they stand?"

"They're not happy. I don't love our Soviet comrades, but I have been sounding them out, as you know. They helped when we needed help—at least, until last year. Now they won't come through with technical assistance so that we can make our own nuclear weapons."

"But they promised," James interjected. "Promised formally. On paper."

"Now they've got the perfect excuse for reneging. Old Mao's too reckless, they say. They're dead set against the Quemoy action. Adventurism, they call it. And they point out the obvious. It's possible . . . just barely possible that we can take Quemoy without bringing in the Americans. But we can't take Taiwan without fighting the Americans—and Taiwan's the real objective, not a pisspot little offshore island. So Moscow's sitting this one out. The first test of the Sino-Soviet alliance since we pulled their chestnuts out of the fire in Korea—and we're already isolated."

"And Moscow feels the Chairman's also reckless at home?"

"They're right. He directly challenges the Russians by declaring we'll reach true Communism before them.

Opium Communism, they call it. Do you expect them to like it?"

"I can see their position," James admitted. "But I don't have to like it either."

"Who likes it? I certainly don't. But it's real. And it's time we faced reality, stopped befuddling ourselves with visions out of the opium-pipe. But we can only wait for the collapse. Then every sane man in the Party will have to pick up the pieces. That's my view."

James took his dismissal from the Defense Minister and faithfully reported his "view" to the Premier. Chou En-lai listened without comment to the warnings of disaster. Unlike the Defense Minister, he understood that the first duty of a statesman was to survive.

"The Marshal may be right or wrong about the consequences," the Premier finally said. "He is certainly right about the choice before us. All we can do is go along for now."

August, September, and October of 1958 were the cruellest and most tumultuous months since the establishment of the People's Republic of China on October 1, 1949. The Great Leap Forward and the Great People's Communes were proclaimed to transfigure both China and the Chinese people. The earthly paradise of true Communism promised by Karl Marx was to be attained in a historical instant, perhaps a year, certainly no more than three to five years. The Chinese people were to awe the world by entering a new epoch of man's life on this earth under the inspired guidance of Chairman Mao Tse-tung.

At the beginning, few of China's millions of cadres shared the Premier's skepticism. Even fewer believed with the Defense Minister that the heroic enterprise must end in catastrophe. The audacity of the endeavor and the apocalyptic language that described the endeavor dazzled the men and women who were charged with transforming the Chairman's vision into reality in the rice-fields of the south, in the wheat fields of the north—and in the impressionable minds of their six hundred million compatriots.

James Sekloong marveled at the magnitude of the Chairman's vision. Dishonesty and strife, greed, lust and envy—indeed all ignoble emotions and actions—were to be destroyed by destroying the evil society that bred them.

Nature herself was to abate her harshness and gracefully yield her favors to the industrious wooing of hundreds of millions of Chinese. The mighty rivers were to become docile servants, and the earth was to surrender its iron to tens of millions of questing hands, the ore to be transformed into steel in millions of backyard blast furnaces. Time itself was to be vanquished when inspired human energy accomplished "twenty years' work in a single day." That "wholly new basis for a perfect new social structure," the Great People's Commune, was not only to supplant the family, but to transcend the individual human being. He was to be idyllically happy, but he was no more to be an independent organism than a single polyp in a coral reef. Instead, he was to live in idyllic collective happiness.

Five hundred million peasants were to own all property in common—except, perhaps, their shoes, the notebooks in which they scrawled political maxims, and, for a few, their toothbrushes. They were not even to possess garden plots, domestic animals, houses, cooking pots—or their own hearth fires. Drawing their clothing from central supply depots, eating in public mess halls, and bathing in public bath-houses, they were to become perfect "producing units." Parents were neither to discipline nor to cherish their children, who would be the Commune's charges. Both parents and children were to cast off the "narrow, selfish bonds of filial love"; all their love was to flow to the Motherland, to the Communist Party, and to Chairman Mao Tse-tung.

No Chinese was to sit in sinful idleness for an instant. Grandmothers were to weave baskets and tie brooms in Halls of Venerable Joy, while mothers and daughters worked in fields or workshops. Perhaps one woman in five was to undertake domestic tasks—looking after children, mending clothing, keeping house, and preparing food. With the disappearance of the family, distinctions between the sexes were to vanish in the crucible of perfect equality. Women would differ from men only in their reproductive functions. Men were neither to assume responsibility for women and children nor to exercise authority over them. Women were neither to adorn themselves nor to exercise their tactful domination over men.

A perfect egalitarian society—perfectly featureless and perfectly responsive to authority—was to emerge when the Communes had destroyed all distinctions between manual and intellectual labor, between agriculture and industry, between city and countryside. Under the sway of the Communist priest-kings, the unitary Golden Age celebrated by Chinese mythology would reappear.

The Special Investigation Teams of the People's Liberation Army discovered a quite different reality when the military were, toward the end of the year 1958, ordered to "pick up the pieces," as the Defense Minister had predicted. The Communist Party had been forced to call in the Liberation Army, the only remaining effective instrument of power, when civil administration virtually collapsed, the economy was verging upon paralysis, and the *lao pai-hsing,* vastly overburdened and pitifully underfed, began to mutter in revolt.

"No one knew what a Great People's Commune was." An intense sixteen-year-old schoolboy described the apotheosis of Sansung Village to James Sekloong, who was in command of the investigation in North China. "But it sounded wonderful. We were to govern ourselves. No foreign cadres were to tell us what to do. Everyone would get more food and better clothing—all free. The Commune would produce everything we needed—hoes and shovels, baskets and plows, cloth and thermos bottles, iron and steel too. We'd even be our own soldiers—to defend the country and enforce the people's will."

James lit another cigarette and listened in brooding silence.

"It sounded all right to get free meals in a mess hall, but no one really believed we couldn't *ever* cook our own food or that all parties and holidays were banned. People were glad that old people and young children would be specially looked after. But who could believe husbands and wives would be separated from their children and from each other? That didn't fit the new slogans the cadres recited: *Today in the Mao Tse-tung Era, heaven is here on earth! The new era of universal, almighty man has arrived!*"

The people of Sansung Village, the schoolboy recalled, found that the Great Peace and Prosperity Commune did not bring more food, less work, and untrammeled liberty. They got much less food and that little badly prepared; forced labor was radically intensified and they lost almost all freedom of choice in their personal lives.

"We worked fourteen to eighteen hours a day for a few mouthfuls of food. They promised four ounces of pork a month, but we never saw meat, eggs—or even bean curd. All our rice went to the Commune, so did our chickens and pigs. If we stole a handful of our own rice or hid an egg, we couldn't cook it. All pots and pans had gone to the iron-and-steel drive to help the Motherland resist American aggression in the Taiwan area."

The travail of the Chinese people in September 1958 was hidden from the outside world. Observers in Hong Kong were not struck by the Great People's Communes and the Great Leap Forward until the middle of that month. Both then appeared no more than repetitions of the unremitting campaigns that had convulsed the People's Republic since its establishment. Heavy artillery bombardment of Quemoy, backed by Peking's full-throated threats to "liberate" first the offshore island and subsequently Taiwan itself, did not divert the Chinese people from their ordeal. The crash of guns and the thunder of propagandists did divert the men who "watched" China from outside because they could not enter the country itself. Besides, the audacity of the

Chairman's new endeavor numbed their perceptions. Like the *lao pai-hsing* themselves, the "China Watchers" could not really believe that Mao Tse-tung was determined to make a wholly new China by totally exploiting the nation's single greatest resource, the Chinese people.

Dewey Miller, Hong Kong correspondent for *Newsweek,* intuitively knew that the two "movements" were transcendent. He read the Communists' literal descriptions of their visionary purposes with fascination, but regretfully postponed the necessarily painstaking analysis of Peking's most extraordinary pronouncements. New York wanted full coverage of the intensifying Quemoy crisis, since direct American involvement could lead to a collision with Peking and, perhaps, with Moscow. Resignedly, Miller boarded a DC-6 of General Claire Chennault's Civil Air Transport to Taipei and ensconced himself in the gray-stone Friends of China Club. Formerly a hostel for the puritanical Officers' Moral Endeavor Association, the Club offered minimal comfort to the foreign press corps that crammed all its facilities. It was, however, centrally located, just across the square from the red-brick Presidential Offices that housed the Ministry of Defense, and its telephones functioned as well as any on the island. The staff was accustomed—if not reconciled—to the correspondents' outrageous professional demands and sometimes equally outrageous personal behavior, while the Club's convenience attracted both senior Chinese officials and foreign diplomats.

His dark hair threaded with gray and his pouched brown eyes mournful, the big American lounged in the coconut-thatch-decorated barroom. Ignoring his colleagues' chatter in eight languages, he divided his attention between his third prelunch martini and his search for a fresh approach to the over-reported crisis. The green-eyed colonel of the Foreigners' Police seated at the bar drew only a bored glance; that Nationalist watch-dog constantly patroled the Friends of China

Club. The big American rose when a stocky figure in a tan uniform marked by four golden stars entered.

"General Sekloong," Miller said, "I hoped to see you here. Your mother asked me to give you her greetings."

"Very good of you, Mr. Miller."

Thomas Sekloong concealed his irritation at encountering one of the few foreign correspondents he respected. It was necessary to talk to correspondents, since their reports could rally support abroad. He would, however, have preferred to talk with any other correspondent. Miller's questions probed too deep, and he was, after Chungking, instinctively skeptical of all Nationalist statements.

"Still around, I see, Mr. Miller," Thomas added with heavy jocularity. "I thought you'd left us. You must be an Old China Hand by now."

"I guess Old China Hands never leave, General. They only fade away—eventually. Maybe we acquire a kind of Chinese toughness and resilience by osmosis."

"You grant us those qualities?"

"Of course, General. Otherwise you Nationalists would've given up long ago. You, for one, would certainly be more comfortable in New York or Hong Kong. I admire your optimism. I wish I could share it."

"And have you seen the paradise the Communists say they've created on the mainland?"

"Not yet," Miller grinned. "Not for a while yet. The State Department's finally said we could go, but Peking's not having any."

"How extraordinary," Thomas jibed.

They fenced for half an hour. Miller tried to pry hard information from the Generalissimo's aide. Thomas was determined to yield nothing, while maintaining outward cordiality. Yet it occurred to him that Miller could prove useful. The Americans wanted to veil the impending major operation, but the Nationalists' interests would be best served by the fullest publicity.

"Mr. Miller, may I offer a suggestion?" Thomas asked. "The *Helena* puts into Keelung tonight and leaves tomorrow. Her voyage could be interesting."

Two days later, the U.S.S. *Helena,* flagship of the U.S. Seventh Fleet, pounded south through the stormy Straits of Taiwan accompanied by two destroyers. When the dawn of September 8, 1958, broke early over the white-crested waves, the crew had been awake for hours, as had Dewey Miller. He had talked himself aboard the heavy cruiser, finally appealing to his old acquaintance, the Commander of the Seventh Fleet. The Captain's refusal to take the correspondent on board had then been over-ruled by Vice-Admiral Wallace Beakley.

"He's here and he knows something's up," the Fleet Commander had decided. "Let him sail with us."

The small Admiral with the thrusting nose was an amiable host over the martinis prohibited by Navy regulations. Though he would face acutely critical decisions in the morning, he appeared the most relaxed man on the cruiser. Beakley's chief-of-staff fretted over the operations plan and speculated on the catastrophic repercussions of that plan's going awry. But the man to whom President Dwight Eisenhower had delegated final authority—and final responsibility—calmly discussed his own expectations with Dewey Miller in his mahogany-paneled quarters.

"We're resupplying Quemoy," Beakley explained. "The Nationalist Navy can't get through Communist artillery and air attacks, so the garrison's running short. *Helena* will stay outside the twelve-mile limit, which we do *not* recognize. The destroyers will convoy Nationalist landing-craft to the three-mile limit off Quemoy we *do* recognize. Coincidentally, three miles off Quemoy is just twelve miles from the Communist shore. A simple operation."

"Very simple, Admiral," Miller rejoined. "Just routine, isn't it? And no back-up force?"

"Well, a couple of flat-tops are lying off the east coast of Taiwan," Beakley smiled. "They need sea room. I don't want them trapped in the narrow Straits if something happens."

"Are they carrying nuclear weapons? Will you use them?"

"Now, Dewey, you know you shouldn't ask me that. All I can say is this: We have a variety of weapons in our arsenal, and we use those weapons appropriate to the tactical situation."

"But it's a strategic decision, isn't it?" Miller persisted. "If the Communists attack us and we use nuclear weapons, the Russians could come in."

"They could," Beakley conceded. "Just figure that we'll use all appropriate force—and no more. Now get out of here and let me get some sleep."

Shielded by the Marine sentry at the door of his cabin, Beakley slept well. Few others aboard the *Helena* did. Dewey Miller prowled the cruiser, chatting with officers and bluejackets until 3:00 A.M. before resorting to his stuffy cabin. He was on the bridge at 5:00 when the jagged hills of Fukien Province reared through the morning mist.

Helena rolled heavily in a beam wind, and choppy seas tossed her eleven thousand tons. The cruiser maneuvered precisely, guided by the bright green images on her radar screens. Beside her slender length, slab-sided gray attack-transports lowered their landing-craft. When the small craft moved off, knife-prowed destroyers flanked the small convoy butting through the waves toward the smudge on the horizon that was Quemoy. Through his binoculars, Dewey Miller saw the sand-flecked, gray-black explosions of the Communist barrage. The pinnacle of Taiwushan was intermittently silhouetted by air bursts opening a hundred feet above the ground like red chrysanthemums. Water-spouts rose from shells exploding in front of the landing-craft.

The loudspeaker of the Talk Between Ships circuit squawked metallically: "The landing-craft are in trouble. Seas are too high for them to run at speed. Artillery barrages on the beaches."

"Tell them to slow down," the Admiral directed. "No point in trying to get there so fast they turn turtle."

"Landing-craft Three broaching to," the TBS reported. "She's going over."

"Slow down," Beakley ordered. "I repeat: Slow down."

"Nationalist Combat Air Patrol overhead," the air-defense officer reported from his post at the high-angle radar. "Thirty-six planes orbiting."

"Good," the Admiral acknowledged. "Though I'd rather have our own planes flying CAP."

"Landing-craft two miles from the beach," squawked the TBS. "Barrage slowing . . . lifting."

"Maybe we're bluffing them out." Beakley allowed himself a thin smile.

"Twelve planes detached from Nationalist CAP," the air-defense officer reported. "Making southwest toward Swatow."

"Tell those idiots to get back here," the Admiral snapped.

"No contact, Sir," the air-defense officer reported after three minutes. "They don't acknowledge our signals."

"The little bastards are looking for trouble," the chief-of-staff said nervously. "They know damned well they're supposed to be overhead."

"I have an unidentified flight on my radar," the air-defense officer reported. "Twenty-two . . . twenty-four . . . thirty-two unidentified aircraft. Their course is northeast, estimated speed four hundred and fifty knots, range one hundred and sixty miles. They're on an interception course. ETA twenty minutes."

"Tell *Midway* to fly off two fighter squadrons. They're to orbit over the Pescadores. Bombers to load weaponry and start engines."

Just two hundred and twenty miles away, the 50,000-ton aircraft-carrier *Midway* was gilded by the morning sunlight reflected from the cliffs of Taiwan's east coast. The carrier's steam-catapults hammered, hurling three jet-fighters into the air each minute. Twenty-four silver jets streaked across the mountains of Taiwan toward their rendezvous over the Pescadore Islets, eighty-five miles east of Quemoy. They could be overhead in nine minutes if the Admiral ordered them to engage the Communists' People's Air Force. Their jet-engines whining, the heavier bombers straddled the flight-deck elevators that lifted light nuclear bombs from the Special Weapons Room deep in *Midway*'s hold.

"Nationalist CAP engaging unidentified aircraft," the air-defense officer reported flat-voiced. "They're drawing the bandits toward our position, veering off and trailing their coats."

"Goddamnit," the chief-of-staff exploded. "They want . . . they really want an incident."

"Prepare to launch bombers," Beakley ordered. "Our fighters to orbit ten miles east of our position."

"Firing off beach intensifying again," the TBS said tinnily. "Ranging toward the destroyers."

Beakley stared through his binoculars at the sandy splotch of Quemoy, which was obscured by waterspouts. The angular landing craft tossed in the billows. The escort destroyers paced the invisible barrier of the three-mile limit, their guns elevated to hurl shells over Quemoy at the Communist batteries.

"Nationalist CAP returning," the air-defense officer reported. "They've knocked down four bandits. The rest are still approaching."

"Bring our fighters to five miles," Beakley snapped.

"Enemy artillery fire slackening," the TBS squawked. "Landing craft approaching the beach."

"Unidentified aircraft veering away," the air-defense officer reported.

"First landing-craft beaching now," the TBS rattled.

"We've faced them down," Beakley exulted, displaying emotion for the first time. "It's all over."

"Second landing-craft on the beach," the tinny voice of the TBS said.

"Unidentified flight going off my screen," the air-defense officer reported.

The chief-of-staff lifted his gold-encrusted cap from his bald head and mopped his red forehad with a blue handkerchief. A messenger shouldered deferentially through the throng of officers. He gave his clipboard to the Admiral, who flipped through the flimsies and handed the board to Miller without comment.

PRIORITY COMSEVFLEET PERSONAL. [MILLER READ.] TASS REPORTS SOVIET PREMIER KHRUSHCHEV SAID IN MOSCOW SOVIET UNION WOULD COME TO THE AID OF PEOPLE'S REPUBLIC OF CHINA UNDER TREATY OF MUTUAL DEFENSE IF REPEAT IF CHINA WERE VICTIM OF AGGRESSION REPEAT AGGRESSION. ITEM ENDS GENERALISSIMO CHIANG KAI-SHEK AGREED IN PRINCIPLE WITH SECSTATE DULLES HE WOULD MAKE SOON PUBLIC STATEMENT RENOUNCING USE OF FORCE TO RETAKE MAINLAND. MESSAGE ENDS.

"The second item's confidential, Dewey," the Admiral admonished. "But both look good. We didn't fire a shot, but Khrushchev's walking away from this mess— and the Gimo's finally giving us the pledge we wanted."

"Would you have used the bomb if they attacked us?" Miller asked.

"You know, Dewey," the Admiral replied deliberately, "I don't really know. But the decision was mine."

Careless of Navy regulations, Dewey Miller lifted a silver flask of cognac to his lips. He had, he knew, almost seen the beginning of World War III. Anything could have happened if the Communist warplanes had not withdrawn after Peking was informed that Moscow would not support its assault on Quemoy. However, Chairman Mao Tse-tung had been deprived of the general war he said he wanted, while his ignominious disengagement would do him no good at home.

The possible long-range consequences of that morning's work were intriguing. It could prove an epochal turning point. Washington had shackled the hands of the Nationalist Chinese and Moscow the Communist Chinese in order to maintain the precarious balance of world peace. Relations between Washington and Moscow could, therefore, improve markedly.

Moreover, Peking would reappraise its own strategy after Nikita Khrushchev's humiliating public repudiation of his commitments to Chairman Mao. American firmness had been demonstrated by the Seventh Fleet's escorting the Nationalist landing-craft, while American restraint would be demonstrated by compelling the Generalissimo to publicly renounce use of force against the mainland. Peking had, in turn, receded from direct confrontation with the United States by lifting its artillery barrage and withdrawing its warplanes. That morning's events could in time lead to reconciliation between the People's Republic of China and the United States of America, which had been vituperatively hostile to each other since the Korean War. But that time was still far distant.

Although he felt the issue had been decided, Dewey Miller's editors instructed him to remain on Taiwan while Peking staged a dramatic performance to save face. The Liberation Army bombarded Quemoy for several weeks, dueling with the resupplied Nationalist artillery. But the ammunition laboriously stockpiled for the Fukien Coastal Command's mixed batteries of captured American and purchased Soviet guns were insufficient for a prolonged siege, even a mock siege. On October 25, 1958, Peking acknowledged the stalemate by announcing that Quemoy would thenceforth be shelled on alternate days in order "to preserve the lives of our oppressed compatriots and to permit the farmers to finish harvesting their crops." Despite their resentment at having been forced to renounce the reconquest of the mainland by force, the Nationalists rejoiced at having turned back the gravest Communist threat since 1949. American officers and diplomats oscillated between relief and bewilderment at the Communists' half-about-turn and finally concluded that they just could not understand the Oriental Mind. Dewey Miller hooted in derision at his countrymen's failure to comprehend the obvious—and wondered if he were losing contact with the Occidental Mind.

In Peking, Deputy Chairman Liu Shao-chi, Premier Chou En-lai, and Defense Minister Peng Teh-huai turned their urgent attention from Quemoy to a nation in turmoil. Chairman Mao's sycophants demanded the Defense Minister's head in retribution for his failure to take Quemoy, while the Premier's practical administrators contended that the Chairman must acknowledge the blatant failure of the Great Leap Forward and the Great People's Communes. The opposing factions were united only in their wrath against the Soviet Union, but neither wanted a public quarrel with Moscow—just yet. Both factions were obsessed with passive resistance in almost every Commune and with violent resistance that verged upon revolt in many Communes.

Wary of challenging the Chairman directly, the three most powerful men in China prepared for the unavoidable confrontation with the assistance of men who, like James Sekloong, were bound to them by personal loyalty. On the basis of his confidential agents' information, James drew an ominous conclusion for Chou En-lai's guidance. The Communist regime was in acute danger because the Chairman had exhausted the people's faith. An unbridgeable gulf yawned between his visions and the reality his policies had created. The Chinese people were laughing at the government that had so spectacularly failed to attain either its internal or its external goals. Ridicule was breaking the Communists' power.

The Premier and Comrade Shao-chi pleaded with the Chairman to halt the rush to disaster. To their remonstrances Mao Tse-tung replied: "Man is a productive animal. He must produce!"

"Man is also a consuming animal," Chou En-lai later observed to James Sekloong. "If the people don't eat, they won't work."

"We *must* move soon." James's advice reflected the Defense Minister's near despair. "Or we won't be able to move at all."

"Not just yet," the Premier cautioned. "But soon, very soon."

The fearful reality of enfeebled adults, exhausted children, rebellious cadres, mutinous troops, and wasted resources finally prevailed over Mao Tse-tung's fantasies. Early in December 1958, the Communist Party's Central Committee met to weigh the dire reports submitted by the Army's Investigation Teams and by emergency conferences of local officials. The triumvirate finally prevailed, and the Central Committee ordered a halt to the quest after the illusory ideal society.

Under intense pressure, Mao Tse-tung resigned as Chairman of the People's Republic. Telephone lines and radio circuits crackled across the great breadth of China to carry the news to local Party Bureaux. Stunned senior cadres mechanically replaced handsets and haltingly informed their subordinates that Chairman Mao would "thenceforth devote himself to theoretical researches." The era of the Chairman's absolute power had ended abruptly.

Like all Hong Kong, the Sekloongs looked forward to a period of relaxation when on February 22, 1959, the New Year's Festival saw out the Year of the Dog. Shaken by a new influx of refugees fleeing the Great Leap Forward, the Colony had been tensely apprehensive. Hong Kong's people had feared for their kindred in China. The authorities had feared the Communists would reinforce their campaign against Quemoy by intensifying pressure on Hong Kong. Though the imagined threat had dissipated by late February, the Colony was still nervous. Tales told by refugees and complaints in letters from the mainland revealed aspects of the People's Republic even the most ardent Nationalist adherents had not previously discerned—and the state of China governed Hong Kong's fate.

"At least there's nothing they can do for an encore, no new lunacy those nuts in Peking can dream up," Albert Sekloong remarked breezily to his grandmother. "They've shot their bolt."

Lady Mary was reluctant to agree. She feared that the illimitable ingenuity of the Chinese leaders, exacerbated by their insatiable passion for intrigue, would impel them to even greater and more destructive fantasies. She was, however, much more concerned with a more immediate and more personal matter. With heavy-footed indirection, Albert had indicated that his friendship with Kazuko Matsuyama, the daughter of the

745

chairman of the Mitsubishi Bank, was no casual flirtation. Lady Mary was too wise to oppose the match as she had vainly opposed Charlotte's marriage to Manfei Way in another age. She was, nonetheless, deeply troubled by the prospect of Albert's marrying not merely a Japanese, but a daughter of the Mitsubishi empire that had allied itself with the Wheatleys before the Great War in the Pacific.

She simply could not, she reflected, reconcile herself to such an un-Chinese match. Startled by her own thoughts, Lady Mary laughed aloud. Only ten years earlier, it would have been inconceivable that she should think in such terms. But, she realized that through the years she had almost imperceptibly come to equate herself with the Chinese. She remembered again the words of the former soldier who had exhorted the angry mob to spare Sarah and her in 1951: "They are not foreigners. They are Sekloongs. They are *our* people."

Lady Mary knew she could not prevent the match. Perhaps Sarah could divert her son Albert, as his grandmother could not. Although she never talked about her humiliation by Japanese soldiers, Sarah hated their nation, refusing even to visit Japan.

But, if the marriage could not be prevented, it must be accepted. Concluding realistically that she could not risk a breach with Albert, Lady Mary resolved to make him Chairman of J. Sekloong and Sons as a wedding present—whomever he married. She would content herself with the title of Honorary Chairman, and she would retain only vestigial power. She was already planning the festivities that would celebrate her eightieth birthday the following year—if she lived that long.

"So there's nothing to fear," Albert was saying. "They've really shot their bolt. Only encore I can think of would be for old Mao to proclaim himself Emperor, and that's not very likely. They'll settle down. And we can get on with business."

"Albert, my lad," Lady Mary replied. "Don't ever underestimate the ability of the Chinese to make problems for themselves—or for others. They've shown again that they can't rule themselves. An encore, an even more spectacular mess? I don't think so, not really. But I do wonder."

Part Eight

Albert and the Red Guards

October 24, 1965–September 26, 1967

October 24, 1965–March 6, 1966

THE Boeing 707 with the blue-and-white globe of Pan-American Airways shining on its tail swept low over dingy Mongkok. The jet-engines' raucous whine rattled the grimy windows of cock-loft sweatshops and egg-crate tenements only two hundred feet beneath the extended landing-gear.

Neither the pale women assembling artificial flowers and cheap transistor radios nor the men tending cutting machines and drill presses raised their heads when the buildings trembled. They were inured to the peril of airlines landing over the world's most densely populated square mile. That constantly repeated shock was just one of the barely endurable strains Hong Kong's drive to transform itself from an entrepôt for others' products into a light manufacturing center imposed on frail human organisms. They worked their twelve-hour days and they slept in fetid cubicles amid unceasing clamor, never out of sight or hearing of at least twenty other persons.

The proprietors of the textile mills, plastic plants, clothing factories, and machine shops were comfortably isolated in their villas on Hong Kong Island or the New Territories. Their balance sheets did not reckon the human cost of their profits. A high birthrate, supplemented by the flow of refugees from China, provided cheap, intelligent labor in apparently inexhaustible profusion. The men, women, and adolescents who toiled in the Colony's workshops could not count the cost in shattered nerves, tuberculous lungs, rickety bones, or chronic exhaustion. Those traumas of the body and the spirit were the price of their survival.

The silver airliner settled like a weary stork on the runway that jutted into Kowloon Bay. The air in the first-class compartment was stale after the four-hour flight from Tokyo, and the stewardesses slumped in their seats, yearning for hot baths before an evening of flirtation at Gaddi's in the Peninsula Hotel. A pair of American businessmen rubbed their stubble-bristled chins and stretched muscles cramped by the nineteen-hour flight from San Francisco. Apparently untouched by fatigue, the two women in seats 1A and 1B peered out the oval window as the 707 taxied into the gathering twilight of October 24, 1965.

Lady Mary Sekloong was, she said, too old at eighty-five to be tired, even after a six-month trip around the world to bid farewell to her widely dispersed family and friends. Opal, her traveling companion, was incapable of fatigue, since at forty-one the vital juices flowed undiminished in her ample body. Only concern for Lady Mary had marred her childlike pleasure in the long voyage of discovery. She was distressed because the older woman would make no concession to either her age or her frailty.

"Hong Kong's utterly different, Opal." Lady Mary's high voice quavered slightly. "I wish I could show you how it was when I first arrived sixty-five years ago. It's a new world now, all the old buildings gone. The Hilton, the Mandarin, Prince's Building, all concrete towers instead of funny, homely, square little buildings with gingerbread cornices and columns."

"And there, something else new." Opal pointed. "Albert's new toy, one of his airplanes."

The 707 halted beside a Lockheed Electra. Above the gold-and-blue stripe on its fuselage the legend *Hong Kong Airlines* was scrolled, while the golden winged dragon reared against a royal-blue shield on its rounded tail.

The front doors of the Rolls-Royce Silver Shadow that drew up beside the 707's boarding ramp displayed the same emblem. Sarah Haleevie Sekloong and her daughter-in-law Kazuko Matsuyama Sekloong waited in the Rolls for the Immigration Officer to clear Lady Mary and Opal. The four women met in a flurry of perfumed kisses and joyful exclamations.

"That was very naughty of you, Sarah," Lady Mary

laughed. "Snatching us off the airplane, instead of letting us go through the normal arrival routine. Willie Evans *will* be annoyed."

"Our terrible-tempered Director of Immigration *is* very annoyed." Sarah smiled with light malice. "He snorted about special privileges, flouting regulations, and so on for half an hour. But his instructions came from Government House."

"Are you very tired, Grandmother?" Kazuko's speech showed no trace of Japanese sibilance. Her mid-Pacific accent bore the British imprint of the Convent of the Sacred Heart in Tokyo and the special American imprint of Radcliffe.

"No, my dear. Not at all. I can't waste the little time I have left being tired. But a glass of champagne will perk me up when we get home."

Kazuko opened a whorled-walnut panel to reveal a miniature refrigerator. Her mouth curved in the complacent pussycat smile of a Saito print, and her small, capable hands stripped the foil from a bottle of Taittinger *blanc de blancs*. A Pucci swirled with a serpentine print in bold primary colors sheathed Kazuko's slender body under her blond mink, and her finely molded ankles were handsomely set off by alligator pumps. An expensively nurtured, late-twentieth-century female, she was the antithesis of the stereotypical dumpy Japanese woman. Kazuko's natural charm and her obvious deep affection for Albert had reconciled both her mother-in-law, Sarah, and Lady Mary to the match they had originally resisted.

"From Albert," Kazuko said. "He apologizes, but he really couldn't get away."

"To your safe return!" As Sarah lifted her tulip glass, her simply coiffed white hair contrasted with her dark eyes and the black sheen of her sable cape. "We've all missed you terribly!"

"Tell me all the news," Lady Mary demanded.

"We've been very quiet, Mother," Sarah replied. "Except for my trip to Israel. I wrote you about that. My Research Institute in Jerusalem is doing exciting

753

work on cancer. I never, never tell the rabbis that I'm sponsoring research in swine genetics here. Trying to produce a super-pig—what a project for a good Jewish girl!"

"And, Kazuko, have you any news?" Lady Mary candidly scrutinized her granddaughter-in-law's slender figure.

"We're rather quiet, too," Kazuko smiled. "Business keeps Albert so busy. And, I'm afraid, the answer to your question is no. No baby coming as yet."

"Doesn't bother me, my dear," Lady Mary said. "I'm not desperately anxious for more great-grandchildren. Too much breeding already—in the family and the entire world."

"Actually," Kazuko confessed, "I've been working with the Family Planning Association. Albert's all for it. Father Romanio never says a word, just gives me that sweet, enigmatic Italian smile, like a male Mona Lisa."

"It was different in my day," Lady Mary recalled. "But so many things were utterly different. It's easier for the women now, but, I think, harder for the men."

"You've never told us how things were about *that* in your youth," Kazuko asked brashly. "What was it like?"

"Children, yes. We need children, but don't let him make you a brood-mare. Why, I remember . . . but that's another story." Lady Mary abruptly veered from the subject in deference to Charles's memory. "Do you know it took us only twenty-two hours to London? I remember just ten or eleven years ago it took me sixty-two hours—and fifty days back in 1900."

"Tell them about the trip, Lady Mary," Opal suggested. "We saw everyone, the Rothschilds and the Sassoons, your brother's grandchildren and Sarah's Henry . . . Major Sir Henry, very handsome. Gwinnie's Blanche and George. Even that terrible son of George's, Chappie Parker. Just everyone."

"Yes, everyone," Mary followed Opal's lead. "Henry's Jonathan and little Mary are terribly country, to the manor born. Only fifteen and fourteen, but they have the self-assurance of centuries of unchallenged privilege. You'd never think . . ."

Mary paused. She did not wish to tarnish the glow of her homecoming by so soon confiding her concern for her great-grandchildren to the three women who were closest to her.

"Look there." She indicated the working-class tenements of Kowloon. "I see the National Day flags are still up. Funny, isn't it? The poor always put out many more Nationalist suns than Communist stars, while the banks and big shops fly so many more red flags. But why aren't the cranes on those half-completed blocks working? Have they stopped building?"

"We wrote you about the bank failures," Sarah recalled. "Five Chinese-owned banks went under, and the construction industry seized up for lack of funds. However, it's picking up again slowly. But you were going to say something about the family, weren't you?"

"Yes, Sarah, I was," Lady Mary replied reluctantly. "I shall if you wish. I'm troubled. They're all so complacent. The entire world's changing, but the grandchildren and their children are too secure, smug and untroubled. It's true, you know. Wealth, particularly great wealth, makes people different. Perhaps you and Kazuko don't really know what I'm talking about. You've always enjoyed great privilege. But Opal and I, we know."

"Different how, Grandmother?" Kazuko prompted.

"We're isolated from the reality most people know. The family, all of us are sheltered from the uncertainties of life. We simply don't know how the other ninety-nine percent of humanity lives and feels. It makes me afraid."

"Afraid?" Sarah was still fascinated by Lady Mary's speculative intellect. "Why afraid?"

"We Sekloongs are vulnerable only to the ills of the flesh, to corruption of the spirit, and to great political storms. But we're able to buy the best medical care, and we can even influence political developments in our favor. We cannot, however, buy spiritual immunity. I smell degeneration, and I'm afraid for the family."

The Rolls-Royce purred onto the vehicular ferry to Hong Kong Island, which was already glowing with a hundred thousand lights in the dusk. Ignoring the curious stares of other passengers, Lady Mary sought the precise words to convey her misgivings.

"We live above humanity, as aloof as tribal deities. It's not like the bitter struggles, the triumphs and disasters the Old Gentleman knew when he created this realm for us. Or even the hopes and disappointments Charles and I knew."

The fiction—or at least half-fiction—was firmly embedded in her mind. She refused to remember that Charles had, for most of his life, contributed appreciably less than she herself to rearing the House of Sekloong.

"The grandchildren can't understand, the great-grandchildren can't even try to understand that it wasn't always so. Today the Sekloongs' troubles are troubles we make for ourselves, the sins of the wayward spirit. We reach too far. We demand too much. In our boredom we seek thrills in artificial danger or silly . . . so-called love affairs."

Lady Mary realized that she had not fully communicated her incipient distress. She waved at the panorama of the Island shimmering in the gray-velvet twilight.

"This is *our* kingdom, this Hong Kong, the center of our power. Even the shape of the land has changed radically, but we reign secure from Sekloong Manor. Look at St. George's Building. Fifteen years ago, it was an old, squat, crenellated block with the dark offices of J. Sekloong and Sons spreading through it like a mole's burrow. Now Albert sits on the nineteenth floor of a glass-and-steel tower and thinks he can control or command everything below him. I wonder if he ever notices the big red-neon characters on the Bank of China: *Hail the Invincible Thought of Mao Tse-tung!*"

Albert Sekloong had not come to the airport because

756

he wanted to avoid the cloyingly scented female reunion and, he acknowledged to himself, because he
wanted to put off seeing his grandmother. Besides, several problems he could neither delegate nor postpone
demanded his attention. His diverse enterprises were
reviving after the shock to the Colony's commercial life
inflicted by the bank failures. But some of his affairs
were still tricky, "temporarily fluid," he conceded in
American business jargon. He had, therefore, stocked
the Rolls with champagne and promised "hopefully" to
leave the office early. That hope was fading, for things
were breaking fast. At 6:00 P.M. in Hong Kong, it was
only 10:00 in the morning in London, while New York
would not begin to stir for another four or five hours.
But one matter he could deal with immediately.

He levered a toggle switch on the communications
center that squatted robotlike beside his desk, flashing
red, green, blue, and yellow lights.

"Try Jiro Matsuyama again. If he's not at his office,
he'll be in his car or at home. And no calls while I'm
waiting."

Albert closed his eyes and sought to clear his mind
with the Zen meditation technique his brother-in-law
had taught him. But "perfectly blank lucidity" eluded
him. He had watched his grandmother's airplane land
from his aerie seventeen stories above the Hong Kong
branch of the Bank of America, the world's largest financial institution. He would be glad to see her, though
he devoutly hoped she would wait a few days before
she began probing. He had, after all, dutifully sent her
reports every two weeks. His affairs were, just temporarily of course, too tangled to describe concisely, and
he dreaded the catechizing to which the old lady might
subject him.

The mahogany connecting door from his corner suite
was a constant reminder that he did not wholly control
the Sekloong empire. The adjoining room was a replica
of Sir Jonathan's office in the original St. George's
Building, even to the twin scrolls on the wall. The black
pedestal telephone still stood on the ebony desk. The

single divergence from the old photographs was the red rose, changed every day, in a small crystal bud vase.

Albert had complained during the uninhibited discussions Lady Mary enjoyed that preserving the Old Gentleman's office was gross sentimentality, made worse by the obtrusive rose in the vase that had once lightened her own dingy cubbyhole. She had replied equably that it was the best investment they could make, since it would constantly remind them of how they had begun. But he wanted to look forward, not backward.

Albert's office was self-consciously ultra-modern, an industrial designer's fantasy of stainless steel, lucite, and leather. The brushed-steel communications console sprouted plastic umbilical cords, and a teletype softly chattered reports from all the world's major share, commodity, and money markets. Above the new computer terminal hung a long gold frame that displayed on a blue silk background the article *Time* magazine had devoted to the new image of the Sekloong enterprises three months earlier. Albert abandoned his unsuccessful Zen meditation and massaged his vanity by reading the words for the twenty-second time.

Lithe, powerful Albert Sekloong, 32, slumps relaxed in his $2,000 elephant-hide chair, his feet in $200 loafers hand-crafted in London (He considers Hong Kong's master cobblers "clumsy.") casually propped on his kidney-shaped, hand-rubbed, *tung*-oiled teak desk. His eyes flash, and the full lips in his bronzed face smile disarmingly as he denies that he has materially altered the style of the world's third largest privately owned commercial empire.

But the smart money and the smart moneymen in London's City, New York's Wall Street, and Hong Kong's own Ice House Street say otherwise. The first of his richly complex Chinese-British-Jewish family to be admitted to the exclusive Hong Kong Club, Albert Sekloong has swept through the tradition-webbed offices of J. Sekloong and Sons like a steel-bristled broom. He has transformed the solid, substantial, once opium-based empire long dominated by his 85-year-old grandmother, Lady Mary Sekloong, into a hard-driving,

hypermodern conglomerate. The emblem of the Sekloong dynasty is still the winged dragon chosen by its
founder, half-Chinese Baronet Sir Jonathan Sekloong.
The emblem of Sir Jonathan's ambitious, American-
trained great-grandson might better be a glitteringly
aggressive Intercontinental Ballistic Missile. Albert
Sekloong's impact on his competitors must be measured
in megatons.

His few intimates and his more numerous enemies
agree that competitiveness is the key to his character—
and his operations.

"Albert," says one rival, "is determined to prove
himself to the whole world, but most of all to himself.
He's not content administering an empire worth almost
$1 billion or presiding over the measured expansion he
initiated eight years ago under Lady Mary's guidance.
He's got to pull off at least one major coup a week to
show that he's the equal—or the superior—of Sir
Jonathan himself."

Albert Sekloong has attacked the citadels of commerce like a *condottiere* captain with an electronic
sword. It's not easy to outshine his high-powered family:
Albert is the nephew of Archbishop (and Cardinal-
apparent) Charles Sekloong; the cousin of cinemactress
Comtesse Alaine d'Alivère; and cousin-by-marriage of
Deputy Under Secretary of State Spencer Taylor Smith.
A new element in the mix: Jiro Matsuyama, considered
the brightest *modan ekuzekutibu* (modern executive) in
the even more tradition-encrusted Mitsubishi empire.
Instant rapport welded the Harvard Business School
classmates, and in 1960 Albert married Jiro's then
23-year-old sister Kazuko (Radcliffe '56, Phi Beta
Kappa).

Albert Sekloong remains an enigma. He appears
more comfortable with Asians than with Americans or
Europeans, despite his entrée to the highest circles in
the West. Some suggest that Albert (one-fifth Chinese,
one-half Jewish) still remembers real or imagined slights
during his long residence in America under the care of
his Aunt Charlotte (married, fourth time, billionaire
Avram Barakian, the Enigmatic Armenian, 1951).
Such speculation right or wrong, he's shown a predis-
position for doing business with such dubious Asian

partners as the Communist regimes of Peking and Hanoi.

Himself no Communist, but a swashbuckling, capitalist free-booter, Albert has put together a dazzling array of new ventures under his own company, Albert Sekloong Associates, Ltd., called Ah Sek along Ice House Street. For the first time, a Sekloong company went public two months ago when Ah Sek offered its shares on the Hong Kong, London, and New York Stock Markets. All were snatched up at the issue price of $15. They're now selling at $45.

A partial list of the new Sekloong ventures: Dragon Plastics and Electronics with a range of products from helmet liners to computer components; 64 percent of Hong Kong Airways, a scrappy feeder line for the Far East and Southeast Asia that's worrying the big carriers by creaming off profitable short-haul and medium-haul business; heavy commitments in grain futures, estimated about $20 million, after successful brokerage of previous Canadian grain sales to Communist China; Borneo South Seas Explorations, which melds Mitsubishi technology with Sekloong connections through the overseas Chinese of Indonesia and has committed an estimated $40 million to leases and prospecting off Borneo; Megalith Housing, which plans mammoth apartment complexes for accommodation-short Hong Kong; China Agencies, a major factor in expanding trade with Peking, while, confirmed report has it, funneling trucks, radios, pharmaceuticals and rubber goods to Hanoi; and Dragon Films, a fledgling of one month, purposes and direction not yet known.

To top it off, Ah Sek recently took options on large quantities of commodities from rubber, tin, and zinc to textiles, steel, and chemicals. One knowledgeable source contends: "Albert thinks a war's coming and remembers the legendary Sekloong killing before the First World War!"

That's just the superstructure. The solid foundation is the old Sekloong holdings in real estate, hotels, shipping, banking, and highly profitable distributorships for mundane necessities ranging from kerosene to sewing-machines. But the superstructure is reaching higher every day. The limits of its growth? Some smart money-men say only the sky.

Though jibes about his unlimited ambition still rankled, rereading the panegyric had done Albert more good than an hour of meditation. He was refreshed, ready to cope with whatever problems his rapid expansion next cast up. If *Time* considered his achievements "breathtaking" and "dazzling," how could he disagree?

The communications center chimed softly, and a green light winked.

"Mr. Sekloong, your wife calling." A secretary's voice spoke from a concealed speaker. "And I have Mr. Matsuyama on the green line."

"Tell her I'll get back to her as soon as I can. Jiro, hello Jiro, where the devil are you? I've been trying to reach you all day."

"In a traffic jam in Roppongi. If the Mercedes weren't fitted with a desk, a dictating machine, and a telephone, I'd lose half my working day."

"Why don't you get a helicopter, one of those two-place Bell jobs?"

"I've thought about it, but it doesn't go with the image. We new *zaibatsu* have to keep a low profile—or catch hell from the press and the unions. I wish we had a nice tight oligarchy that keeps everything under control like Hong Kong."

"You do all right," Albert said dryly. "Japan Incorporated isn't cracking. And I know who runs Japan Incorporated."

"I've told you that's a damned exaggeration. If only you knew how much time I waste placating this one, cajoling that one, and. . . . But you didn't call to discuss the eco-sociology of Japan. What's on your mind?"

"Borneo and oil," Albert replied succinctly. "I don't like the way it smells. After that half-assed Communist coup failed last September, our people've been getting pushed around. Sukarno himself's shaky, can't last as President. Subandrio'll fall with him—and there goes the five million dollars we 'contributed' to the Foreign Minister's 'special fund.' If the generals take over . . ."

". . . we're in the shit," Matsuyama completed the

sentence. "And they're beginning to wrap up all your buddies. My people tell me all Chinese are going to get hit. The students are calling Subandrio *Peking Anjing*, the Peking dog."

"The whole deal could unravel, couldn't it?"

"It's not that bad yet. We can make new connections . . ."

". . . and pay new bribes."

"I'm afraid so. But that's better than letting the whole thing go down the drain. Look, Albert, just keep cool."

"I'm not steaming, not yet. But it's damned bad timing with this Hong Kong slump."

"I thought you were coming out of it."

"We are, but it's slow. Construction's way off, and cash is tight. I've had to move funds . . . some of them yours . . . out of Ah Sek to cover other commitments. All legitimate, of course, but I'm beginning to feel a cold breath on my neck."

"Albert, I'll check on Borneo. But look at it like this. It can't go completely sour. The Indonesians need our technology and the oil income too badly. If worse comes to worst, we'll just have to pull in our horns for a while—wait them out."

"That's a little comfort, Jiro, but not much. And *really* look around. We may need cash in a hurry."

"You don't want me to bullshit you, old buddy, do you? Hand you a lot of optimistic talk that isn't worth a damn? Just keep cool on Borneo. And I *will* look around. But what set you off? The old lady back yet?"

"Today," Albert answered glumly. "She just got back."

"Oh, I get it," Jiro laughed. "Look, don't let her spook you. You're still her blue-eyed boy, and she *is* eighty-five, even if she is sharper than most big operators half her age. The big firm's still solid, isn't it? Nothing wrong with J. Sekloong and Sons?"

"No trouble there," Albert conceded. "I guess I'm just edgy."

"We'll talk again soon. My love to Kazuko. Tell her I want to be an uncle."

"She's not that anxious to be a mother," Albert laughed. "But I'll give her your message. Thanks, Jiro."

The Porsche Targa flicked its canary-yellow tail insouciantly around the curves of the road winding up The Peak. Albert gunned the motor as he downshifted under the winged-dragon arch, and the twin exhaust pipes rumbled throatily. Jiro, who was deliberately unobtrusive in his dark suits and black Mercedes, mocked his tear-drop sports car as "Al's Adolescent Fantasy Machine." But Albert grinned at the jibe.

The two spoke the same language, the hard-boiled, Americanized argot of the new international marketplace, and Albert trusted Jiro as he did no other. Jiro was one of the family, and the two self-consciously emancipated Asians still knew in their bones that only family ties were, ultimately, dependable. But Jiro was not a Sekloong. He was not burdened by the ingrained reverence for the Old Gentleman or the responsibility for the unproductive members of the clan that, Albert felt, hampered his own initiative and restricted his individuality. Radial tires skidding on flying gravel, the Targa stopped before the iron-bound double doors of The Castle.

The closed shutters of the Second Small House cheered Albert by their mute demonstration that Sir Jonathan had not been infallible. Kazuko and he had moved into the First Small House, originally Mary and Charles's, when the three Dowager Empresses chose to live together in The Castle. Together was not quite the right word: Lady Mary, Sarah, and Opal maintained three distinct households in the stone pile that lacked only arrow slits and machicolations to make it a medieval fortress. The Second Small House was, however, tenanted only by an occasional relation spending a few months in Hong Kong. Sir Jonathan, that compulsive builder of monuments to himself, had never imagined a time when too few Sekloongs were permanently resident in Hong Kong to fill all the clan's dwellings.

Albert strode through the circular marble reception hall and bounded up the stairs to the study, where, the Number One Boy told him, the ladies were "taking tea." He brushed his grandmother's crumpled-velvet cheek with his lips, careful not to jar her tulip glass of champagne. He kissed his mother, who was sipping a brandy-and-soda. His hand trailed affectionately across his wife's shoulders. Kazuko alone was actually "taking tea," green tea from a handleless Japanese cup. The old girls liked their nip, but his modern wife preferred the conventional lady's beverage because, she complained, alcohol made her flush bright red.

"At last, Albert," Lady Mary smiled affectionately. "You've been busy, have you?"

"Sorry, Grandma. I just couldn't get away earlier. It must have been easier in the old days. No telephones and Telexes to chain you to your desk."

"Less frenetic, perhaps," Lady Mary replied. "But easier? I think not. However, we didn't make such a great splash in the press."

Here it comes, Albert warned himself. She's back just five minutes, and the inquisition is starting.

"Oh, you mean the *Time* piece. They were going to do it anyway. I thought I'd get a better shake if I cooperated. Besides, publicity's good for business nowadays. The rules've changed."

"I won't debate modern business practices or the sweet lure of publicity with you. I can appreciate its practical value, even if the greatest value is to your own ego." Lady Mary's smile drew the sting from her words. "I'm not happy at public identification with my friend Chou En-lai's erratic regime. However, it *is* China, so there's no help for it. But Hanoi? I *suppose* you know what you're doing."

"I do," he replied. "Besides, *Time* erred, as they say. Our share of the Hanoi trade is practically nonexistent. Mostly it's Mitsubishi."

Albert poured a jigger of Glenlivet over the ice cubes

in his glass. He was surprised and relieved. He had expected Lady Mary to seize upon the hard commercial aspects of his expansion, rather than the political ramifications. She asked only two more questions.

"I take it you haven't touched the foundation, the established operations of J. Sekloong and Sons. Not made any fundamental changes, *Time* to the contrary notwithstanding?"

"No, I haven't, Grandma," he could reply in good conscience.

"And your own new company, though it's not strictly my concern? The shareholders are protected, aren't they?"

"No greater than any commercial risk, and less than many. Of course, there's always an element . . ."

"But no more than normal? Albert Sekloong Associates, Ltd., is still a Sekloong enterprise. Our name won't be smirched?"

"No, I assure you. No monkey business. No risk the shareholders take that I don't. I can show you."

"Fine, Albert. Perhaps we can look at the books another day."

Albert Sekloong raised his glass in a silent toast. He'd forgotten how reasonable the old girl could be when she chose.

In bed that night, he asked Kazuko with elaborate casualness, "Lady Mary seems content with my affairs. Did she cross-question you and Mother?"

"A little, but no more than she did you. I got the impression she's more concerned about our producing another great-grandchild for her."

"Fine," he whispered into the hollow of her throat. "Let's see if we can't oblige her."

His fingers gently peeled back the skirt of her lace nightdress. Albert was the first naturally monogamous Sekloong male; his passions were divided between his delightfully uninhibited wife and his spiraling business affairs. The latter passion, normally greater, was soon submerged in the first.

Albert Sekloong had, to the best of his knowledge, told his grandmother the literal and complete truth. In late October 1965, the Sekloong empire was vigorously producing goods and services, as well as profits. He had taken no greater risks than his competitors in Hong Kong, the twentieth century's last stronghold of commercial buccaneers. He had scrupulously obeyed the minimal regulations of the Colony's laws, and he had adroitly slipped through their numerous loopholes. Recalling Lady Mary's tales of his great-grandfather's adventures, he could sincerely affirm that he had not sailed as close to the wind as had Sir Jonathan when his ships were beginning to bring their rich cargoes into harbor.

"Venture capital" meant just that. Albert had to venture widely to utilize the opportunities offered by an increasingly unsettled Asia—and he fully expected some losses. Some of his ventures might raise eyebrows in the City of London or on Wall Street. But even the more adventurous financiers, merchants, and industrialists of London and New York had always lifted their eyebrows at Hong Kong's daring. His conscience was clear, and his accounts were healthy, though somewhat short of liquid cash because of the constant drain of Borneo South Seas Explorations.

A month later, Albert would have hesitated before assuring Lady Mary that all was well. Two months later, he could not have offered that assurance without perjuring himself.

January 1966 brought a disastrous sequence of apparently unrelated setbacks. Albert could almost smell the sour stench of his own fear when he pored over the files in his showcase office, just as Sir Jonathan had reviewed his dispositions at the blackwood desk that stood in the adjoining office before counterattacking the Wheatleys forty-eight years earlier. Had his upbringing behind the unbreakable walls of Sekloong wealth not imbued him with immense self-confidence, Albert might have panicked. Even so, he wondered if he were becoming paranoid. The assaults from every quarter appeared deliberately orchestrated. Though he had taken no greater risks than were customary in *laissez-faire* Hong Kong, the unparalleled misfortunes threatened to bear him down.

Poor quality control and, perhaps, sabotage at Dragon Plastics and Electronics had resulted in purchasers' rejecting goods worth almost $3 million. The new art of ultra-miniaturization had rendered obsolete an additional $1.2 million worth of transistors and computer components assembled by deft-handed girls peering through microscopes to solder wires one-hundredth of a hair's diameter. Assisted by Jiro Matsuyama, Albert was negotiating for licenses to manufacture printed circuits and micro-sliced quartz chips. But his greatest advantage, cheap and skilled labor, would be sharply reduced by the new automated manufacturing processes, while initial fees and new equipment would cost $5 million.

The alternative was dismaying and, ultimately, not very helpful. He could sell out Dragon's inventory and capital equipment at a heavy discount in order to obtain cash to shore up his other enterprises. However, both his pride and his business sense counseled against that course. The loss would be great, and the receipts would be rapidly dissipated.

His most prized possession, Hong Kong Airways, had been virtually snatched away from him, though he retained his 64 percent interest in the six Lockheed Electras standing idle on the tarmac at Kaitak. Hong Kong Airways was no longer functioning. Glorying in his lone-wolf image, Albert had failed to protect his flanks by making allies in London. He had, therefore, been humiliatingly outmaneuvered. A "routine route reallocation" by Whitehall had cut Hong Kong Airways back to two flights a week to Taipei and a single flight to Bangkok. The old British *hongs* had manipulated the politicians. In collaboration with British Overseas Airways, Derwent's had taken over Albert's routes for their new Sino-British Airlines, which flew chartered BOAC jets flown by BOAC crews. For its future independent operations, Sino-British had hired Albert's unemployed air crews and, in a deliberate gesture of contempt, had offered $150,000 for each of the six Electras. He was still stubbornly rejecting that derisory offer.

Borneo South Seas' oil ventures were at a standstill. The right-wing generals who were consolidating their control of Indonesia had suspended all drilling "for technical reasons," imposed confiscatory taxes on his overseas Chinese associates—and were threatening outright expropriation. Nonetheless, the payroll and maintenance costs had to be met, as did contracted fees to the Indonesian Government. The alternative was loss of his entire investment.

Political upheavals had also struck at his China trade by virtually paralyzing all Peking's foreign commerce. No official of a state-trading corporation dared approve a sale or place a firm order for fear that he might subsequently be pilloried for sabotaging the revolution by trading with the "capitalist-imperialists." Albert was, nonetheless, bound to pick up $18 million in wheat futures—and pay hard cash—in two months' time. Besides, he was overcommitted to an inventory of general goods for the China market. Hanoi would gladly have taken his commodities at bargain prices, but the North Vietnamese lacked cash. Moreover, a mild-mannered commercial attaché from the American Consulate-General had warned Albert that he would be blacklisted if he did not withdraw entirely from the Hanoi trade. He could not sacrifice his relations with American firms for the chimera of a North Vietnamese market. Worse, Mitsubishi and the other *zaibatsu* had virtually monopolized that market. The U.S. Government, anxious to avoid offending Tokyo, turned a judiciously blind eye to those transactions through dummy corporations.

Washington was already locked into a massive military commitment to the defense of South Vietnam. The Administration's economists, seeing further than the generals, had preempted a rise in the prices of raw materials like the zinc, rubber, and tin Albert had bought

768

on the futures market by releasing measured quantities from their own vast stockpiles. If the war lasted long enough, he might possibly recoup. But he would in three months' time be forced to take delivery, warehouse, and pay for large quantities of raw materials for which he could find no market. He had never planned to touch what the trade called "physical commodities," but to sell his paper options on a rising market.

The single hopeful area was Megalith Housing. Swollen with refugees and the staffs of foreign firms, Hong Kong badly needed more dwellings. But the market was sluggish, construction costs were rising, and money was still tight. The financial community had not recovered from the bank failures, and sensible financiers were waiting to see how the American involvement in Vietnam developed. Albert, nonetheless, rejected offers to sell his Megalith stock at a reasonable profit, since he was confident that the housing market would rebound.

The extraordinary reverses had shaken his self-confidence and almost pushed Albert Sekloong Associates, Ltd. to the wall. The day in late February 1966 when Ah Sek shares dropped to $4.55 was his worst, for he began to believe in the conspiracy he had earlier dismissed as a fantasy. But he forced himself to examine his position dispassionately. Many of his difficulties stemmed from unanticipated technological and political changes. He knew that he had not given due attention to those vital factors because they seemed a dull diversion from his fast-moving commercial operations. He had, he realized, built a towering corporate structure, as *Time* had noted with admiration. Though constructed in accordance with normal Hong Kong business practices, that structure was flimsy. He had used loans, mortgages, share sales, and pledges to raise new funds for each successive venture. As a result, he was chronically short of cash, though his actual assets had expanded in quantity and increased in value. His splendid edifice was, therefore, extremely vulnerable to shifts in the winds.

Besides, he had angered the Hong Kong trading community by his determination to go it alone. If his competitors had in truth united to attack him, they had been provoked by his obvious disregard for the complex Sino-British network that dominated the Colony through its subtle exchange of favors.

Yet his single gesture to that network was also causing him acute concern. The stock market's evaluation of Ah Sek shares accurately reflected its current cash position, if not its prospects. By a strict accounting, Albert Sekloong Associates, Ltd. was on the verge of bankruptcy. Most of the receipts from the stock sold to the public had gone to shore up Dragon Plastics and to maintain Borneo Explorations.

How, Albert wondered, could he explain to an angry meeting of shareholders in mid-March why a company that could not pay its first scheduled dividend had disbursed $1.2 million to its Board of Directors for fees, entertainment, club bills, travel, chauffeured automobiles, luxury housing, and "miscellaneous expenses"? He had thought to insure the good will of a predominantly British Board seeded with influential Chinese. Such lavish rewards were acceptable on the part of a high-profit company. They were intolerable in a new firm whose assets had dwindled alarmingly. The payments were legal, but unquestionably irregular.

At the beginning of March 1966, Albert Sekloong sat in his glittering office and contemplated the collapse of all his hopes. If Ah Sek were forced into bankruptcy, it would take his entire personal fortune with it. He would retain only the small, inviolable trust fund Sir Jonathan had provided. He would be destroyed as a businessman and maimed emotionally, since the core of his self-esteem was his confidence in his commercial acumen. Moreover, the family would empty the vials of its wrath on the head of the man who had lost so much money.

Albert slumped in his elephant-hide chair and gazed at the hills of Kowloon cast into dark relief by the violet rays of the twilight sun retreating into China. The red-and-green navigation lights of airliners flashed into the incandescent beams of landing lights as the jets took off and landed on the long concrete runway bisecting Kowloon Bay. Nathan Road in Tsimshatsui was a pyrotechnical extravaganza of winking neon signs with red-and-white streams of automobile lights flowing between them. From Tsimshatsui to Kaitak, yellow lights flickered in a thousand factories and ten thousand tenements. He lifted his hand in a rueful salute to the realm that had, only six months earlier, seemed his undisputed kingdom.

Jiro Matsuyama had done his best, but Jiro could raise no more than $2.5 million, a ludicrous sum in view of Albert's needs. Jiro was too tightly constrained by the silk-covered steel-cable conventions of Japanese business to offer more than that pittance and his sympathy. Albert could not go to the Hong Kong banks without confessing that, as their managers suspected, he was being driven onto the rocks. He could not obtain refinancing in London or New York unless he pledged the full resources of J. Sekloong and Sons, and he was debarred from that desperate step both legally and morally. The company was not his, but the family's. He could not offer it as collateral without the family's approval.

He reluctantly flicked a switch and spoke to his harried secretary.

"Get me Avram Barakian," he directed. "His yacht's somewhere between the Persian Gulf and Bombay."

He swiveled his chair to face the wall adorned with the framed article from *Time* and waited. Twice his hand crept toward the switch to countermand his instructions, and twice it fell inertly to his side. The Enigmatic Armenian was his last hope, but he hated to appeal to his Aunt Charlotte's husband. Although he could be as generous in personal matters as a latter-day Maecenas when the whim took him, the super-tycoon was habitually tight-fisted in business dealings. Albert still remembered the Christmas vacation during which he had polished Avram Barakian's Bentley and Cadillac twice each day. At sixteen, that was the only way he could repay "Uncle Avram" for the damages inflicted by his own Chevrolet convertible in a drunken accident he wanted neither his Aunt Charlotte nor his mother to know about. Albert dreaded pleading with Barakian, but he had no choice.

The chimes of the communications center sounded, and his secretary said: "On line 5, Mr. Sekloong. He's coming to the phone."

"Hello, Uncle Avram, how are you?" His lips twisted in a forced smile, which he hoped would infuse his voice with relaxed bonhommie.

Forty-eight minutes later Albert replaced the handset with the gingerly relief of a zoo-keeper returning a coral snake to its cage. After spending more than three-quarters of an hour and $800, he was totally exhausted, prickly with self-loathing, cringing in humiliation—and not a penny better off. He felt soiled and battered. He needed a triple whiskey and a steaming shower.

Avram Barakian had cross-examined him with voluble curiosity. Avram Barakian had expressed willingness to assist his nephew-by-marriage "to the limit of my resources." He had hedged his generosity with only one condition: effective control of both Albert Sekloong Associates, Ltd., and J. Sekloong and Sons. When Albert protested that he could not bind J. Sekloong, Avram Barakian had explained in detail how he could do so "completely within the law." Realizing that the Armenian had been plotting that takeover strategy while awaiting his appeal, Albert had forced himself to end the conversation casually: "I'll think about it, Uncle Avram, and get back to you. Give my love to Aunt Charlotte."

When the direct line from The Castle flashed its silent summons, he lifted the handset resignedly. He had already been steeling himself to appeal to the court of last resort, his grandmother.

"Albert, it's time we had a serious talk." Lady Mary's high voice was commanding. "I'd like you to come and see me alone after dinner, say nine-thirty.

And, Albert, please don't have more than two drinks."

His grandmother's Victorian courtesy was even more humiliating than Avram Barakian's smooth rapaciousness.

For the first time in his life, Albert Sekloong found his formidable grandmother indecisive. Lady Mary hesitated to broach the subject she had summoned him to discuss. For the first time, he fully apprehended the great age of the frail figure in the quilted, red-silk robe. She was almost eighty-six. Her skin was flaccid over her cheekbones; her full mouth was bloodless; and her violet eyes were dim. Even the jade butterfly in her hair drooped dispiritedly. For the first time, he was primarily aware of his responsibility to the House of Sekloong, rather than his determined effort to create a legend surpassing that of Sir Jonathan.

Lady Mary was an old woman in need of reassurance.

"Give me a small glass of champagne, my dear," she said. "And pour yourself a whiskey. A small one, if you will."

"No, thank you." His answer surprised even himself. "I'd better not."

Her eyes lifted in slow appraisal and shone again.

"You don't want a drink?" she asked.

"I do, but I'd better not. It's time I grew up."

"Yes, it *is* high time. By the way, you didn't tell me Kazuko was pregnant."

"She wanted to tell you herself. And I've been obsessed with . . . with other things."

"Poor Albert!" Lady Mary's spirit flared. "All that and impending fatherhood too. You've truly played the fool, haven't you?"

"All the way, the whole hog."

"So I gather." She gestured toward the sheaf of telegrams on the coffee table. "The entire family's screaming in anguish."

"They might have spared *you* their complaints."

"They couldn't very well, could they? They all say you haven't answered repeated inquiries."

"That's not completely true," he protested defensively. "I've talked with some. I had Alaine, Mademoiselle la Comtesse, on the phone for half an hour today. She was raging. Not only her income, her *rightful* income reduced, but no backing for her new film, either."

"She's quite astigmatic where her own interests are concerned, isn't she? Her *rightful* income is an allowance I chose to make her. She has no legal claim. What is the new film?"

"Much like the others." Albert squirmed. "A little sex and nudity, a sprinkling of politics. The usual."

"Also anti-American and anti-capitalist, as usual?"

"Well, Grandma, about the same. You remember the one on Dienbienphu? The heroic French nurse who was captured and then saw the light."

"Yes," Lady Mary said dryly. "She ended in Algeria helping the National Liberation Front, and the French secret service tortured her. She looked fetching squirming half-naked. I know I'm old-fashioned, but for a granddaughter of mine to . . ."

"It made money." Albert was defensively casual. "And the next one was a blockbuster. The poor French model taken up by a multimillionaire megalomaniacal American publisher, exploited and cast aside."

"And this one?"

"It's called *Love and Death in Saigon*. Alaine plays a half-Vietnamese girl who is corrupted by the Americans. But she turns against the Americans and redeems herself."

"Very pretty!" Lady Mary's voice was contemptuous. "*Someone* will certainly provide the money to complete it, perhaps the KGB. And it'll be a triumph. The simple-minded love anti-Americanism."

"It sells, Grandma," Albert protested, wondering why he'd felt the old lady was losing her grip.

"It sells all right. Lenin said something apropos: 'When the time comes for the Bolsheviks to hang the bourgeoisie, the bourgeoisie will sell their executioners the rope.' Why are we determined to destroy ourselves?"

"It's the vogue, Grandma. Perhaps it'll pass."

"Please God!" Coldly vehement, she picked up the telegrams. "And all the others are complaining about your cutting their dividends. Your Uncle Thomas, your brother Henry, your cousins George and Blanche, the whole lot boiling. Only your Uncle James hasn't added his voice. And your Uncle Charles, of course. He cabled he was praying for you and asked if we needed him here."

"I don't see how he could help. I need cash, not prayers."

"Don't underestimate prayer. You obviously need prayer too. It *is* interesting. The only ones not whining like sick puppy-dogs are James and Charles—the commissar and the priest. And, of course, your Aunt Charlotte, who can't tell six pence from six guineas."

"I've spoken to Barakian," Albert admitted. "Nothing there. Nothing at all. Oh, he offered unlimited help, all right. In exchange for total control, that is."

"What did you expect? How do you feel, by the way?"

"Like a fool!" Albert was startled into bitter candor by Lady Mary's abrupt question. "A damned adolescent fool!"

"That's a good sign." She contemptuously dropped the telegrams onto the table. "As for this lot, they'll just have to manage, make do with last year's Lincolns and Rollses."

"And what am *I* to do?" Albert reverted to his life-long conviction that she would always find a solution.

"What are *we* to do, now that you've finally confided in me, as you should in the first place."

"I'm sorry, but I couldn't till now. I did think of foreclosing Albert Sekloong Associates . . ."

"Bankruptcy, you mean?"

"I suppose so. I'd be letting my own shares go down

the drain. Potentially ten million dollars. But at least I'd be off the hook. It is a limited company."

"You'll do as you think best." Her tone was severe. "I have no financial interest in Ah Sek, but I would advise most strongly against letting it go into bankruptcy."

"It's my only hope. With Ah Sek off my back, perhaps I can salvage the other . . ."

"And be branded forever as a bankrupt."

"It doesn't work that way, nowadays, Grandma. Look at Sir Dougal MacFadzean. He let his holding company go into bankruptcy, and today he's at the top of the heap again."

"Perhaps I'm behind the times," Mary conceded. "But I can think of other overwhelming reasons. Apart from what it would do to you, letting Ah Sek go bankrupt would reflect on *all* the Sekloong companies. Think what they'd say at the Bank or Derwent's. 'The Sekloongs are on the way down!' "

"They're already talking, Grandma. Letting Ah Sek go would help the other enterprises, show we're still ruthless enough."

"Albert, the shareholders *must* come first. They bought Ah Sek because of the Sekloong name. My own amah has two hundred shares. Can you really impoverish thousands like her for your convenience?"

"They'll lose anyway. Only a miracle can pull Ah Sek out."

"Then a miracle is necessary. The Old Gentleman would have raged at a Sekloong enterprise going into voluntary bankruptcy. Your father would have been ashamed, deeply ashamed. You cannot abandon the stockholders. Albert, you simply cannot. Besides, it doesn't fit *my* plans."

"*Your* plans."

"I have been thinking about the best way to clear up this mess, you know. Though the final responsibility's yours."

"I brought the books." Albert opened his attaché case. "Do you want to glance at . . ."

"By all means," she replied sweetly. "I'd very much like to check your figures against my own."

Lady Mary's white head bent over the yellow accountants' work sheets, and the frivolous jade butterfly quivered on its golden spring, ruby eyes flashing. Albert's dark head was still as his square fingers indicated the key figures, and he jotted brief notes on a foolscap pad. They groped slowly through the labyrinthine problems of the interlinked companies. After three hours, Albert sat upright and rubbed his cramped neck.

"All right, then," he said. "We have category A, the enterprises where we'll concentrate our resources. Category B, where we'll cut back or, if absolutely necessary, let go. Category C, well, we can only hope political or economic conditions will change if we hold on."

"Then we're agreed, Albert?" Lady Mary's question was rhetorical. "Dragon Films are definitely B. No more money for Alaine?"

"It's not important, Grandma, not in the total picture. Just a sideline. But let me reprise."

"Just one more thing, Albert." Lady Mary's excessively sweet tone was an admonition. "Hong Kong Airways must go too."

"But . . ." he protested.

"Oh, you'll get the cash," she interrupted. "I'll talk to some people in London, perhaps Washington. We can dispose of the Electras, pay the debts, and still have a small surplus. But you must learn you cannot play a lone hand against the very big boys, and particularly not against governments. Losing those routes was sheer foolishness, just because you couldn't be bothered to make the proper friends. However, you can't keep your toy."

Albert bristled at being reprimanded like a schoolboy, but prudently subsided.

"And the grain futures, the commodities," Lady Mary continued in the same schoolmistress's tone. "I think we can manage to dispose of them at a profit, a good profit."

"How can we possibly? The market's falling, and no one's buying."

"But they will. The harvest in Russia looks bad, I hear. And the Chinese, they'll be needing grain again soon. Let me drop a few words to Dewey Miller, point out a few obvious facts. The word will spread rapidly enough once the press takes it up."

"I hadn't thought of that," Albert confessed.

"Business, my dear, is not simply a matter of balance sheets and headlong expansion. You must never overlook the human factors, the political factors. Politics is more than half the game. I learned that a long time ago."

"And that's why you've always been so immersed in politics?"

"For its own sake, too. Albert. Politics is just people, and people *are* interesting. But let's finish your reprise."

"All right. Dragon Plastics are Category A. Rather than sell at a loss or close down temporarily, we'll modernize rapidly. Since you insist, we'll realize on the Electras and let Hong Kong Airways go. They're definitely Category B. Megalith Housing and Borneo Explorations are C, worth holding on to until the political and economic situations change. But they'll need a substantial cash input to keep them going."

"We'll see the Hong Kong Shanghai Bank tomorrow, as we agreed," Lady Mary summed up. "They'll provide the few millions we'll need. If we paint the picture slightly blacker than it is, the Bank will have no choice at all. If the Sekloongs are imperiled, the Bank *can't* let them go. Not after the Chinese-owned banks' failures. A serious crack in the Sekloong enterprises would shake Hong Kong's economy to the foundations."

"Well," Albert said heavily, "you've shown me the way out. I never dreamed . . ."

"So busy building you forgot to consolidate, were you? Some things they didn't teach at Harvard or Pennsylvania."

"I guess so, Grandma. Now I will have that drink. Then I'll let you get some sleep."

"Perhaps a drop of champagne for me. I feel rather invigorated, my dear. It's good to be back in the thick of things again."

Albert marveled at his grandmother's resilience. The frail old woman had been replaced by the decisive executive. She was actually enjoying the challenge, glorying in pitting herself against fate. She had almost persuaded him that he was bestowing an inestimable favor by forcing her to return to the struggles of the marketplace.

"I'm very grateful, Grandma," he said gruffly, busying himself with glasses, bottles, and ice. "It's really not your responsibility."

"Who else's, my dear? Don't be stuffy. You sound like your grandfather. I'm enjoying this."

"I'll enjoy it more when we're out of the woods."

"Speaking of woods," Lady Mary observed with seeming irrelevance, "do you keep an eye on China?"

"I haven't lately. You know I've been rather busy."

"It might repay your attention. The economic picture could change totally. Another cataclysmic upheaval is apparently starting. Dewey Miller says he doesn't know just what yet, but feels it could be even more turbulent than the Great Leap Forward. Peking is talking about a Great Proletarian Cultural Revolution."

June 8, 1966–September 26, 1967

BOMBARD THE HEADQUARTERS OF THE MEN IN POWER FOLLOWING THE CAPITALIST ROAD! Shih Tou-tou stepped back to admire the slashing brushstrokes of her big-character poster.

DESTROY ALL DEMONS AND MONSTERS IN THE COMMUNIST PARTY! The twenty-eight-year-old daughter of General Shih Ai-kuo thrilled again to a *frisson* of exultation and fear at daring to champion the invincibly correct policy line of Chairman Mao Tse-tung against the bourgeois-imperialist agents who dominated both Peking and Ching Hua University on the edge of the capital.

The irony was double-edged. Ching Hua had been a seedbed of progressive thought and revolutionary activists ever since its endowment with funds originally paid by China to foreign powers as indemnity for the Boxers' misdeeds in 1900. Tou-tou knew that the University owed its existence to the foreigners' having returned those funds, though she dismissed the gesture as "cultural imperialism." She did not know that she owed her own existence to Mary Philippa Osgood's decision to marry Charles Sekloong instead of the British officer who had been brutalized by his own role in suppressing the Boxer Rising.

THE UNIVERSITY IS RULED BY COUNTERREVOLUTIONARY TRAITORS! THE REVOLUTIONARY STUDENTS DEMAND THEIR DISMISSAL! HAIL EXTENSIVE DEMOCRACY! HAIL TRUE SOCIALISM! ALL HAIL TO CHAIRMAN MAO!

James Sekloong's younger child, an instructor in history, was dressed in the uniform blue tunic and trousers that clothed all students and faculty members. She deliberately suppressed her awareness that the cotton fabric was finer than that worn by others, while the skilful tailoring accentuated her rounded hips and full breasts. Tou-tou preferred to forget the external marks of the privilege she enjoyed because of her father's rank as a full general in the People's Liberation Army and his position as Deputy Commander of the multiprovincial Peking Military Region. But her hazel eyes glowed with righteous joy at her own leading role in the climactic struggle between the true revolutionary line and the corrupt bureaucracy championed by her own father.

Tou-tou hefted the hammer she had snatched from the University carpenter's shop and emphatically drove six more nails through the thick cardboard poster into the wooden lintel of the library doors. Her declaration of faith, the first to appear at Ching Hua, was too important to risk its being torn away by the winds that blustered across the campus on the late afternoon of June 8, 1966.

She briefly delighted in the provocative figure she presented. Her pale skin, flushed with emotion, was set off by the glossy plaits all the girl students wore. She was, she realized with a rush of pride, truly a Heroine of the Revolution like the martyrs whose exploits she recounted to inspire her students to greater zeal. She pictured herself, hammer raised before the poster that was a declaration of war, at the focal point of a mural painted by some future revolutionary artist to commemorate the moment that would live in the annals of People's China. But she suppressed that stirring of selfish individualism, and she admonished herself that she fought for the revolution, not for personal glorification.

The campus was hushed as the golden dusk cast its shadows among the groves of young pine trees that had risen again on the ochre North China plain, planted at the Chairman's command to conserve the powder-fine soil after its centuries of denudation by fuel-hungry farmers. The ball of the sun glowed red through the dust haze over the temples on the green Western Hills. The wild ducks scrawling their immensely feathered V-formations against the darkening sky called hoarsely to each other.

Diverted by the idyllic prospect, Tou-tou marveled that semblance and reality could differ so totally. In the unearthly peace of the closing day, the University might have been the serene center of ancient learning it appeared, rather than the first battlefield of the most violent struggle to convulse China since the establishment of the People's Republic seventeen years earlier. The struggle had already toppled the fourth-ranking man in the hierarchy of the Communist Party and all his henchmen. The Chairman had already declared that the struggle would continue for years, becoming ever more violent as it developed.

The clashing of cymbals and the shouting of slogans

startled the green-black ducks bobbing on the lake, and Tou-tou shrank into the shadows of the pines. Ching Hua, her own university, was enemy territory still, though she had just signaled the counterattack of the loyal left against the usurping right. A column of students waving banners marched six abreast across the playing field between the library and the men's dormitory. Their broadly gesticulating figures were silhouetted against the dusk like an ink-brush painting of an immemorial peasant army advancing against its oppressors.

The appearance was, once again, totally deceptive. Tou-tou knew the slight woman leading the procession as the embodiment of evil, the chief agent of the traitorous men in power following the capitalist road who plotted to destroy all the accomplishments of almost two decades of revolutionary rule in China. Disguised in the plain blue clothing of the revolutionary masses, that woman minced across the rough grass as if she were still wearing the decadent high-heeled shoes, the violet-silk *cheongsam,* and the ostentatious many-stranded pearl necklace she had flaunted when she traveled abroad as the representative of China—and disgraced the Chinese people by her vulgarly bourgeois behavior.

The woman was Wang Kwang-mei, wife of Chairman Liu Shao-chi of the People's Republic of China. Her chanting followers were the Cultural Revolution Team that her renegade husband had ordered to transform the University into a citadel of reaction. Tou-tou knew that the struggle, which was just erupting into violence, had begun in earnest more than eight years earlier, when the deliberate sabotage and blundering inefficiency of so many cadres halted the Great Leap Forward short of total success. Mao Tse-tung had then resigned as Chairman of the People's Republic in order to concentrate upon the profound analysis of Chinese society essential to remolding that society. Shortly thereafter, in April 1959, the deluded Central Committee of the Communist Party had chosen the man called with unctuous affection Comrade Shao-chi to be Chairman of the Republic. Tou-tou's own father had cast his vote for that retrogressive appointment.

The balance had been partially righted in September 1959, when Chairman Mao forced the wavering Central Committee to depose the Minister of Defense called "Great General" Peng Teh-huai and replace him with Field Marshal Lin Piao. Her own father, a witting henchman of the reactionaries, still spoke of Lin Piao, his first company commander, as "an inveterately ambitious careerist, a poisonous snake masquerading as a benevolent dragon." For eight years, Liu Shao-chi had striven to turn the clock back and restore capitalism in China. But the vigorous revolutionary tempo was finally being revived by the tumultuous, glorious spring and summer of 1966. Having outwaited and outwitted his enemies, the Chairman was taking the offensive against their bureaucratic fortress in Peking, while Lin Piao, his loyal disciple, marshaled the revolutionary forces for the final assault on the reactionaries' citadel. Tou-tou and her "rebel revolutionary" followers were the vanguard of that attack in Peking. Chairman Mao, Defense Minister Lin, and Chiang Ching, who was the Chairman's wife, were completing their own preparations in loyal Shanghai.

The reactionaries' procession stormed past the men's dormitory where Tou-tou's Struggle Group was assembling to plan in secret the next phase of the battle to wrest Ching Hua University from the class enemy. She was not scheduled to appear for another half-hour. Like the heroic underground agents in the White Areas during the wars against the Japanese and the Kuomintang, the young activists staggered their arrivals to evade the enemy's vigilance. She had herself just issued an open challenge to the enemy by defiantly nailing up her big-character poster, but correct strategy still required the rebel revolutionaries to avoid direct confrontations with the numerically superior forces of reaction.

The long procession strutted behind the diminutive figure of Wang Kwang-mei toward the auditorium behind the library. Still another kangaroo-court would be convened—on no authority except that delegated by the usurper Chairman of the People's Republic—to persecute the loyal followers of Chairman Mao. Tou-tou could as yet do little for those martyrs except plan to avenge their suffering. She hid in the shadows, waiting for the procession to move off. But she felt a thrill of fear when thirty-odd broke away from the main column to march on the men's dormitory. The Chairman's revolutionary tactics clearly prescribed her duty; she must save herself by leaving the campus rapidly and inconspicuously. But she was, she acknowledged with a twinge of guilt, not yet sufficiently disciplined. She lingered behind the screen of pine trees in order to see for herself that her own Struggle Group escaped the invading Cultural Revolution Team.

The twilight haze was blurring the outlines of the square buildings, and the red sun was a half-disc behind the Western Hills. The wild ducks still streamed overhead searching for a resting place for the night. Distracted by their staccato calls, Tou-tou did not consciously register the harsh shouts resounding from the fourth story of the dormitory for half a minute. She was, however, tensely alert when small black figures began pouring out of the doorway pursued by other figures waving clubs. It was like a shadow play, she reflected irrelevantly before yielding to profound relief. Her Struggle Group had been surprised, but was escaping. Kneeling behind the pine trees, she counted the small figures who were outdistancing their pursuers.

Thirteen . . . fourteen . . . fifteen. Only two of her revolutionary rebels remained uncounted, and she might have miscounted in the uncertain light. She shuddered when the foremost counterrevolutionaries flung themselves at the rearmost of her followers and dragged his stocky body to earth. Who, she wondered, had been captured by the enemy? The heavy build could belong only to her second-in-command, Rabbit Wu, or their secretary, Big Chang. Whoever it was, he would be tempered by suffering before her Struggle Group could

784

rescue him. Renewing her oath of vengeance, Tou-tou edged through the deepening darkness toward the edge of the screen of pines.

An anguished shriek from the sky disoriented her totally, and she stood rooted for twenty seconds before frantically scanning the heavens. The gray sky was empty of even the squawking ducks. A second shriek set her nerves trembling. This time she located the source of the shriek. The big window on the fourth floor of the dormitory had been flung wide to emit a broad beam of yellow light. Silhouetted like actors in a spotlight, four shadow figures were holding a fifth suspended halfway out the window. Their victim shrieked again, and Tou-tou watched in helpless anger the torture inflicted on her follower.

"Flying the Airplane," they called it, this swinging a captured enemy around and around at a great height to terrify him. The suspended figure whirled faster and faster, his tormentors leaning further out the window with each swoop. He shrieked again and again, each cry shriller and more despairing. Tou-tou resolved that, whoever the victim was, he must be taught self-discipline. The enemy strove above all to destroy the resolution of the loyal Maoists by terrorizing them so that they would shrink from their avowed mission: *Dare to Rebel! Dare to Make Revolution!* She had herself commanded the same punishment of captured reactionaries to impress upon them the ruthless will of the people's warriors. But the reactionaries must surely be tiring. They must soon cease their inhuman sport.

The figures were whirling so fast in a mad ballet that Tou-tou could not distinguish individuals. She saw only a black mass gyrating in the yellow light, an arm or leg suddenly flung out like the branch of a blasted tree. The mass exploded, and a single figure hurtled through the window to tumble twisting through the air. Trailing a last cry like a banner, he plummeted to the hard ground and lay unmoving, a black heap amid the enveloping darkness.

Kneeling behind the pines, her forehead touching the

yellow earth, Tou-tou unconsciously assumed the age-old Chinese woman's posture of grief. Sobs racked her throat, and she retched in anguish. She was only half-aware of the reactionary Cultural Revolution Team debouching amid harsh laughter from the dormitory. But she heard with piercing clarity their taunts as they passed the crumpled heap midway between the dormitory and the library.

"Fly now, you son of a turtle-bitch! Dare to fly! Dare to make revolution! You won't spit on the people again!"

When the enemy had left the field empty except for its macabre memorial to their vicious cowardice, Tou-tou trudged across the grass toward the dormitory. Her head drooped, and each step required a conscious effort of will. When she came to the sprawled figure, she instinctively averted her eyes. Finally daring to look, she saw, illuminated by the moonlight, the still features of her second-in-command, Rabbit Wu, fixed forever in a grimace of mortal terror.

Sheltering in his staff car like a wounded bear, James Sekloong peered warily through the filmy curtains. Green-painted trucks crammed with armed infantrymen raised the yellow dust on Peking's broad Boulevard of Protracted Peace, and sentries posted at fifty-foot intervals punctiliously saluted his Red Flag limousine. Never had the General received such excessive honors, and never had he felt quite as powerless as he did at seven on the morning of July 20, 1966. Though the streets swarmed with armed men in the tan summer uniform of the People's Liberation Army, most were not his own troops. The Deputy Commander of the Peking Military Region could no more direct their movements than could a rear-rank private with six months' service.

Ten times the number of soldiers patroled the streets than Peking's citizens had seen at any one time since the Liberation Army's triumphal march into the ancient city in January 1949. The metropolis that had endured so many sieges over the millennia was once again besieged—this time from within. The beleaguered and the defenders wore the same uniform, but obeyed conflicting orders. The high command of the Liberation Army was split, as was the Central Committee of the Communist Party. The siege of Peking was directed by Chairman Mao Tse-tung and Defense Minister Lin Piao from their headquarters in Shanghai. The capital was defended by Chairman Liu Shao-chi of the People's Republic and, somewhat less vigorously, by Premier Chou En-lai. Power in China still grew from the barrel of the gun, as the Chairman had observed. Marshal Lin Piao had deployed his own divisions to seize the city and depose the legal government by a military *coup d'état*.

James belched and choked on the sweet smoke of a Tien An Men cigarette, his twelfth since awakening three hours earlier. His morning rice gruel, flavored with shredded pork and peanuts, had as usual been accompanied by lengths of fried bread. But those *yu-tiao* had been greasy, and his sour stomach aggravated his sour mood. His own household was already wracked by political dissension. Careless of the listening servants, he had slammed the gray door of the courtyard behind him after shouting: "We've already got a miniature civil war right here. Heaven help China when a man can find no peace in his own home!"

He had then fled the biting retorts of his wife Lu Ping and his daughter Tou-tou. His women displayed enthusiastic approbation of the Great Proletarian Cultural Revolution, but little understanding. He was burdened with too much knowledge, but they knew little more than the grandiloquent panegyric in the Peking *People's Daily*: "It is a profound revolution that will completely eradicate all old ideology, thinking, and culture, all the old customs, habits, and behavior that have for centuries poisoned the minds of the Chinese people."

Lu Ping and Tou-tou, who were dangerously involved with the Maoists, did not know, as he did, that scores of senior officials had already been swept into limbo. They did know that the Mayor of Peking, the fourth man in the Communist Party and the czar of Chinese culture, was under house arrest. But his women could not be diverted from their mindless devotion to Chairman Mao, who was once again promising to transform China into the perfect Communist society that had somehow evaded the Great Leap Forward. They derided James's warning: "The Cultural Revolution could become an uncontrollable fire that consumes the Communist Party—even a civil war."

"You're still a bourgeois, still a treaty-port Sekloong," his wife charged. "You simply don't understand Chairman Mao's transcendental insights. The greater the disorder, the greater the final victory. We shall build a magnificent new world on the ruins of the old."

"Don't talk jargon to me," James replied coldly. "I was a Communist when you were still tending pigs in Kiangsi. We can't build Communism on a battlefield strewn with corpses. If this Cultural Revolution spreads, it'll put China back a generation."

"Your thoughts are manacled by the old ideas," Tou-tou retorted. "At Ching Hua we've already won a great victory over the revisionist Soviet-line traitor Liu Shao-chi. Every comrade expresses his own opinions in big-character posters. This's true democracy, extensive democracy—not fake, bourgeois democracy. We are using words and weapons to break the rigid, reactionary rule of the concealed capitalist agents in our midst."

James had risen from the breakfast table and pulled on his comfortably shapeless cloth cap with the red star embroidered on its front. Stalking from the courtyard, he realized that he might just have concluded the last frank discussion he would ever have with his wife and daughter. Candor was not merely imprudent, but dangerous in a divided household.

His sour forebodings were interrupted when his driver braked hard at Wangfuching Street. An abrupt halt was rarely necessary, since Peking's sparse motor-traffic was still limited to official, public, and diplomatic motor-vehicles almost eighteen years after the city's

Liberation. A column of young men and women was flowing onto the Boulevard of Protracted Peace. Some were obviously students in their blue tunics; others from farming communes wore home-tailored trousers and shirts. All displayed brassards scrawled with the spiky characters: *Hung Wei Ping*—Red Guard. Chairman Mao and Defense Minister Lin were bringing up their shock troops, deploying the doctrine-intoxicated youths to outflank the regular troops of the Liberation Army. The Red Guards' martial chant reverberated: "We shall level the old world! We shall destroy all old things!"

James stroked his baggy cotton tunic, which was adorned only by red collar flashes. In 1964, Lin Piao's Defense Ministry had taken cognizance of China's public quarrel with the Soviet Union by abolishing formal ranks in the Liberation Army and discarding the gold-braid-encrusted, Soviet-style uniforms. James wondered whether the uniforms would change again if the limping talks with the United States at Warsaw finally led to reconciliation between Washington and Peking. That radical change was not immediately in prospect. But how many would have predicted ten years earlier that the Chairman would turn against the Soviet Union, which he had hailed as China's Big Brother in 1950? Talking with the Americans might avert the threat that haunted James Sekloong and most other professional soldiers—confrontation with the formidable forces the Americans were committing to South Vietnam. China was virtually defenseless, since the Defense Minister believed that seas of guerrillas could overwhelm any modern enemy. The Chief-of-Staff who had advocated a technological build-up was in disgrace, already marked for sacrifice to the great purge that was gathering momentum.

James shivered in the hot, dry air. He realized that his right hand was stroking his Adam's apple, and he pressed his palm against the seat. His hand, it seemed, possessed its own independent will and was deeply concerned for his throat. He might himself be the next senior officer consigned to a Labor Reform Camp.

The staff car halted at the Eastern Entrance to the Great Hall of the People, and the alien sentries before the towering doors saluted perfunctorily. James involuntarily stroked his throat again, but relaxed fractionally when he saw that his staff was at work in his new offices beside the Premier's suite. The adjacent offices of Chairman Liu of the People's Republic of China were vacant. Comrade Shao-chi had prudently retreated to his residence on the Central South Lake behind the walls of the Inner City, where he was protected by his personal bodyguard.

"This is ridiculous," James had remarked to the Premier. "What is happening when the Chief-of-State feels threatened in his own office?"

"Ridiculous, Ai-kuo?" The Premier's reply had been heavily ironic. "We live in ridiculous times. But very sensible on Comrade Shao-chi's part. And I like it. I like a little distance between me and Comrade Shao-chi at this moment."

Sipping green tea and lighting his fifteenth cigarette of the morning, James wondered who was the humorist on his staff. An unknown hand had hung the obligatory colored photograph of a benevolent Chairman Mao between paired classical scrolls that lauded familial and national harmony, the very qualities the Chairman denounced as the greatest obstacles to "progress through struggle." Levity was nowhere encouraged in the New China; levity regarding politics was a grave "error"; and even the hint of levity toward Mao Tse-tung was a heinous offense. The Peking Municipal Committee of the Communist Party had just been dismissed *en masse* because of its newspapers' heavy-handed satire of the Chairman.

The General bolted the door, clambered up on a chair, and removed the scrolls. Rolling them tight, he tucked them behind a filing cabinet. He might, he reflected, be suffering from incipient paranoia, but better paranoid than purged.

James Sekloong returned to his desk and lit his sixteenth cigarette with fingers that quivered. He was as absurdly ashamed of his stealthy removal of the old scrolls as an adolescent leafing through pornographic pictures behind a locked bathroom door. But the atmosphere of Peking in late July 1966 was itself absurd. Chairman Mao had proclaimed a war of extermination against all the customs, the thinking, and the material works of the old civilization that had been China's proudest possession, the civilization that had, in a wider sense, been China itself. The apparently innocuous scrolls on his wall were, therefore, a direct threat to James Sekloong.

Mao Tse-tung, the man, had grown far larger than his office. Transcendent reverence for the Chairman, greater than the supernatural awe that had invested the Emperors, paralyzed the will of the senior members of the Communist hierarchy. None of the nearly two hundred men and women who in theory ruled the vast nation of almost seven hundred million persons was free of the pervasive fear, and none could trust any other. The Premier's discreet drawing away from the embattled Chairman of the People's Republic, his old comrade-in-arms Liu Shao-chi, was symptomatic of the terror Chairman Mao had deliberately inspired. The Shanghai Rebel Revolutionary Group's success in setting the oldest friends against each other was its most powerful weapon.

James's desk was heaped with files marked URGENT. "The terrifying efficiency of the bureaucracy," the Premier had remarked, "is in full operation. The frightened cadres throw up heaps of paper without meaning, most as relevant to our problems as the classical 'eight-legged essays' of the Imperial Civil Service Examinations. Just words, words, and more words—beautifully and symmetrically organized—but meaningless."

The reports from the Intelligence Section of the Peking Military Region were, however, highly relevant, particularly the *Daily Situation Report*. Their terse language, unburdened by the customary political jargon, in itself attested to the severity of the tremors that were shaking the People's Republic.

James turned to the folders without enthusiasm. His interest was low, though he knew their contents could in the long run determine his own fate. The reports had already been overtaken by events. Late the preceding night, his orderly had brought him a note abruptly canceling the plenary meeting of the Central Committee originally scheduled for that morning by the Premier, Comrade Liu Shao-chi, and the Secretary-General of the Communist Party, the abrasive Teng Hsiao-ping, whose administrative talents had won him his nickname, The Organizer. The pro-Liu majority of the Central Committee, which had assembled in Peking, dared not convene under the threat of Red Guard violence and Lin Piao's guns.

The operations reports graphically set forth the reasons for Lin Piao's successful use of terror. Though most of the generals of the Liberation Army were loyal to the legitimate authority represented by Comrade Shao-chi, the removal of the Chief-of-Staff had immobilized them while Lin Piao's armies occupied key road and railway junctions commanding ingress to the capital and then marched into Peking unopposed. Signal after signal offered variations on the same theme: "We set out as ordered, but found no logistical support. . . . My division was incapacitated by an epidemic of influenza. . . . There was no transport." The stumbling excuses—and the absence of any communications whatsoever from some major commanders—were a grim record of the irresolute inaction that had permitted Lin Piao's *coup d'état* to triumph.

When he returned to his dissension-torn household that evening, James Sekloong's spirits were at their lowest ebb. He wrapped himself in the protective silence that was to cloak his despair during the next ten days while he watched the dissolution of the vision of a perfect China that had inspired him since 1926.

The Maoists seized the propaganda machinery that conveyed the wishes of their rulers to both the cadres and the people. By late July, the Maoists had purged the Party's Propaganda Bureau and taken over the *People's Daily,* the Central Broadcasting Station, and the New China News Agency. Power, they knew, sprang from the pen and the microphone, as well as the gun. The Maoists controlled those weapons, and they had neutralized most of China's guns.

Having secured the capital physically, the Maoists finally launched their formal political attack. Four Ilyushins landed at Peking Airport on July 28, 1966, to discharge the Chairman, his disciple Lin Piao, his wife Chiang Ching, and the Maoist minority of the Central Committee of the Communist Party. The "bombardment of the headquarters of the men in power following the capitalist road," the preparatory attack Tou-tou had initiated, was intensified on July 29. Hundreds of thousands of zealots, led by students and shepherded by the Defense Minister's troops, surged through the streets. They chanted their loyalty to the Chairman and raged against his opponents. Tou-tou marched among them, exulting in her personal triumph. Her Red Guards had broken Liu Shao-chi's Cultural Revolution Teams on the campus of Ching Hua University in pitched fights with clubs, hammers, and chains. At that moment, the actual power of the obscure twenty-eight-year-old instructor in history was appreciably greater than her high-ranking father's.

The men (and the few women) who met two days later in the Great Hall of the People to decide China's fate had been winnowed by Lin Piao's troops and intimidated by the street mobs. They numbered less than half the one hundred and ninety-three members of the Central Committee, and those who questioned the new order prudently kept silent.

James Sekloong was seated among his wary peers under the stardust lights of the small auditorium. The lining of his mouth was puckered and acrid with the nicotine-and-tar detritus of his daily intake of ninety-odd cigarettes. Though the session had begun only half an hour earlier the auditorium was already hung with smoke, and the light beams shining from the ceiling were twined with writhing gray spirals. Around him James saw nervous faces haggard with fatigue, their set mouths sucking on cigarettes. The men and women who were in theory supreme in China had been exhausted by the turmoil of the preceding weeks. James felt as if he were seated among an assembly of phantoms drained of mortal will.

Nonetheless, it was marginally better to be present than to be absent; it was preferable to face the menacing stares of the Defense Minister's storm troopers, who paced the aisles, than to have already been cast into the outer darkness. Faithful to the Premier's wry advice, James had adroitly avoided committing himself irrevocably to either faction. He was seated in the middle ranks of the Central Committee, neither too close to the front nor too far to the rear. The impassive Premier sat among the Political Bureau behind a long table on the stage, the rhythmic clenching and unclenching of his stiffly cocked right hand revealing his inner tension. Comrade Shao-chi was pale and distant as a gray ghost. The Chairman smiled blandly from the seat of honor, but did not speak. The satraps of China, themselves cowed into silence, had already heard reports that the Chairman was suffering from Parkinsonism, which severely impeded his speech.

"We are going to dismiss a number of people, promote a number, and keep some in their present posts," the wax-white Disciple Lin Piao announced shrill-voiced and vitriolic. "Those who are incorrigible will be relieved of their posts immediately."

The rulers of China stealthily regarded each other under lowered eyelids like terminal-cancer patients wondering who would go next. The Deputy Commander of the Peking Military Region disciplined his features into a noncommittal mask. Never in his adult life had he felt such paralyzing fear. The Defense Minister's tirade, veering from harsh assertion to near-hysterical self-justification, eroded the convictions that had sustained James's courage through forty years of battle and intrigue. Without the Communist Party, he himself was nothing—and the Party for which he had lived was being destroyed. The Chairman, whose authority derived from the consent of the Central Committee, was imposing his personal will on the Central Committee by force.

Mao Tse-tung beamed vacuously, as if presiding over a ceremonial dinner. Comrade Shao-chi shrank physically under the verbal assault against himself and all his works. The Premier's face was fixed in closed rigidity, and his hands lay like flexed claws on the table.

"Recently my heart has been quite heavy." At his moment of triumph, Lin Piao still paraded the mock humility that had so long concealed his illimitable ambition. "I am not equal to my task, and I may fail in my duties. . . . But I am doing all I can to minimize my mistakes. I shall rely upon the Chairman, upon my comrades of the Standing Committee of the Political Bureau, and upon the comrades just appointed to the new Task Force Directing the Great Proletarian Cultural Revolution."

James suppressed his involuntary start. The Task Force included the Chairman's termagant wife, who was irremediably bitter. She had, she felt, been systematically slighted by the Party's intellectual establishment ever since her unsuccessful struggles to become a star of left-wing motion-pictures in Shanghai in the mid-1930s. He feared she would be a new, more vengeful Empress Dowager.

"Chairman Mao is the central axis, and we are the mill-stones that revolve on that axis and grind fine," Lin Piao declaimed. "We must in all our deeds adhere to the brilliant thought of Mao Tse-tung. There cannot be two policy lines or two proletarian headquarters. Only the Chairman can command, and we must unswervingly obey his every command. . . . I never interfere with the Chairman on major matters, nor do I trouble him with minor matters."

The public pretence of "socialist legality," James noted, was discarded in that last sentence, as was, finally, Lin Piao's personal pretence of humility. His former company commander had asserted his personal supremacy over the Cultural Revolution—and all China.

Personal dictatorship was supplanting collective rule, but not one delegate dared object. The vacant chairs of those who had resisted Lin Piao's *coup d'état* mutely enjoined obedience. The armed soldiers standing along the walls overwhelmingly demonstrated that the ultimate source of all power was naked force. The militant Red Guard activists, the "rebel revolutionary" students and workers, roared in the gallery behind James. Their wild chanting heralded the violent anarchy the Chairman and the Minister of Defense were releasing upon the nation.

The rump Central Committee carried Lin Piao's "proposals" by acclamation. The enormity of the planned Great Proletarian Cultural Revolution so shocked James Sekloong that he automatically jotted notes he later read with startled disbelief: "Create entire new society after destroying—totally—all old ideas, culture, customs, and habits. Dismiss *all* erring officials *throughout* the nation. Erect new government structures called Revolutionary Committees to replace *all* existing Government and Party organs. Establish reformed educational system and create *totally* new culture. License adolescent Red Guards to rampage through China— burning and killing to impose new order."

In a moment of eerie clarity, James distinctly heard his own daughter's voice shrieking in the gallery: "All hail to Deputy Chairman Lin! Hail, hail, hail the thought of Mao Tse-tung! Destroy all demons and monsters!"

Lin Piao was thus acclaimed as Chairman Mao's heir-apparent and the sole Deputy Chairman of the Communist Party, replacing the four incumbent Vice-Chairmen. Comrade Shao-chi was degraded from first Vice-Chairman to eighth rank in the Political Bureau, just beneath Secretary-General Teng Hsiao-ping, The Organizer. One omission permitted James to hope still for the future of China as he walked numbly toward the Eastern Exit of the Great Hall of the People among his silent, shuffling peers. Though no longer second Vice-Chairman, Chou En-lai remained the third-ranking member of the Communist Party. Even Lin Piao did not yet dare dispense with the man who had been his teacher at the Whampoa Academy forty years earlier.

The first assignment given an apprehensive James Sekloong by the new master of China paradoxically bestowed uneasy peace upon his household. He directed the Liberation Army's support for the first mass rally of Red Guards. Some 900,000 "rebel revolutionaries" from Peking were to be joined by an additional 100,000 transported by airplane, truck, and railroad from the far corners of the nation. The preparations only the military could carry out imposed a logistical burden far greater than moving several army corps. James was assisted in his labors by his daughter Tou-tou, when she was not diverted by her ideological duties as one of the five chief leaders of all China's Red Guards. Though Tou-tou assumed that she was virtually running China, father and daughter worked well together. Their intense concentration upon their practical tasks left them neither energy nor time to quarrel.

James was deterred from taunting her as much by fear of the harridan his daughter had become as by his preoccupation with the staff work. Soaring high on the thermal currents of elation, Tou-tou could not descend to the personal disputes with her father that had made their home life acrimonious for months.

The spectacle they had stage-managed astonished both father and daughter on the morning of August 18, 1966. Beyond counting in their multitudes, red banners danced in demoniac frenzy over the Plaza of the Gate of Heavenly Peace. The sun's radiance, diffused by the powdered dust borne on the wind from Central Asia, ignited the clouds of scarlet bunting. The rebel revolutionaries sang the old favorite, "The East Is Red," and the refrain swelled from a million throats: "Mao Tse-tung is the red, red sun in our hearts!" They beat time with booklets bound in red plastic, and crimson waves lashed the broad Plaza. The red booklets flipped open, and a million Red Guards chanted in unison from *The Quotations of Chairman Mao* as selected and edited by Deputy Chairman Lin Piao.

"We must distinguish between our friends and our enemies; we must defend our friends and crush our enemies. . . ."

The war chants reverberated from the red-brick walls of the fifteenth-century Gate of Heavenly Peace, where the Emperors had once received the homage of their people. Above the Gate's central arch beamed a portrait of Mao Tse-tung fifty times lifesize. Red banners hanging like classical scrolls on either side were indited in enormous gold characters: HAIL THE PEOPLE'S REPUBLIC OF CHINA! HAIL THE GREAT UNITY OF THE COMMON PEOPLE OF ALL THE WORLD! The upswept eaves of the two-tiered roof shone pale yellow in the morning haze—and the Red Guards waited, as they had all night.

At ten in the morning they were finally rewarded for their patience and their ardor. Remote as wooden figures on a medieval clock tower, a miniature procession appeared on the Gate of Heavenly Peace. Emerging into the sunlight, the leading figure raised his hand in an angular, awkward salute. He leaned heavily on his shorter companion, and his ponderous head turned from side to side like a clockwork doll's. He walked with the shuffling robotic gait characteristic of Parkinsonism. When Chairman Mao appeared in the uniform of the People's Liberation Army for the first time in a decade, mass ecstasy transfigured the Red Guards. A million young men and women were transported from frenzied anticipation to mindless rapture.

"*Mao Chu-hsi! Mao Chu-hsi! Mao Chu-hsi!*" The rebel revolutionaries chanted "Chairman Mao!"—and their words merged into cataracts of joyful sound that transcended literal meaning: "*Chu-hsi Mao Chu-hsi Mao Chu-hsi . . .*" The wild cataracts rose and

798

swelled and broke to rise and swell and break time and time again. Girls jumped high into the air, tears streaming down their contorted faces. Youths bounded up and down, pummeling each other in their transports. The red banners swirled in the bright morning breeze. The little red books rose and fell in the demented, broken rhythms of storm-born breakers. All individual identity and all individual feelings were swept away by the torrents of mass emotion.

The sanctified Chairman was the redeemer, the savior of a generation brutally frustrated in its expectations of infinite proletarian blessings. Like a Renaissance king appealing to the new bourgeoisie to join him against the wicked nobles, Chairman Mao was inviting the revolutionary masses to join him in crushing the wicked "capitalist-line" bureaucracy of the Communist Party that had contrived such bitter frustration. The most unruly youths of China were exhorted: "Dare to rebel! Rebellion is good! Dare to create disorder! Dare to make a total revolution!"

James Sekloong watched in mute astonishment and Tou-tou was moved to ecstasy beyond words when Deputy Chairman Lin Piao issued his orders to his Red Guards. The heir-apparent's drawn features were chalky, and clear-framed spectacles bestrode his hooked nose. Slight in his olive-green tunic, he looked like a frail scholar. But his commands, echoing through a hundred loudspeakers, were as impassioned as a barbarian Mongol chieftain's exhortation to slaughter and pillage.

"The Great Proletarian Cultural Revolution is aimed at eliminating bourgeois ideology and establishing proletarian ideology—remolding men's souls, revolutionizing their ideology, plucking out the roots of Soviet-style revisionism, and developing the Socialist system."

Wild shouts drowned Lin Piao's voice. The Disciple raised his eyes and paused. Mao Tse-tung shuffled to his side and peered amiably over his shoulder.

"We will strike down those men in authority who are taking the capitalist road! We will strike down the reactionary academic savants! We will strike down all bourgeois royalists! We will strike down all demons and monsters!"

Torrents of cheers again overwhelmed his shrill voice. The Disciple looked up in mild surprise. The Chairman nodded like an indulgent uncle acknowledging thanks for a birthday present.

James Sekloong felt himself far older than his fifty-nine years when the first mass rally ended. He watched with anguish the subsequent rallies that assembled additional millions of Red Guards in order to consecrate them to the revolutionary crusade. Tou-tou exulted as more than twenty million Red Guards marched out to overthrow the previously all-powerful Communist Party Secretaries of schools, factories, Communes, and government organs. Except for Lin Piao's toadies, the generals of the Liberation Army, which was the only remaining organized power in China, refused to intervene. Like James Sekloong, they found reason to hope the insane storm would blow itself out. Though the nation's spiritual regeneration demanded mass violence, that violence was initially directed at insensate objects, rather than living human beings. When James read the New China News Agency's file on August 25, 1966, he felt renewed confidence that the symbolic cataclysm would be limited:

PEKING—A revolutionary fire was ignited on the campus of the Central Institute of Arts yesterday to destroy the sculptures of Buddha, the niches of Buddha, and sculptures of emperors, kings, ministers, generals, scholars, beauties, and demons of Greek and Roman origins or of ancient, feudal China.

The masses of revolutionary students and teachers were in high spirits. They cast out the sculptures of the Goddess of Mercy, princes, and the fierce-looking gods Shu Yu and Yu Lu which they had collected from various temples in China; the stone horses and tigers they had collected from Imperial tombs; the sculptures of King David of Israel—the "hero" David in the Bible; the "Goddess of Love and Beauty"—the Venus of Greek legends; Apollo; and others purchased abroad. All these were burned and smashed in broad daylight.

Tou-tou mocked her father's complacency when he laid the file down and incautiously observed, "They've cleansed the Party thoroughly, and they've destroyed the old objects. Now's the time to consolidate and advance."

"It's just beginning," she replied with ardent malice. "The Cultural Revolution is no simple reshuffling of chairs in the Central Committee. It will shake every Party member like an earthquake. It will destroy all who dare defy Chairman Mao's revolutionary line—whether they are members of the Politburo or low-level cadres on rural communes."

James resigned himself to hearing her out.

"We Red Guards," Tou-tou declared, "will smash not only the outward semblances of the old world. We will totally destroy all bourgeois vestiges—and all the remaining bourgeoisie."

During the next few months James concluded with sorrow that his daughter had understated, rather than exaggerated the violence of the eruption. Not only senior officials, but minor cadres like the Party secretaries of middle schools were deposed by the roving Red Guards. Chairman Mao's children's crusade spared neither the obscure nor the powerful. A ninety-two-year-old former Imperial Mandarin was frog-marched through the streets of Tientsin in a dunce cap for refusing to destroy a seven-hundred-year-old scroll. An internationally renowned philosopher was compelled to write confession after confession until the Red Guards finally felt that he had reformed his "evil thoughts," the fruit of forty years of intense study in China, Europe, and America. Even the aged widows of "counterrevolutionaries" were terrorized.

As Tou-tou had predicted, the Cultural Revolution became ever more violent. She herself marched among the Red Guards who roamed China to "exchange revolutionary experiences" and to intimidate the enemies of the sanctified Chairman. School was out, and school was to remain out for years as the Red Guards reveled in destruction and slaughter. Regional Party secretaries and provincial governors were beaten with fists, clubs, and chains. Hundreds of officials were killed, and thousands were maimed. Red Guards broke into bourgeois homes to destroy their "decadent, old possessions." Many so-called bourgeoisie were beaten to death, while others killed themselves. Their bodies were burned on the pyres of their belongings.

The deeds appeared mindless, but their purpose was political, always political. Only by terrifying his opponents could Defense Minister Lin Piao establish his absolute personal power.

In December 1966 the Deputy Chairman ordered his adolescent storm troopers to attack his highest opponents. All China trembled before Lin Piao when he deposed Chairman Liu Shao-chi of the People's Republic and The Organizer Teng Hsiao-ping, Secretary-General of the Communist Party. The Organizer was paraded through the streets of Peking wearing placards that proclaimed him: THE ENEMY OF THE PEOPLE! THE SECOND MAN IN POWER IN THE ANTI-SOCIALIST BLACK GANG! The Red Guards pelted him with rotten fruit and human excrement.

James Sekloong stayed close to Premier Chou En-lai, who was also under attack, but agilely evading a potentially fatal confrontation with Lin Piao and his Red Guards. The Premier was even able to preserve the hard core of his powerless administration by protecting the best of his protégés. James survived, as did the Foreign Minister, a People's Marshal who had been dragged from his office and harangued by Red Guards while he stood among the looted files of his ministry.

The old Marshal gestured toward the strewn papers and warned, "You are revealing state secrets."

"State secrets, your mother's," a Red Guard leader replied. "Who gives a shit for state secrets? Everything must be open to all!"

The first six months of the Cultural Revolution were

the ecstatic culmination of Tou-tou's life, the glorious fulfilment of all her dreams. In early January 1967 she revenged herself upon Wang Kwang-mei, the wife of Comrade Liu Shao-chi, who had led the reactionary Cultural Revolution Teams at Ching Hua University. On a rain-bleak winter afternoon, Tou-tou set in train her "strategy to outflank and capture" the woman who still enjoyed a certain immunity from frontal attack. Tou-tou's weapon was the telephone in the hospital originally established by the American-supported Peking Union Medical College.

"This is Peking Number One Hospital." She spoke urgently into the mouthpiece. "We regret we have bad news for you."

"What is it?" asked Wang Kwang-mei tremulously. "Tell me what's wrong. Please tell me."

"Your daughter Liu Ping-ping has been injured in an automobile accident. You must come immediately."

"How badly is she hurt?" asked the distraught mother. "Her life is not . . ."

"I'm sorry. I can give you no further information. Come at once."

Tou-tou replaced the handset and turned to her waiting subordinates.

"That's caught the turtle-bitch," she said. "We'll drag her out."

Wang Kwang-mei, who had not left the shelter of her residence for a month, drove up to the hospital in a Red Flag limousine twenty minutes later. She was accompanied by a single burly bodyguard, whom the Red Guards seized.

"Forget about your daughter," Tou-tou told the astonished woman. "She may live or she may die. More important, it's time for you to settle your accounts with the people."

Wang Kwang-mei's ordeal lasted for twenty-eight hours. Taken to Ching Hua University, she was reviled by shifts of Red Guards who demanded that she confess her sins against the people of China. She was mauled by girl students who forced her to wriggle into the violet-silk *cheongsam* and slip on the high-heeled pumps she had worn on her state visits to Indonesia and Burma. Tou-tou laughed venemously when Wang Kwang-mei complained that the shoes were too small to fit over her heavy socks and pleaded with the Red Guards to return to her home, where they had found the *cheongsam,* and bring her a pair of nylon stockings. That was bourgeois vanity indeed. Instead, the shameless traitress was confronted with a detailed record of her own lies and her husband's thefts of the people's property. A tireless Tou-tou presided over the interrogation that pressed Wang Kwang-mei time after time to acknowledge that her husband, Comrade Shao-chi, had disputed Chairman Mao's decisions and sabotaged Chairman Mao's policies.

Wang Kwang-mei finally confessed to her personal sins. Though she was close to hysteria because of her anxiety for her daughter and her own physical exhaustion, she stubbornly refused to admit that her husband had deliberately deceived the Chairman by plotting to restore capitalism in China. Seated on the gritty staircase of the library, she alternately wept and pleaded to be allowed to sleep. Finally, Tou-tou gave the signal. from the chair where she had brooded like an indefatigable Fury throughout her rival's long torment.

"Let her go," Tou-tou said flatly. "She's suffered enough—for the moment. Next time, she'll confess *all* her sins."

Before Tou-tou allowed herself to sleep on the floor of her office, she reflected that her revenge had been all the more satisfactory because of Wang Kwang-mei's obdurate refusal to implicate Liu Shao-chi. She herself had contemptuously tossed Wang Kwang-mei aside like a gutted fish. Since the traitress's humiliation was not yet finished, the next interrogation, which must break her totally, would be completely satisfactory.

By late January 1967, Chairman Mao's Red Guards had split into bitterly opposed factions contending for local power amid national anarchy. They fought with crowbars, home-made pistols, daggers, cleavers, and crude spears. They shot each other with rifles and submachine guns seized from passive Liberation Army soldiers who had been ordered not to interfere with the violent course of the Cultural Revolution. Literal reports from China were so bizarre that a stunned outside world rejected them, just as it had refused to credit the initial pronouncements of the Great Leap Forward eight years earlier. Few foreigners could bring themselves to believe that Mao Tse-tung had unloosed forces that threatened to destroy his own People's Republic of China or that those forces had already shattered the structure of the People's Government and the Communist Party. Even fewer could understand that the pent resentment of Chinese youth was defying the directives of both Chairman Mao and Deputy Chairman Lin Piao. Outsiders simply could not comprehend events that appeared wholly irrational to them.

Dewey Miller of *Newsweek* was appalled at the mindless violence sweeping China. He could not dismiss the graphic dispatches of the *People's Daily,* the New China News Agency, the provincial broadcasting stations—and the hundreds of broadsides and pamphlets issued by mutually hostile Red Guard groups in a flowering of freedom of publication unprecedented in the People's Republic. He accordingly reported that China was in turmoil. Though themselves normally hungry for sensation, his less experienced colleagues accused him of gross exaggeration. Miller flatly asserted during a discussion on Hong Kong television that the Cultural Revolution was verging upon chaos. The movement, he said, had virtually destroyed the Communist Party. He warned that Lin Piao, the sorcerers' disciple, had conjured up forces he could not control, while the half-senile Mao Tse-tung was a compliant figurehead.

A French correspondent, reinsuring his next visa to China, confidently refuted Miller: "Chairman Mao himself has planned the Cultural Revolution. Lin Piao is only his agent. And the two know exactly what they're doing. The Cultural Revolution is a mass movement controlled by the Communist Party. It will be a glorious success!"

At that point Miller realized that it would be worse than pointless to discuss the grand design he had discerned behind the apparently aimless nation-wide violence. His editors had finally agreed—despite their own skepticism—to run a long takeout on the ideological concepts motivating the destructive antics of the Red Guards. His colleagues were unprepared even to consider that audacious purpose, which had been described in detail by Peking's doctrinal journal *Red Flag*.

The Task Force Directing the Cultural Revolution, Dewey Miller concluded, sought to alter the fundamental character of the Chinese people. Moreover, the Maoists envisioned nothing less than mankind's first perfect government, so perfect it transcended formal government. Their model was the egalitarian Paris Commune of 1871, which Karl Marx had described as "history's first true proletarian government."

Dewey Miller realized with half-incredulous awe that the Chairman was determined to transform China from a nation-state into a popular confederation. The new Revolutionary Committees were to exercise all legislative, executive, and judicial functions, while their functionaries were to be chosen from among the proletariat by a mystical consensus far more "democratic" than direct elections. Not only provinces, cities, and villages, not only factories, universities, and newspapers were to be run by the new political organisms. The Central People's Government and the Communist Party itself were to be replaced by those Revolutionary Committees. All China was to be one Great People's Commune. The Red Guards were seeking to destroy existing Chinese society by mass violence in order to make way for a seamlessly perfect, quintessentially new Chinese society.

Dewey Miller despaired of discussing his insight with his fellow correspondents. They were so self-consciously cynical that they somewhat paradoxically ended by applauding—without understanding—the

Chairman's every action. Instead, he retired to the blue-carpeted bar of the Foreign Correspondents' Club atop the Hilton Hotel to nurse his wounds and drench his anger.

Jaunty in a cashmere jacket and cordovan loafers, thirty-four-year-old Lachlan Wheatley, the new *taipan* of Derwent's, slipped onto the adjoining stool to await the Japanese associates with whom he was dining. In 1967, the Correspondents' Club was the In-place among the In-people.

"Miller, you're wrong, you know," Wheatley said with measured sympathy. "Of course all you pressmen exaggerate. But you talked twaddle on television. Business with China is good. They're buying lorries, wheat, and fertilizer. How can you say things are out of control?"

"That's the way it goes, Wheatley," Dewey replied and finished his martini in silence.

Lady Mary was less complacent than Lachlan Wheatley. Though she made her own peace with the Chinese people years earlier, her tough-minded realism was unimpaired. Like Dewey Miller, she had read the voluminous literature of the Cultural Revolution and had talked with Red Guards who had fled from China. Those early defectors from the Cultural Revolution were revolted by their own deeds and fearful of the future.

"You're probably *understating* events," she told Miller. "I fear civil war."

The first pitched battle between the storm troopers of idealistic nihilism and the neo-Stalinist defenders of the established order was fought in Shanghai, the city of seven million on the mudflats where the Woosong and Hwangpoo Rivers join before disgorging into the Yangtze River and the East China Sea. The mortal confrontation was historically and dramatically inevitable. Both capitalism and Communism had come to China through Shanghai, and, after seventeen years of the

Communists' People's Republic, those antagonistic forces still contended in the great port.

By mid-January 1967 the excesses of the Red Guards had alienated Shanghai's working class. The longshoremen and factory workers whose fathers had seized the city in 1927 under Chou En-lai's leadership turned against the Maoist zealots of the Shanghai Revolutionary Committee that had "seized power" from the former municipal government. Led by their old cadres, the workers staged mass strikes. Electricity and water flowed only intermittently, and trains halted on their tracks. Mills and foundries stood idle, while ocean-going ships were as effectively stranded when longshoremen refused to unload cargoes as if they had run aground. Angry farmers in the surrounding countryside choked the city's food supplies to a trickle. The revolt of the masses precipitated the armed struggle that was called the "January Storm."

Tou-tou came to Shanghai in mid-January to lead the Red Guards from Peking who battled for the Chairman's supernal ideals. The granddaughter Lady Mary had never seen was convinced that her father was a vicious counterrevolutionary. James, in turn, despaired of diverting his daughter from the path he feared would lead to her destruction, though her mother Lu Ping was wavering in her dedication to the Cultural Revolution.

Having survived many intra-Party struggles, Lu Ping could no longer delude herself regarding the latest and most destructive struggle. She quailed at the barbarism of the rampaging adolescents, and she realized that her husband's warnings against irrevocable commitment to the Cultural Revolution were but prudent. Three decades of Party life had taught her the cardinal virtue of self-preservation: She knew that her fate was directly linked to his, despite the Party's cant about "perfect equality between male and female."

But Lu Ping could influence her daughter neither by political logic nor by maternal admonition. Tou-tou was as obstinate as her great-grandfather, Bandmaster John

Philip Osgood, who had refused to attend his only daughter's wedding to a "blasted chink."

Tou-tou's chief target was the striking railway workers. They not only demanded higher wages, but refused to operate trains overloaded when visiting Red Guards pushed into carriages reserved for the workers of the Third Iron and Steel Works. The revolution therefore demanded that the politically conscious Red Guards, themselves the privileged children of senior officials and intellectuals, instruct the manual laborers in their "proletarian duties."

Chanting revolutionary songs, Tou-tou led the march of three hundred and fifty Peking Red Guards on the railway workers' apartment complex. Her unit was challenged by a defensive phalanx of three hundred Shanghai Red Guards, who were the railway workers' children. The leaders confronted each other while the massed ranks behind them waved little red books and shouted Chairman Mao's slogans.

"We stand with our fathers, with the working class!" The cheeks of the eighteen-year-old Shanghai leader were scarlet in anger. "We are the true proletariat, while you, you rotten eggs from Peking, are fake proletarians."

"We must distinguish clearly between our enemies and our friends." Tou-tou countered with the appropriate quotation from Chairman Mao. "You Shanghai people are rotten with bourgeois thinking. The railways must run again to serve the people."

"What do you know about serving the people?" the Shanghai youth retorted. "You foreigners have created chaos—devoured our food and stolen our rights. You've made Shanghai a jungle. Serve the people, you say! Because of you, the people don't even have enough food!"

"We must reason together," Tou-tou replied. "We must reconcile our views by struggle, criticism, and reform. We must . . ."

"If it's struggle you want . . ." The Shanghai leader hefted a crowbar.

A barrage of bricks soared over the rival leaders' heads into the defensive phalanx. The Shanghailanders growled in their throats and surged forward, trapping Tou-tou and their own leader between the converging front ranks. The youth's iron bar caught Tou-tou in the solar plexus, and she doubled over. The Shanghai Red Guards' pounding feet pummeled her defenseless body while girls' shrill screams rose above youths' enraged rumbling.

Two of her followers dragged Tou-tou from under the writhing knots of combatants. She motioned them to return to the battle and shouted: "Struggle! Struggle harder! A revolution is not a tea party!"

Shaken by the Shanghailanders' fierce defense of their parents and their homes, the Peking Red Guards retreated from the concrete battlefield. But they rallied and returned to the attack. The rival groups skirmished for five days, mauling each other in fierce melees. The Peking detachment counted seven dead and twenty-eight hospitalized; the defenders' casualties were even higher. Yet the trains still stood unmanned in their marshaling yards.

Tou-tou was in the thick of battle for almost a month. Her hair hung lank; her face was deeply scratched; her body was bruised and battered purple. Still she led her followers into the fray, hurling her most vehement taunts at the soldiers who cordoned off the struggling Red Guards.

"Son of a bitch-turtle," she screamed at a portly major whose superior calm recalled her father. "You're worse than the counterrevolutionaries. The People's Army *must* support the people's cause."

The astonished major regarded her blankly. Tou-tou rushed at him, whirling a heavy iron chain. When his men fended her off with rifle butts, she sobbed in frustration.

She knew the rot went deep, as Chairman Mao had warned, since the People's Liberation Army itself was infected with the deadly virus of bourgeois thought. Socialism was obviously in mortal peril when peasants from suburban truck farms marched into the city. Armed with rifles and shotguns by their reactionary cadres, the peasants joined the workers on February 6 to besiege the Kiangsi Street offices of the Shanghai People's Commune, the "ultra-left" successor to the Shanghai Revolutionary Committee. Tou-tou and sixteen lesser Red Guard leaders from Peking stood behind the bespectacled First Secretary of the Commune when he fearlessly faced the mob.

"You've taken over the factories and production has stopped." A bearded peasant leader brandished an old Japanese rifle. "We won't send a grain of rice or a leaf of cabbage to Shanghai until the factories start up again —until you grant our just demands. The peasants and workers demand more food, higher pay, and an end to oppression."

Tou-tou glowed with admiration for the First Secretary's courage. He patiently explained that even peasants and workers must sacrifice immediate benefits for the ultimate good of all the people. He did not blanch when the old peasant shouted, "We *are* the people— and you are sucking *our* blood!" He firmly told the dupes of the capitalist-roaders that the evil days of landlord-capitalist exploitation would return if they did not support the Shanghai People's Commune. The misguided peasants stubbornly repeated their demands for more food, lower taxes, higher wages, and shorter working hours.

"I can't do anything about your problems at this time," the First Secretary said reasonably. "It's a matter of national policy, a question for the Party Center."

The First Secretary retired with dignity into the dilapidated stone-faced building, but the infuriated peasants and workers would not disperse. Six hundred reactionaries advanced on the Commune's offices, every tenth man armed with a fowling piece, an old rifle, or a shotgun. But guards carrying submachine guns stood before the wrought-iron gates. As the door closed behind the First Secretary, they fired at the ground in front of the peasants' feet.

Watching through a window, Tou-tou marveled at the guards' restraint. Their commander shouted to the peasants to halt, but the tide of angry men flowed toward the building. The guards fired a second volley, careful not to hit the peasants.

"Cease firing," the wiry old peasant cried, "or we shoot back."

"Halt!" the guard commander shouted. "One more step and we'll shoot you down!"

The peasants and workers surged forward, and the commander ordered his men to fire.

They shot directly into the mob. Though twelve peasants fell, their fellows still moved forward. Their ancient weapons blasted the guards, felling five. The guards retreated into the building.

"This is counterrevolution," Tou-tou cried. "The reactionaries are trying to seize power!"

A volley from the mob shattered the windows, and dank air poured into the building. The guards' submachine guns fired prolonged bursts, and the peasants fell back. Her voice thick with indignation, Tou-tou shouted encouragement to the brave defenders of the new-born Shanghai Commune. Skulking in doorways across the road, the peasants raked the building with shots. Shouting louder, Tou-tou leaned out the window to brandish her little red book at the counterrevolutionaries. An impact hurled her to the floor of the cold room. She was crawling back to the window, determined to rejoin the struggle, when delayed shock overcame her.

Tou-tou did not see the belated arrival of the police of the Public Security Corps or their clash with the peasants. She did not see cordons of Liberation Army soldiers isolate both the rioters and the police. Insolently neutral, the soldiers actually opened their ranks to allow the peasants and workers to withdraw when their ammunition was exhausted. Throughout the protracted fight, Tou-tou lay unconscious on the floor amid broken glass.

She opened her eyes to see an intent young man

bending over her. He wore the red-starred cap of the Liberation Army. When his fingers probed her wound a lance of pain impaled her, and she sank back into unconsciousness.

"It's a pity," the young Army doctor said. "I'll need X-rays, but I'm pretty sure her spine's broken. Those hammered slugs are fearful. With luck she'll live. But she'll never walk again."

On the other side of the world, a declining former imperial capital embarked on another evening of gaiety. The London night was unseasonably warm for mid-April, and the police horses pawed restively at the unyielding pavement. A mounted constable swabbed his red forehead with his handkerchief.

"No way to spend the English summer, is it, Fred?" His partner offered the obligatory jest. "But it'll be over tomorrow."

"Rather be me and you, Bert, than those poor sods on foot." Fred nodded toward the arm-linked ranks of foot constables holding back the massed crowds that filled the Haymarket from Piccadilly Circus to Pall Mall.

"You think we've got aggro now," Bert warned. "Wait'll the nobs start coming out."

"Yanks quit Vietnam! Yanks quit Vietnam! Yanks go home!"

The throng chanted without passion, mesmerized by the monotonous beat of its own voices. Flags fluttering on long poles obscured the blue-tiled façade of Finland House. The American stars-and-stripes was scrawled with the taunt: SHAME. The red star of the Vietnam National Liberation Front fluttered vigorously beside the golden star of the Democratic Republic of (North) Vietnam. The three red stripes on the yellow flag of the Republic of (South) Vietnam were defaced by the black words: AMERICAN PUPPETS.

Placards held high demanded: FREEDOM FOR SOUTH VIETNAM. UP THE LIBERATION FRONT. YANK MURDERERS QUIT VIETNAM. University students waved the little red book of *Chairman Mao's Quotations* and shouted: "Without a people's army, the people have nothing."

The floodlit marquee of the Theatre Royal proclaimed in red letters four feet high: *Life and Death in Saigon*. Three-foot-high yellow letters blazoned the magic name: Alaine d'Alivère.

Before retiring seven hours earlier in Hong Kong, Albert Sekloong had smiled over the Telexed guest list for the premiere and the receipts for forward bookings. Dragon Films, he estimated, would clear $3 million on *Life and Death*, and his own outlay was no more than $200,000. Forced to withhold further financing in order to salvage Ah Sek, Albert retained his original financial interest in the project he had thought defunct.

Two days after *The Guardian* carried a sympathetic interview with Alaine lamenting the demise in midproduction of her *chef d'oeuvre*, the Friends of the Vietnamese People had offered to guarantee costs up to $2 million. Their loan was to bear a reasonable interest of 4 percent. If the finished film lived up to their confident expectations, they said, they would remit the interest "as a contribution to culture."

The Friends of the Vietnamese People had alarmed Alaine by "tentatively suggesting minor changes to make the film more realistic by graphically portraying American brutality and the valor of the People's Forces." But Alaine in all artistic conscience found no reason to object. The Friends had even provided actual footage of the Vietcong operating in the Mekong Delta. The stark black-and-white scenes contrasted dramatically with the gaudy color depicting the degenerate Americans and their Vietnamese puppets. The film told the story of a half-Vietnamese prostitute: first, her sexual exploitation by a sadistic American colonel, and, later, her arduous but honorable life after she stabbed him and joined the People's Liberation Forces, carrying the master plan for the infamous Operation Phoenix that assassinated Vietcong cadres.

The London premiere sponsored by the Friends of the Vietnamese People was proving a commercial and artistic coup. The intellectual community had contended for invitations, and the Friends had, quite remarkably, secured the 146-year-old Theatre Royal, which normally presented only stage plays. The first-night audience included authors and journalists, actors and actresses, television celebrities and university dons, compassionate clergymen and Labour life-peers, as well as militant American scriptwriters and motion-picture stars living in civilized exile in London. The American Ambassador had declined, but the French Ambassador, wearing all his decorations with his tailcoat, was seated beside three delegates of the National Liberation Front in funereal black.

London was only the beginning. Premieres followed by long runs were already booked for Paris, Munich, Tokyo, and Stockholm. The United States, still gripped by war hysteria, the Friends advised, was more difficult to book. But *avant garde* theaters, anti-war activists, and student groups were keenly interested.

"Ho . . . Ho . . . Ho Chi Minh! Ho . . . Ho . . . Ho Chi Minh!" The crowd chanted as the Theatre Royal's doors opened and the critics scurried to make their deadlines. "Ho . . . Ho . . . Ho Chi Minh! Ho . . . Ho . . . Ho Chi Minh!"

The portly critic of *The Times* paused on the pavement for a word with the bright young man *The Washington Post* had flown to London for the premiere.

"You know, Jake," the Englishman mused, "if I simply *had* to sum up this film in one word . . . thank God I don't. . . . But, if I had to, that word would be *integrity*."

"It took guts to make this one, Lionel," the man from *The Washington Post* replied. "Real guts to blast the Establishment just by telling the truth. It really tells it like it is."

"You chaps who've been in Vietnam, you do know," *The Times* observed. "It must have been Hell. How long were you there?"

"Actually I never . . . too busy at home. But I've talked with our guys who were there. Real guts, that's

815

what it took to make this movie. And that Alaine—what a dame!"

"Quite dishy, isn't she?"

A slender, dark-haired girl wearing red-velvet trousers and a black-velvet jacket over a frilled white blouse smiled dreamily at the overheard conversation. Her violet eyes were unfocused, and their pupils were pinpoints. Mary Henriette Philippa Sekloong was floating in euphoria induced by her cousin's triumph and by the four pipes of opium she had smoked before the performance. Wholly self-assured at sixteen, Little Lady Mary disdained the marijuana and amphetamines her seventeen-year-old brother Jonathan III favored. She contemptuously spurned the LSD her eighteen-year-old cousin George Chapman Parker III urged upon her.

"Opium was good enough for great-great-grandpapa," she said firmly. "It must be good enough for me."

The cousins could not believe that Sir Jonathan had never smoked a single pipe of opium. Jonathan III, who was drawing on a joint, had insouciantly dismissed his father Sir Henry's heated denial that the Old Gentleman was an opium addict. The equally skeptical George Chapman Parker III, who wore a stained jeans jacket over a tee-shirt emblazoned DEATH TO ALL PIGS, squinted into the floodlights, which his disoriented brain perceived as an oscillating, unearthly rainbow.

"Don't hand me that crap, man!" Chappie had sneered at his father when that strait-laced Air Force Brigadier General pleaded with him to give up drugs. "Don't I know it? Grandpa Jonnie peddled opium on Shanghai streets. And great-great-grandpa . . . the Old Man, Sir Jonathan, for Chris' sake. He shoveled the stuff into China. Why donchya stop preaching to me? Go back to Vietnam and drop napalm on babies!"

"Ho . . . Ho . . . Ho Chi Minh! Ho . . . Ho . . . Ho Chi Minh!" The crowd chanted, surging forward. "Ho . . . Ho . . . Ho Chi Minh!"

The constables struggled to clear a lane for the Daimlers, Jaguars, Bentleys, and Rolls-Royces of the audience. The bejeweled women waiting between the marble pillars designed by Thomas Nash for King George IV had already repaired make-up ravaged by their tears for the oppressed South Vietnamese peasantry. The three cousins paused indecisively amid the chattering filmgoers.

"Whyn't we go back to that great club with the horse and acid?" Chappie Parker suggested. "Skip Alaine's party. Nobody but old deadbeats there."

"I think not, Chappie," Jonathan replied judiciously. "Let's go back to Belgrave Square. I've got some new hash hidden behind the Picasso."

"Hash, man!" Chappie snorted. "That's for kids. Why not the club, real action?"

"We'll never make the ten o'clock plane if we don't get a bit of sleep," Mary admonished her wavering brother. "And it's a two-hour drive from Zurich to St. Moritz. I want to be on the slopes tomorrow afternoon."

"You're a real tough doll, ain't you?" Her cousin was admiring. "Okay, if that's the way you want it."

"Ho . . . Ho . . . Ho Chi Minh!" The raucous chanting was aggressive. "Ho . . . Ho . . . Ho Chi Minh!"

Alaine d'Alivère emerged from the Theatre Royal to pose for avid photographers between the white pillars. Her blond beauty framed by the ermine stole draped over her cloth-of-gold gown, Alaine was as radiant as her sapphire-and-diamond necklace. She raised her clenched fist in salute.

"Ah . . . laine! Ah . . . laine! Ah . . . laine!" The spaced syllables were a counterpoint to the rhythmic chant: "Ho . . . Ho . . . Ho Chi Minh!"

Kissing her hands to the demonstrators, Alaine entered her waiting Daimler. Distracted by the by-play, the rank of gawking constables broke under the crowd's renewed assault. A pole knocked a mounted constable from his horse. The foot constables drew their truncheons, but their thin line was overborne by the weight of the throng.

"Pigs!" Chappie shouted. "Kill the pigs!"

Dragging Jonathan along, he hurled himself into the melee. After hesitating momentarily, Little Lady Mary followed. It looked as much fun as schussing straight from the Corvatch to the Palace Hotel in St. Moritz. She slithered through the battling throngs toward her brother and cousin, who were bearing down a struggling constable.

"Kill . . . the . . . pigs! Kill . . . the . . . pigs!" Chappie chanted to the rhythm of a metronome ticking within his own brain. "Kill . . . the . . . pigs!"

"Ho . . . Ho . . . Ho Chi Minh!" Jonathan's lighter voice responded. "Long live Chairman Mao! Long live Chairman Mao!"

Flung wide in the struggle, the constable's hand struck Mary in the face. She bit down reflexively, and the constable screamed. Mary unlocked her teeth and echoed her brother's cry: "Long live Chairman Mao!"

The mounted constables forced the crowd back, their disciplined horses gradually channeling the writhing mass of screaming youths. A knife jabbed a velvet flank, and a horse reared. The crowd shrank from the flailing hooves, leaving the three young Sekloongs isolated. Four constables converged to imprison them in blue-clad arms.

"Kill . . . the . . . pigs!" Chappie chanted, jerking his knee at a constable's groin. "Kill . . . the . . . pigs!"

"No, you don't, you little Yank bastard!" The constable slammed his truncheon down on Chappie's thigh.

The Black Maria and the bleakly utilitarian police station, redolent of Dettol, subdued the cousins. Despite his relief at having slipped his last two joints behind the Black Maria's hard bench, Jonathan's fingers trembled. He thrust his hands deep into his pockets and, elation departed, considered his predicament, above all, his father's reaction.

"I think my leg's broken." Chappie was still flying high on LSD. "Goddamned pigs won't let you live. But don't worry. I've had this scene before. The slammer's not that bad."

He perked up when a stout wardress led Mary away.

"Watch that one," he stage-whispered. "She looks like a bull dike, and she's got eyes for you."

A subdued Jonathan gratefully accepted the opportunity to telephone his father's solicitor, his cousin John Philip Duane Osgood, who was Lady Mary's nephew.

"Not to worry," John Osgood reassured him. "I'll have you out in time to make your plane. Good thing your parents are abroad. But, do tell me, old chap, what was the exercise in aid of? What was the point?"

Mid-July of 1967 was unbearably hot—steaming, miserably hot even for Hong Kong. The daytime temperature had not dropped below 92° for two months, while the humidity, inexorably linked to the thermometer, ranged between 88 and 97 percent. The low of 88° during the hours of darkness brought no relief to millions sweltering in the tenements of Wanchai and Kowloon. Those were the readings at the breezy eminence of the Royal Observatory in Kowloon. The asphalt melted in downtown Victoria, and thermometers read 110° in the sun on posh Shouson Hill Road, where the privileged complained that their air conditioners labored to bring the temperature down 10°. Working-class families gasped like landed fish in minuscule bed-alcoves in Mongkok and Kuntong. The red lines on their cheap Chinese thermometers reached 120° and could rise no higher.

Haggard with physical and nervous exhaustion, all Hong Kong's people scanned the weather forecasts and prayed for a typhoon. The vicious tropical storms that intermittently scourged the Colony in June often brought floods and landslides, but they also filled the reservoirs and drove temperatures down. In 1967, however, typhoons Queenie and Rita maddeningly veered away to savage Taiwan and Hainan Islands. No rain had fallen for eight months, and the Colony's reservoirs were great baked mud pits.

The desperate shortage of water was the ultimate torture, and the authorities were compelled to enforce rationing by closing the valves on the mains. For just two hours once every four days, taps tantalizingly yielded brackish trickles to half-fill bathtubs and plastic buckets. The pressure was too low to carry water above the sixth floor of jerry-built high rises that lacked elevators. The unfortunates above that divide labored up narrow staircases carrying slopping kerosene tins filled at public taps where hundreds waited. Sweat-soaked garments unlaundered for weeks covered sweating bodies caked with salt.

Nature had conspired with diplomatic protocol to afflict the Colony. Failure of the normal spring rains had invariably required water-rationing in the 1950s. But the Colony had not suffered rationing for almost ten years, not since Kwangtung Province contracted to provide supplementary water through new pipelines. Unfortunately, the agreement stipulated that Hong Kong would not draw on Chinese water from mid-June through mid-September. Civil servants, diplomats, and newspapermen, all drenched in their own sweat, wondered whether the Chinese would actually reopen their enormous valves when mid-September came. Kwangtung was still shipping the pigs, the chickens, and the vegetables that fed Hong Kong. But the timorous feared that the failure to provide emergency water was an extension of the militant Cultural Revolution, a deliberate attempt to exert indirect but powerful pressure on the Colony.

The actual reason was less subtle and less ominous. The managers of the Kwangtung Waterworks dared not depart from the letter of the contract by opening their valves. It was, they felt, better to do nothing, rather than render themselves vulnerable to political criticism by acting positively.

The Castle and the demi-mansions of Sekloong Manor possessed their own holding tanks. Since those rooftop tanks stored only three days' normal supply for the Manor's hundred-odd inhabitants, Lady Mary reluctantly ordered new pumps for the well that had served Sekloong Manor before water mains came to The Peak. But she insisted upon stringent water discipline. July 1967 was no time to flaunt one's privileges. The Sekloongs would maintain a very low posture amid Hong Kong's manifold troubles.

"Water, water everywhere, nor any drop to drink," Archbishop Charles Sekloong observed plaintively to his mother. "And hardly a drop to wash in."

Charles had arrived four days earlier to assess the Great Proletarian Cultural Revolution's implications for the Church and to counsel the Colony's large Catholic population in its fearful perplexity. The Roman Curia preferred to rely upon Charles, who was one of their own, rather than heed the astringent Belgian Jesuit who had devoted eighteen years to analyzing the People's Republic. Charles had, however, already decided that he must depend largely upon that Jesuit, as well as the diplomats and newspapermen the world called China Watchers.

Though happy to return home, the Archbishop felt slightly uncomfortable in The Castle, where even the water shortage seemed a self-abnegating pretence. He could, however, hardly spurn his aged mother's hospitality. She had passed her eighty-seventh birthday on June 28, 1967, and he could not hope that the Lord God in His mercy would grant her many more years.

"Water, water everywhere, particularly here." He laughed, and Lady Mary suddenly saw the mischievous Little Mandarin of half a century ago in the heavy-set churchman.

"You're getting fat," she twitted. "If you don't look out, you'll be one of the fattest archbishops, as well as one of the youngest. And do stop going on about water."

"Would you rather I talked about wine?" he asked. "The pleasures of the table, Mother, are all that are left to me."

"And the pleasures of power, Charles. No Sekloong could ever resist power."

"But power exercised with discretion, and for the common good." The Archbishop was suddenly serious. "Not for self-glorification."

"So they all say, Charles, everyone who loves power. At least you've given up trying to convert me."

"Never tried, you know. A doctor doesn't treat his own family. Anyway, you'll do. You'll be waiting in Heaven for me—if you don't outlive us all."

"I may outlive your mad grandnephews and grandniece if they don't stop their nonsense. And perhaps your brother James as well."

"This is the year of the riots, Mother," Charles said. "The madness is everywhere—Paris, Hong Kong, New York and, of course, all China. I heard about that escapade in London. Any more news of Tou-tou or James?"

"Nothing more than James's one brief letter," she sighed. "He wrote that Tou-tou had been severely injured, perhaps crippled. But not a word about himself."

"We can't expect that, can we? If he's in difficulties, he'd only make them worse by broadcasting them. But James will survive. I'm worried about the younger ones."

"What *has* got into the children, Charles? Sometimes I fear they're all mad."

"Not mad, just terribly self-indulgent and, though it sounds an unlikely combination, overzealous. Youth is always too zealous, age, perhaps, too tolerant."

"Charles, you're being obscure."

"I mean, Mother, that the children are muddleheaded. As Christians, they know that good and evil exist. But they can't really distinguish between them. Nor can they, as Chairman Mao teaches, distinguish clearly between their friends and their enemies."

"Nor distinguish their own interests," Mary said tartly. "They are allying themselves with people who want to destroy everything the Old Gentleman built."

"That's more your province than mine. I shudder at their misguided moral fervor. And they see everything in hard-edged black and white."

"Not when they're flying high, as they say, on drugs."

"That, too? I feared as much. What can *we* do?"

"I'm having them out in August, Mary, Jonathan, and that unspeakable Chappie. I can, at least, talk with them. I don't think their parents ever try."

"This August, Mother?"

"Yes, Charles. They'll learn more from Hong Kong in turmoil than in tranquility."

"With the riots and the threat from China?"

"Fiddle-faddle, Charles. You sound like that fool Lachlan Wheatley, the new *taipan*. He's bleating nonsense all over the Colony: 'What could we do if half a million Red Guards pour across the border?' "

"What *could* we do?"

"Nothing, because they *won't*. The Liberation Army has already turned back twenty thousand Red Guards who wanted to march on Hong Kong. Probably knew they'd never come back."

"And our own local Red Guards?"

"They're pink pussycats, not red tigers. Anyway, the people have made their choice. And, I suspect, so has Peking. All the sound and fury is just face-saving."

"Are you quite sure?"

"As sure as I can be. Hong Kong Chinese don't like the British. We're stuffy and self-righteous and venal. But they like the Communists even less. They're stuffy, self-righteous, venal—and brutal."

"But the riots and the bombs? Hong Kong's hardly reassuring just now."

"Neither is it terrifying. Tell me, Charles, what have you learned about our little Cultural Revolution? I think the children can learn from it. You might too."

"Not much yet. I've only just arrived, you know. Naturally, I've chatted with a few people, read the local press, and . . ."

"The local press, indeed! May I tell you how it's looked to me? I'll try not to bore you."

"You never could, my dear."

Charles congratulated himself. He placed much higher value on Lady Mary's views than those of the bureaucrats, but he had wanted her to volunteer her account.

"It all began in April with a gaggle of labor disputes." Lady Mary spoke rapidly, and her violet eyes were animated. "The workers were right, of course, but that became a side issue. Our local Maoists—most of them fat-cat capitalists, by the way—didn't really know what Peking wanted, but saw the chance to prove their militant loyalty by bringing the Cultural Revolution to Hong Kong. And what better pretext than labor disputes?

"Early in May, a few thousand students and workers were marching through the streets waving their little red books, chorusing the Chairman's quotations, and demanding justice for the striking workers. Occasionally, the proletariat's leaders alighted from their Mercedeses and Rollses to chant slogans."

Charles was amused by his mother's acerbic acuity.

"Albert was caught in an incident on Connaught Road. The rioters hurled bricks and paving stones. But the police stood firm behind their wicker shields. Their confidence was, no doubt, enhanced by their steel helmets. Nonetheless, three constables were hospitalized. But they didn't savage the rioters. *Too* patient, perhaps.

"Then it turned nasty. The rioters sallied out to attack the police from their fortresses: the China Products Emporiums, which sell mainland goods; the Bank of China, which virtually enjoys extra-territorial rights; and the trades union headquarters in high buildings. Some wielded stolen revolvers. Most had knives, crowbars, clubs, and bicycle chains.

"The China Products stores and the Bank were out of bounds politically, and it was suicidal to climb the narrow stairways to the union offices with missiles raining down. By the time the riot company reached the top, the rioters had escaped across the rooftops to another fortress. But someone used his head. Helicopters dropped onto the rooftops to discharge the riot companies. Attacked from above and below, the Maoists were trapped.

"Then the slogans began to change. The Maoists demanded 'justice' for their imprisoned comrades, which meant letting them go free. They also demanded the end of British imperialism. 'Limeys, go home!' as Albert might say. It got terribly sticky when someone on the other side decided to join in. The border police were pinned down by machine-gun fire from the Chinese side, and the Gurkhas had to rescue them. For a few days, we had a mini-border war. But Canton finally told the hotheads to cool down.

"Government House was besieged by demonstrators bearing petitions. The police finally winkled them out of Lower Albert Road, and that was the prelude to the real confrontation.

"About one thousand rioters massed around the Hilton. Some tourists got a nasty shock. One minute they were happily watching our quaint natives demonstrate. The next minute, the Maoists shattered the big plate-glass windows and poured into the Coffee Shop. I'm told one American matron's blue hair turned white with fright. Actually, it wasn't funny. Three of the old dears were badly cut by flying glass.

"I saw the confrontation from Kennedy Road through binoculars. A thousand or so rioters were trying to force their way up the hill to Government House. A few hundred policemen faced them. The Maoists swore terrible oaths I couldn't possibly repeat. They kicked the constables in the groin, gouged at their eyes, and thrust fingers up constables' noses. But our little Cantonese boys stood firm.

"I wish the foreigners had been as firm. Almost all the big *taipans* and the little *taipans,* Chinese *and* foreign, discovered pressing business elsewhere. Simply *had* to fly off for urgent medical attention. It was disgraceful, my dear.

"At any rate, I watched those policemen stand in the fearfully hot sun for two hours, abused and mauled. Their discipline was almost unbelievable. What those stocky little chaps put up with. A sergeant's skull was fractured, and those hell-cat female comrades stabbed a corporal. He was almost emasculated.

"When the rioters charged the police, the superintendent finally gave the order, and the constables waded into the demonstrators. I can't say that they were gentle, though they never unslung their rifles. In ten minutes, the battle of the Hilton Hotel was won.

"Since then, it's been downhill, though the police have had to use tear-gas and rubber bullets several times since. We still have amateurish small bombs exploding here and there. Most hurt the poor Chinese— curious workers or children who pick up packages left at bus stops. Very amateurish, though I shouldn't like to be the chap who defuses the bombs."

"You make it sound like a jolly Christmas entertainment, Mother," Charles protested.

"It wasn't my dear, I assure you. Reminded me of the riots in 1900 and 1909, particularly the political riots in 1900. It's frightening the way these clashes between Chinese and British recur. In 1900 the Boxers besieged the Legations in Peking. In 1967 the Red Guards besieged the Russian Embassy and burnt the British Embassy. Chinese and foreigners just can't seem to get along. The Maoists in Hong Kong again stuck up placards demanding: CRUSH BRITISH IMPERIALISM. KILL THE WHITE-SKINNED PIGS. One couldn't *really* leave then, could one? Besides, our own people were in danger."

"Our *own* people, Mother?"

"Yes, our own people. Millions of decent, hardworking Chinese who've been exploited for generations by both foreigners and their wealthy blood-brothers. One simply couldn't leave them to the gentle mercy of the Communists. But it's really over now. I'm buying land as fast as I can, before everyone realizes the threat is finished and prices rise again."

The Archbishop coughed to keep from laughing aloud. How, he wondered, could he ever understand the human soul when he could not understand the soul of the one human being who had given him life? His mother apparently saw no moral incongruity in affirming her responsibility to the people of Hong Kong in one sentence and in the next discussing her plans to profit from their suffering.

He was touched by her loyalty to the Chinese and wryly amused by the automatic reflex of a commercial mind trained by the old master Sir Jonathan. How, he wondered, could the Old Gentleman have put his impress so deeply on Mary Philippa Osgood, an alien woman from an alien culture? Sir Jonathan, too, had striven to help the poor Chinese, and Sir Jonathan, too, had consistently profited from the political upheavals that tormented the poor.

Was it really all over, Charles wondered, Hong Kong's ordeal by its own small Cultural Revolution?

Neither Hong Kong nor China itself was to emerge from the violence of the Great Proletarian Cultural Revolution for some time. Hong Kong was to suffer another five months, China almost two years longer. The tide of disorder in the Colony, having reached its height in June 1967, was slowly receding. The high-tide swept China in July 1967, and the immensely greater turmoil in the People's Republic was to wreak vastly greater damage before it subsided into troubled half-peace.

Charles Sekloong and Dewey Miller later pieced together the story of the climactic Wuhan Revolt. From July 13 through July 23, they concluded, limited civil war had ravaged the industrial plexus of Central China. The Wuhan Revolt was the most violent rejection of Chairman Mao's commands.

Neighboring Kiangsi Province was already aflame. Well organized, heavily armed former soldiers of the Liberation Army fought pitched battles against Maoists and regular troops. Three rival Red Guard factions, each more than 100,000 strong, struggled in the streets of Canton. Antagonistic Red Guards dueled with artillery and tanks in Chungking. Soviet trains carrying arms to Hanoi through Kwangsi Province were hijacked, and their North Vietnamese guards were killed.

Dispatched by Premier Chou En-lai to mediate, James Sekloong pleaded with the leaders of Kwangsi's hostile factions: "Keep the rifles, machine guns, and mortars, if you must. But for Heaven's sake give back the anti-aircraft missiles. Neither of you has an air force."

The commanding general sealed off Nanking and ignored all Peking's orders. He feared the shattered Party Center less than the angry workers who demanded that he crush the Maoists.

Only in Wuhan, however, did combat units of the Liberation Army inflict severe casualties on each other. Thousands of anti-Maoist workers of the Wuhan Iron and Steel Works precipitated those battles by organizing a paramilitary force called the Million Heroes, which included thousands of disillusioned Red Guards. The general commanding the Wuhan Military Region was already demoralized by Maoist-incited anarchy. He permitted his 8201st Division to support the Million Heroes when the irregulars seized the Yangtze River railway bridge and severed China's main line of north–south communication. But his 8199th Division, which was loyal to the Maoists, counterattacked to retake the bridge.

Only one man could cut through the Gordian complexity of doctrine, power, and emotion. On July 21, 1969, Chou En-lai, accompanied by General Shih Ai-kuo, landed at a People's Air Force base near the embattled city. The Premier summarily relieved the Regional Commander and delivered an ultimatum to the leaders of the opposing factions and the commanders of the 8201st and 8199th Divisions.

"I am bringing up two artillery divisions," Chou stormed. "A flotilla of gunboats will reach Wuhan this time tomorrow. Bomber Command is on alert. If all fighting does not stop in two days' time, those forces will bombard Wuhan. General Shih Ai-kuo will remain to carry out my orders."

When James Sekloong escorted the exhausted Premier to his airplane, Chou En-lai was uncharacteristically candid.

"I must get back before Peking, too, explodes," he said. "I rely upon you to make these idiots stop fighting each other. Use *all* necessary force."

"All *necessary* force, Comrade Premier? Can you be more precise?"

"More precise? How could I? It's in your hands. You *must* pull this one off or civil war will sweep the country. But I will tell you one thing: When this madness ends, we'll never let the wild children anywhere near power again—and Lin Piao will go."

On July 23 fighting ceased. James collapsed onto a camp bed, having cajoled and threatened, pleaded and warned for a sleepless forty-eight hours. When he woke fourteen hours later, the silence startled him. For the first time in a month, no shots resounded in Wuhan. He wondered if he would have bombarded the city, and grimly concluded that he would have done so if the troops and the Red Guards had not observed the cease-fire. He had come a long, weary way from the Whampoa Academy and the siege of Shanghai forty years earlier. He had, perhaps, come too far on the road that had forked decisively when he fired his Beretta pistol at his Uncle Harry.

On August 1, 1967, China signally failed to celebrate the fortieth anniversary of the Nanchang Rising that had given birth to the People's Liberation Army. The generals were still striving to reestablish their authority by suppressing almost universal civil disorder; the countryside was cut off from the turbulent cities; and Peking was itself virtually isolated from the provinces. Just a year after the rump Central Committee of the Communist Party had decreed the Great Proletarian Cultural Revolution, the nation was disintegrating. Though barely averted once, a major civil war still threatened. Much time was needed to impose civil order, much more time to heal the wounds of the body politic. Chou En-lai knew it would require not months or years, but at least half a decade to re-create a stable administration in a peaceful country—if that feat was, indeed, possible.

The direct threat to Hong Kong ended in September, though random bombs still shook the Colony. Common danger had drawn together the Colony's Chinese and European inhabitants as had common suffering under the Japanese invasion. The British believed that true unity forged in the mutual ordeal joined the two communities in harmony. The Chinese, who knew better, did not disillusion their alien rulers.

Most were otherwise concerned. Better times were coming as the escalating war in Vietnam pumped American dollars into Hong Kong's economy. The timorous bureaucrats of Kwangtung Province, adhering strictly to the letter of the agreement, turned on the water promptly at midnight of September 14. The practical politicians who were regaining power in Peking obviously believed that British Hong Kong was still useful to Communist China. The Colony happily returned to the traditional functions that had made it indispensable and rich—trading with all who wished to trade and taking its due profits.

Albert Sekloong was still elated by his personal exploit. Driving past the Country Club on Wong Chuk Hong Road, he saw two young boys from the nearby farm village poking bamboo poles at a brown-paper parcel. Shouting to the boys to run, he hurtled out of his canary-yellow Porsche and threw the parcel into the underbrush. The bomb exploded in midair, peppering his right arm with metal fragments. The pain of his wounds was allayed by fulsome praise from the newspapers and near adulation from his grandmother, his mother, and, best of all, his wife. Lieutenant Colonel Sir Henry Sekloong and Brigadier General George Parker were not the only men of action in his generation. Since all others hailed his heroism, Albert could disregard his Uncle Charles's dry observation that the plaudits might have been less enthusiastic if the Sekloongs were not automatically news in Hong Kong.

The resurgence of confidence after a half-year of terror was invigorating the Colony's business—and stimulating Albert's own enterprises. He was particularly pleased by the one venture that was inherently glamorous, though negligible financially beside his other interests. Delighted by the receipts from *Life and Death in Saigon,* which was still filling theaters in Japan, Europe, and Southeast Asia, he was planning a new production by Dragon Films. That costume epic of the Ming Dynasty would offend neither his grandmother's Victorian moral sensibilities nor her conservative political sensitivities.

More important, Albert could rejoice without reservation at the results of the drastic operation Lady Mary and he had mounted two years earlier to rescue his foundering major enterprises. But a more mature Albert reflected with new humility that his grandmother's perspicacity had been even more critical to the success of that endeavor than had his own energy and agility. He further realized that luck had been a determining factor. Luck or "good fortune with a little prodding," as Lady Mary described it. Luck or "a merciful Providence," as his Uncle Charles insisted. He gave thanks to that Providence for teaching him that more than acumen and drive were required to assure success in business or any other human enterprise. He was learning that ruthlessness might occasionally be necessary, but that ruthlessness was in itself neither a particular virtue nor a guarantee of success. He reminded himself that he must never again forget the imponderables of human irrationality and human emotions, whether writ large in politics or writ fine in relations between individuals.

Nonetheless, Albert was justifiably pleased with himself. After Lady Mary's contacts prepared the way, he had sold the six Electras of Hong Kong Airways to Air America, the private airline of the American Central Intelligence Agency. Dragon Plastics and Electronics Ltd. was amassing substantial profits from sales of its printed and quartz-chip circuits in the United States and Japan. Wheat and commodity futures had risen dramatically after Lady Mary called Dewey Miller's attention to the probability of Soviet and Chinese shortages. Peking was buying hundreds of thousands of tons of grain to alleviate the shortages following upon the disruption of the Cultural Revolution and, in particular, to feed the Liberation Army and the Security Forces. Megalith Housing had already sold flats that would not come into existence until 1970. Best of all, judicious "gifts" to the generals who ruled Indonesia had regained the drilling concessions of Borneo South Seas Exploration, and he was momentarily expecting confirmation of the major oil strike his geologists confidently promised. The shares of his holding company, Ah Sek, were rising rapidly, while J. Sekloong and Sons was exuberantly profitable. Albert had, he felt, proved himself in adversity.

He was therefore not particularly put out by his grandmother's wry tone when she asked Kazuko and him to join his Uncle Charles and his mother, Sarah, for dinner at her table.

"I suppose champagne is in order," Lady Mary said. "But I'd be still happier, Albert, if you truly recognized that someone has to look after the next generation. Not just your boy and girl. They're only babies. But little Mary and Jonathan. Even the unspeakable Chappie. That someone, Albert, I'm afraid, is you."

"I'm loaded down already, Grandma." Albert protested automatically. "I know I've been lucky and I'd have gone under without you. But now's the time to make a real killing."

"Albert, money is for use," Sarah said, "not just for making more money."

"You've got two sides to your brain, Albert, and you've got two hands," Lady Mary added. "You must find time for the family and for those others who need help. Otherwise all your killings will be meaningless. Why your great-grandfather . . ."

"Not another lecture on the Old Gentleman,

Grandma, please," Albert smiled. "I know all the great things he did, and, I promise, I'm trying."

"Yes, another lecture, whether you like it or not." Lady Mary's smile paid reluctant tribute to Albert's charm. "Money is all important to those who don't have it. It means freedom and power. But money should be no more than a tool to those who possess large quantities. Otherwise, it means enslavement."

"We almost didn't have it, Grandma," Albert said. "My fault, but we were all worried, weren't we?"

"Do stop preening yourself," Lady Mary rejoined tartly. "It requires near genius to *begin* making a fortune when one starts with nothing. Already possessing large sums, one must be very clever indeed *not* to make more. One must be a veritable genius of ineptitude to lose a fortune."

"And, Albert, you must make your money work for you and for others," his mother reminded him. "So many things need to be done here and elsewhere."

Albert was nonplussed by the new demands imposed at his moment of triumph. Archbishop Charles Sekloong hid a smile behind his damask napkin. Some day, he reflected, Albert might rise to the almost impossibly high standards set by his mother, his grandmother, and his great-grandfather.

"What," Albert finally asked, "do you expect of me now?"

"You are now *the* Sekloong," his grandmother replied. "You must *willingly* assume total responsibility for the entire clan. You must preserve not only the Sekloong fortunes, but the Sekloong reputation. Our name means more than wealth. It means intelligent charity and wide awareness of the effect of our actions on other human beings. It means generously recompensing—in all manner of ways, not just financially—those whose brains and hands have given you your wealth. Above all, it means responsibility for the less fortunate, as your father, your grandfather, and your great-grandfather understood."

"I can only try, after I've tried to understand exactly

what you mean." Albert joked to cover his embarrassment, but reverted to seriousness. "And, I promise you, I *will* try."

"You may say grace, now, Charles." Lady Mary relented. "Please give profound thanks for our survival —and pray the Lord to preserve the Sekloongs from their greatest failing, pride."

Postlude

June 28, 1970

THE deserted offices of J. Sekloong and Sons on the nineteenth floor of St. George's Building swayed slightly each time the raging wind hurled solid rain against their sheet-glass windows. At 1:04 on the morning of Sunday, June 28, 1970, Typhoon Linda was gathering herself to leave Hong Kong and storm into China. One propeller-shaft snapped like a bamboo wand, the 8,000-ton freighter *Oriental Monarch* pounded herself into a jagged wreck against the airport runway. When its hillside foundation gave way, the twelve-story Alexandra Mansion on Stubbs Road subsided into a tumulus of concrete, mud, and twisted automobiles that entombed thirty-seven corpses. The Colony's ordeal was not yet over; the typhoon's lashing tail was still to wreak great damage and sweep away many lives.

Within the darkened suite, the single rose in the crystal bud vase beside the upright telephone dropped two petals on Sir Jonathan's ebony desk. The shining leather and bright steel womb Albert Sekloong had made his adjoining room reverberated with the repeated impacts, and the framed article from *Time* magazine rattled against the chased-gold Japanese wallpaper. Albert's communications center shrilled peremptorily for three full minutes. But no intelligence perceived the signal, and no hand lifted the telephone. Precisely upon the 181st second, an orange light glowed on the brushed-steel console beside the kidney-shaped desk. A relay tripped automatically, and, fifteen seconds later, a green light flashed. Faithful to its designer's intent, Albert's expensive toy was transferring urgent calls over great distances without human intercession.

The Colony's internal communications had been short-circuited by flood-waters seeping into cables and junction-boxes. Under Secretary Spencer Taylor Smith could not communicate with the boxlike United States

Consulate-General on Garden Road, which was still linked to the web of cables and satellites the American military had spun around the globe. No more could General Shih Ai-kuo telephone the sealed building in grimy North Point where the New China News Agency, the Peking regime's unofficial embassy, maintained its own telecommunications center. But the two private cables from Sekloong Manor to the Sekloong offices were still operating, as were the heavily shielded cables from St. George's Building to the computers of Cable and Wireless that fed electronic pulses into underseas cables to Washington and land-lines to Peking.

For the next three hours, those impromptu links were to carry scrambled telephone calls from the two antagonistic capitals to their senior emissaries confined in The Castle by Typhoon Linda's furious departure. The protracted negotiations between the People's Republic of China and the United States of America in Warsaw were culminating in an urgent dialogue in Hong Kong. The great storm admirably suited Lady Mary's purpose, since it forced the American diplomat and the Chinese general to talk face to face. Moreover, the rapid escalation of the crisis denied them the evasions and procrastination of normal diplomatic usage.

Peking forced the pace. At 12:20 on that Sunday morning—its clocks an hour behind Hong Kong's—the Chinese capital was arid and hot. Miniature whirlwinds of yellow dust from Central Asia swirled under the dim streetlights of the Boulevard of Protracted Peace, and the solitary wail of a train bound for Sinkiang 1,600 miles to the northwest echoed in the silence of the dark city. But beams of light from the Premier's offices in the Great Hall of the People and from the Headquarters of the People's Liberation Army twelve miles distant welcomed the limousines of senior officials.

Premier Chou En-lai was warily approaching a head-on confrontation with his nominal superior in the Communist Party and his nominal subordinate in the Central Government—Deputy Chairman Lin Piao, who was also First Vice Premier and Minister of Defense.

Though he knew that attacking Nationalist-held Taiwan could bring China and the United States into armed collision, the Premier could not countermand the assault Lin Piao had ordered. The Deputy Chairman planned to establish his supreme power—and to overthrow Chou En-lai—by using his troops to "liberate" the island, an achievement that had eluded the Premier's diplomacy for two decades. That feat would make Lin Piao's power unchallengeable by solidifying the support of the victorious generals behind him. His personal victory would lead to radical oppression at home, ending almost inevitably in popular rebellion; it would, further, commit a militant China to adventurism abroad that must eventually result in a nuclear clash with the United States. Yet, even the Premier would be vilified as a "traitor to the revolution" by the Deputy Chairman's sycophants if he directly opposed the operation.

Chou En-lai had, however, won the Politburo's approval for a final test of the diplomatic option even before he sent James Sekloong to Hong Kong to face Spencer Taylor Smith. The astute Chou En-lai had noted Washington's conciliatory signals—most obviously the gradual dismantling of American restrictions on trade and travel between the two countries. If the United States were seriously prepared to discuss improving relations with the People's Republic, he could still avert the assault. Lin Piao was, however, calculatedly impatient—committed by temperament and self-interest to the military solution, whatever the cost. He argued that the resolution of the United States, the power that must finally defend Taiwan, had been broken by American inability to bring the horrifying war in Vietnam to a victorious conclusion.

"There will never be a better opportunity, never," Lin Piao told Chou En-lai by telephone at 12:46 A.M. "It's Sunday, and Taiwan is disrupted by the typhoon. We'll bypass Quemoy to hit Taiwan directly. The bombers of the 6121st Air Division are arming, and the Navy is embarking the assault force. The Chairman himself has authorized the assault."

"Of course, Comrade Deputy Chairman." The Premier did not allude to their common knowledge that the enfeebled Chairman Mao Tse-tung, who was virtually sequestered by Lin Piao, almost invariably agreed with the last person who spoke to him. "If the American spy-planes and satellites saw no movement, the threat wouldn't be credible. The Chairman, as always, sees further than you or I—toward a diplomatic solution."

"Only if the Americans give way," Lin Piao concluded. "The Occidental Mind understands only one thing—force."

In the air-conditioned situation room in the basement of the White House, junior officers were transferring the latest intelligence reports of the Liberation Army's deployments against Taiwan to the talc overlays on maps of East China that had preempted the slots normally occupied by large-scale maps of Vietnam. The time was 12:52 P.M. on June 27, 1970, since Washington was thirteen hours behind Hong Kong and twelve hours behind Peking. The junior officers suppressed their annoyance at being deprived of a relaxed Saturday afternoon in deference to the President and his Assistant for National Security Affairs. The two men who controlled the world's most powerful military machine were attended by a constellation of generals and admirals. The officers' stars and ribbons were gaudily theatrical beside the seersucker jackets of the sandy-haired Assistant Secretary of State for the Far East and the tall, dark Asian specialist of the National Security Council. The Americans had not anticipated the triangular crisis quite so soon, though they knew Lin Piao and Chou En-lai were contending for power—and they had prepared detailed military and political plans to meet a Communist threat to Taiwan.

"The damned Chinese are screwing us up." The President was aggrieved. "Here we've been signaling we were ready to talk turkey—and suddenly they put a gun at our heads. And those shit-assed students've got me in a bind. It's too soon after the raid into Cambodia.

I'd hate to tangle with Peking right now. The agitators'd make life hell."

"We *must* help Chou En-lai, Mr. President," the Security Adviser observed. "If we are not firm, Lin Piao will strike, I believe."

"But it's my frigging decision, *mine,* not yours." The President irritably emphasized his responsibility. "And how much do we really know?"

"Dick?" The Security Adviser nodded to the young professor. "What's your appreciation?"

"Everything indicates it's a bluff—as far as Chou is concerned." The Security Council's Asian specialist measured his words. "But Lin Piao's going for broke. If we stand up to them, they *should* back down. If we don't, they'll certainly go all the way."

"Marshall?" the Security Adviser asked.

"I believe, Mr. President," the Assistant Secretary added, "that a diplomatic solution is still possible. But we've got to give Chou En-lai something concrete, a real prospect of our disengaging from Taiwan and relaxing Sino-American tension. Chou needs a victory— or Lin Piao and his hawks take over."

The President brooded darkly, his prognathous jaws clenched.

"We retain many military options, Mr. President," the Security Adviser counseled. "A range of responses from local defensive action to conventional bombing of Chinese staging points—escalating to industrial facilities and Peking itself. The Soviet dilemma is worse than our own. Which side to help?"

"The Sovs," interposed the Chief of Naval Operations, "have no significant forces in the area—and their bases are too far from Taiwan. I'd say they'd sit this one out."

"I believe Chou En-lai understands the nuances within our common conceptual framework," the Security Adviser continued. "He knows we can't give Taiwan away overnight. He must also know we can't cling forever to a spent force like the Nationalists. To me, the

841

Foreign Ministry's message relayed by General Shih Ai-kuo is basically conciliatory."

"But Chou En-lai's not running the show?" the President asked. "That's the problem?"

"Yes, Sir," the Asian specialist agreed. "And Lin Piao hasn't got the smarts. He thinks a spectacular victory'd really fix him up—all power for life. His threat's for real. The guns are moving, and he's playing for keeps—not bluffing."

"We've already told Spence Smith to feed them the usual crap—we'd view gravely any provocative action, all that crap?" the President asked.

"Yes, Sir," the Security Adviser confirmed. "And more: the United States cannot countenance the flagrant use of force against a friendly nation that has itself categorically renounced use of force against the Chinese mainland. We've also told Smith to request highly specific clarification of General Shih's offer to negotiate."

The President withdrew into himself, isolated by invisible but almost palpable walls from the ordered bustle in the situation room. He communed with his inner Furies for three minutes before announcing his decision.

"All right then. Move major Seventh Fleet units toward Taiwan and the China Coast. Yellow alert for SAC. Get some big bombers into the air and crank the missiles up. That'll warn the Russians off."

The generals and admirals hurried to the telephones that would set the American war-machine in motion half a world away. The four civilians were isolated, and the President wondered if he had already yielded too much authority to the men in uniform.

"The diplomatic option is still open." The National Security Adviser sensed his chief's misgivings. "We've already determined how far we can go—and how fast."

"Assuming," the President said, "we're dealing with Chou En-lai."

"That's the $64,000 question," agreed the Security Adviser. "Can we make it so?"

While the civilians pondered, the military of both sides moved. Teletypes chattered in Omaha, the headquarters of the Strategic Air Command. Ninety seconds later, B-52s carrying nuclear and conventional bombs climbed into orbit over Okinawa. Jet-engines whined on airfields in China's Fukien Province as pilots tested their Ilyushin-28 bombers. Five minutes later, combat-armed Marines filed into C-141s bound from Okinawa to Taiwan, and Chinese infantrymen carrying AK-47 assault rifles braced themselves as their east-bound landing-craft rolled in the billows of the Taiwan Straits. Spraddle-legged on the flag bridge of the heavy cruiser *Long Beach,* the vice-admiral commanding the U.S. Seventh Fleet squinted into the windy night and spoke quietly. Two minutes later, the aircraft-carrier *Enterprise* on Yankee Station off North Vietnam altered course, and her four nuclear-powered engines drove her northeast through the long swells of the South China Sea at thirty-eight knots. At the same moment, the carrier *Oriskany* pointed her gray bow toward the Taiwan Straits, trailing a light cruiser and four destroyers through the ten-foot waves of Typhoon Linda's wake in the East China Sea. The first Chinese convoy, carrying 9,000 men and shepherded by high-speed patrol-boats, was already sixteen miles from the Fukien coast, pounding due east to cover the ninety-four miles that separated it from Taiwan.

The quiet eye of the storm of Chinese and American military movements was The Castle in Sekloong Manor. The interface (as the new technology called the point of contact) between those two great forces was two men actually facing each other on either side of the azalea-banked fireplace of the study. Neither Spencer Taylor Smith nor James Sekloong rejoiced at having suddenly attained the pinnacle of power toward which he had clambered all his life. Each was awed by the terrifying responsibility he discerned from his new eminence. The domestic setting intensified the negotiators' unease. Neither could concentrate properly upon the hazardous confrontation while the unruly family milled about him. Even Lady Mary had yielded to the temptation to draw her son aside and offer unsought counsel.

"James, this is your opportunity," she had said. "You know I haven't always approved of your deeds or your associates. Too much killing. You can either crown your life by this night's work—or loose greater bloodshed and devastation. Incidentally, Charlotte tells me Avram Barakian is in touch with the Americans. They are interested in providing China with technology to develop offshore oil. It's your only hope, you know."

"At a great profit, no doubt," her son replied. "Always the greedy capitalists."

James's snap rejoinder masked his perturbation. He was dismayed by the outside world's knowledge of both China's vast offshore oil reserves and Peking's hope that their exploitation would resolve the nation's great economic and strategic problems. The Premier's "practical production faction" and the Deputy Chairman's "struggle faction," which were contending for supreme power, disagreed strongly on the development of those petroleum deposits. The Premier believed that foreign, particularly American, technological expertise under Chinese control was essential to their development. The Deputy Chairman argued that China would sacrifice both her Socialist purity and her freedom of action by utilizing foreign technicians and foreign equipment.

James's own loyalties were divided. As a soldier, he was directly subordinate to Lin Piao, who had been his first commander. As a Chinese and a Communist, he owed equal loyalty to his first teacher of Marxism, Chou En-lai. He would normally have supported the Premier's more rational policies regarding both national development and "liberating" Taiwan. But he was disturbed by the Premier's apparent acquiescence in the degradation of his wife Lu Ping. Besides, his military instinct preferred the hard line—a quick, overwhelming attack while the enemy was in disarray. But, remembering his son dead in Korea and his daughter maimed by

Lin Piao's Cultural Revolution, he shrank from further bloodshed.

Though Spencer Taylor Smith's loyalties were not divided, he too resented the family's pressure. Lady Mary had approached the Under Secretary too.

"Spencer," she had said, her hand resting on the bannister of the great Y-shaped staircase, "you must be patient with the Chinese. They are difficult. No one knows that better than I."

"Of course, Lady Mary," Spencer Taylor Smith answered impatiently.

"But they are too important to your country to overlook," she continued càlmly. "I've found they are sometimes so much more intelligent—or more stupid—than others. They are very, shall I say, vital—and they overdo things, go to excess. They're all extremists, even James. Be patient, Spencer—and be careful."

The Under Secretary was still pondering that enigmatic advice when his wife's Uncle Thomas approached him.

"Remember Quemoy, Spencer," the Nationalist General said. "We Nationalists don't give up easily. We just don't give up at all. *You* can block whatever treachery Washington and Peking are planning. Your hand is on the lever. And remember Quemoy!"

"The situation's not really analogous, Tom."

"Look, Spencer, we'll survive—no matter what dirty deals you make. We'll survive even if the Communists strike tomorrow morning."

"They're not likely," the American parried, "to do that."

"Spencer, don't take me for a fool. We have our sources and we know what the game is tonight. We'll survive—even if we have to fight alone. Maybe the Russians'll help us. You don't know what agreements we've made with them. And don't think you can force us to march into a grave you dig for us."

Thomas turned away contemptuously. His hauteur gave way to haste when he saw his niece Blanche Taylor descending the staircase, and he withdrew.

"What did that little creep want, Spence?" she asked. "He's a horror Don't believe a word he says. Aunt Charlotte says so—and she's his own sister."

"That'll do, Blanche!" Taylor Smith snapped at the one person to whom he need never pretend diplomatic courtesy. "I've had about enough. I'm engaged in grave negotiations—and you pass on messages from your dizzy Aunt Charlotte. This isn't a family matter."

"Don't be too sure, Spence." Blanche gathered her green-brocade skirt and swept away. "It's a big family."

The Under Secretary's black shoes scuffed against the polished teak treads as he climbed the Y-shaped staircase. The fatigue induced by tension was, he realized, compounded by his irritation at his wife's intrusive family. Thank God, he thought, the younger generation had not weighed in, particularly the unbearable Chappie Parker. As he reached the top of the staircase he smiled in grim derision of his own optimism. Little Lady Mary and her brother Jonathan were bearing down on him along the broad corridor.

Spencer Taylor Smith reflected that he was to be spared no conceivable annoyance during the hours that tested to the utmost all his diplomatic skills forged by the experience of a lifetime. His young cousins were the outward semblance of propriety: she in an ankle-length orange-silk dress with a cowl neckline and long sleeves, he in a tailcoat cut to understated perfection by Henry Poole of Cork Street. But their way of life and, he feared, their political views belied their appearance.

Still at Cambridge, Jonathan rode his father's horses in steeplechases and drove his Maserati on the Grand Prix circuit with the same wild zest. Little Lady Mary, who possessed the best mind of the fourth generation, was studying physics at Oxford, and Spencer Taylor Smith had heard her exclaim in exasperation to her great-grandmother: "No, Granny, generating electricity by fusion, *not* fission—*im*plosion, not *ex*plosion." She was, however, known among her contemporaries not as a "brain," but for her amours; and she had been hounded by the press only six months earlier for "having driven to suicide" the abstract-impressionist poet Alvin Gutmacher.

The American diplomat consoled himself that the passage of time would undoubtedly win the brother and sister to the solid bourgeois virtues he himself exemplified. But, remembering their arrest in London in 1967 and subsequent incidents, he turned away in haste.

"They probably want to tell me to give away not only Taiwan, but Hawaii and Catalina too," he muttered to himself.

His escape was blocked by two male figures: Jonathan and Little Lady Mary's father, brevet Brigadier Sir Henry Sekloong, dashing in the dark-blue dress uniform of the 17/21 Lancers; and George Chapman Parker, Jr., imposing in the light-blue of a United States Air Force major general. The two soldiers, above all the others, should know better than to interfere, and the diplomat was in no mood to talk with them. From earlier conversations, he assumed they would urge him to fire atomic missiles at Peking. Gratefully, he opened the door of the study and slipped into that sanctuary.

Those encounters distracted Spencer Taylor Smith as he watched James Sekloong settle into the worn, red-leather chair Dr. Sun Yat-sen had occupied in December 1911 shortly after the Republican Revolution. James, too, was distracted. He knew he must unavoidably "lean to one side," in the Chairman's phrase, by serving either the Premier or the Deputy Chairman. The direction in which he leaned could mean peace or war, as well as his own survival or eclipse.

"Mr. Smith," he said, "we've heard all these threats before. The United States cannot countenance the flagrant use of force, et cetera, et cetera, et cetera. We've heard it all before."

"And we've acted before, General Shih. I urge you to advise your principals not to be hasty. The United States is no paper tiger."

"No paper tiger? You've been bogged down in Vietnam for five years, Mr. Smith."

"We're not talking about guerrillas, General, or limited war. The Seventh Fleet is moving aircraft-carriers into the Taiwan area. Nuclear-armed bombers are in the air, and our missiles are in the firing position. Be careful how you loose the holocaust."

"You wouldn't dare. We, too, possess nuclear weapons. The American people are firmly opposed to your aggression in Vietnam. The entire world is angry at American arrogance."

"General Shih, my President is a great man, a daring man, no more to be judged by ordinary standards than your Chairman Mao. Neither you nor I can predict how he will react. We can obliterate your industry and your cities in ten minutes—and you have *no* allies. But we are willing to talk. Just what do you have in mind when you speak of negotiations that contain hope of successful compromise?"

"Mr. Smith, China's leaders do not always agree, as you may know. But all are determined to liberate Taiwan. The only question is how. Peacefully or by force —the choice is yours."

"General Shih, could you clarify that remark?" The Under Secretary of State was unaware that the Deputy Political Commissar of the People's Liberation Army was being forced toward a perilous personal choice. "I find your rhetoric obscure."

"I shall be very candid, Mr. Smith. China does not want war, and we are prepared to be reasonably patient regarding Taiwan. But *no* Chinese government—and *certainly* not Premier Chou En-lai's—can survive unless it can show a realistic prospect of liberating Taiwan."

"I take your point, General Shih. Perhaps we should both talk with our principals. After you, Sir."

"Perhaps we should. But let me stress one point again. The attack will come within hours unless we are convinced that that realistic prospect exists. Otherwise, I can't stop it. Even Premier Chou cannot stop it."

After posting his bodyguard at the door, James used the scrambler in the library to speak with the acting Chief-of-Staff of the Liberation Army. Neither the Deputy Chairman nor the Premier was immediately available.

"Comrade Shih, the first assault wave has sailed, and the bombers know their targets," his nominal superior added. "It will be costly, but we are *not* bluffing. You must impress that fact upon the Americans."

In the broad corridor, James Sekloong again met Spencer Taylor Smith hurrying toward the morning-room. The American scrambler had been installed in the incongruously cozy chintz setting, where James's sister Gwinnie had told Mary of her determination to make the marriage with Dr. George Parker that produced the Under Secretary's wife, Blanche. James's elation at Chinese troops' finally moving against Taiwan and, if need be, the Americans inflamed his constantly simmering anger at American arrogance.

"You may be too late, Mr. Smith," he warned. "Our troops have sailed. It will very soon be too late to avoid a collision. We are *not* bluffing. Ask your superman President if he wants war with China. Ask him that!"

"I'll get back to you as soon as I have word, General Shih. Meanwhile, I'd advise my principals to caution if I were you."

James saw no need to pass on the reiterated threat. Instead, he drifted into the drawing-room for a brandy, discovering too late to withdraw that his sister Charlotte, his sister-in-law Sarah, and his brothers Thomas and Charles were chatting with Lady Mary. His mother had resigned herself to the impossibility of sleeping until the wracking tension abated. But she was wispy frail in exhaustion, her pallor other-worldly. The new *taipan* Albert Sekloong and his wife Kazuko sat outside the circle of their elders, watching Lady Mary with open concern.

"Join us, James," Sarah invited. "It's the first time in decades all our generation is together. I hope not the last."

"I hope not, Sarah. Believe me, I've often thought about you."

James yielded to the appeal to family solidarity,

though he required privacy to analyze the intensifying crisis. His acceptance of Sarah's sentimental invitation surprised the Communist General, who believed he had long ago burned away such bourgeois weaknesses as personal affection.

"We've been talking about time," his mother said lightly. "Having you all here again may have deranged me, but one thinks about such things at my age. I now know how time moves."

"An emendation to Einstein's Theory of General Relativity?" Charles Cardinal Sekloong jested. "Even the scientists now admit it doesn't answer *all* questions."

"I'm not joking, Charles," Lady Mary replied. "I'm now convinced there is eternal life. The generations of mankind . . . the generations of a family . . . endure forever. Time doesn't move—in a straight line or a circle. Time is a fixed point, never changing, that we human beings go round in eternal succession. There is our immortality."

"A gentle heresy," the Cardinal murmured. "But you'll find in due time there is *personal* immortality."

"Not for some years, I hope," the Communist General mused over his brandy-snifter. "But, Mother, your notion's Confucian and anti-progressive. Taking the successive generations of the family as the center of human life sanctions all the old loyalties. Corrupt personal loyalties are still the greatest barrier to China's progress."

Albert suddenly felt himself far older than his middle-aged uncles. Their responsibilities and their power were, ultimately, impermanent abstractions; capriciously bestowed by circumstances and by other men, their tasks and their influence could be stripped away as abruptly by the same external forces. But he was, he realized viscerally for the first time, *the* Sekloong, his responsibilities and his power deriving from his own independent position. Though the world might consider the men who spoke for great institutions like antagonistic nations and the Church more powerful than even the grandest merchant, he was, finally, responsible for them and for all the family. From that responsibility sprang his own power, ultimately greater and more enduring than theirs.

"The family *is* at the center." Albert spoke in the new consciousness of his own authority. "Not in the metaphysical old way Grandma means, but the center of all your politics. What are we talking about except human beings gathered together by God into families? I, for one, intend to keep faith with *all* my loyalties."

"Loyalty to the family and the legitimate leader *is* the center of our lives," Thomas assented. "Without loyalty we are nothing."

"Your loyalty to Old Chiang, I suppose," James jibed. "That's helped everybody a lot, hasn't it?"

"Without such loyalty, China would be infinitely worse off." The Nationalist General had not stinted the whiskey, the rice wine, the champagne, or the brandy. "There would be no hope for the future—only your soulless materialism."

"Unquestioning loyalty ruins China." The Communist General spoke softly, his customary fire extinguished in thoughtfulness. "Yours to Chiang Kai-shek, of course. Perhaps my loyalty too. All men and all systems are flawed. Absolute loyalty to any man or system is ultimately destructive evil."

"I never thought I'd hear you speak those words, James," the Cardinal interjected. "But, then, you speak from bitter experience."

"I do," James acknowledged. "And I have myself done some things that were wrong, perhaps evil."

"Like what?" Thomas taunted. "You've always acted as if your damned Communist Party was infallible. Now you admit error. Like what bad things?"

"We've all done things we regret," Charlotte interposed. "I repent of . . ."

"Now, dear, that's all past, well behind . . ." Sarah soothed.

Preoccupied with his brother's question, James ignored the women's soft-spoken exchange. It was the first time in decades he had seriously considered anything Thomas said.

"The cult of the steel Bolshevik," the Communist General finally said. "The conviction that an infallible doctrine justifies all actions—however vicious. Above all, glorying in revolutionary brutality."

"Just exactly what do you mean, James?" The Nationalist General responded instinctively to his brother's mood, and the wordless communication that had linked them as young men revived to inspire his next question. "Can you tell us more about Harry Sekloong's death? I know *we* didn't kill him, though the Generalissimo considered it. So it must have been you . . . your people."

"It wasn't . . . wasn't my *people*." James spoke so faintly the others leaned forward to hear him. "It wasn't just my people. God help me, it was . . . was . . . I who . . ."

"James, not really?" Charlotte gasped. "Your own . . . your own uncle? *You* shot him?"

"I'm afraid so, Charlotte. It was for China . . . for the cause. But now I wonder. Too many killings, too much blood."

"James, *you! You yourself*?" Lady Mary's voice was so thin it might have come from behind the curtain of the eternity she pondered. "*You,* James?"

"Yes, Mother, I did. I'm no longer proud that . . ."

"James, I'm suddenly exhausted," Lady Mary half-whispered. "Please help me to my bedroom."

"Mother, can I . . ." Sarah fluttered in concern.

"No, no one else. Just James. I'll see you all in the morning."

Leaning heavily on James's arm, Lady Mary climbed the great Y-shaped staircase she had eagerly descended on Thomas's arm six hours earlier.

"I'm sorry, Mother!" James's words stumbled. "Deeply sorry I told you, profoundly sorry for what I did. But I shouldn't have told you."

Lady Mary did not speak until they entered her bedroom.

"Sit down, James," she directed without passion. "There is something I must tell you. Something I alone know."

He obediently seated himself on the chaise-longue and gazed into his brandy-snifter.

"James," his mother said, "Harry Sekloong was *not* your uncle, but . . ."

"What are you saying, Mother? Harry *not* my uncle! It's wonderful, your trying to console me, but . . ."

"James, Harry Sekloong was . . . was . . . your father. You should know Harry was your father."

"My father? That's impossible . . . ridiculous."

"Nonetheless, true! Who should know better than I? I'm sorry, but you had to know before I . . ."

"My *father?"* James echoed. *"Harry*—my father?"

"Yes, James. I hope you can forgive me. I'm too old for anger at your . . . at what you did. But you had to know. I pray there'll be no more senseless killing of those we love—or others."

James Sekloong's hand clenched, and the splintered brandy-snifter gashed his palm. Groping for a handkerchief to stanch the blood, he strode blindly from the bedroom. He was enraged at the entire world—at his mother's frailty, at his brother's probing, and at his superiors' ruthlessness. He was, above all, enraged at himself. His lifelong loyalties, already battered by the power struggle in China, tossed in an emotional maelstrom.

Harry Sekloong his father! Unknowing, he had rendered the Party the greatest sacrifice he could make—a far greater sacrifice than his own life, which he had cheerfully hazarded a score of times. He had killed his own father.

Bewildered, enraged, and revolted, momentarily demented with shame and sorrow, he stumbled into the storm-torn garden. The wind hurled him against the gray-stone wall of The Castle, and a spear of pain pierced the scar tissue on his left shoulder, which had been torn by the *Kempei*'s bullet in Peking thirty-three years earlier.

The same gust rattled the windows of Sir Jonathan's darkened office. In the baleful lightning's flare, the last petals fell from Lady Mary's rose onto the ebony desktop.

The destroyer-leader U.S.S. *Sampson* pitched south-southwest through the stormy night seventy-six miles west of Nationalist Taiwan, forty-three miles east of Communist Fukien. *Sampson* probed the darkness with invisible fingers, but spume rising from the post-typhoon waves clouded her surface-radar. The sailor peering at the green screen monotonously reported: "No contact. No contact."

Sampson rolled to starboard, bringing her surface-radar antenna to bear on the sea.

"Two targets," the bluejacket reported. "Two targets: bearing 272, course 46, range 3,000 yards, estimated speed 36 knots."

The radar of the high-speed patrol-boats of the Communist East Seas Flotilla registered *Sampson*'s bulk a half minute later. They were pitching wildly, and their antennae were much lower. Nonetheless, the Chinese captains reacted before the American. They had been ordered to fire on any unidentified craft that might threaten the heavy laden landing-ships behind them. The rapid-fire cannon of *East Seas 234* and *East Seas 249* chattered, and water-spouts rose eighty yards from *Sampson*'s starboard bow.

"Return fire," the American captain ordered. "Main battery, rapid fire under radar control."

Orange flame billowed from *Sampson*'s two 5-inch guns, and her surface-to-surface Tartar missiles trained on the patrol-boats.

"Yeoman," the captain directed. "In plain voice to ComSevFleet, CincPac, and DOD: Fired on by two unidentified small vessels at approximately . . ."

". . . 24'58" north, 119'42" east," the navigating officer supplied.

"Targets' course approximately 46. I have taken them under fire with main battery. Request instructions."

Relayed automatically to the loudspeaker, the signalman's Texas drawl echoed in the White House situation room. The President flushed in anger when the Chief of Naval Operations added: "Heading for the northwest coast of Taiwan."

"Get the little bastards," he directed.

"Turn them aside for the moment, perhaps, Mr. President," the Security Adviser suggested deferentially.

"All right, Henry," the President said. "Turn them aside. But kill them if they won't divert or there's immediate danger to the destroyer. Use the missiles."

East Seas 234 and *East Seas 249* maintained their high-speed base course through the 2 A.M. darkness of the Taiwan Straits, while zigzagging to evade *Sampson*'s fire. Six 40-millimeter shells penetrated the thin armor of the destroyer's starboard quarter to explode in the after emergency-steering compartment. A sailor screamed and clutched his mangled arm. Another slumped silently to the deck, dying before he felt the shell-splinter pierce his brain. *Sampson*'s captain made his own decision as the Chief of Naval Operations' voice began relaying the President's instructions.

"Fire the Tartars," he commanded.

Four rockets arched their fiery trails against the night-black sky. *East Seas 234* was obliterated forty-three seconds later, and *East Seas 249* dodged erratically.

"Let him go," the captain directed. "But track him. Damage report?"

The Chinese convoy slowed and turned north at the urgent command of the captain of *East Seas 249*. At least fifteen minutes would elapse before his action report reached Peking and an additional fifteen before he could receive new orders—if the decision were taken immediately. The less sophisticated Chinese communications system and the cumbersome decision-making process in Peking had fortuitously given the Chinese almost an hour's grace before resuming the engagement. Close air-support would be necessary if the vanguard were to proceed to Taiwan, and the Chinese were not adept in the highly technical art of fighting an air-sea battle at night. The critical decision had, therefore, been effectively postponed by several hours. First light was at 4:57 A.M.

In Washington, the Assistant Secretary for the Far East told the President and his Security Adviser: "I've got Smith on the phone."

"Put him on the speaker," the President directed.

"This is Smith," the loudspeaker rattled. "General Shih informs me that the Chicoms' first wave has sailed and . . ."

"We know, Smith," the President said. "A destroyer's just had a brush with their patrol-boats. She got one after taking some shells. She's tracking now. Tell the Reds we'll retaliate against their land bases if there's any further molestation of our vessels."

"Yes, Sir," the voice from Hong Kong replied. "Shih also says the Premier will fall if he can't come up with a credible, realistic prospect of gradual American withdrawal from Taiwan. Lin Piao's determined to press the attack. Shih says only such a concession can prevent his doing so."

"We'll blow them out of the water," the President snapped. "Are they all nuts?"

"I don't know, Sir," the Under Secretary replied. "But the Chicom military seem absolutely determined."

The Security Adviser spoke into his chief's ear. After two minutes, the President nodded agreement and spoke into the microphone again.

"I'm told you know the minimum conditions we can accept. Go back and talk to the Commie General. But, remember, any more frigging around and we hit them hard. Tell him that."

Pondering his next move, Spencer Taylor Smith returned to the study. He carried thousands—perhaps hundreds of thousands—of lives in his hands; the President's testy directions from faraway Washington could not relieve him of that burden. He started when he found James Sekloong seated in the same leather chair wearing an open-necked shirt and cream-linen trousers that had belonged to his father Charles. James's red-rimmed eyes stared unseeing into the fireplace from haggard features.

"My government, General Shih," Smith spoke formally, "views with the gravest alarm the commencement of hostilities by your government. Your patrol-boats have inflicted damage on an American destroyer. We have destroyed one boat. Any further hostile action will be countered by attacks on your land bases."

"If that's true, it alters the situation," James replied automatically. "It's exactly what I warned about. Next the bombers and then . . ."

"For God's sake, man, how do we stop this insanity?" the American appealed. "It's up to us, it seems!"

The urbane Spencer Taylor Smith's outburst pushed James Sekloong over the threshold. Already shaken by the awful revelation of his paternity, his equilibrium collapsed. The rashness he had fought to suppress all his life reasserted itself, for once enlisted in the service of moderation. Out of his profound humiliation, his rage, shame, and self-loathing, James Sekloong spoke to his nephew by marriage and assumed the ultimate responsibility he had shunned. He would, he decided in that instant, do it his own way—if necessary sacrificing himself to save hundreds of thousands of other lives.

"Look here, Spencer, I shouldn't say this," he exclaimed. "But I will. I won't haggle. I can't haggle. I'll give you our minimal conditions. We *must* have agreement to further negotiations at the highest level—first Kissinger, later Nixon. And we *must* have general agreement *right now*. Agreement to disengage from Taiwan . . . to let us handle it our own way. We won't—I can promise you—be hasty or use force, except in the last extremity. Not for several years, at any rate. In return, we offer better relations, trade, access to our oil reserves, and a broad understanding to act in concert against Soviet imperialism whenever possible. But you *must* accept our minimal conditions right now."

"I understand your minimal conditions," Smith countered. "Can you assure me personally, General . . . ah . . . James . . . that you're wholly sincere, not just playing for time?"

"For God's sake, Spencer, I'm not fooling with you. It's the only way we can turn the invasion around. Otherwise, there *will* be war. Lin Piao *will* win and . . ."

"I'll convey your message. But I can—personally, not officially—tell you that, in broad outline, your conditions appear acceptable. Now, let's both get on the telephone."

Apprehension gnawed at James Sekloong's new resolution, but he insisted upon being put through to the Premier. If he had misjudged Chou En-lai's position, he would certainly be purged. The Premier himself would probably be purged, and the People's Republic of China would be at war with the United States of America. After eighteen minutes, at 3:32 A.M., Hong Kong time, he finally heard the Premier's familiar crackling Kiangsu accent.

"Well, Ai-kuo, what can you tell me?"

"I understand, Comrade Premier, that our patrolboats have clashed with an American destroyer."

"Correct. I've just heard."

"And the Americans claim one was destroyed."

"I hadn't heard that. I'll have the report checked."
James waited while Chou En-lai spoke to an aide.

"Now," the Premier resumed, "what else have you to
tell me? Any cracks, any openings? It's getting very
tight."

James summarized his last discussion with Spencer
Taylor Smith. The Premier listened without comment.
When James had finished, there was a long pause on
the static-blurred line. After more than two minutes,
when James feared he had lost the connection, Chou
En-lai spoke slowly.

"Tell them: Yes. We can make detailed arrangements later. But we can live with your agreement. I can
halt the troop movements. Yes, we can all live with
those terms—*almost* all of us. You've done well. Now
let me get to work. I'll call you later."

Trembling with relief for himself and his world,
James walked slowly to the study to await Spencer Taylor Smith. When the American returned, the Chinese
spoke wearily.

"It's all right, Spencer. My people can live with it.
The details must be worked out, but the general outline's acceptable."

"And mine, too, James. A small drink, perhaps, before we discuss those details and report again to our
governments. I'll need something a little more concrete."

James Sekloong took the younger man's arm pater-
nally as they walked down the hall. The strained faces
in the drawing-room brightened on beholding the gesture.

"It's all right," James told the Sekloongs. "There'll
be no war. You can tell Mother Sino-American relations should improve markedly. And ask her to forgive
me for . . . for everything."

Charlotte, Sarah, and Kazuko carried his message to
Lady Mary, who lay waxen frail in the high bed of the
big bedroom that had been Sir Jonathan's. Her violet

eyes sparkled before fluttering closed, and her translucent hand fondled the winged-dragon plaque.

"I'm glad, very glad," Mary Philippa Osgood Sekloong murmured. "It won't be easy or always pleasant. But it is a beginning. Now, I think, I shall rest for a while—perhaps a long, long time."

About the Author

A student of Asia for almost three decades, Robert Sampson Elegant has been most recently Visiting Professor in Journalism and International Studies at the University of South Carolina. A distinguished foreign correspondent who has covered most of the major events in Asia since 1951, Mr. Elegant is fluent in Chinese and Japanese. Before leaving daily reporting to devote himself to writing novels and longer studies of the international scene he was foreign-affairs columnist for the *Los Angeles Times*—his columns syndicated to over 300 newspapers in the United States and abroad.

Born in New York, Mr. Elegant was educated at the University of Pennsylvania and Columbia University, where he received an M.A. in Chinese and Japanese and an M.S. in journalism. Over the years he has written for such diverse publications as *Foreign Affairs, Commentary, The Nation, The National Review, Reader's Digest,* and *Look.*

Author of six nonfiction works on China and Asia, Mr. Elegant has received the Edgar Allan Poe Award for his novel of suspense, *A Kind of Treason,* and *The Seeking,* set in Central Asia in 100 B.C., was hailed as a remarkably poetic evocation of the past. For his journalistic work he has been the recipient of many awards, including one from Sigma Delta Chi and four from the Overseas Press Club. He and his wife, the former Moira Clarissa Brady of Sydney, Australia, presently live in Ireland with their two children.

BESTSELLERS

HELEN MacINNES

Helen MacInnes's bestselling suspense novels continue to delight her readers and many have been made into major motion pictures. Here is your chance to enjoy all of her exciting novels, by simply filling out the coupon below.

☐	ABOVE SUSPICION	23101-1	1.75
☐	AGENT IN PLACE	23127-5	1.95
☐	ASSIGNMENT IN BRITTANY	22958-0	1.95
☐	DECISION AT DELPHI	C2790	1.95
☐	THE DOUBLE IMAGE	23512-2	1.95
☐	FRIENDS AND LOVERS	23538-6	1.95
☐	HORIZON	23434-7	1.75
☐	I AND MY TRUE LOVE	23303-0	1.75
☐	MESSAGE FROM MALAGA	X2820	1.75
☐	NEITHER FIVE NOR THREE	23566-1	1.95
☐	NORTH FROM ROME	23285-9	1.75
☐	PRAY FOR A BRAVE HEART	22907-6	1.75
☐	REST AND BE THANKFUL	23621-8	1.95
☐	THE SALZBURG CONNECTION	23611-0	1.95
☐	THE SNARE OF THE HUNTER	23502-5	1.95
☐	THE VENETIAN AFFAIR	23667-6	1.95
☐	WHILE STILL WE LIVE	23099-6	1.95

Buy them at your local bookstores or use this handy coupon for ordering:

Taylor Caldwell

☐	NEVER VICTORIOUS, NEVER DEFEATED	08435-9	1.95
☐	TENDER VICTORY	08298-4	2.25
☐	THIS SIDE OF INNOCENCE	08434-0	1.95
☐	YOUR SINS AND MINE	00331-6	1.25
☐	THE ARM AND THE DARKNESS	23616-1	2.25
☐	CAPTAINS AND THE KINGS	23069-4	2.25
☐	DIALOGUES WITH THE DEVIL	Q2768	1.50
☐	THE FINAL HOUR	23670-6	2.25
☐	GLORY AND THE LIGHTNING	23515-7	2.25
☐	GRANDMOTHER AND THE PRIESTS	C2664	1.95
☐	GREAT LION OF GOD	22445-7	1.95
☐	THE LATE CLARA BEAME	23157-7	1.50
☐	MAGGIE—HER MARRIAGE	23119-4	1.50
☐	NO ONE HEARS BUT HIM	23306-5	1.75
☐	ON GROWING UP TOUGH	23082-1	1.50
☐	A PILLAR OF IRON	23569-6	2.25
☐	THE ROMANCE OF ATLANTIS	23787-7	1.95
☐	TESTIMONY OF TWO MEN	23212-3	2.25
☐	WICKED ANGEL	23310-3	1.75
☐	TO LOOK AND PASS	13491-1	1.75

Buy them at your local bookstores or use this handy coupon for ordering: